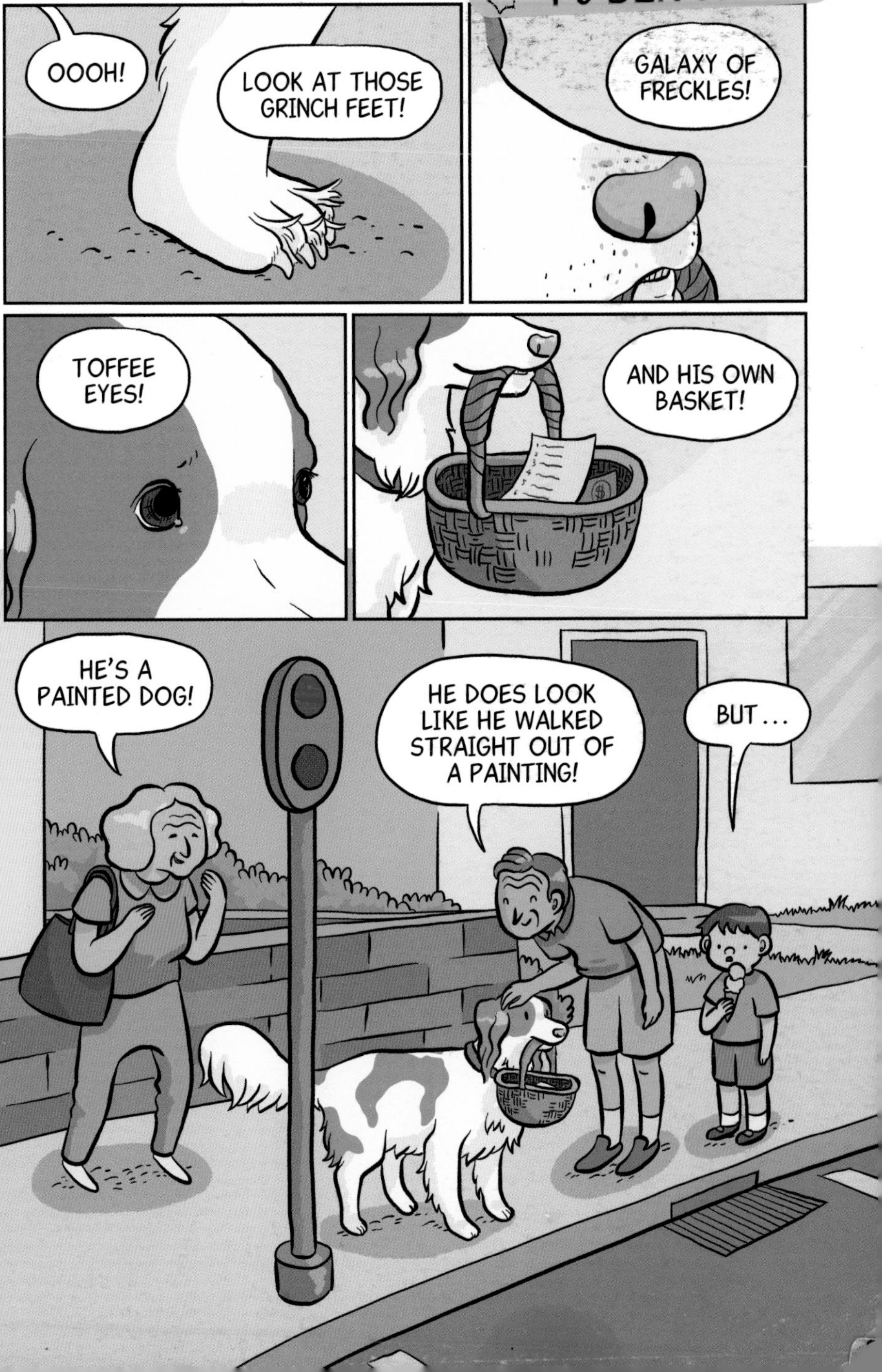
OOOH!
LOOK AT THOSE GRINCH FEET!
GALAXY OF FRECKLES!
TOFFEE EYES!
AND HIS OWN BASKET!
HE'S A PAINTED DOG!
HE DOES LOOK LIKE HE WALKED STRAIGHT OUT OF A PAINTING!
BUT . . .

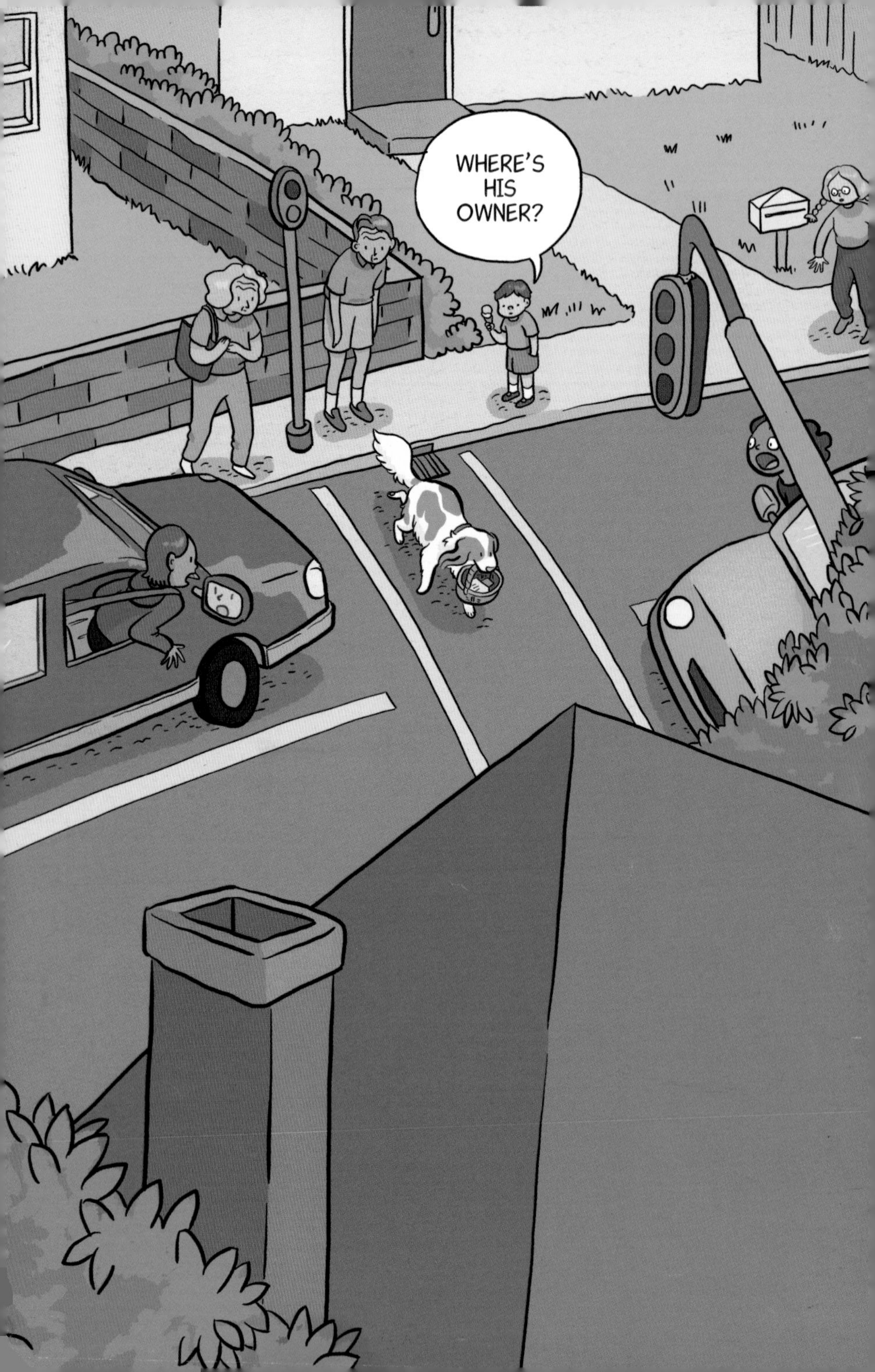
WHERE'S HIS OWNER?

Pawcasso

by Remy Lai

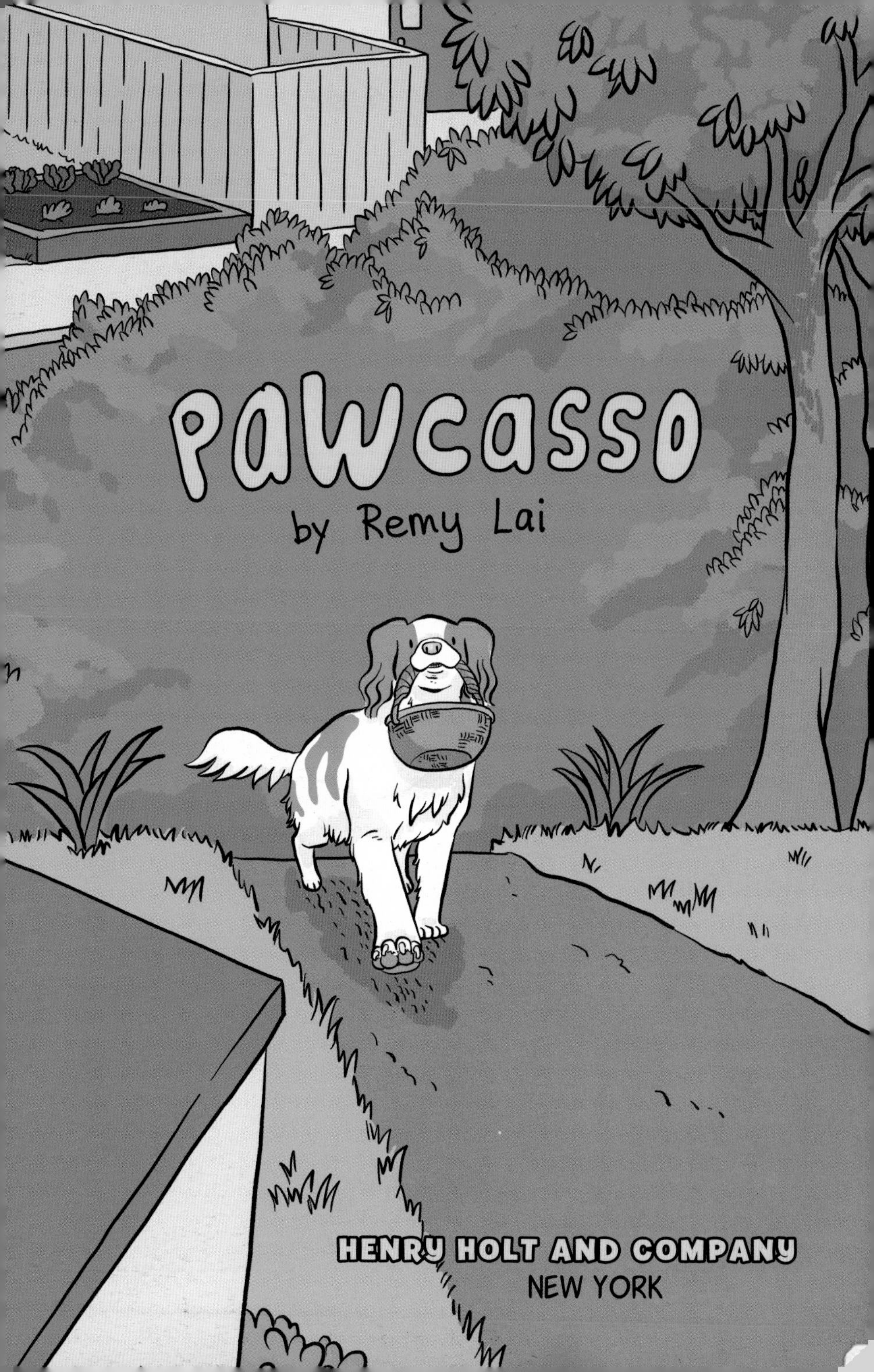

HENRY HOLT AND COMPANY
NEW YORK

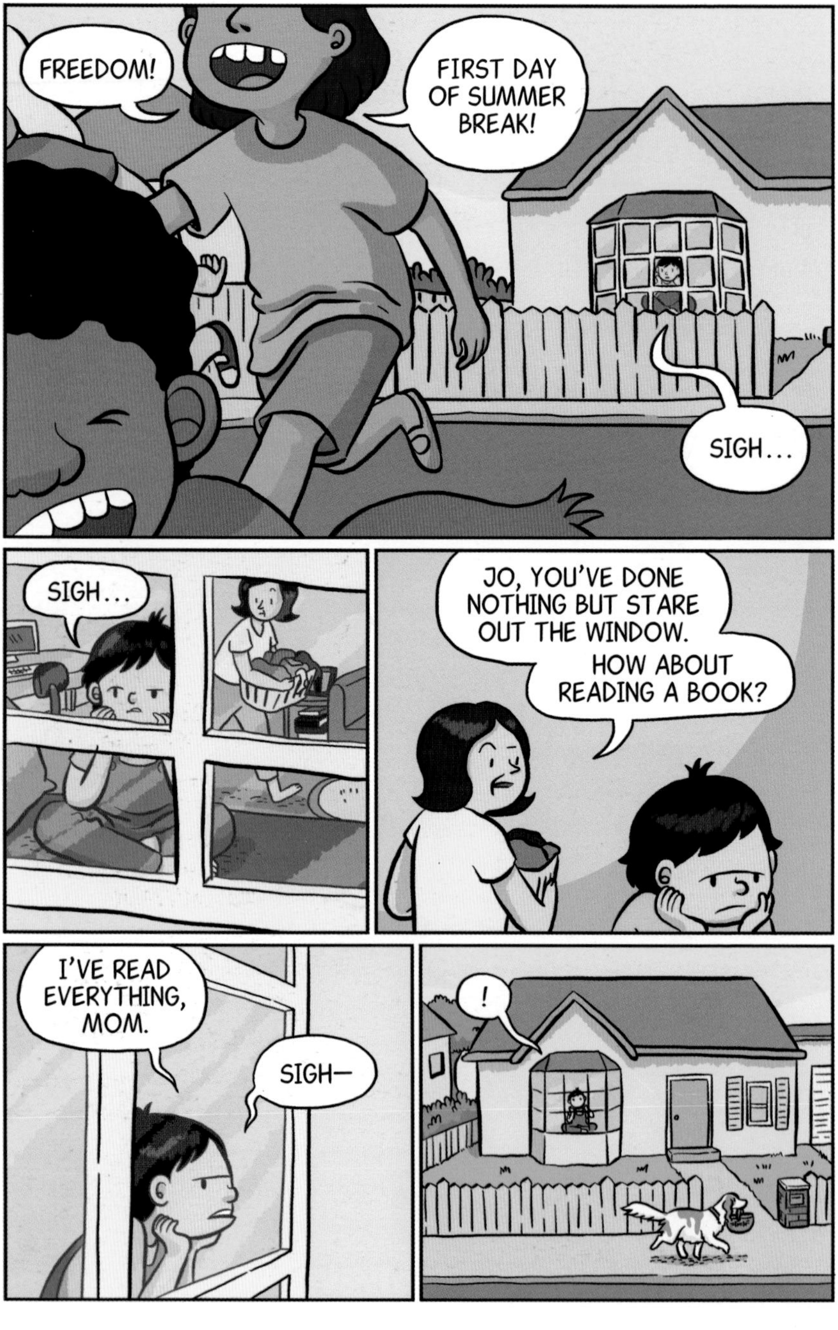
FREEDOM!
FIRST DAY OF SUMMER BREAK!
SIGH...
SIGH...
JO, YOU'VE DONE NOTHING BUT STARE OUT THE WINDOW.
HOW ABOUT READING A BOOK?
I'VE READ EVERYTHING, MOM.
SIGH—
!

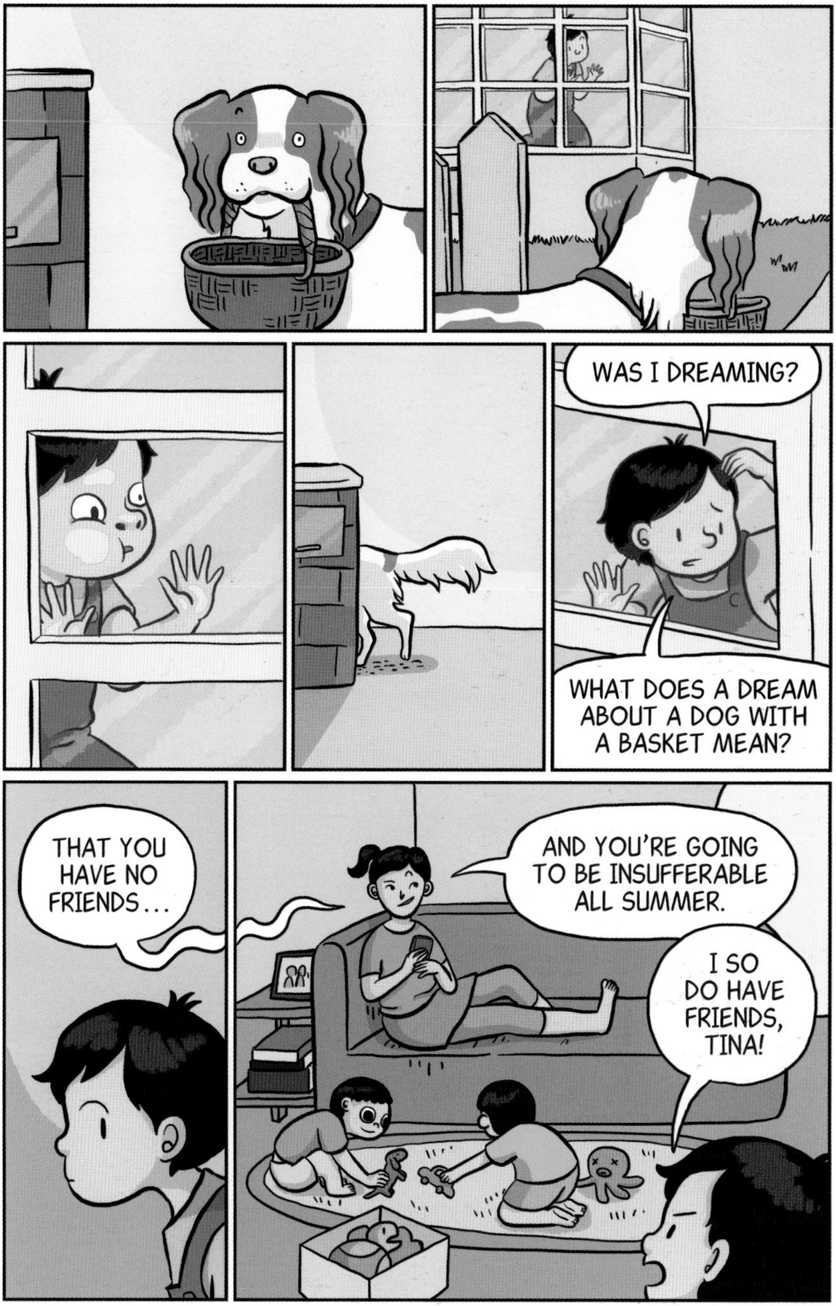
WAS I DREAMING?
WHAT DOES A DREAM ABOUT A DOG WITH A BASKET MEAN?
THAT YOU HAVE NO FRIENDS...
AND YOU'RE GOING TO BE INSUFFERABLE ALL SUMMER.
I SO DO HAVE FRIENDS, TINA!

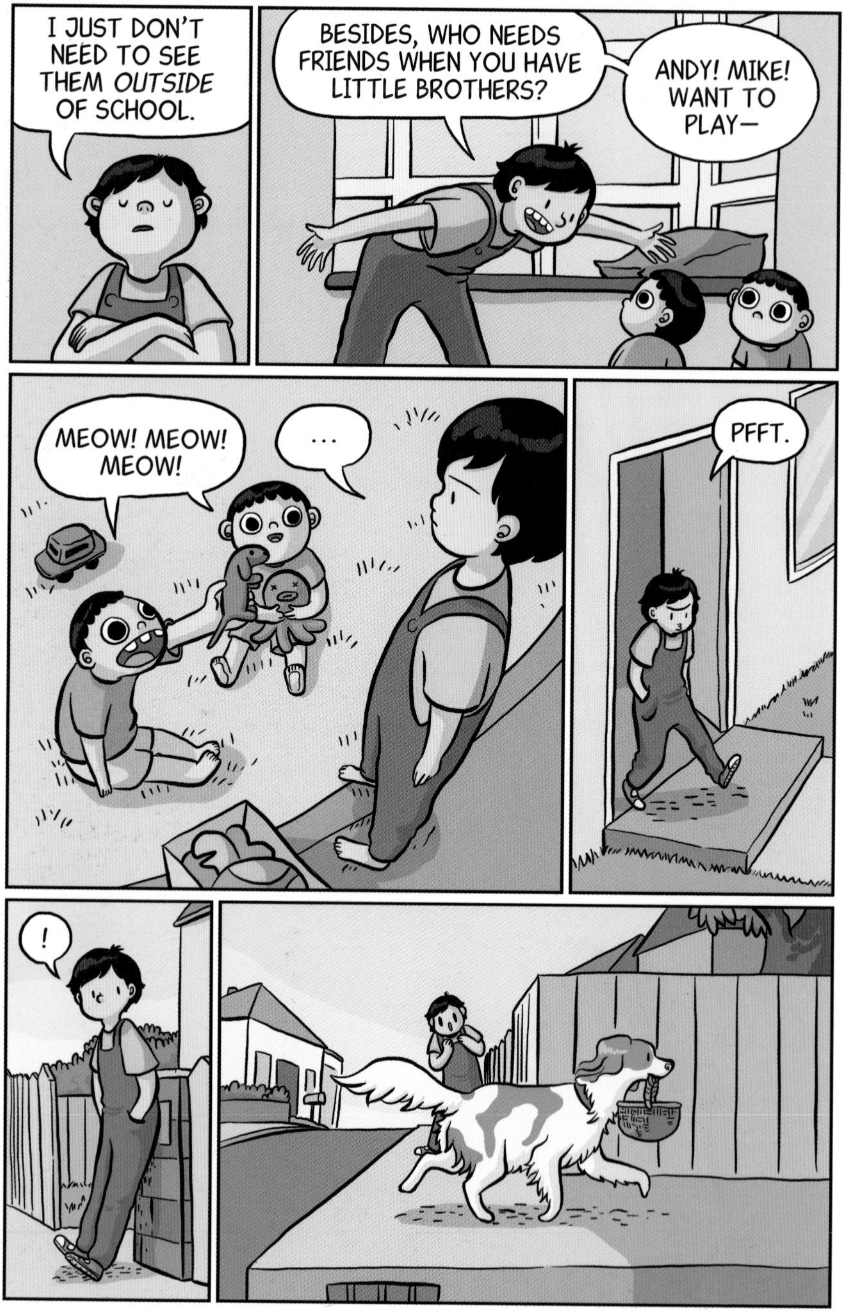
I JUST DON'T NEED TO SEE THEM *OUTSIDE* OF SCHOOL.
BESIDES, WHO NEEDS FRIENDS WHEN YOU HAVE LITTLE BROTHERS?
ANDY! MIKE! WANT TO PLAY—
MEOW! MEOW! MEOW!
...
PFFT.
!

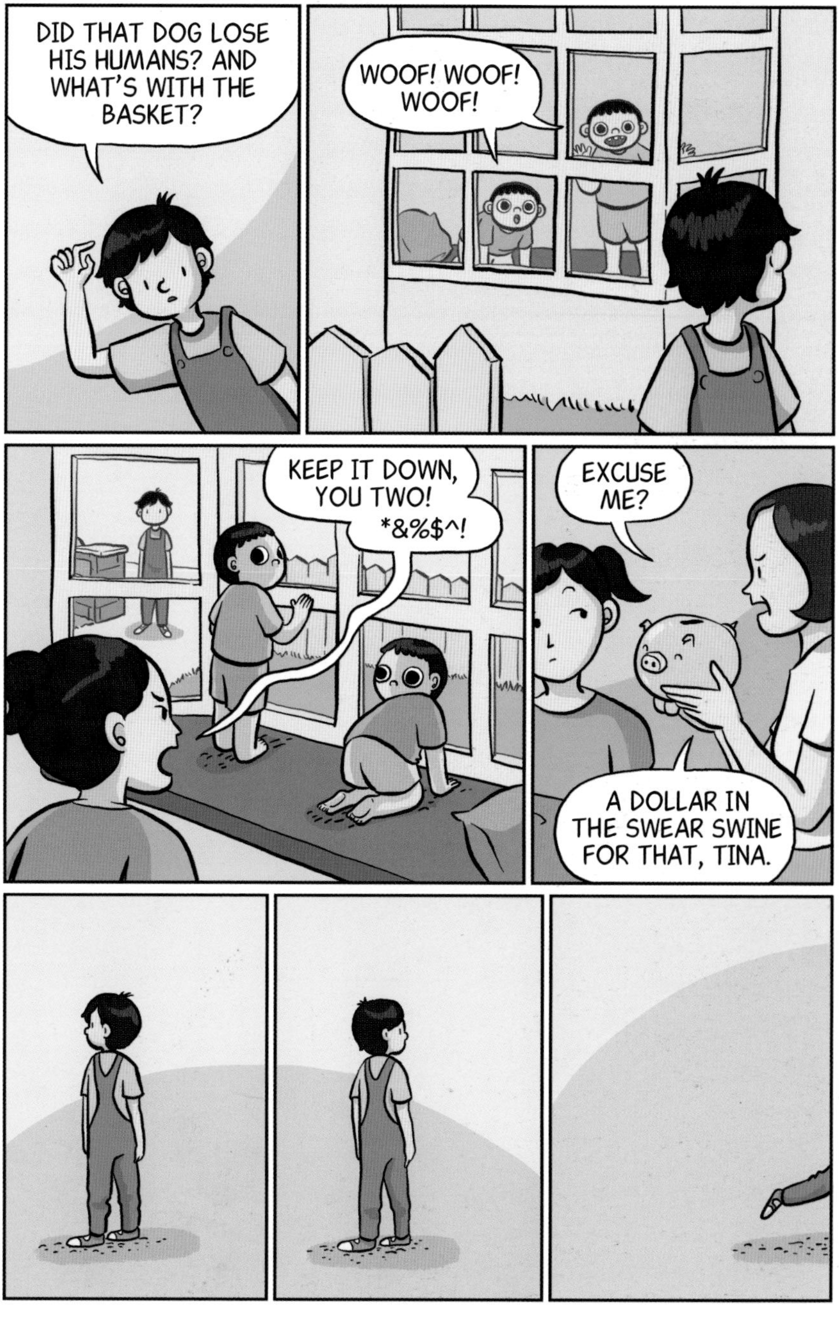
DID THAT DOG LOSE HIS HUMANS? AND WHAT'S WITH THE BASKET?
WOOF! WOOF! WOOF!
KEEP IT DOWN, YOU TWO! *&%$^!
EXCUSE ME?
A DOLLAR IN THE SWEAR SWINE FOR THAT, TINA.

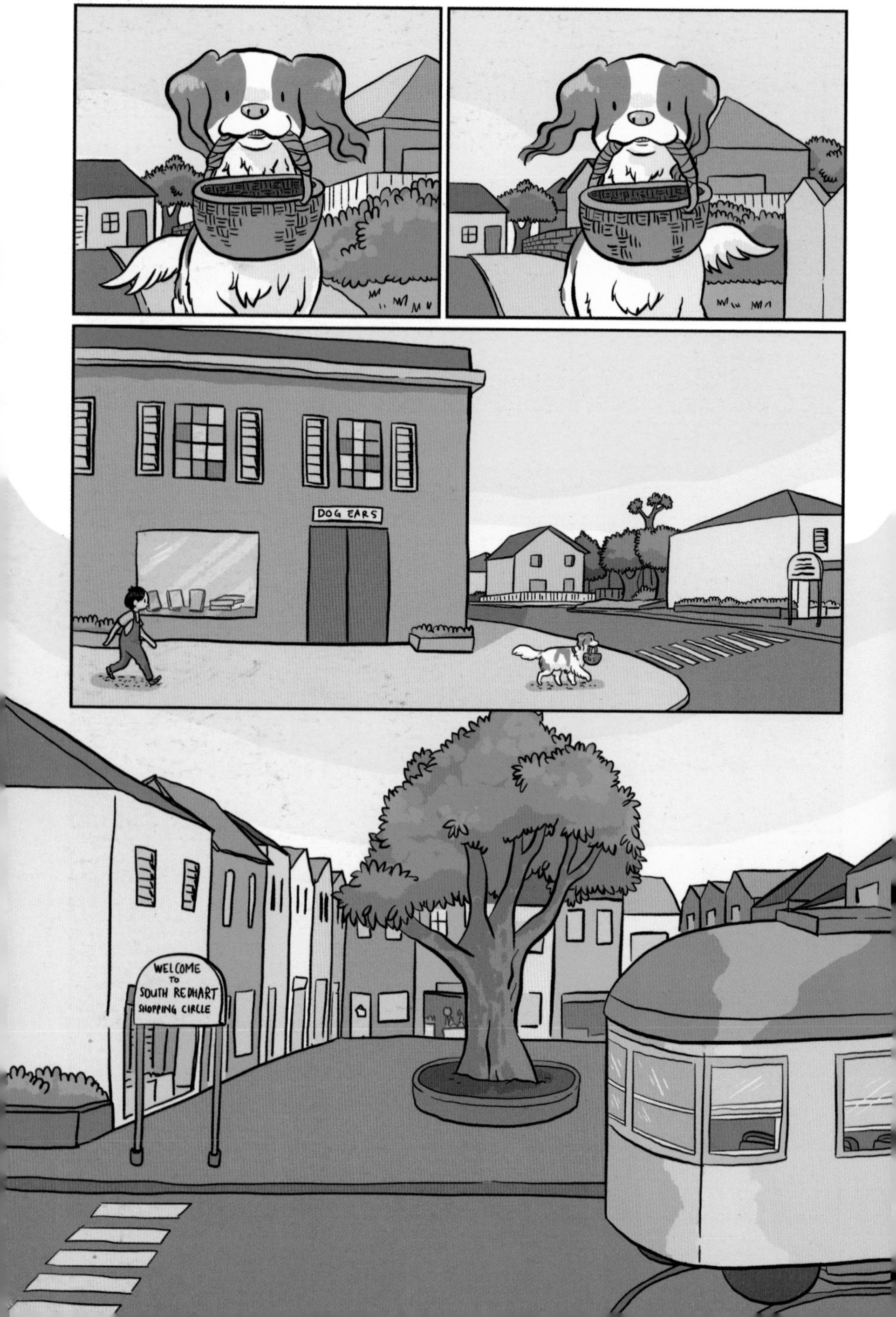
DOG EARS
WELCOME TO SOUTH REDHART SHOPPING CIRCLE

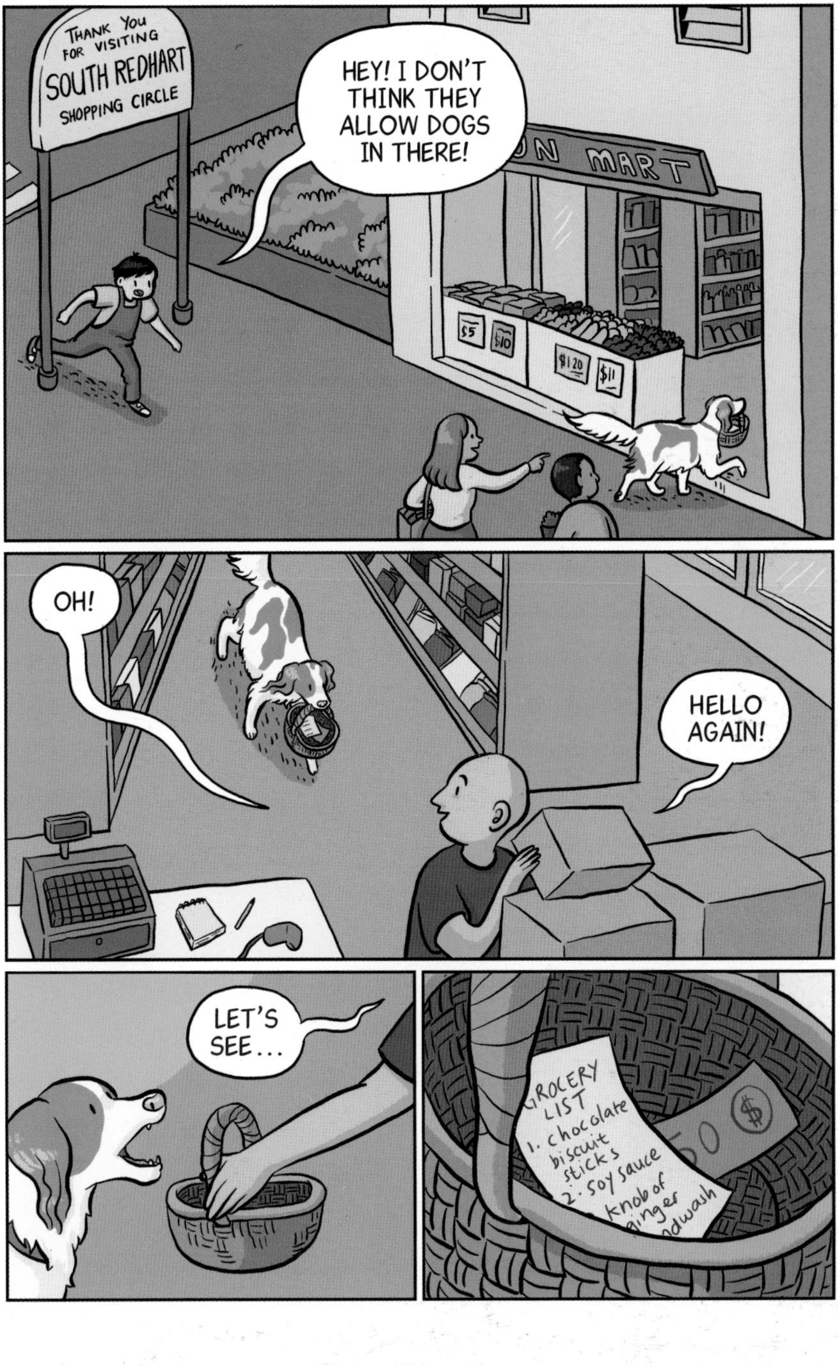
THANK YOU FOR VISITING SOUTH REDHART SHOPPING CIRCLE
HEY! I DON'T THINK THEY ALLOW DOGS IN THERE!
MART
$5
$10
$1.20
$11
OH!
HELLO AGAIN!
LET'S SEE...
GROCERY LIST
1. chocolate biscuit sticks
2. Soy sauce
knob of ginger

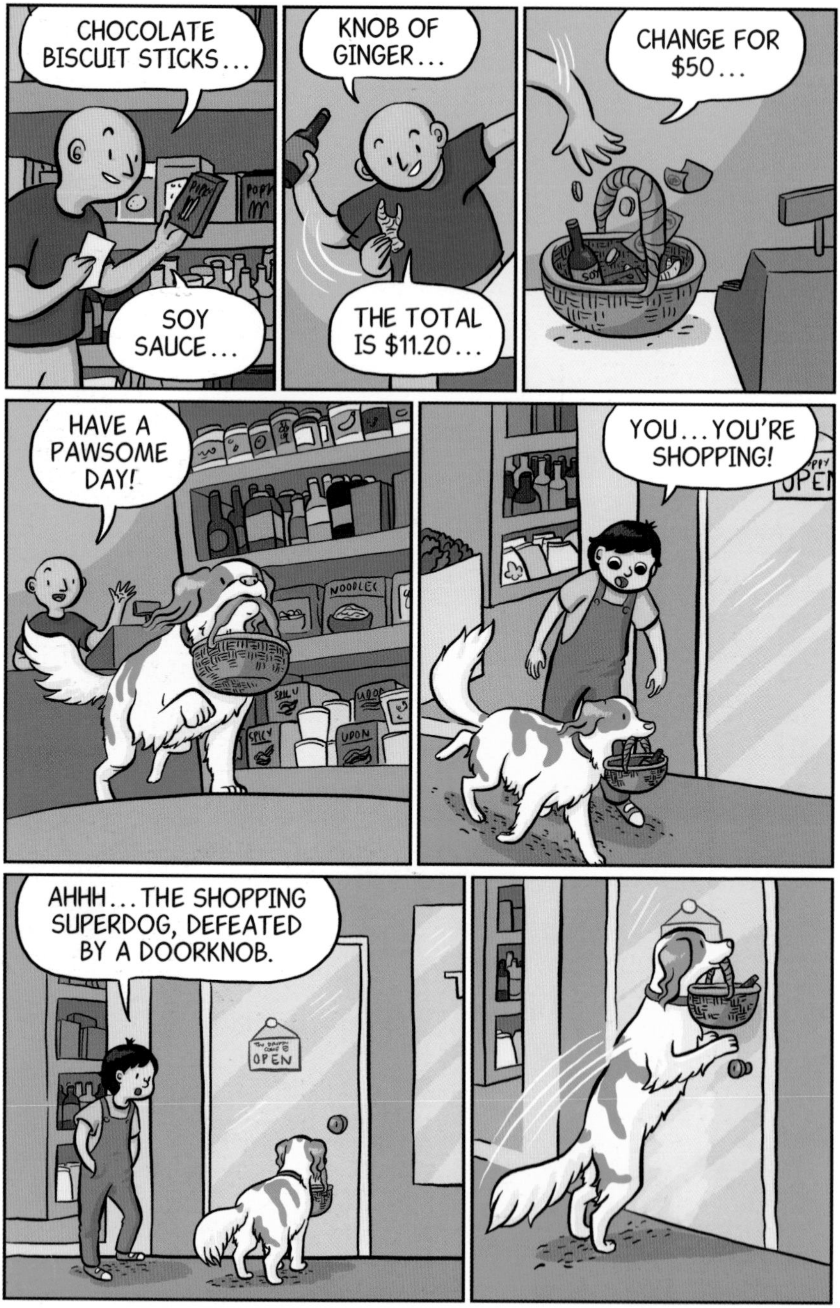
CHOCOLATE BISCUIT STICKS...
SOY SAUCE...
KNOB OF GINGER...
THE TOTAL IS $11.20...
CHANGE FOR $50...
HAVE A PAWSOME DAY!
YOU...YOU'RE SHOPPING!
OPEN
AHHH...THE SHOPPING SUPERDOG, DEFEATED BY A DOORKNOB.
OPEN

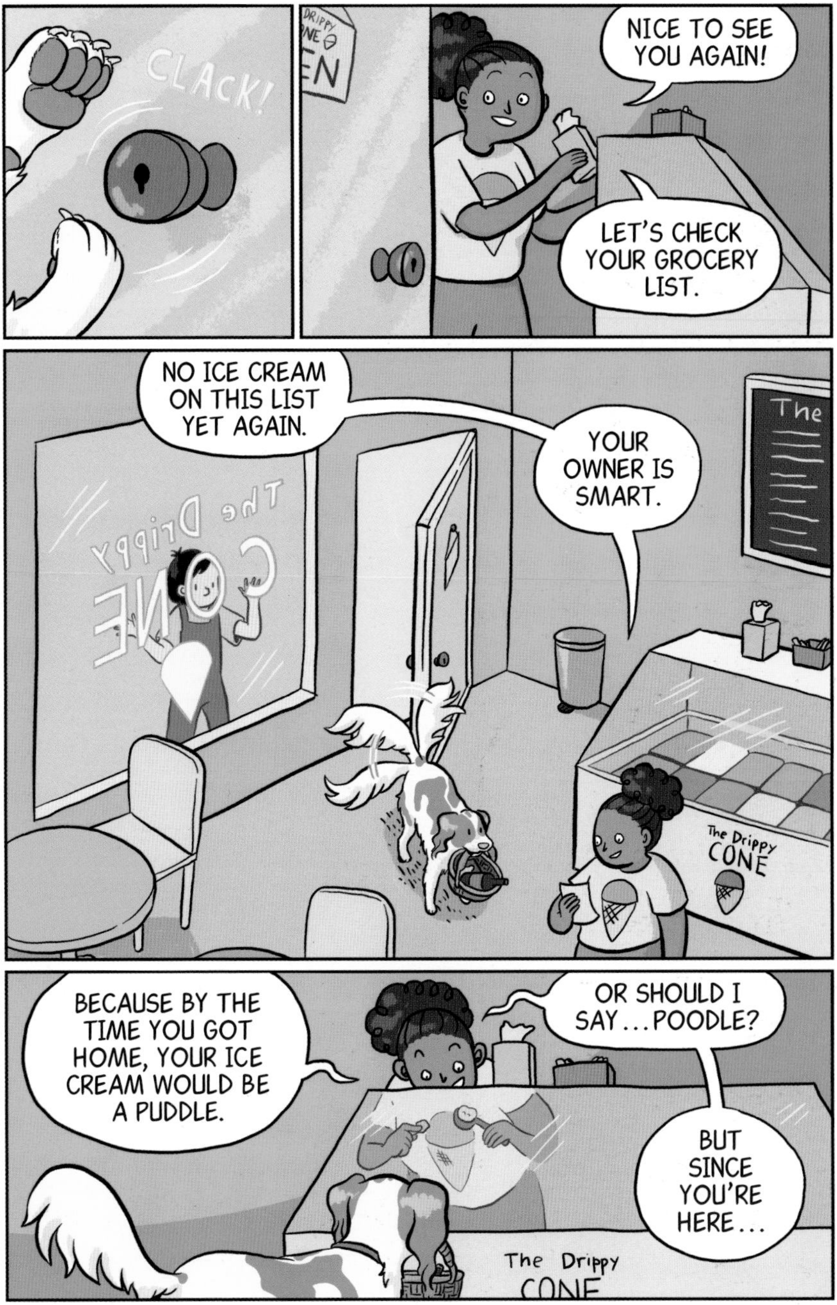
CLACK!
NICE TO SEE YOU AGAIN!
LET'S CHECK YOUR GROCERY LIST.
NO ICE CREAM ON THIS LIST YET AGAIN.
YOUR OWNER IS SMART.
The
The Drippy CONE
BECAUSE BY THE TIME YOU GOT HOME, YOUR ICE CREAM WOULD BE A PUDDLE.
OR SHOULD I SAY...POODLE?
BUT SINCE YOU'RE HERE...
The Drippy

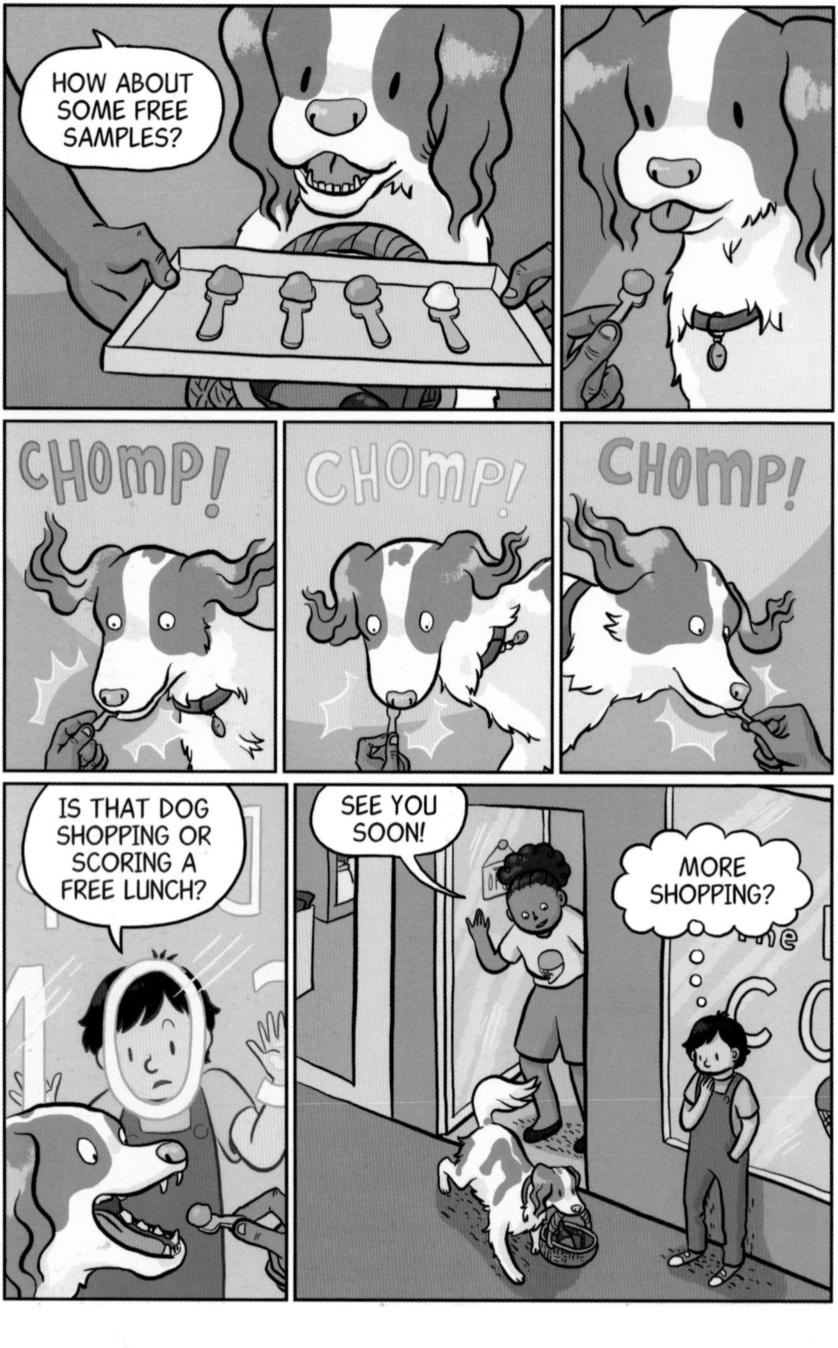
HOW ABOUT SOME FREE SAMPLES?
CHOMP!
CHOMP!
CHOMP!
IS THAT DOG SHOPPING OR SCORING A FREE LUNCH?
SEE YOU SOON!
MORE SHOPPING?

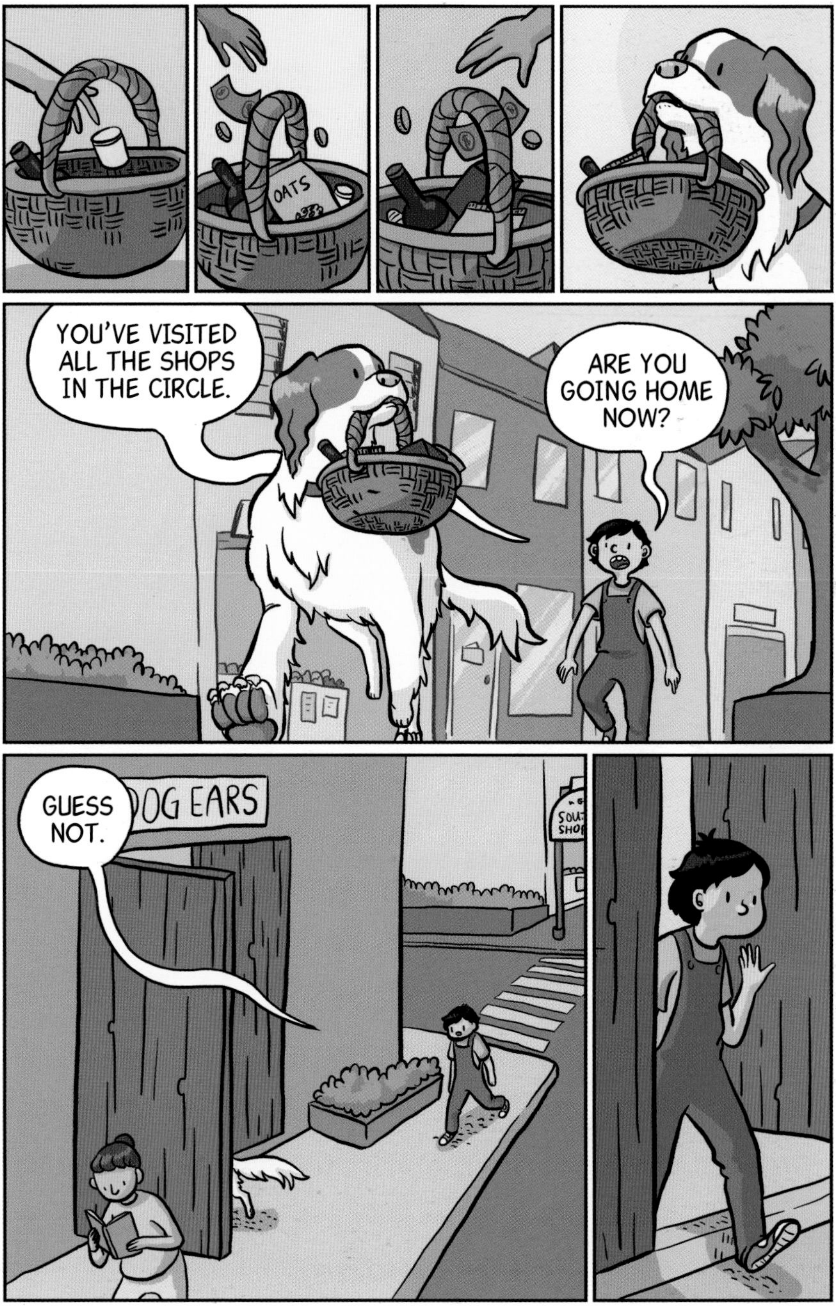
OATS
YOU'VE VISITED ALL THE SHOPS IN THE CIRCLE.
ARE YOU GOING HOME NOW?
GUESS NOT.
DOG EARS

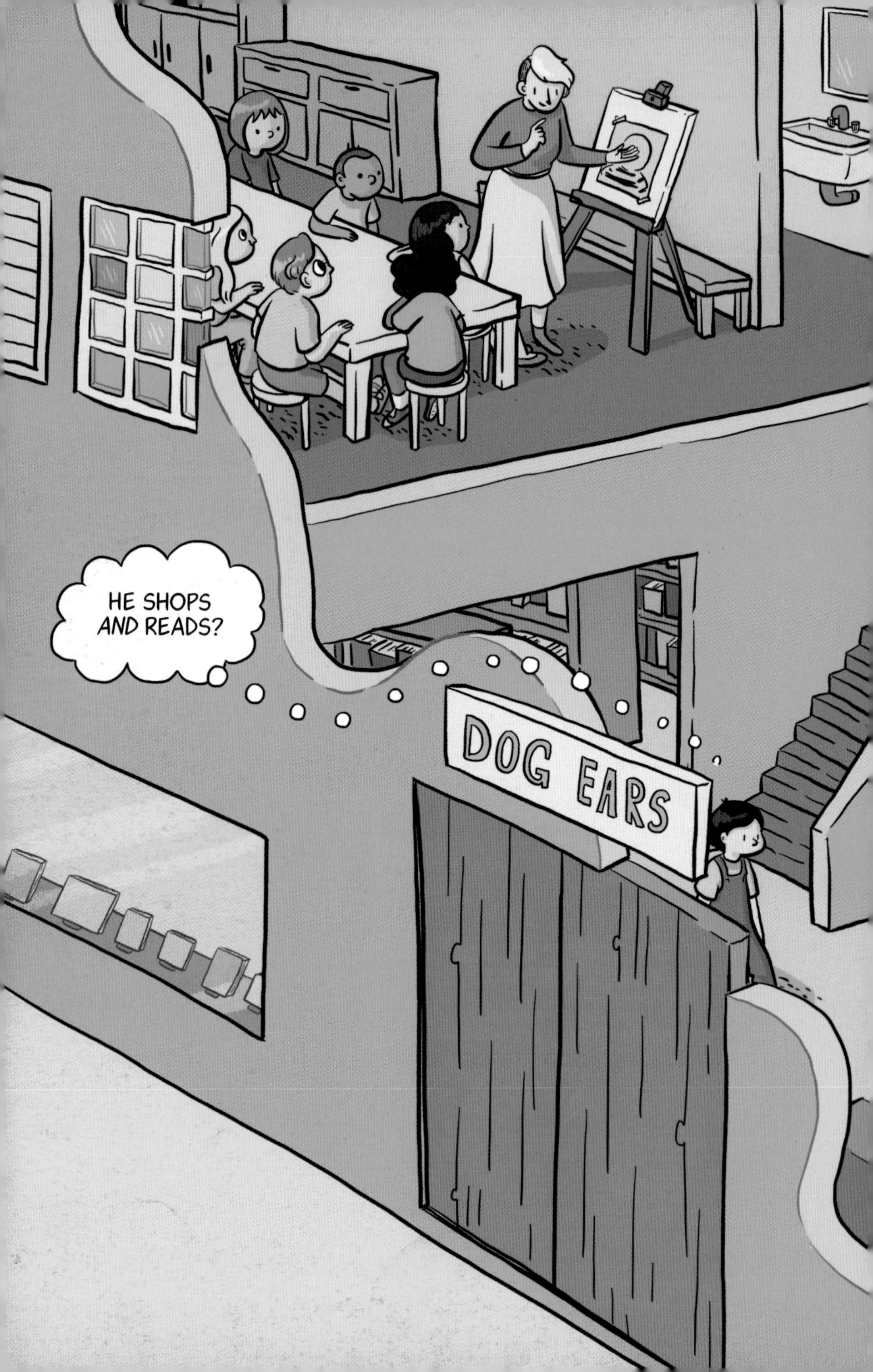
HE SHOPS
AND READS?
DOG EARS

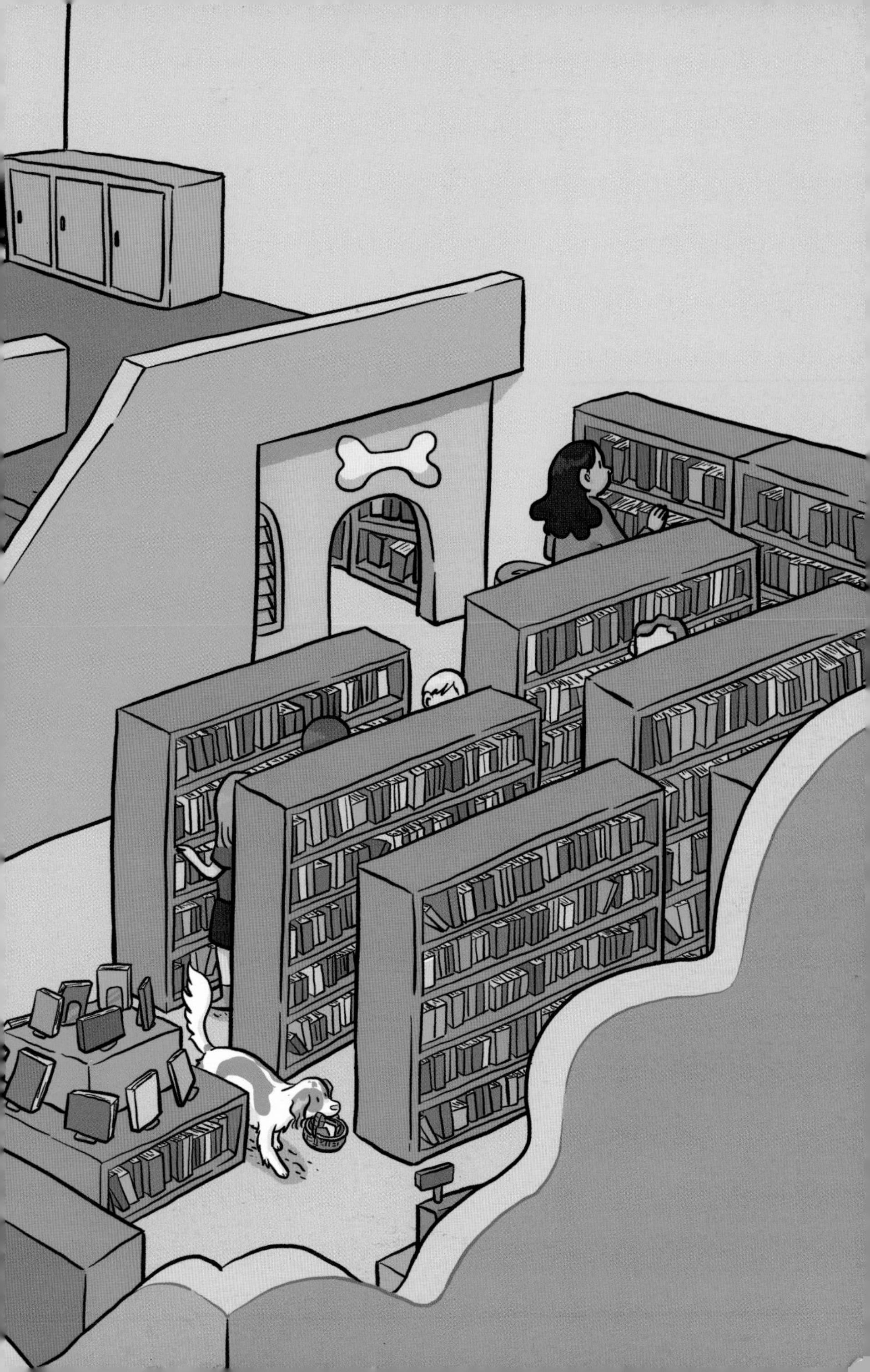

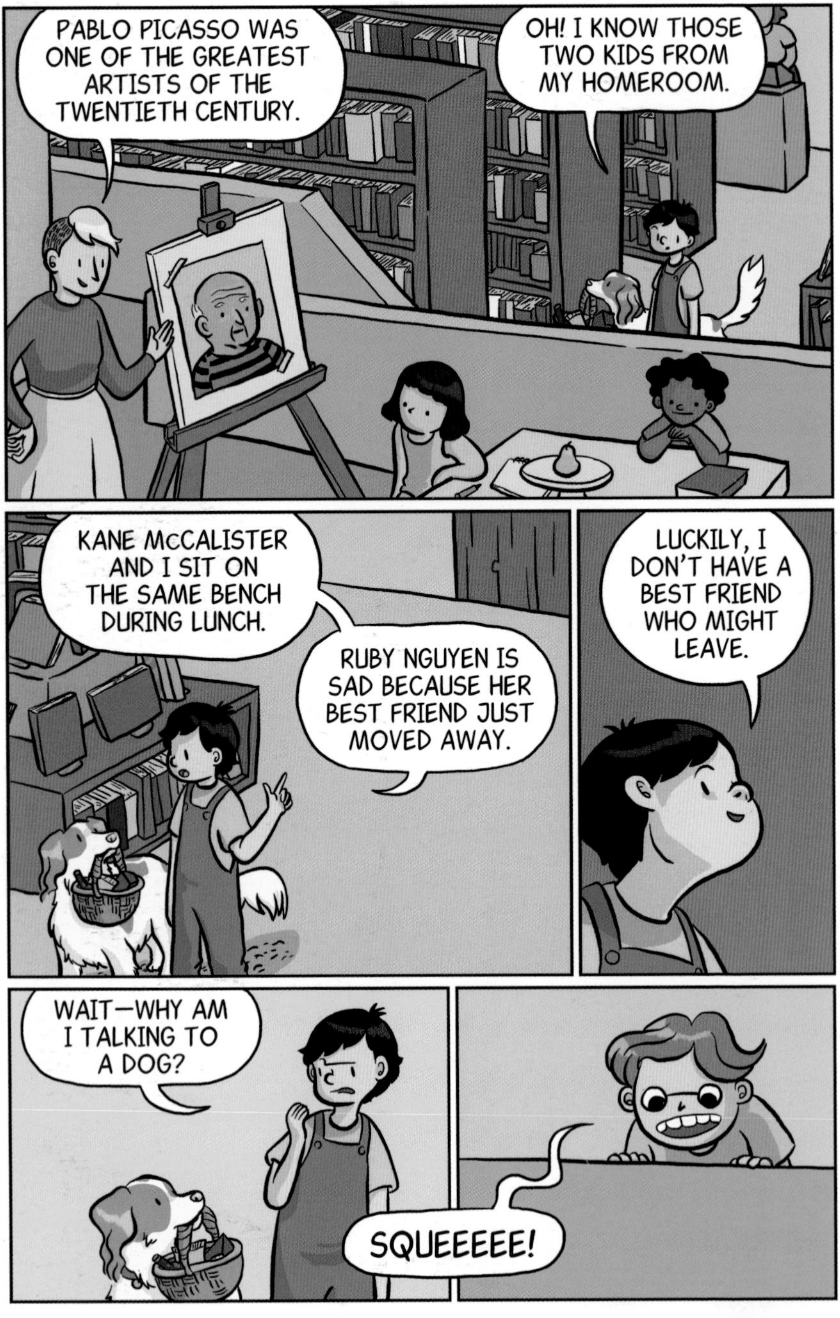
PABLO PICASSO WAS ONE OF THE GREATEST ARTISTS OF THE TWENTIETH CENTURY.
OH! I KNOW THOSE TWO KIDS FROM MY HOMEROOM.
KANE McCALISTER AND I SIT ON THE SAME BENCH DURING LUNCH.
RUBY NGUYEN IS SAD BECAUSE HER BEST FRIEND JUST MOVED AWAY.
LUCKILY, I DON'T HAVE A BEST FRIEND WHO MIGHT LEAVE.
WAIT—WHY AM I TALKING TO A DOG?
SQUEEEEEE!

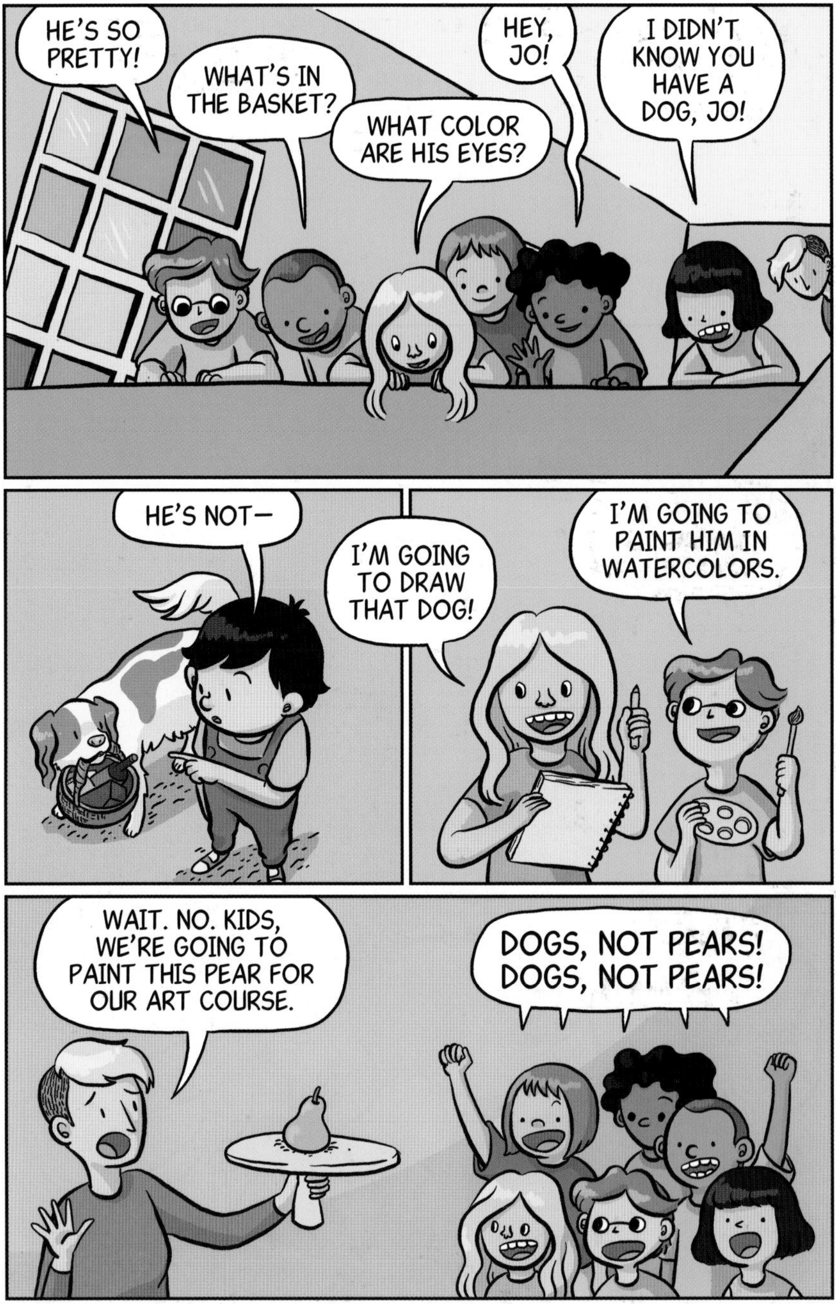
HE'S SO PRETTY!
WHAT'S IN THE BASKET?
WHAT COLOR ARE HIS EYES?
HEY, JO!
I DIDN'T KNOW YOU HAVE A DOG, JO!
HE'S NOT—
I'M GOING TO DRAW THAT DOG!
I'M GOING TO PAINT HIM IN WATERCOLORS.
WAIT. NO. KIDS, WE'RE GOING TO PAINT THIS PEAR FOR OUR ART COURSE.
DOGS, NOT PEARS! DOGS, NOT PEARS!

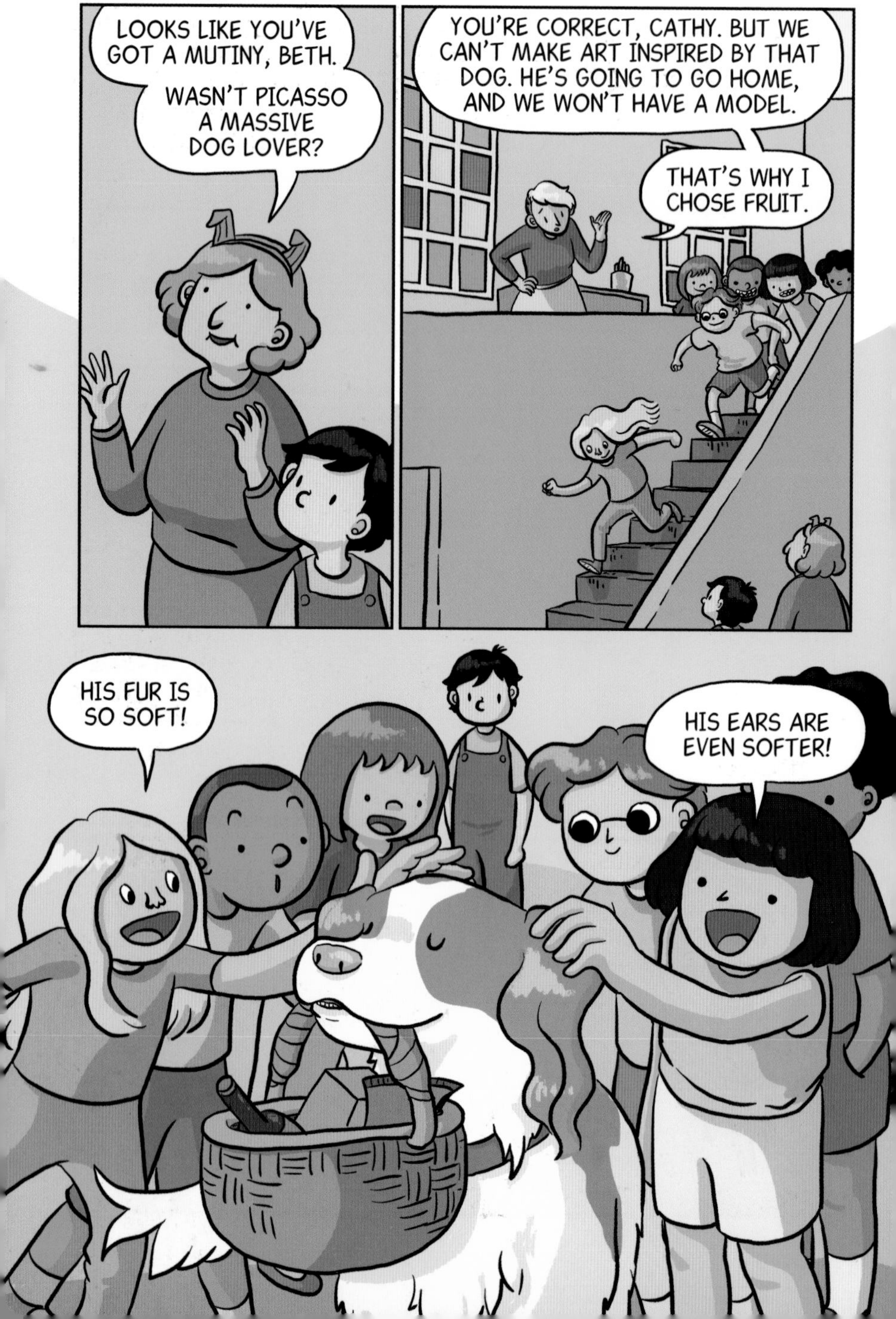
LOOKS LIKE YOU'VE GOT A MUTINY, BETH.
WASN'T PICASSO A MASSIVE DOG LOVER?
YOU'RE CORRECT, CATHY. BUT WE CAN'T MAKE ART INSPIRED BY THAT DOG. HE'S GOING TO GO HOME, AND WE WON'T HAVE A MODEL.
THAT'S WHY I CHOSE FRUIT.
HIS FUR IS SO SOFT!
HIS EARS ARE EVEN SOFTER!

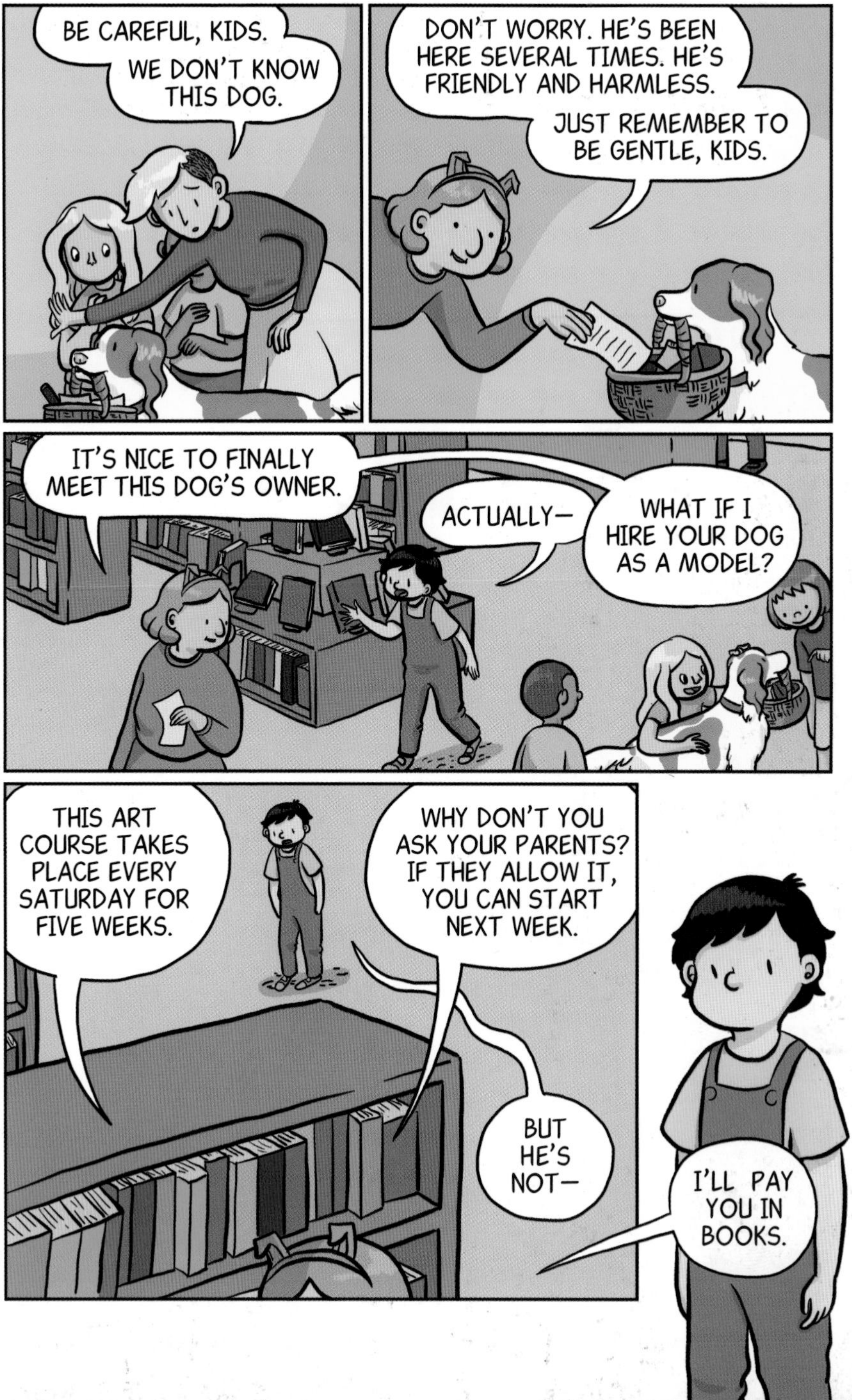
BE CAREFUL, KIDS.
WE DON'T KNOW THIS DOG.
DON'T WORRY. HE'S BEEN HERE SEVERAL TIMES. HE'S FRIENDLY AND HARMLESS.
JUST REMEMBER TO BE GENTLE, KIDS.
IT'S NICE TO FINALLY MEET THIS DOG'S OWNER.
ACTUALLY—
WHAT IF I HIRE YOUR DOG AS A MODEL?
THIS ART COURSE TAKES PLACE EVERY SATURDAY FOR FIVE WEEKS.
WHY DON'T YOU ASK YOUR PARENTS? IF THEY ALLOW IT, YOU CAN START NEXT WEEK.
BUT HE'S NOT—
I'LL PAY YOU IN BOOKS.

ONE PER ART CLASS. AND YOU'RE WELCOME TO ATTEND THE COURSE.
I'M NO PICASSO. AND THE DOG—
HERE'S THE BOOK ON YOUR GROCERY LIST. YOU HAVE GREAT TASTE IN COMICS.
THE DOG IS NOT—
JO, WHAT'S YOUR DOG'S NAME?
BYE, JO'S DOG!
WOOF!
I MEAN "WAIT!"

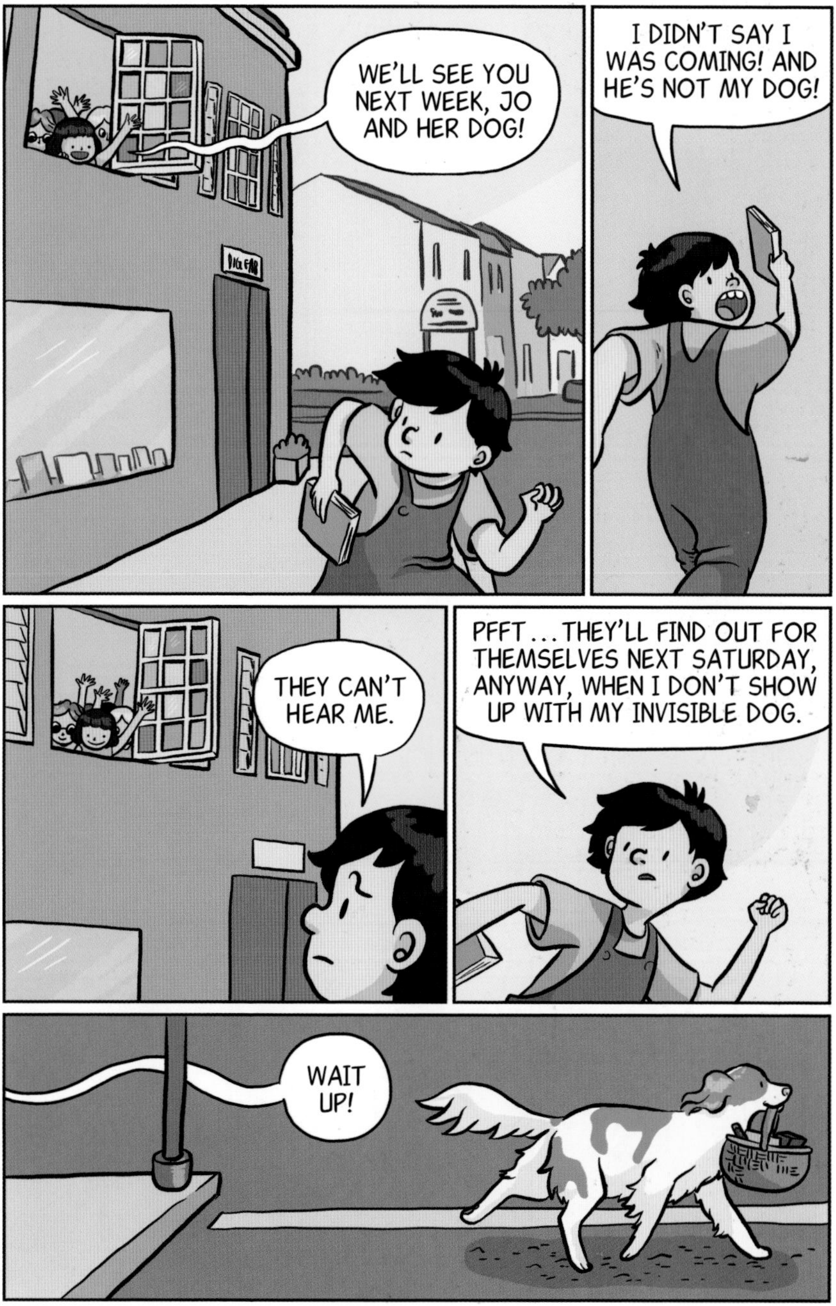
WE'LL SEE YOU NEXT WEEK, JO AND HER DOG!
I DIDN'T SAY I WAS COMING! AND HE'S NOT MY DOG!
THEY CAN'T HEAR ME.
PFFT...THEY'LL FIND OUT FOR THEMSELVES NEXT SATURDAY, ANYWAY, WHEN I DON'T SHOW UP WITH MY INVISIBLE DOG.
WAIT UP!

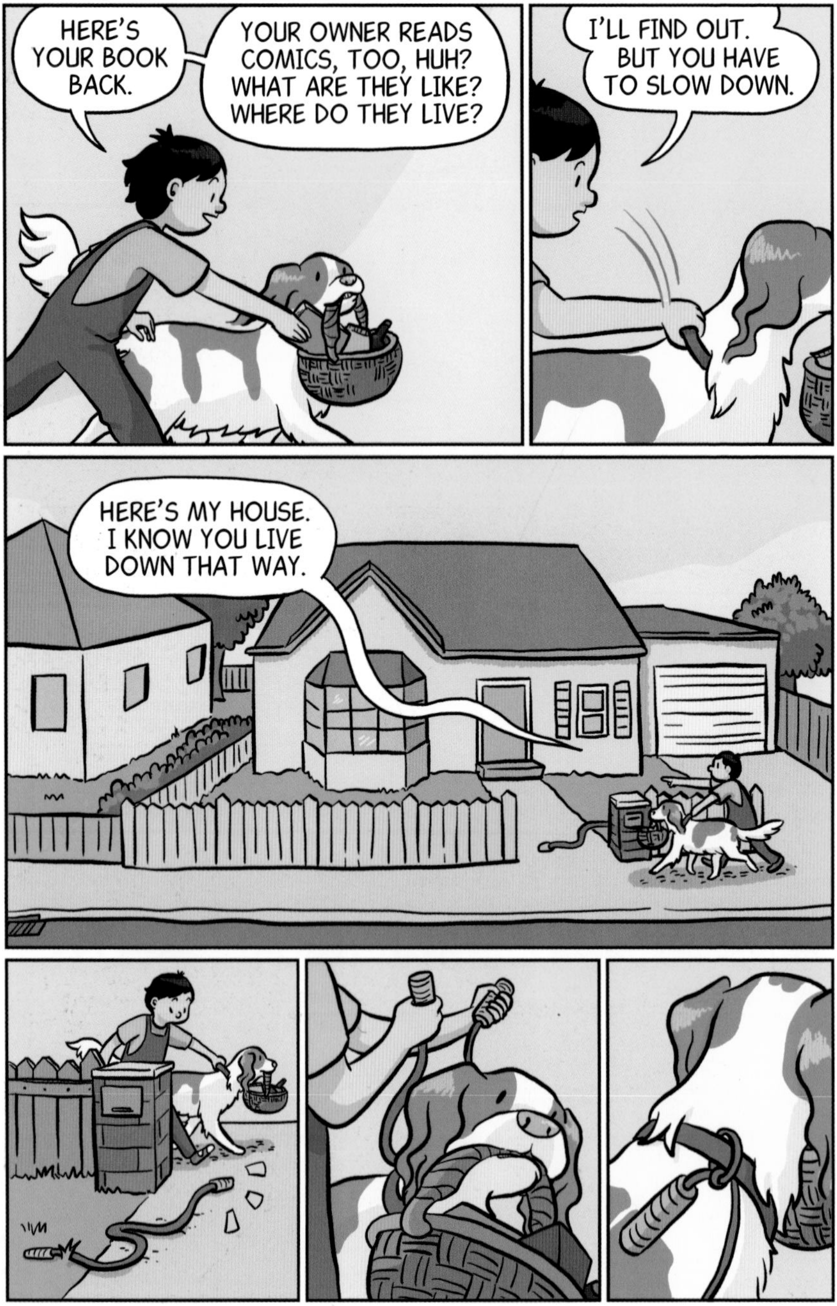
HERE'S YOUR BOOK BACK.
YOUR OWNER READS COMICS, TOO, HUH? WHAT ARE THEY LIKE? WHERE DO THEY LIVE?
I'LL FIND OUT. BUT YOU HAVE TO SLOW DOWN.
HERE'S MY HOUSE. I KNOW YOU LIVE DOWN THAT WAY.

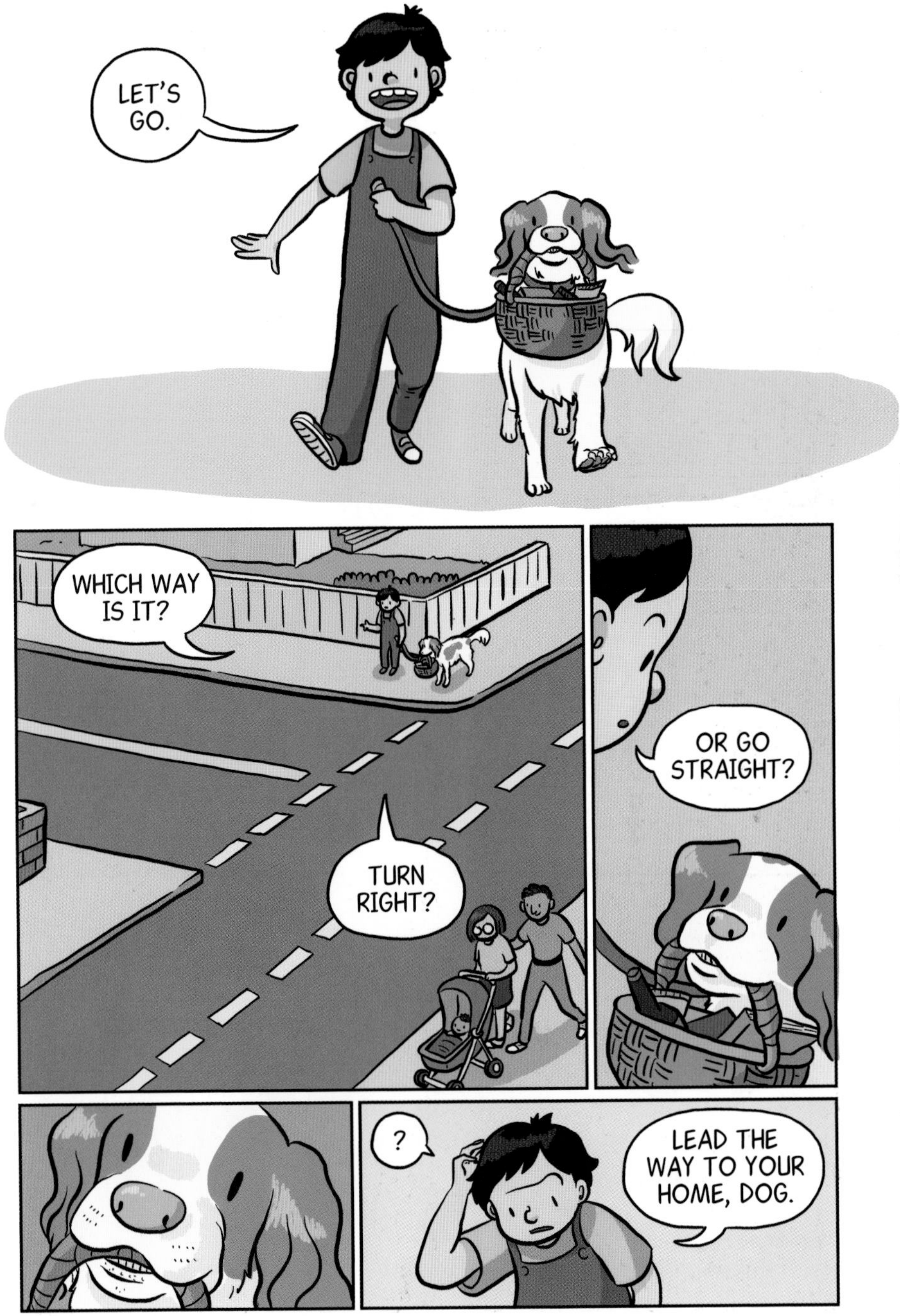
LET'S GO.
WHICH WAY IS IT?
TURN RIGHT?
OR GO STRAIGHT?
?
LEAD THE WAY TO YOUR HOME, DOG.

?

ARE YOU FOLLOWING ME BECAUSE YOU'RE LEASHED? HMM...

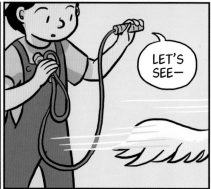

LET'S SEE—

???

MAYBE HIS NAME IS CHEETAH.

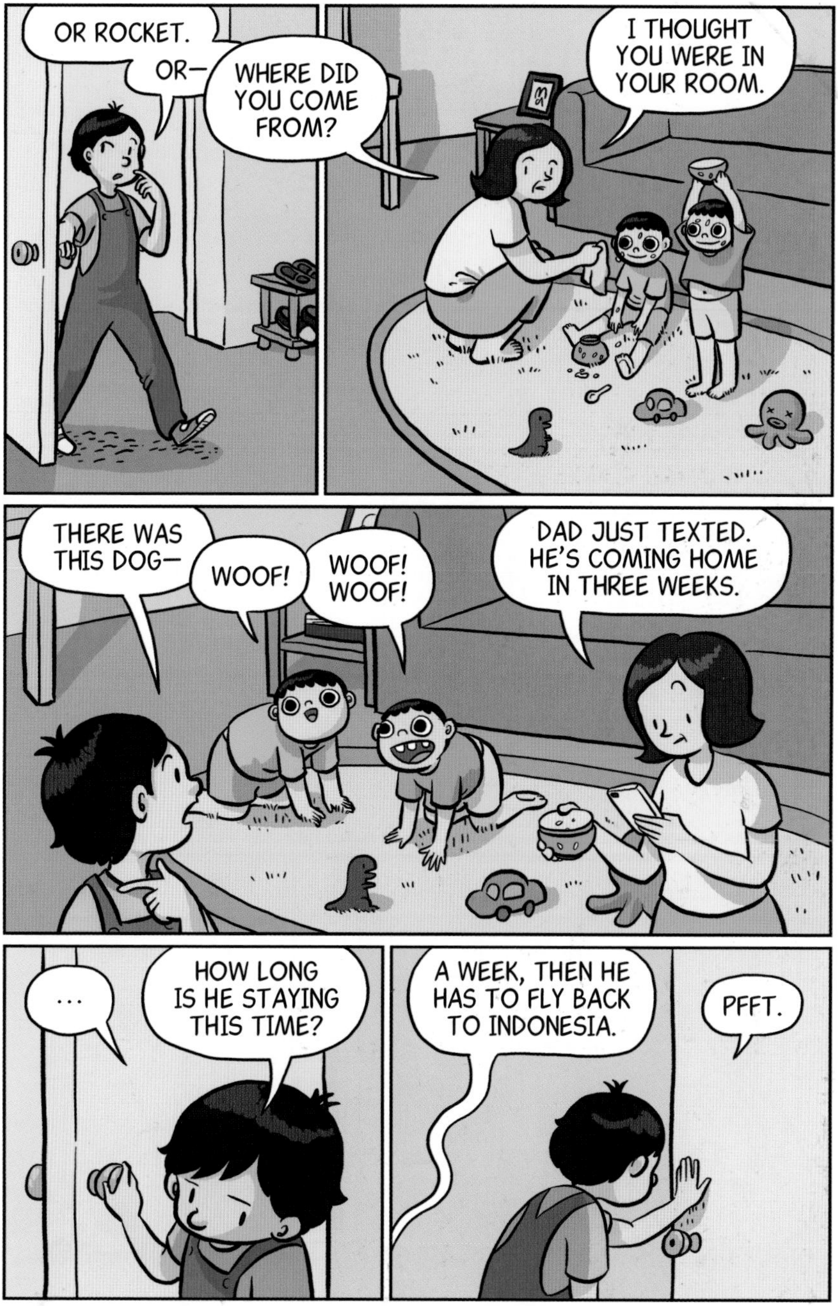
OR ROCKET.
OR—
WHERE DID YOU COME FROM?
I THOUGHT YOU WERE IN YOUR ROOM.
THERE WAS THIS DOG—
WOOF!
WOOF! WOOF!
DAD JUST TEXTED. HE'S COMING HOME IN THREE WEEKS.
...
HOW LONG IS HE STAYING THIS TIME?
A WEEK, THEN HE HAS TO FLY BACK TO INDONESIA.
PFFT.

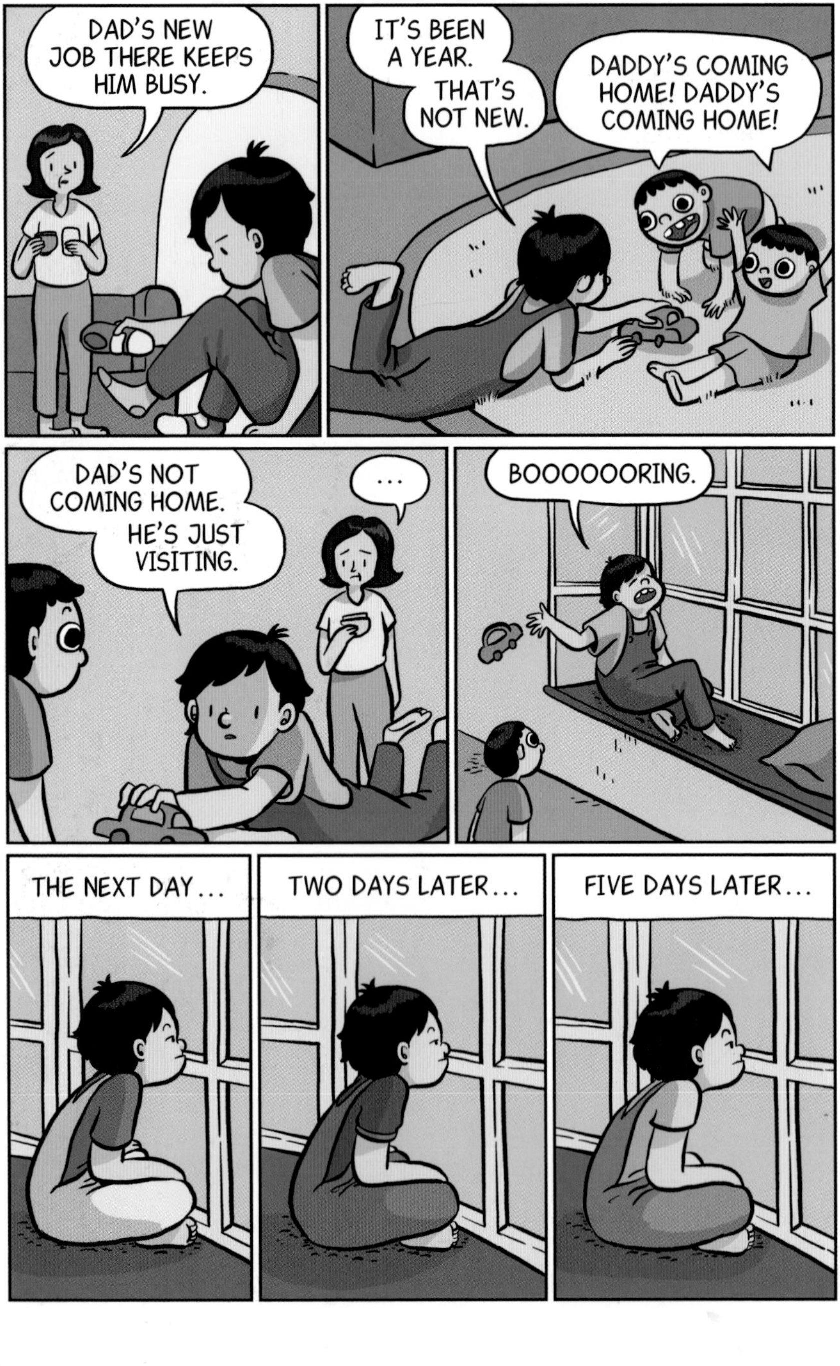
DAD'S NEW JOB THERE KEEPS HIM BUSY.
IT'S BEEN A YEAR.
THAT'S NOT NEW.
DADDY'S COMING HOME! DADDY'S COMING HOME!
DAD'S NOT COMING HOME.
HE'S JUST VISITING.
...
BOOOOOORING.
THE NEXT DAY...
TWO DAYS LATER...
FIVE DAYS LATER...

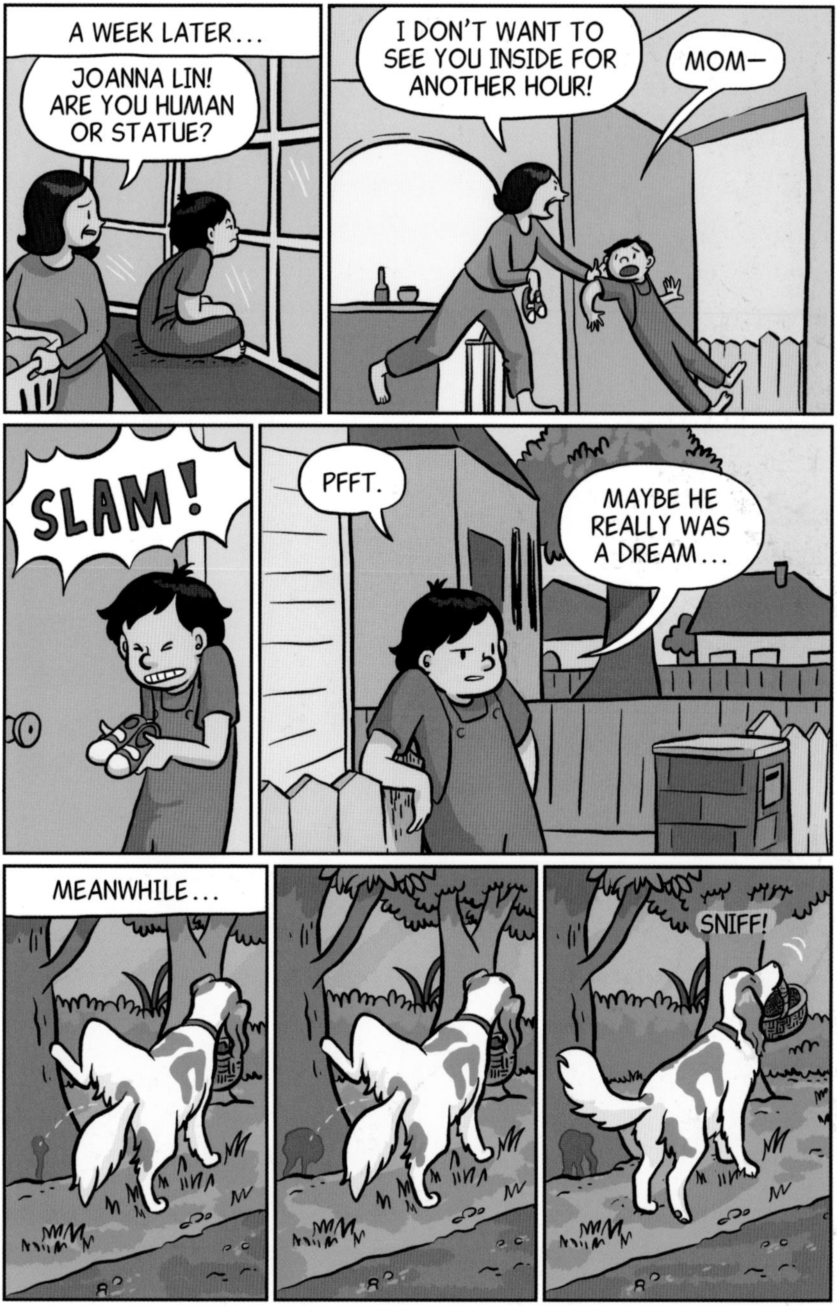
A WEEK LATER...
JOANNA LIN! ARE YOU HUMAN OR STATUE?
I DON'T WANT TO SEE YOU INSIDE FOR ANOTHER HOUR!
MOM—
SLAM!
PFFT.
MAYBE HE REALLY WAS A DREAM...
MEANWHILE...
SNIFF!

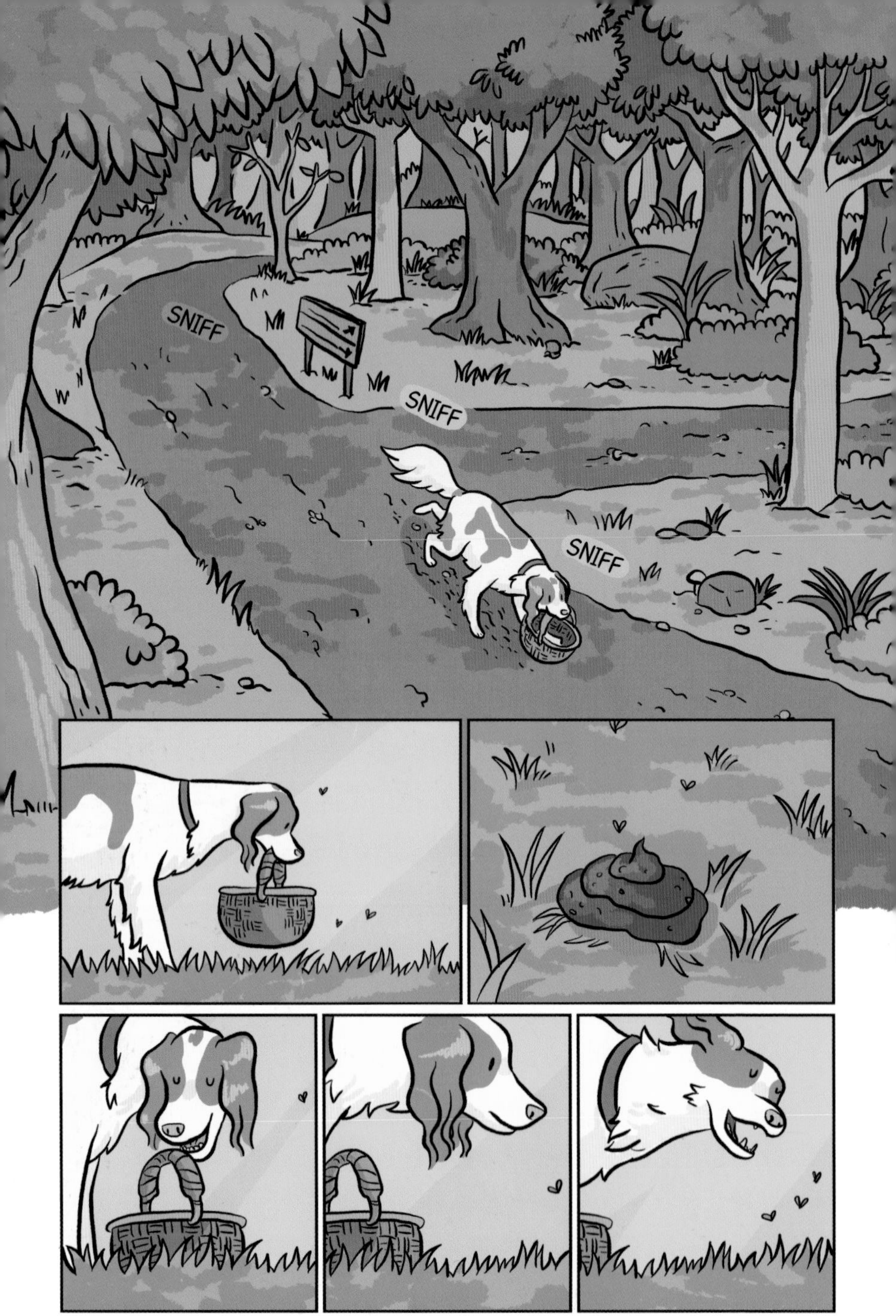
SNIFF
SNIFF
SNIFF

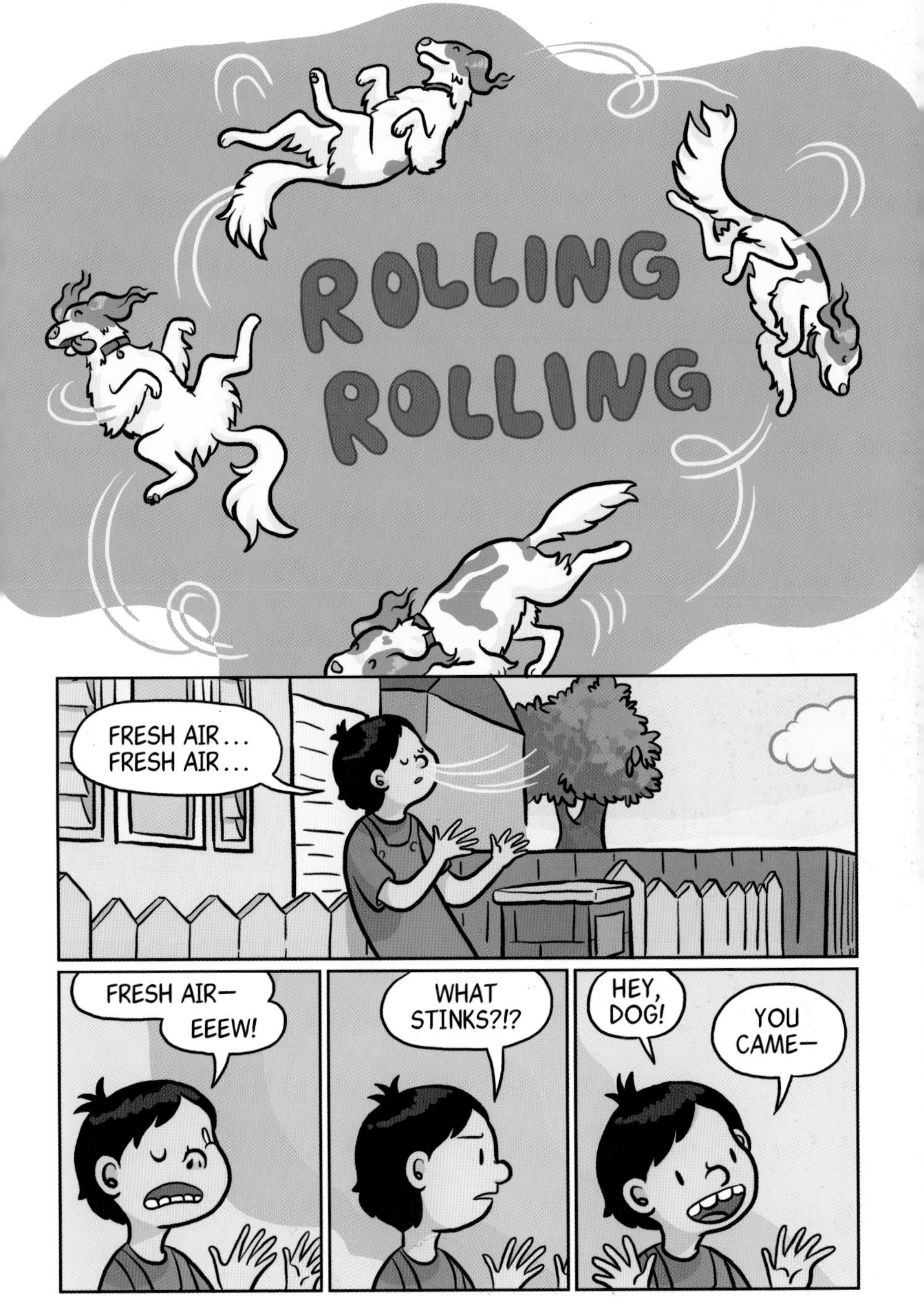
ROLLING
ROLLING
FRESH AIR...
FRESH AIR...
FRESH AIR—
EEEW!
WHAT
STINKS?!?
HEY,
DOG!
YOU
CAME—

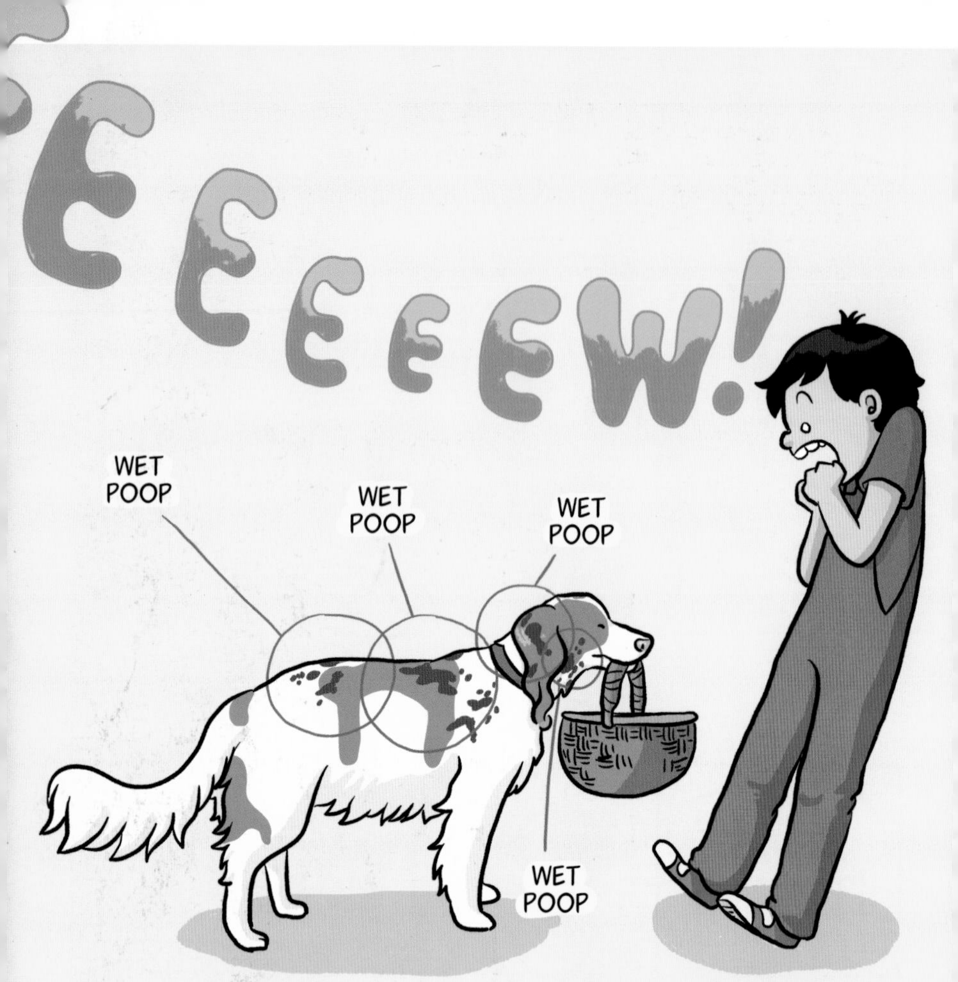
EEEEEEW!
WET POOP
WET POOP
WET POOP
WET POOP

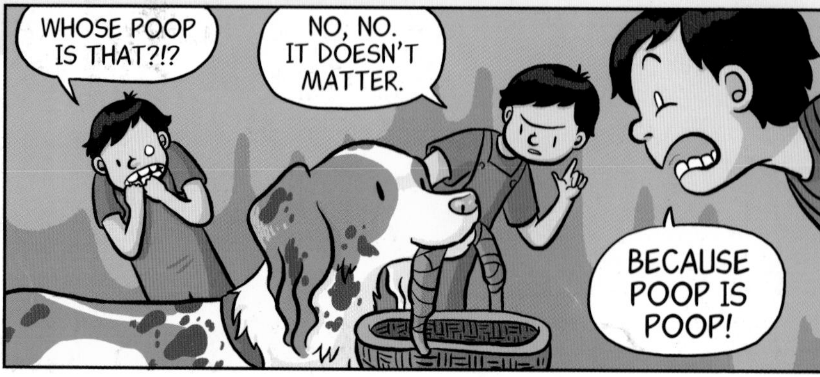
WHOSE POOP IS THAT?!?
NO, NO. IT DOESN'T MATTER.
BECAUSE POOP IS POOP!

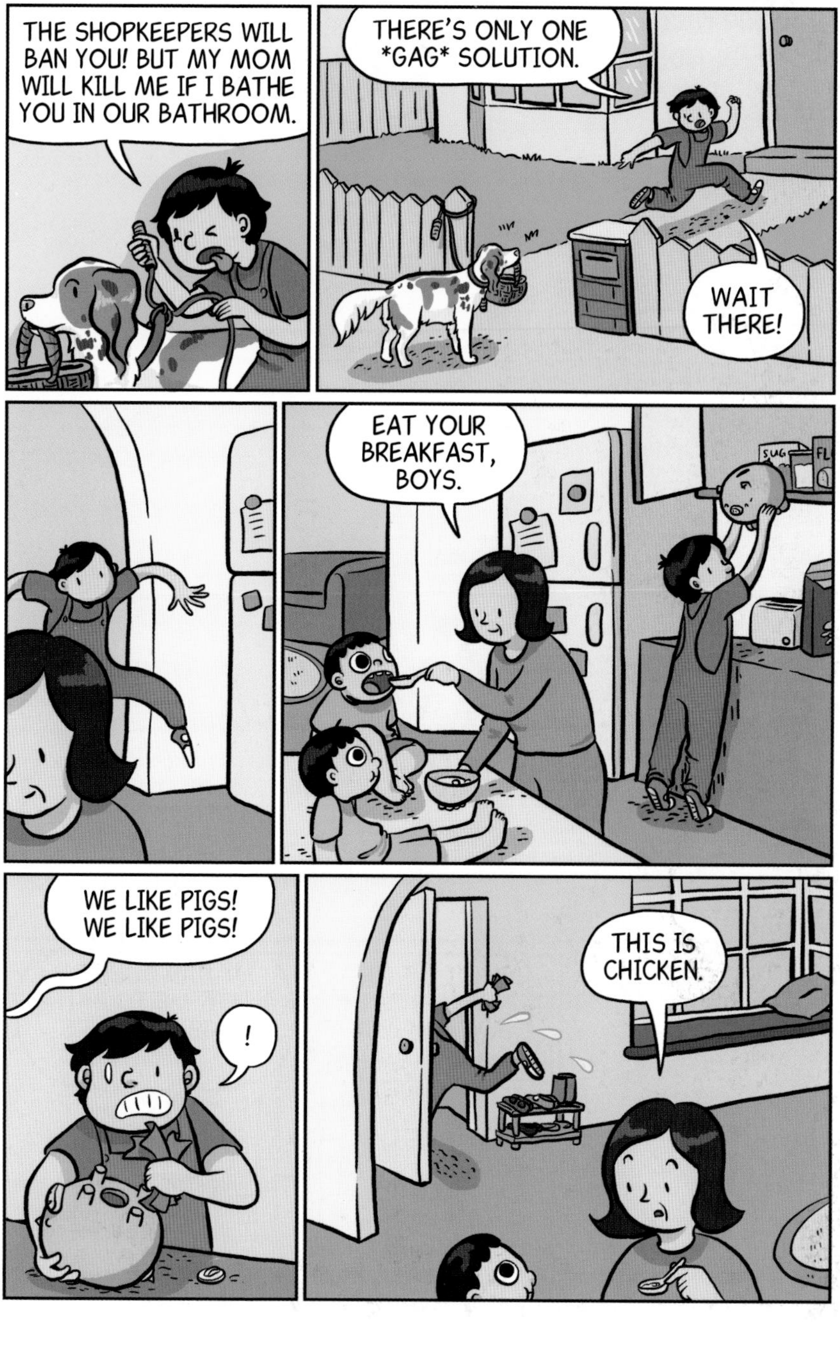

THE SHOPKEEPERS WILL BAN YOU! BUT MY MOM WILL KILL ME IF I BATHE YOU IN OUR BATHROOM.
THERE'S ONLY ONE *GAG* SOLUTION.
WAIT THERE!
EAT YOUR BREAKFAST, BOYS.
WE LIKE PIGS! WE LIKE PIGS!
!
THIS IS CHICKEN.

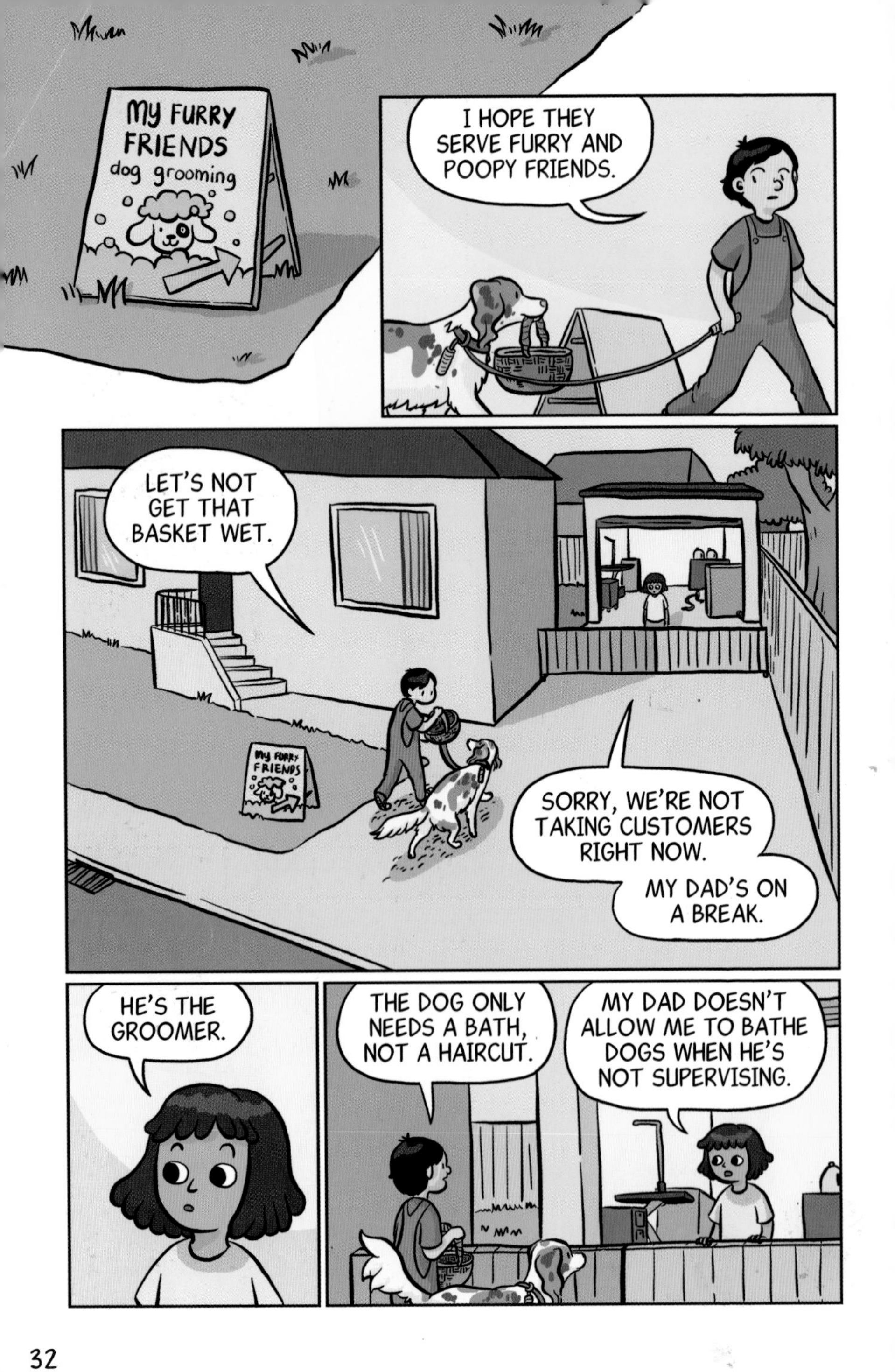
MY FURRY FRIENDS
dog grooming
I HOPE THEY SERVE FURRY AND POOPY FRIENDS.
LET'S NOT GET THAT BASKET WET.
MY FURRY FRIENDS
SORRY, WE'RE NOT TAKING CUSTOMERS RIGHT NOW.
MY DAD'S ON A BREAK.
HE'S THE GROOMER.
THE DOG ONLY NEEDS A BATH, NOT A HAIRCUT.
MY DAD DOESN'T ALLOW ME TO BATHE DOGS WHEN HE'S NOT SUPERVISING.

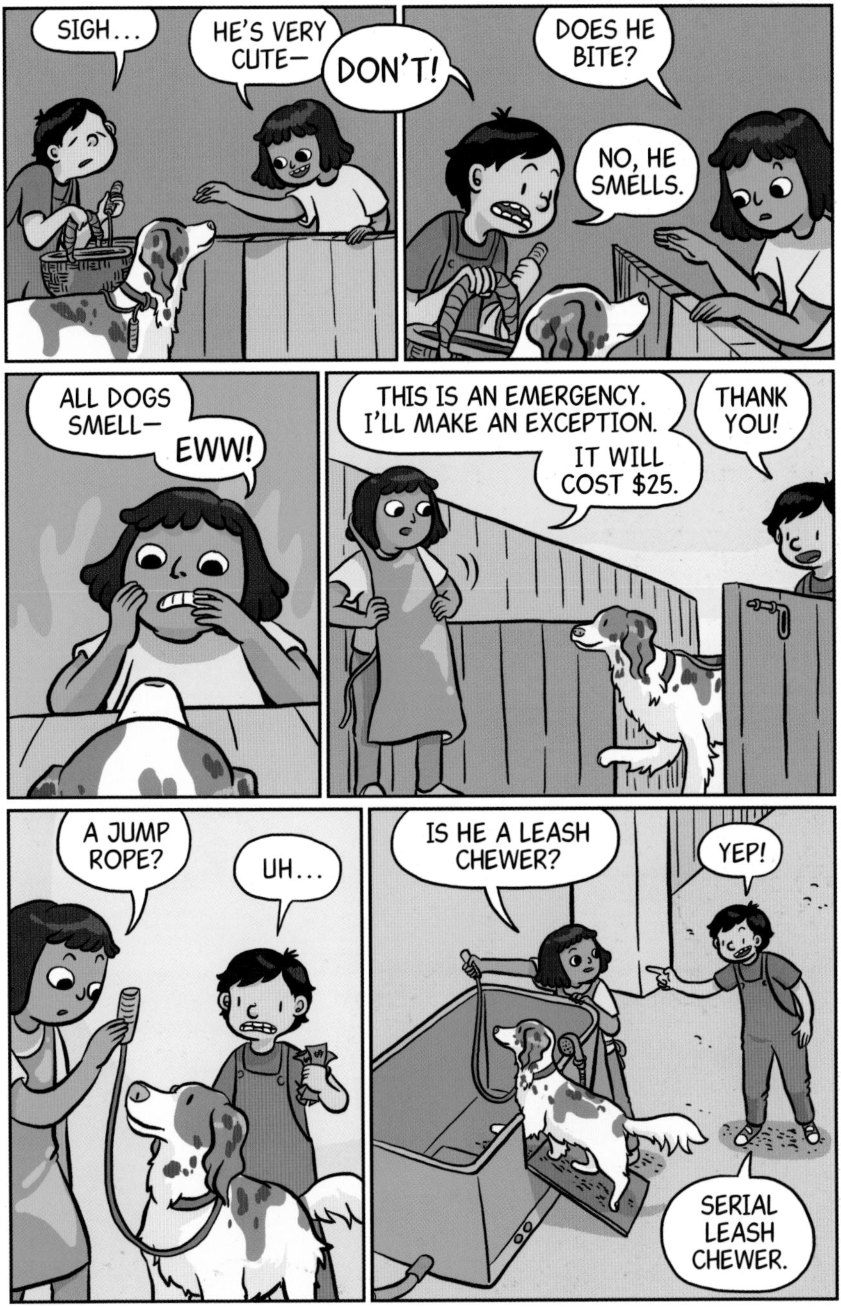
SIGH...
HE'S VERY CUTE—
DON'T!
DOES HE BITE?
NO, HE SMELLS.
ALL DOGS SMELL—
EWW!
THIS IS AN EMERGENCY. I'LL MAKE AN EXCEPTION.
IT WILL COST $25.
THANK YOU!
A JUMP ROPE?
UH...
IS HE A LEASH CHEWER?
YEP!
SERIAL LEASH CHEWER.

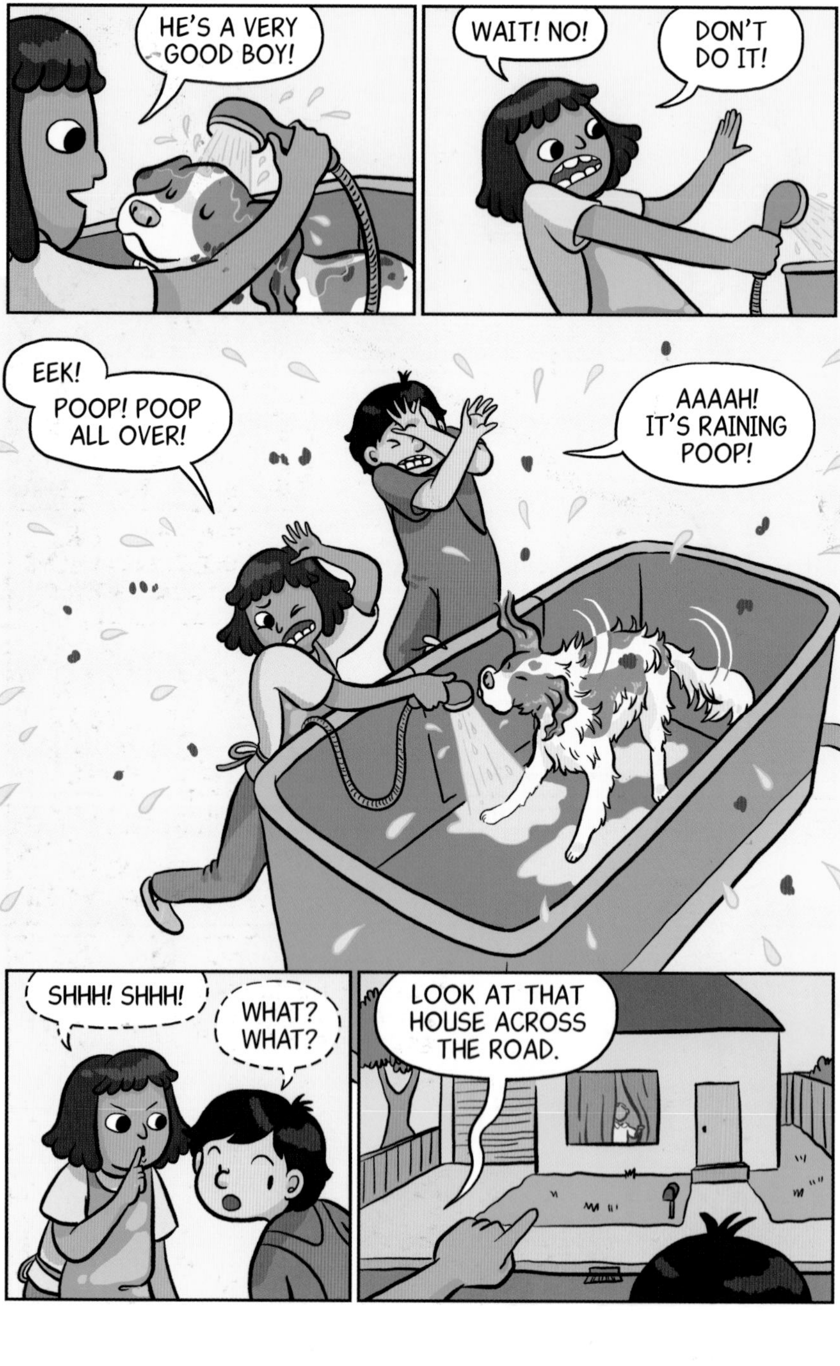
HE'S A VERY GOOD BOY!
WAIT! NO!
DON'T DO IT!
EEK!
POOP! POOP ALL OVER!
AAAAH! IT'S RAINING POOP!
SHHH! SHHH!
WHAT? WHAT?
LOOK AT THAT HOUSE ACROSS THE ROAD.

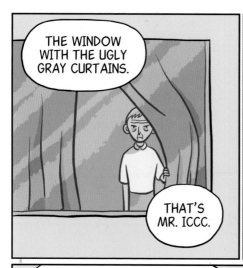

THE WINDOW WITH THE UGLY GRAY CURTAINS.

THAT'S MR. ICCC.

IT'S PRONOUNCED "ICK" BUT IT'S SPELLED I-C-C-C.

AS IN "I'LL COMPLAIN TO THE CITY COUNCIL."

THAT CRANKY MAN IS ALWAYS MAKING COMPLAINTS ABOUT MY FURRY FRIENDS.

COMPLAINTS!

YEAH, LIKE...OH, THE DOGS ARE MAKING TOO MUCH NOISE!

OH, THE DOGS SMELL LIKE WET DOGS!

OH, THEIR DOG SHAMPOOS SMELL TOO FLOWERY!

I'D LOVE TO BE A FLY ON THE WALL WHEN THE COUNCIL GETS A CALL ABOUT TWO GIRLS SCREAMING "POOP! POOP!"

HA!

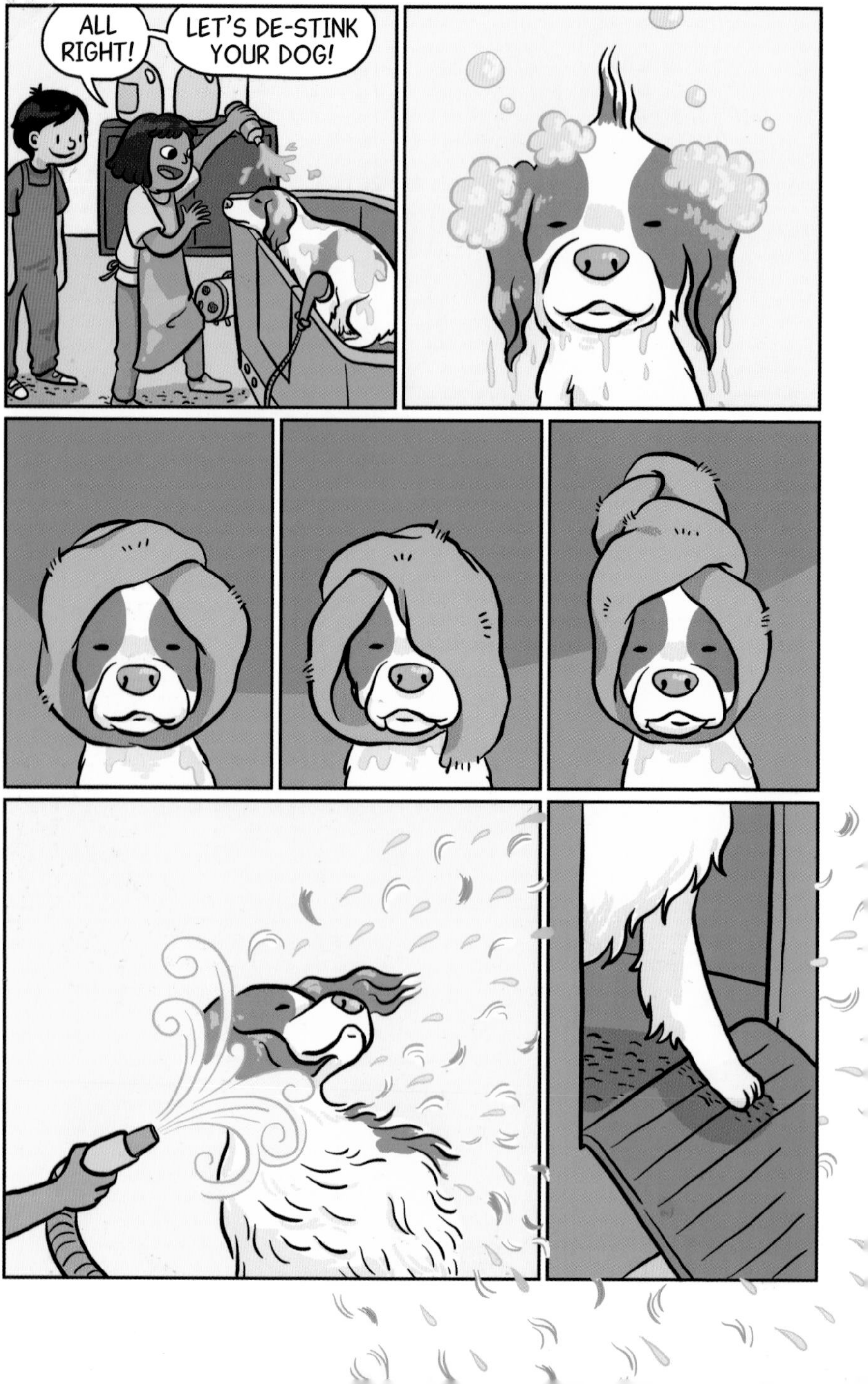
ALL RIGHT!
LET'S DE-STINK YOUR DOG!

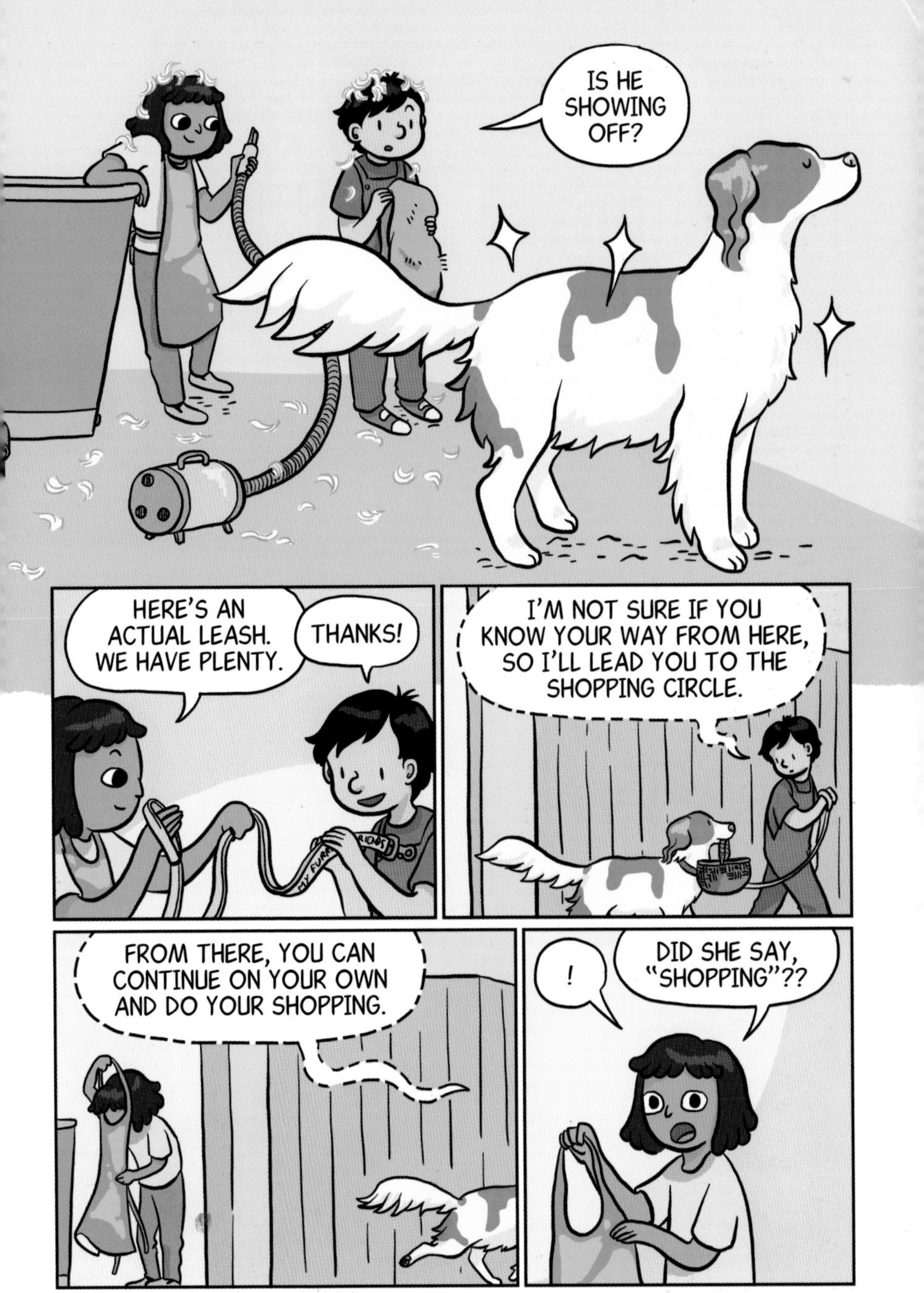
IS HE SHOWING OFF?
HERE'S AN ACTUAL LEASH. WE HAVE PLENTY.
THANKS!
I'M NOT SURE IF YOU KNOW YOUR WAY FROM HERE, SO I'LL LEAD YOU TO THE SHOPPING CIRCLE.
FROM THERE, YOU CAN CONTINUE ON YOUR OWN AND DO YOUR SHOPPING.
!
DID SHE SAY, "SHOPPING"??

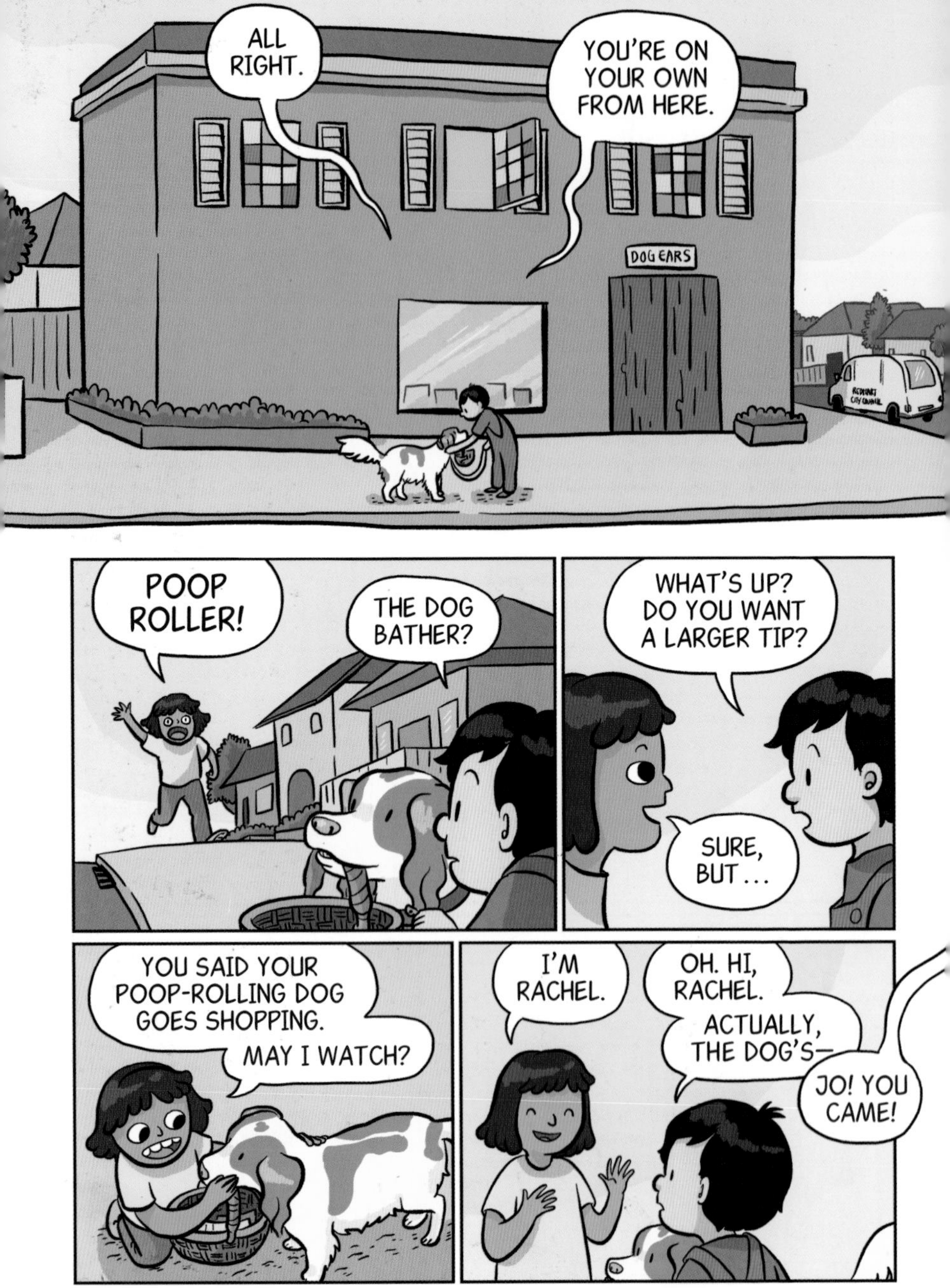
ALL RIGHT.
YOU'RE ON YOUR OWN FROM HERE.
DOG EARS
POOP ROLLER!
THE DOG BATHER?
WHAT'S UP? DO YOU WANT A LARGER TIP?
SURE, BUT . . .
YOU SAID YOUR POOP-ROLLING DOG GOES SHOPPING.
MAY I WATCH?
I'M RACHEL.
OH. HI, RACHEL.
ACTUALLY, THE DOG'S—
JO! YOU CAME!

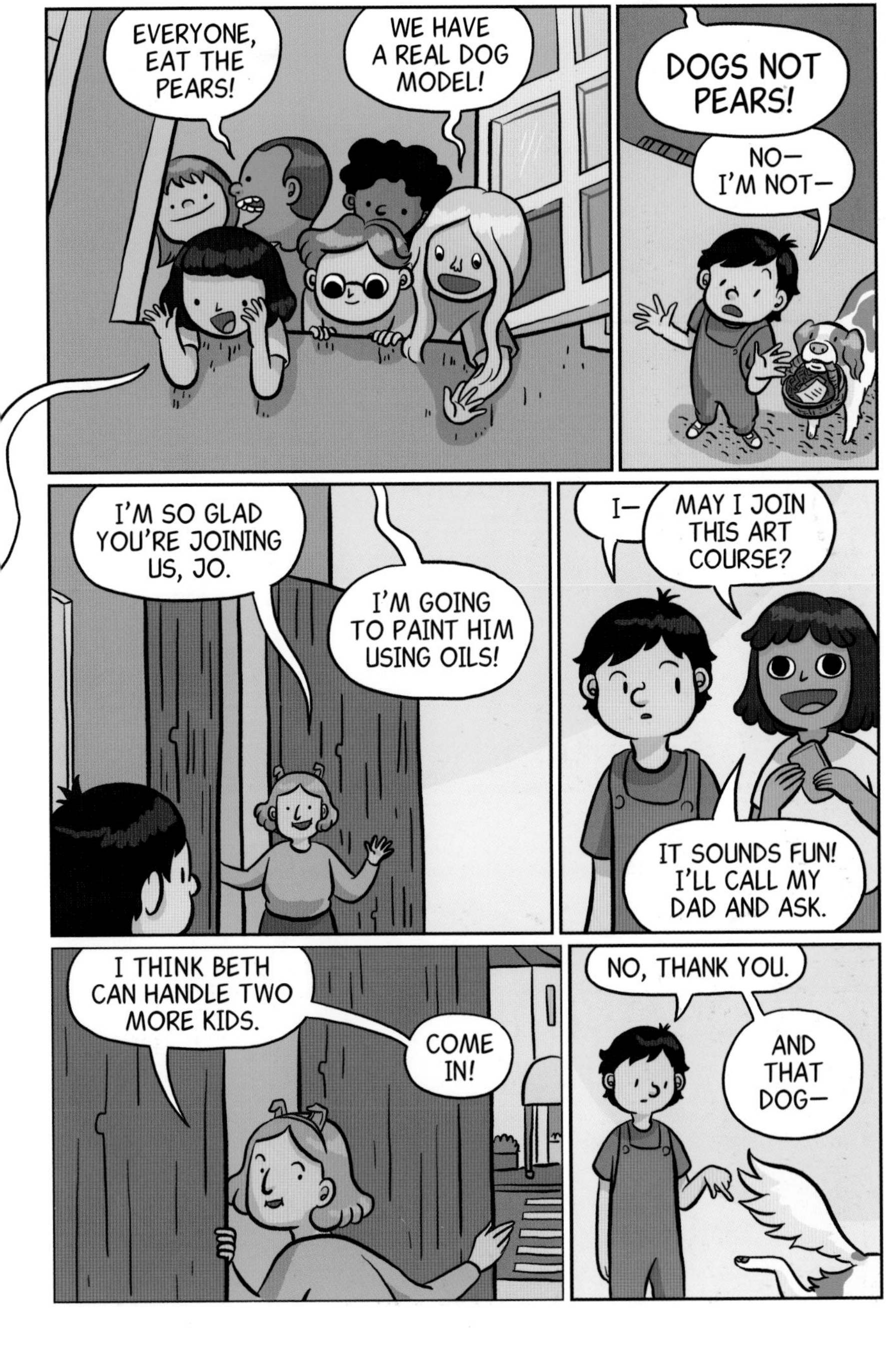
EVERYONE, EAT THE PEARS!
WE HAVE A REAL DOG MODEL!
DOGS NOT PEARS!
NO— I'M NOT—
I'M SO GLAD YOU'RE JOINING US, JO.
I'M GOING TO PAINT HIM USING OILS!
I—
MAY I JOIN THIS ART COURSE?
IT SOUNDS FUN! I'LL CALL MY DAD AND ASK.
I THINK BETH CAN HANDLE TWO MORE KIDS.
COME IN!
NO, THANK YOU.
AND THAT DOG—

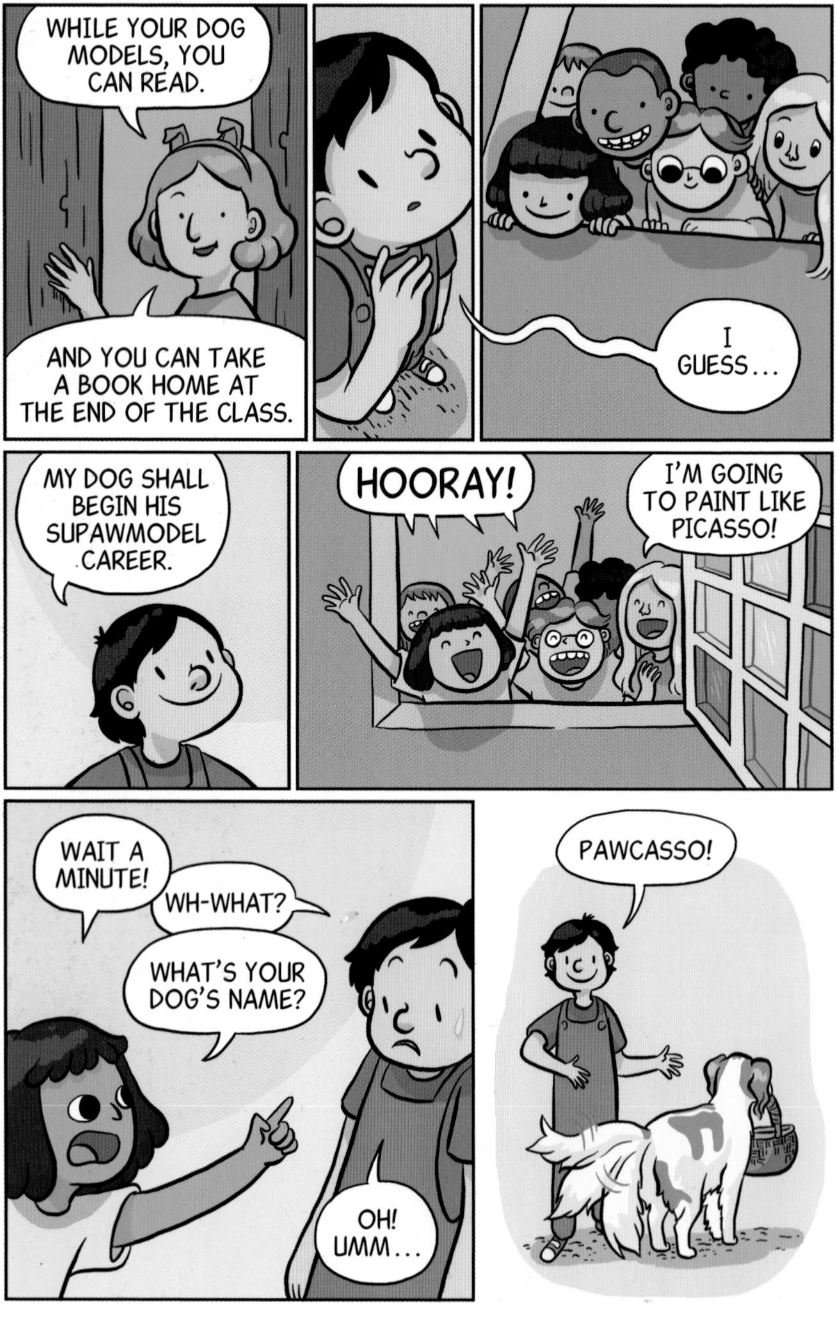
WHILE YOUR DOG MODELS, YOU CAN READ.
AND YOU CAN TAKE A BOOK HOME AT THE END OF THE CLASS.
I GUESS...
MY DOG SHALL BEGIN HIS SUPAWMODEL CAREER.
HOORAY!
I'M GOING TO PAINT LIKE PICASSO!
WAIT A MINUTE!
WH-WHAT?
WHAT'S YOUR DOG'S NAME?
OH! UMM...
PAWCASSO!

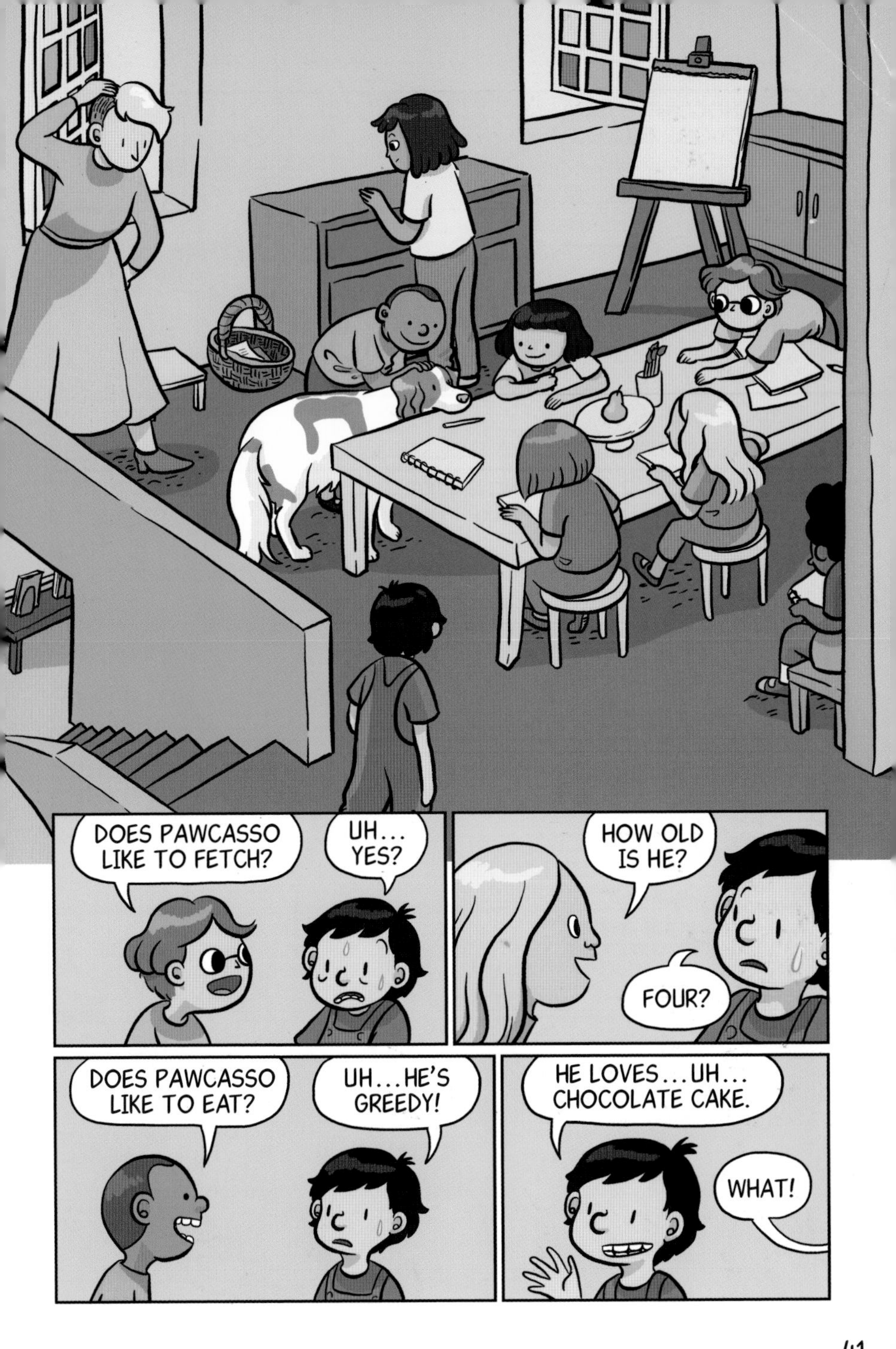
DOES PAWCASSO LIKE TO FETCH?
UH... YES?
HOW OLD IS HE?
FOUR?
DOES PAWCASSO LIKE TO EAT?
UH...HE'S GREEDY!
HE LOVES...UH... CHOCOLATE CAKE.
WHAT!

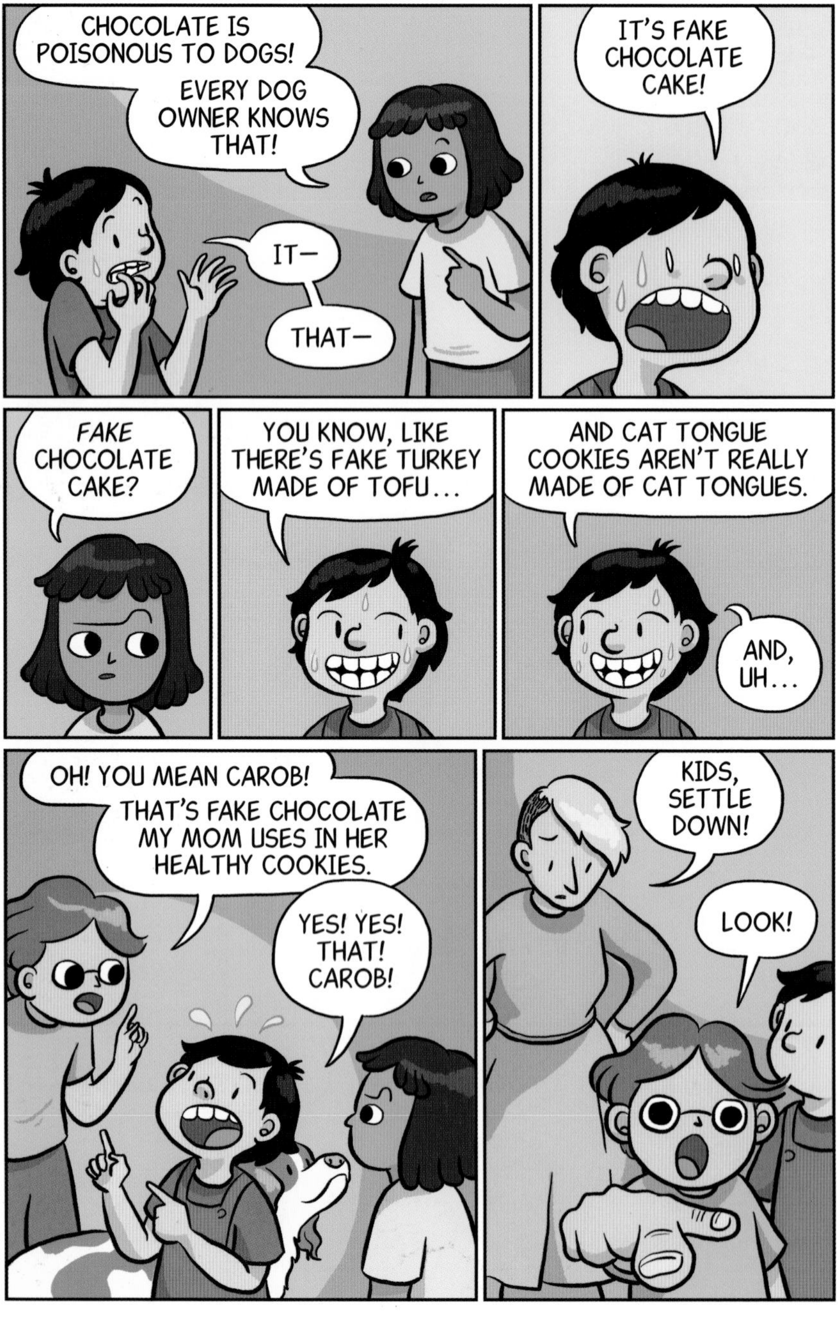
CHOCOLATE IS POISONOUS TO DOGS!
EVERY DOG OWNER KNOWS THAT!
IT—
THAT—
IT'S FAKE CHOCOLATE CAKE!
FAKE CHOCOLATE CAKE?
YOU KNOW, LIKE THERE'S FAKE TURKEY MADE OF TOFU...
AND CAT TONGUE COOKIES AREN'T REALLY MADE OF CAT TONGUES.
AND, UH...
OH! YOU MEAN CAROB!
THAT'S FAKE CHOCOLATE MY MOM USES IN HER HEALTHY COOKIES.
YES! YES! THAT! CAROB!
KIDS, SETTLE DOWN!
LOOK!

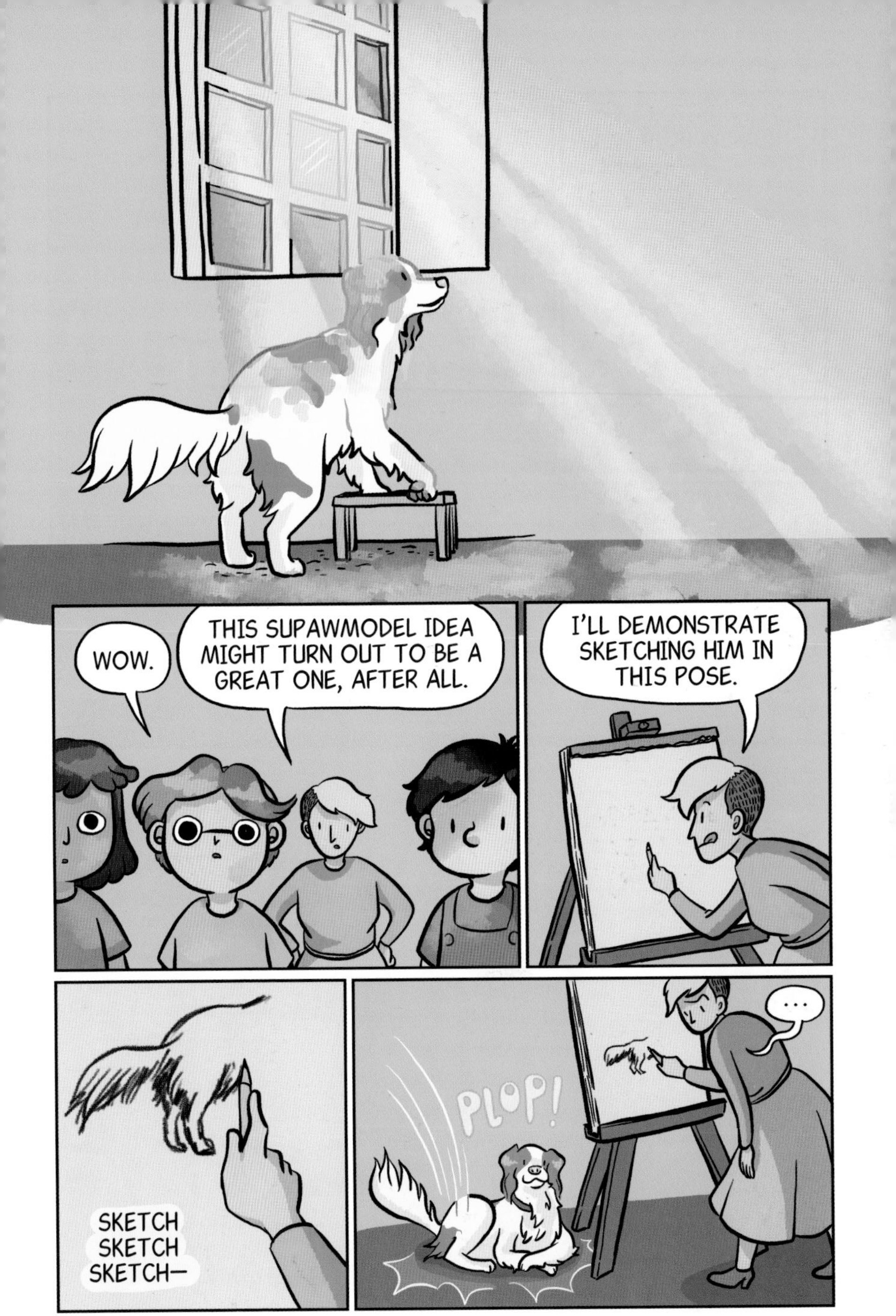
WOW.
THIS SUPAWMODEL IDEA MIGHT TURN OUT TO BE A GREAT ONE, AFTER ALL.
I'LL DEMONSTRATE SKETCHING HIM IN THIS POSE.
SKETCH SKETCH SKETCH—
PLOP!
. . .

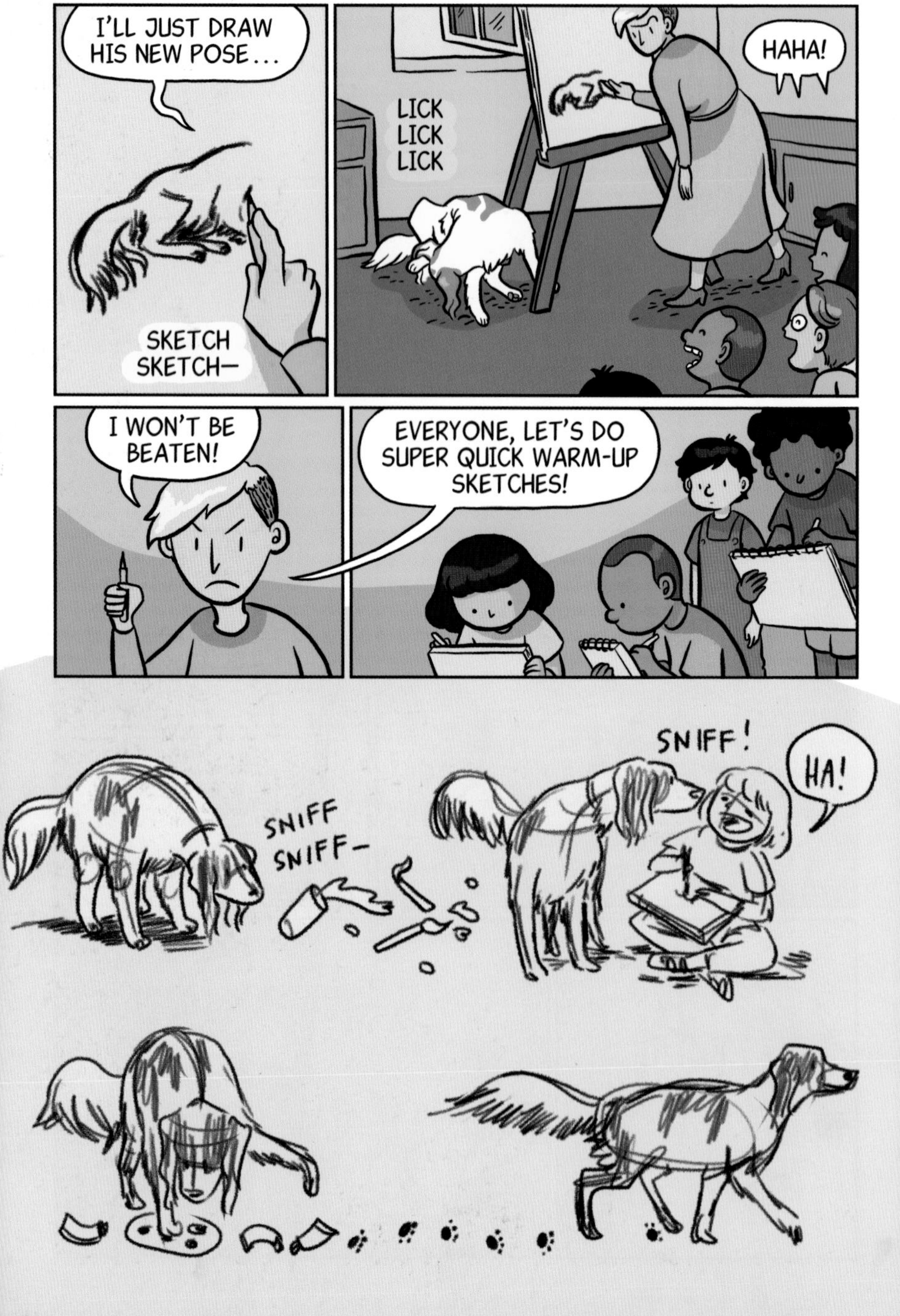
I'LL JUST DRAW HIS NEW POSE...
SKETCH SKETCH—
LICK LICK LICK
HAHA!
I WON'T BE BEATEN!
EVERYONE, LET'S DO SUPER QUICK WARM-UP SKETCHES!
SNIFF SNIFF—
SNIFF!
HA!

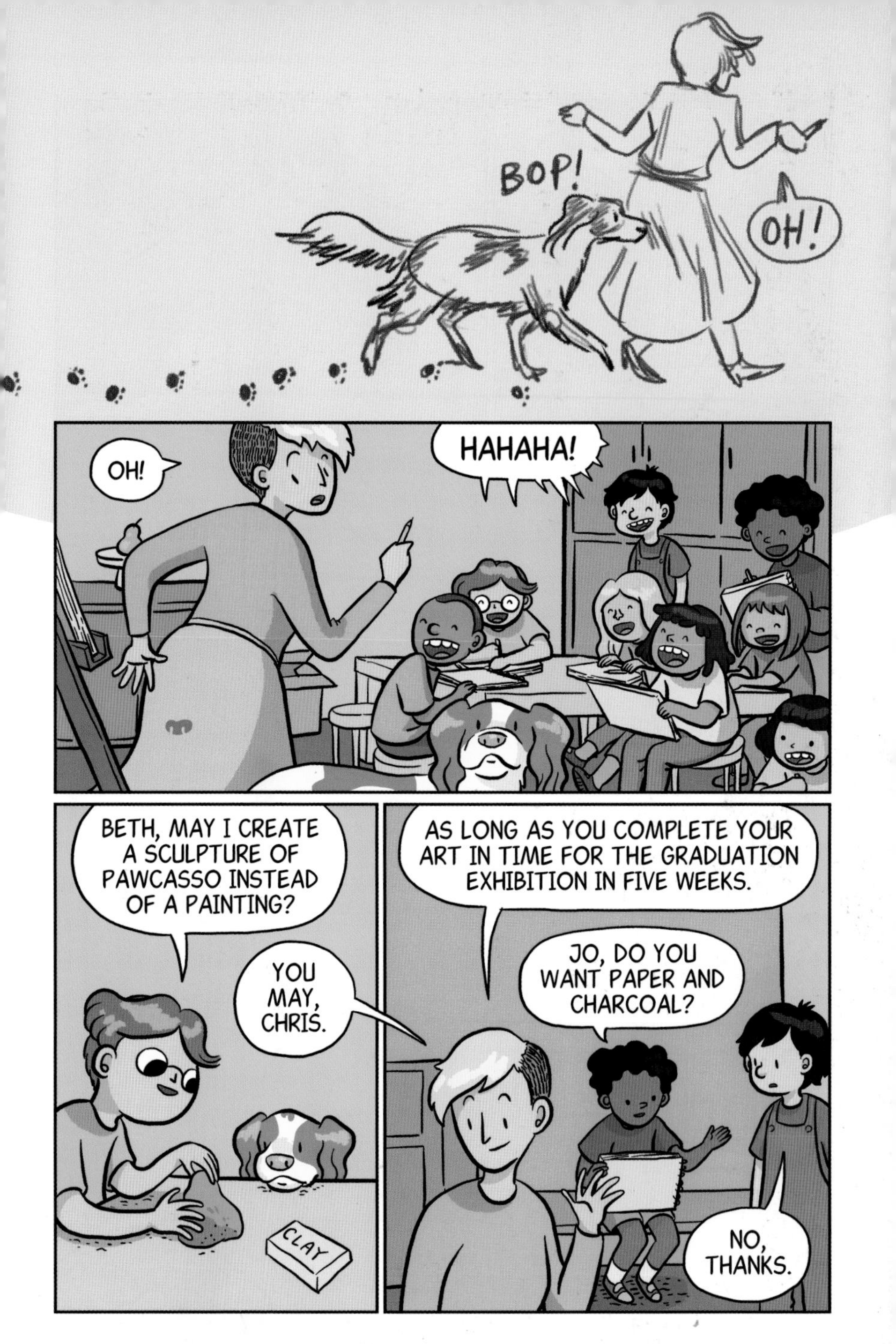
BOP!
OH!
OH!
HAHAHA!
BETH, MAY I CREATE A SCULPTURE OF PAWCASSO INSTEAD OF A PAINTING?
YOU MAY, CHRIS.
CLAY
AS LONG AS YOU COMPLETE YOUR ART IN TIME FOR THE GRADUATION EXHIBITION IN FIVE WEEKS.
JO, DO YOU WANT PAPER AND CHARCOAL?
NO, THANKS.

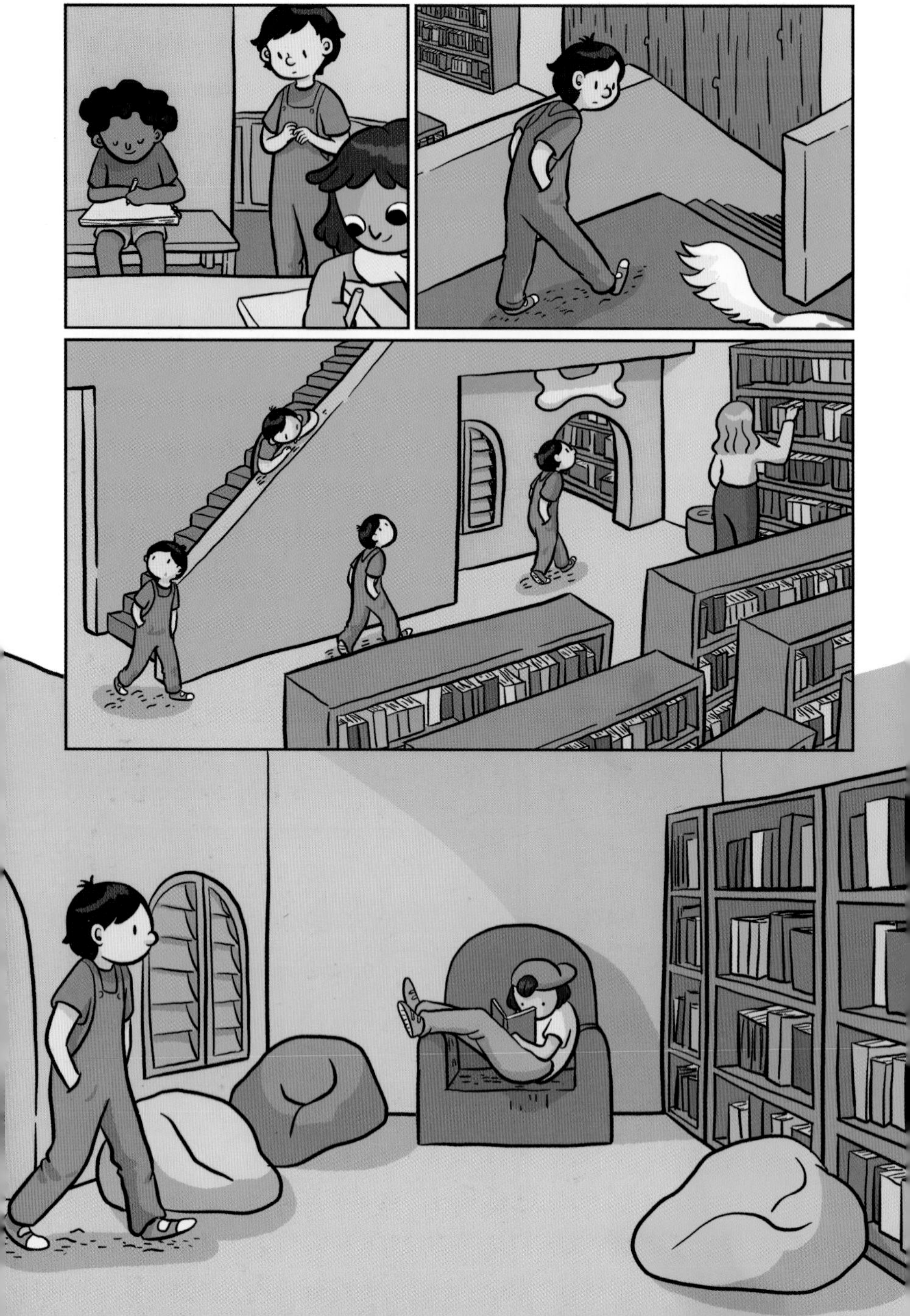

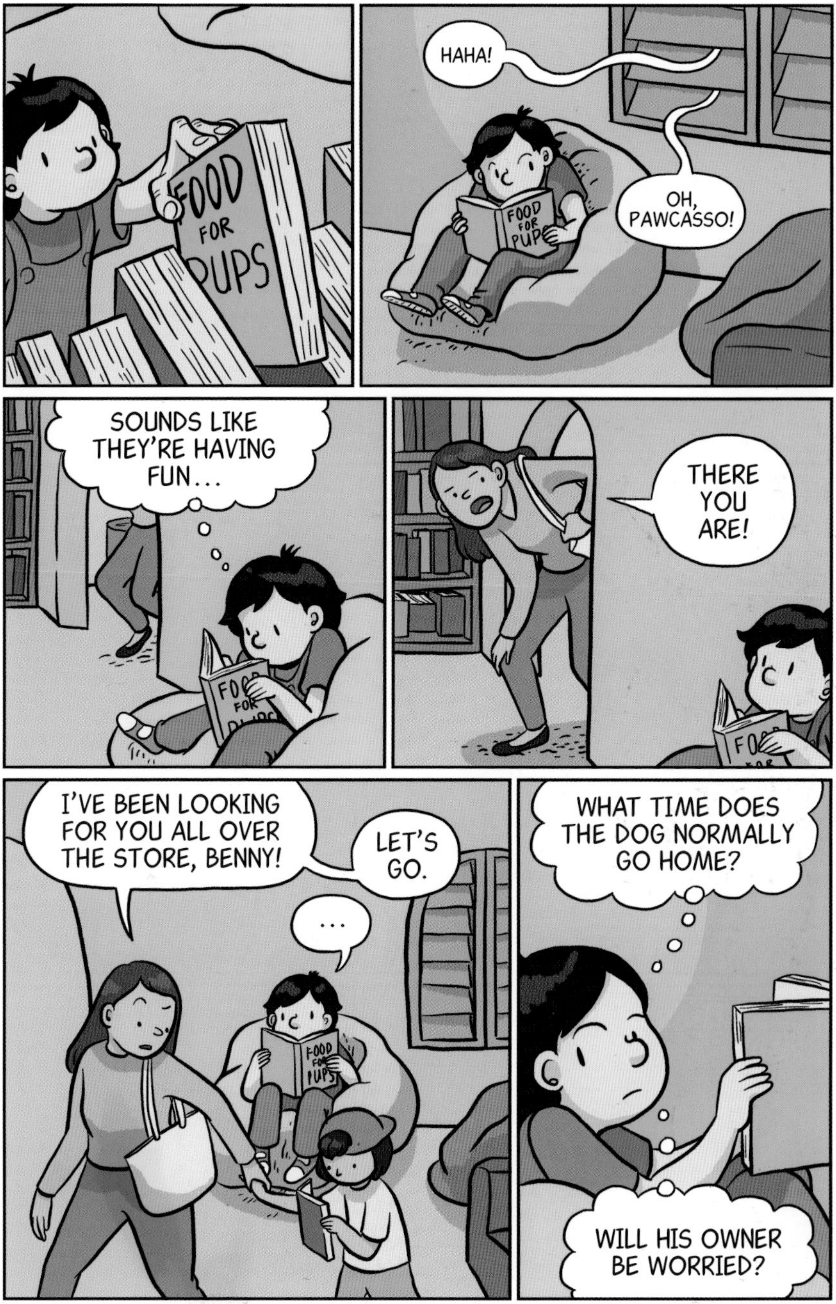
FOOD FOR PUPS
HAHA!
OH, PAWCASSO!
FOOD FOR PUPS
SOUNDS LIKE THEY'RE HAVING FUN...
THERE YOU ARE!
I'VE BEEN LOOKING FOR YOU ALL OVER THE STORE, BENNY!
LET'S GO.
...
FOOD FOR PUPS
WHAT TIME DOES THE DOG NORMALLY GO HOME?
WILL HIS OWNER BE WORRIED?

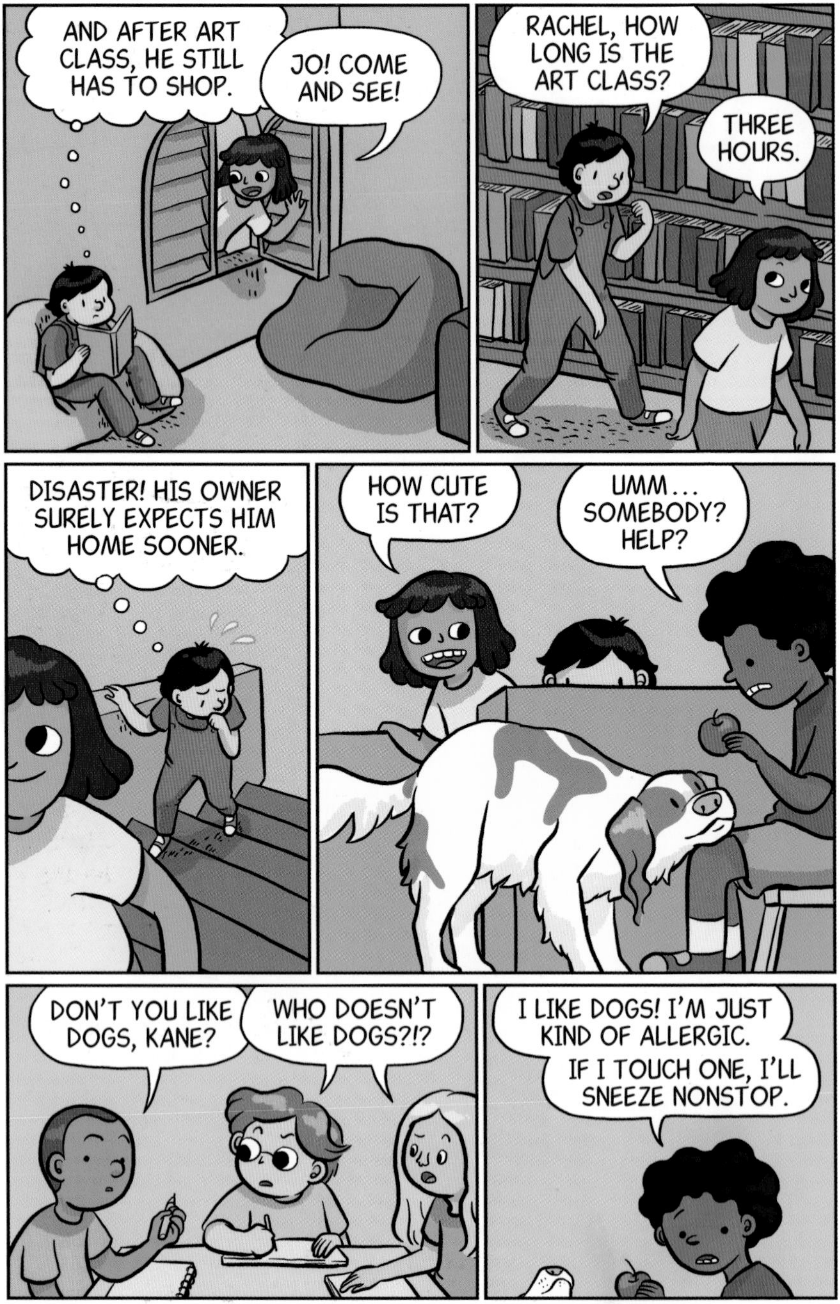
AND AFTER ART CLASS, HE STILL HAS TO SHOP.
JO! COME AND SEE!
RACHEL, HOW LONG IS THE ART CLASS?
THREE HOURS.
DISASTER! HIS OWNER SURELY EXPECTS HIM HOME SOONER.
HOW CUTE IS THAT?
UMM... SOMEBODY? HELP?
DON'T YOU LIKE DOGS, KANE?
WHO DOESN'T LIKE DOGS?!?
I LIKE DOGS! I'M JUST KIND OF ALLERGIC.
IF I TOUCH ONE, I'LL SNEEZE NONSTOP.

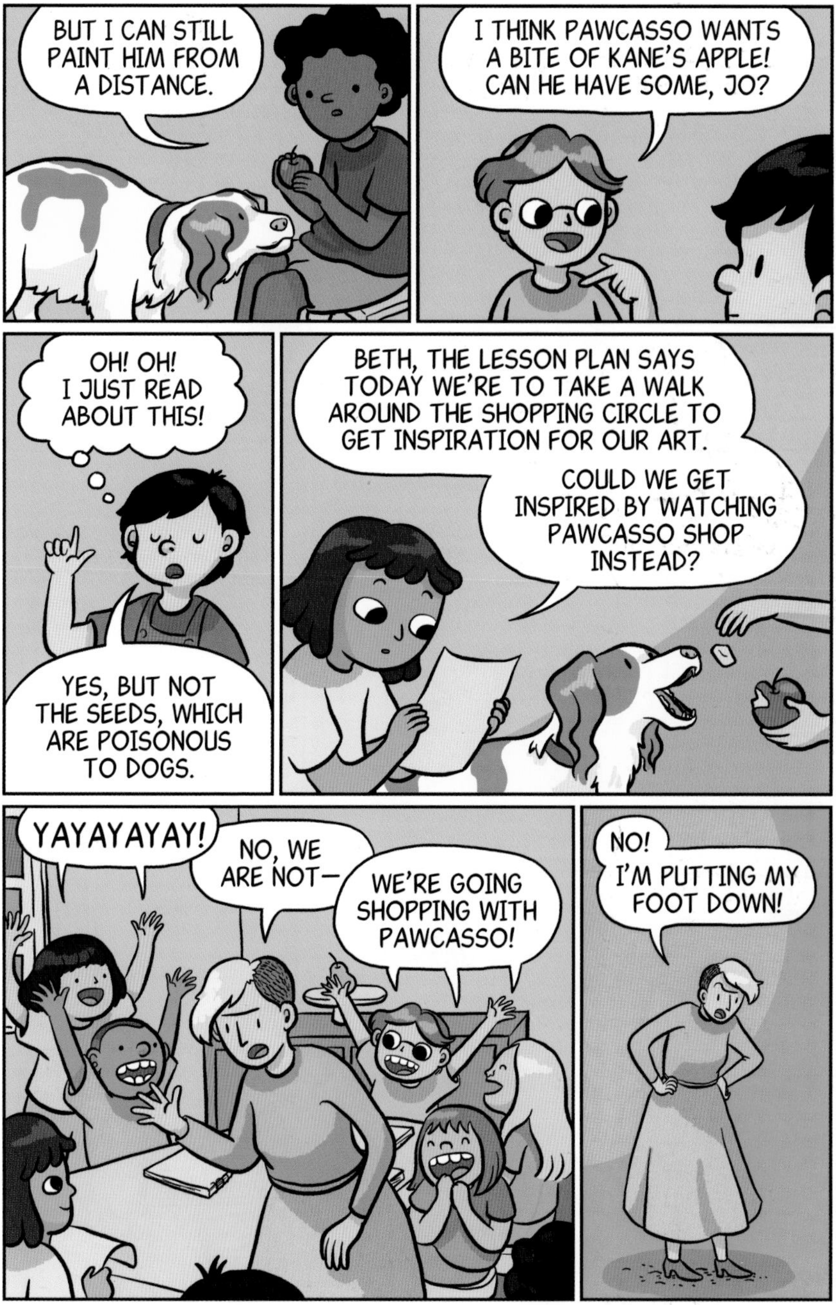
BUT I CAN STILL PAINT HIM FROM A DISTANCE.
I THINK PAWCASSO WANTS A BITE OF KANE'S APPLE! CAN HE HAVE SOME, JO?
OH! OH! I JUST READ ABOUT THIS!
YES, BUT NOT THE SEEDS, WHICH ARE POISONOUS TO DOGS.
BETH, THE LESSON PLAN SAYS TODAY WE'RE TO TAKE A WALK AROUND THE SHOPPING CIRCLE TO GET INSPIRATION FOR OUR ART.
COULD WE GET INSPIRED BY WATCHING PAWCASSO SHOP INSTEAD?
YAYAYAYAY!
NO, WE ARE NOT—
WE'RE GOING SHOPPING WITH PAWCASSO!
NO!
I'M PUTTING MY FOOT DOWN!

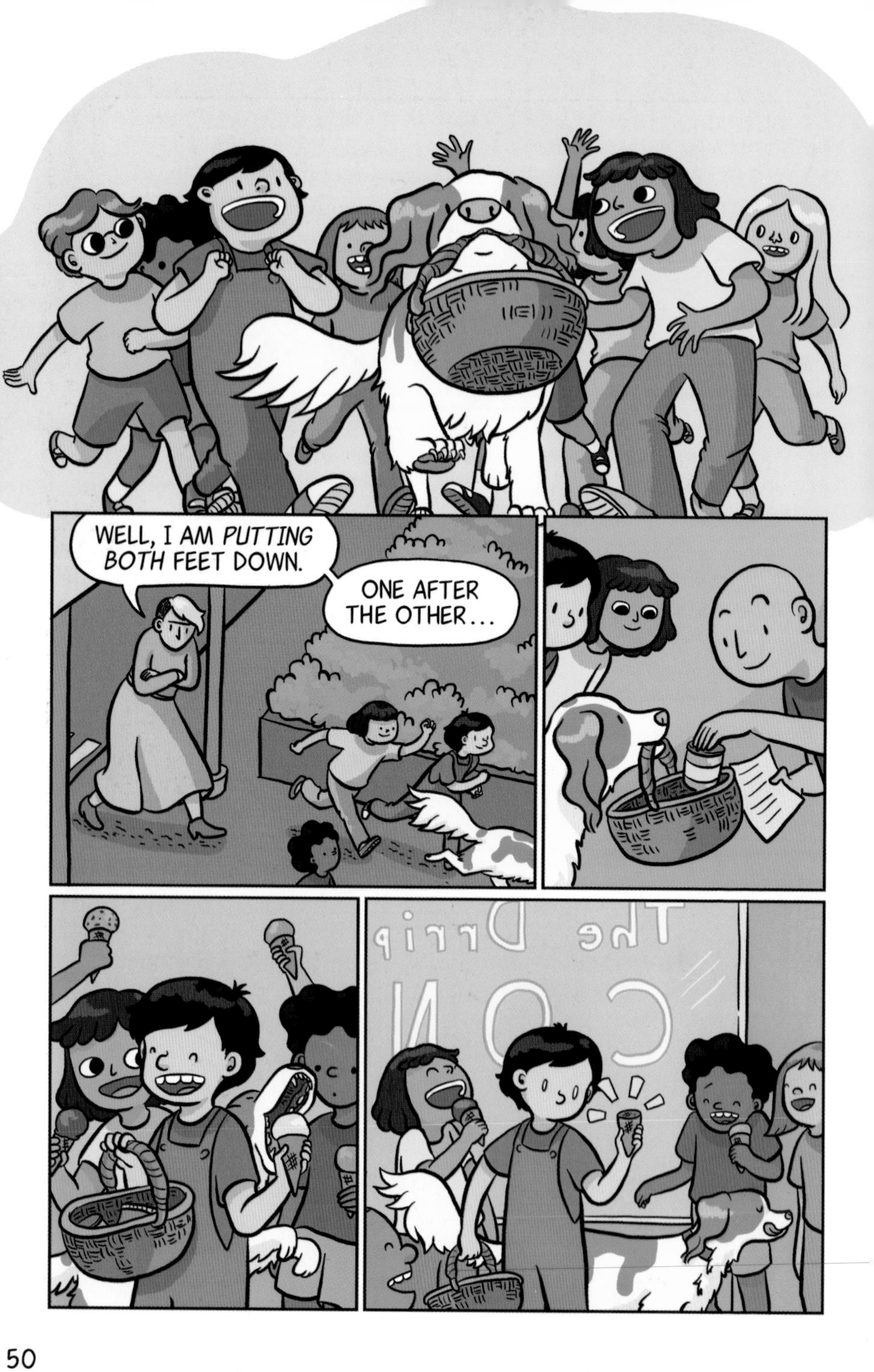
WELL, I AM *PUTTING* *BOTH* FEET DOWN.
ONE AFTER THE OTHER...

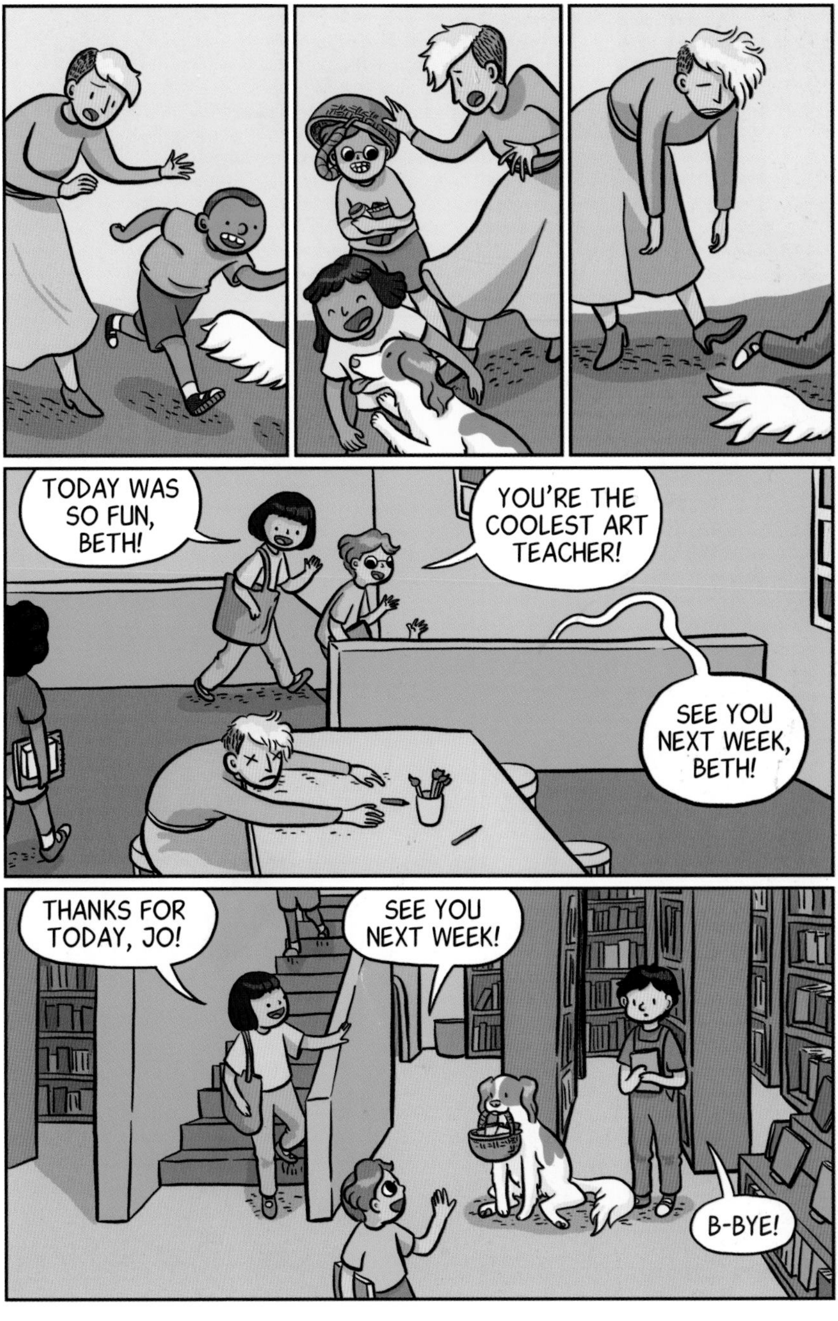
TODAY WAS SO FUN, BETH!
YOU'RE THE COOLEST ART TEACHER!
SEE YOU NEXT WEEK, BETH!
THANKS FOR TODAY, JO!
SEE YOU NEXT WEEK!
B-BYE!

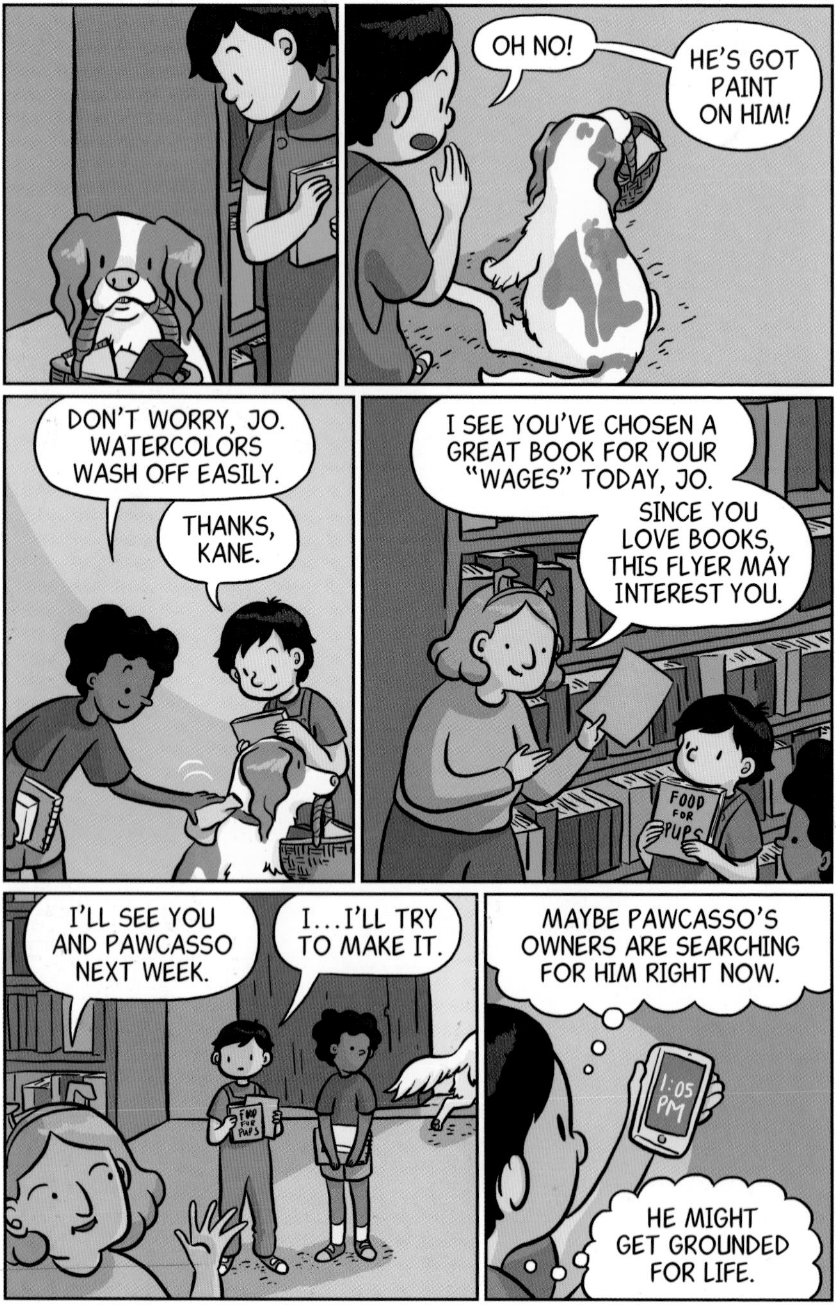
OH NO!
HE'S GOT PAINT ON HIM!
DON'T WORRY, JO. WATERCOLORS WASH OFF EASILY.
THANKS, KANE.
I SEE YOU'VE CHOSEN A GREAT BOOK FOR YOUR "WAGES" TODAY, JO.
SINCE YOU LOVE BOOKS, THIS FLYER MAY INTEREST YOU.
FOOD FOR PUPS
I'LL SEE YOU AND PAWCASSO NEXT WEEK.
I...I'LL TRY TO MAKE IT.
FOOD FOR PUPS
MAYBE PAWCASSO'S OWNERS ARE SEARCHING FOR HIM RIGHT NOW.
1:05 PM
HE MIGHT GET GROUNDED FOR LIFE.

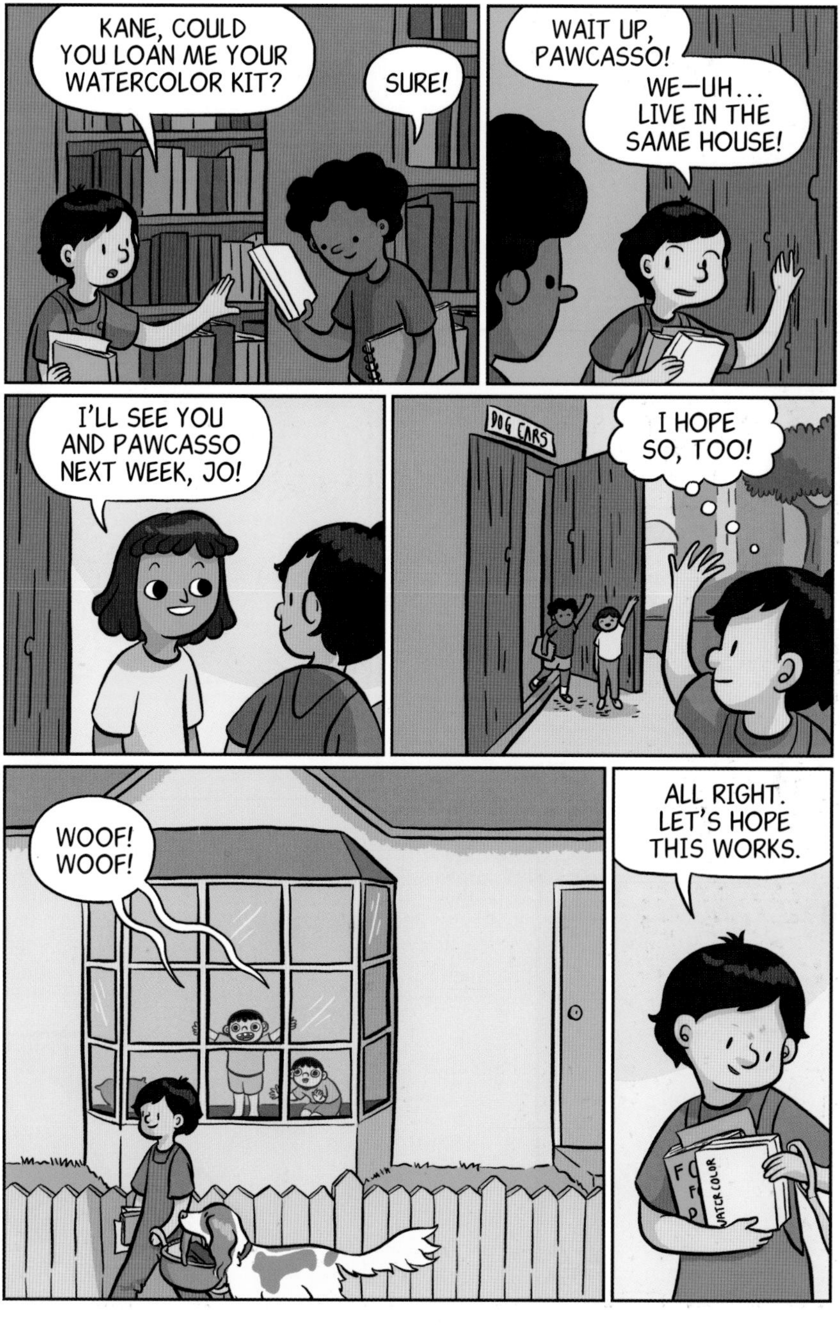
KANE, COULD YOU LOAN ME YOUR WATERCOLOR KIT?
SURE!
WAIT UP, PAWCASSO!
WE—UH... LIVE IN THE SAME HOUSE!
I'LL SEE YOU AND PAWCASSO NEXT WEEK, JO!
DOG CARS
I HOPE SO, TOO!
WOOF! WOOF!
ALL RIGHT. LET'S HOPE THIS WORKS.
WATERCOLOR

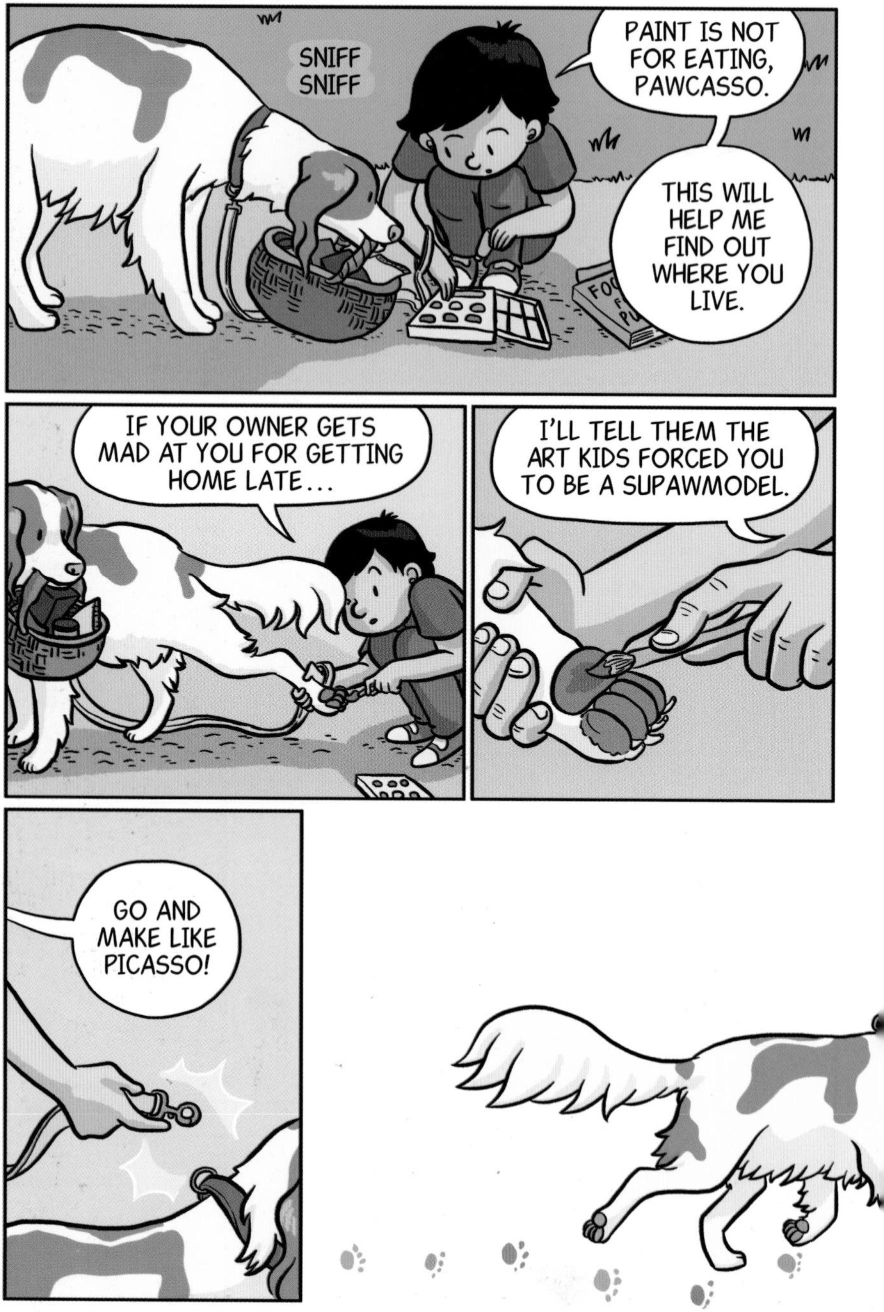
SNIFF
SNIFF
PAINT IS NOT FOR EATING, PAWCASSO.
THIS WILL HELP ME FIND OUT WHERE YOU LIVE.
IF YOUR OWNER GETS MAD AT YOU FOR GETTING HOME LATE...
I'LL TELL THEM THE ART KIDS FORCED YOU TO BE A SUPAWMODEL.
GO AND MAKE LIKE PICASSO!

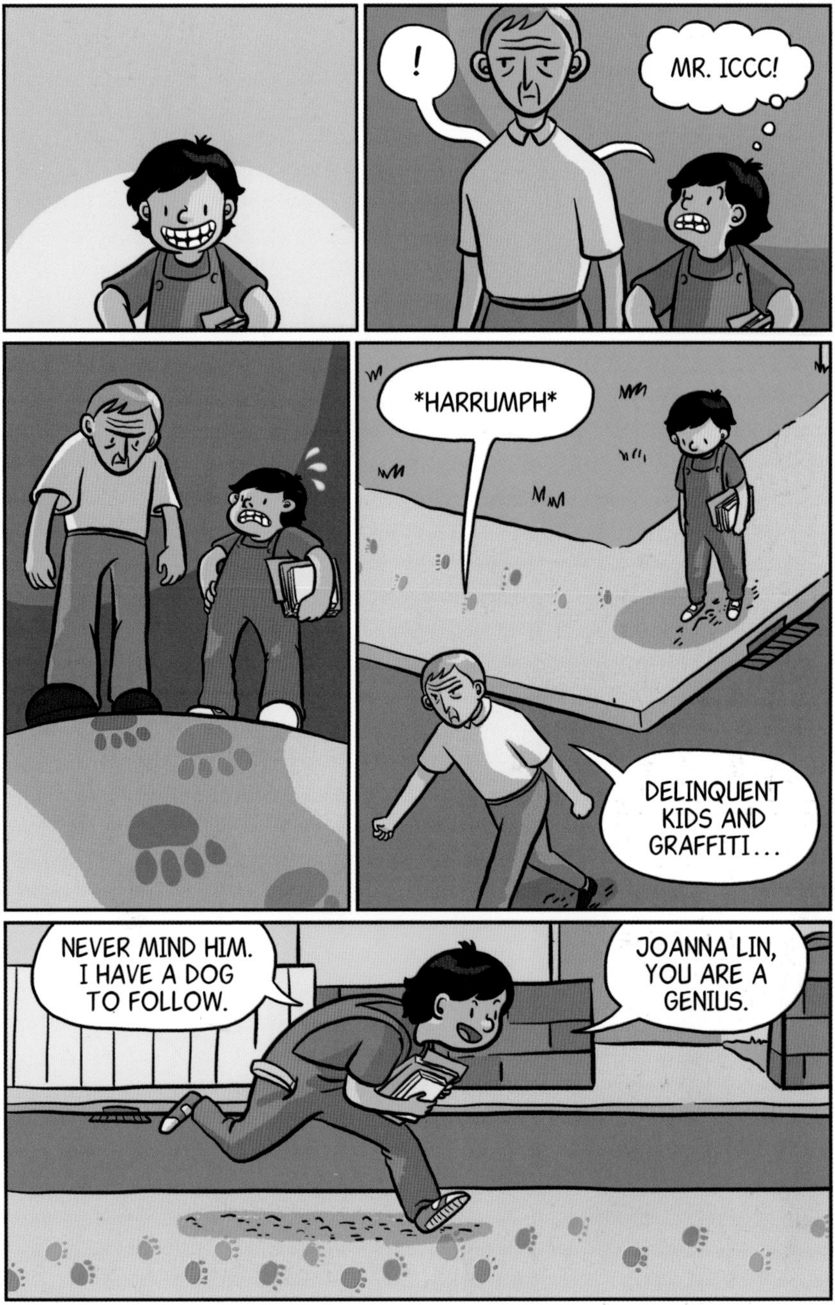
!
MR. ICCC!
HARRUMPH
DELINQUENT KIDS AND GRAFFITI...
NEVER MIND HIM. I HAVE A DOG TO FOLLOW.
JOANNA LIN, YOU ARE A GENIUS.

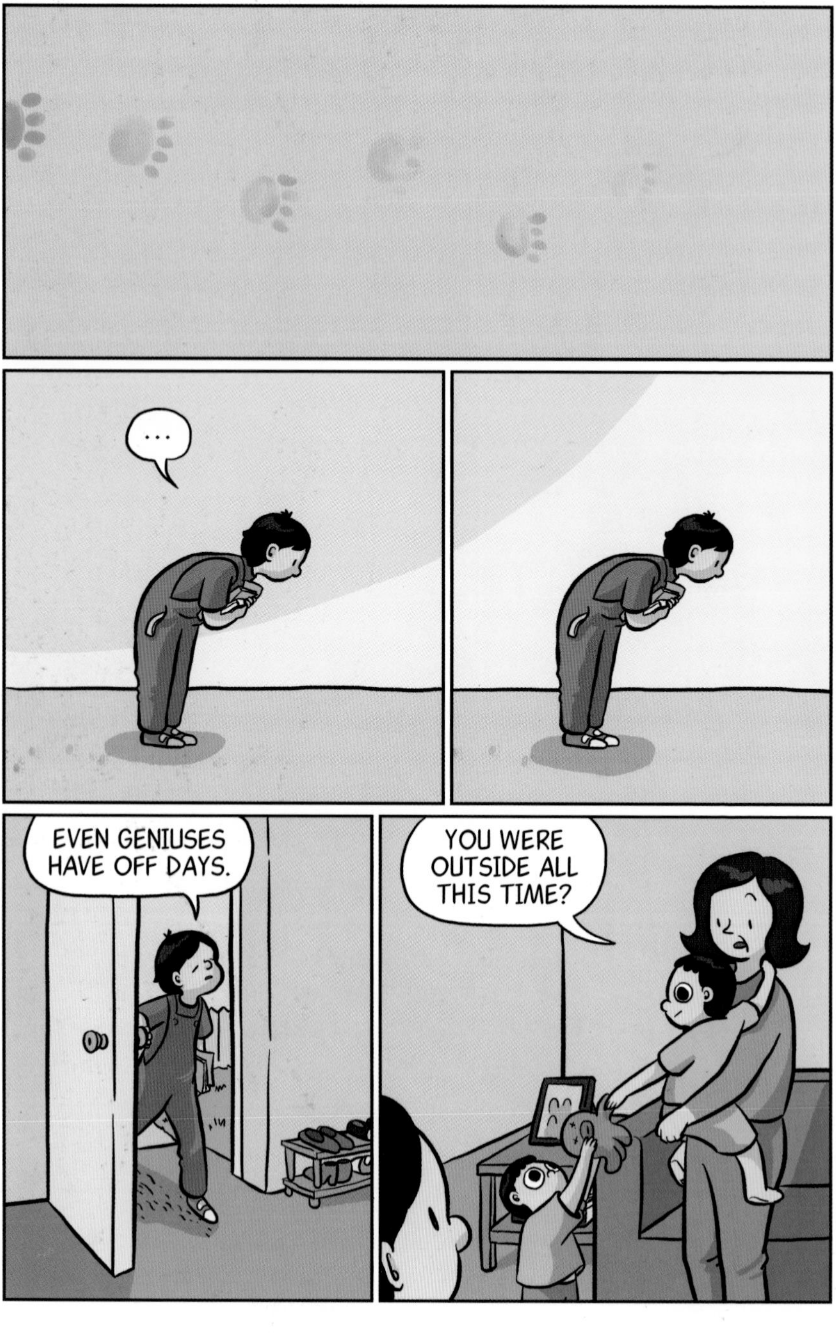
...
EVEN GENIUSES HAVE OFF DAYS.
YOU WERE OUTSIDE ALL THIS TIME?

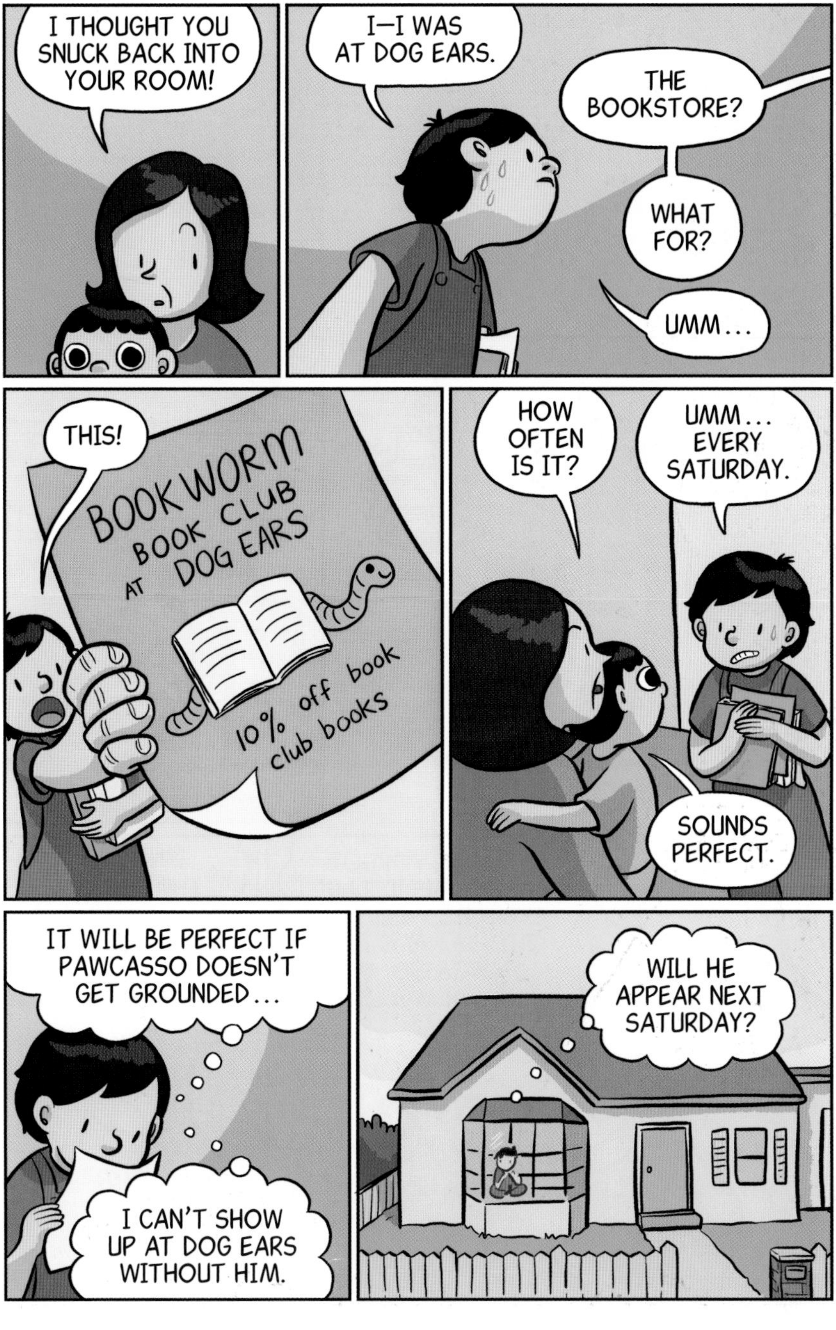

I THOUGHT YOU SNUCK BACK INTO YOUR ROOM!
I—I WAS AT DOG EARS.
THE BOOKSTORE?
WHAT FOR?
UMM...
THIS!
BOOKWORM BOOK CLUB AT DOG EARS
10% off book club books
HOW OFTEN IS IT?
UMM... EVERY SATURDAY.
SOUNDS PERFECT.
IT WILL BE PERFECT IF PAWCASSO DOESN'T GET GROUNDED...
I CAN'T SHOW UP AT DOG EARS WITHOUT HIM.
WILL HE APPEAR NEXT SATURDAY?

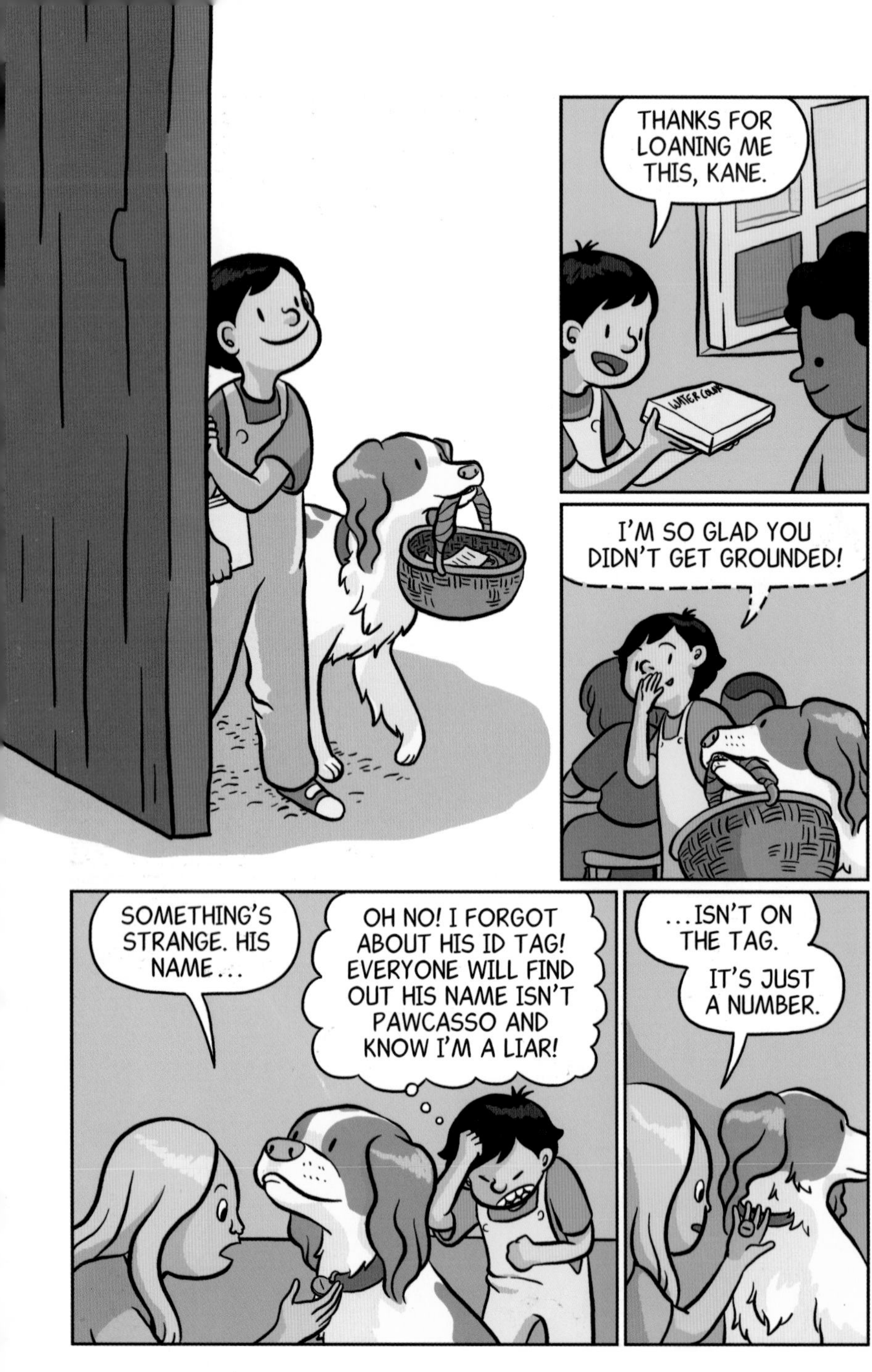
THANKS FOR LOANING ME THIS, KANE.
WATER COLOR
I'M SO GLAD YOU DIDN'T GET GROUNDED!
SOMETHING'S STRANGE. HIS NAME...
OH NO! I FORGOT ABOUT HIS ID TAG! EVERYONE WILL FIND OUT HIS NAME ISN'T PAWCASSO AND KNOW I'M A LIAR!
...ISN'T ON THE TAG.
IT'S JUST A NUMBER.

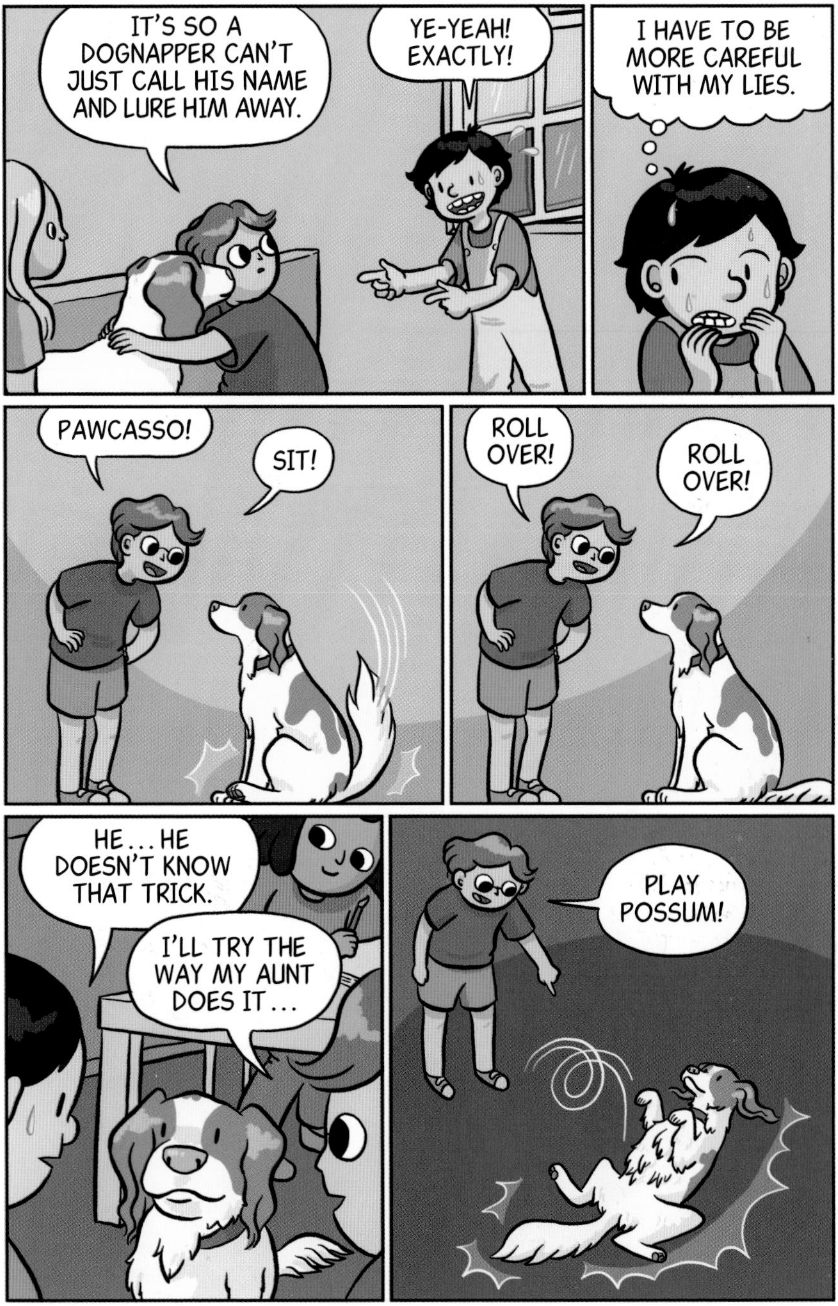
IT'S SO A DOGNAPPER CAN'T JUST CALL HIS NAME AND LURE HIM AWAY.
YE-YEAH! EXACTLY!
I HAVE TO BE MORE CAREFUL WITH MY LIES.
PAWCASSO!
SIT!
ROLL OVER!
ROLL OVER!
HE... HE DOESN'T KNOW THAT TRICK.
I'LL TRY THE WAY MY AUNT DOES IT...
PLAY POSSUM!

AH YES. I—I FORGOT HE DOES KNOW THAT TRICK.

HOW DID YOU TEACH HIM TO ROLL OVER?

UMM... BY SHOWING HIM?

HOW?

BY... UMM... GETTING ON THE GROUND...

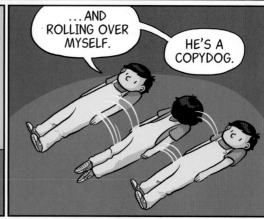

...AND ROLLING OVER MYSELF.

HE'S A COPYDOG.

I'VE NEVER HEARD OF THAT METHOD...

GULP

DOG TRAINING SOUNDS LIKE FUN!

I WANT TO TRY, TOO!

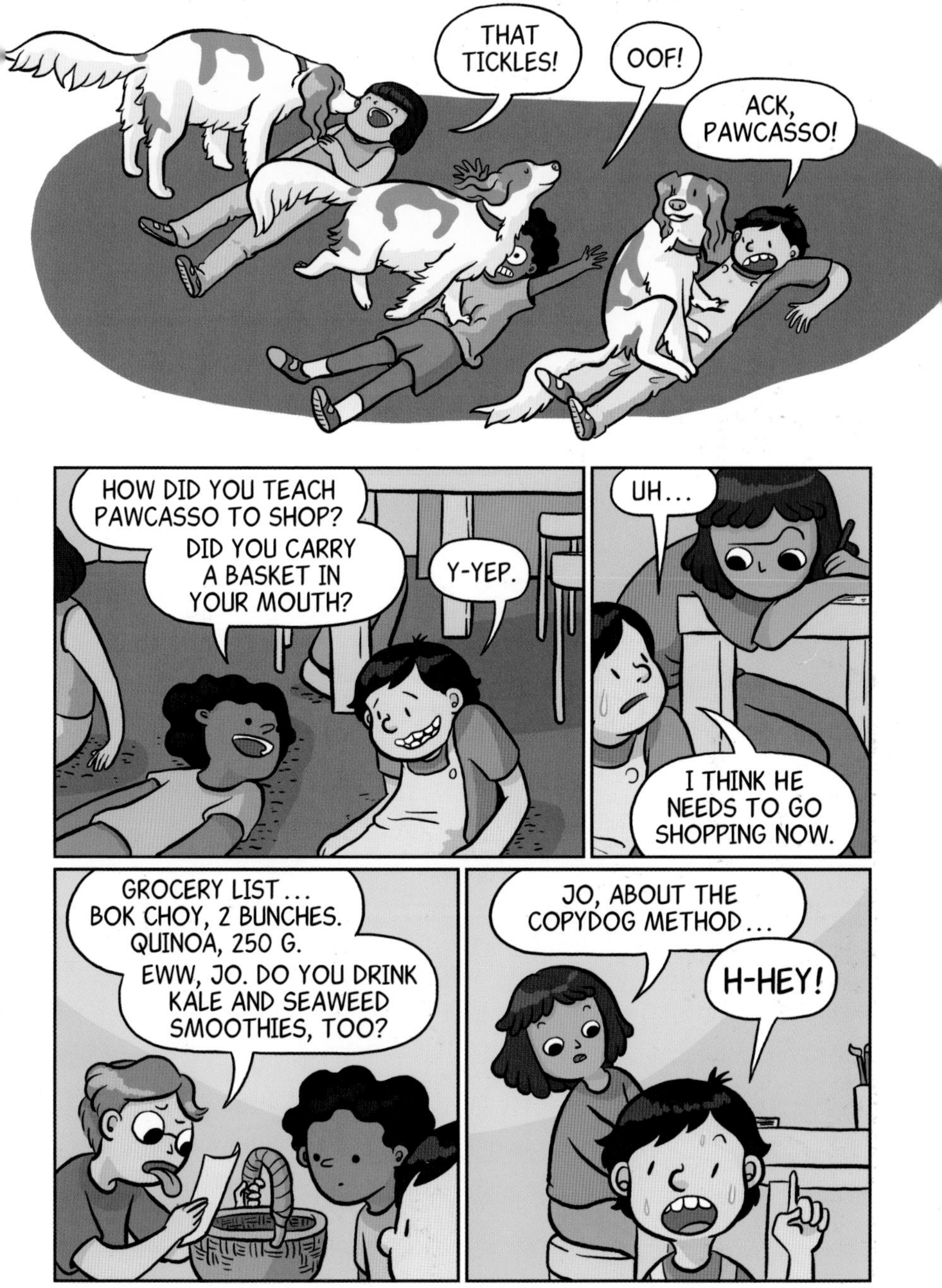
THAT TICKLES!
OOF!
ACK, PAWCASSO!
HOW DID YOU TEACH PAWCASSO TO SHOP?
DID YOU CARRY A BASKET IN YOUR MOUTH?
Y-YEP.
UH...
I THINK HE NEEDS TO GO SHOPPING NOW.
GROCERY LIST... BOK CHOY, 2 BUNCHES. QUINOA, 250 G.
EWW, JO. DO YOU DRINK KALE AND SEAWEED SMOOTHIES, TOO?
JO, ABOUT THE COPYDOG METHOD...
H-HEY!

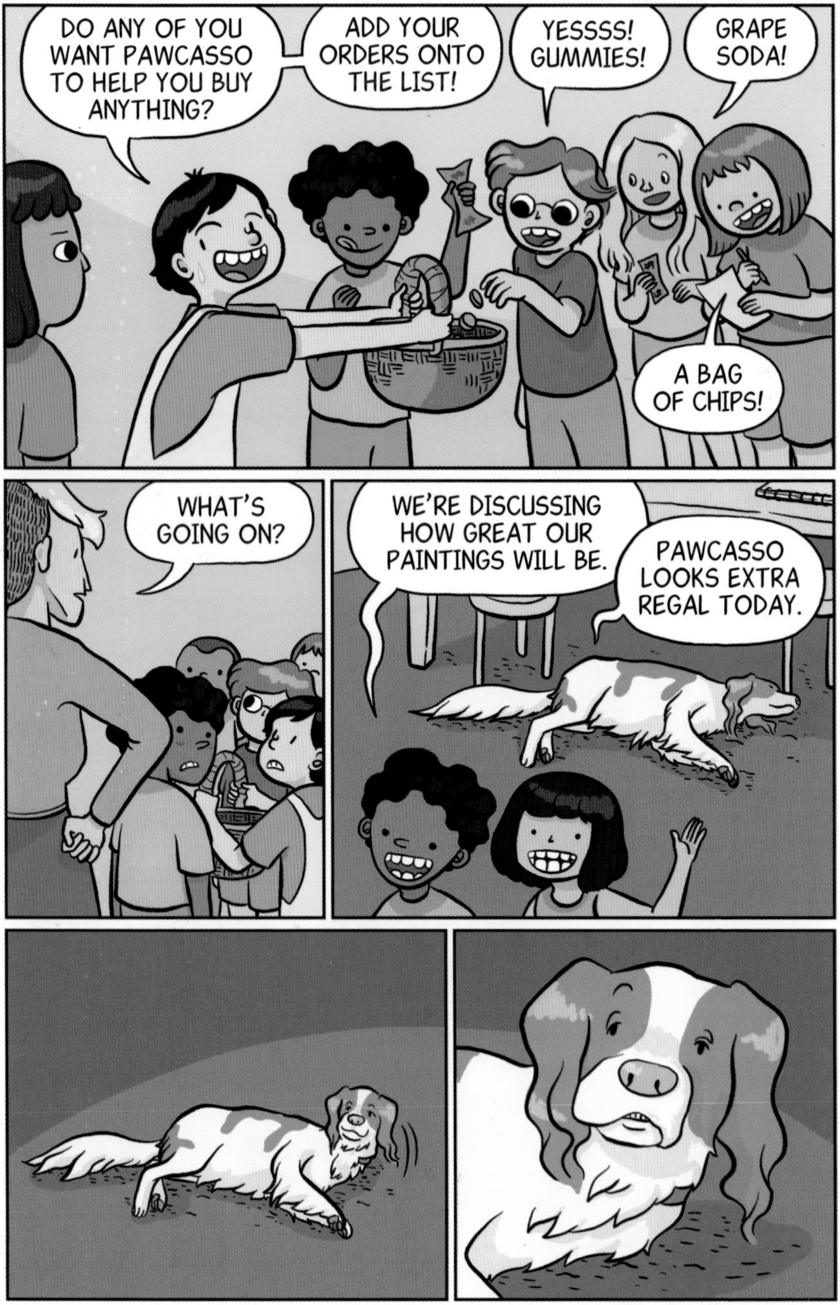
DO ANY OF YOU WANT PAWCASSO TO HELP YOU BUY ANYTHING?
ADD YOUR ORDERS ONTO THE LIST!
YESSSS! GUMMIES!
GRAPE SODA!
A BAG OF CHIPS!
WHAT'S GOING ON?
WE'RE DISCUSSING HOW GREAT OUR PAINTINGS WILL BE.
PAWCASSO LOOKS EXTRA REGAL TODAY.

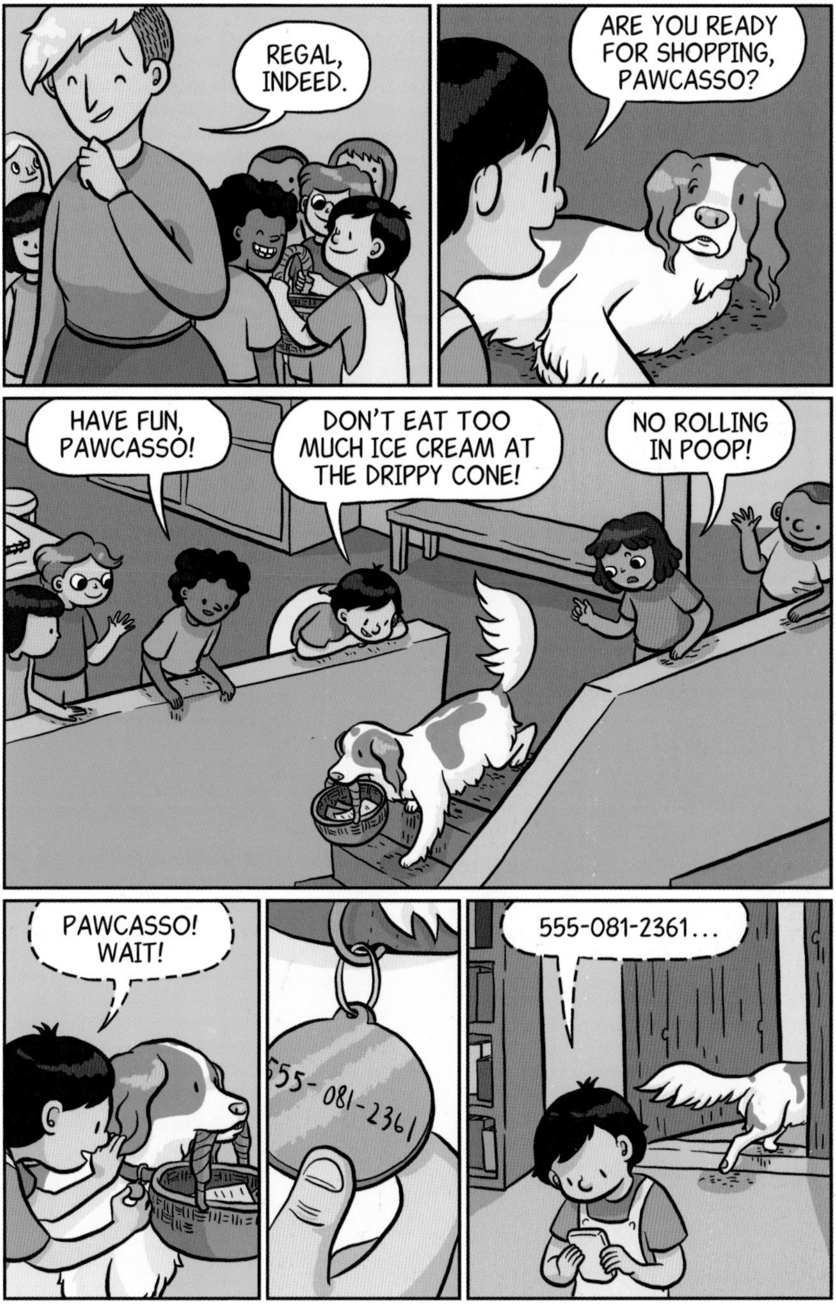
REGAL, INDEED.
ARE YOU READY FOR SHOPPING, PAWCASSO?
HAVE FUN, PAWCASSO!
DON'T EAT TOO MUCH ICE CREAM AT THE DRIPPY CONE!
NO ROLLING IN POOP!
PAWCASSO! WAIT!
555-081-2361
555-081-2361...

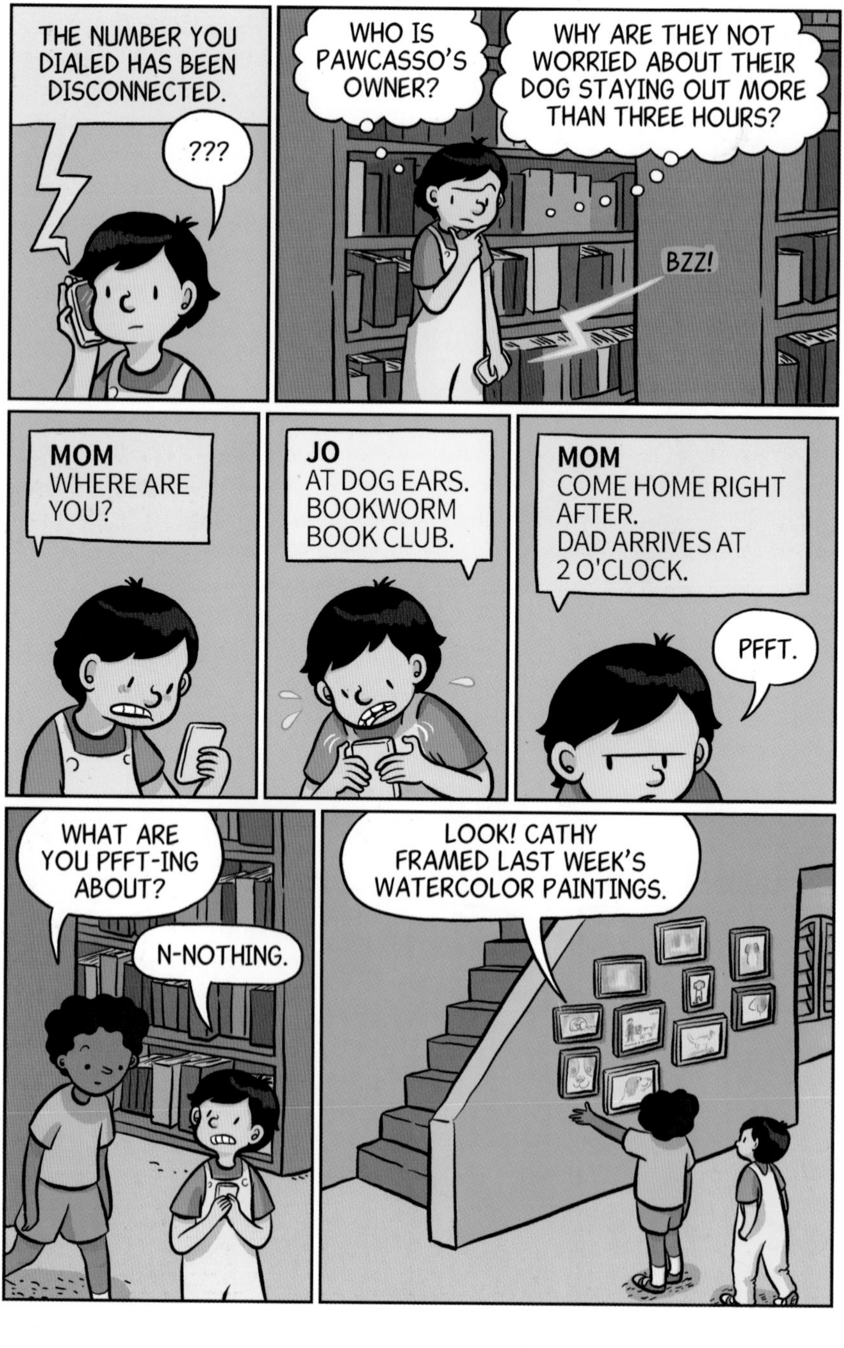
THE NUMBER YOU DIALED HAS BEEN DISCONNECTED.
???
WHO IS PAWCASSO'S OWNER?
WHY ARE THEY NOT WORRIED ABOUT THEIR DOG STAYING OUT MORE THAN THREE HOURS?
BZZ!
MOM
WHERE ARE YOU?
JO
AT DOG EARS. BOOKWORM BOOK CLUB.
MOM
COME HOME RIGHT AFTER. DAD ARRIVES AT 2 O'CLOCK.
PFFT.
WHAT ARE YOU PFFT-ING ABOUT?
N-NOTHING.
LOOK! CATHY FRAMED LAST WEEK'S WATERCOLOR PAINTINGS.

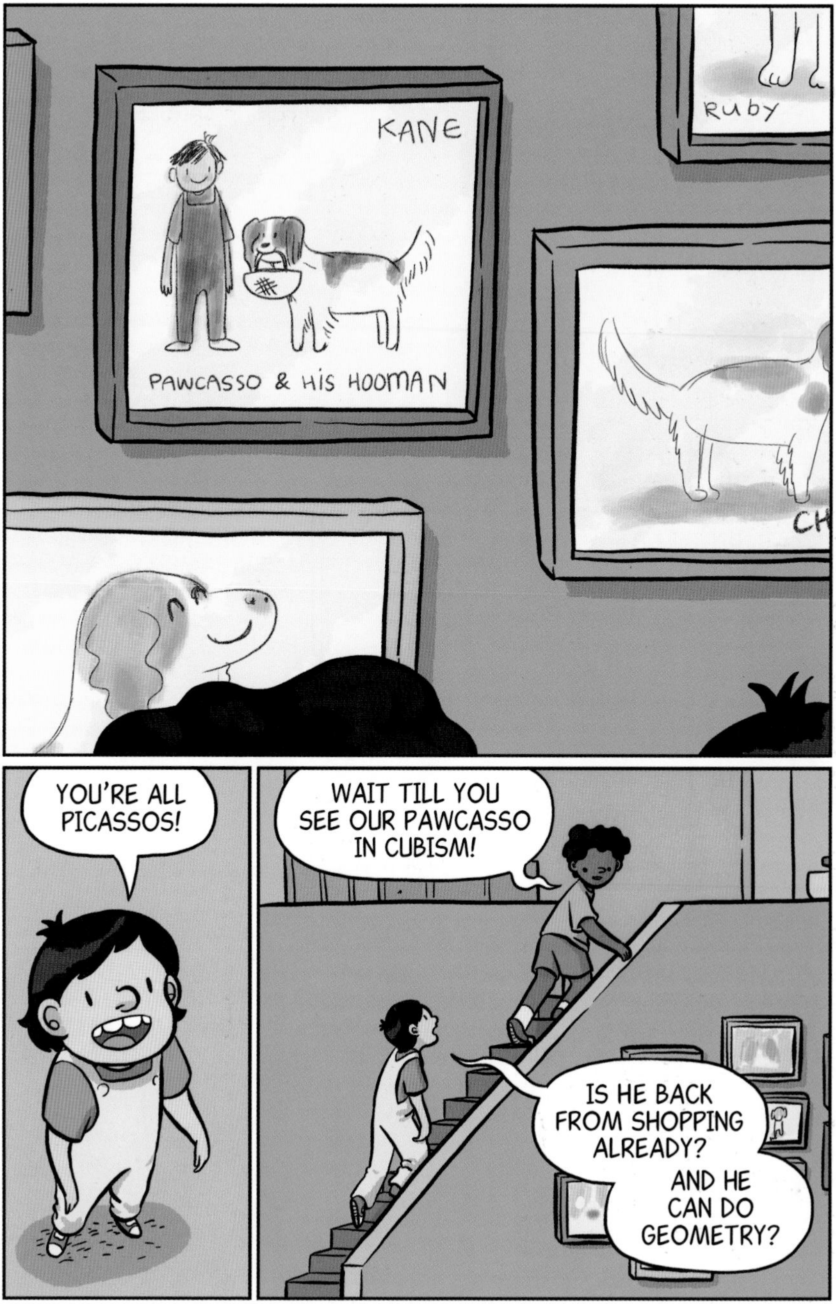
RUBY
KANE
PAWCASSO & HIS HOOMAN
YOU'RE ALL PICASSOS!
WAIT TILL YOU SEE OUR PAWCASSO IN CUBISM!
IS HE BACK FROM SHOPPING ALREADY?
AND HE CAN DO GEOMETRY?

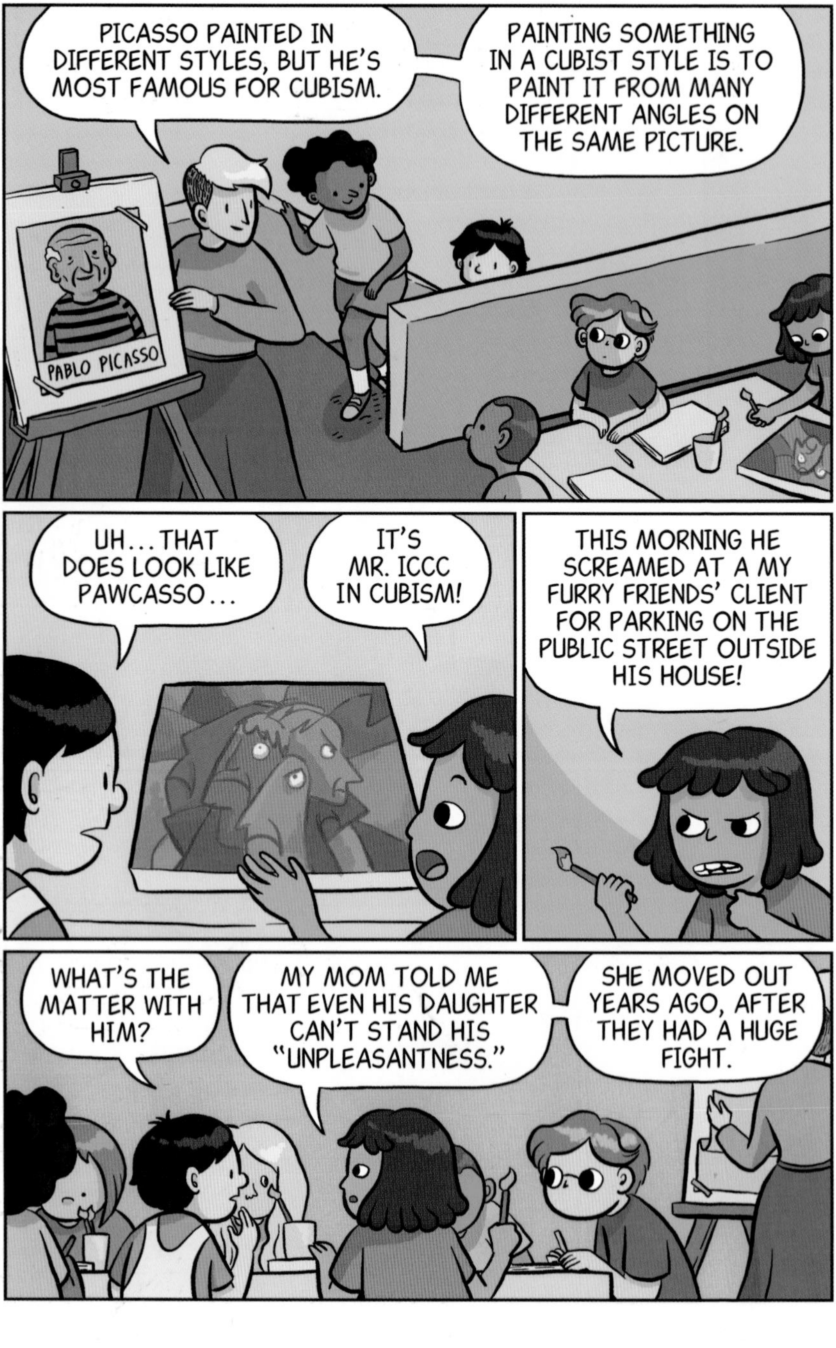
PICASSO PAINTED IN DIFFERENT STYLES, BUT HE'S MOST FAMOUS FOR CUBISM.
PAINTING SOMETHING IN A CUBIST STYLE IS TO PAINT IT FROM MANY DIFFERENT ANGLES ON THE SAME PICTURE.
PABLO PICASSO
UH... THAT DOES LOOK LIKE PAWCASSO...
IT'S MR. ICCC IN CUBISM!
THIS MORNING HE SCREAMED AT A MY FURRY FRIENDS' CLIENT FOR PARKING ON THE PUBLIC STREET OUTSIDE HIS HOUSE!
WHAT'S THE MATTER WITH HIM?
MY MOM TOLD ME THAT EVEN HIS DAUGHTER CAN'T STAND HIS "UNPLEASANTNESS."
SHE MOVED OUT YEARS AGO, AFTER THEY HAD A HUGE FIGHT.

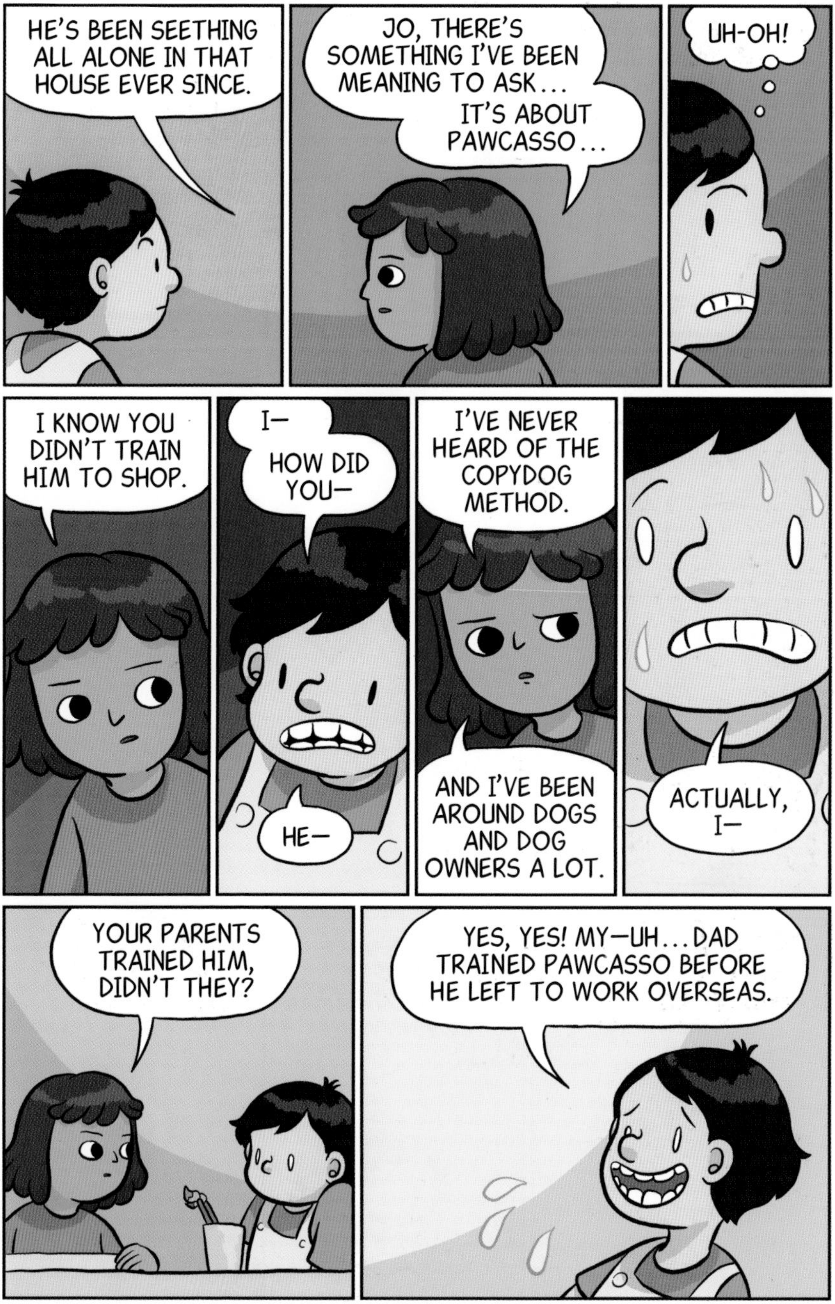
HE'S BEEN SEETHING ALL ALONE IN THAT HOUSE EVER SINCE.
JO, THERE'S SOMETHING I'VE BEEN MEANING TO ASK...
IT'S ABOUT PAWCASSO...
UH-OH!
I KNOW YOU DIDN'T TRAIN HIM TO SHOP.
I—
HOW DID YOU—
HE—
I'VE NEVER HEARD OF THE COPYDOG METHOD.
AND I'VE BEEN AROUND DOGS AND DOG OWNERS A LOT.
ACTUALLY, I—
YOUR PARENTS TRAINED HIM, DIDN'T THEY?
YES, YES! MY—UH...DAD TRAINED PAWCASSO BEFORE HE LEFT TO WORK OVERSEAS.

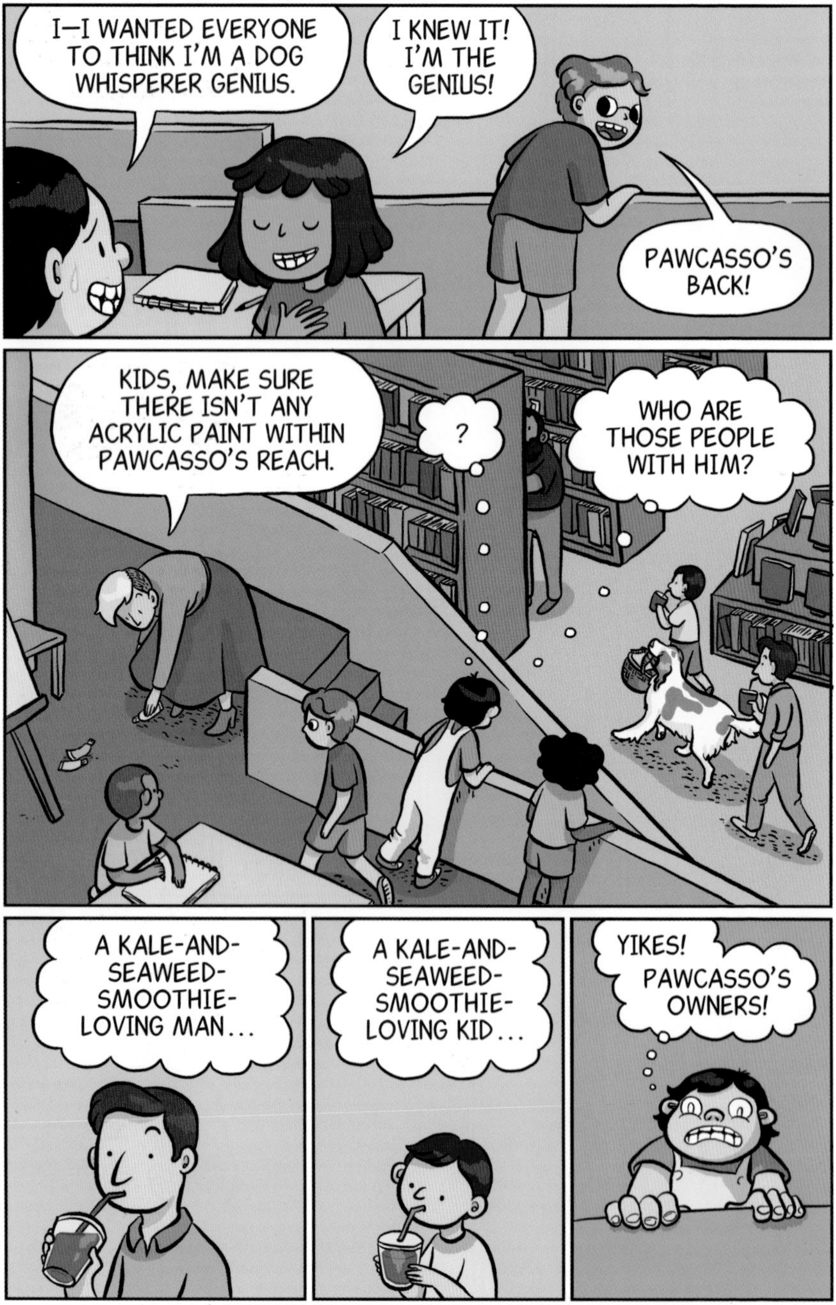
I—I WANTED EVERYONE TO THINK I'M A DOG WHISPERER GENIUS.
I KNEW IT! I'M THE GENIUS!
PAWCASSO'S BACK!
KIDS, MAKE SURE THERE ISN'T ANY ACRYLIC PAINT WITHIN PAWCASSO'S REACH.
?
WHO ARE THOSE PEOPLE WITH HIM?
A KALE-AND-SEAWEED-SMOOTHIE-LOVING MAN...
A KALE-AND-SEAWEED-SMOOTHIE-LOVING KID...
YIKES! PAWCASSO'S OWNERS!

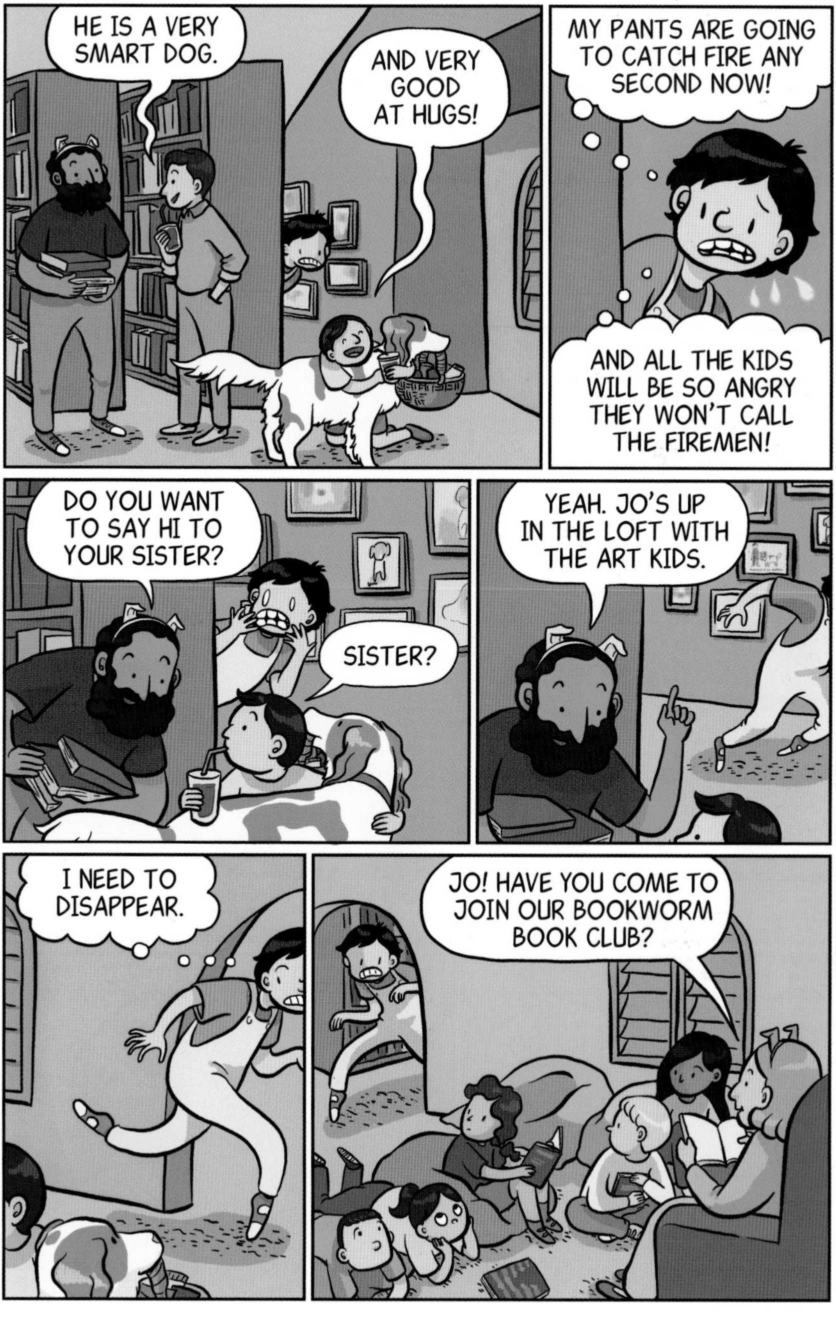
HE IS A VERY SMART DOG.
AND VERY GOOD AT HUGS!
MY PANTS ARE GOING TO CATCH FIRE ANY SECOND NOW!
AND ALL THE KIDS WILL BE SO ANGRY THEY WON'T CALL THE FIREMEN!
DO YOU WANT TO SAY HI TO YOUR SISTER?
SISTER?
YEAH. JO'S UP IN THE LOFT WITH THE ART KIDS.
I NEED TO DISAPPEAR.
JO! HAVE YOU COME TO JOIN OUR BOOKWORM BOOK CLUB?

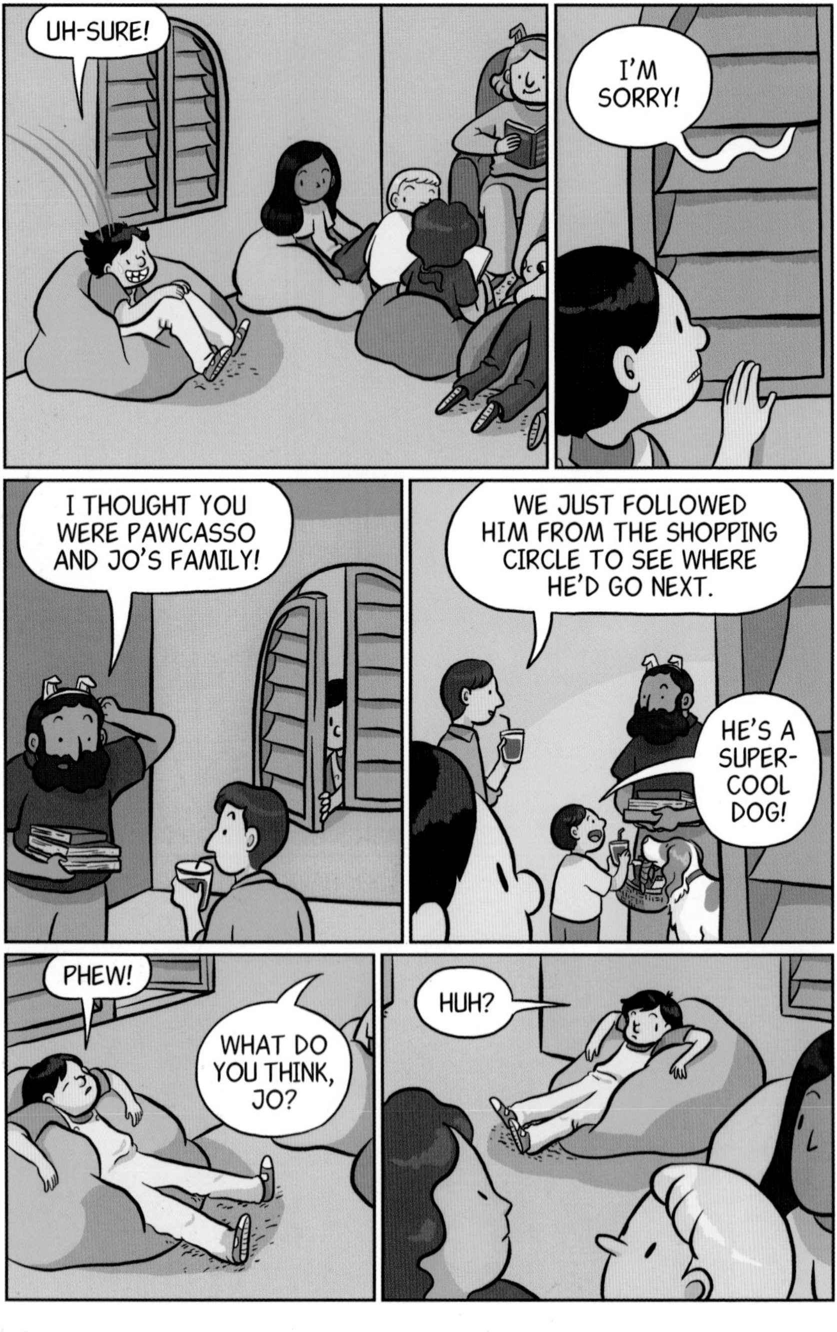
UH-SURE!
I'M SORRY!
I THOUGHT YOU WERE PAWCASSO AND JO'S FAMILY!
WE JUST FOLLOWED HIM FROM THE SHOPPING CIRCLE TO SEE WHERE HE'D GO NEXT.
HE'S A SUPER-COOL DOG!
PHEW!
WHAT DO YOU THINK, JO?
HUH?

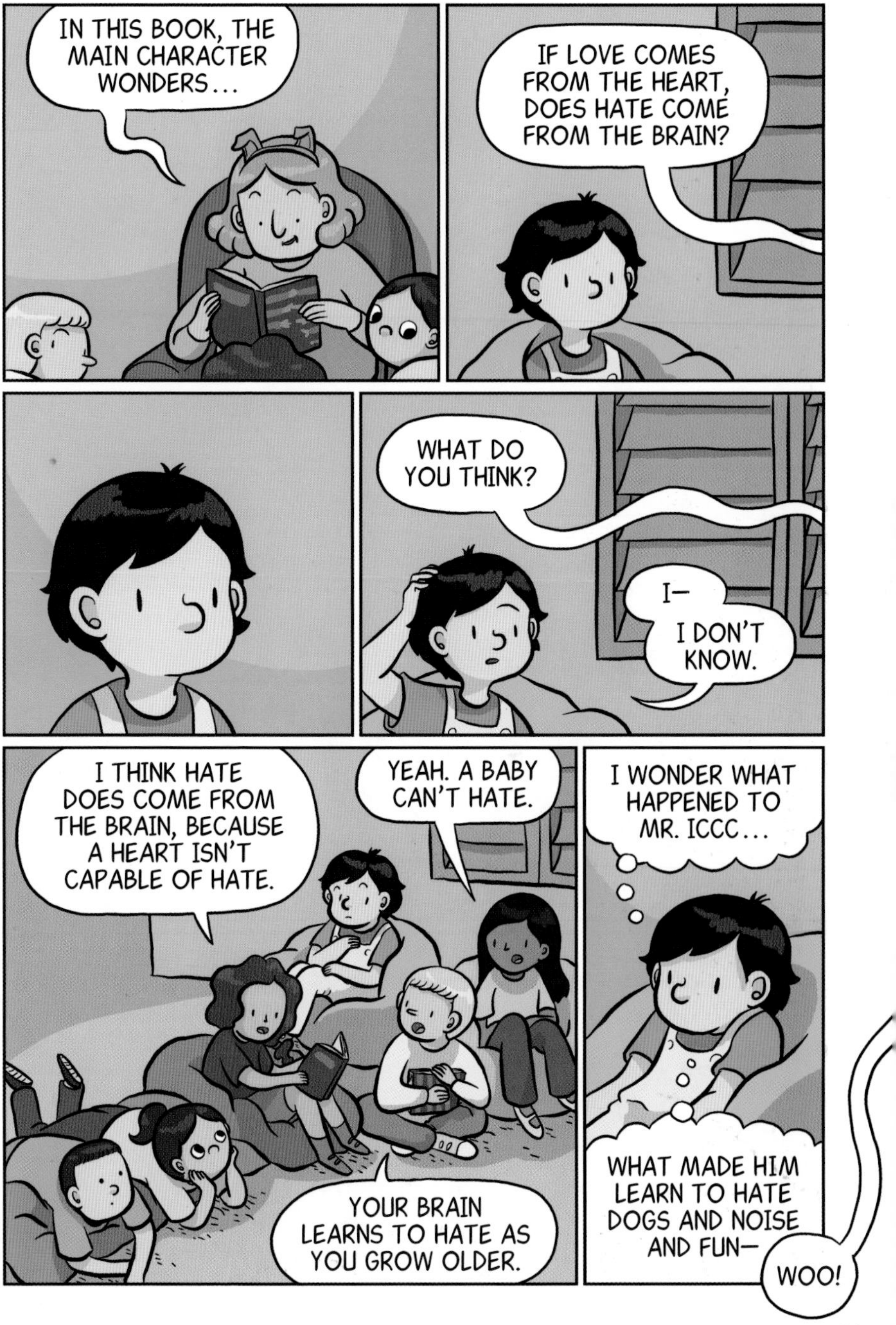
IN THIS BOOK, THE MAIN CHARACTER WONDERS...
IF LOVE COMES FROM THE HEART, DOES HATE COME FROM THE BRAIN?
WHAT DO YOU THINK?
I—
I DON'T KNOW.
I THINK HATE DOES COME FROM THE BRAIN, BECAUSE A HEART ISN'T CAPABLE OF HATE.
YEAH. A BABY CAN'T HATE.
YOUR BRAIN LEARNS TO HATE AS YOU GROW OLDER.
I WONDER WHAT HAPPENED TO MR. ICCC...
WHAT MADE HIM LEARN TO HATE DOGS AND NOISE AND FUN—
WOO!

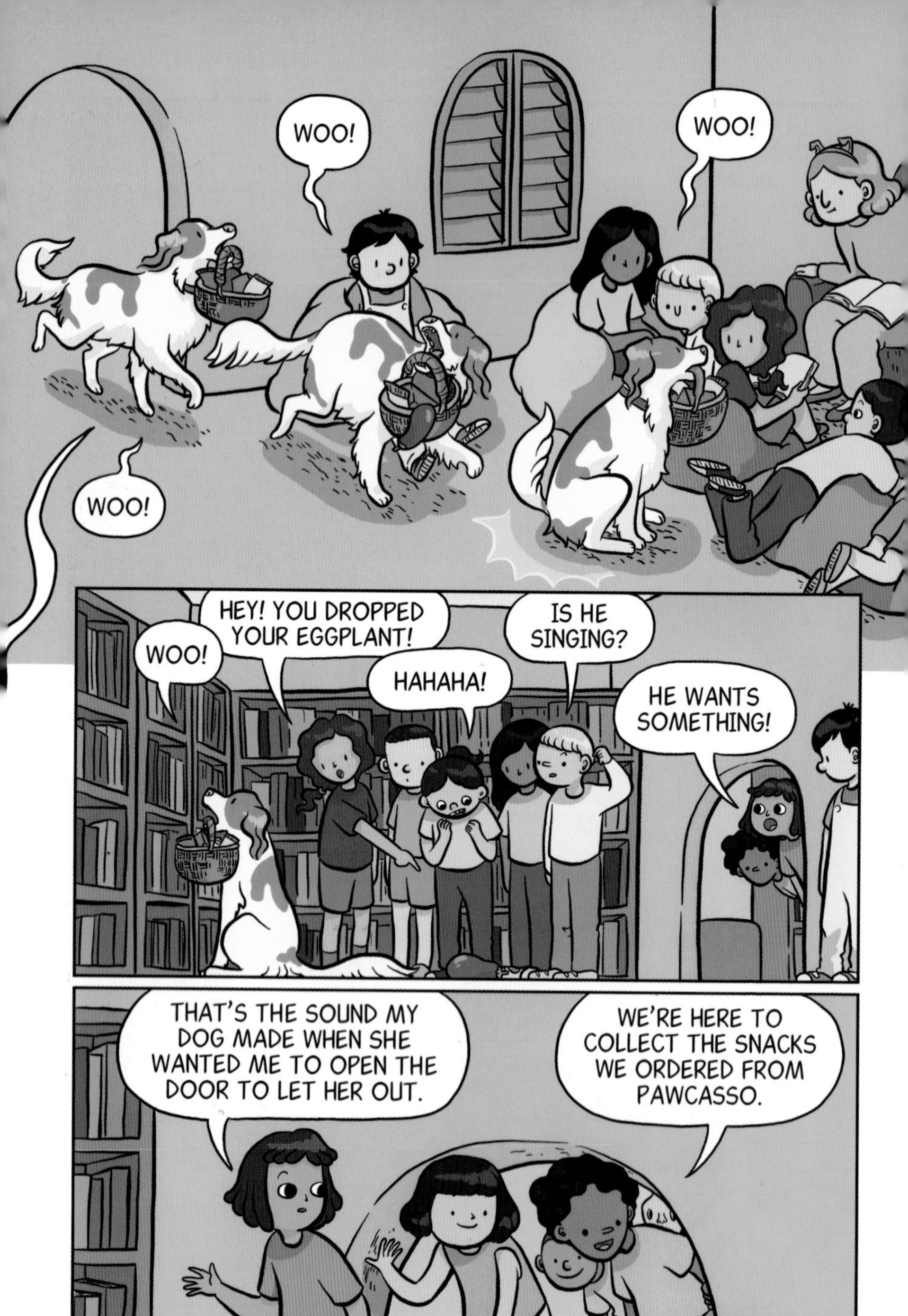
WOO!
WOO!
WOO!
WOO!
HEY! YOU DROPPED YOUR EGGPLANT!
HAHAHA!
IS HE SINGING?
HE WANTS SOMETHING!
THAT'S THE SOUND MY DOG MADE WHEN SHE WANTED ME TO OPEN THE DOOR TO LET HER OUT.
WE'RE HERE TO COLLECT THE SNACKS WE ORDERED FROM PAWCASSO.

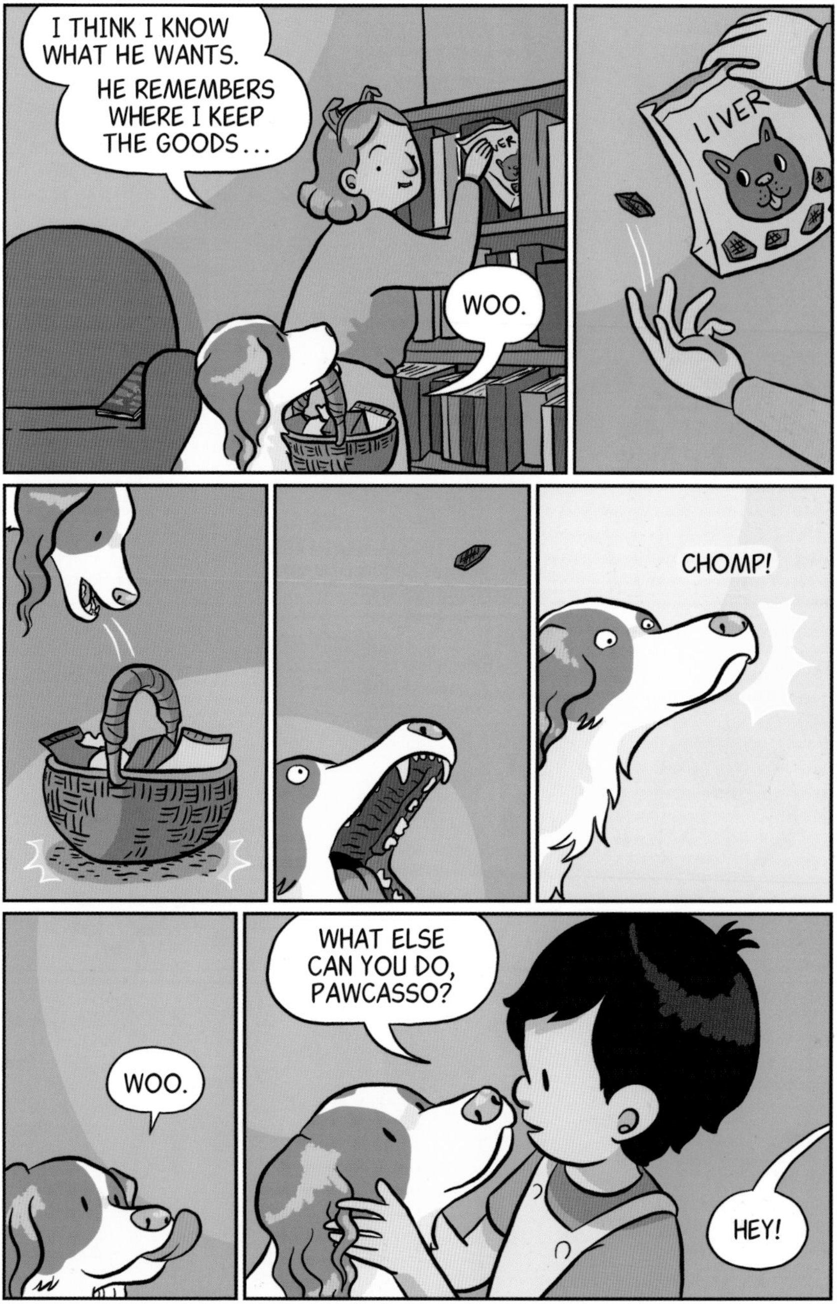
I THINK I KNOW WHAT HE WANTS.
HE REMEMBERS WHERE I KEEP THE GOODS...
WOO.
LIVER
CHOMP!
WOO.
WHAT ELSE CAN YOU DO, PAWCASSO?
HEY!

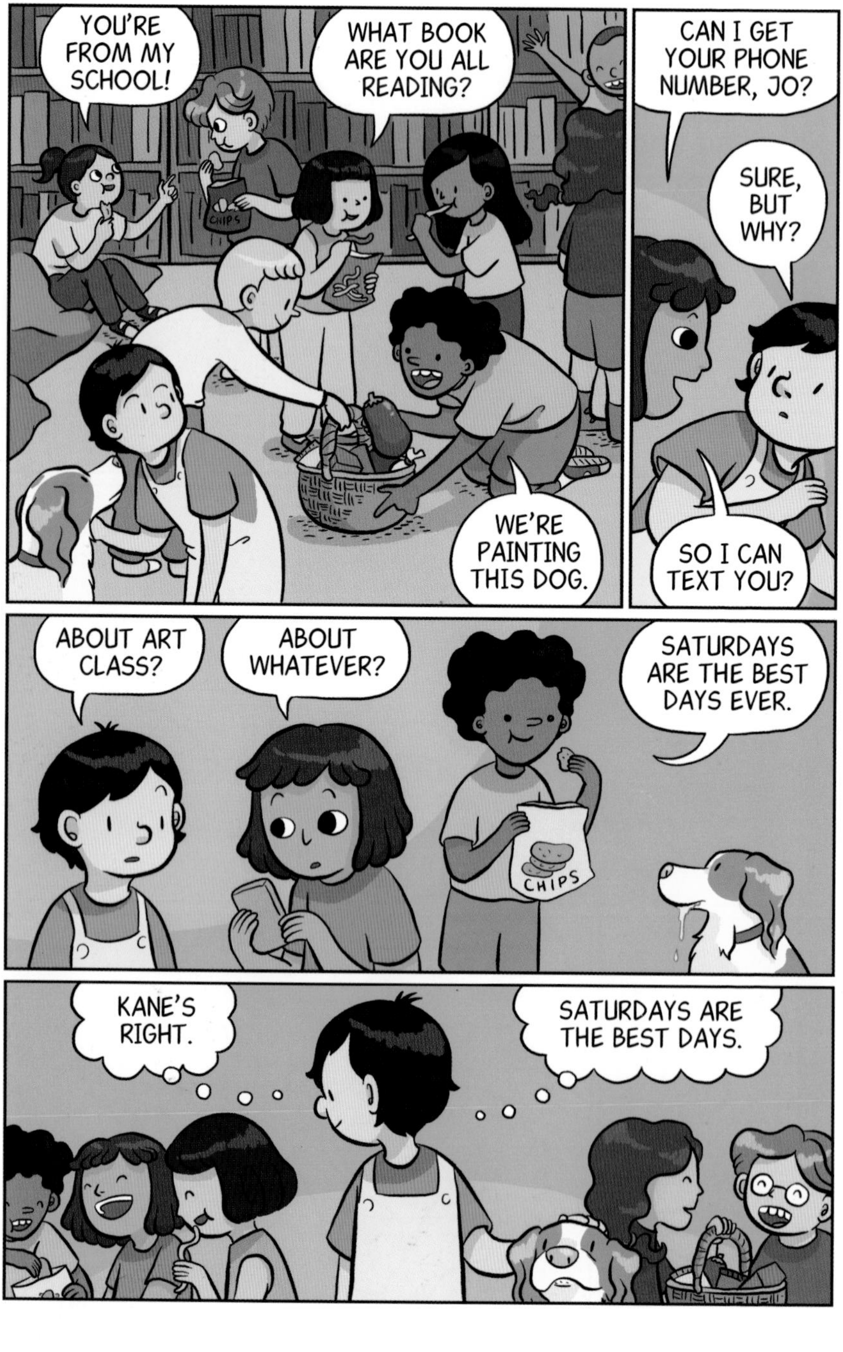
YOU'RE FROM MY SCHOOL!
WHAT BOOK ARE YOU ALL READING?
WE'RE PAINTING THIS DOG.
CAN I GET YOUR PHONE NUMBER, JO?
SURE, BUT WHY?
SO I CAN TEXT YOU?
ABOUT ART CLASS?
ABOUT WHATEVER?
SATURDAYS ARE THE BEST DAYS EVER.
CHIPS
KANE'S RIGHT.
SATURDAYS ARE THE BEST DAYS.

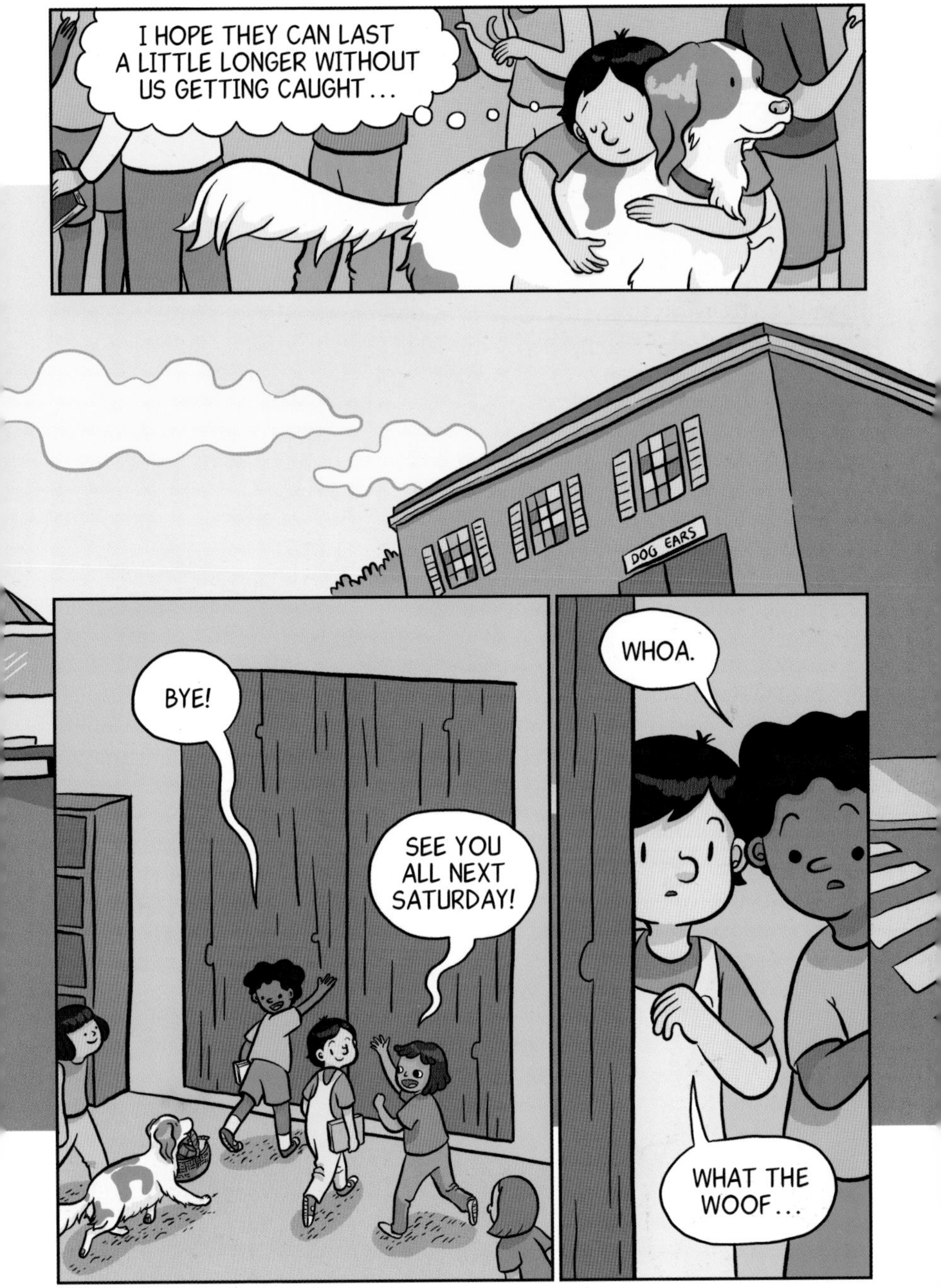
I HOPE THEY CAN LAST A LITTLE LONGER WITHOUT US GETTING CAUGHT...
DOG EARS
BYE!
SEE YOU ALL NEXT SATURDAY!
WHOA.
WHAT THE WOOF...

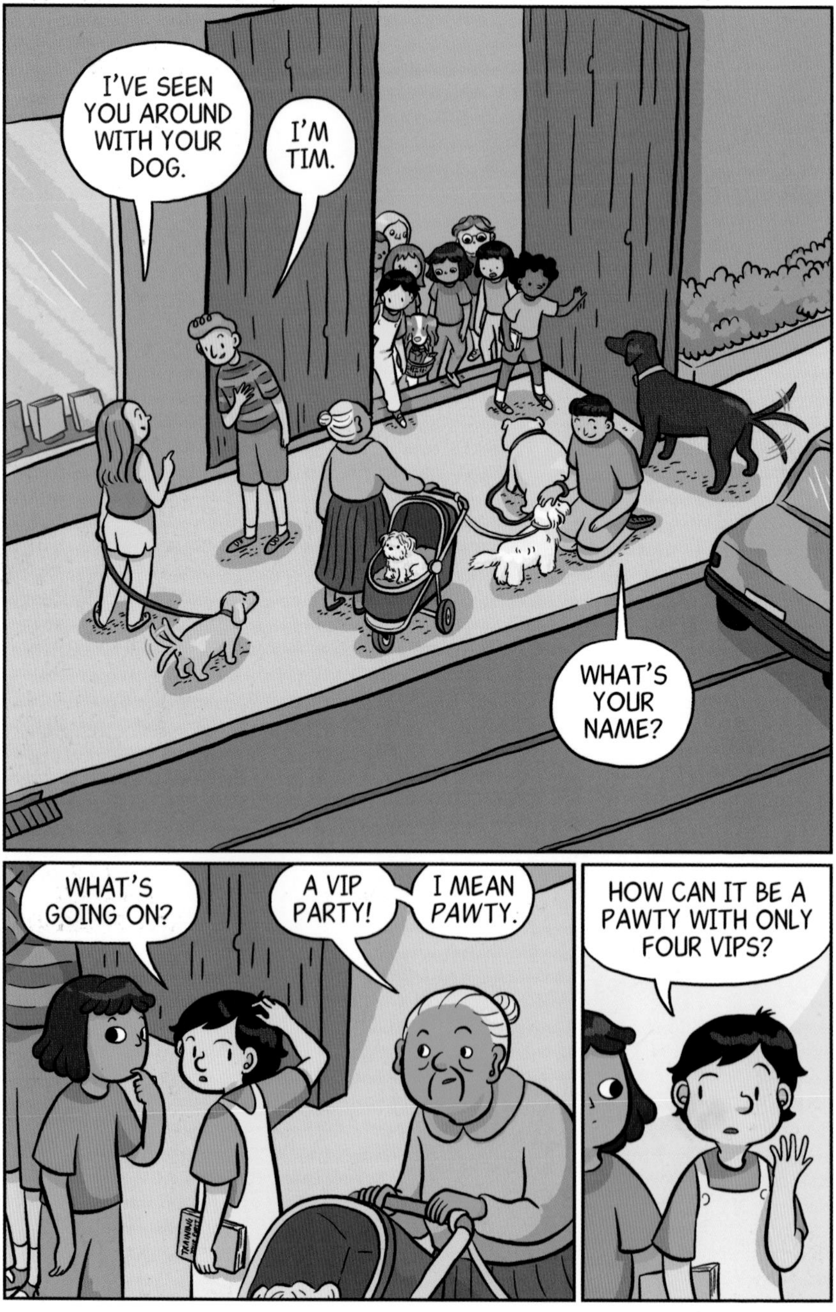
I'VE SEEN YOU AROUND WITH YOUR DOG.
I'M TIM.
WHAT'S YOUR NAME?
WHAT'S GOING ON?
A VIP PARTY!
I MEAN PAWTY.
HOW CAN IT BE A PAWTY WITH ONLY FOUR VIPS?

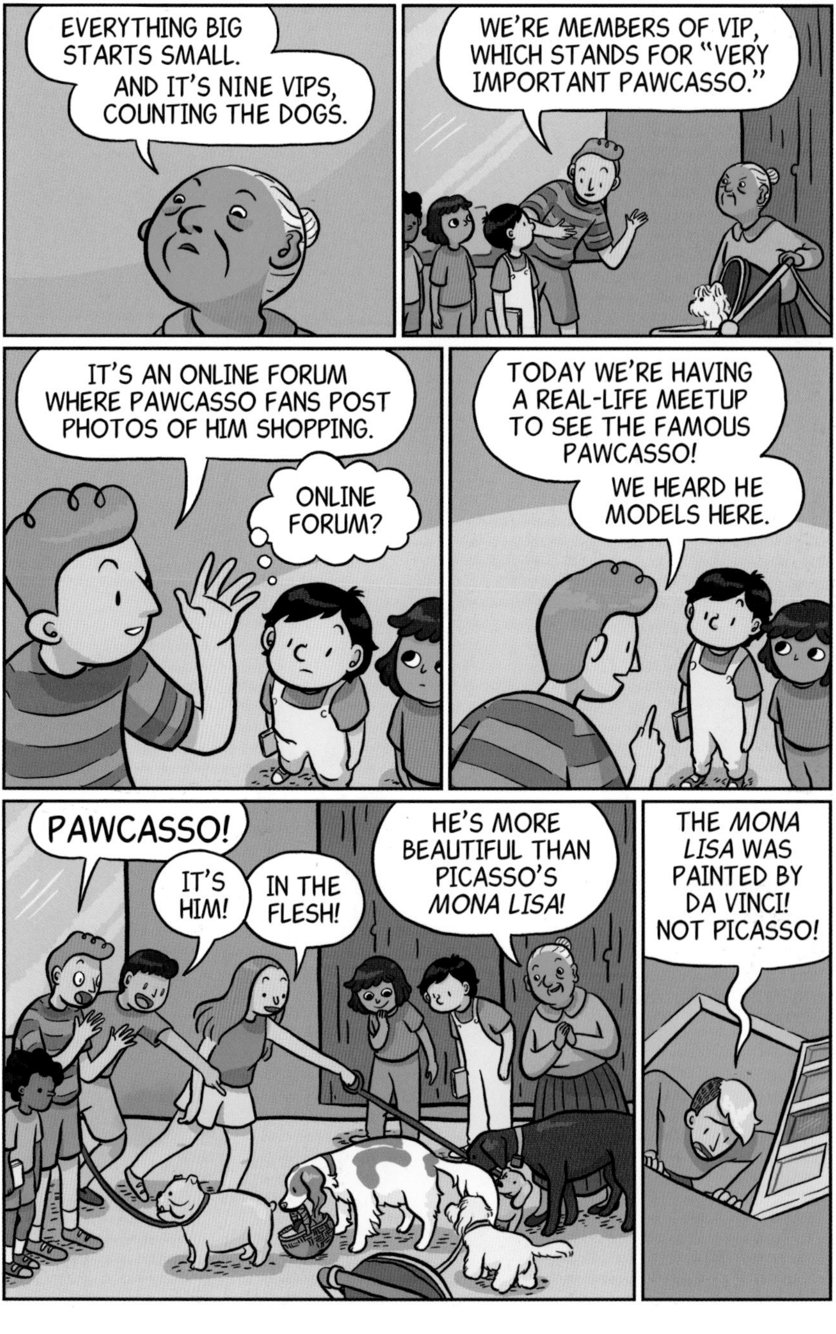
EVERYTHING BIG STARTS SMALL.
AND IT'S NINE VIPS, COUNTING THE DOGS.
WE'RE MEMBERS OF VIP, WHICH STANDS FOR "VERY IMPORTANT PAWCASSO."
IT'S AN ONLINE FORUM WHERE PAWCASSO FANS POST PHOTOS OF HIM SHOPPING.
ONLINE FORUM?
TODAY WE'RE HAVING A REAL-LIFE MEETUP TO SEE THE FAMOUS PAWCASSO!
WE HEARD HE MODELS HERE.
PAWCASSO!
IT'S HIM!
IN THE FLESH!
HE'S MORE BEAUTIFUL THAN PICASSO'S *MONA LISA*!
THE *MONA LISA* WAS PAINTED BY DA VINCI! NOT PICASSO!

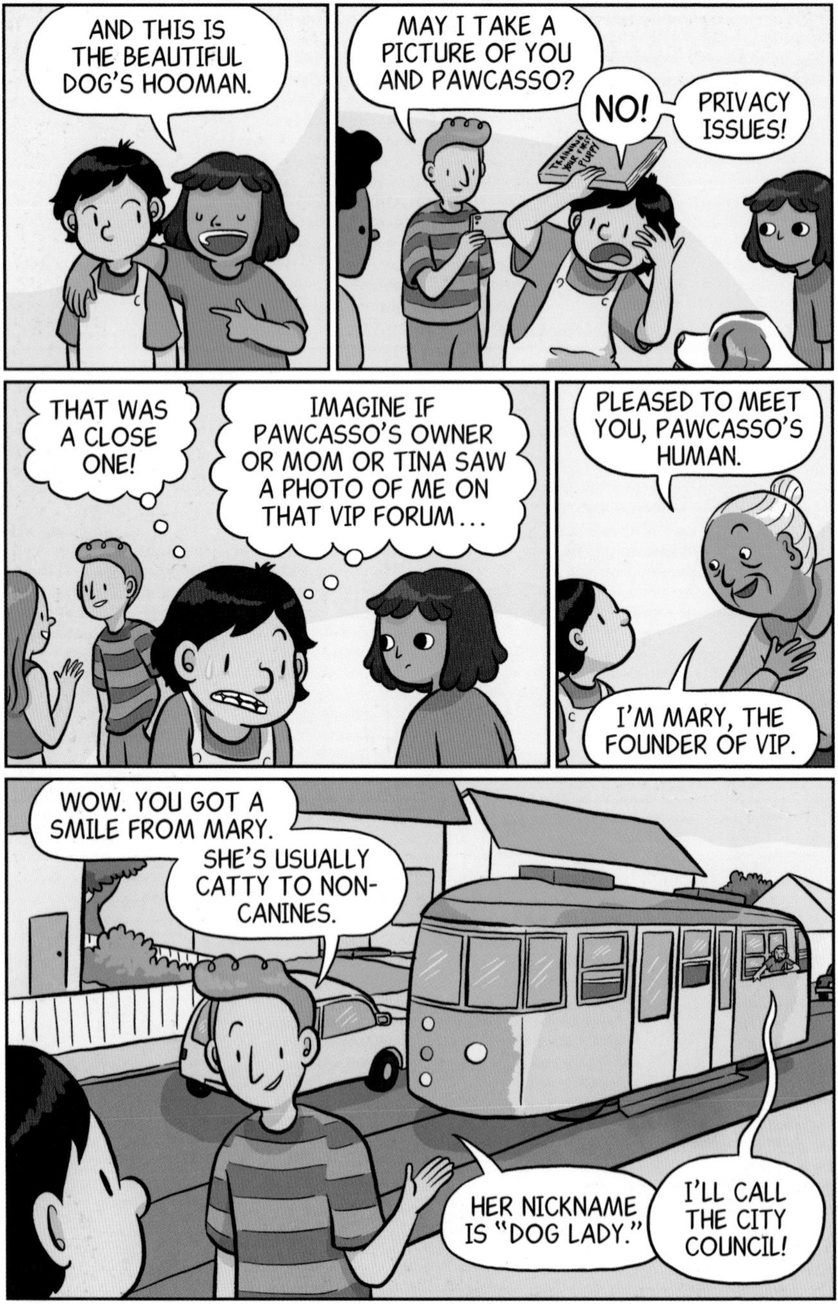
AND THIS IS THE BEAUTIFUL DOG'S HOOMAN.
MAY I TAKE A PICTURE OF YOU AND PAWCASSO?
NO!
PRIVACY ISSUES!
THAT WAS A CLOSE ONE!
IMAGINE IF PAWCASSO'S OWNER OR MOM OR TINA SAW A PHOTO OF ME ON THAT VIP FORUM...
PLEASED TO MEET YOU, PAWCASSO'S HUMAN.
I'M MARY, THE FOUNDER OF VIP.
WOW. YOU GOT A SMILE FROM MARY.
SHE'S USUALLY CATTY TO NON-CANINES.
HER NICKNAME IS "DOG LADY."
I'LL CALL THE CITY COUNCIL!

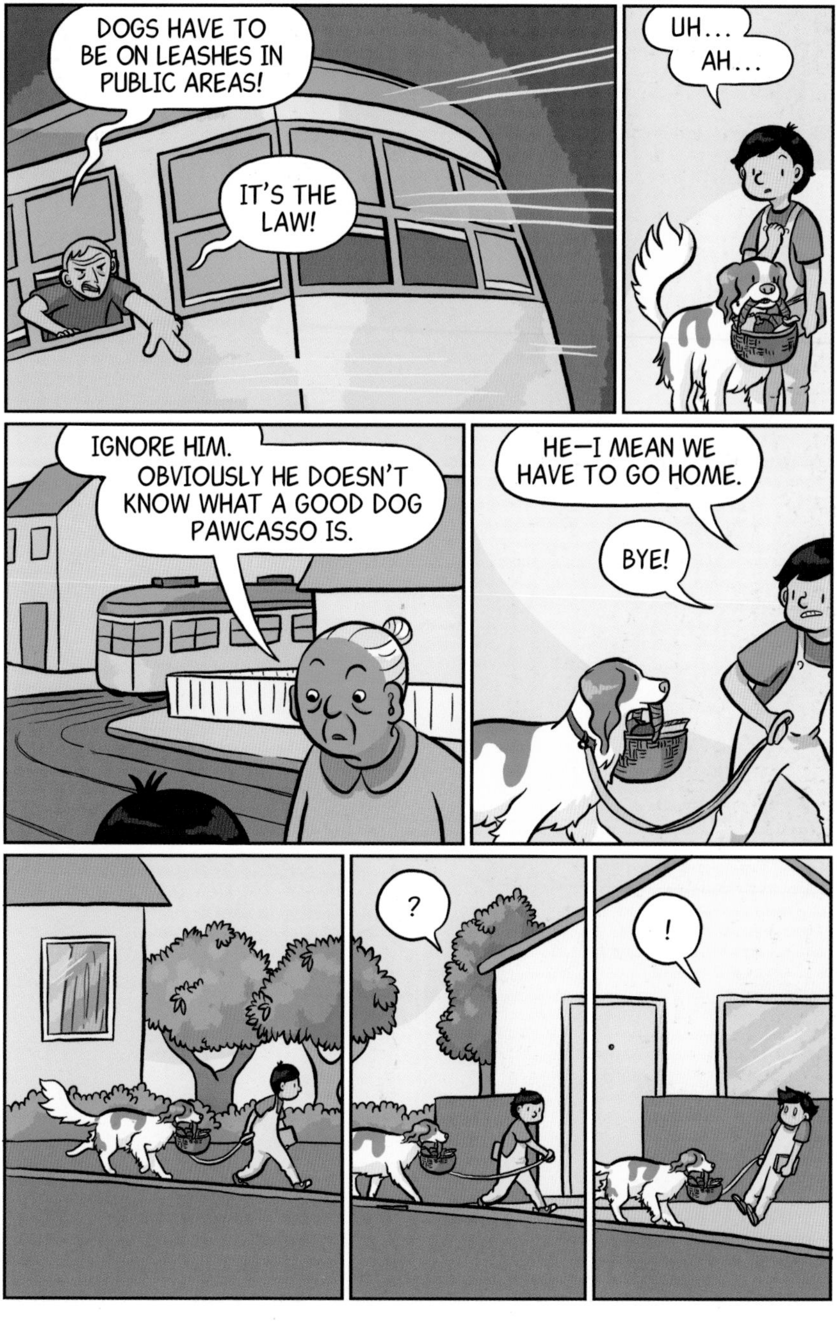
DOGS HAVE TO BE ON LEASHES IN PUBLIC AREAS!
IT'S THE LAW!
UH...
AH...
IGNORE HIM.
OBVIOUSLY HE DOESN'T KNOW WHAT A GOOD DOG PAWCASSO IS.
HE—I MEAN WE HAVE TO GO HOME.
BYE!
?
!

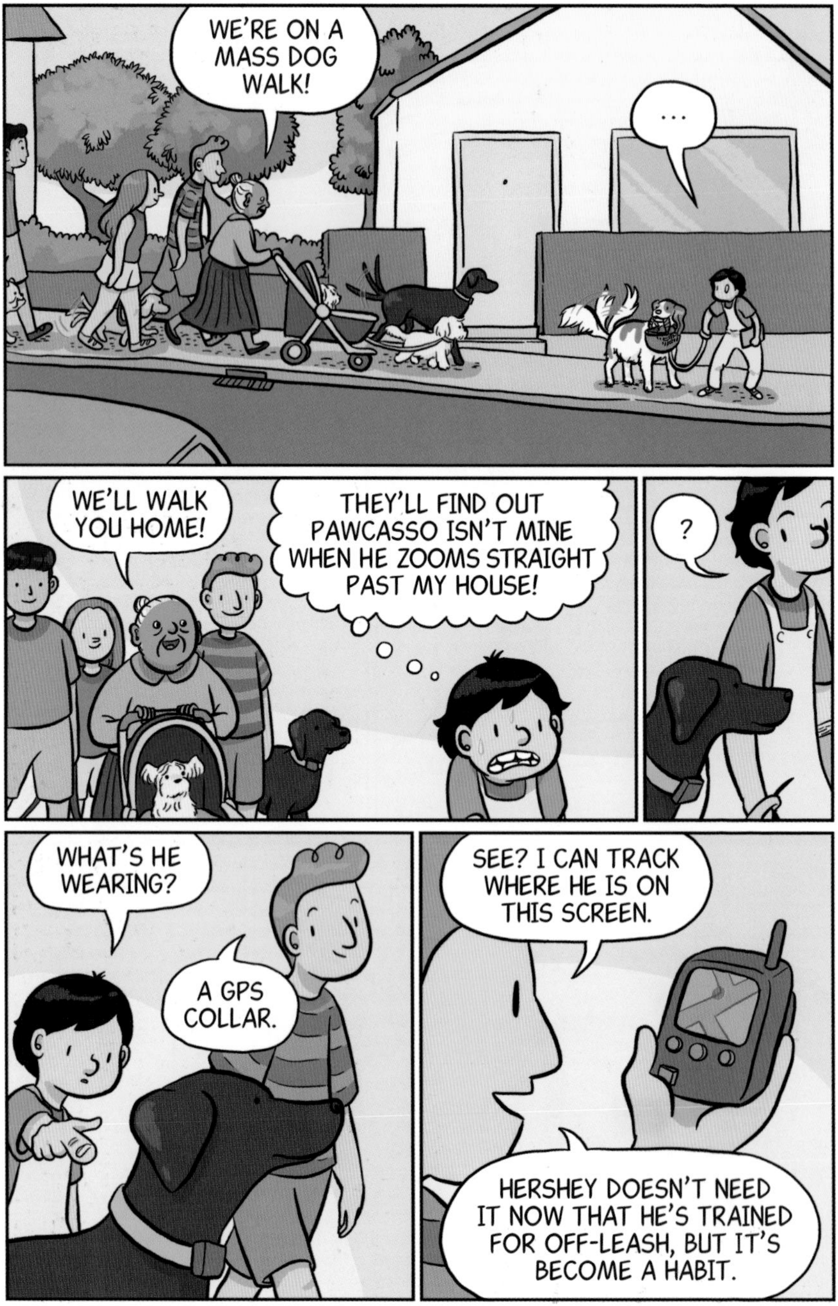
WE'RE ON A MASS DOG WALK!
...
WE'LL WALK YOU HOME!
THEY'LL FIND OUT PAWCASSO ISN'T MINE WHEN HE ZOOMS STRAIGHT PAST MY HOUSE!
?
WHAT'S HE WEARING?
A GPS COLLAR.
SEE? I CAN TRACK WHERE HE IS ON THIS SCREEN.
HERSHEY DOESN'T NEED IT NOW THAT HE'S TRAINED FOR OFF-LEASH, BUT IT'S BECOME A HABIT.

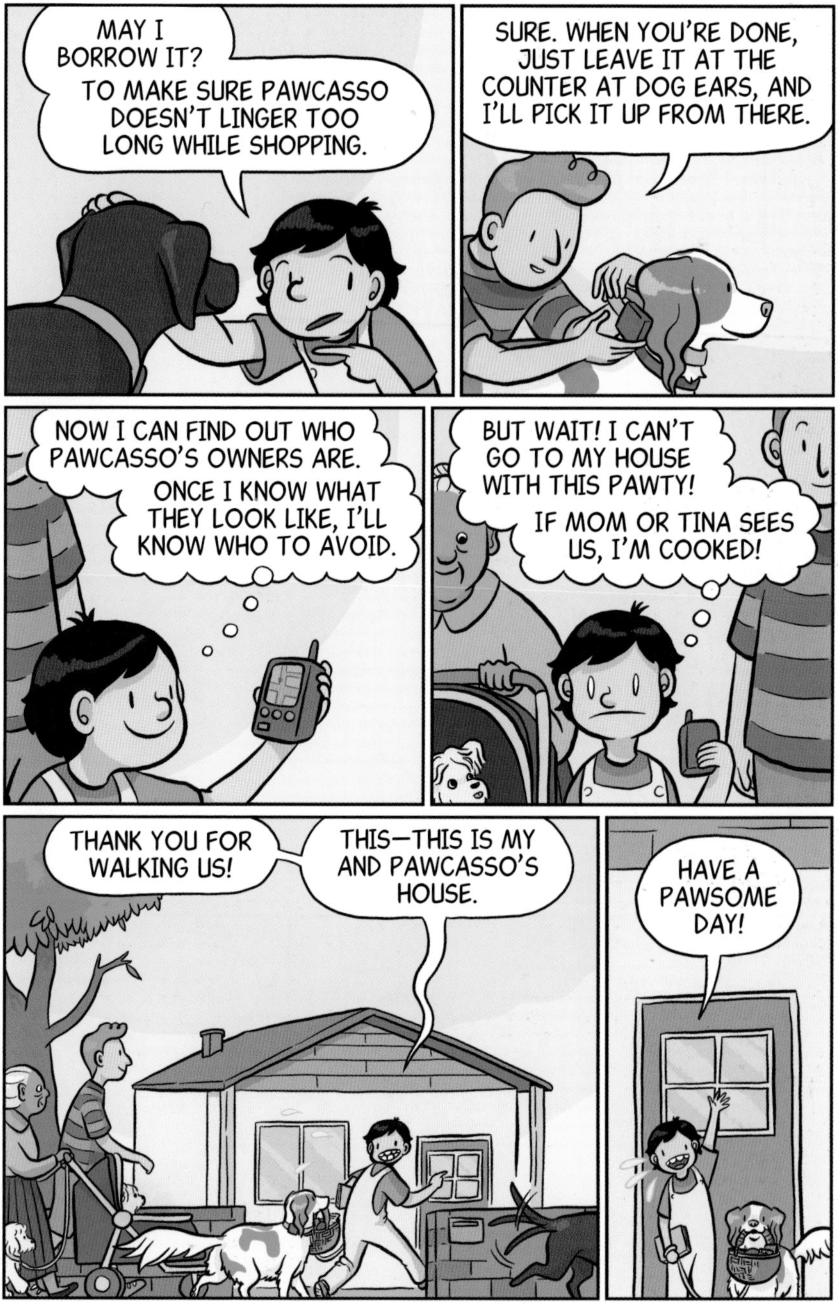
MAY I BORROW IT?
TO MAKE SURE PAWCASSO DOESN'T LINGER TOO LONG WHILE SHOPPING.
SURE. WHEN YOU'RE DONE, JUST LEAVE IT AT THE COUNTER AT DOG EARS, AND I'LL PICK IT UP FROM THERE.
NOW I CAN FIND OUT WHO PAWCASSO'S OWNERS ARE.
ONCE I KNOW WHAT THEY LOOK LIKE, I'LL KNOW WHO TO AVOID.
BUT WAIT! I CAN'T GO TO MY HOUSE WITH THIS PAWTY!
IF MOM OR TINA SEES US, I'M COOKED!
THANK YOU FOR WALKING US!
THIS—THIS IS MY AND PAWCASSO'S HOUSE.
HAVE A PAWSOME DAY!

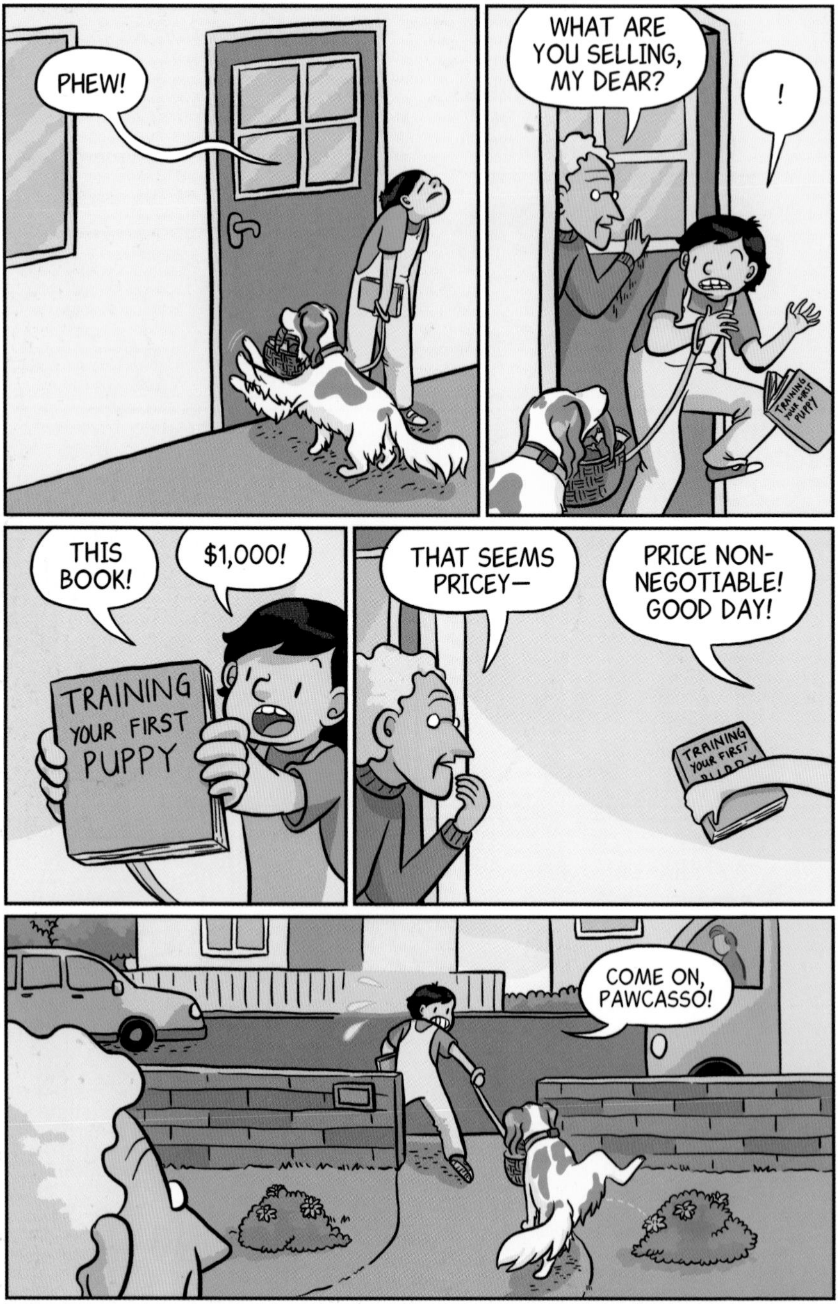
PHEW!
WHAT ARE YOU SELLING, MY DEAR?
!
TRAINING YOUR FIRST PUPPY
THIS BOOK!
$1,000!
TRAINING YOUR FIRST PUPPY
THAT SEEMS PRICEY—
PRICE NON-NEGOTIABLE! GOOD DAY!
COME ON, PAWCASSO!

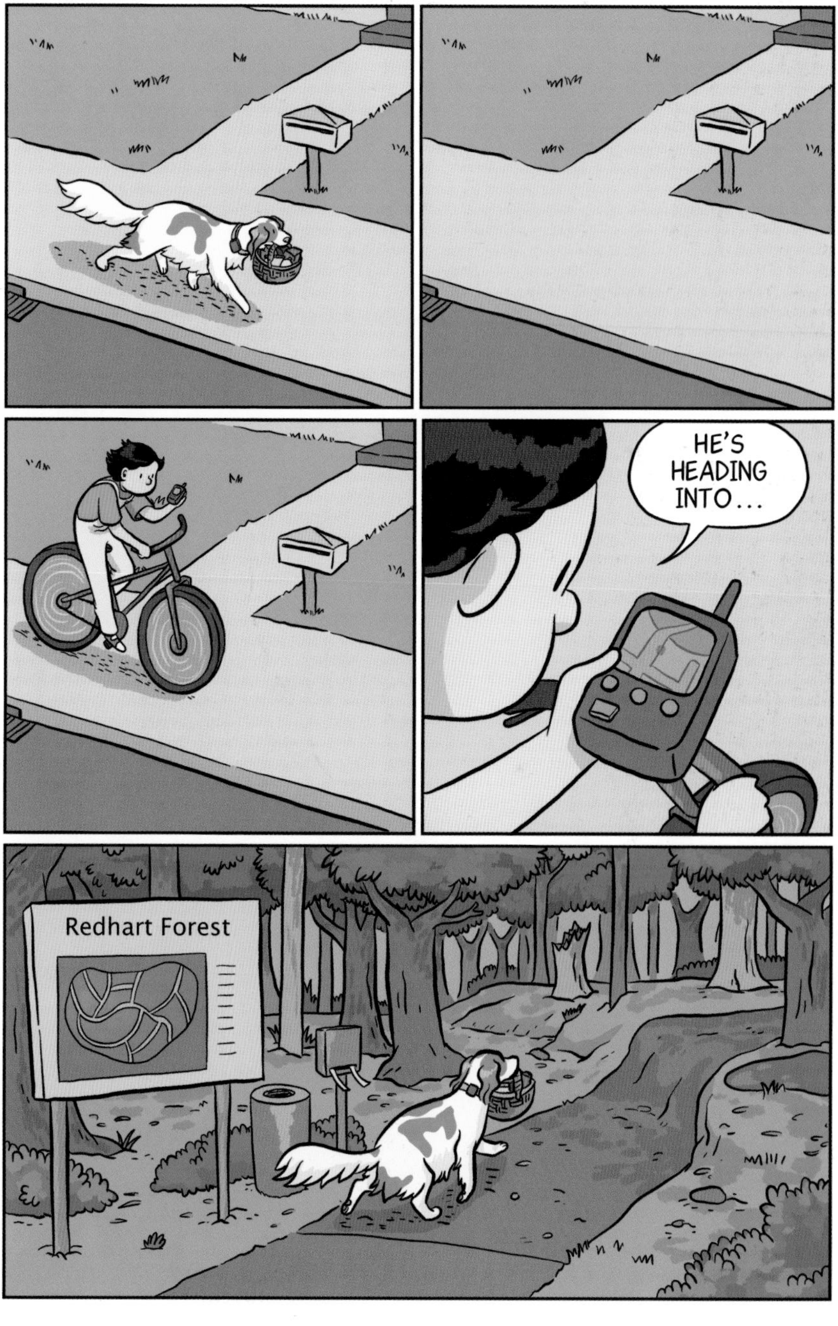
HE'S HEADING INTO...
Redhart Forest

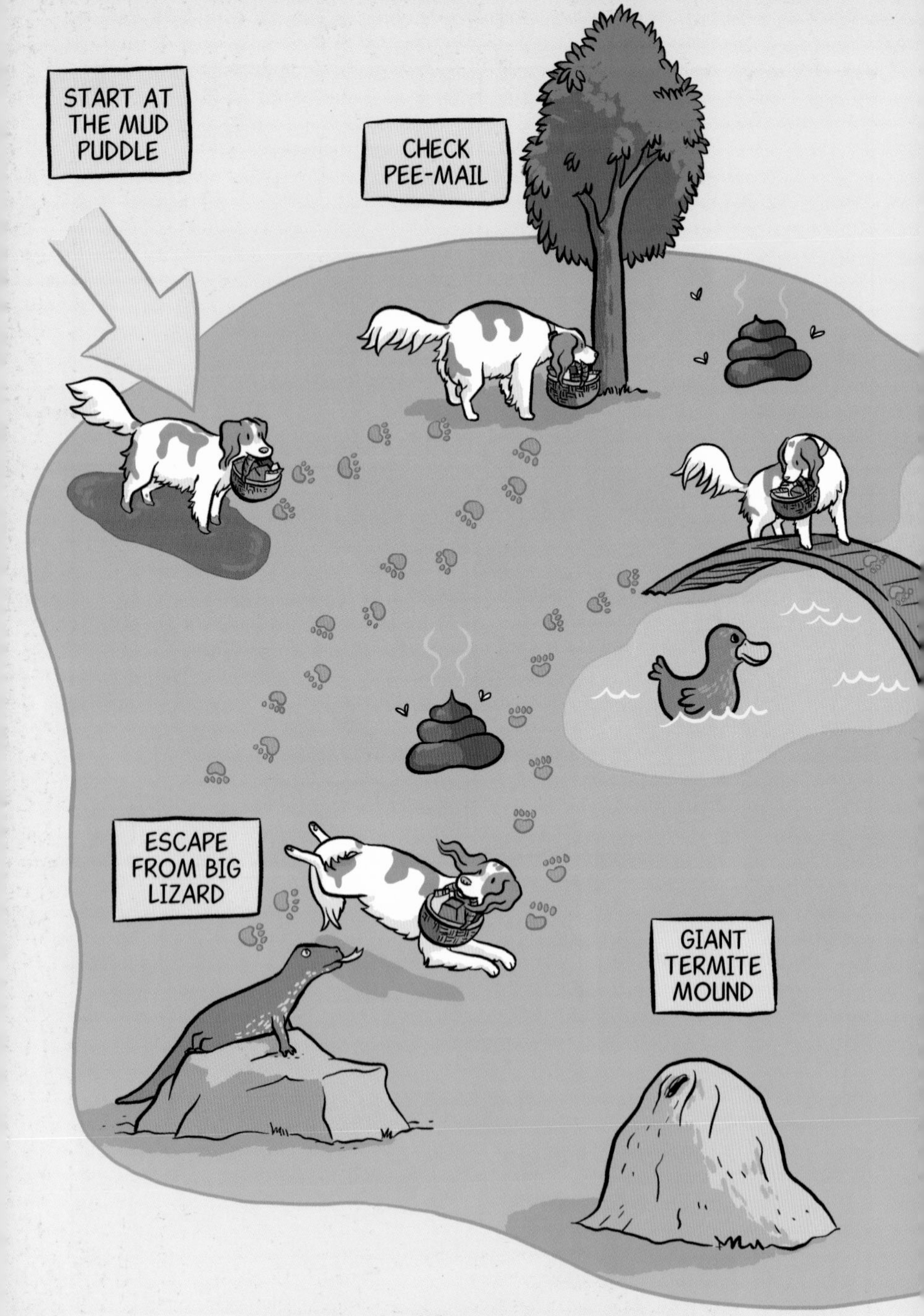
START AT THE MUD PUDDLE
CHECK PEE-MAIL
ESCAPE FROM BIG LIZARD
GIANT TERMITE MOUND

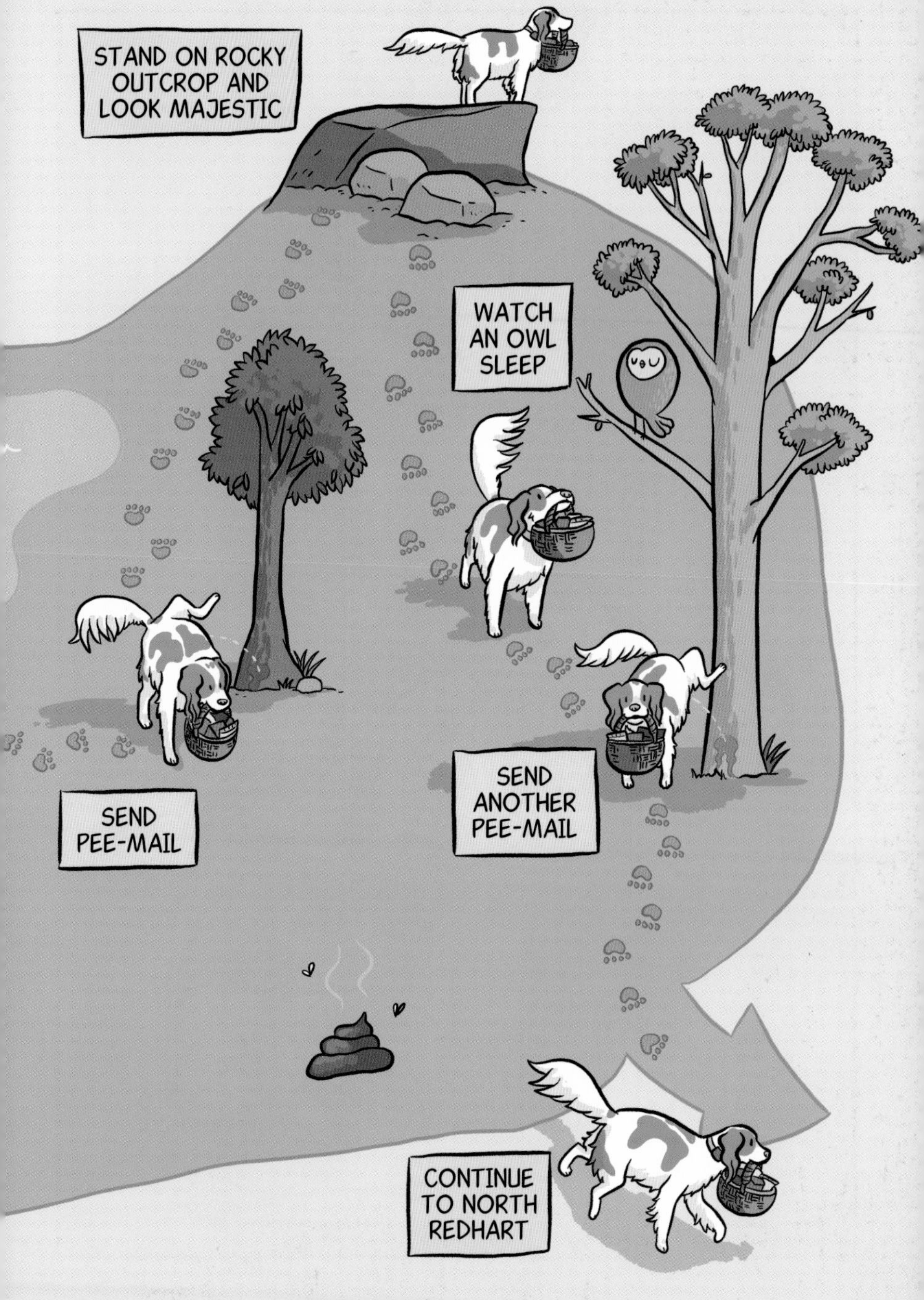
STAND ON ROCKY OUTCROP AND LOOK MAJESTIC
WATCH AN OWL SLEEP
SEND PEE-MAIL
SEND ANOTHER PEE-MAIL
CONTINUE TO NORTH REDHART

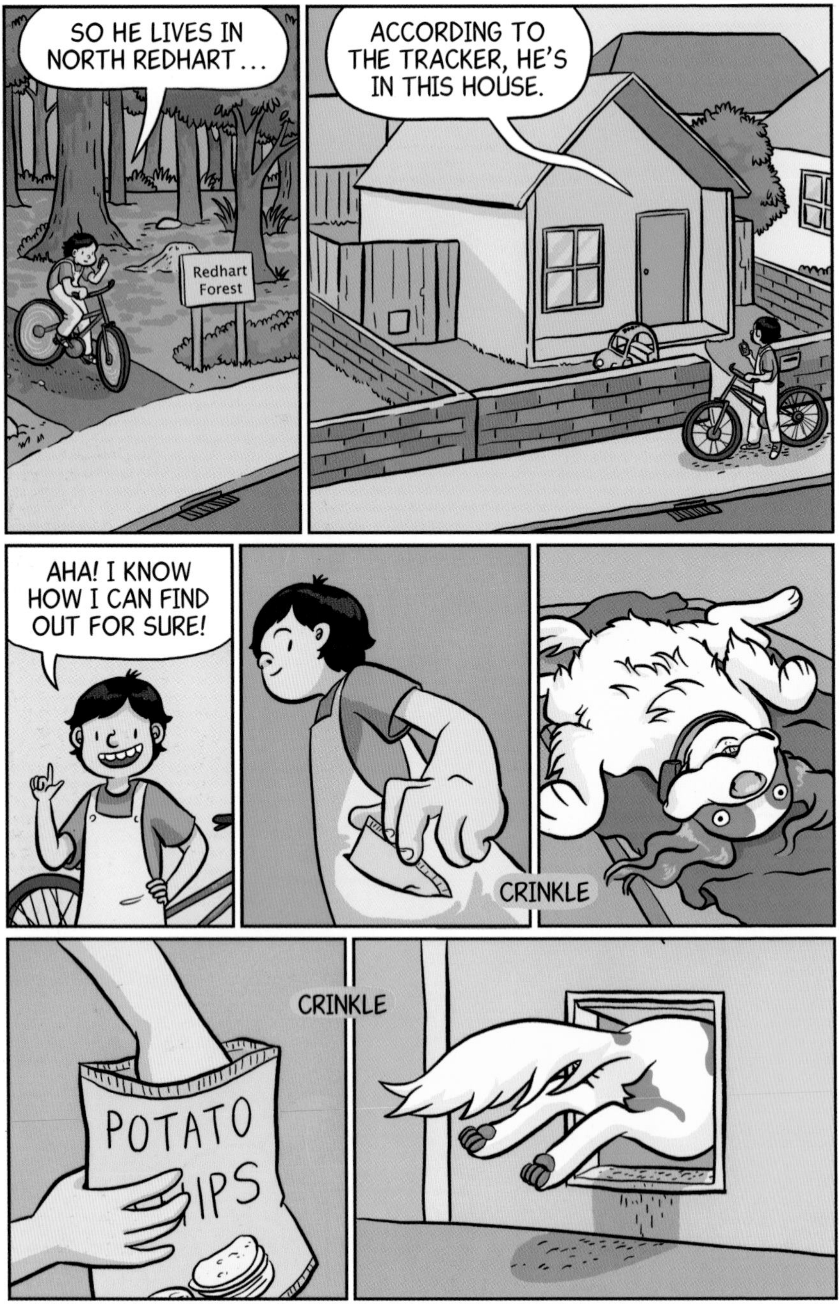
SO HE LIVES IN NORTH REDHART...
Redhart Forest
ACCORDING TO THE TRACKER, HE'S IN THIS HOUSE.
AHA! I KNOW HOW I CAN FIND OUT FOR SURE!
CRINKLE
CRINKLE
POTATO
IPS

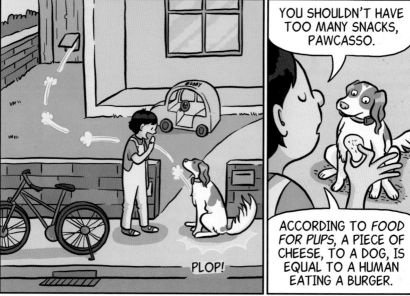

PLOP!

YOU SHOULDN'T HAVE TOO MANY SNACKS, PAWCASSO.

ACCORDING TO *FOOD FOR PUPS*, A PIECE OF CHEESE, TO A DOG, IS EQUAL TO A HUMAN EATING A BURGER.

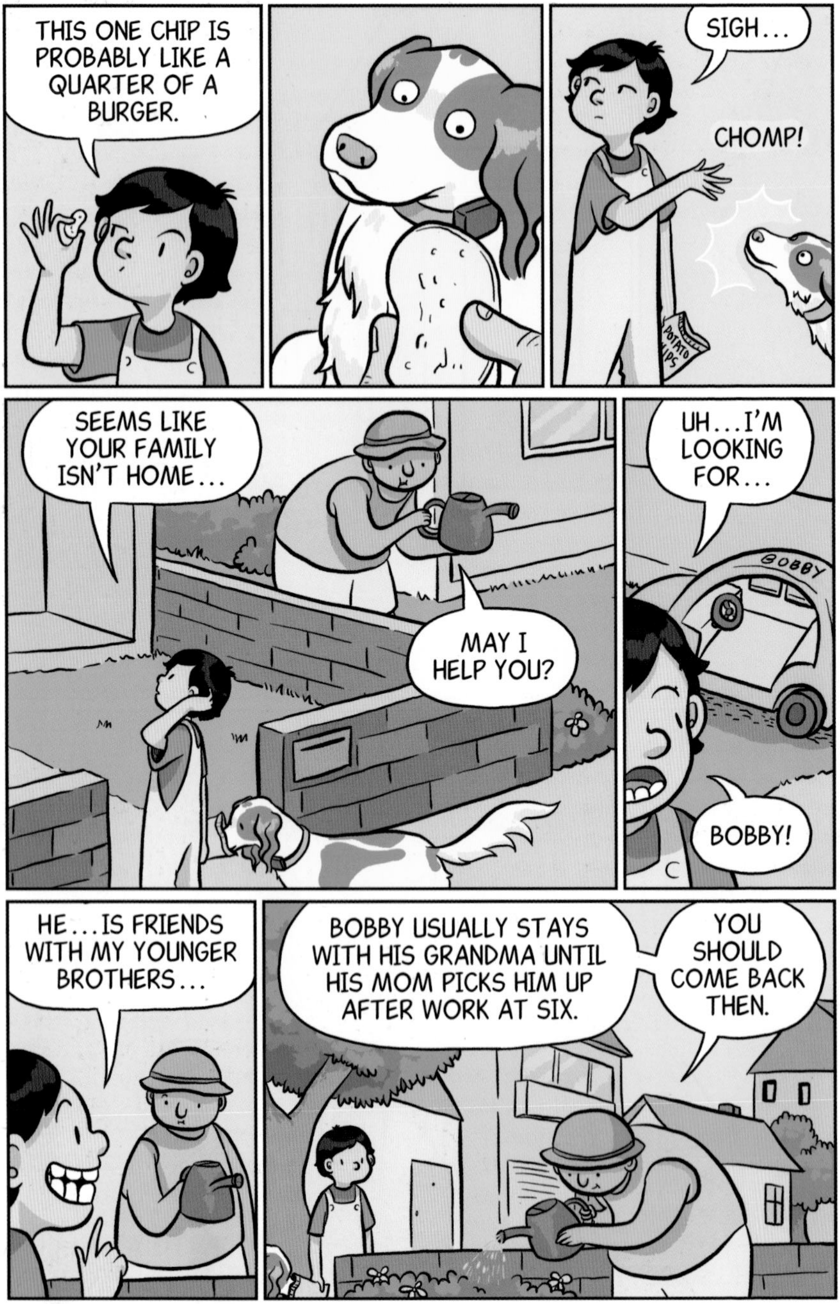
THIS ONE CHIP IS PROBABLY LIKE A QUARTER OF A BURGER.
SIGH...
CHOMP!
POTATO CHIPS
SEEMS LIKE YOUR FAMILY ISN'T HOME...
MAY I HELP YOU?
UH...I'M LOOKING FOR...
BOBBY
BOBBY!
HE...IS FRIENDS WITH MY YOUNGER BROTHERS...
BOBBY USUALLY STAYS WITH HIS GRANDMA UNTIL HIS MOM PICKS HIM UP AFTER WORK AT SIX.
YOU SHOULD COME BACK THEN.

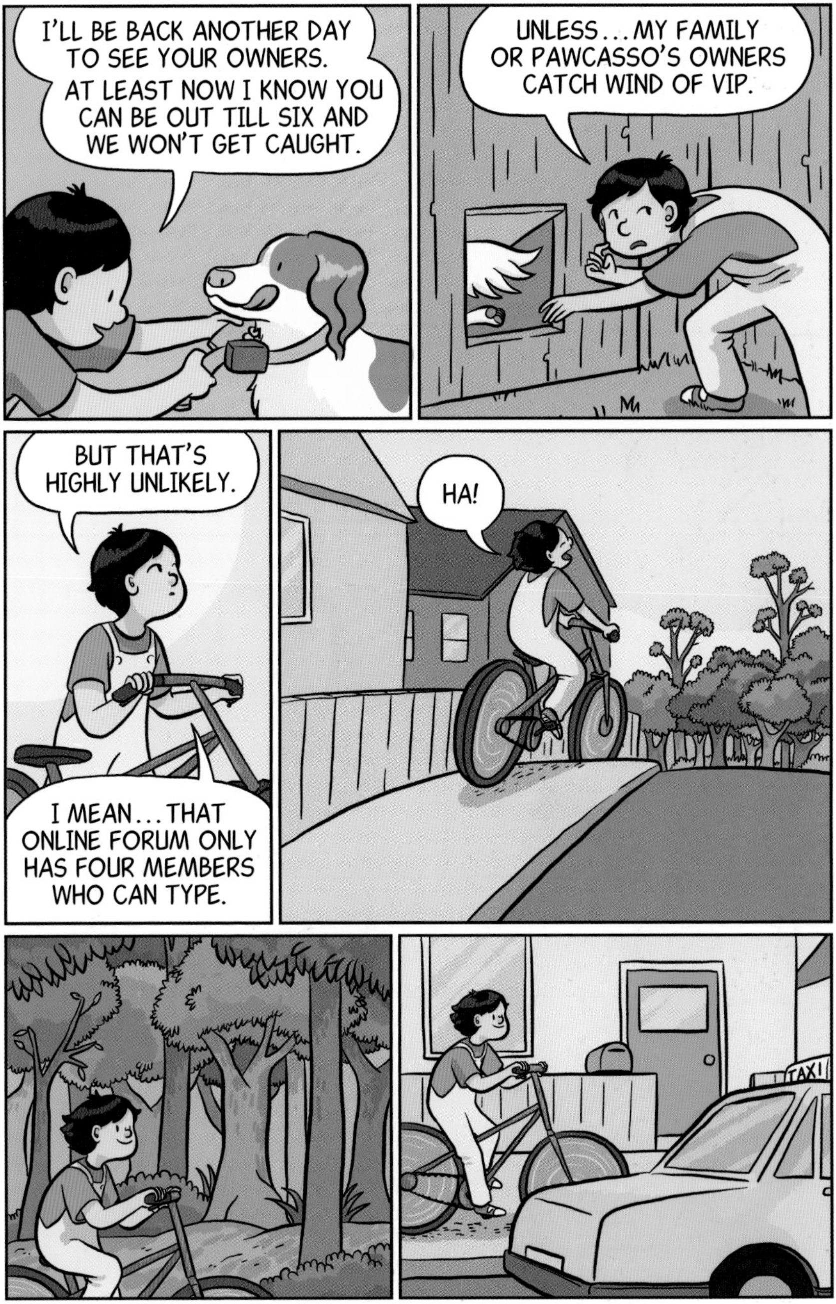
I'LL BE BACK ANOTHER DAY TO SEE YOUR OWNERS.
AT LEAST NOW I KNOW YOU CAN BE OUT TILL SIX AND WE WON'T GET CAUGHT.
UNLESS... MY FAMILY OR PAWCASSO'S OWNERS CATCH WIND OF VIP.
BUT THAT'S HIGHLY UNLIKELY.
I MEAN... THAT ONLINE FORUM ONLY HAS FOUR MEMBERS WHO CAN TYPE.
HA!
TAXI

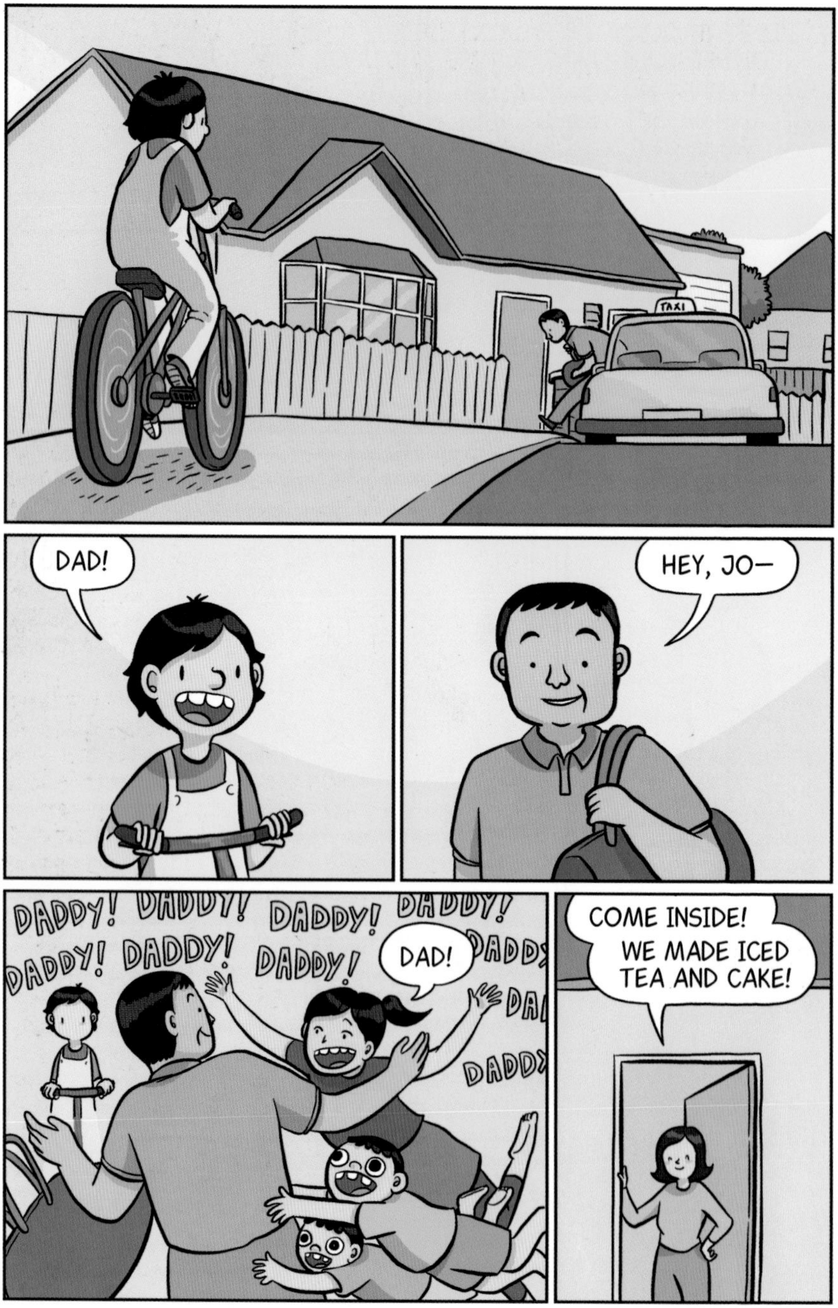
TAXI
DAD!
HEY, JO—
DADDY! DADDY! DADDY! DADDY!
DADDY! DADDY! DADDY!
DAD!
COME INSIDE! WE MADE ICED TEA AND CAKE!

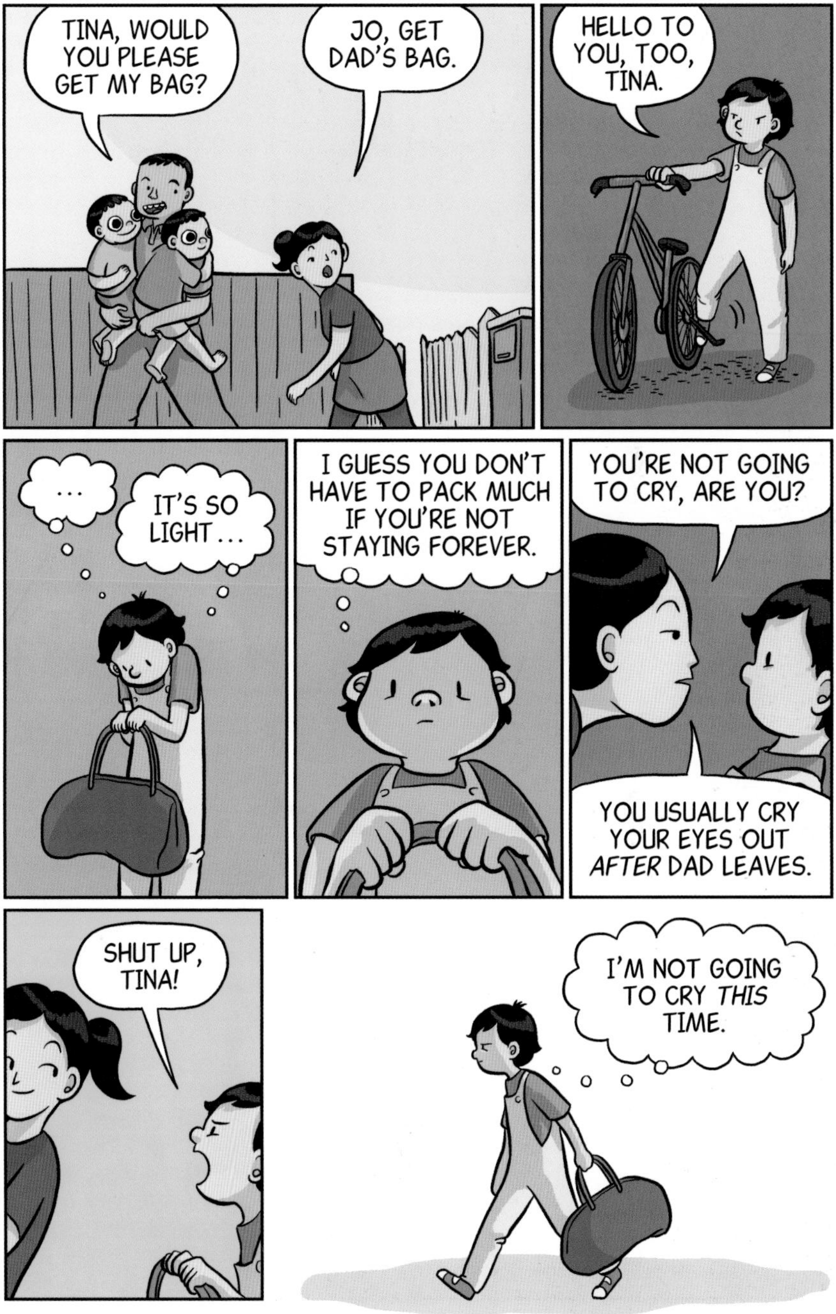
TINA, WOULD YOU PLEASE GET MY BAG?
JO, GET DAD'S BAG.
HELLO TO YOU, TOO, TINA.
...
IT'S SO LIGHT...
I GUESS YOU DON'T HAVE TO PACK MUCH IF YOU'RE NOT STAYING FOREVER.
YOU'RE NOT GOING TO CRY, ARE YOU?
YOU USUALLY CRY YOUR EYES OUT *AFTER* DAD LEAVES.
SHUT UP, TINA!
I'M NOT GOING TO CRY *THIS* TIME.

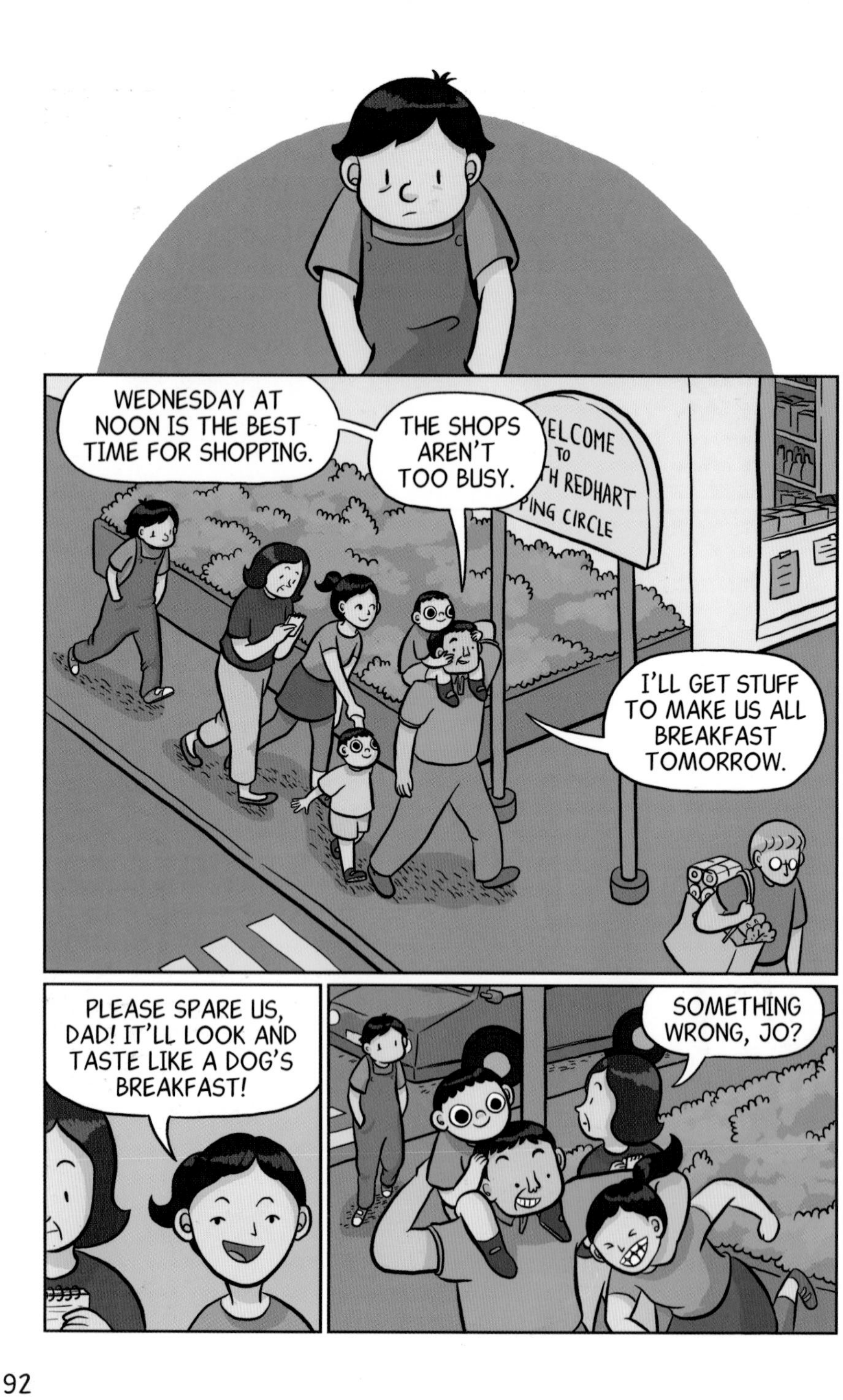
WEDNESDAY AT NOON IS THE BEST TIME FOR SHOPPING.
THE SHOPS AREN'T TOO BUSY.
I'LL GET STUFF TO MAKE US ALL BREAKFAST TOMORROW.
PLEASE SPARE US, DAD! IT'LL LOOK AND TASTE LIKE A DOG'S BREAKFAST!
SOMETHING WRONG, JO?

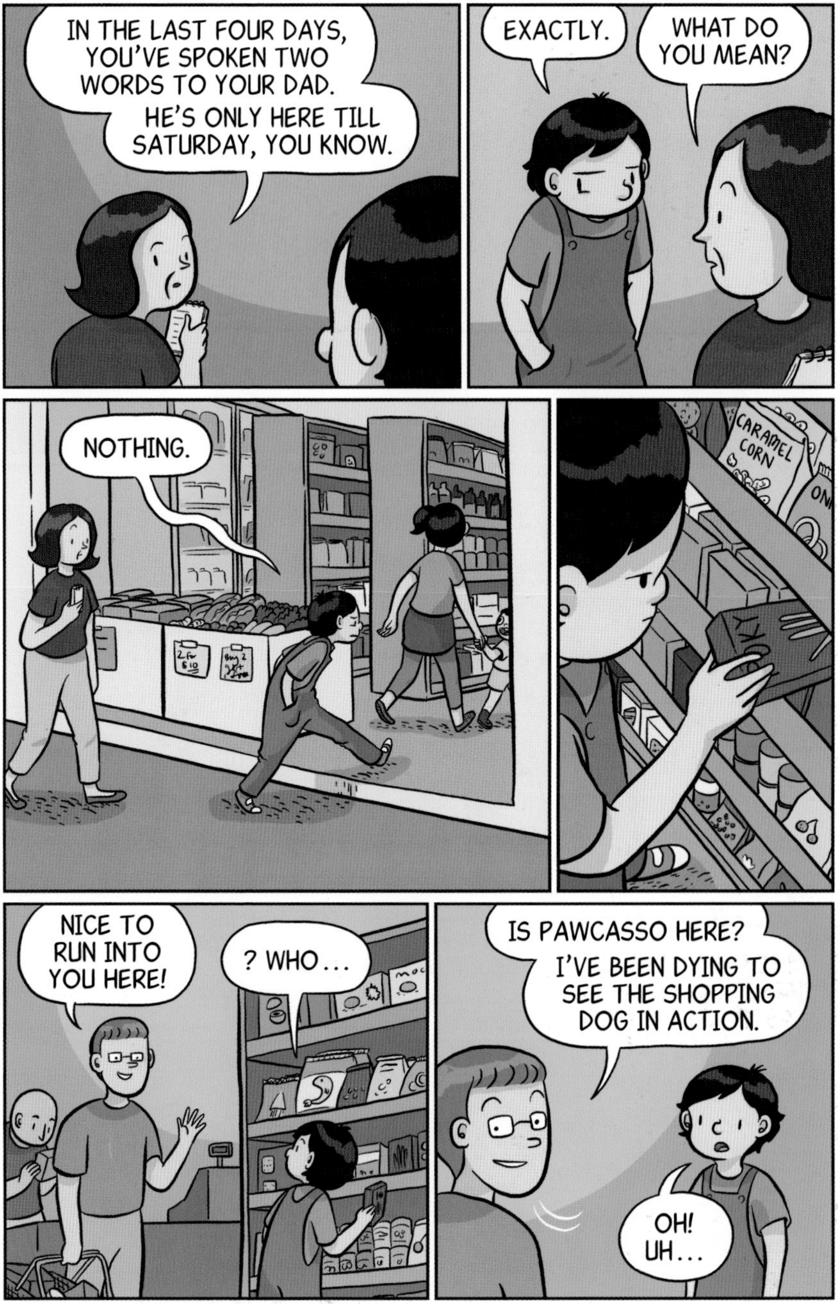
IN THE LAST FOUR DAYS, YOU'VE SPOKEN TWO WORDS TO YOUR DAD.
HE'S ONLY HERE TILL SATURDAY, YOU KNOW.
EXACTLY.
WHAT DO YOU MEAN?
NOTHING.
CARAMEL CORN
NICE TO RUN INTO YOU HERE!
? WHO...
IS PAWCASSO HERE?
I'VE BEEN DYING TO SEE THE SHOPPING DOG IN ACTION.
OH! UH...

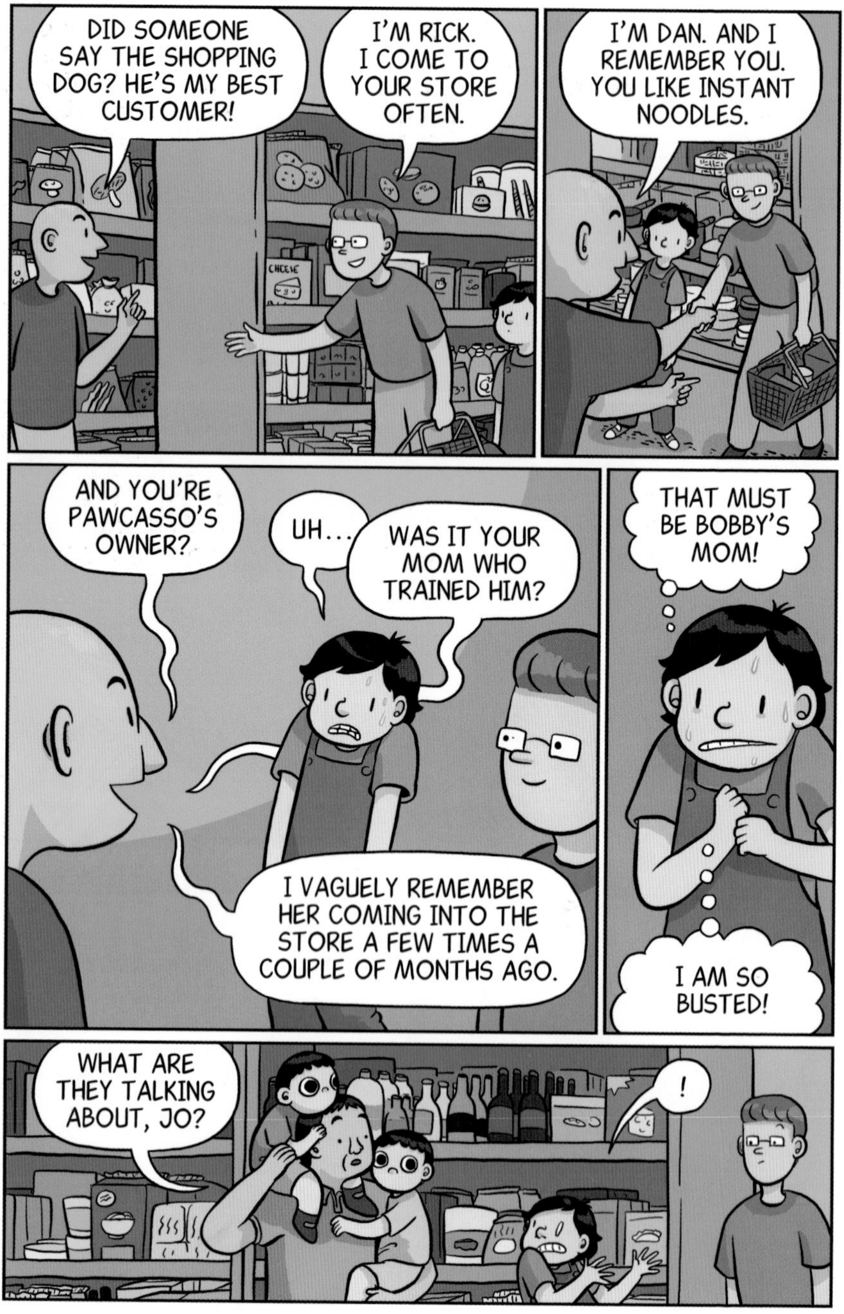
DID SOMEONE SAY THE SHOPPING DOG? HE'S MY BEST CUSTOMER!
I'M RICK. I COME TO YOUR STORE OFTEN.
CHEESE
I'M DAN. AND I REMEMBER YOU. YOU LIKE INSTANT NOODLES.
AND YOU'RE PAWCASSO'S OWNER?
UH...
WAS IT YOUR MOM WHO TRAINED HIM?
I VAGUELY REMEMBER HER COMING INTO THE STORE A FEW TIMES A COUPLE OF MONTHS AGO.
THAT MUST BE BOBBY'S MOM!
I AM SO BUSTED!
WHAT ARE THEY TALKING ABOUT, JO?
!

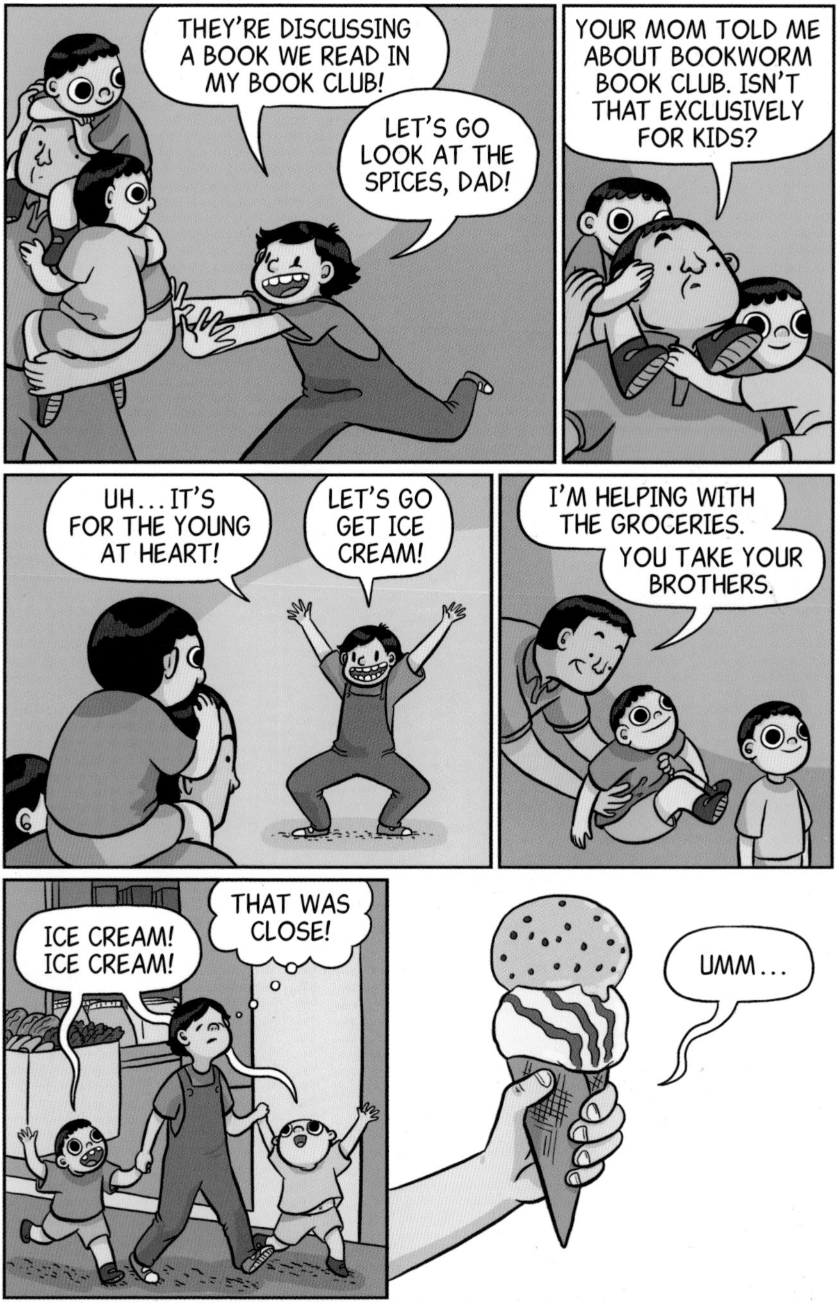

THEY'RE DISCUSSING A BOOK WE READ IN MY BOOK CLUB!
LET'S GO LOOK AT THE SPICES, DAD!
YOUR MOM TOLD ME ABOUT BOOKWORM BOOK CLUB. ISN'T THAT EXCLUSIVELY FOR KIDS?
UH... IT'S FOR THE YOUNG AT HEART!
LET'S GO GET ICE CREAM!
I'M HELPING WITH THE GROCERIES.
YOU TAKE YOUR BROTHERS.
ICE CREAM! ICE CREAM!
THAT WAS CLOSE!
UMM...

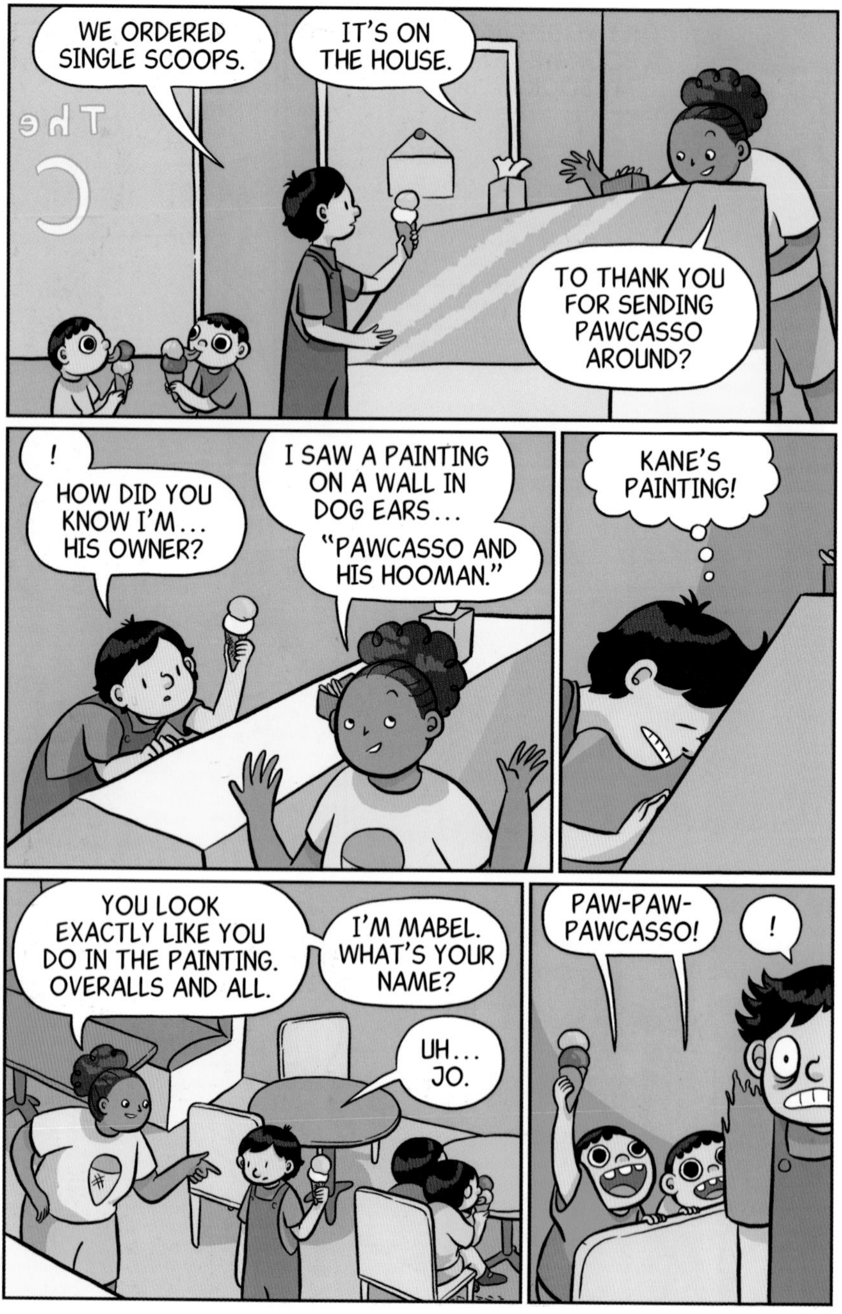
WE ORDERED SINGLE SCOOPS.
IT'S ON THE HOUSE.
The
TO THANK YOU FOR SENDING PAWCASSO AROUND?
!
HOW DID YOU KNOW I'M... HIS OWNER?
I SAW A PAINTING ON A WALL IN DOG EARS...
"PAWCASSO AND HIS HOOMAN."
KANE'S PAINTING!
YOU LOOK EXACTLY LIKE YOU DO IN THE PAINTING. OVERALLS AND ALL.
I'M MABEL. WHAT'S YOUR NAME?
UH... JO.
PAW-PAW-PAWCASSO!
!

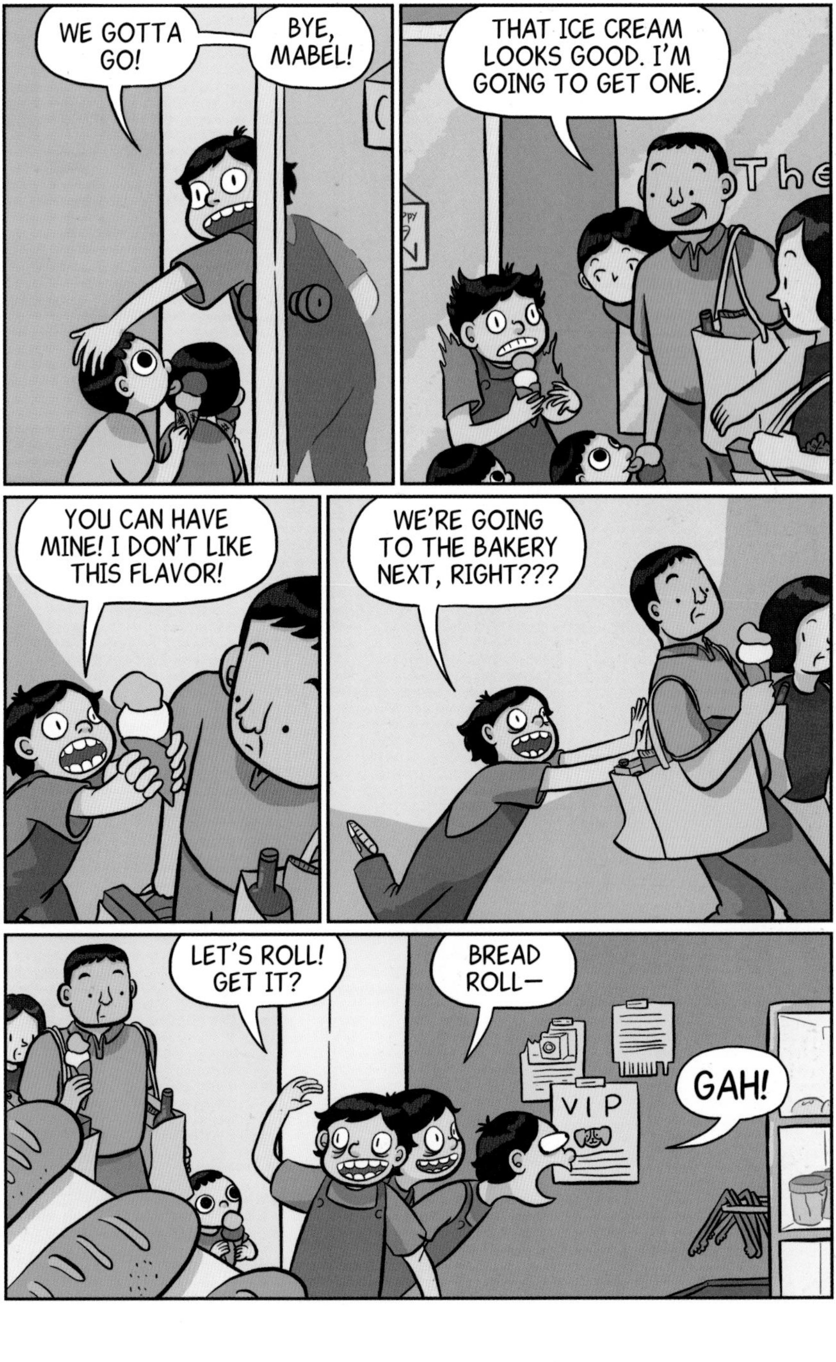
WE GOTTA GO!
BYE, MABEL!
THAT ICE CREAM LOOKS GOOD. I'M GOING TO GET ONE.
YOU CAN HAVE MINE! I DON'T LIKE THIS FLAVOR!
WE'RE GOING TO THE BAKERY NEXT, RIGHT???
LET'S ROLL! GET IT?
BREAD ROLL—
VIP
GAH!

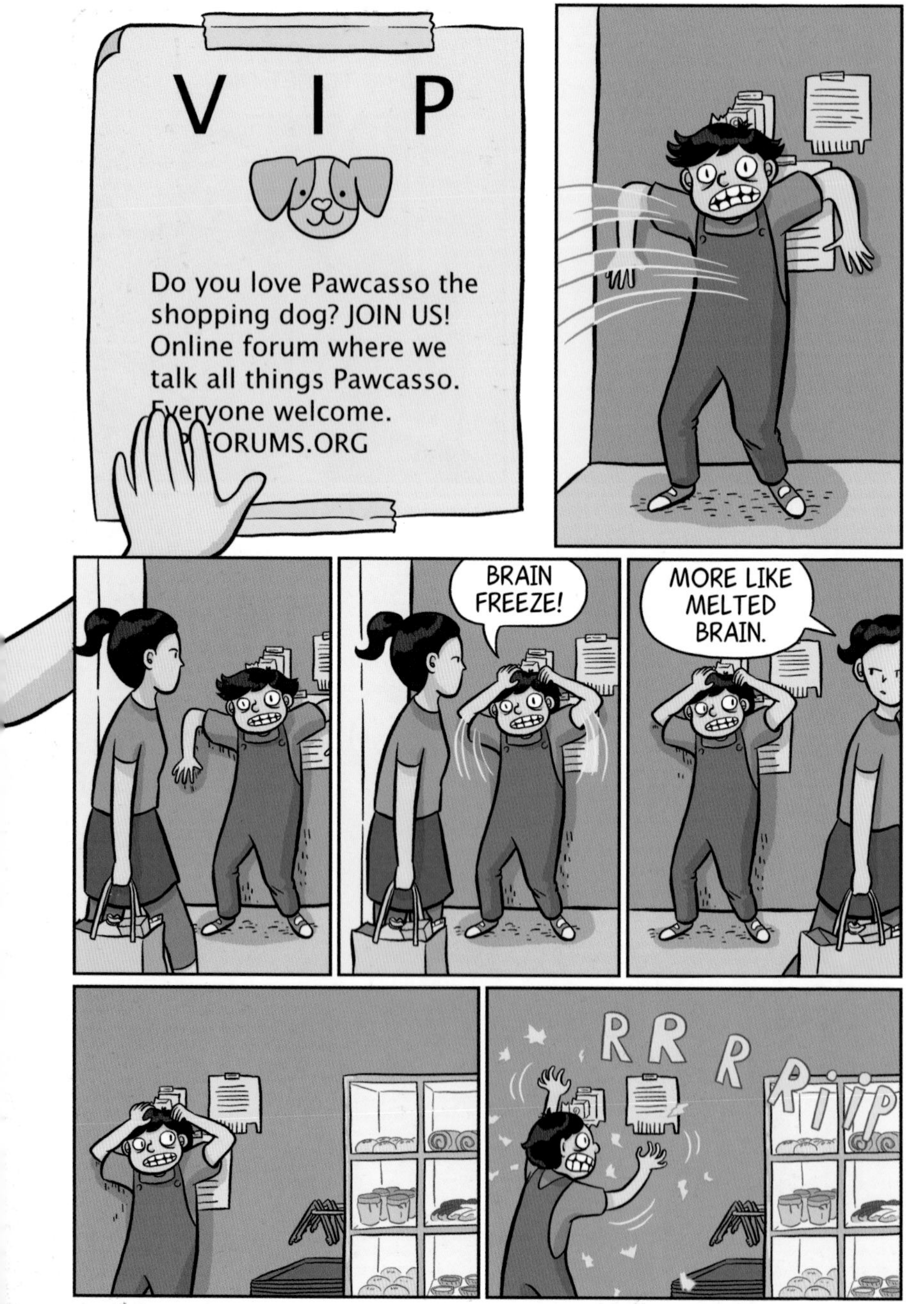
VIP
Do you love Pawcasso the shopping dog? JOIN US! Online forum where we talk all things Pawcasso. Everyone welcome.
ORUMS.ORG
BRAIN FREEZE!
MORE LIKE MELTED BRAIN.
R R R
RIIP

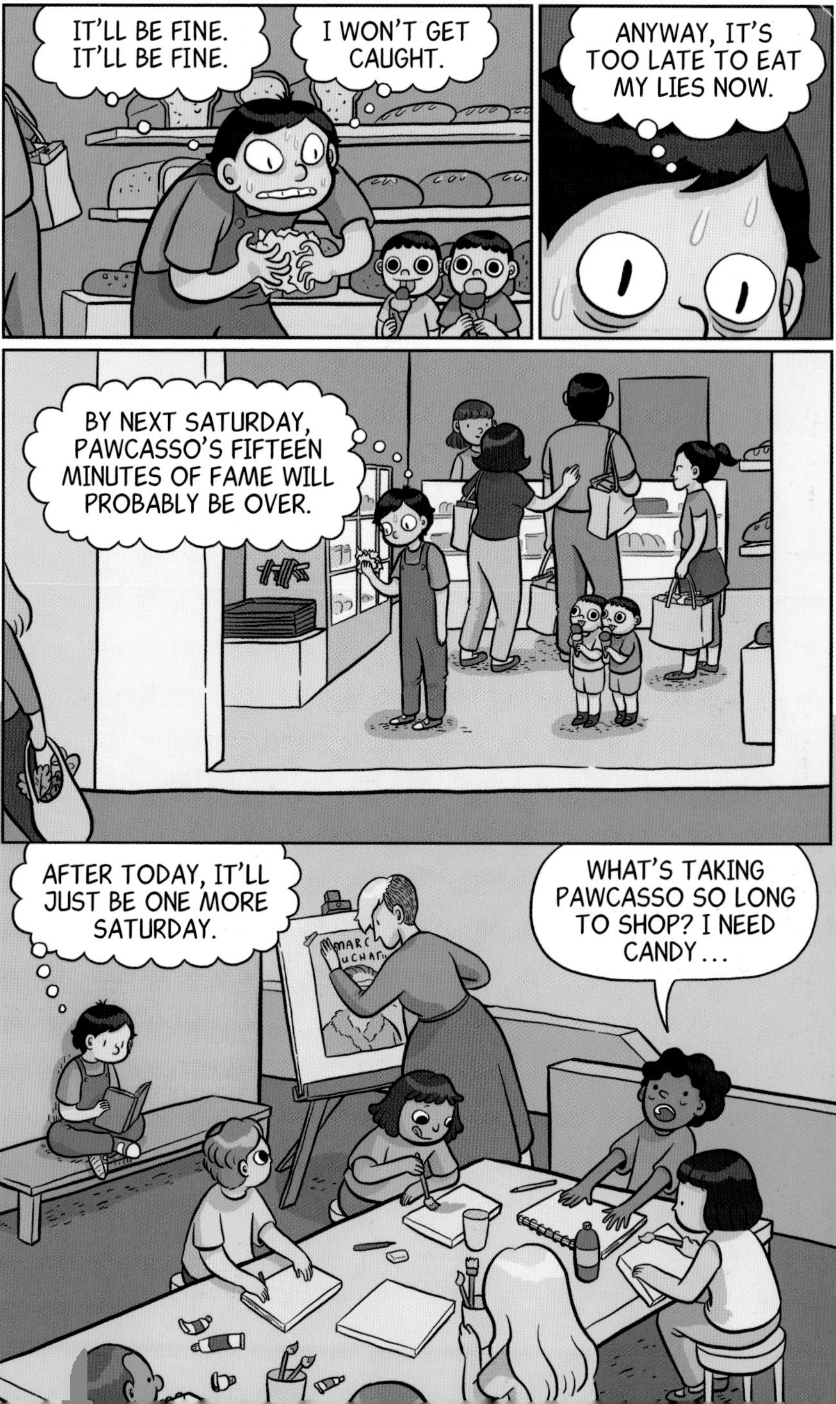
IT'LL BE FINE. IT'LL BE FINE.
I WON'T GET CAUGHT.
ANYWAY, IT'S TOO LATE TO EAT MY LIES NOW.
BY NEXT SATURDAY, PAWCASSO'S FIFTEEN MINUTES OF FAME WILL PROBABLY BE OVER.
AFTER TODAY, IT'LL JUST BE ONE MORE SATURDAY.
WHAT'S TAKING PAWCASSO SO LONG TO SHOP? I NEED CANDY . . .

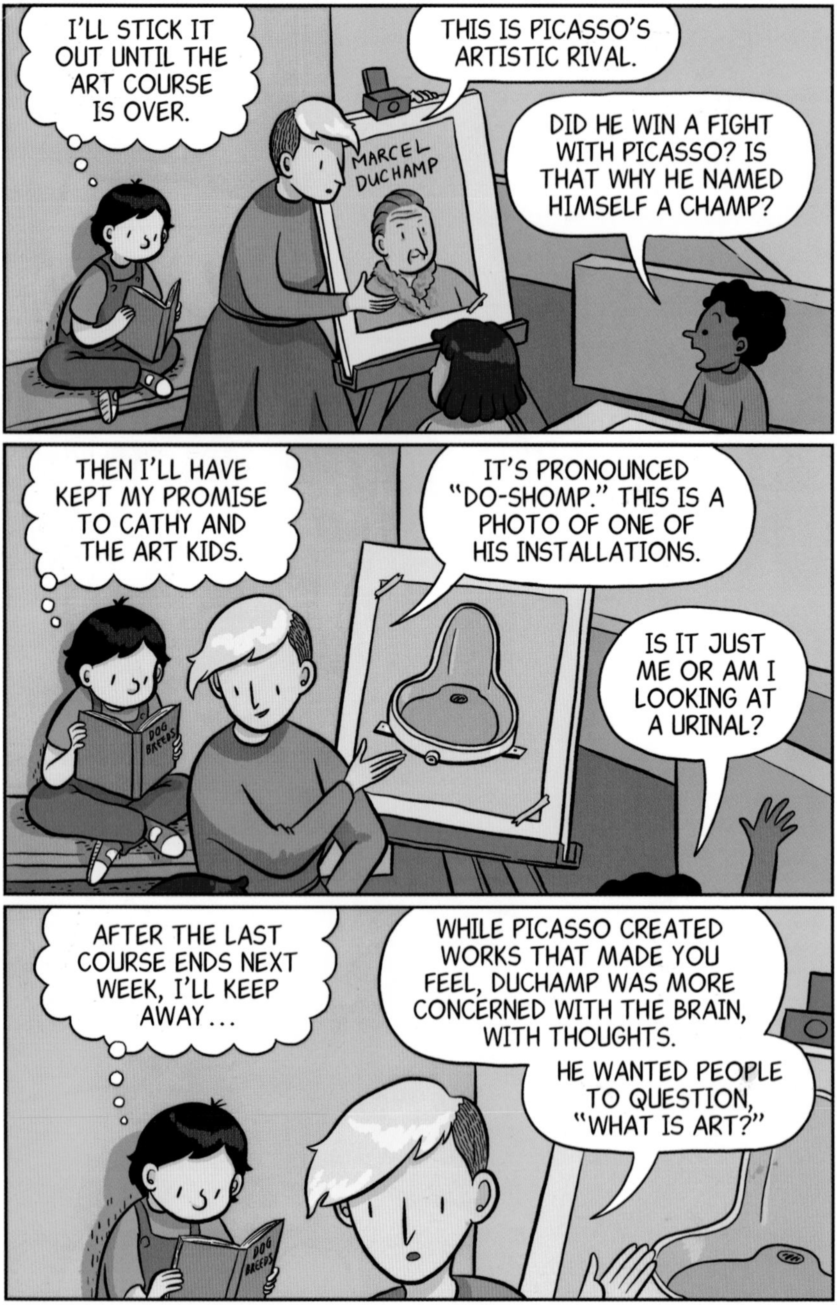
I'LL STICK IT OUT UNTIL THE ART COURSE IS OVER.
THIS IS PICASSO'S ARTISTIC RIVAL.
MARCEL DUCHAMP
DID HE WIN A FIGHT WITH PICASSO? IS THAT WHY HE NAMED HIMSELF A CHAMP?
THEN I'LL HAVE KEPT MY PROMISE TO CATHY AND THE ART KIDS.
IT'S PRONOUNCED "DO-SHOMP." THIS IS A PHOTO OF ONE OF HIS INSTALLATIONS.
DOG BREEDS
IS IT JUST ME OR AM I LOOKING AT A URINAL?
AFTER THE LAST COURSE ENDS NEXT WEEK, I'LL KEEP AWAY...
WHILE PICASSO CREATED WORKS THAT MADE YOU FEEL, DUCHAMP WAS MORE CONCERNED WITH THE BRAIN, WITH THOUGHTS.
HE WANTED PEOPLE TO QUESTION, "WHAT IS ART?"
DOG BREEDS

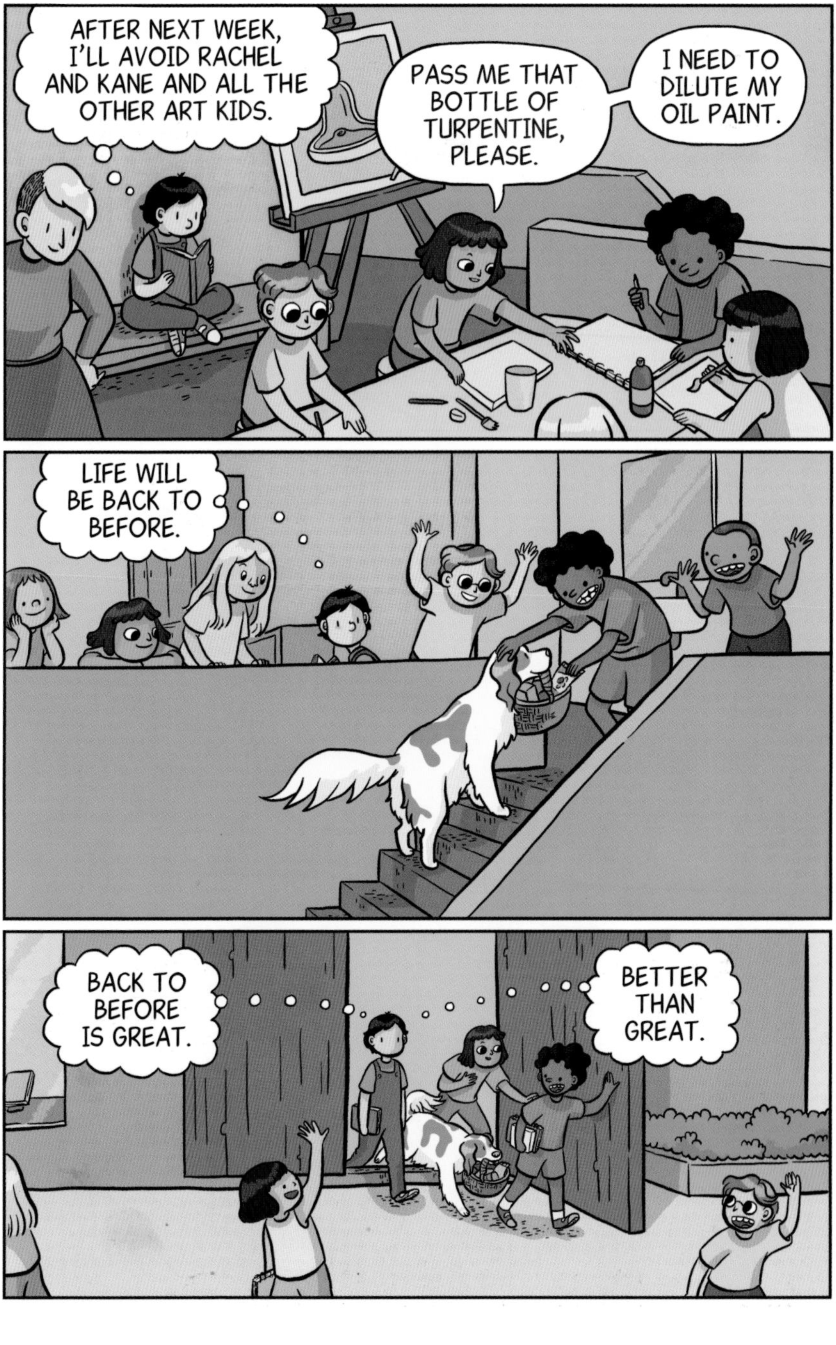
AFTER NEXT WEEK, I'LL AVOID RACHEL AND KANE AND ALL THE OTHER ART KIDS.
PASS ME THAT BOTTLE OF TURPENTINE, PLEASE.
I NEED TO DILUTE MY OIL PAINT.
LIFE WILL BE BACK TO BEFORE.
BACK TO BEFORE IS GREAT.
BETTER THAN GREAT.

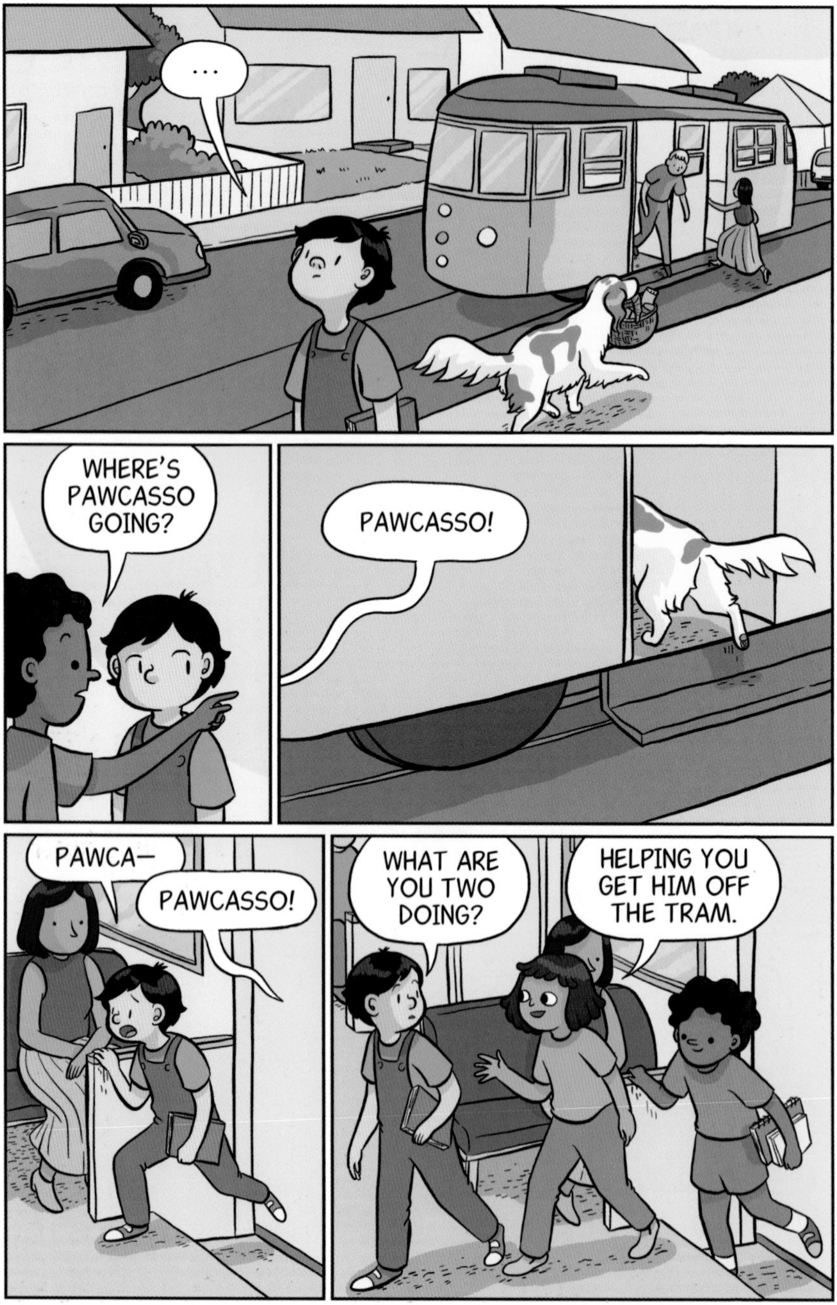
...
WHERE'S PAWCASSO GOING?
PAWCASSO!
PAWCA—
PAWCASSO!
WHAT ARE YOU TWO DOING?
HELPING YOU GET HIM OFF THE TRAM.

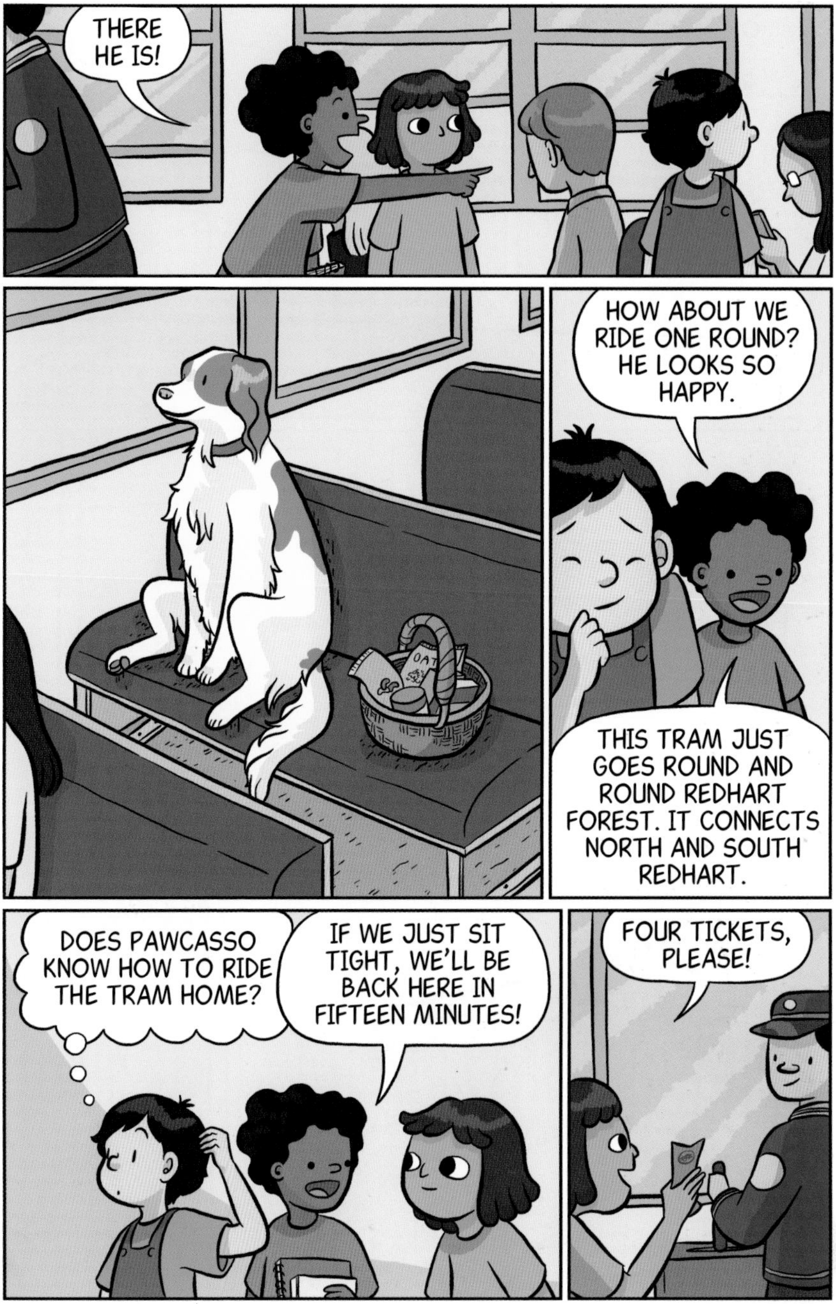
THERE HE IS!
HOW ABOUT WE RIDE ONE ROUND? HE LOOKS SO HAPPY.
THIS TRAM JUST GOES ROUND AND ROUND REDHART FOREST. IT CONNECTS NORTH AND SOUTH REDHART.
DOES PAWCASSO KNOW HOW TO RIDE THE TRAM HOME?
IF WE JUST SIT TIGHT, WE'LL BE BACK HERE IN FIFTEEN MINUTES!
FOUR TICKETS, PLEASE!

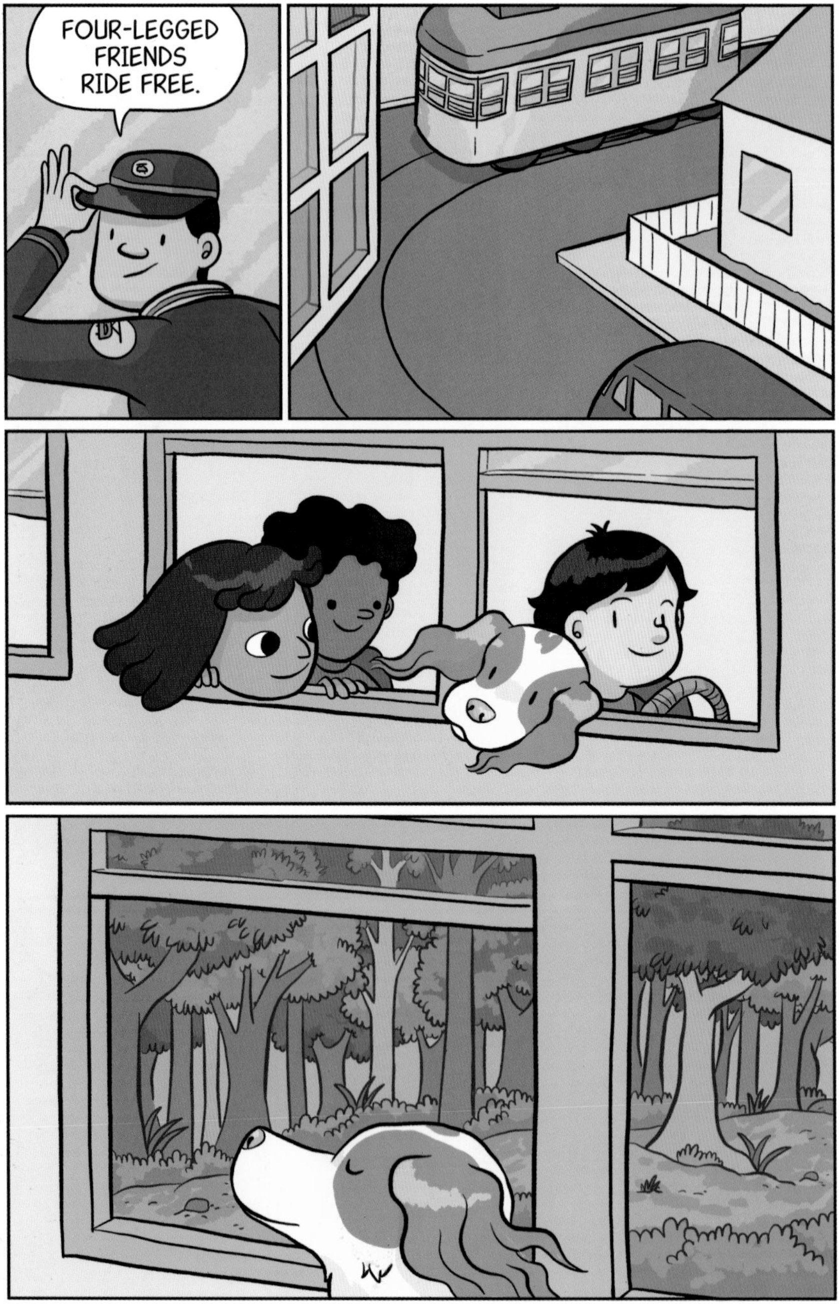
FOUR-LEGGED FRIENDS RIDE FREE.

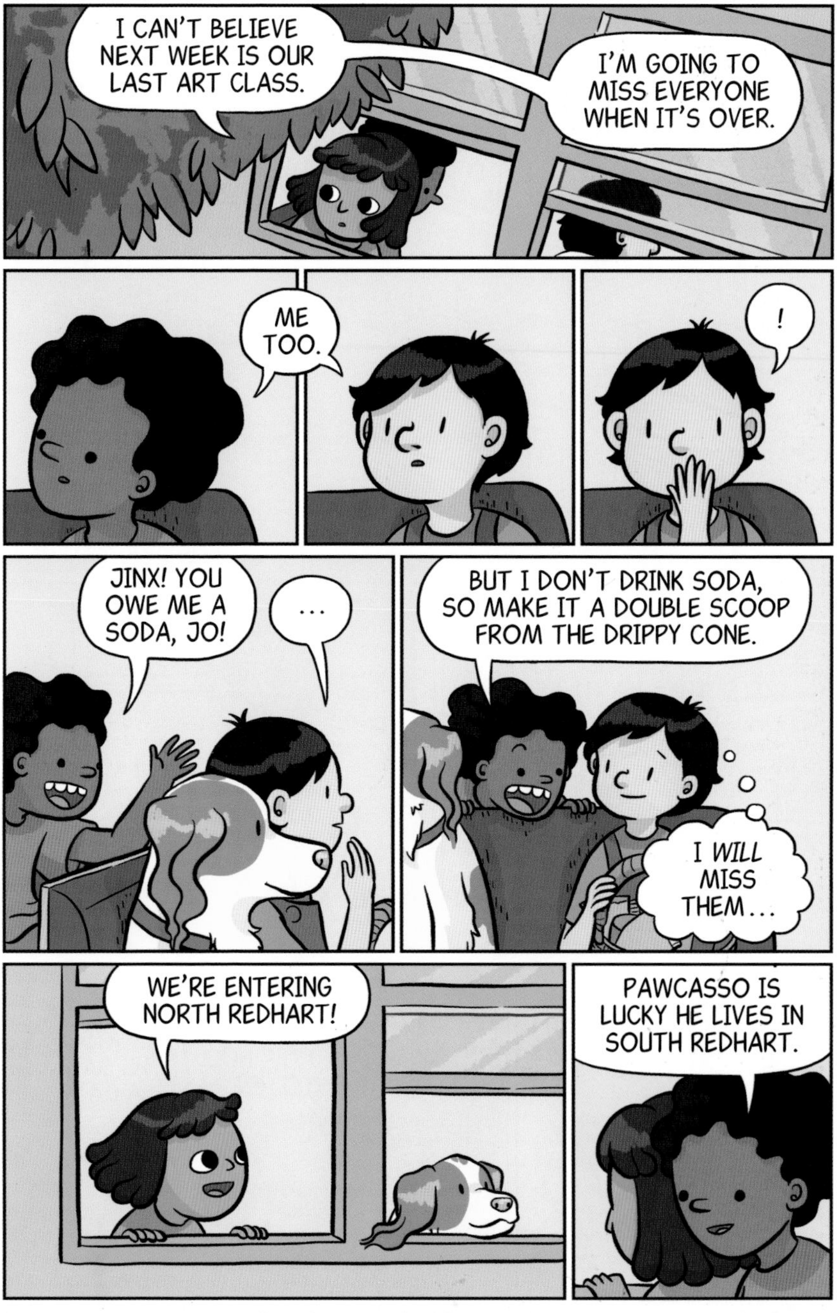
I CAN'T BELIEVE NEXT WEEK IS OUR LAST ART CLASS.
I'M GOING TO MISS EVERYONE WHEN IT'S OVER.
ME TOO.
!
JINX! YOU OWE ME A SODA, JO!
...
BUT I DON'T DRINK SODA, SO MAKE IT A DOUBLE SCOOP FROM THE DRIPPY CONE.
I *WILL* MISS THEM...
WE'RE ENTERING NORTH REDHART!
PAWCASSO IS LUCKY HE LIVES IN SOUTH REDHART.

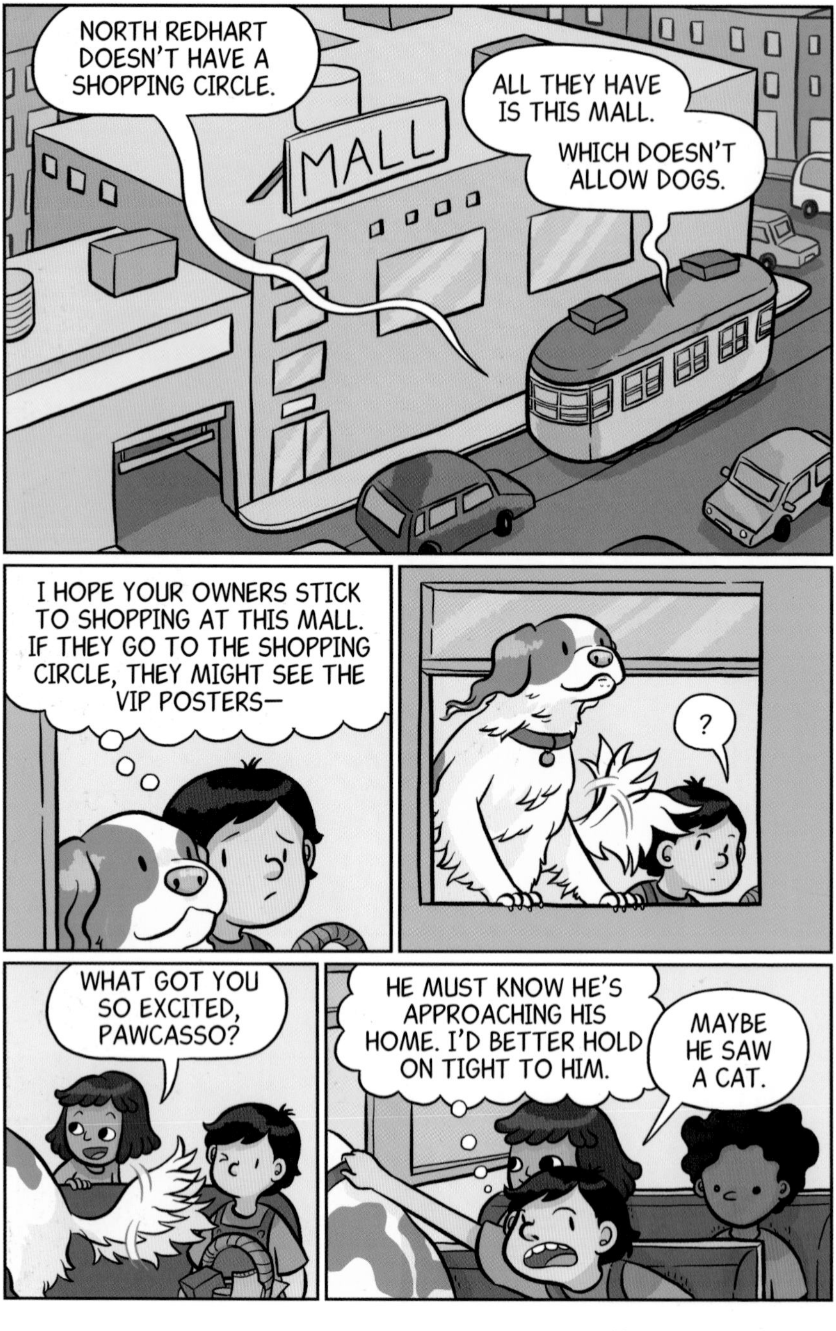
NORTH REDHART DOESN'T HAVE A SHOPPING CIRCLE.
ALL THEY HAVE IS THIS MALL.
WHICH DOESN'T ALLOW DOGS.
MALL
I HOPE YOUR OWNERS STICK TO SHOPPING AT THIS MALL. IF THEY GO TO THE SHOPPING CIRCLE, THEY MIGHT SEE THE VIP POSTERS—
?
WHAT GOT YOU SO EXCITED, PAWCASSO?
HE MUST KNOW HE'S APPROACHING HIS HOME. I'D BETTER HOLD ON TIGHT TO HIM.
MAYBE HE SAW A CAT.

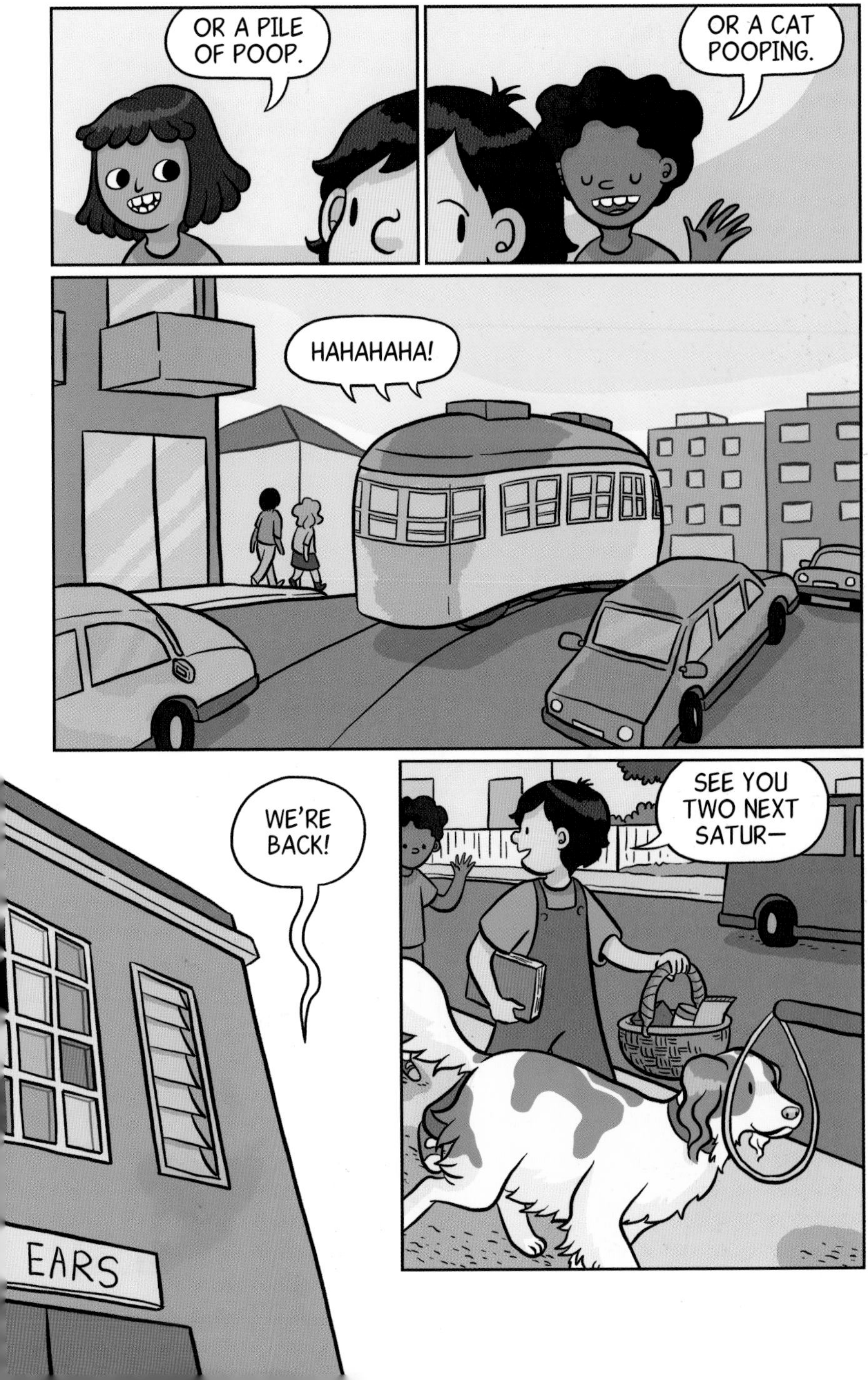
OR A PILE OF POOP.
OR A CAT POOPING.
HAHAHAHA!
WE'RE BACK!
SEE YOU TWO NEXT SATUR—
EARS

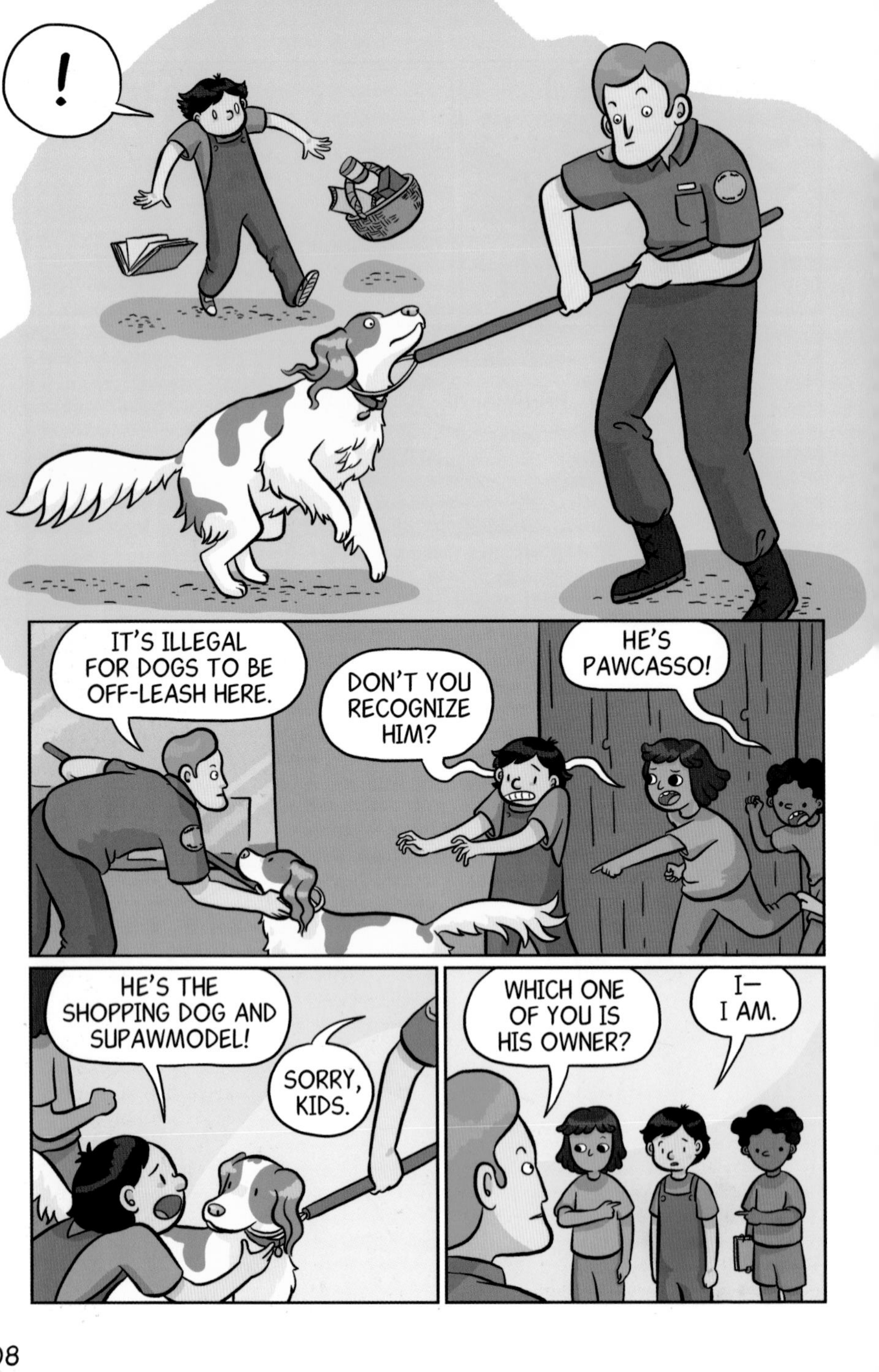
!
IT'S ILLEGAL FOR DOGS TO BE OFF-LEASH HERE.
DON'T YOU RECOGNIZE HIM?
HE'S PAWCASSO!
HE'S THE SHOPPING DOG AND SUPAWMODEL!
SORRY, KIDS.
WHICH ONE OF YOU IS HIS OWNER?
I— I AM.

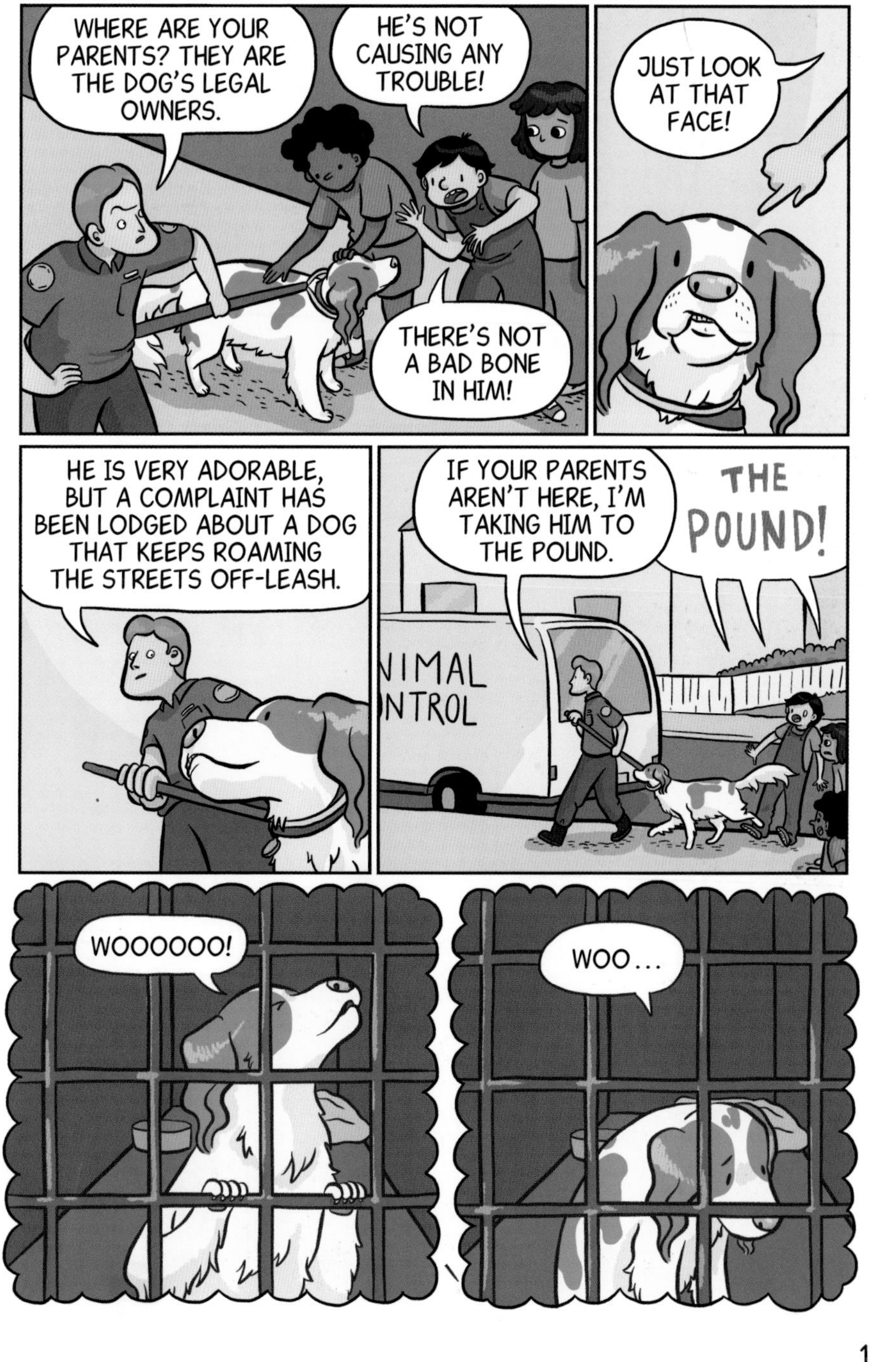

WHERE ARE YOUR PARENTS? THEY ARE THE DOG'S LEGAL OWNERS.
HE'S NOT CAUSING ANY TROUBLE!
THERE'S NOT A BAD BONE IN HIM!
JUST LOOK AT THAT FACE!
HE IS VERY ADORABLE, BUT A COMPLAINT HAS BEEN LODGED ABOUT A DOG THAT KEEPS ROAMING THE STREETS OFF-LEASH.
IF YOUR PARENTS AREN'T HERE, I'M TAKING HIM TO THE POUND.
THE POUND!
NIMAL NTROL
WOOOOOO!
WOO...

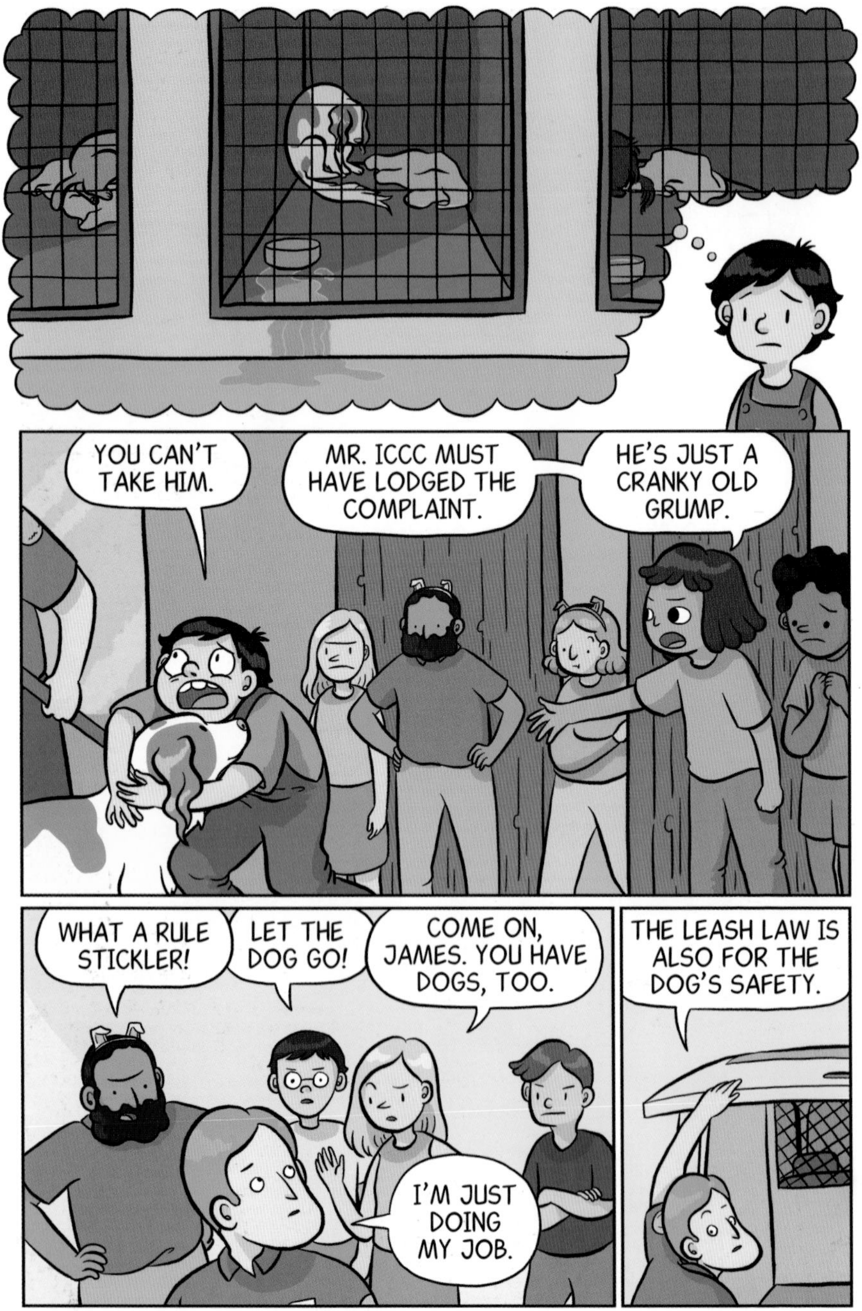
YOU CAN'T TAKE HIM.
MR. ICCC MUST HAVE LODGED THE COMPLAINT.
HE'S JUST A CRANKY OLD GRUMP.
WHAT A RULE STICKLER!
LET THE DOG GO!
COME ON, JAMES. YOU HAVE DOGS, TOO.
I'M JUST DOING MY JOB.
THE LEASH LAW IS ALSO FOR THE DOG'S SAFETY.

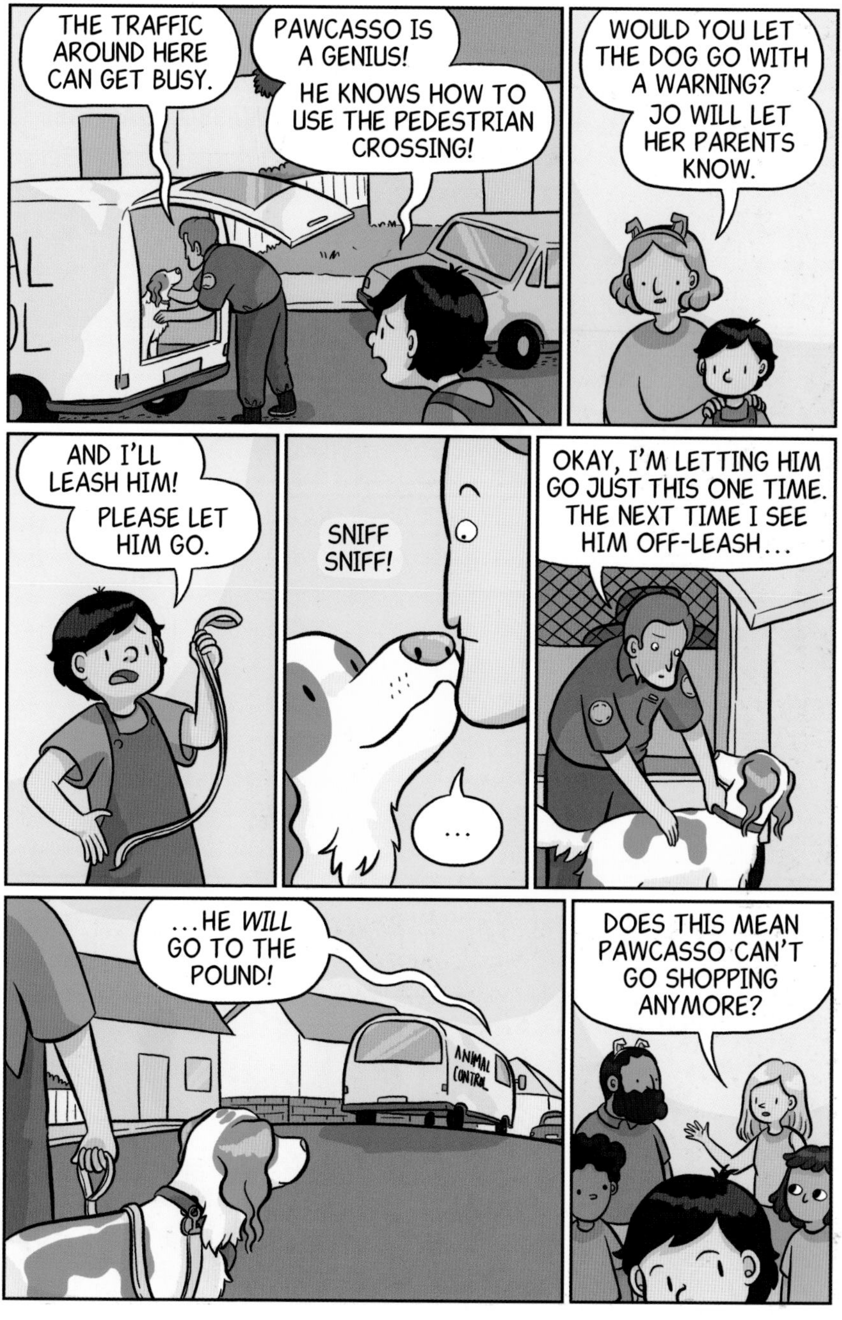
THE TRAFFIC AROUND HERE CAN GET BUSY.
PAWCASSO IS A GENIUS!
HE KNOWS HOW TO USE THE PEDESTRIAN CROSSING!
WOULD YOU LET THE DOG GO WITH A WARNING?
JO WILL LET HER PARENTS KNOW.
AND I'LL LEASH HIM!
PLEASE LET HIM GO.
SNIFF SNIFF!
...
OKAY, I'M LETTING HIM GO JUST THIS ONE TIME. THE NEXT TIME I SEE HIM OFF-LEASH...
...HE *WILL* GO TO THE POUND!
ANIMAL CONTROL
DOES THIS MEAN PAWCASSO CAN'T GO SHOPPING ANYMORE?

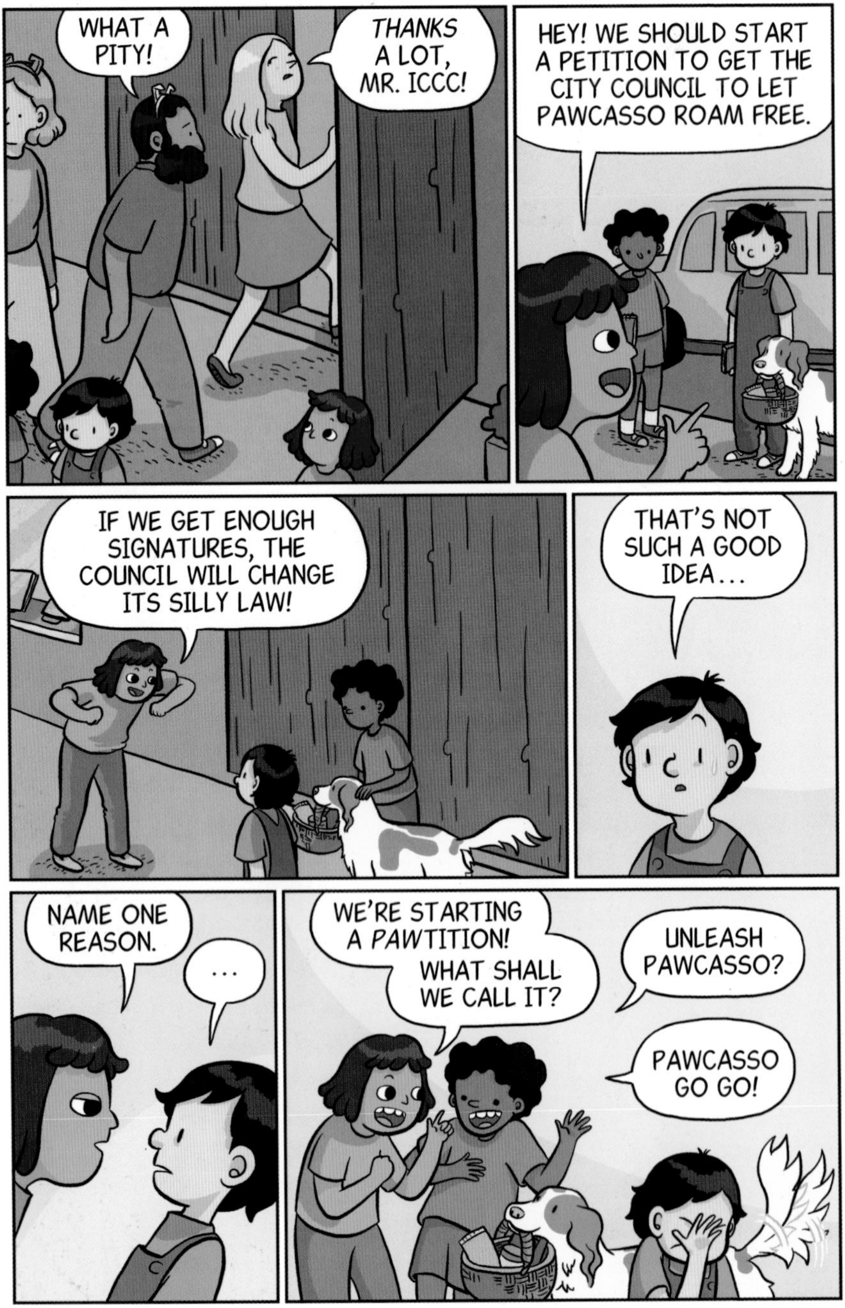
WHAT A PITY!
THANKS A LOT, MR. ICCC!
HEY! WE SHOULD START A PETITION TO GET THE CITY COUNCIL TO LET PAWCASSO ROAM FREE.
IF WE GET ENOUGH SIGNATURES, THE COUNCIL WILL CHANGE ITS SILLY LAW!
THAT'S NOT SUCH A GOOD IDEA...
NAME ONE REASON.
...
WE'RE STARTING A *PAW*TITION!
WHAT SHALL WE CALL IT?
UNLEASH PAWCASSO?
PAWCASSO GO GO!

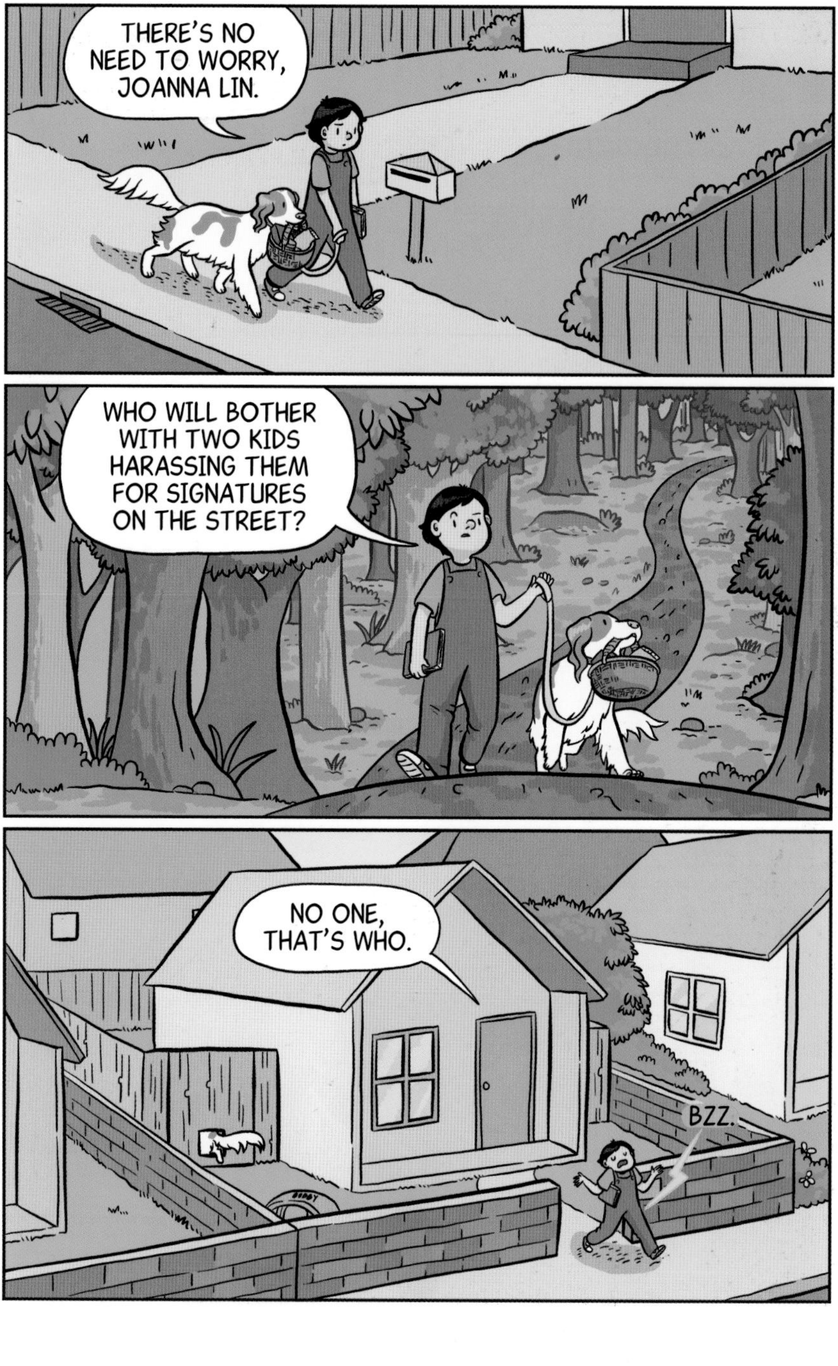
THERE'S NO NEED TO WORRY, JOANNA LIN.
WHO WILL BOTHER WITH TWO KIDS HARASSING THEM FOR SIGNATURES ON THE STREET?
NO ONE, THAT'S WHO.
BZZ.

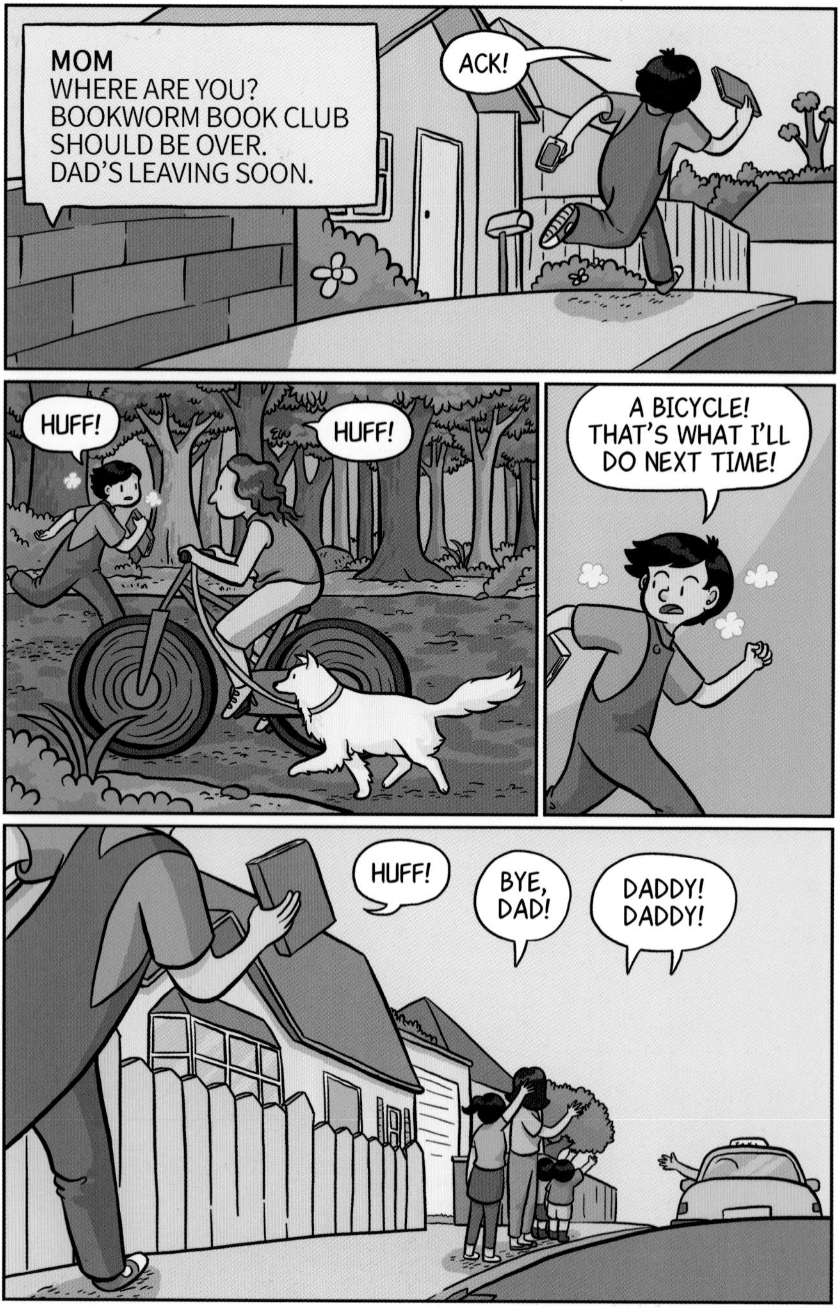
MOM
WHERE ARE YOU? BOOKWORM BOOK CLUB SHOULD BE OVER. DAD'S LEAVING SOON.
ACK!
HUFF!
HUFF!
A BICYCLE! THAT'S WHAT I'LL DO NEXT TIME!
HUFF!
BYE, DAD!
DADDY! DADDY!

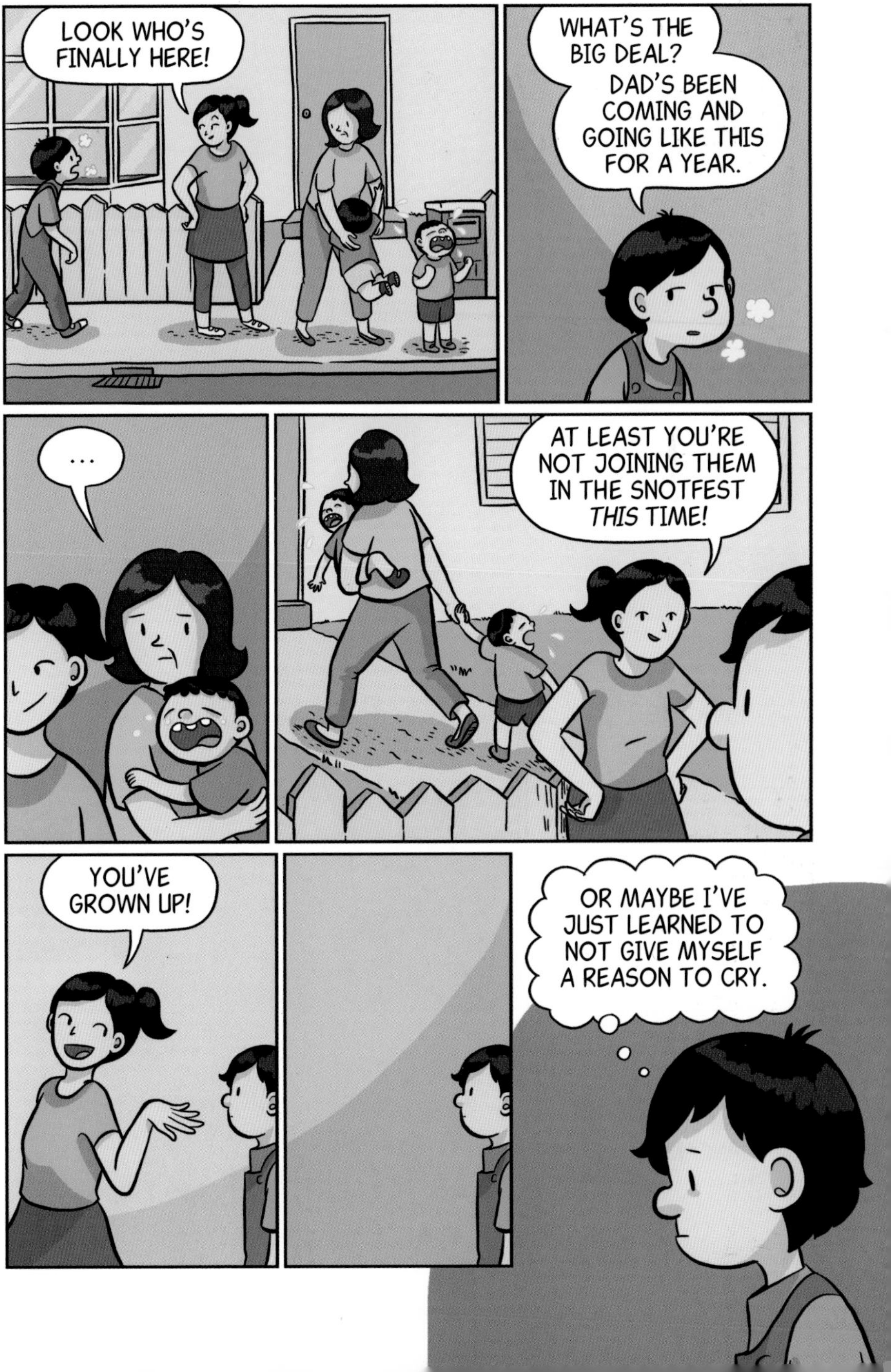
LOOK WHO'S FINALLY HERE!
WHAT'S THE BIG DEAL?
DAD'S BEEN COMING AND GOING LIKE THIS FOR A YEAR.
...
AT LEAST YOU'RE NOT JOINING THEM IN THE SNOTFEST *THIS* TIME!
YOU'VE GROWN UP!
OR MAYBE I'VE JUST LEARNED TO NOT GIVE MYSELF A REASON TO CRY.

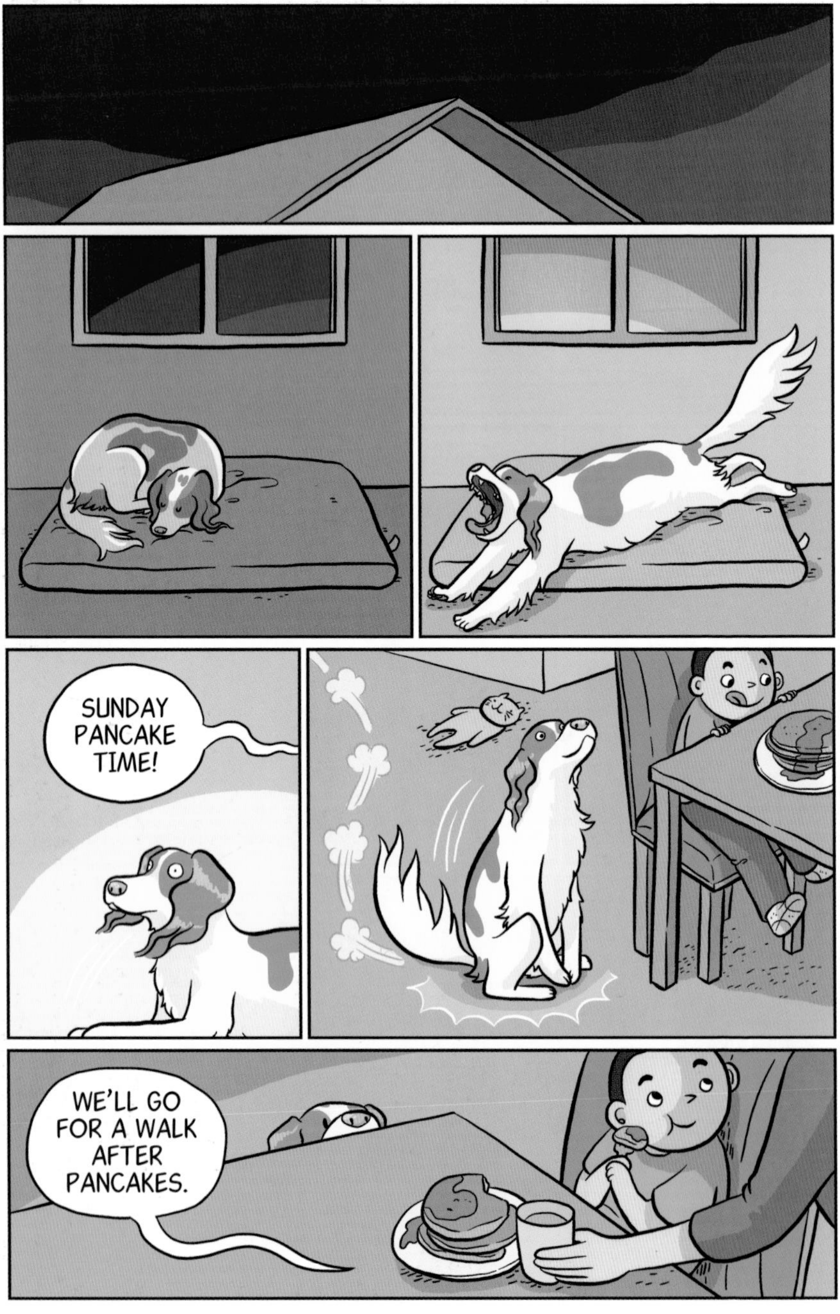
SUNDAY PANCAKE TIME!
WE'LL GO FOR A WALK AFTER PANCAKES.

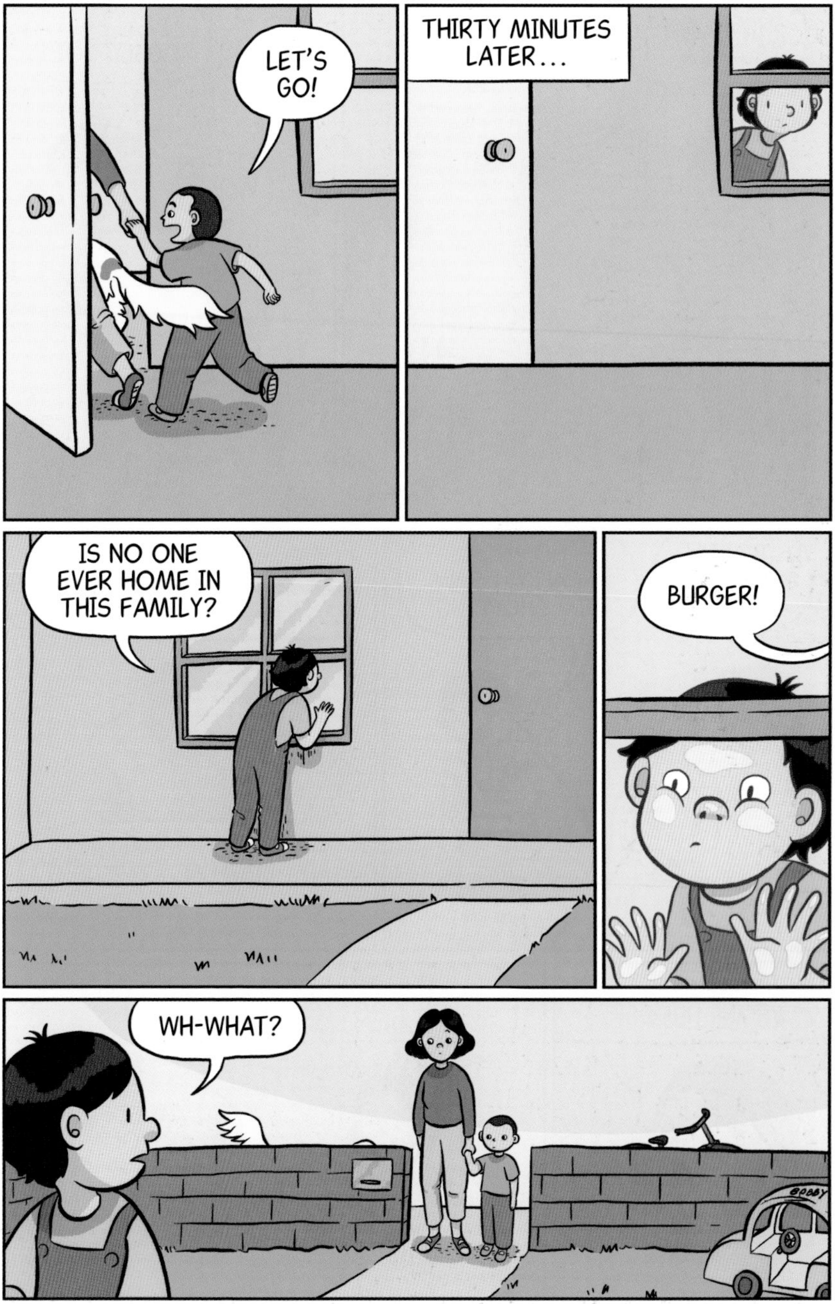
LET'S GO!
THIRTY MINUTES LATER...
IS NO ONE EVER HOME IN THIS FAMILY?
BURGER!
WH-WHAT?

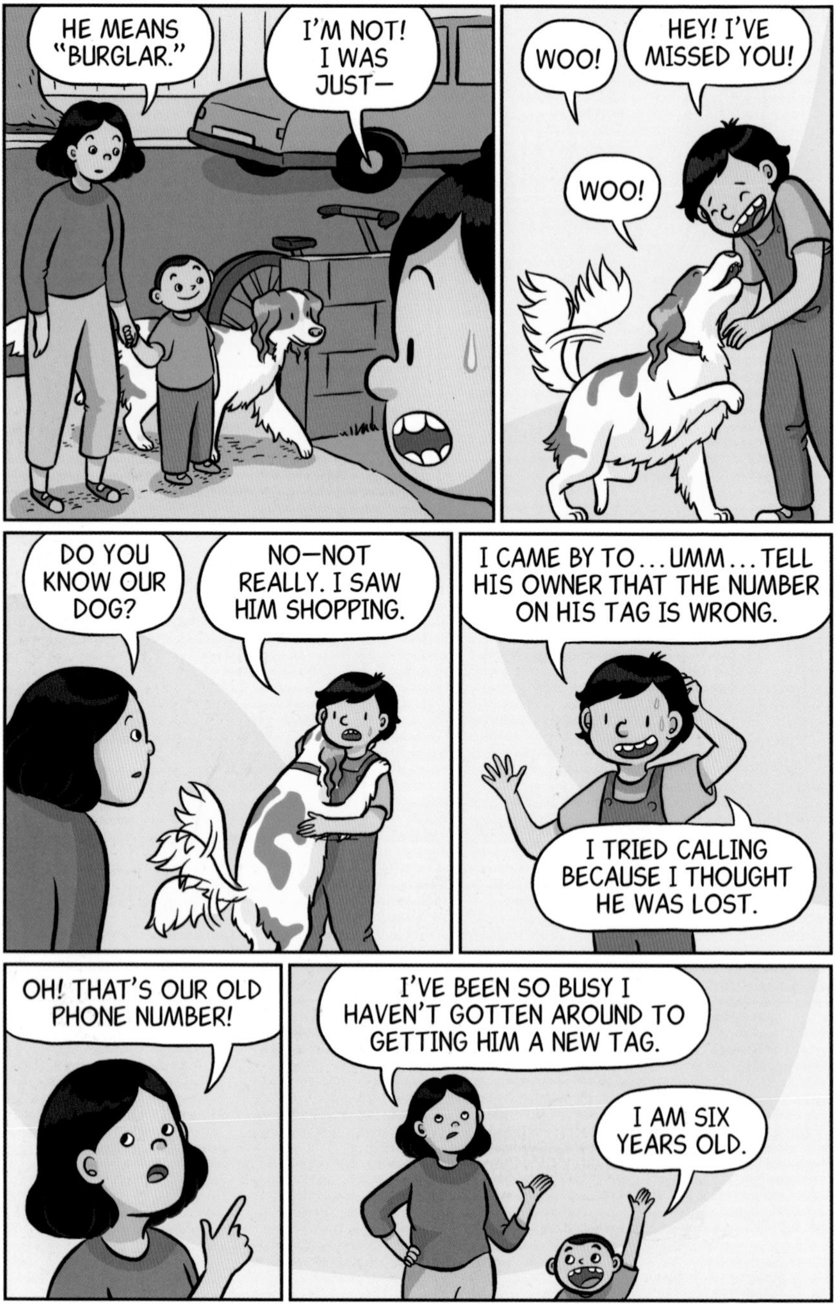
HE MEANS "BURGLAR."
I'M NOT! I WAS JUST—
WOO!
HEY! I'VE MISSED YOU!
WOO!
DO YOU KNOW OUR DOG?
NO—NOT REALLY. I SAW HIM SHOPPING.
I CAME BY TO . . . UMM . . . TELL HIS OWNER THAT THE NUMBER ON HIS TAG IS WRONG.
I TRIED CALLING BECAUSE I THOUGHT HE WAS LOST.
OH! THAT'S OUR OLD PHONE NUMBER!
I'VE BEEN SO BUSY I HAVEN'T GOTTEN AROUND TO GETTING HIM A NEW TAG.
I AM SIX YEARS OLD.

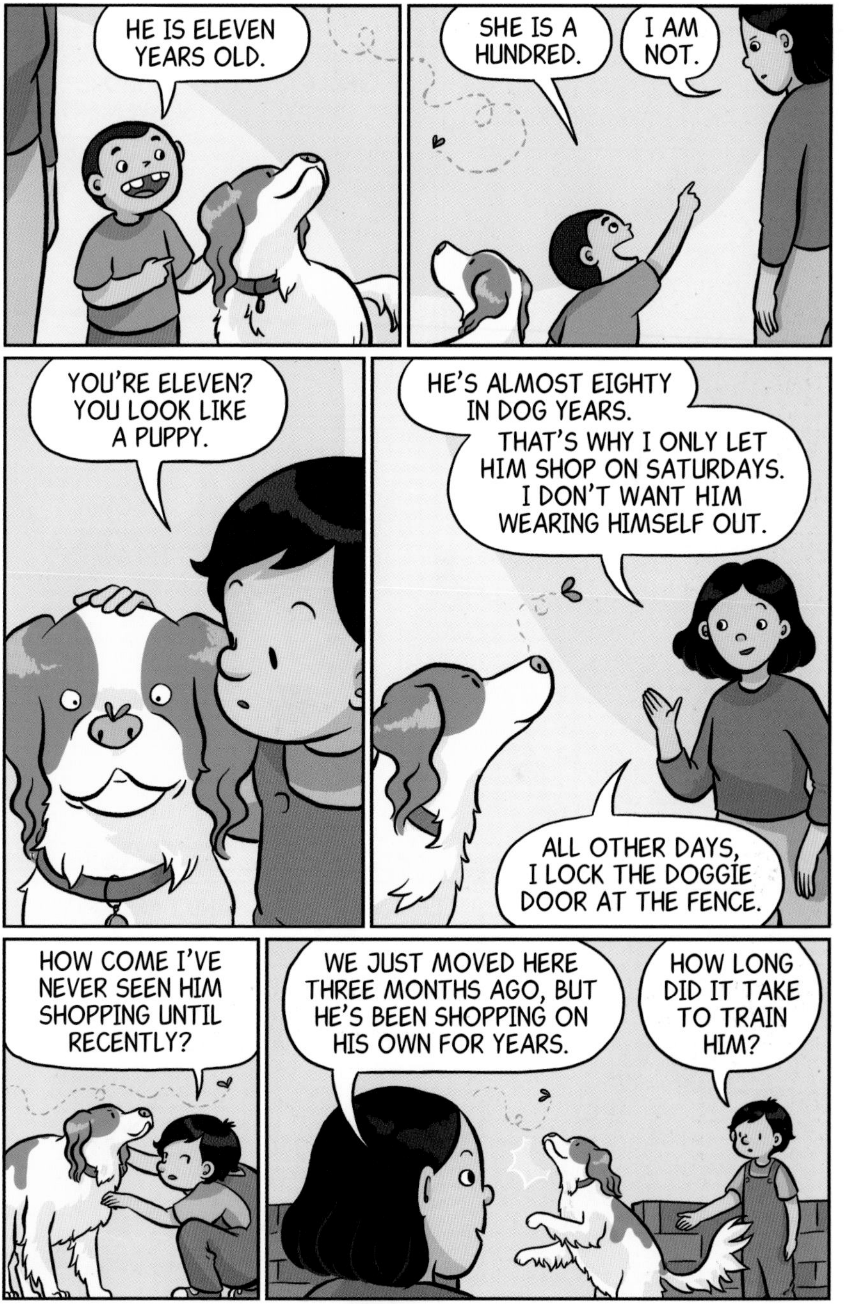
HE IS ELEVEN YEARS OLD.
SHE IS A HUNDRED.
I AM NOT.
YOU'RE ELEVEN? YOU LOOK LIKE A PUPPY.
HE'S ALMOST EIGHTY IN DOG YEARS.
THAT'S WHY I ONLY LET HIM SHOP ON SATURDAYS. I DON'T WANT HIM WEARING HIMSELF OUT.
ALL OTHER DAYS, I LOCK THE DOGGIE DOOR AT THE FENCE.
HOW COME I'VE NEVER SEEN HIM SHOPPING UNTIL RECENTLY?
WE JUST MOVED HERE THREE MONTHS AGO, BUT HE'S BEEN SHOPPING ON HIS OWN FOR YEARS.
HOW LONG DID IT TAKE TO TRAIN HIM?

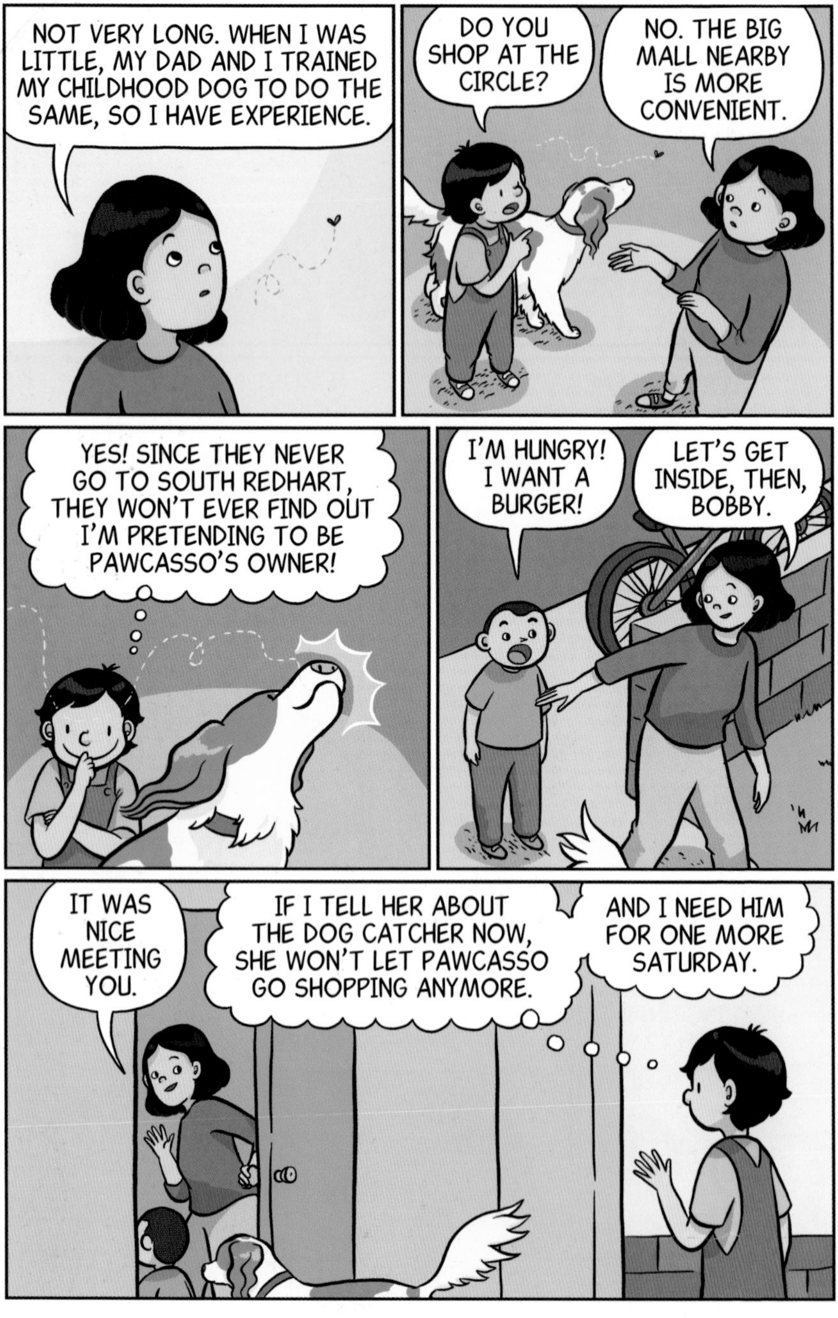
NOT VERY LONG. WHEN I WAS LITTLE, MY DAD AND I TRAINED MY CHILDHOOD DOG TO DO THE SAME, SO I HAVE EXPERIENCE.
DO YOU SHOP AT THE CIRCLE?
NO. THE BIG MALL NEARBY IS MORE CONVENIENT.
YES! SINCE THEY NEVER GO TO SOUTH REDHART, THEY WON'T EVER FIND OUT I'M PRETENDING TO BE PAWCASSO'S OWNER!
I'M HUNGRY! I WANT A BURGER!
LET'S GET INSIDE, THEN, BOBBY.
IT WAS NICE MEETING YOU.
IF I TELL HER ABOUT THE DOG CATCHER NOW, SHE WON'T LET PAWCASSO GO SHOPPING ANYMORE.
AND I NEED HIM FOR ONE MORE SATURDAY.

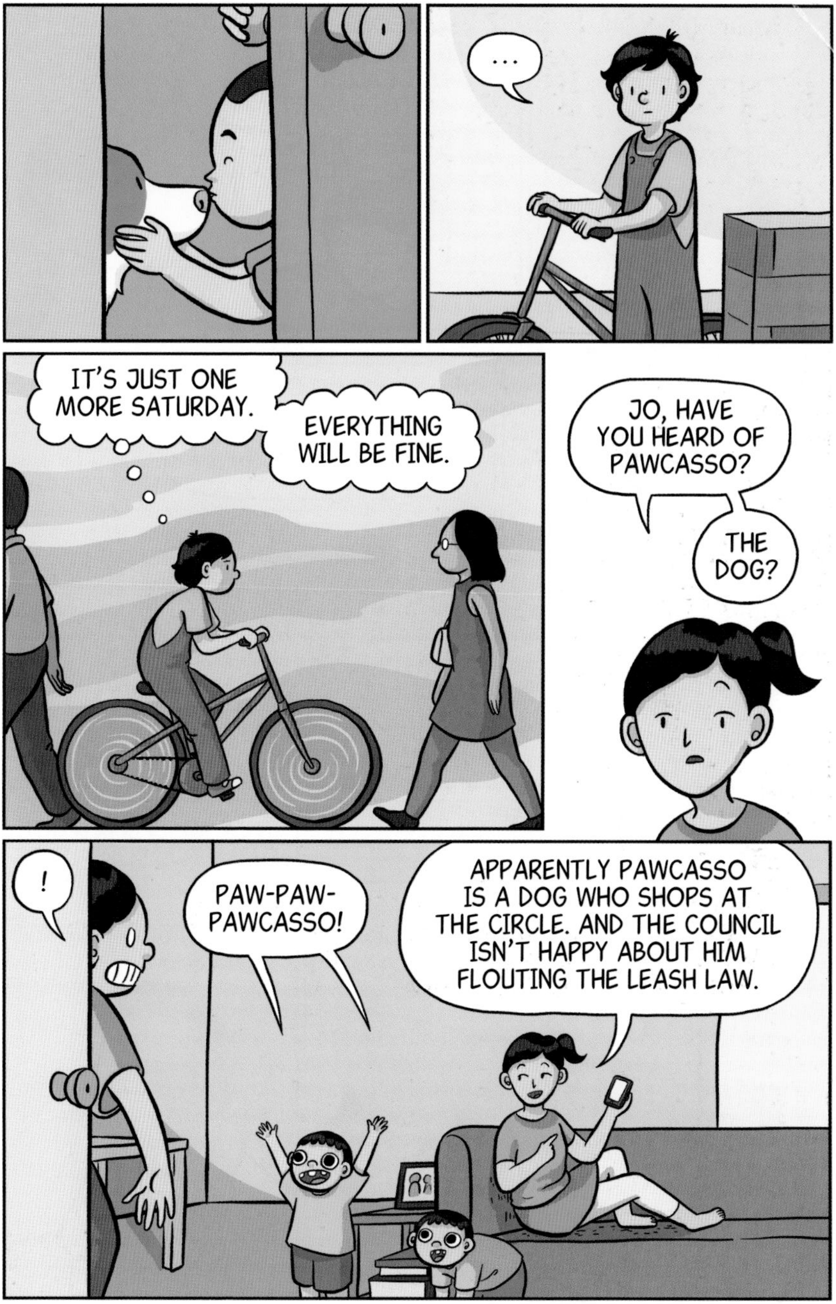
...
IT'S JUST ONE MORE SATURDAY.
EVERYTHING WILL BE FINE.
JO, HAVE YOU HEARD OF PAWCASSO?
THE DOG?
!
PAW-PAW-PAWCASSO!
APPARENTLY PAWCASSO IS A DOG WHO SHOPS AT THE CIRCLE. AND THE COUNCIL ISN'T HAPPY ABOUT HIM FLOUTING THE LEASH LAW.

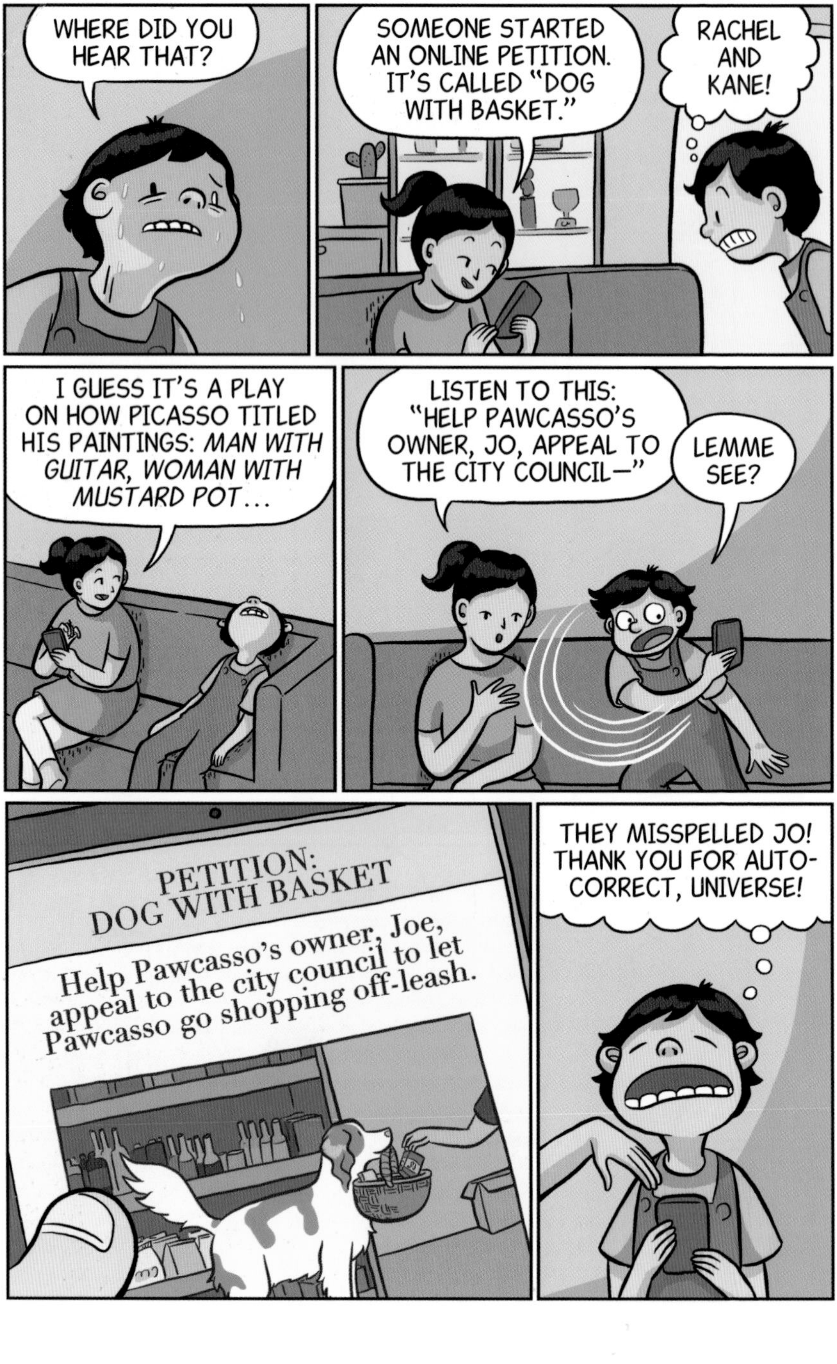
WHERE DID YOU HEAR THAT?
SOMEONE STARTED AN ONLINE PETITION. IT'S CALLED "DOG WITH BASKET."
RACHEL AND KANE!
I GUESS IT'S A PLAY ON HOW PICASSO TITLED HIS PAINTINGS: *MAN WITH GUITAR, WOMAN WITH MUSTARD POT*...
LISTEN TO THIS: "HELP PAWCASSO'S OWNER, JO, APPEAL TO THE CITY COUNCIL—"
LEMME SEE?
PETITION: DOG WITH BASKET
Help Pawcasso's owner, Joe, appeal to the city council to let Pawcasso go shopping off-leash.
THEY MISSPELLED JO! THANK YOU FOR AUTO-CORRECT, UNIVERSE!

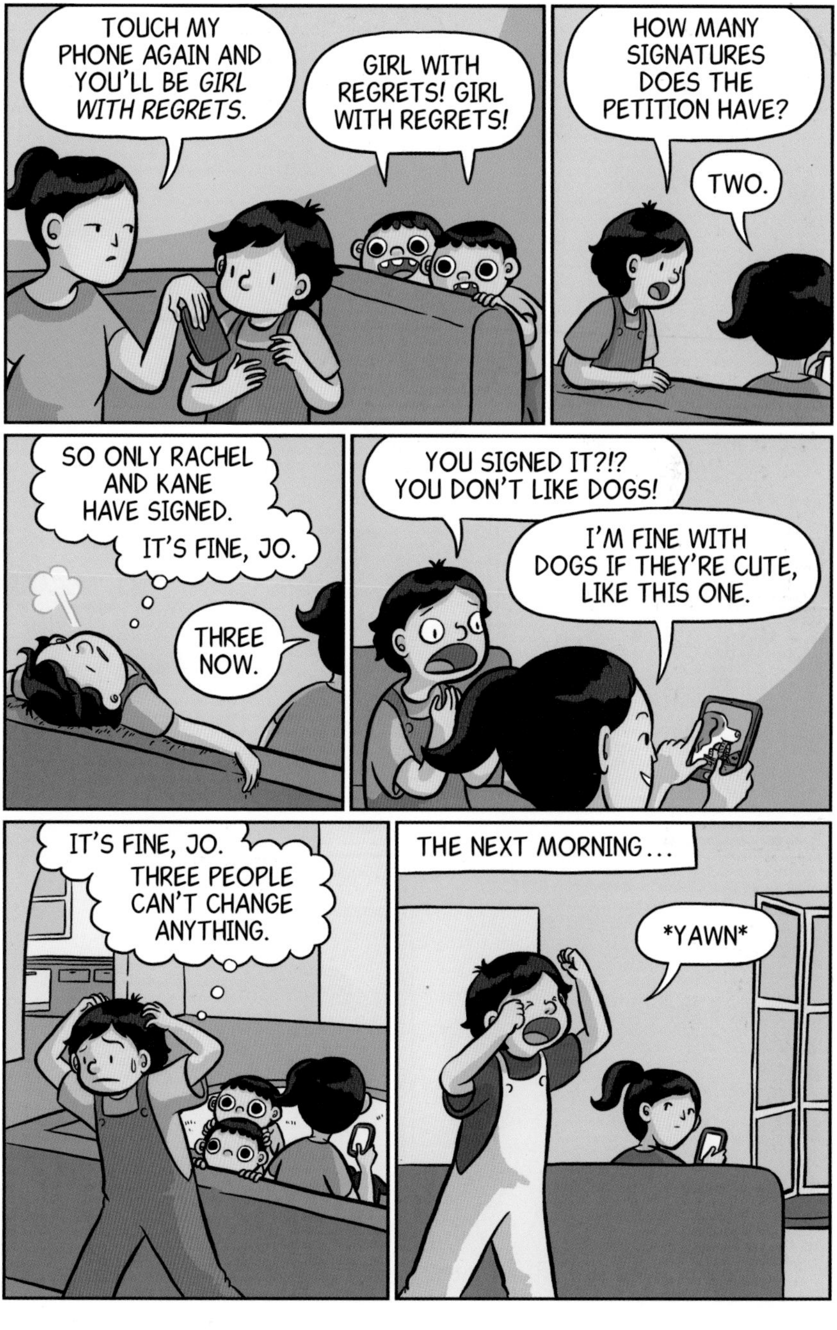
TOUCH MY PHONE AGAIN AND YOU'LL BE *GIRL WITH REGRETS.*
GIRL WITH REGRETS! GIRL WITH REGRETS!
HOW MANY SIGNATURES DOES THE PETITION HAVE?
TWO.
SO ONLY RACHEL AND KANE HAVE SIGNED.
IT'S FINE, JO.
THREE NOW.
YOU SIGNED IT?!? YOU DON'T LIKE DOGS!
I'M FINE WITH DOGS IF THEY'RE CUTE, LIKE THIS ONE.
IT'S FINE, JO.
THREE PEOPLE CAN'T CHANGE ANYTHING.
THE NEXT MORNING...
YAWN

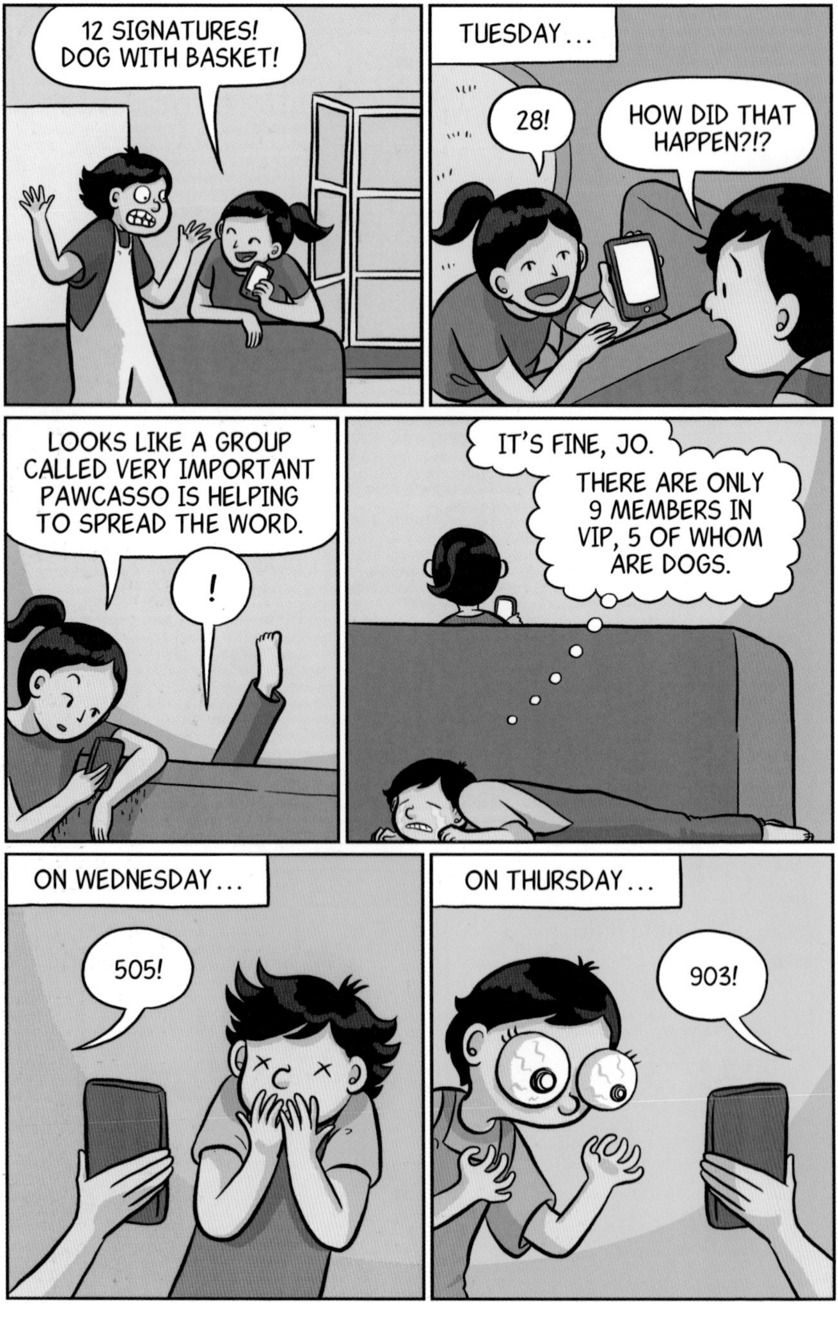
12 SIGNATURES! DOG WITH BASKET!
TUESDAY...
28!
HOW DID THAT HAPPEN?!?
LOOKS LIKE A GROUP CALLED VERY IMPORTANT PAWCASSO IS HELPING TO SPREAD THE WORD.
!
IT'S FINE, JO.
THERE ARE ONLY 9 MEMBERS IN VIP, 5 OF WHOM ARE DOGS.
ON WEDNESDAY...
505!
ON THURSDAY...
903!

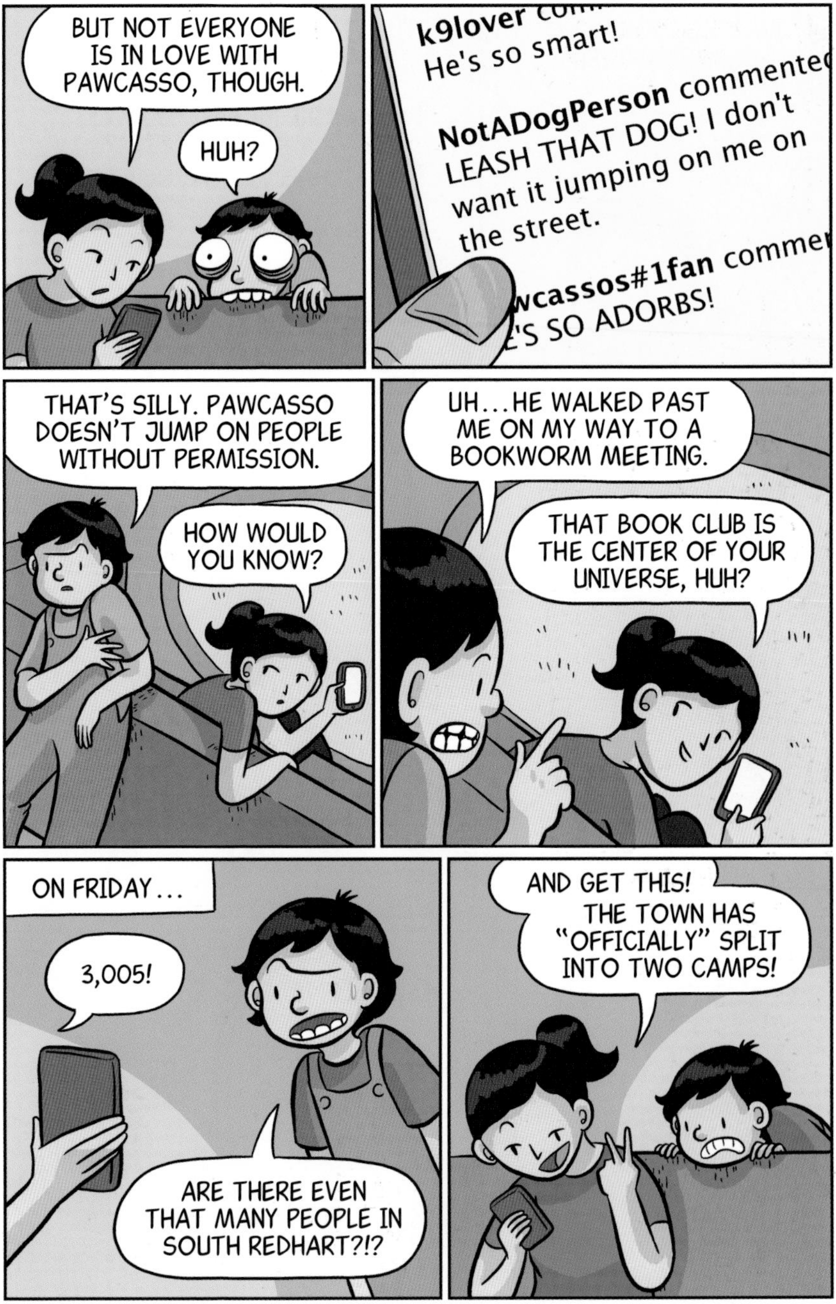
BUT NOT EVERYONE IS IN LOVE WITH PAWCASSO, THOUGH.
HUH?
k9lover
He's so smart!
NotADogPerson commented
LEASH THAT DOG! I don't want it jumping on me on the street.
wcassos#1fan
'S SO ADORBS!
THAT'S SILLY. PAWCASSO DOESN'T JUMP ON PEOPLE WITHOUT PERMISSION.
HOW WOULD YOU KNOW?
UH...HE WALKED PAST ME ON MY WAY TO A BOOKWORM MEETING.
THAT BOOK CLUB IS THE CENTER OF YOUR UNIVERSE, HUH?
ON FRIDAY...
3,005!
ARE THERE EVEN THAT MANY PEOPLE IN SOUTH REDHART?!?
AND GET THIS! THE TOWN HAS "OFFICIALLY" SPLIT INTO TWO CAMPS!

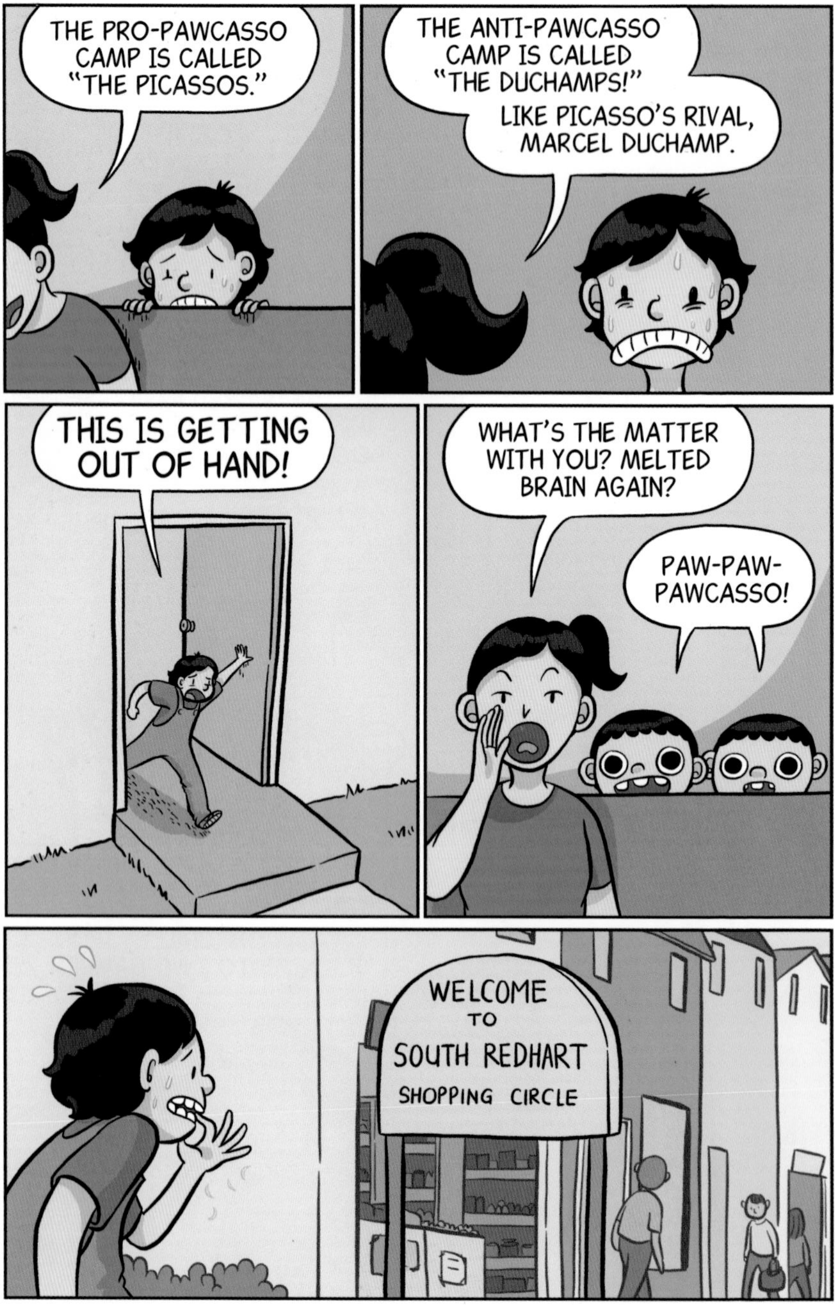
THE PRO-PAWCASSO CAMP IS CALLED "THE PICASSOS."
THE ANTI-PAWCASSO CAMP IS CALLED "THE DUCHAMPS!"
LIKE PICASSO'S RIVAL, MARCEL DUCHAMP.
THIS IS GETTING OUT OF HAND!
WHAT'S THE MATTER WITH YOU? MELTED BRAIN AGAIN?
PAW-PAW-PAWCASSO!
WELCOME TO SOUTH REDHART SHOPPING CIRCLE

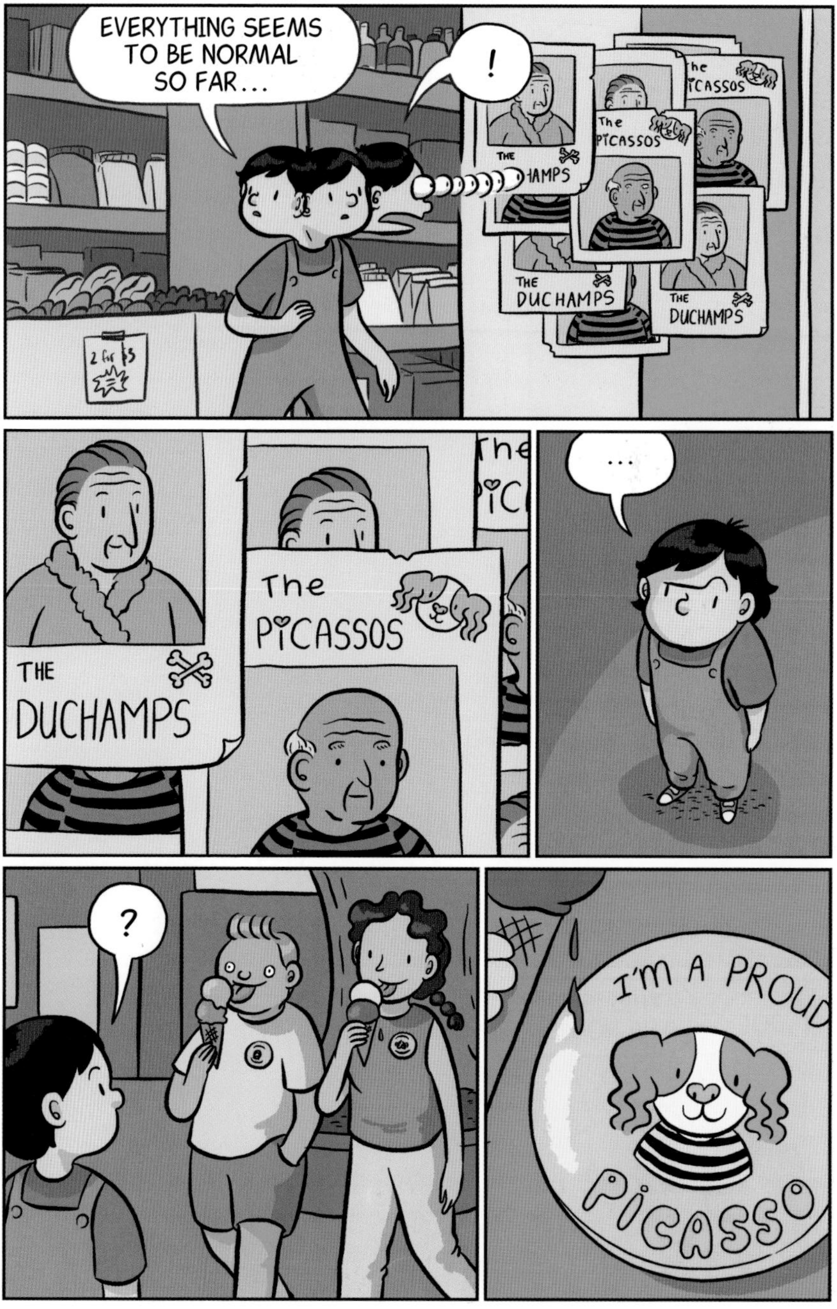
EVERYTHING SEEMS TO BE NORMAL SO FAR...
!
2 for $3
THE DUCHAMPS
The PICASSOS
THE DUCHAMPS
The PICASSOS
...
?
I'M A PROUD PICASSO

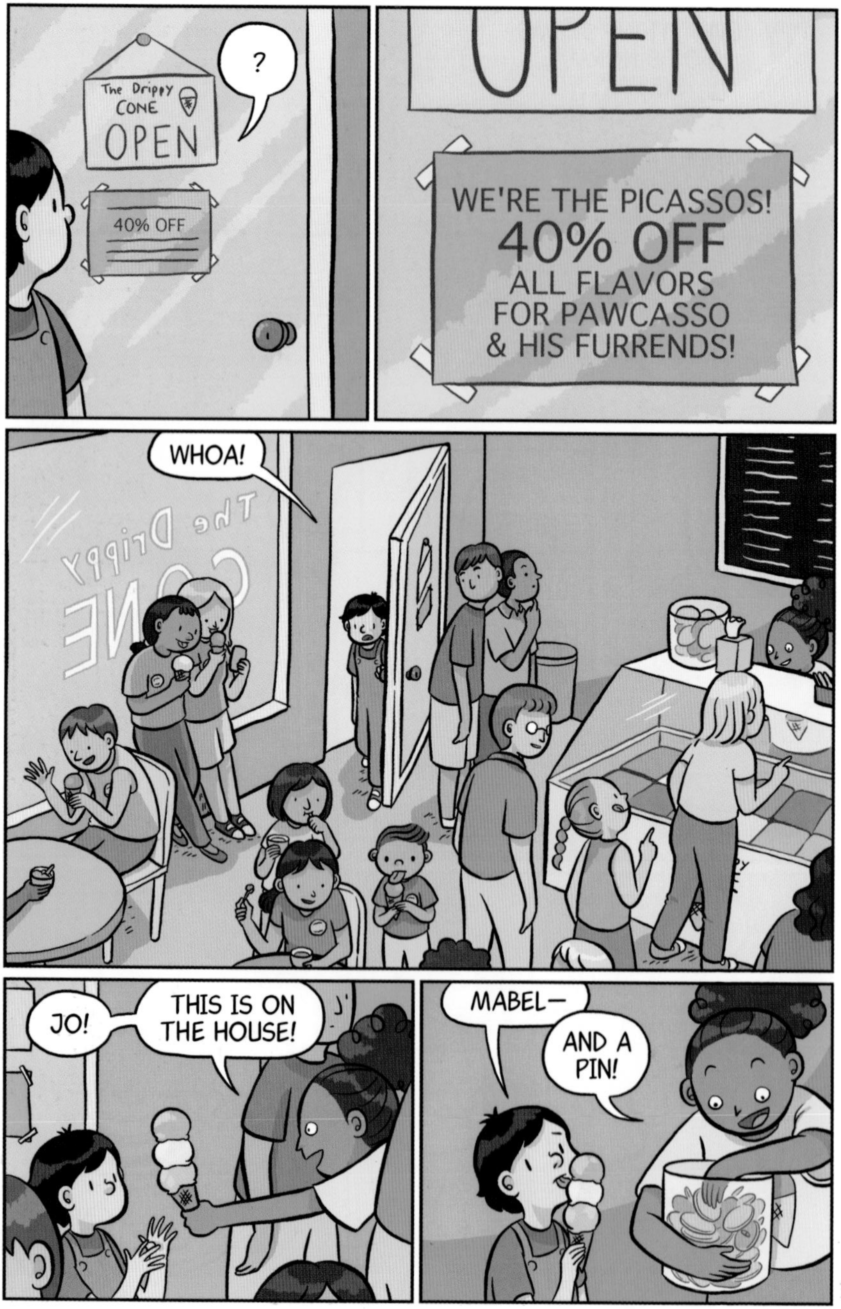
The Drippy CONE
OPEN
40% OFF
?
OPEN
WE'RE THE PICASSOS!
40% OFF
ALL FLAVORS
FOR PAWCASSO
& HIS FURRENDS!
WHOA!
The Drippy CONE
JO!
THIS IS ON THE HOUSE!
MABEL—
AND A PIN!

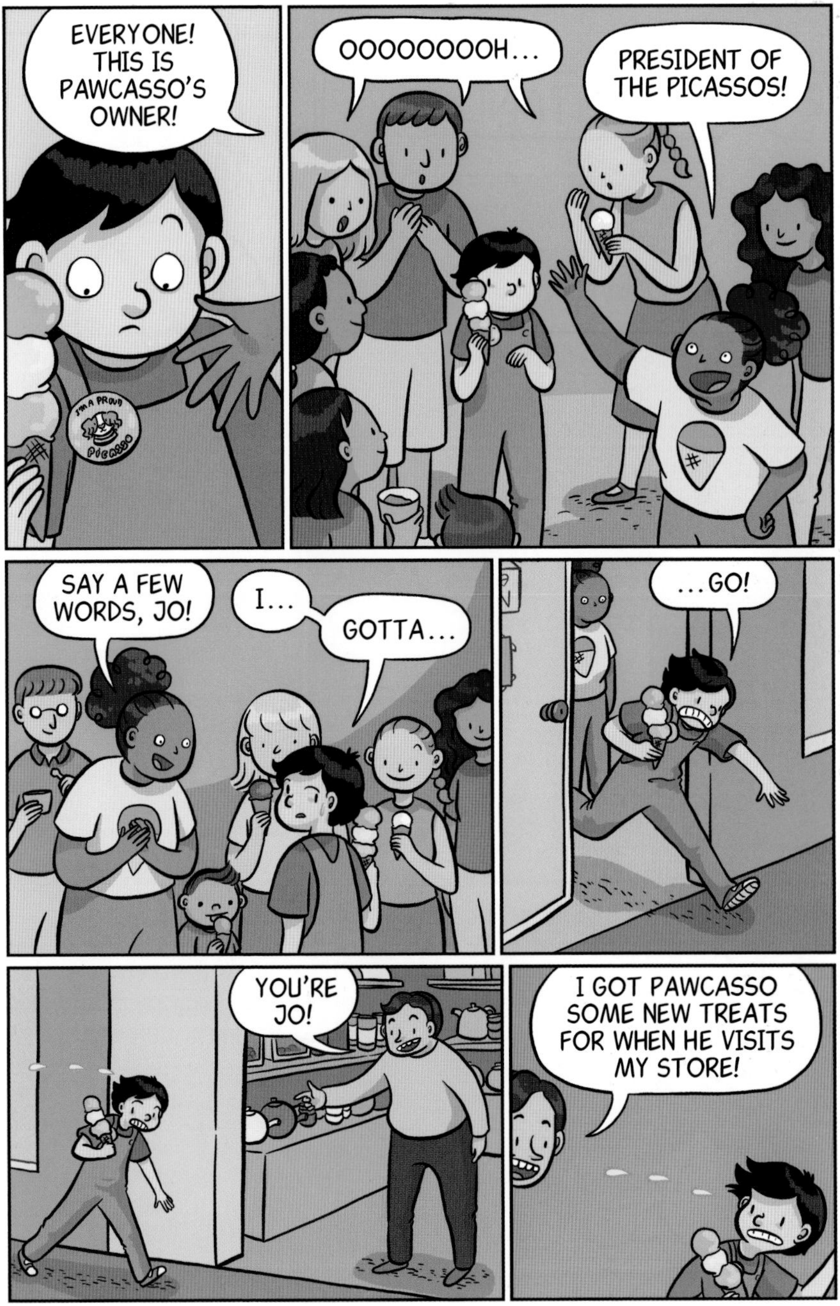
EVERYONE! THIS IS PAWCASSO'S OWNER!
I'M A PROUD PICASSO
OOOOOOOOH...
PRESIDENT OF THE PICASSOS!
SAY A FEW WORDS, JO!
I...
GOTTA...
...GO!
YOU'RE JO!
I GOT PAWCASSO SOME NEW TREATS FOR WHEN HE VISITS MY STORE!

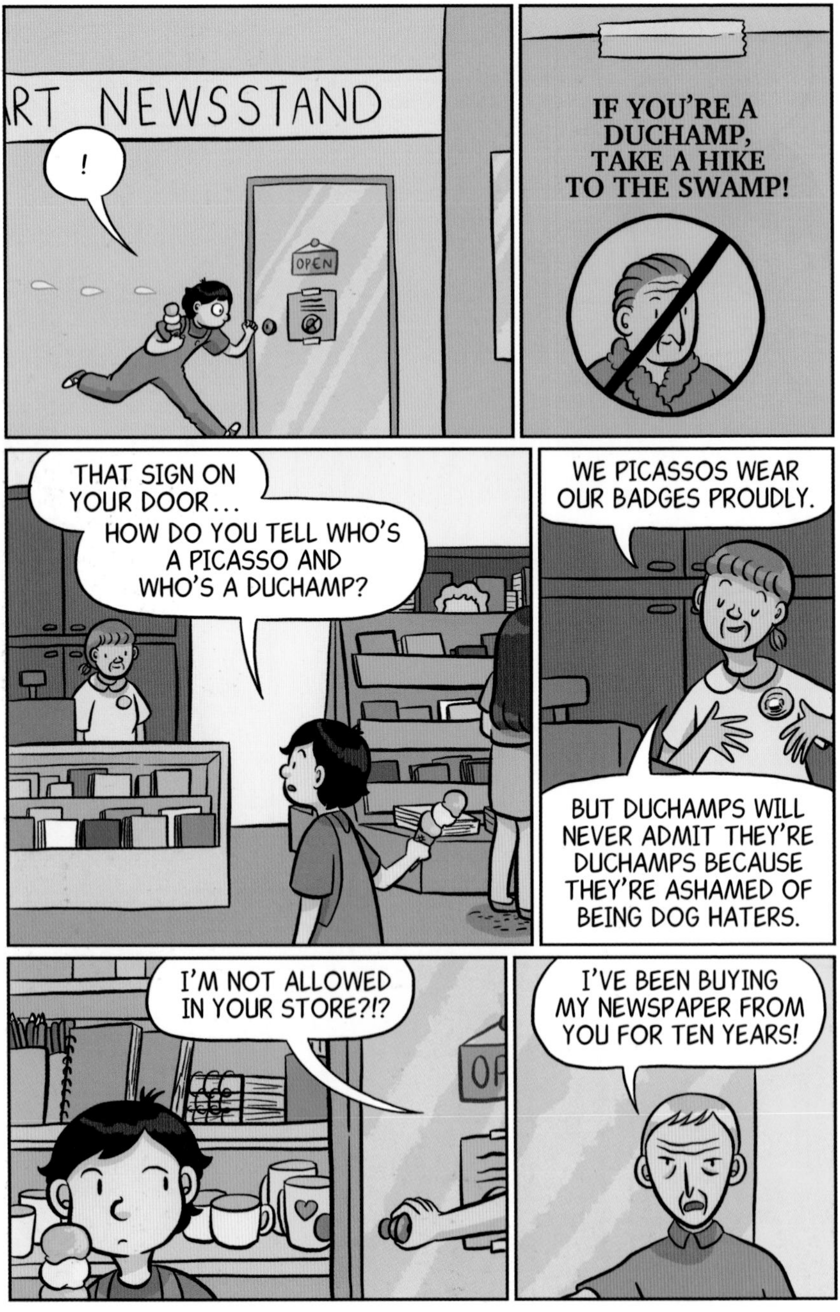

RT NEWSSTAND
!
OPEN
IF YOU'RE A DUCHAMP, TAKE A HIKE TO THE SWAMP!
THAT SIGN ON YOUR DOOR...
HOW DO YOU TELL WHO'S A PICASSO AND WHO'S A DUCHAMP?
WE PICASSOS WEAR OUR BADGES PROUDLY.
BUT DUCHAMPS WILL NEVER ADMIT THEY'RE DUCHAMPS BECAUSE THEY'RE ASHAMED OF BEING DOG HATERS.
I'M NOT ALLOWED IN YOUR STORE?!?
I'VE BEEN BUYING MY NEWSPAPER FROM YOU FOR TEN YEARS!

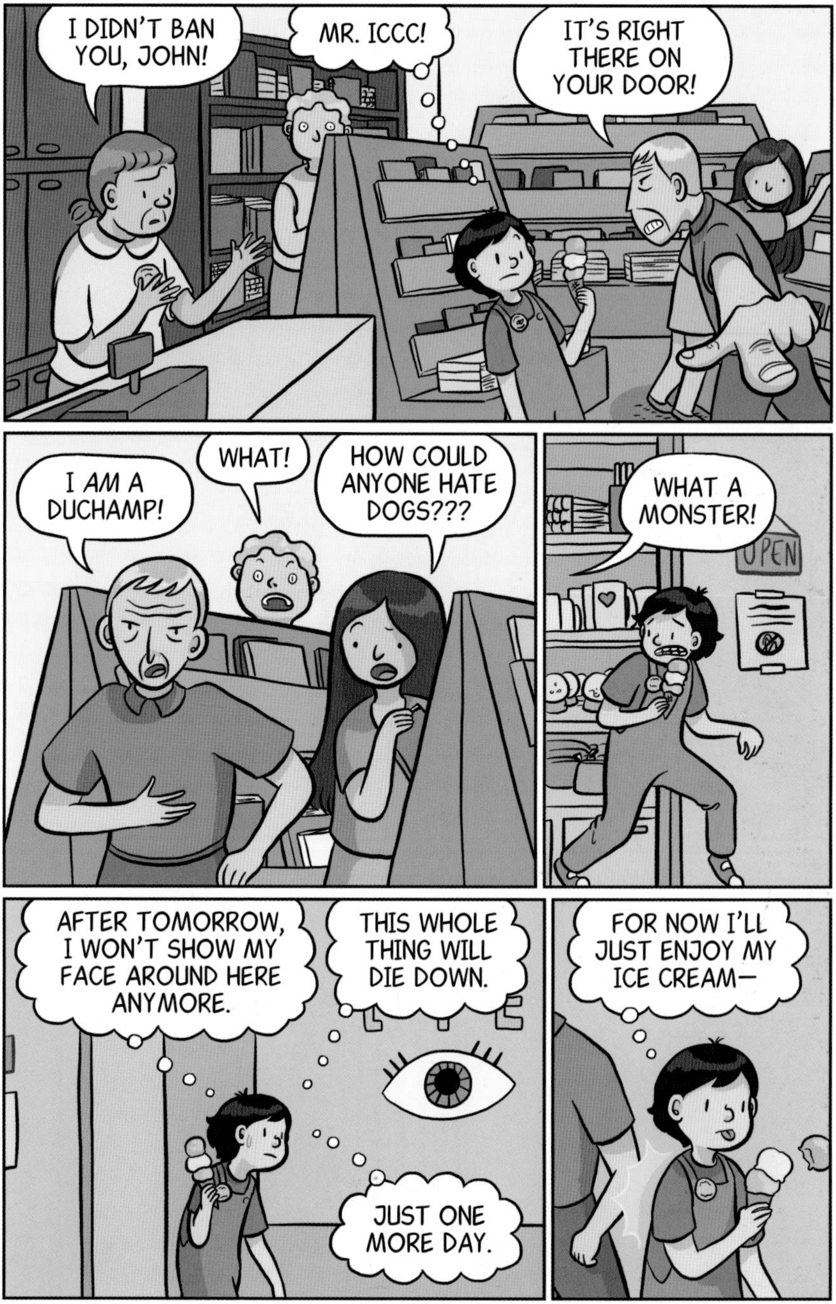
I DIDN'T BAN YOU, JOHN!
MR. ICCC!
IT'S RIGHT THERE ON YOUR DOOR!
I *AM* A DUCHAMP!
WHAT!
HOW COULD ANYONE HATE DOGS???
WHAT A MONSTER!
OPEN
AFTER TOMORROW, I WON'T SHOW MY FACE AROUND HERE ANYMORE.
THIS WHOLE THING WILL DIE DOWN.
JUST ONE MORE DAY.
FOR NOW I'LL JUST ENJOY MY ICE CREAM—

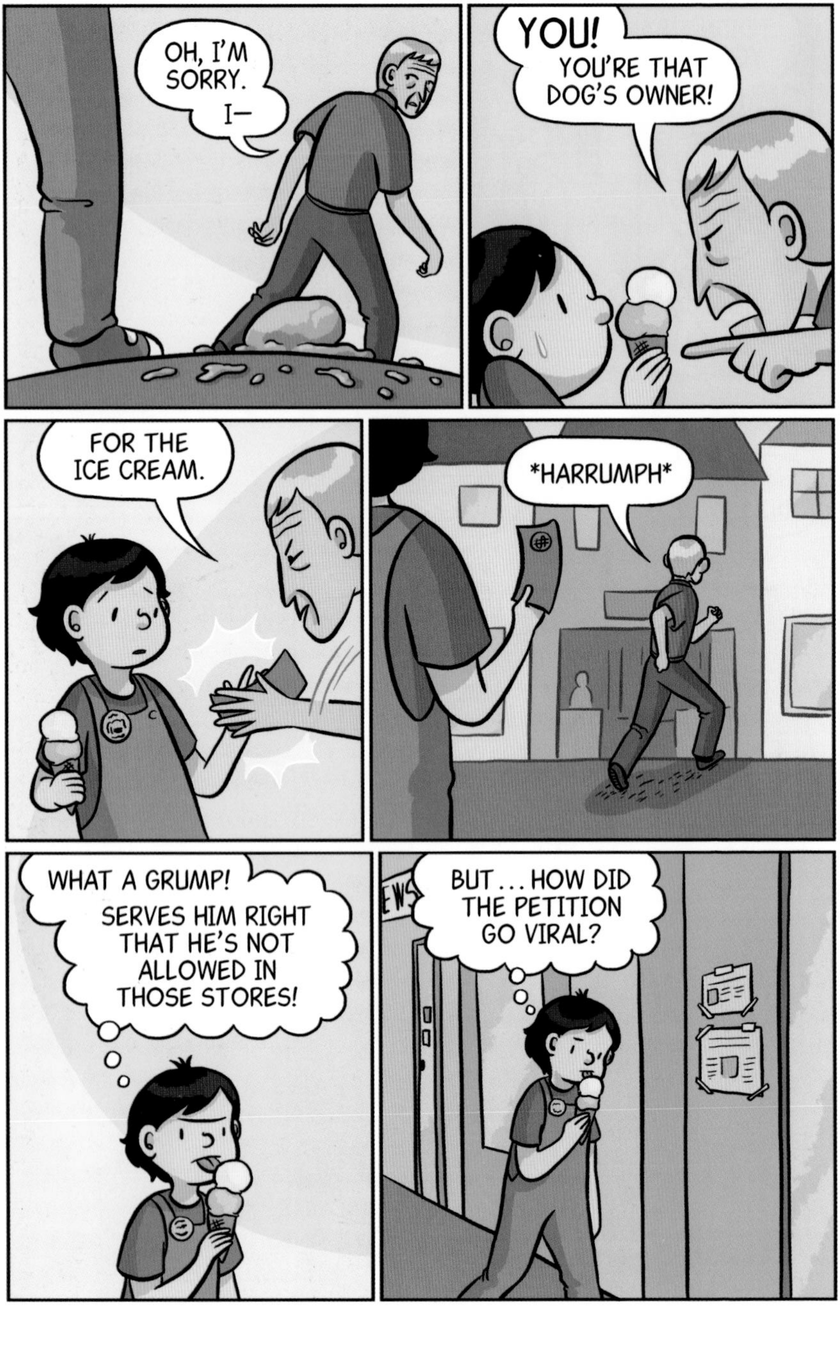
OH, I'M SORRY.
I—
YOU!
YOU'RE THAT DOG'S OWNER!
FOR THE ICE CREAM.
HARRUMPH
WHAT A GRUMP!
SERVES HIM RIGHT THAT HE'S NOT ALLOWED IN THOSE STORES!
BUT . . . HOW DID THE PETITION GO VIRAL?

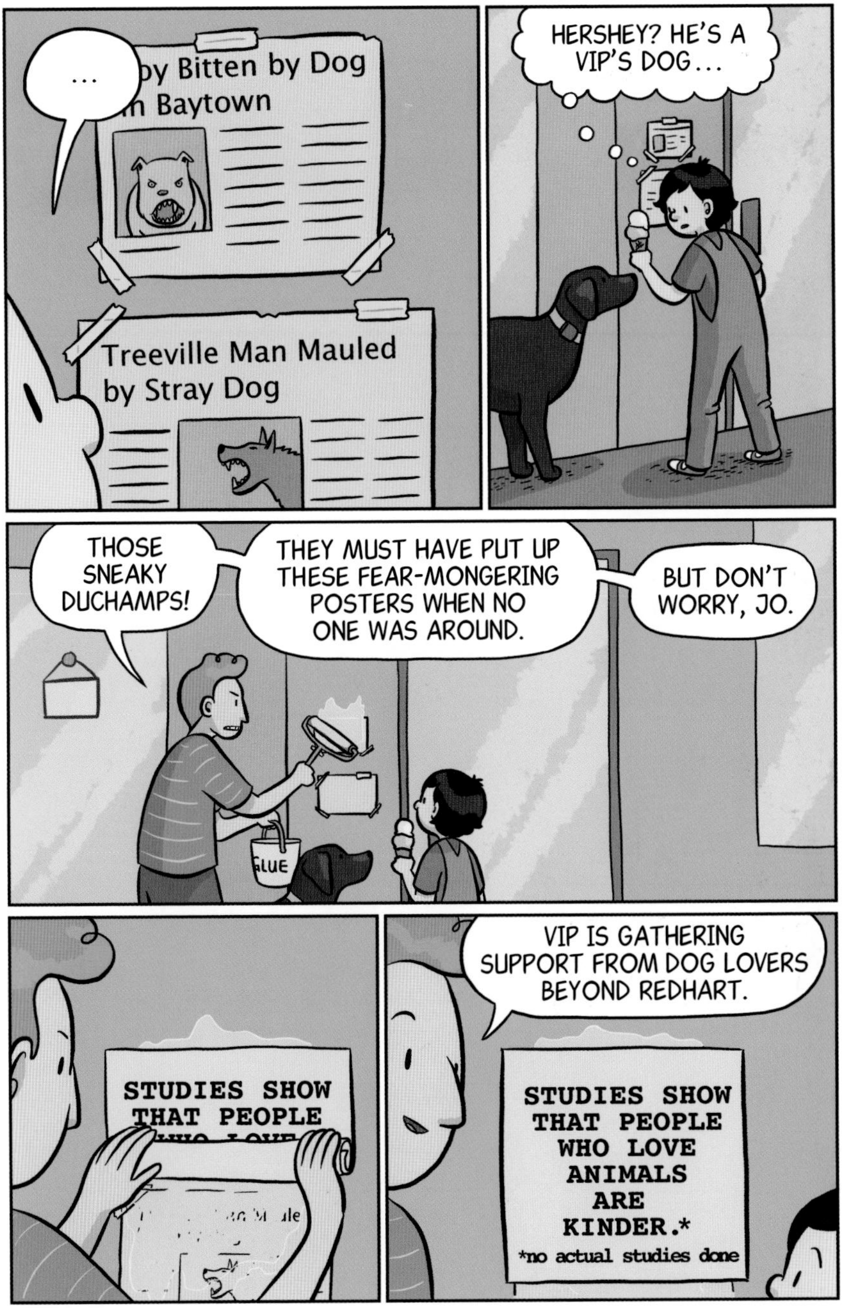
...
Treeville Man Mauled by Stray Dog
HERSHEY? HE'S A VIP'S DOG...
THOSE SNEAKY DUCHAMPS!
THEY MUST HAVE PUT UP THESE FEAR-MONGERING POSTERS WHEN NO ONE WAS AROUND.
BUT DON'T WORRY, JO.
GLUE
STUDIES SHOW THAT PEOPLE
VIP IS GATHERING SUPPORT FROM DOG LOVERS BEYOND REDHART.
STUDIES SHOW THAT PEOPLE WHO LOVE ANIMALS ARE KINDER.*
*no actual studies done

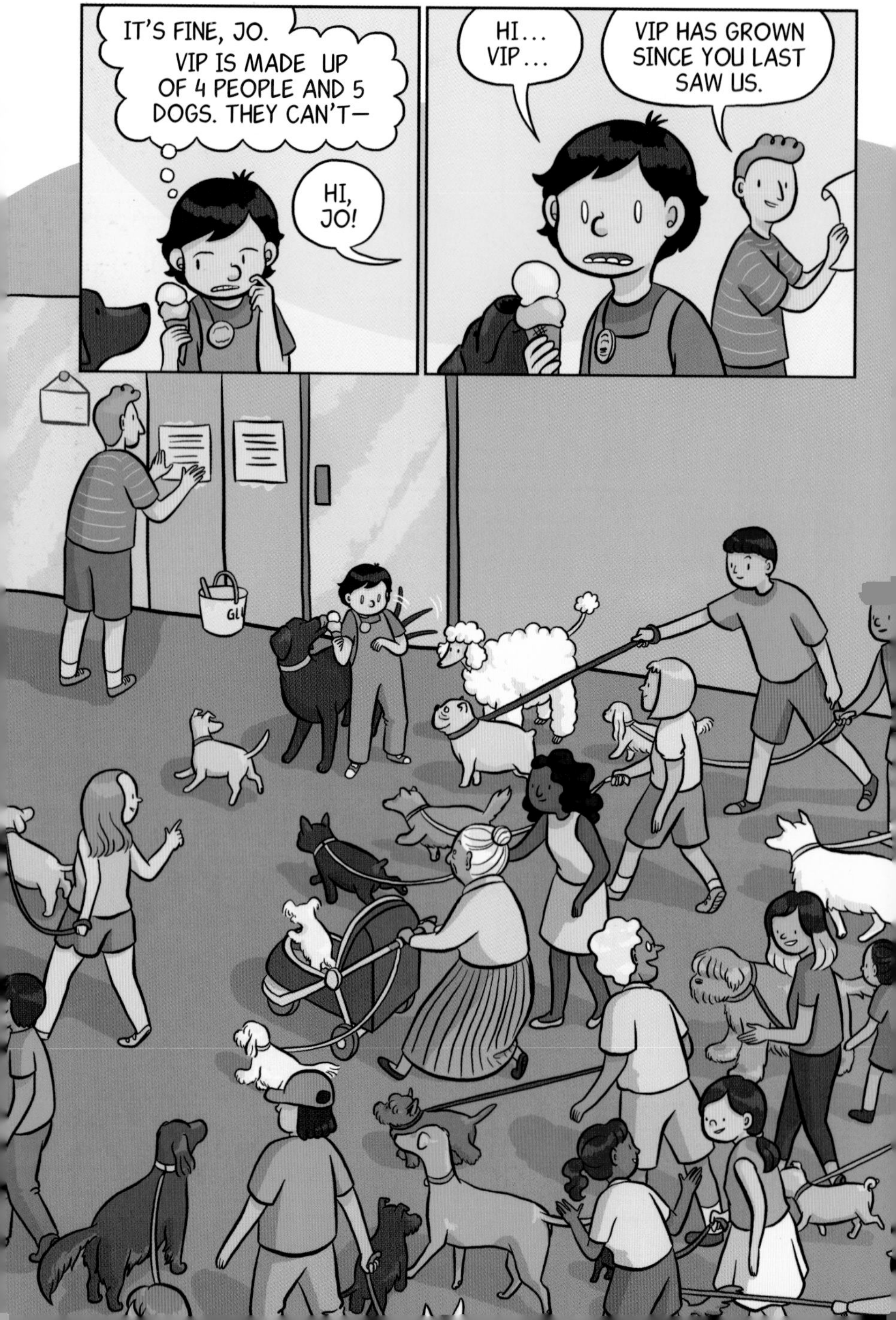
IT'S FINE, JO.
VIP IS MADE UP OF 4 PEOPLE AND 5 DOGS. THEY CAN'T—
HI, JO!
HI... VIP...
VIP HAS GROWN SINCE YOU LAST SAW US.
GL

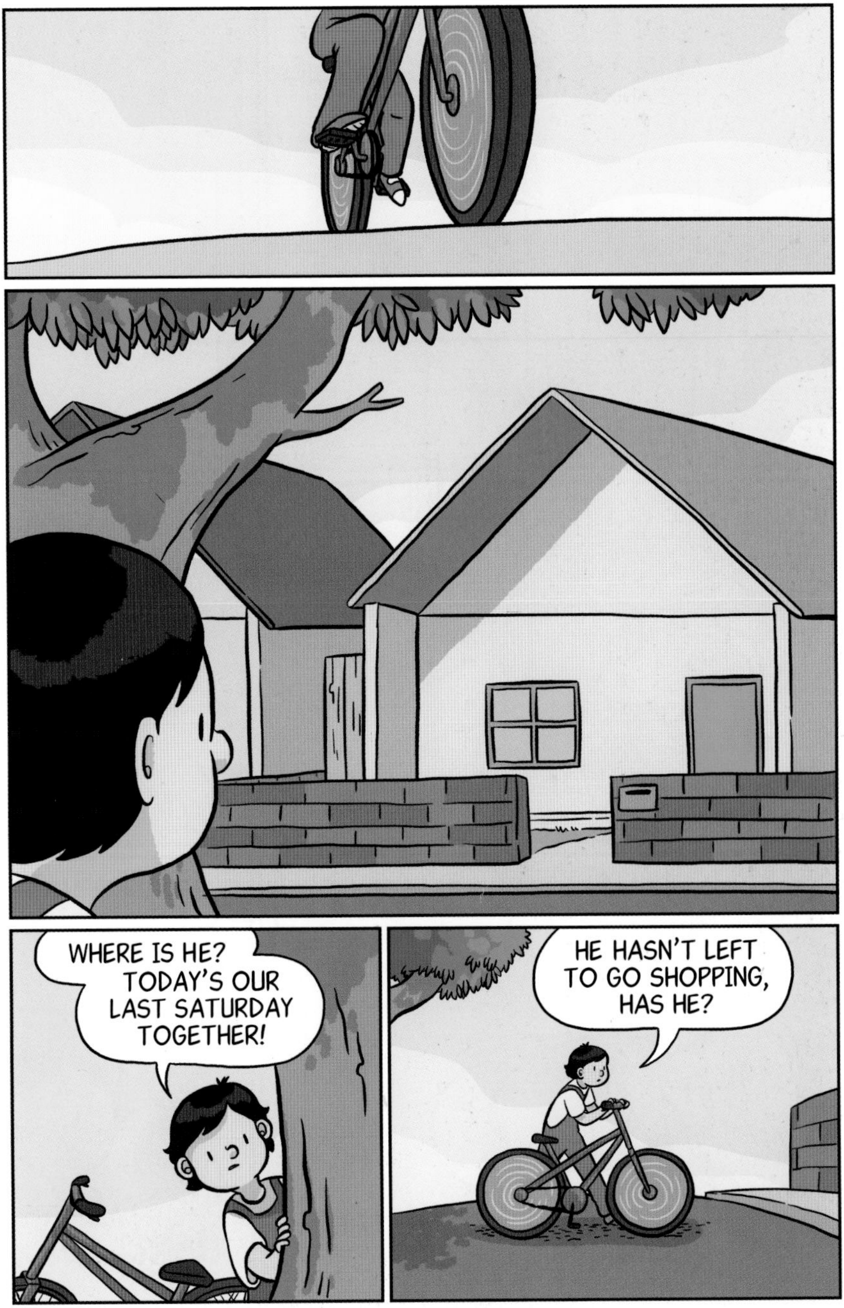
WHERE IS HE? TODAY'S OUR LAST SATURDAY TOGETHER!
HE HASN'T LEFT TO GO SHOPPING, HAS HE?

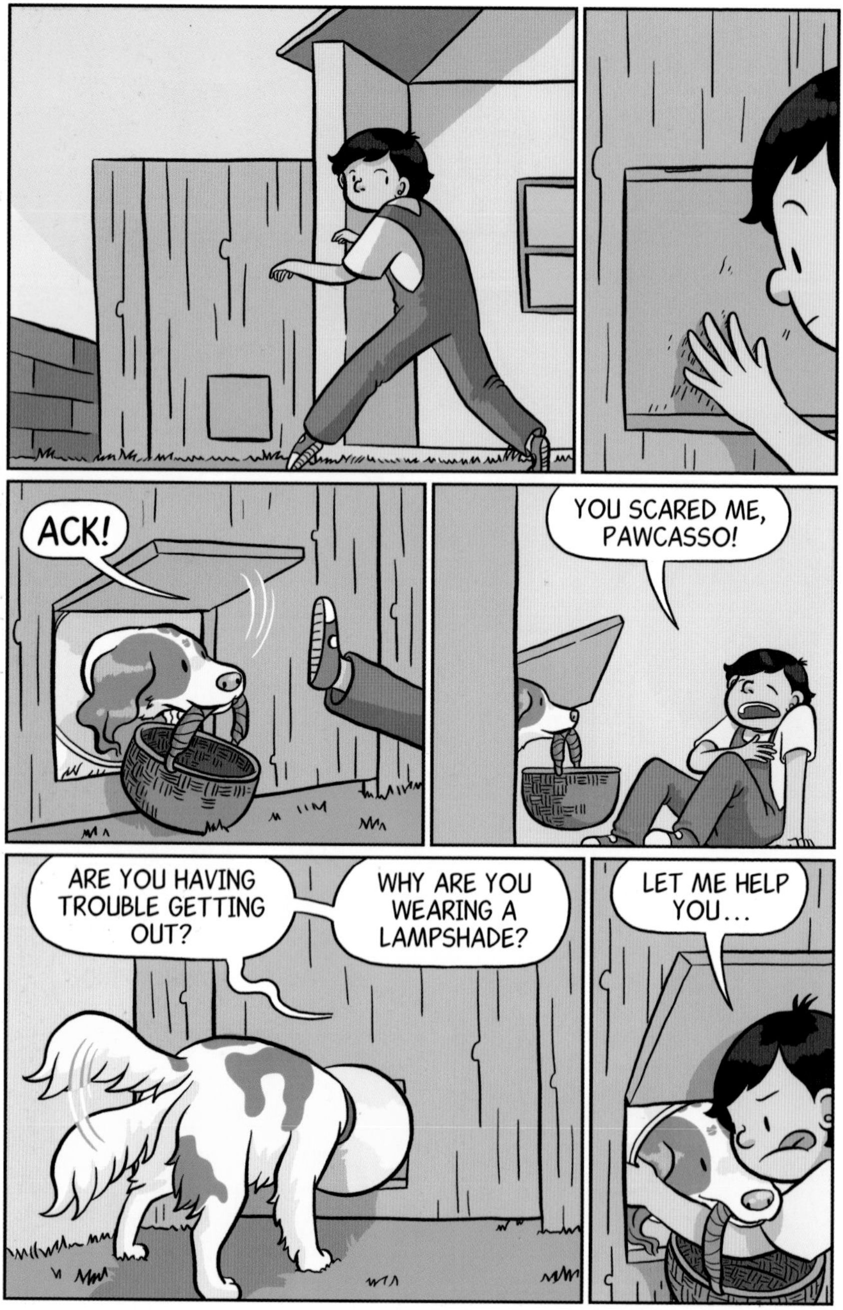
ACK!
YOU SCARED ME, PAWCASSO!
ARE YOU HAVING TROUBLE GETTING OUT?
WHY ARE YOU WEARING A LAMPSHADE?
LET ME HELP YOU...

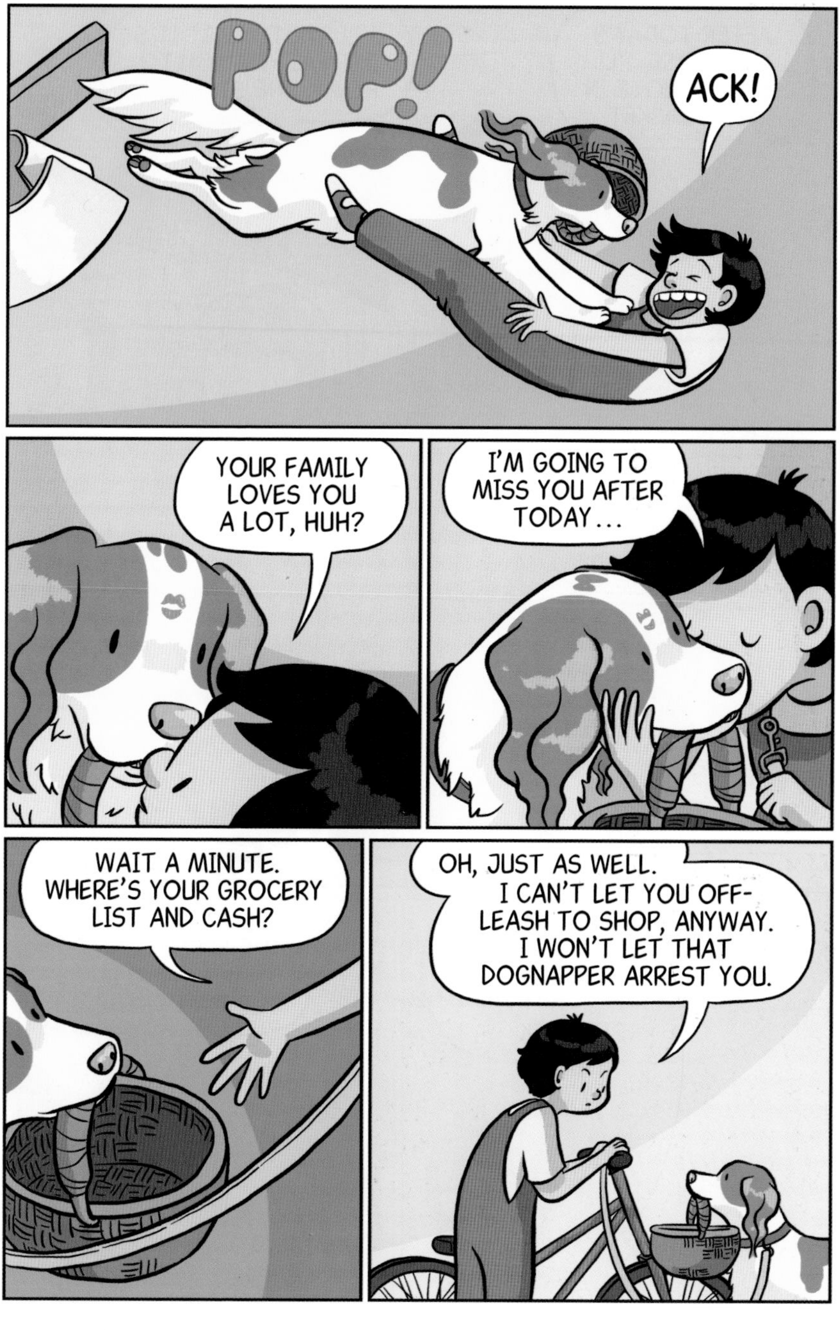
POP!
ACK!
YOUR FAMILY LOVES YOU A LOT, HUH?
I'M GOING TO MISS YOU AFTER TODAY...
WAIT A MINUTE. WHERE'S YOUR GROCERY LIST AND CASH?
OH, JUST AS WELL. I CAN'T LET YOU OFF-LEASH TO SHOP, ANYWAY. I WON'T LET THAT DOGNAPPER ARREST YOU.

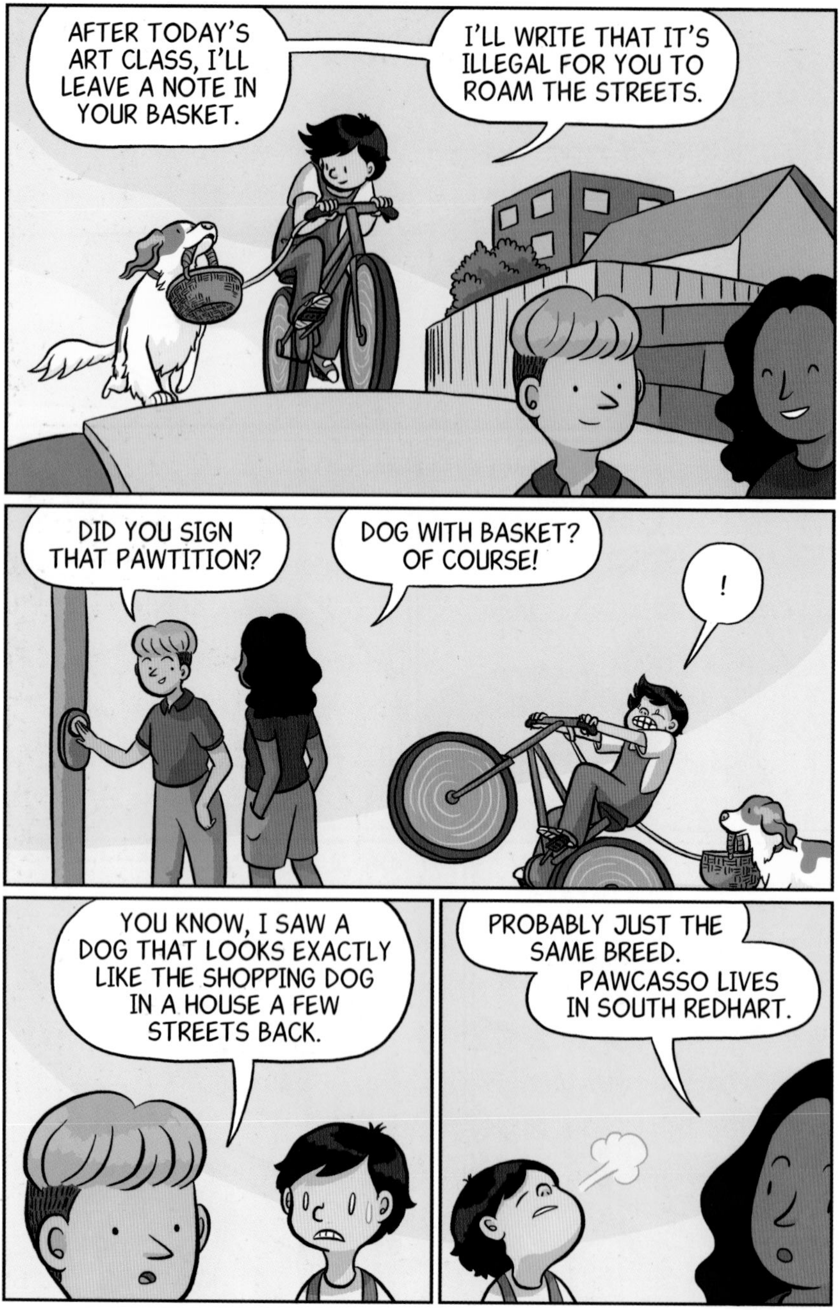
AFTER TODAY'S ART CLASS, I'LL LEAVE A NOTE IN YOUR BASKET.
I'LL WRITE THAT IT'S ILLEGAL FOR YOU TO ROAM THE STREETS.
DID YOU SIGN THAT PAWTITION?
DOG WITH BASKET? OF COURSE!
!
YOU KNOW, I SAW A DOG THAT LOOKS EXACTLY LIKE THE SHOPPING DOG IN A HOUSE A FEW STREETS BACK.
PROBABLY JUST THE SAME BREED.
PAWCASSO LIVES IN SOUTH REDHART.

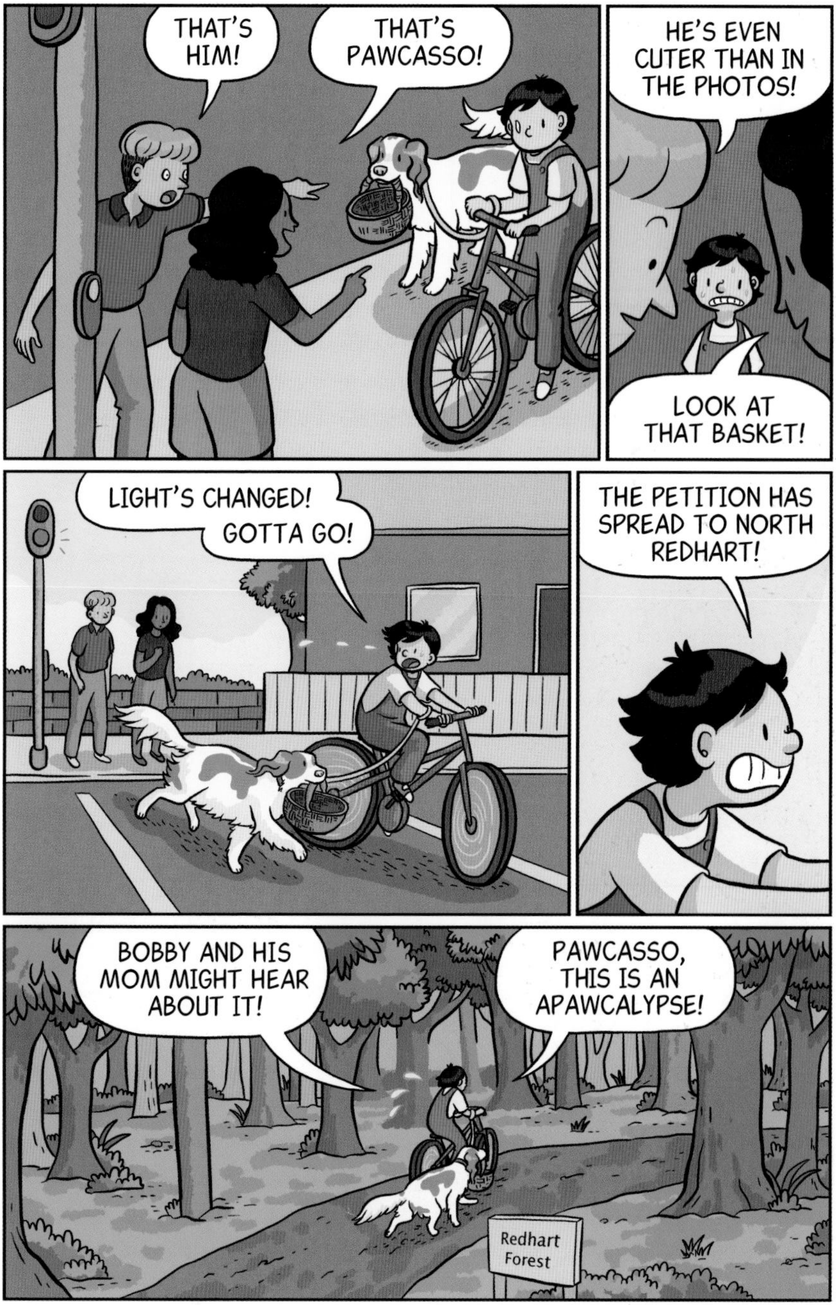
THAT'S HIM!
THAT'S PAWCASSO!
HE'S EVEN CUTER THAN IN THE PHOTOS!
LOOK AT THAT BASKET!
LIGHT'S CHANGED!
GOTTA GO!
THE PETITION HAS SPREAD TO NORTH REDHART!
BOBBY AND HIS MOM MIGHT HEAR ABOUT IT!
PAWCASSO, THIS IS AN APAWCALYPSE!
Redhart Forest

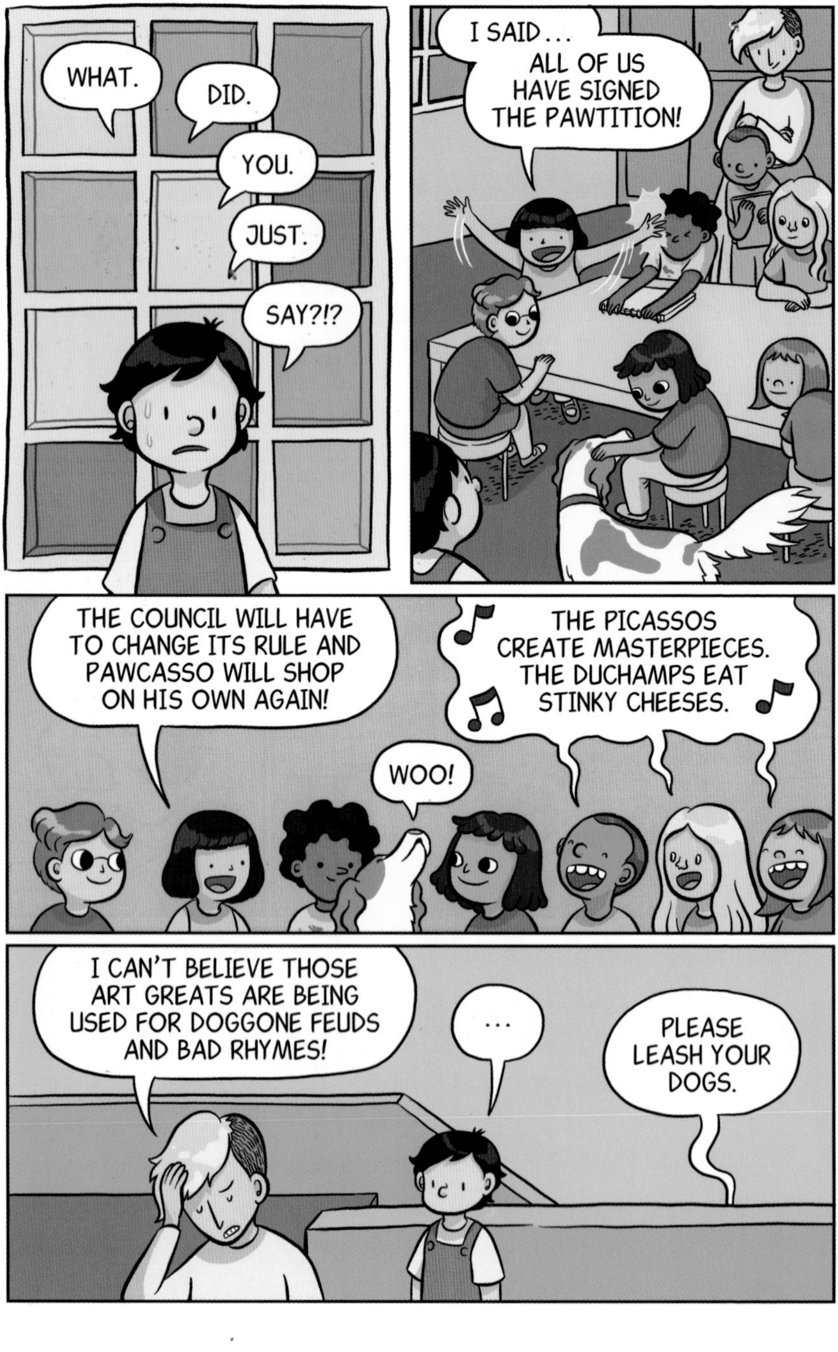
WHAT.
DID.
YOU.
JUST.
SAY?!?
I SAID... ALL OF US HAVE SIGNED THE PAWTITION!
THE COUNCIL WILL HAVE TO CHANGE ITS RULE AND PAWCASSO WILL SHOP ON HIS OWN AGAIN!
THE PICASSOS CREATE MASTERPIECES. THE DUCHAMPS EAT STINKY CHEESES.
WOO!
I CAN'T BELIEVE THOSE ART GREATS ARE BEING USED FOR DOGGONE FEUDS AND BAD RHYMES!
...
PLEASE LEASH YOUR DOGS.

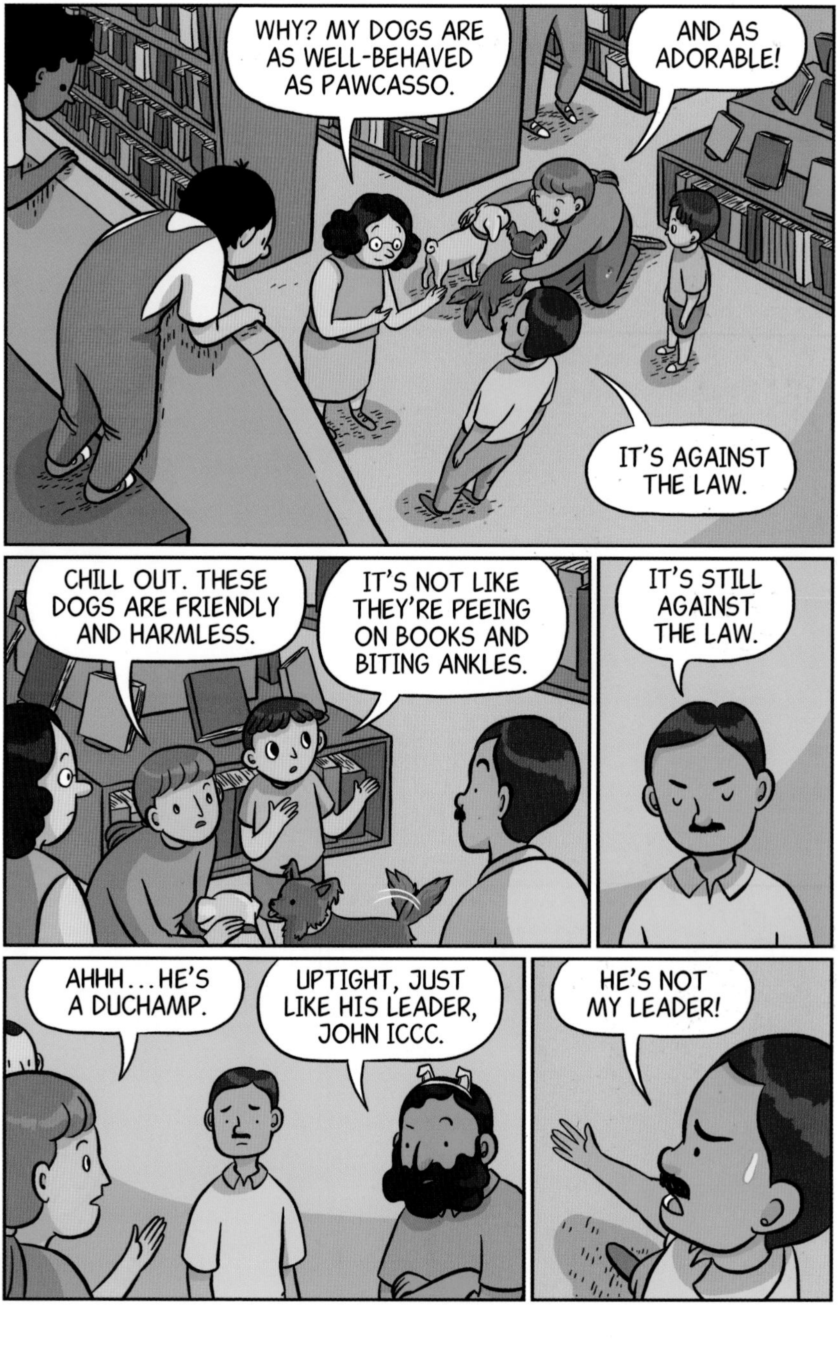
WHY? MY DOGS ARE AS WELL-BEHAVED AS PAWCASSO.
AND AS ADORABLE!
IT'S AGAINST THE LAW.
CHILL OUT. THESE DOGS ARE FRIENDLY AND HARMLESS.
IT'S NOT LIKE THEY'RE PEEING ON BOOKS AND BITING ANKLES.
IT'S STILL AGAINST THE LAW.
AHHH...HE'S A DUCHAMP.
UPTIGHT, JUST LIKE HIS LEADER, JOHN ICCC.
HE'S NOT MY LEADER!

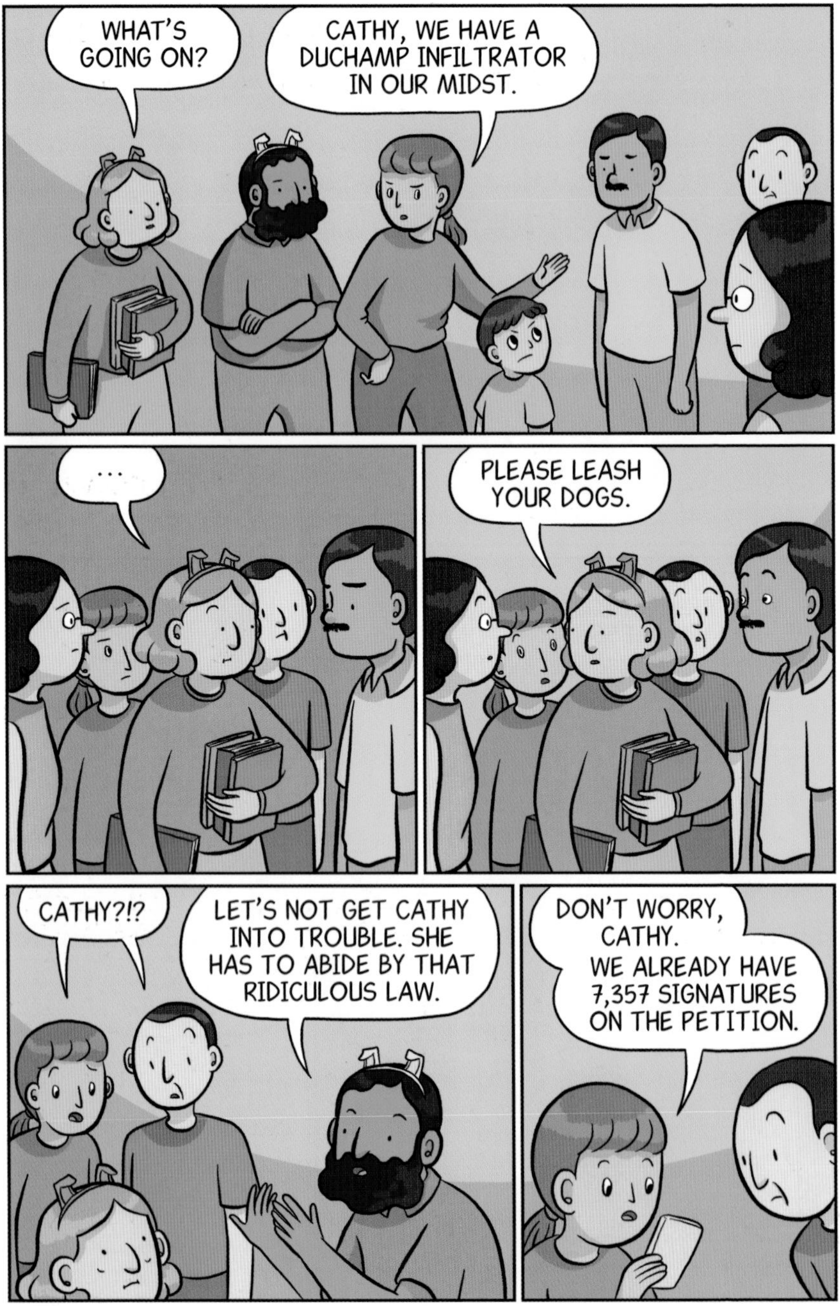
WHAT'S GOING ON?
CATHY, WE HAVE A DUCHAMP INFILTRATOR IN OUR MIDST.
...
PLEASE LEASH YOUR DOGS.
CATHY?!?
LET'S NOT GET CATHY INTO TROUBLE. SHE HAS TO ABIDE BY THAT RIDICULOUS LAW.
DON'T WORRY, CATHY.
WE ALREADY HAVE 7,357 SIGNATURES ON THE PETITION.

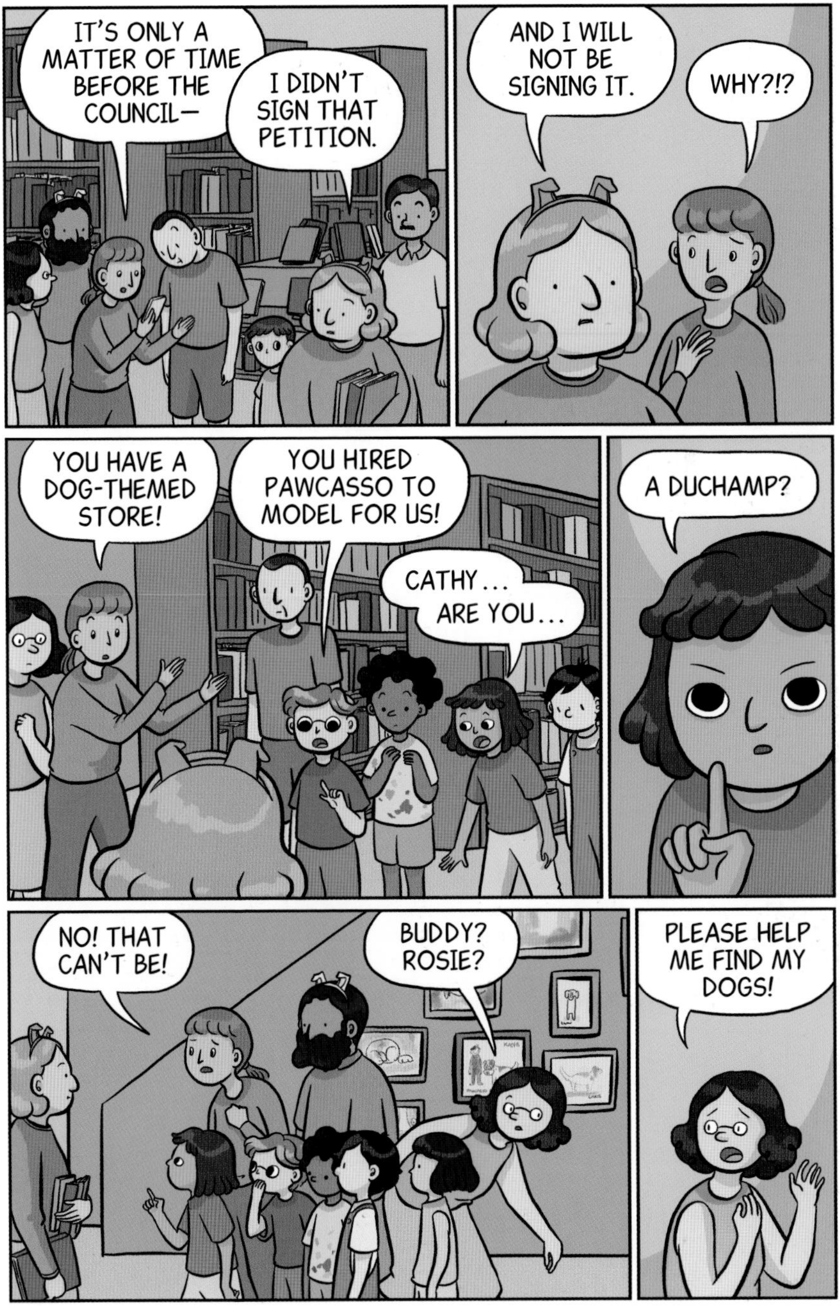
IT'S ONLY A MATTER OF TIME BEFORE THE COUNCIL—
I DIDN'T SIGN THAT PETITION.
AND I WILL NOT BE SIGNING IT.
WHY?!?
YOU HAVE A DOG-THEMED STORE!
YOU HIRED PAWCASSO TO MODEL FOR US!
CATHY... ARE YOU...
A DUCHAMP?
NO! THAT CAN'T BE!
BUDDY? ROSIE?
PLEASE HELP ME FIND MY DOGS!

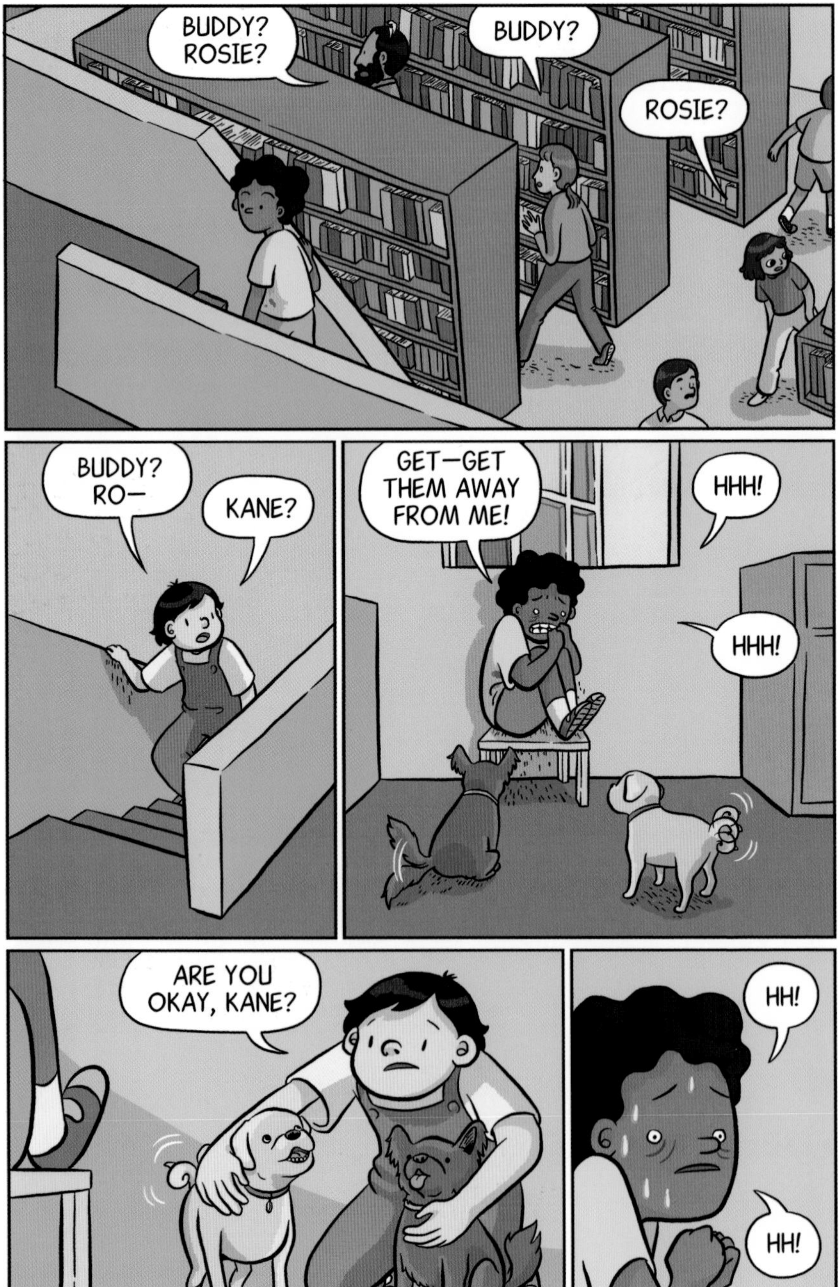
BUDDY? ROSIE?
BUDDY?
ROSIE?
BUDDY? RO—
KANE?
GET—GET THEM AWAY FROM ME!
HHH!
HHH!
ARE YOU OKAY, KANE?
HH!
HH!

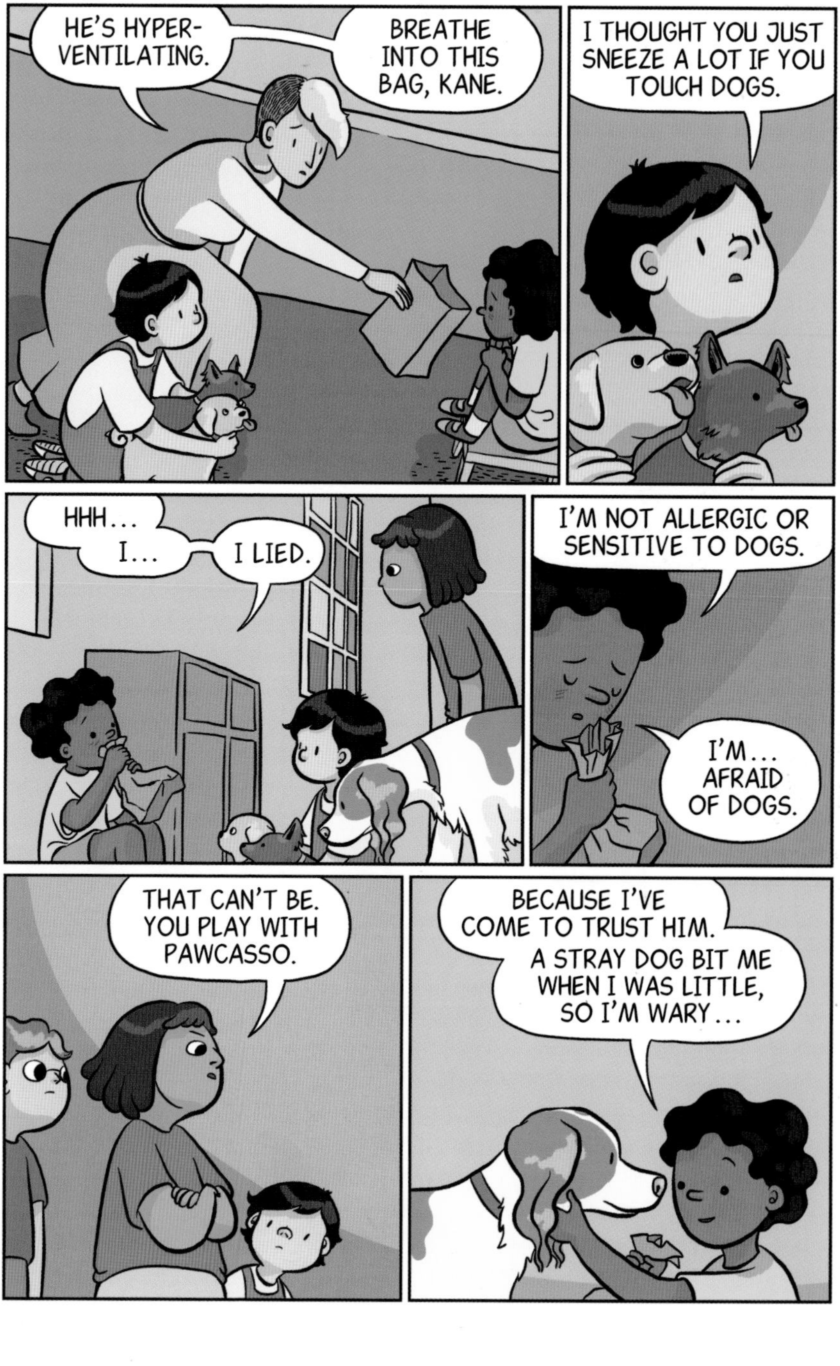
HE'S HYPER-VENTILATING.
BREATHE INTO THIS BAG, KANE.
I THOUGHT YOU JUST SNEEZE A LOT IF YOU TOUCH DOGS.
HHH...
I...
I LIED.
I'M NOT ALLERGIC OR SENSITIVE TO DOGS.
I'M... AFRAID OF DOGS.
THAT CAN'T BE. YOU PLAY WITH PAWCASSO.
BECAUSE I'VE COME TO TRUST HIM.
A STRAY DOG BIT ME WHEN I WAS LITTLE, SO I'M WARY...

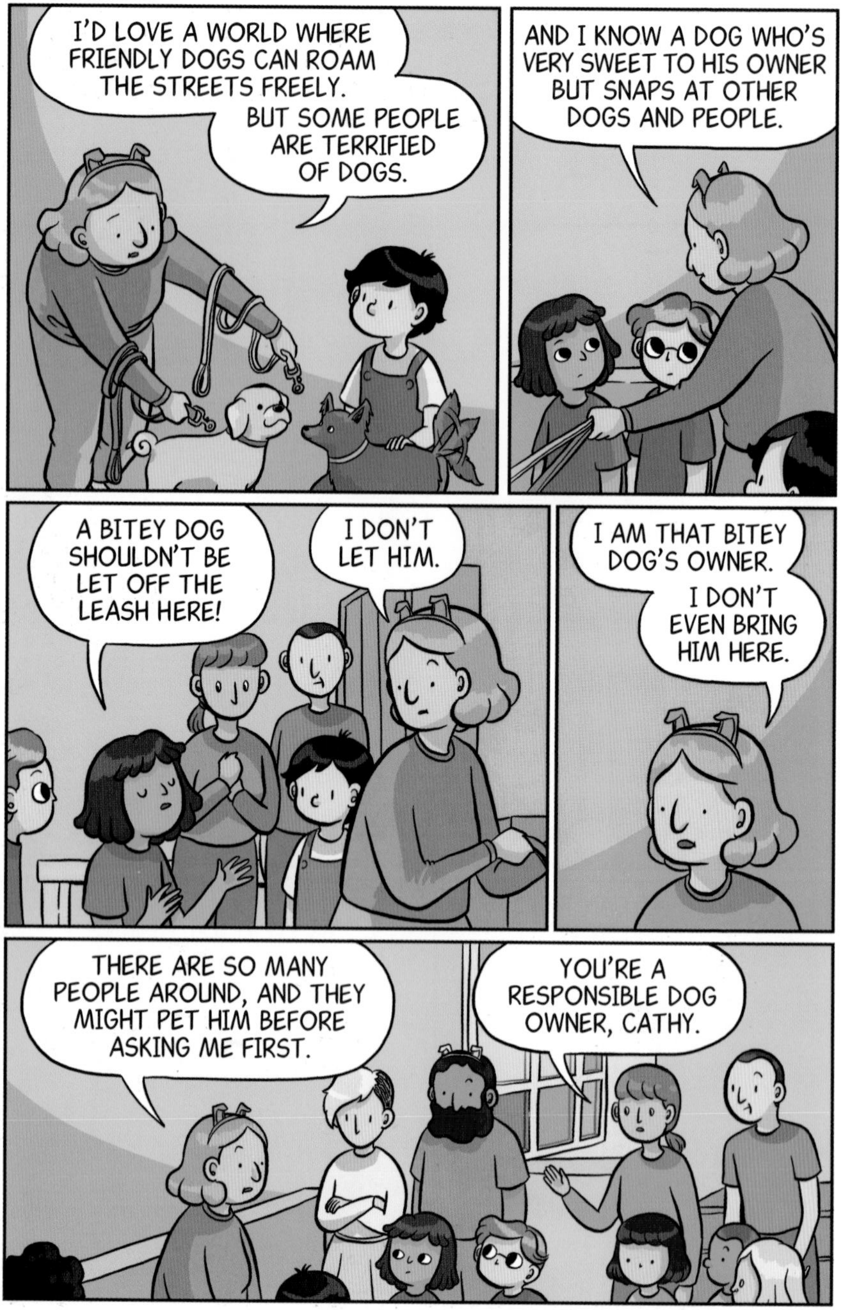
I'D LOVE A WORLD WHERE FRIENDLY DOGS CAN ROAM THE STREETS FREELY.
BUT SOME PEOPLE ARE TERRIFIED OF DOGS.
AND I KNOW A DOG WHO'S VERY SWEET TO HIS OWNER BUT SNAPS AT OTHER DOGS AND PEOPLE.
A BITEY DOG SHOULDN'T BE LET OFF THE LEASH HERE!
I DON'T LET HIM.
I AM THAT BITEY DOG'S OWNER.
I DON'T EVEN BRING HIM HERE.
THERE ARE SO MANY PEOPLE AROUND, AND THEY MIGHT PET HIM BEFORE ASKING ME FIRST.
YOU'RE A RESPONSIBLE DOG OWNER, CATHY.

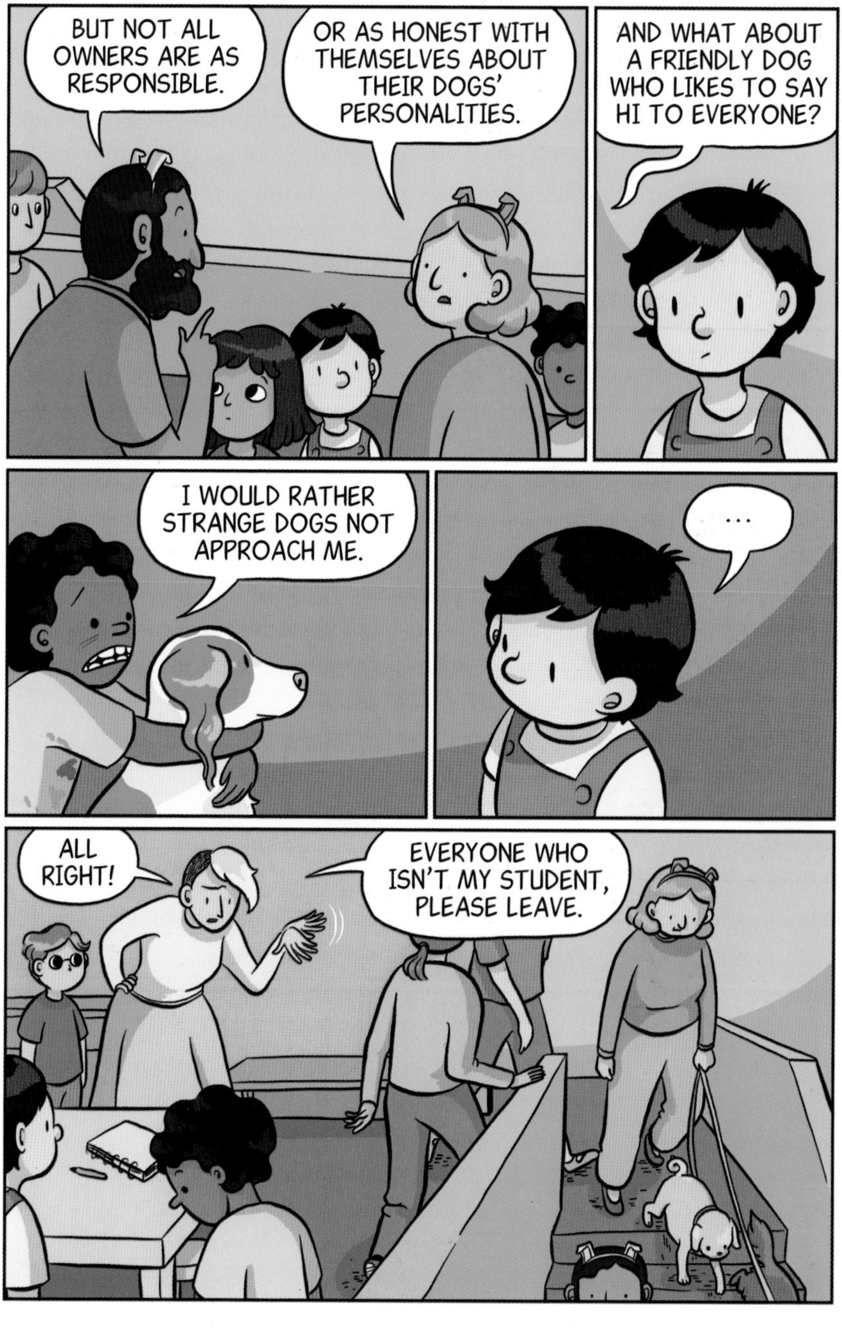
BUT NOT ALL OWNERS ARE AS RESPONSIBLE.
OR AS HONEST WITH THEMSELVES ABOUT THEIR DOGS' PERSONALITIES.
AND WHAT ABOUT A FRIENDLY DOG WHO LIKES TO SAY HI TO EVERYONE?
I WOULD RATHER STRANGE DOGS NOT APPROACH ME.
...
ALL RIGHT!
EVERYONE WHO ISN'T MY STUDENT, PLEASE LEAVE.

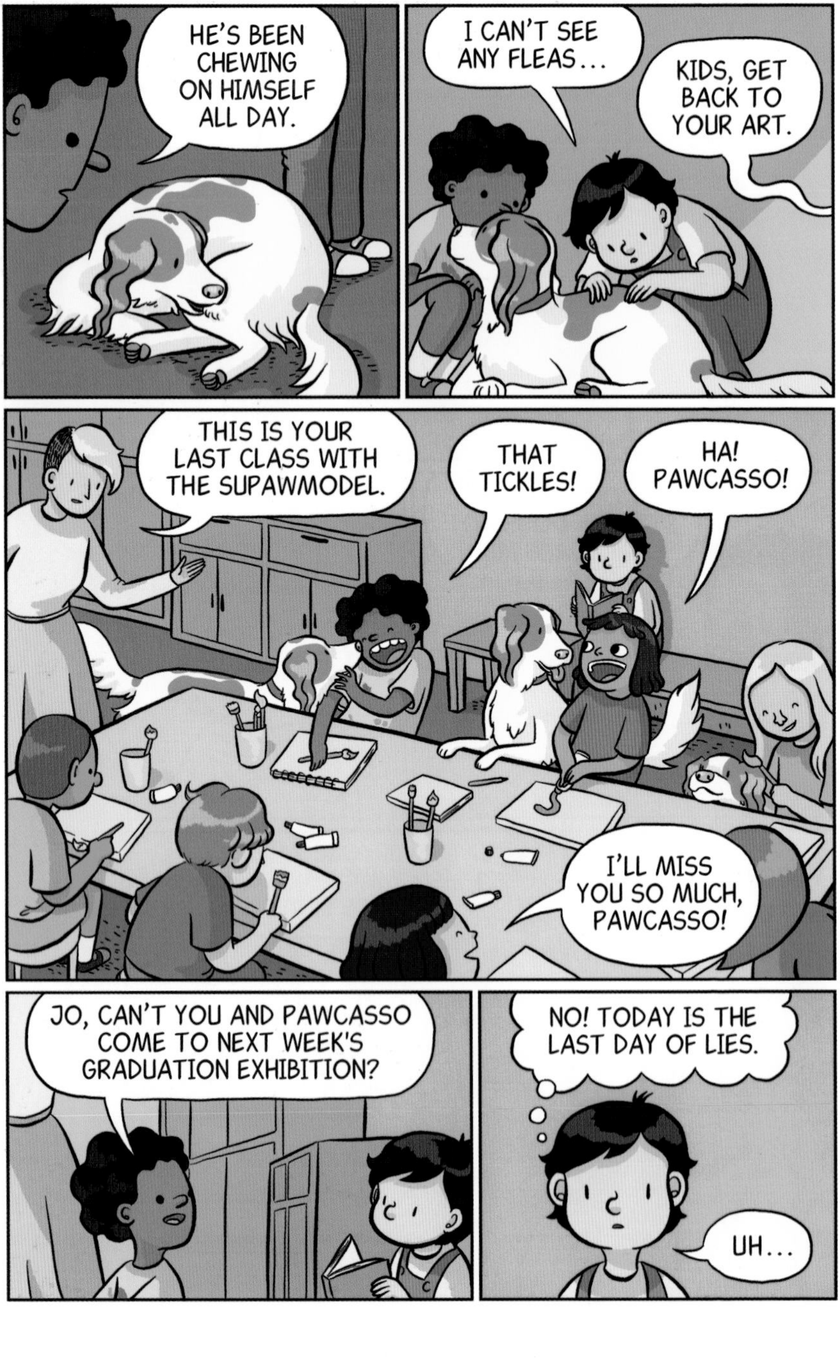
HE'S BEEN CHEWING ON HIMSELF ALL DAY.
I CAN'T SEE ANY FLEAS...
KIDS, GET BACK TO YOUR ART.
THIS IS YOUR LAST CLASS WITH THE SUPAWMODEL.
THAT TICKLES!
HA! PAWCASSO!
I'LL MISS YOU SO MUCH, PAWCASSO!
JO, CAN'T YOU AND PAWCASSO COME TO NEXT WEEK'S GRADUATION EXHIBITION?
NO! TODAY IS THE LAST DAY OF LIES.
UH...

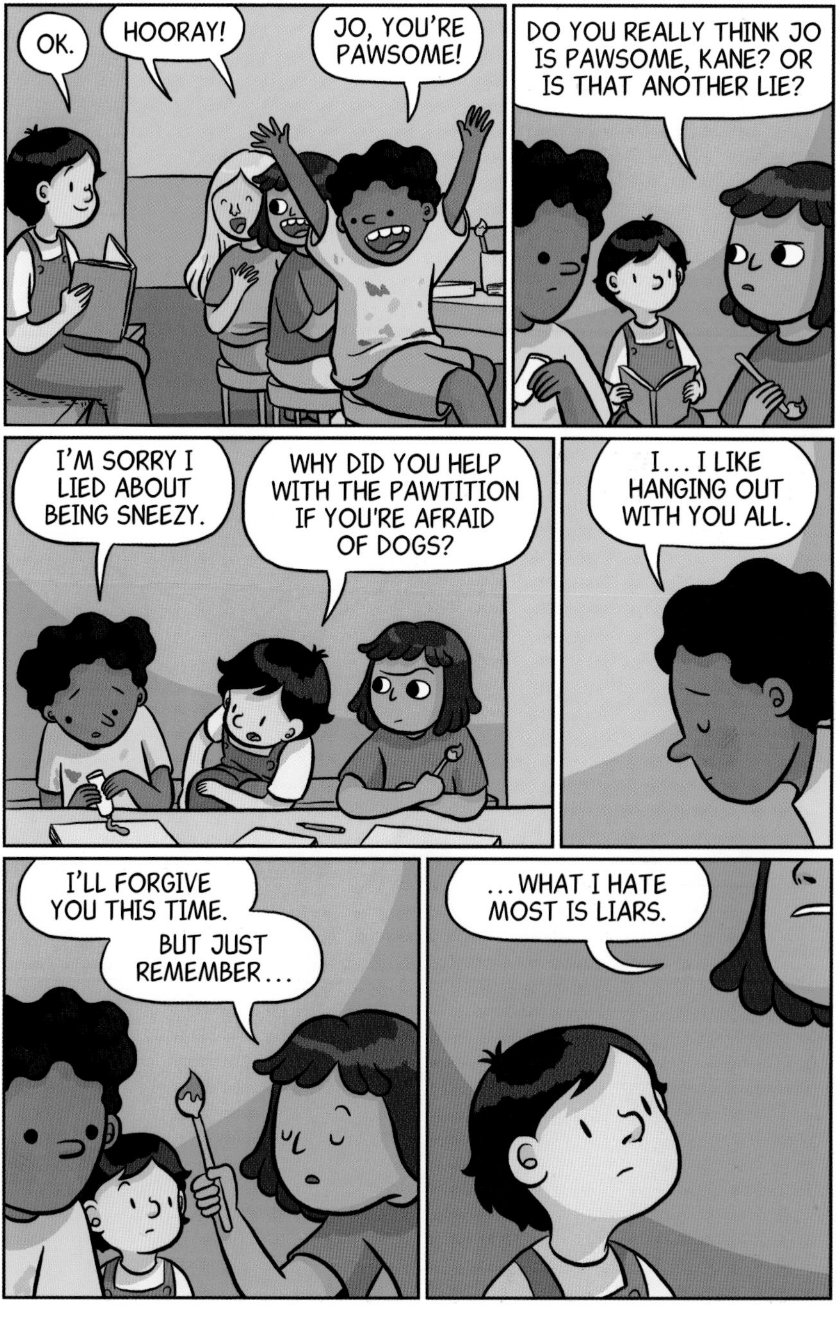
OK.
HOORAY!
JO, YOU'RE PAWSOME!
DO YOU REALLY THINK JO IS PAWSOME, KANE? OR IS THAT ANOTHER LIE?
I'M SORRY I LIED ABOUT BEING SNEEZY.
WHY DID YOU HELP WITH THE PAWTITION IF YOU'RE AFRAID OF DOGS?
I... I LIKE HANGING OUT WITH YOU ALL.
I'LL FORGIVE YOU THIS TIME.
BUT JUST REMEMBER...
...WHAT I HATE MOST IS LIARS.

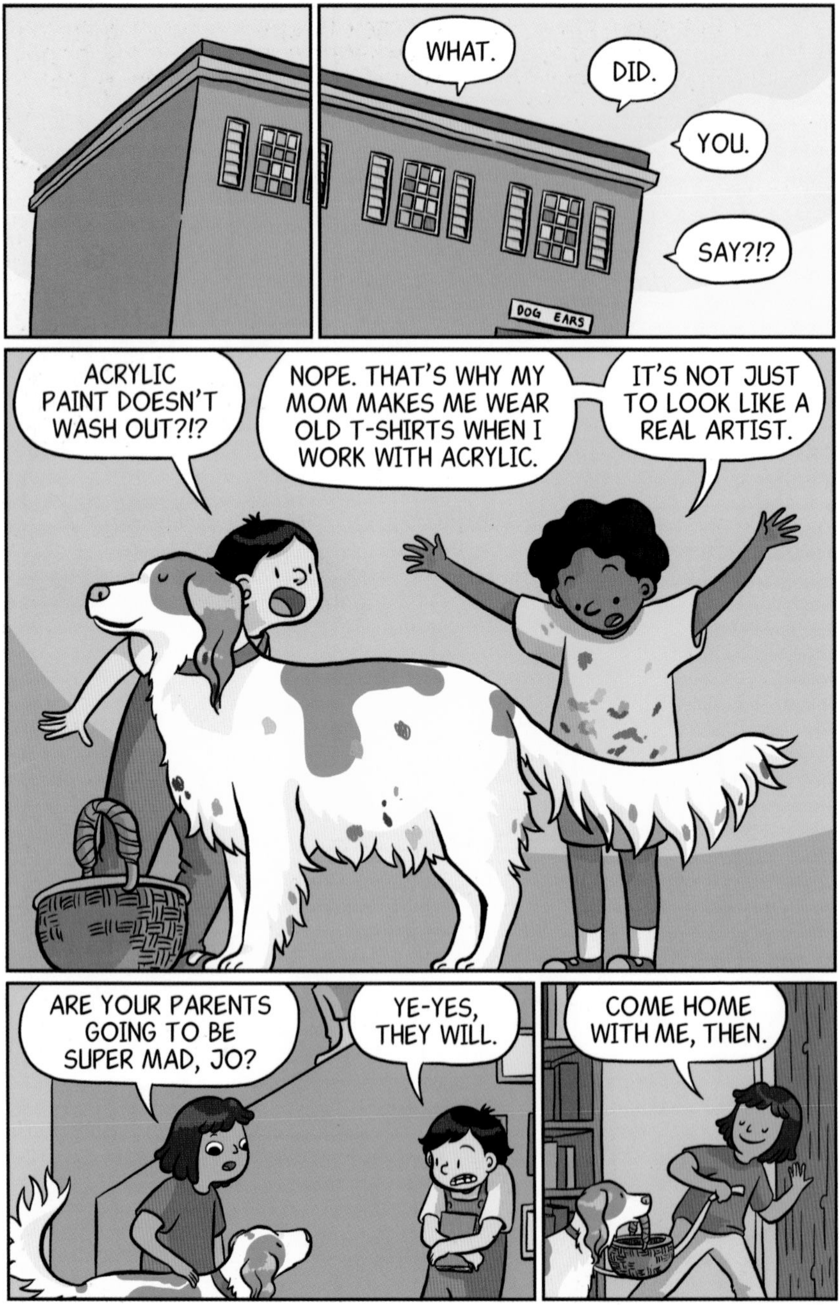
WHAT.
DID.
YOU.
SAY?!?
DOG EARS
ACRYLIC PAINT DOESN'T WASH OUT?!?
NOPE. THAT'S WHY MY MOM MAKES ME WEAR OLD T-SHIRTS WHEN I WORK WITH ACRYLIC.
IT'S NOT JUST TO LOOK LIKE A REAL ARTIST.
ARE YOUR PARENTS GOING TO BE SUPER MAD, JO?
YE-YES, THEY WILL.
COME HOME WITH ME, THEN.

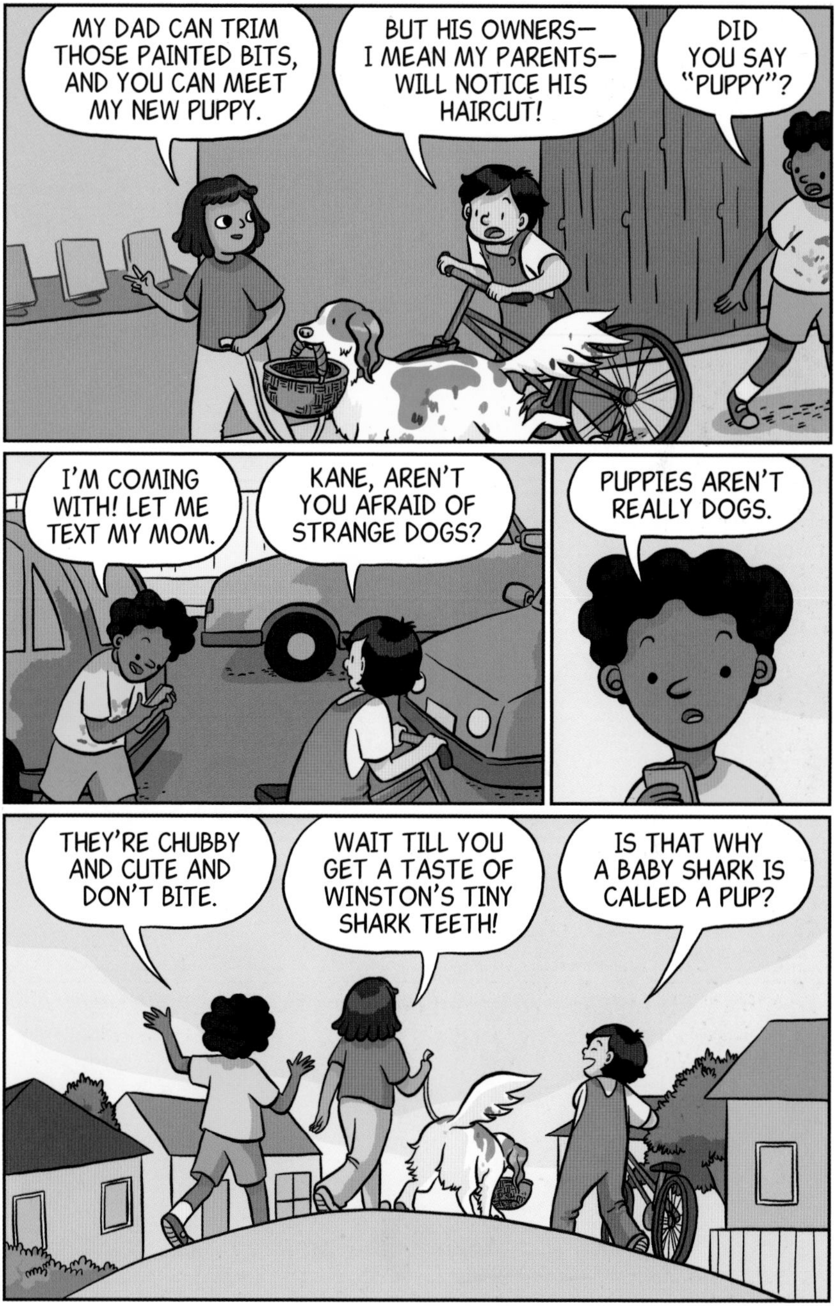
MY DAD CAN TRIM THOSE PAINTED BITS, AND YOU CAN MEET MY NEW PUPPY.
BUT HIS OWNERS— I MEAN MY PARENTS— WILL NOTICE HIS HAIRCUT!
DID YOU SAY "PUPPY"?
I'M COMING WITH! LET ME TEXT MY MOM.
KANE, AREN'T YOU AFRAID OF STRANGE DOGS?
PUPPIES AREN'T REALLY DOGS.
THEY'RE CHUBBY AND CUTE AND DON'T BITE.
WAIT TILL YOU GET A TASTE OF WINSTON'S TINY SHARK TEETH!
IS THAT WHY A BABY SHARK IS CALLED A PUP?

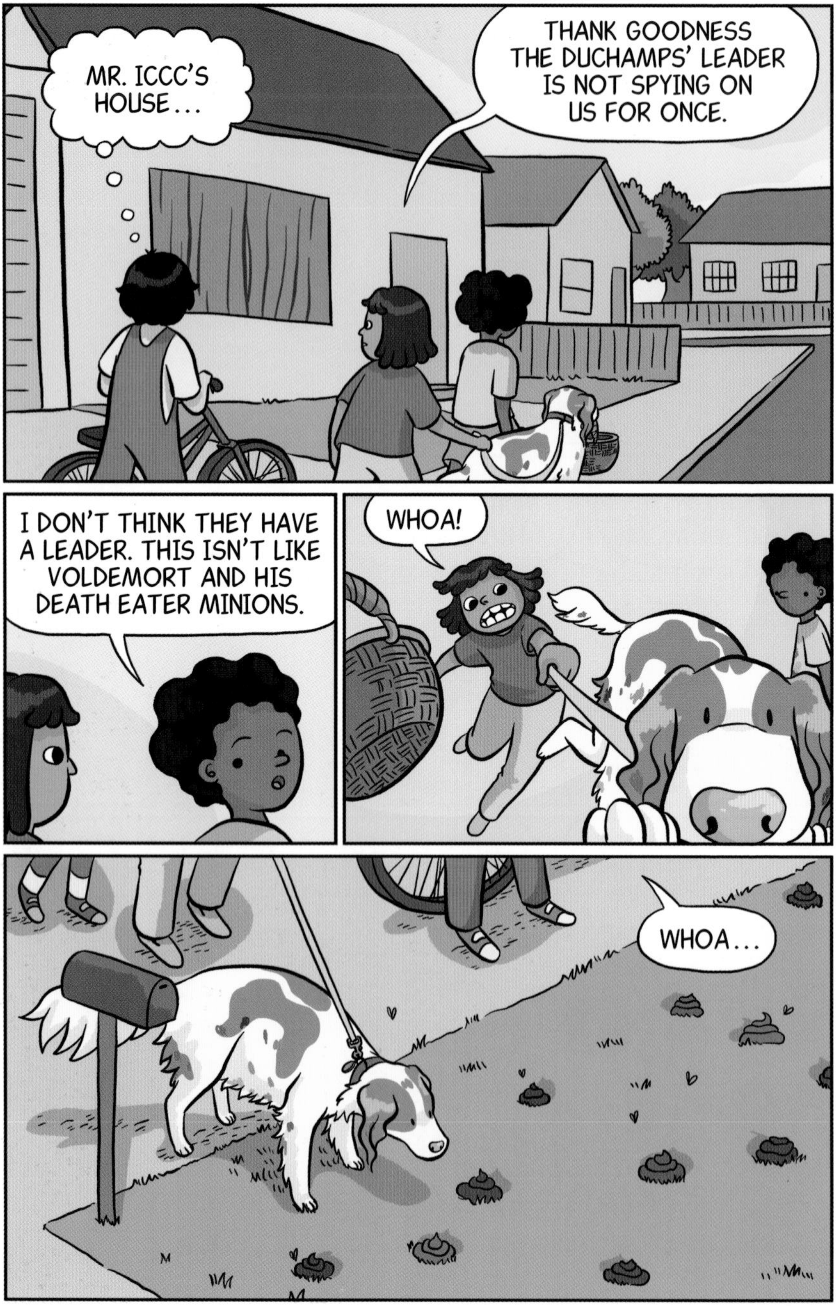
MR. ICCC'S HOUSE...
THANK GOODNESS THE DUCHAMPS' LEADER IS NOT SPYING ON US FOR ONCE.
I DON'T THINK THEY HAVE A LEADER. THIS ISN'T LIKE VOLDEMORT AND HIS DEATH EATER MINIONS.
WHOA!
WHOA...

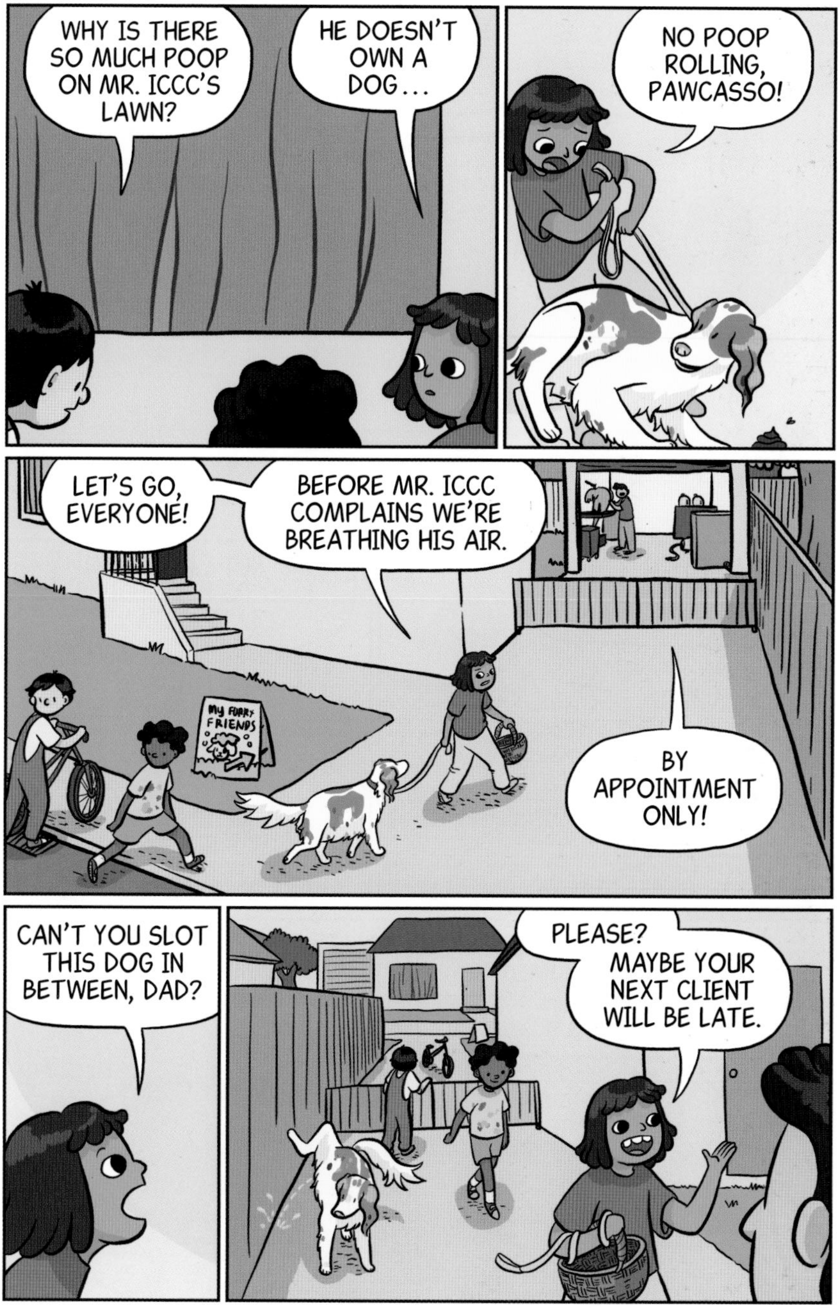
WHY IS THERE SO MUCH POOP ON MR. ICCC'S LAWN?
HE DOESN'T OWN A DOG...
NO POOP ROLLING, PAWCASSO!
LET'S GO, EVERYONE!
BEFORE MR. ICCC COMPLAINS WE'RE BREATHING HIS AIR.
MY FURRY FRIENDS
BY APPOINTMENT ONLY!
CAN'T YOU SLOT THIS DOG IN BETWEEN, DAD?
PLEASE?
MAYBE YOUR NEXT CLIENT WILL BE LATE.

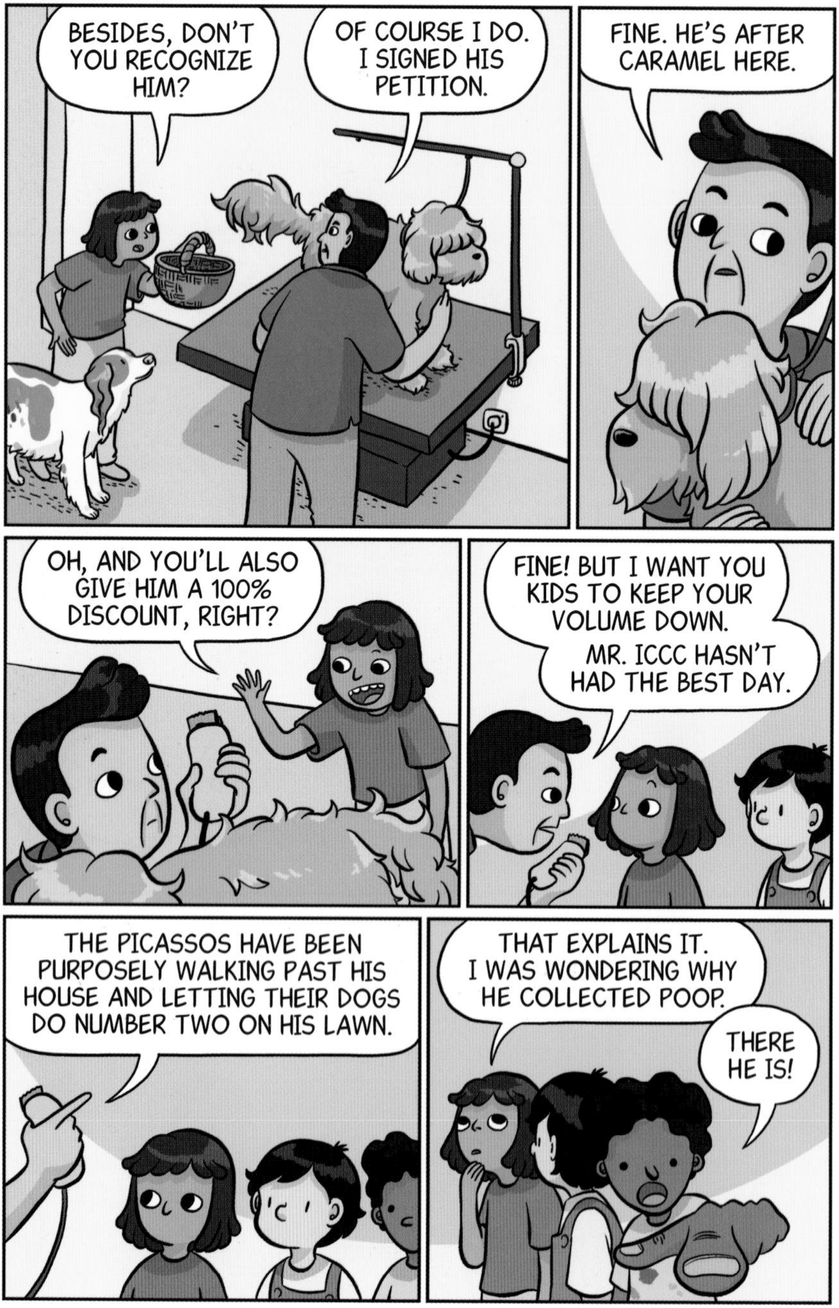
BESIDES, DON'T YOU RECOGNIZE HIM?
OF COURSE I DO. I SIGNED HIS PETITION.
FINE. HE'S AFTER CARAMEL HERE.
OH, AND YOU'LL ALSO GIVE HIM A 100% DISCOUNT, RIGHT?
FINE! BUT I WANT YOU KIDS TO KEEP YOUR VOLUME DOWN.
MR. ICCC HASN'T HAD THE BEST DAY.
THE PICASSOS HAVE BEEN PURPOSELY WALKING PAST HIS HOUSE AND LETTING THEIR DOGS DO NUMBER TWO ON HIS LAWN.
THAT EXPLAINS IT. I WAS WONDERING WHY HE COLLECTED POOP.
THERE HE IS!

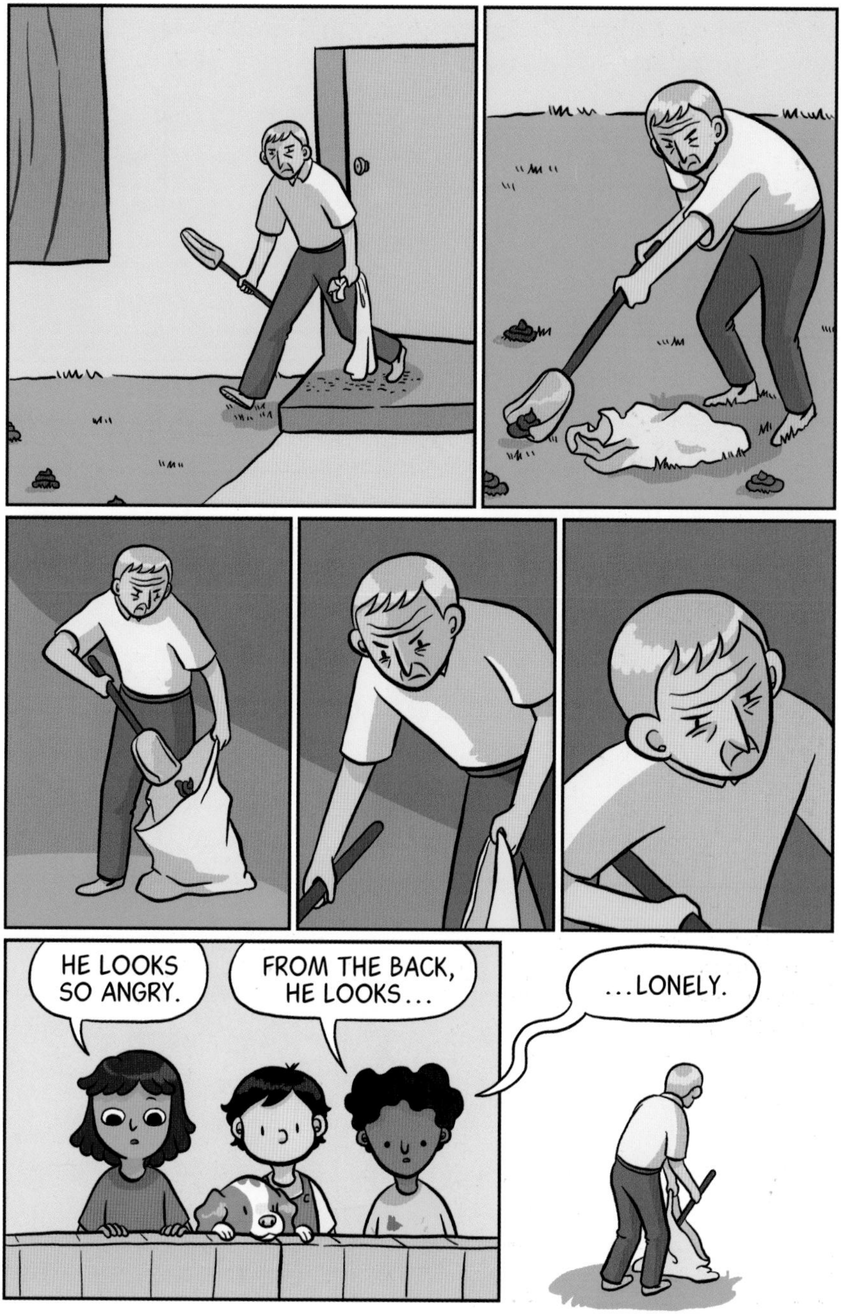
HE LOOKS SO ANGRY.
FROM THE BACK, HE LOOKS...
...LONELY.

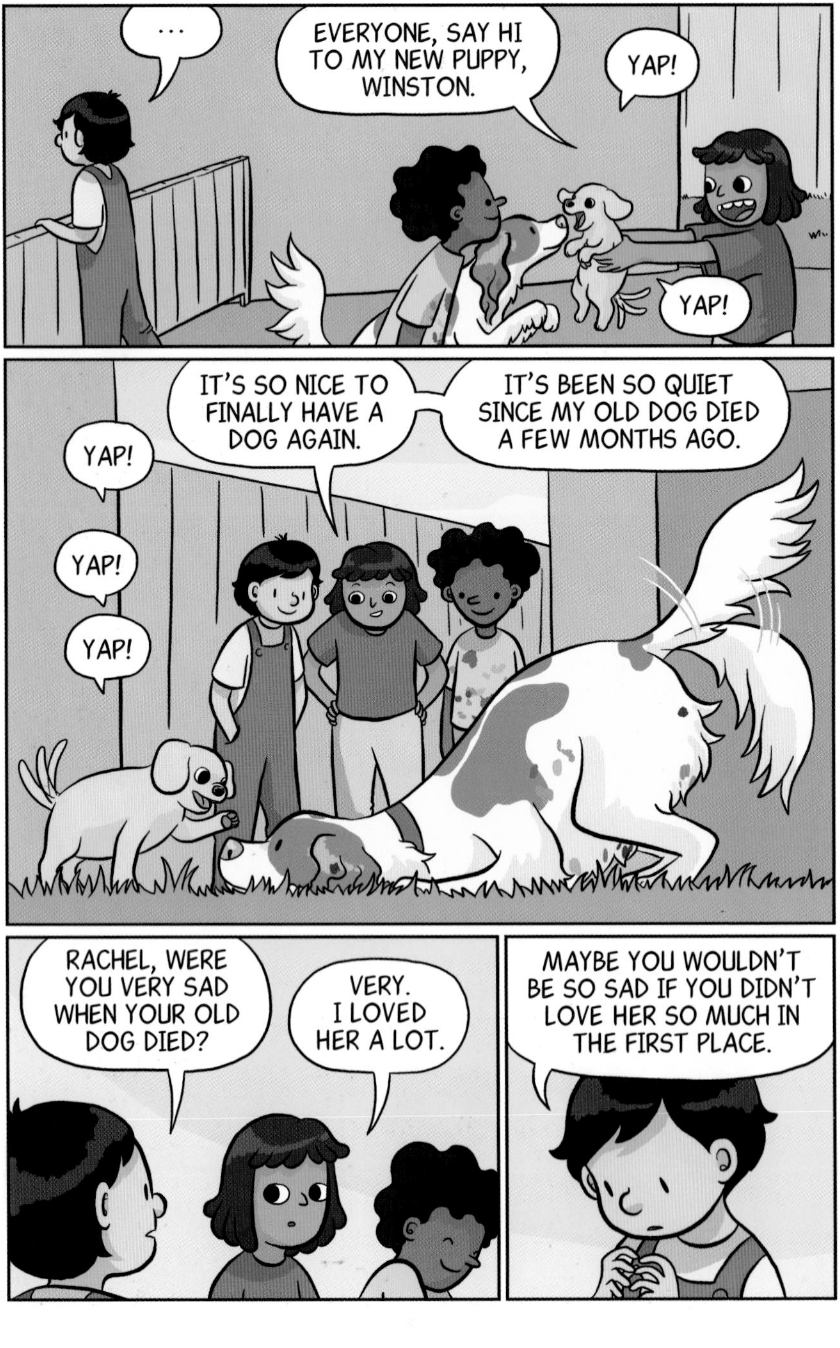
...
EVERYONE, SAY HI TO MY NEW PUPPY, WINSTON.
YAP!
YAP!
IT'S SO NICE TO FINALLY HAVE A DOG AGAIN.
IT'S BEEN SO QUIET SINCE MY OLD DOG DIED A FEW MONTHS AGO.
YAP!
YAP!
YAP!
RACHEL, WERE YOU VERY SAD WHEN YOUR OLD DOG DIED?
VERY. I LOVED HER A LOT.
MAYBE YOU WOULDN'T BE SO SAD IF YOU DIDN'T LOVE HER SO MUCH IN THE FIRST PLACE.

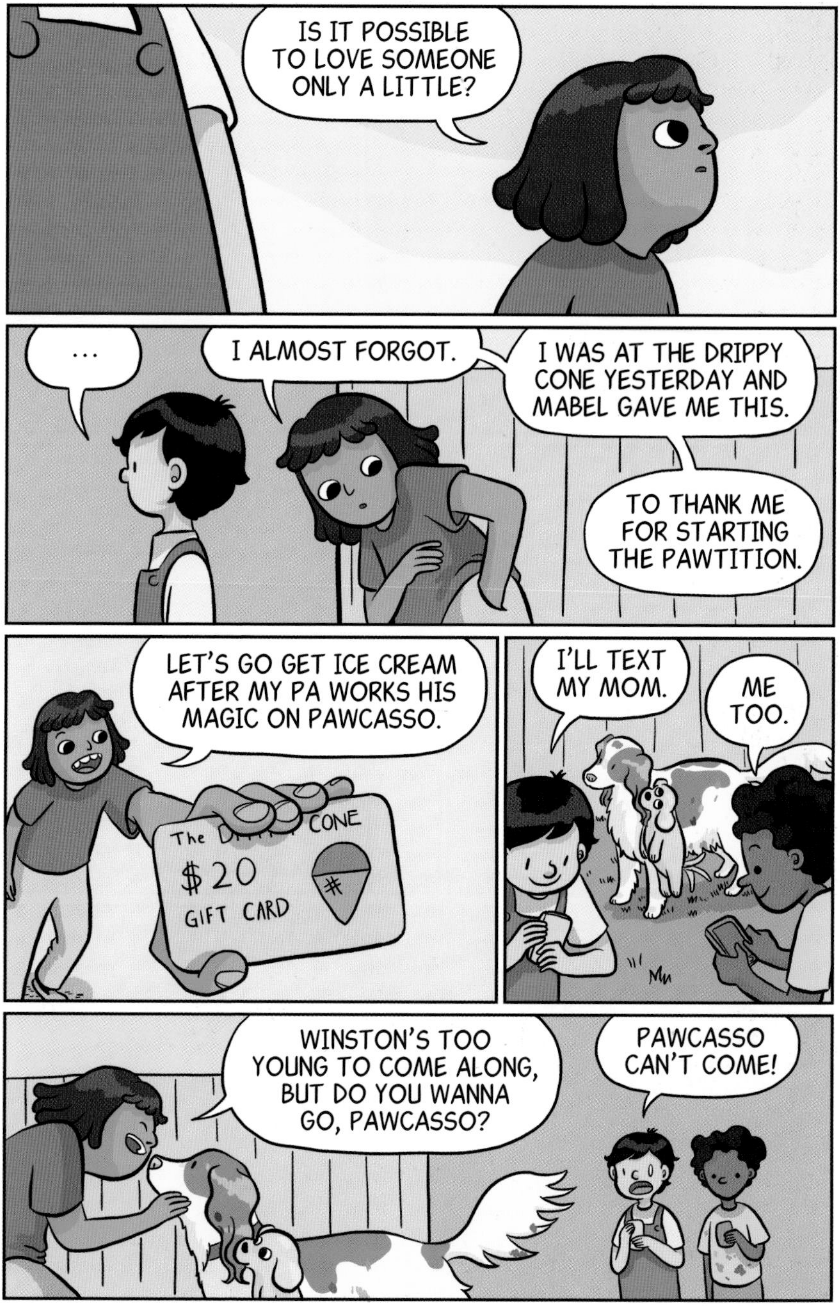
IS IT POSSIBLE TO LOVE SOMEONE ONLY A LITTLE?
...
I ALMOST FORGOT.
I WAS AT THE DRIPPY CONE YESTERDAY AND MABEL GAVE ME THIS.
TO THANK ME FOR STARTING THE PAWTITION.
LET'S GO GET ICE CREAM AFTER MY PA WORKS HIS MAGIC ON PAWCASSO.
The CONE
$20
GIFT CARD
I'LL TEXT MY MOM.
ME TOO.
WINSTON'S TOO YOUNG TO COME ALONG, BUT DO YOU WANNA GO, PAWCASSO?
PAWCASSO CAN'T COME!

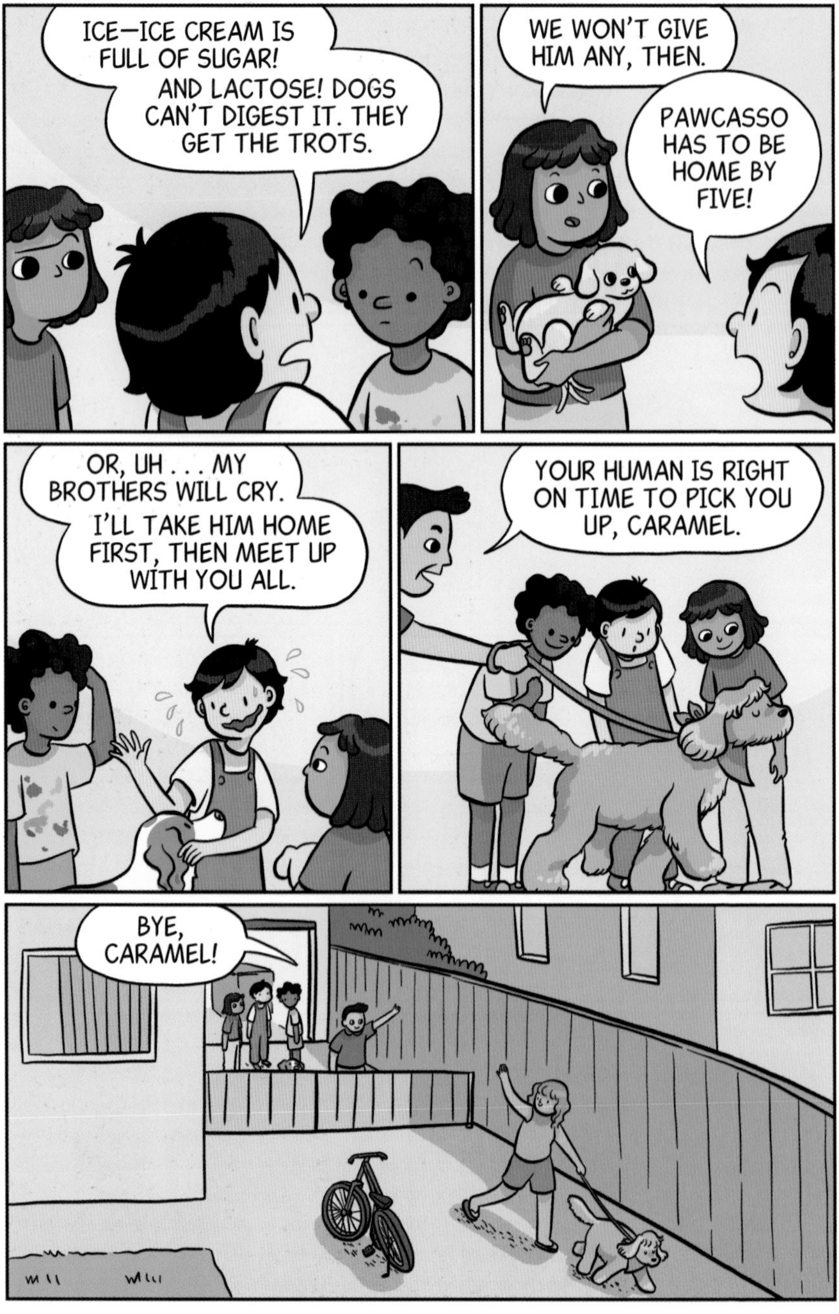
ICE—ICE CREAM IS FULL OF SUGAR!
AND LACTOSE! DOGS CAN'T DIGEST IT. THEY GET THE TROTS.
WE WON'T GIVE HIM ANY, THEN.
PAWCASSO HAS TO BE HOME BY FIVE!
OR, UH . . . MY BROTHERS WILL CRY.
I'LL TAKE HIM HOME FIRST, THEN MEET UP WITH YOU ALL.
YOUR HUMAN IS RIGHT ON TIME TO PICK YOU UP, CARAMEL.
BYE, CARAMEL!

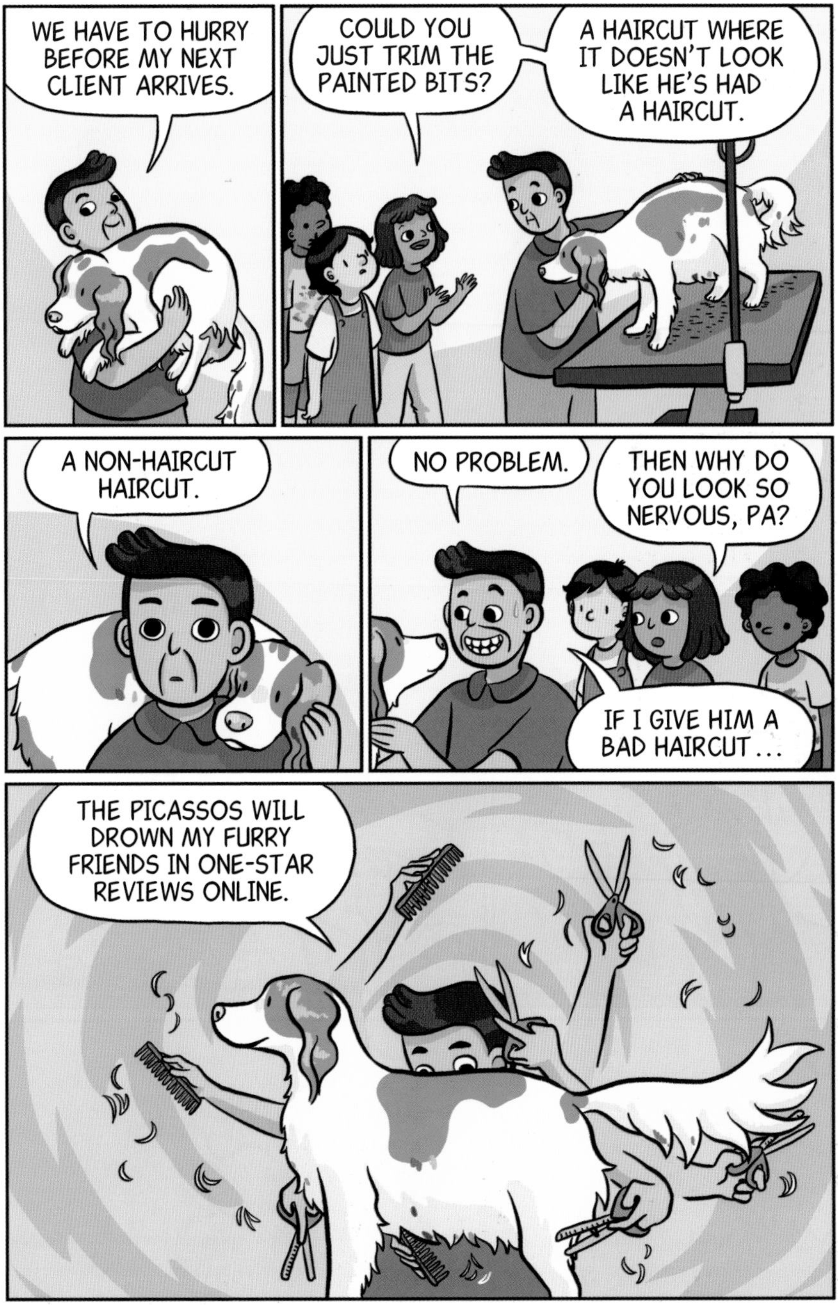
WE HAVE TO HURRY BEFORE MY NEXT CLIENT ARRIVES.
COULD YOU JUST TRIM THE PAINTED BITS?
A HAIRCUT WHERE IT DOESN'T LOOK LIKE HE'S HAD A HAIRCUT.
A NON-HAIRCUT HAIRCUT.
NO PROBLEM.
THEN WHY DO YOU LOOK SO NERVOUS, PA?
IF I GIVE HIM A BAD HAIRCUT...
THE PICASSOS WILL DROWN MY FURRY FRIENDS IN ONE-STAR REVIEWS ONLINE.

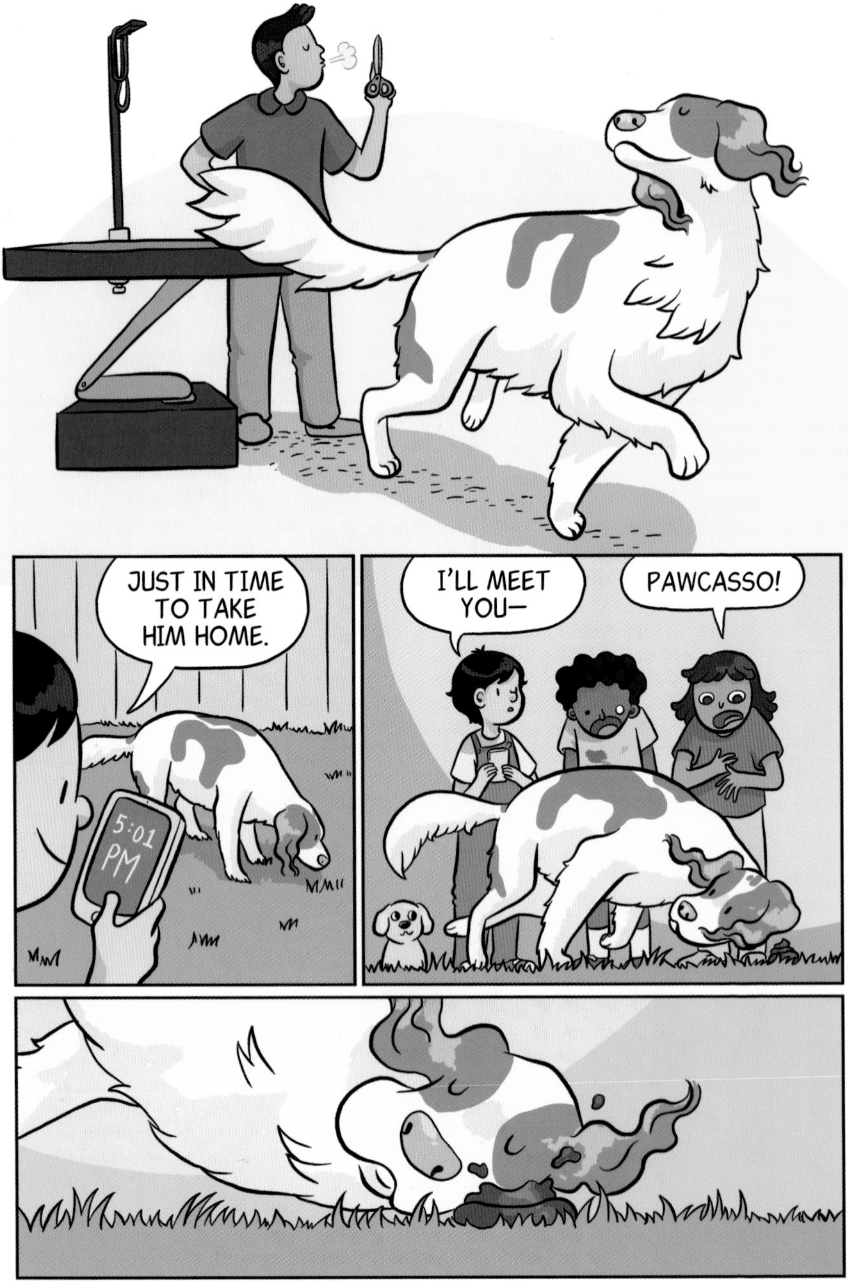
JUST IN TIME TO TAKE HIM HOME.
5:01 PM
I'LL MEET YOU—
PAWCASSO!

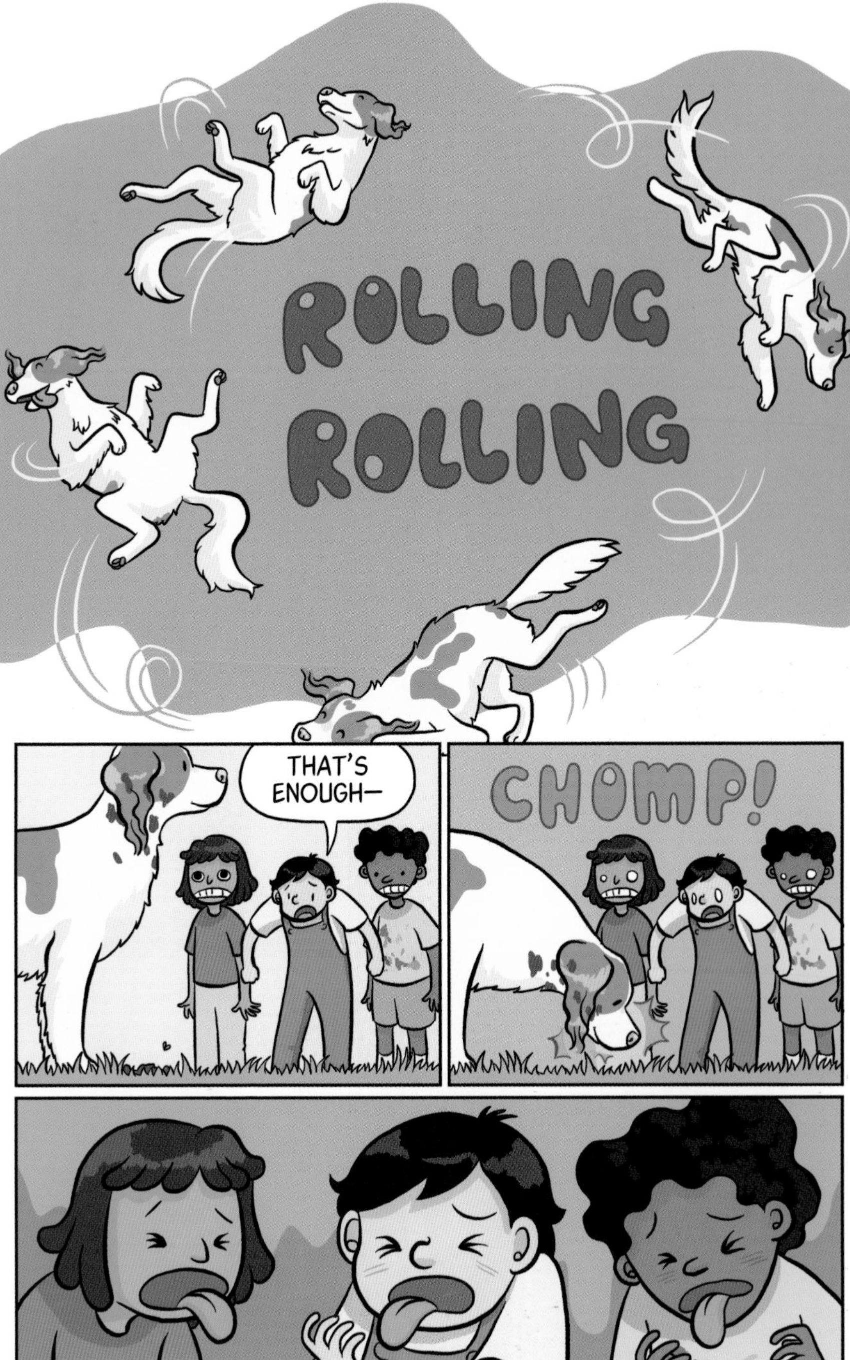
ROLLING
ROLLING
THAT'S ENOUGH—
CHOMP!

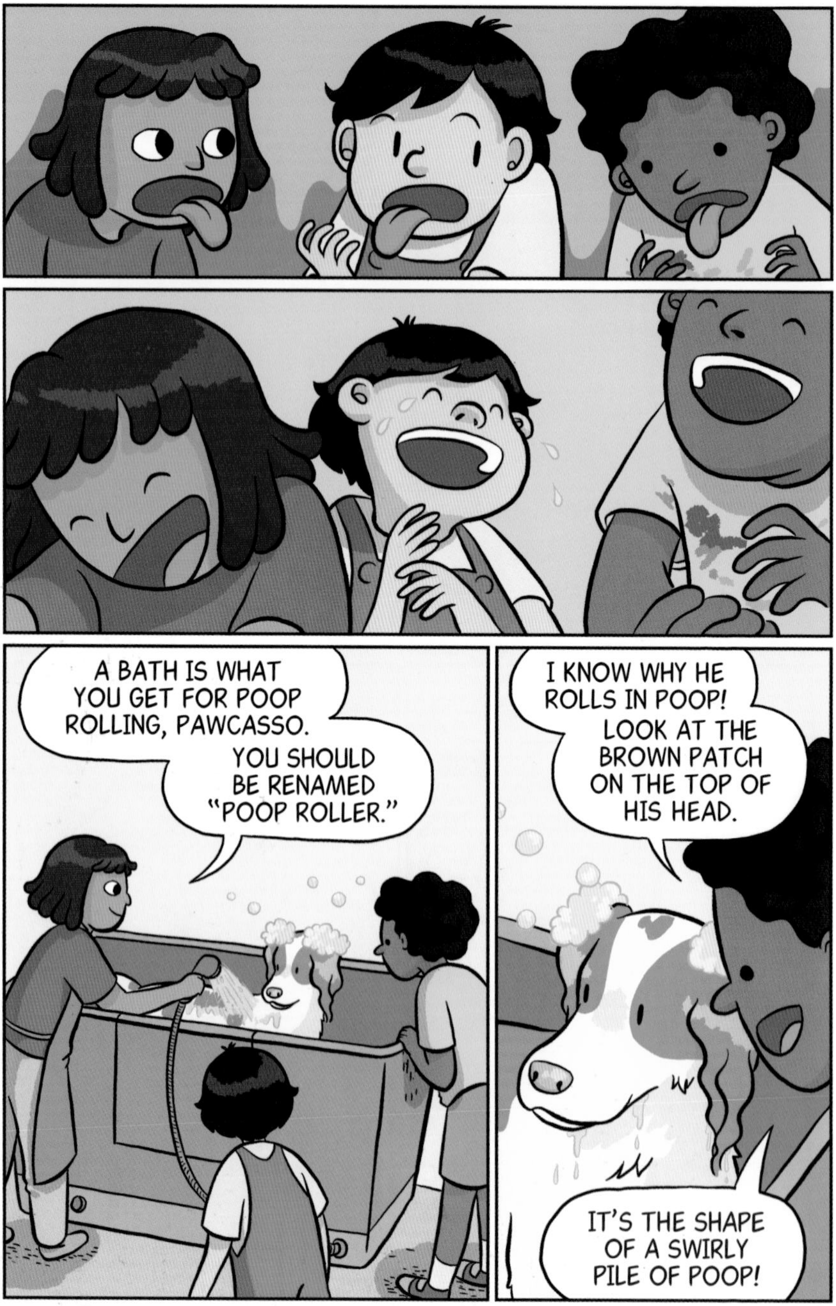
A BATH IS WHAT YOU GET FOR POOP ROLLING, PAWCASSO.
YOU SHOULD BE RENAMED "POOP ROLLER."
I KNOW WHY HE ROLLS IN POOP!
LOOK AT THE BROWN PATCH ON THE TOP OF HIS HEAD.
IT'S THE SHAPE OF A SWIRLY PILE OF POOP!

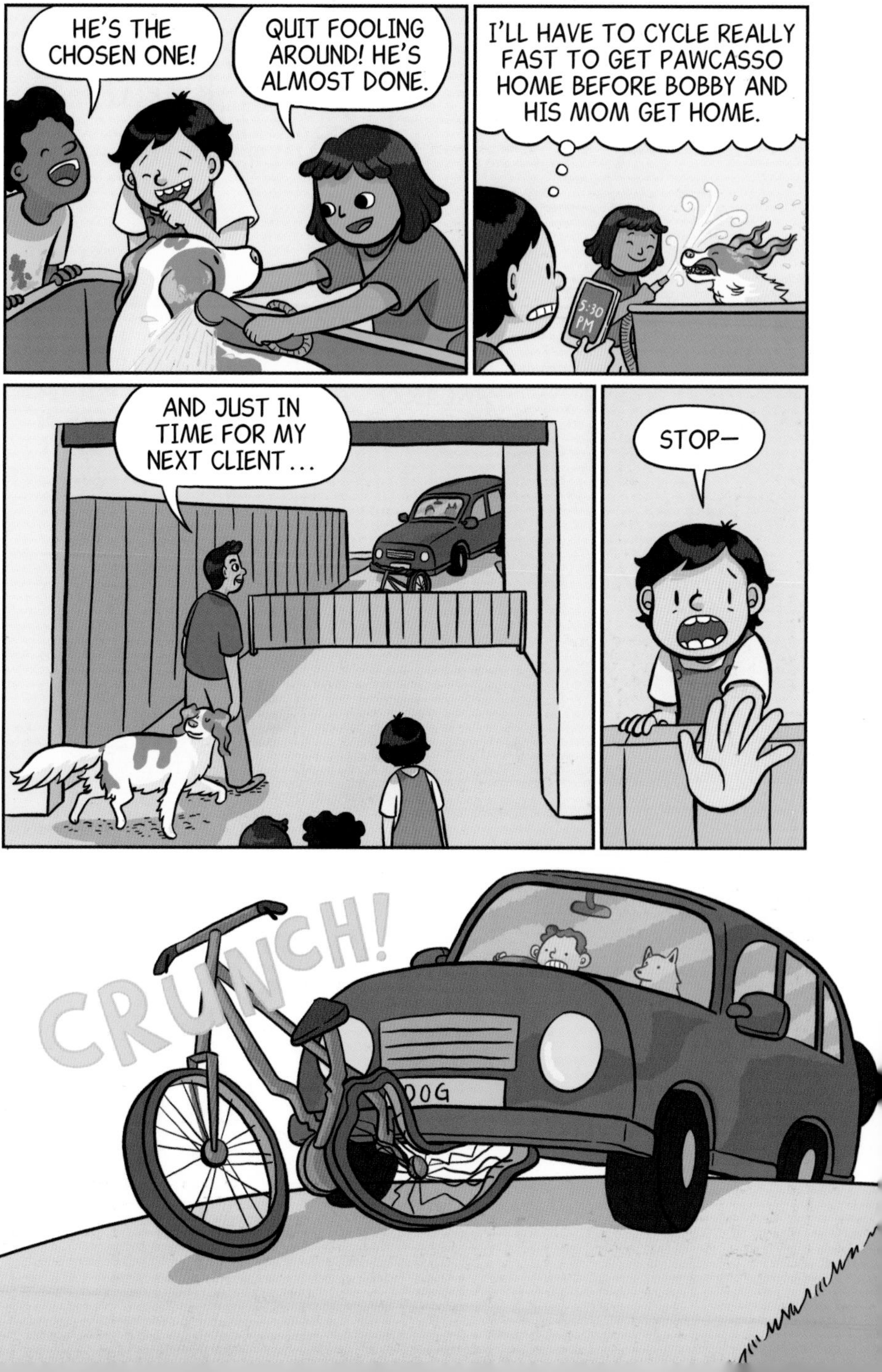
HE'S THE CHOSEN ONE!
QUIT FOOLING AROUND! HE'S ALMOST DONE.
I'LL HAVE TO CYCLE REALLY FAST TO GET PAWCASSO HOME BEFORE BOBBY AND HIS MOM GET HOME.
5:30 PM
AND JUST IN TIME FOR MY NEXT CLIENT...
STOP—
CRUNCH!
DOG

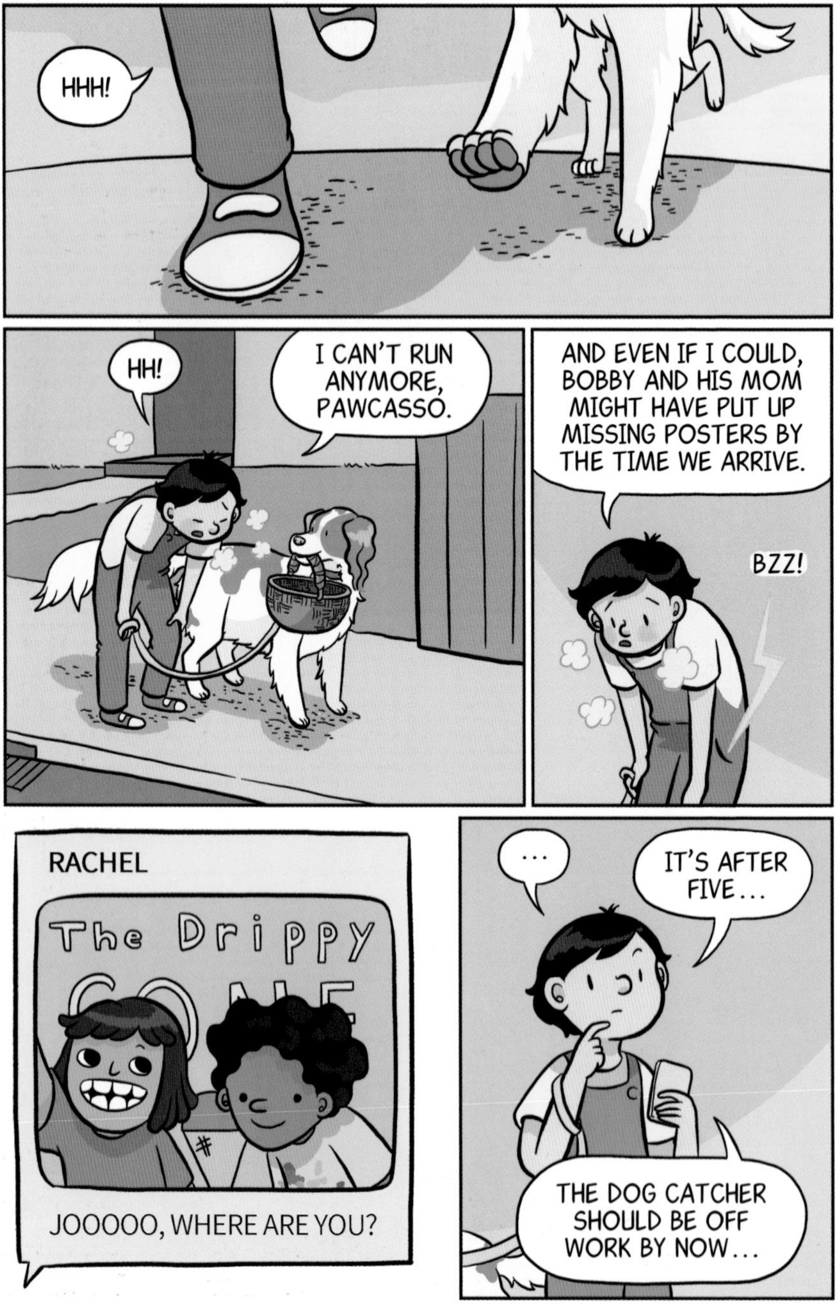
HHH!
HH!
I CAN'T RUN ANYMORE, PAWCASSO.
AND EVEN IF I COULD, BOBBY AND HIS MOM MIGHT HAVE PUT UP MISSING POSTERS BY THE TIME WE ARRIVE.
BZZ!
RACHEL
The Drippy
JOOOOO, WHERE ARE YOU?
...
IT'S AFTER FIVE...
THE DOG CATCHER SHOULD BE OFF WORK BY NOW...

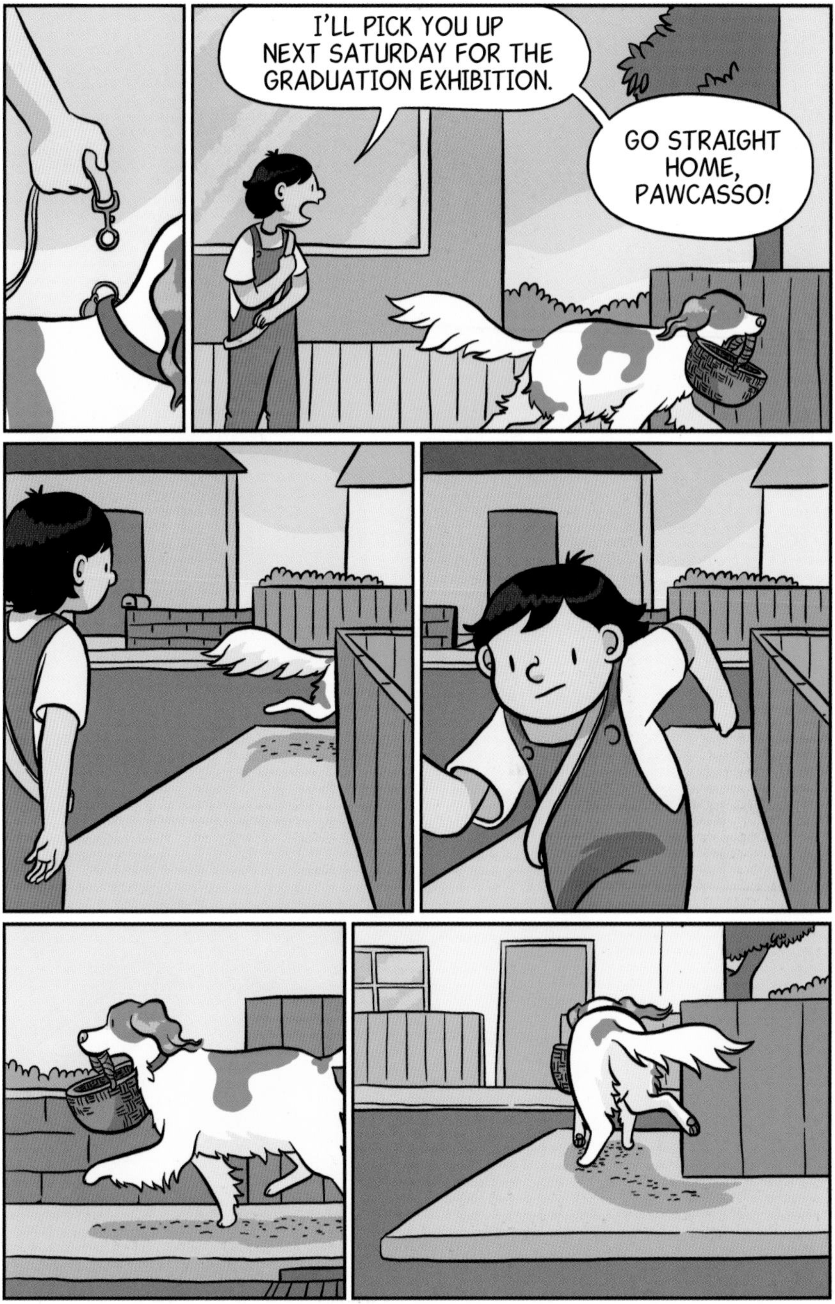
I'LL PICK YOU UP NEXT SATURDAY FOR THE GRADUATION EXHIBITION.
GO STRAIGHT HOME, PAWCASSO!

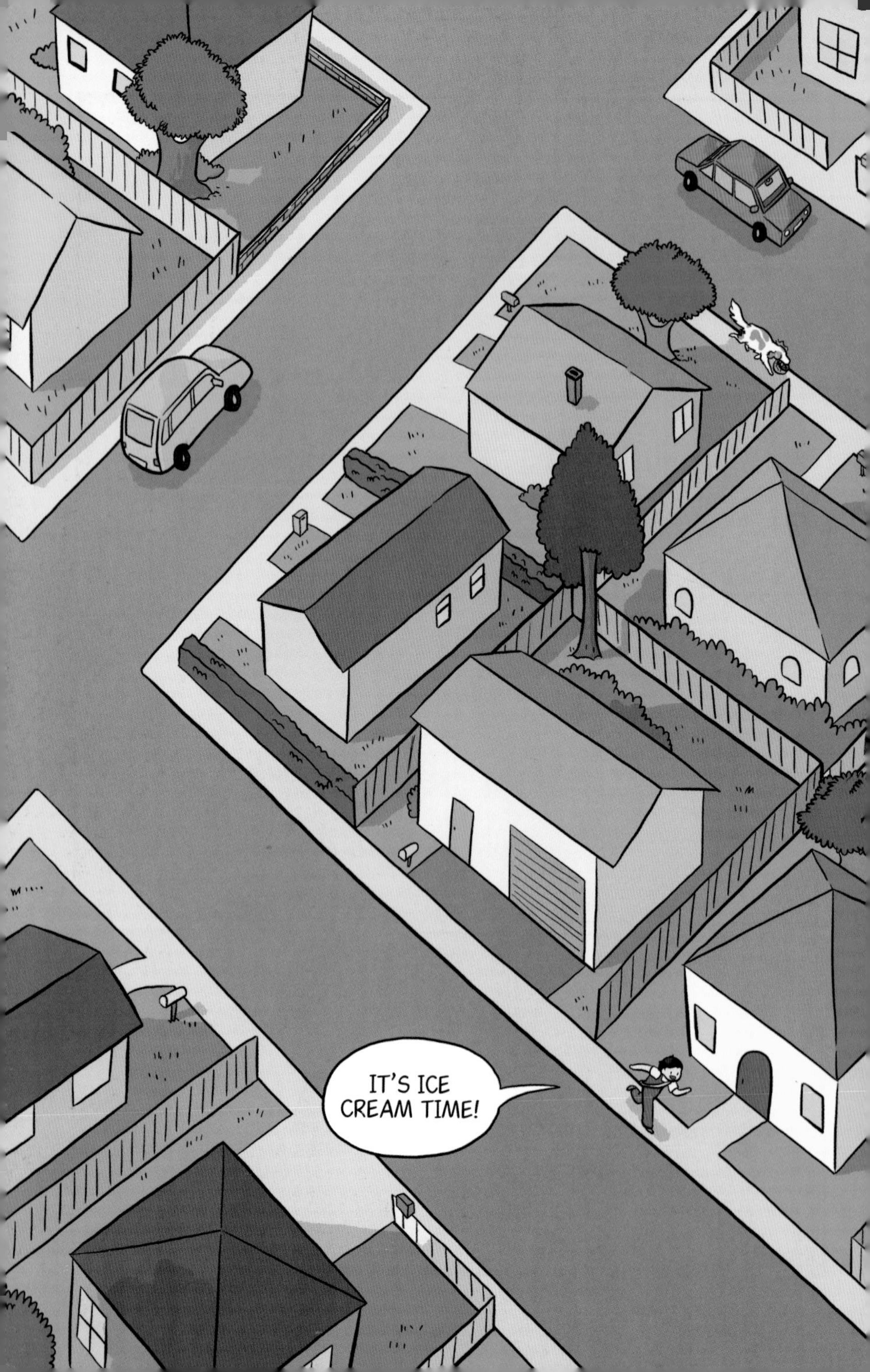
IT'S ICE CREAM TIME!

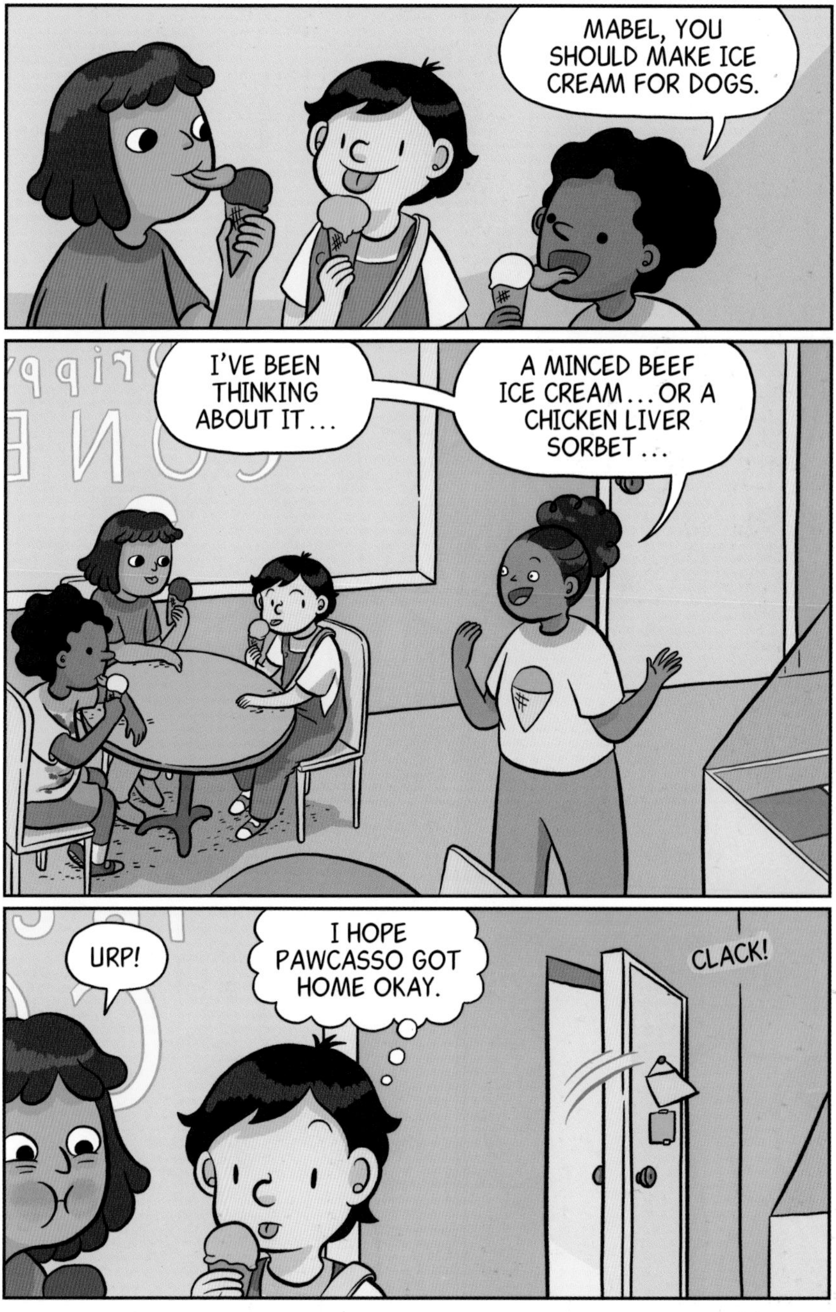
MABEL, YOU SHOULD MAKE ICE CREAM FOR DOGS.
I'VE BEEN THINKING ABOUT IT . . .
A MINCED BEEF ICE CREAM . . . OR A CHICKEN LIVER SORBET . . .
URP!
I HOPE PAWCASSO GOT HOME OKAY.
CLACK!

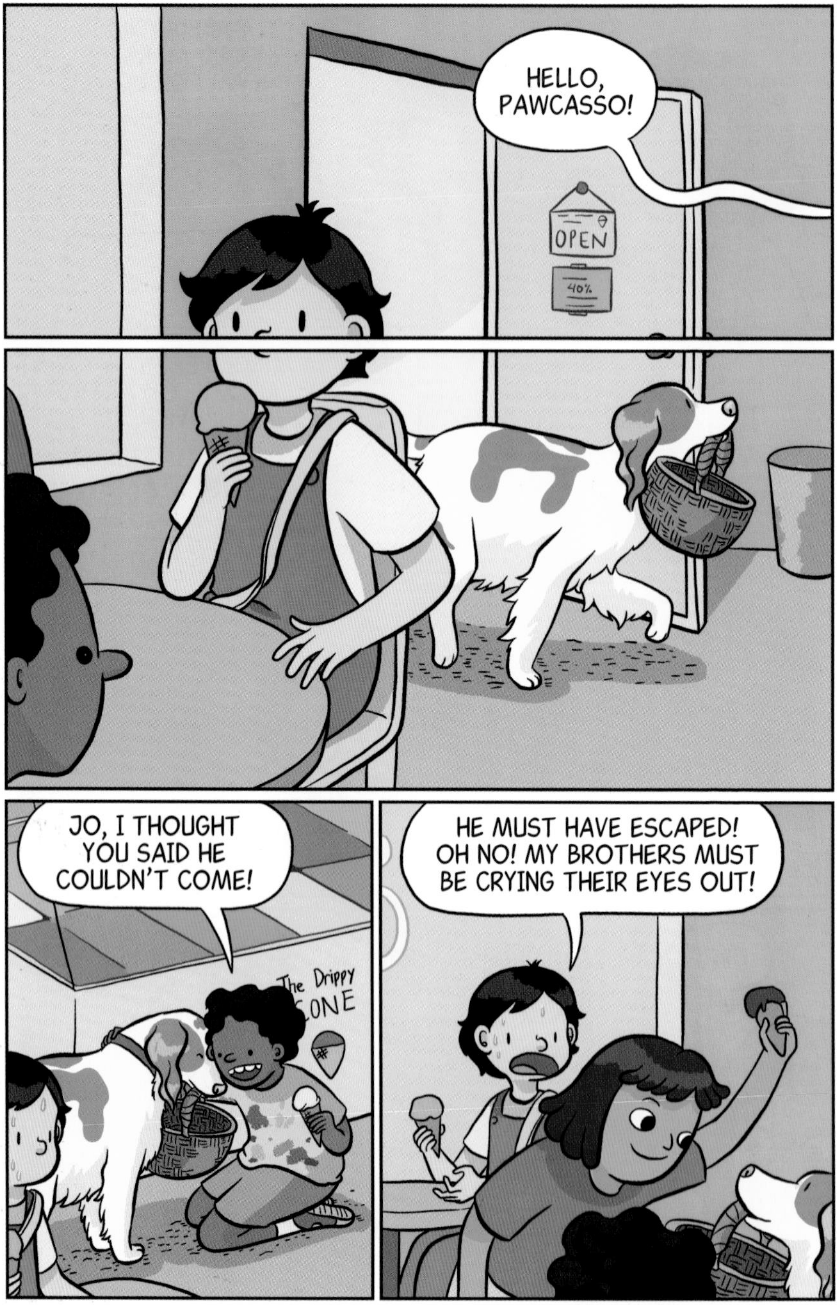
HELLO, PAWCASSO!
OPEN
40%
JO, I THOUGHT YOU SAID HE COULDN'T COME!
The Drippy CONE
HE MUST HAVE ESCAPED! OH NO! MY BROTHERS MUST BE CRYING THEIR EYES OUT!

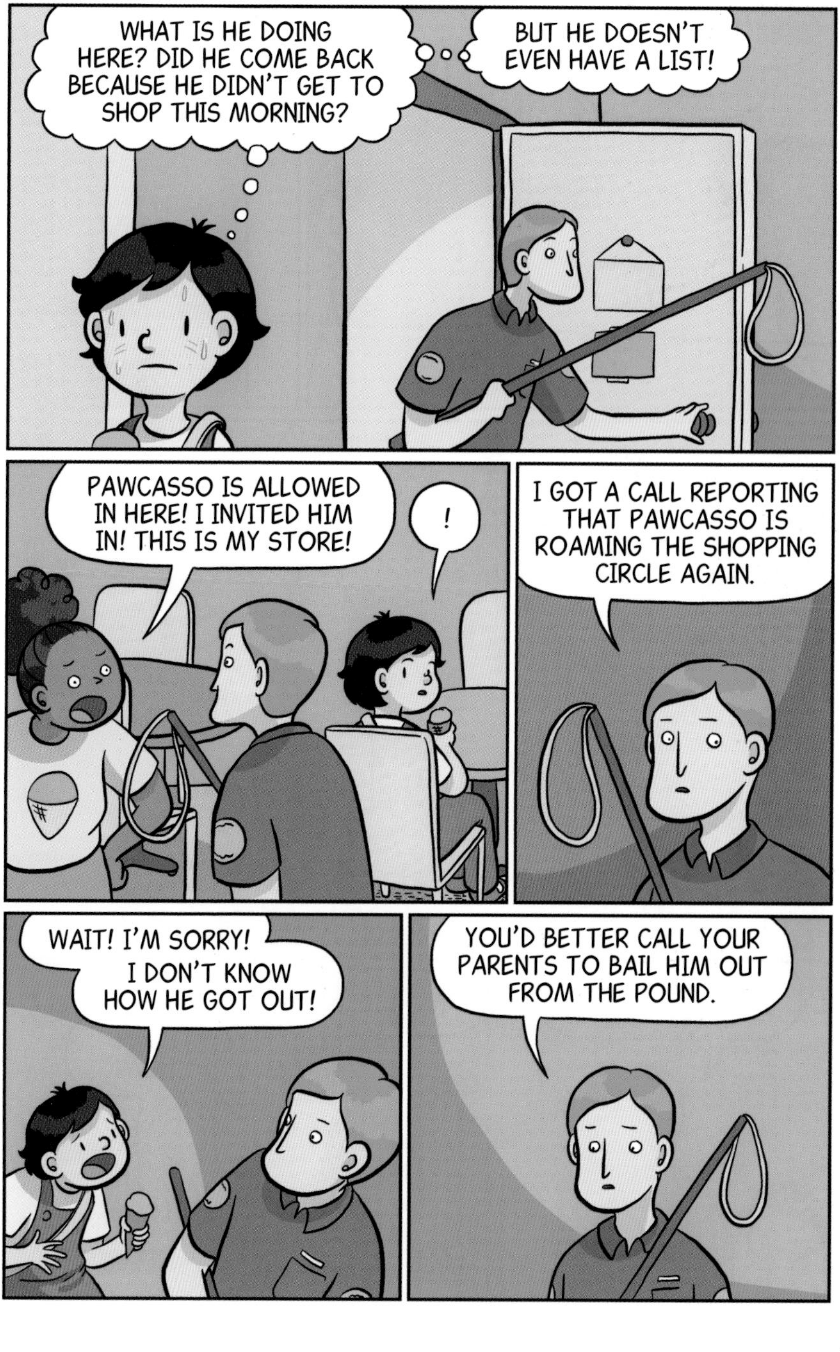
WHAT IS HE DOING HERE? DID HE COME BACK BECAUSE HE DIDN'T GET TO SHOP THIS MORNING?
BUT HE DOESN'T EVEN HAVE A LIST!
PAWCASSO IS ALLOWED IN HERE! I INVITED HIM IN! THIS IS MY STORE!
!
I GOT A CALL REPORTING THAT PAWCASSO IS ROAMING THE SHOPPING CIRCLE AGAIN.
WAIT! I'M SORRY!
I DON'T KNOW HOW HE GOT OUT!
YOU'D BETTER CALL YOUR PARENTS TO BAIL HIM OUT FROM THE POUND.

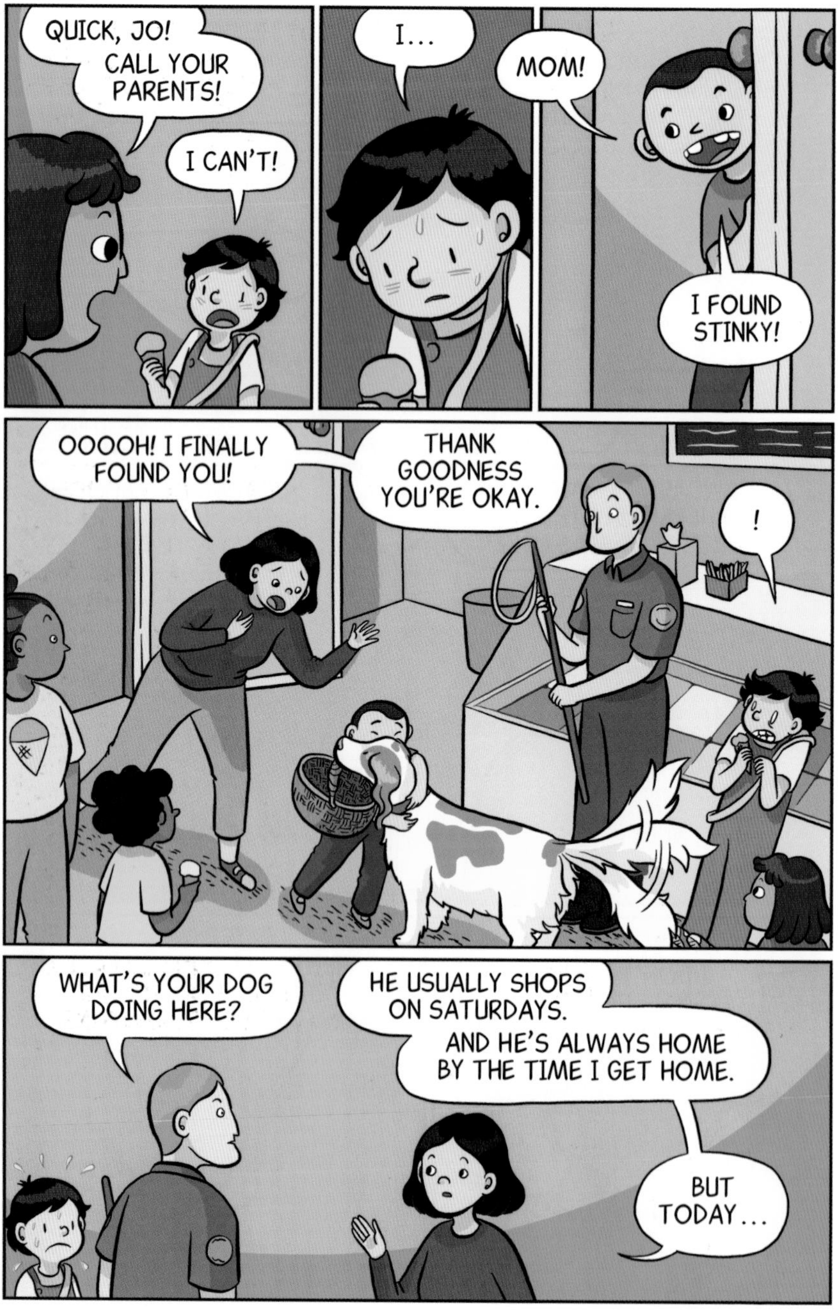
QUICK, JO!
CALL YOUR PARENTS!
I CAN'T!
I...
MOM!
I FOUND STINKY!
OOOOH! I FINALLY FOUND YOU!
THANK GOODNESS YOU'RE OKAY.
!
WHAT'S YOUR DOG DOING HERE?
HE USUALLY SHOPS ON SATURDAYS.
AND HE'S ALWAYS HOME BY THE TIME I GET HOME.
BUT TODAY...

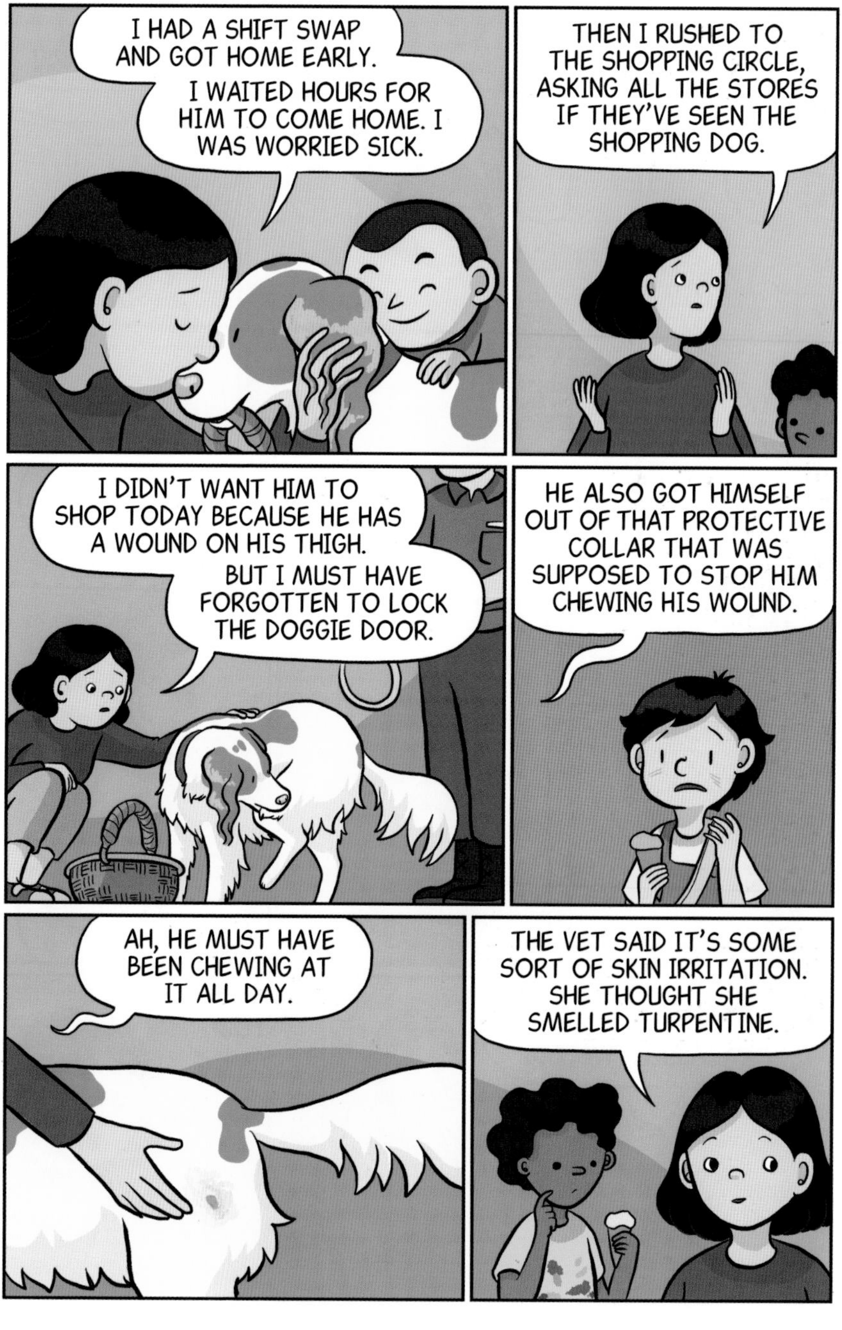
I HAD A SHIFT SWAP AND GOT HOME EARLY.
I WAITED HOURS FOR HIM TO COME HOME. I WAS WORRIED SICK.
THEN I RUSHED TO THE SHOPPING CIRCLE, ASKING ALL THE STORES IF THEY'VE SEEN THE SHOPPING DOG.
I DIDN'T WANT HIM TO SHOP TODAY BECAUSE HE HAS A WOUND ON HIS THIGH.
BUT I MUST HAVE FORGOTTEN TO LOCK THE DOGGIE DOOR.
HE ALSO GOT HIMSELF OUT OF THAT PROTECTIVE COLLAR THAT WAS SUPPOSED TO STOP HIM CHEWING HIS WOUND.
AH, HE MUST HAVE BEEN CHEWING AT IT ALL DAY.
THE VET SAID IT'S SOME SORT OF SKIN IRRITATION. SHE THOUGHT SHE SMELLED TURPENTINE.

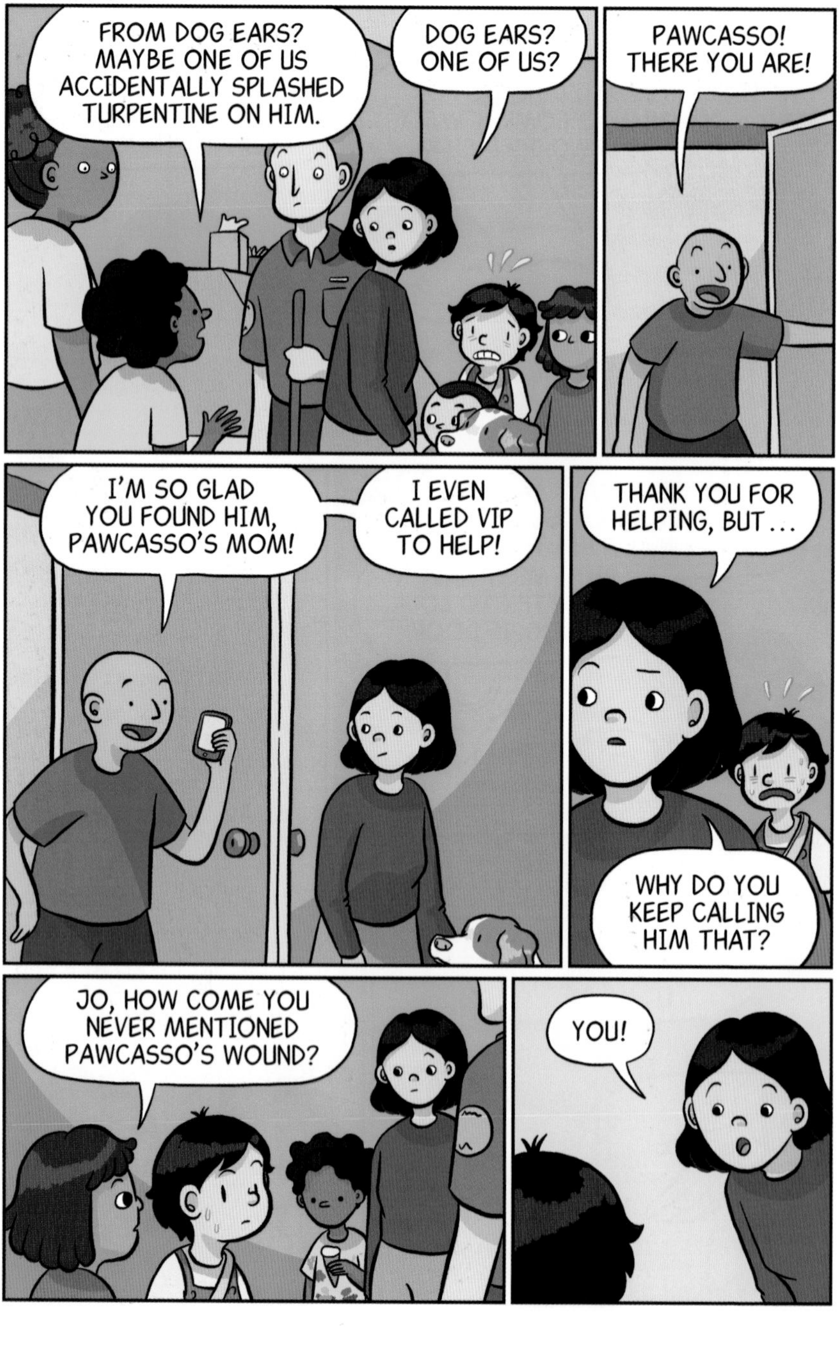
FROM DOG EARS? MAYBE ONE OF US ACCIDENTALLY SPLASHED TURPENTINE ON HIM.
DOG EARS? ONE OF US?
PAWCASSO! THERE YOU ARE!
I'M SO GLAD YOU FOUND HIM, PAWCASSO'S MOM!
I EVEN CALLED VIP TO HELP!
THANK YOU FOR HELPING, BUT . . .
WHY DO YOU KEEP CALLING HIM THAT?
JO, HOW COME YOU NEVER MENTIONED PAWCASSO'S WOUND?
YOU!

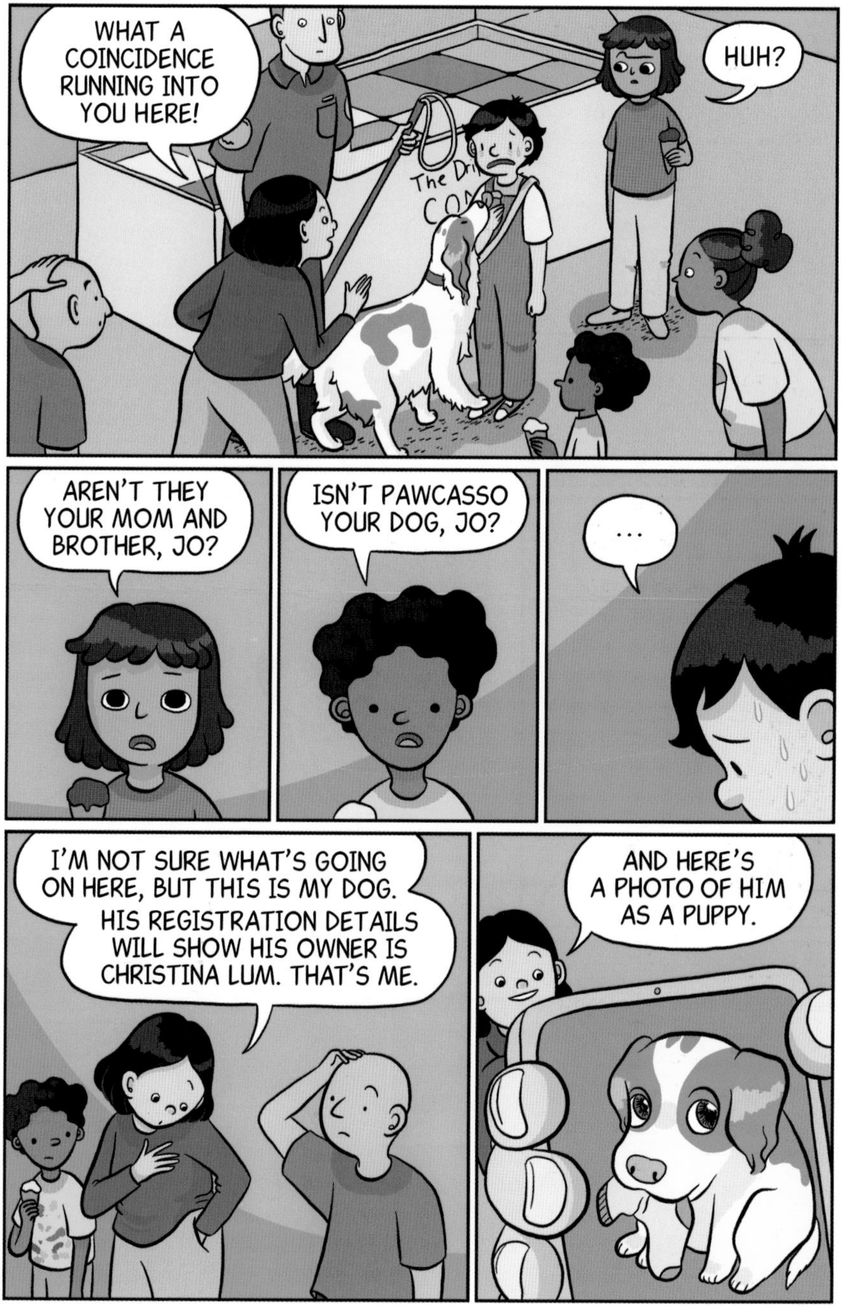
WHAT A COINCIDENCE RUNNING INTO YOU HERE!
HUH?
AREN'T THEY YOUR MOM AND BROTHER, JO?
ISN'T PAWCASSO YOUR DOG, JO?
...
I'M NOT SURE WHAT'S GOING ON HERE, BUT THIS IS MY DOG.
HIS REGISTRATION DETAILS WILL SHOW HIS OWNER IS CHRISTINA LUM. THAT'S ME.
AND HERE'S A PHOTO OF HIM AS A PUPPY.

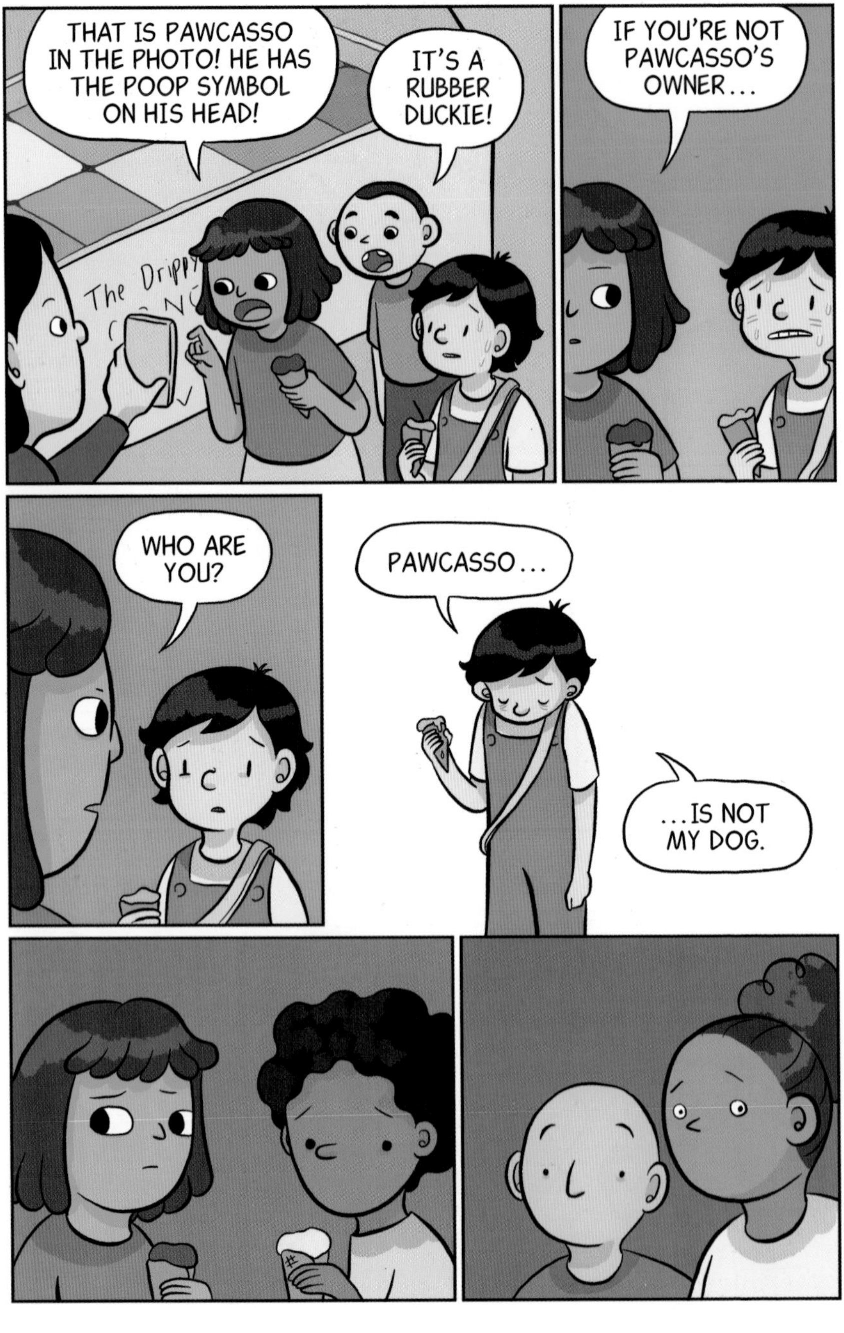
THAT IS PAWCASSO IN THE PHOTO! HE HAS THE POOP SYMBOL ON HIS HEAD!
IT'S A RUBBER DUCKIE!
The Drippy
IF YOU'RE NOT PAWCASSO'S OWNER...
WHO ARE YOU?
PAWCASSO...
...IS NOT MY DOG.

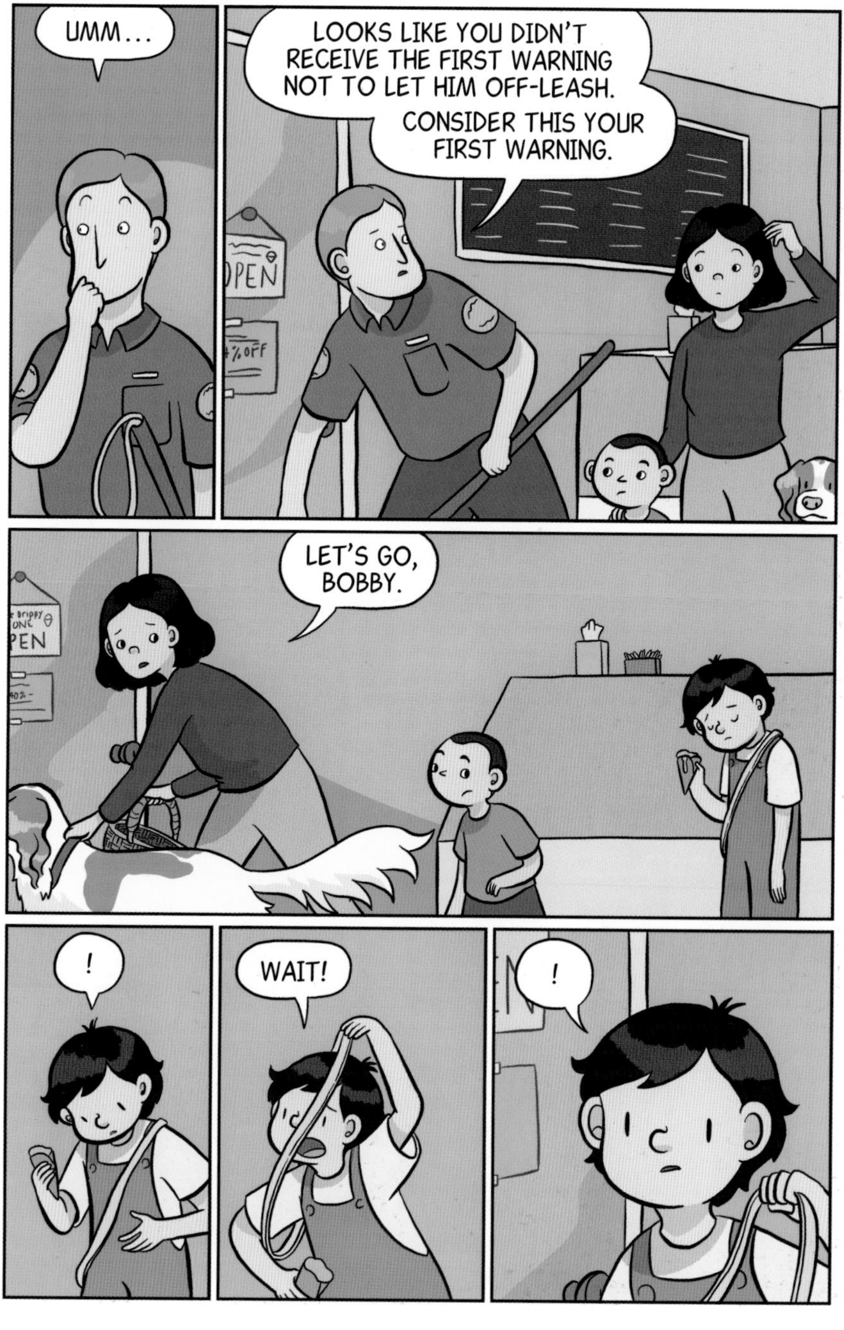
UMM...
LOOKS LIKE YOU DIDN'T RECEIVE THE FIRST WARNING NOT TO LET HIM OFF-LEASH.
CONSIDER THIS YOUR FIRST WARNING.
OPEN
LET'S GO, BOBBY.
!
WAIT!
!

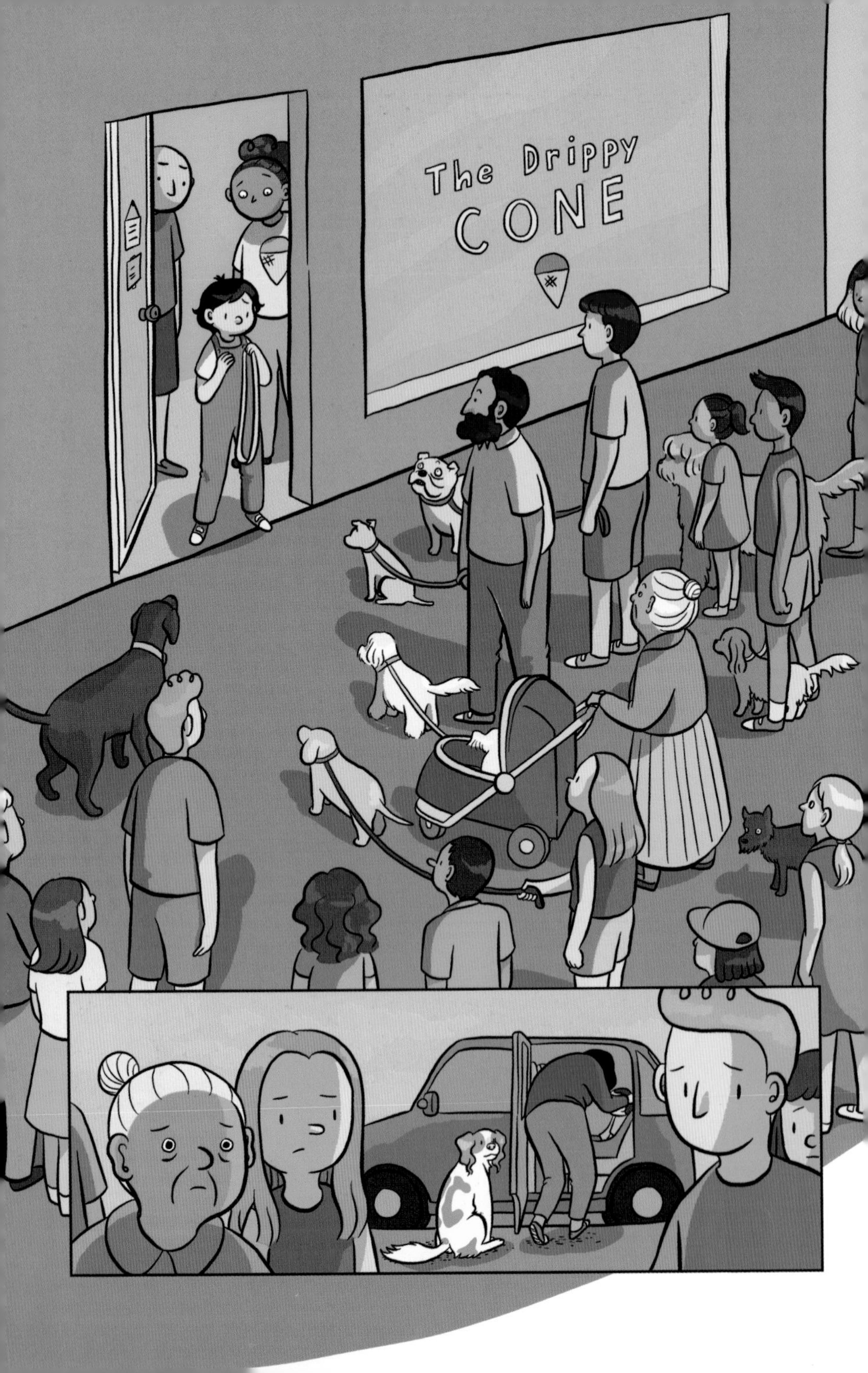
The Drippy
CONE

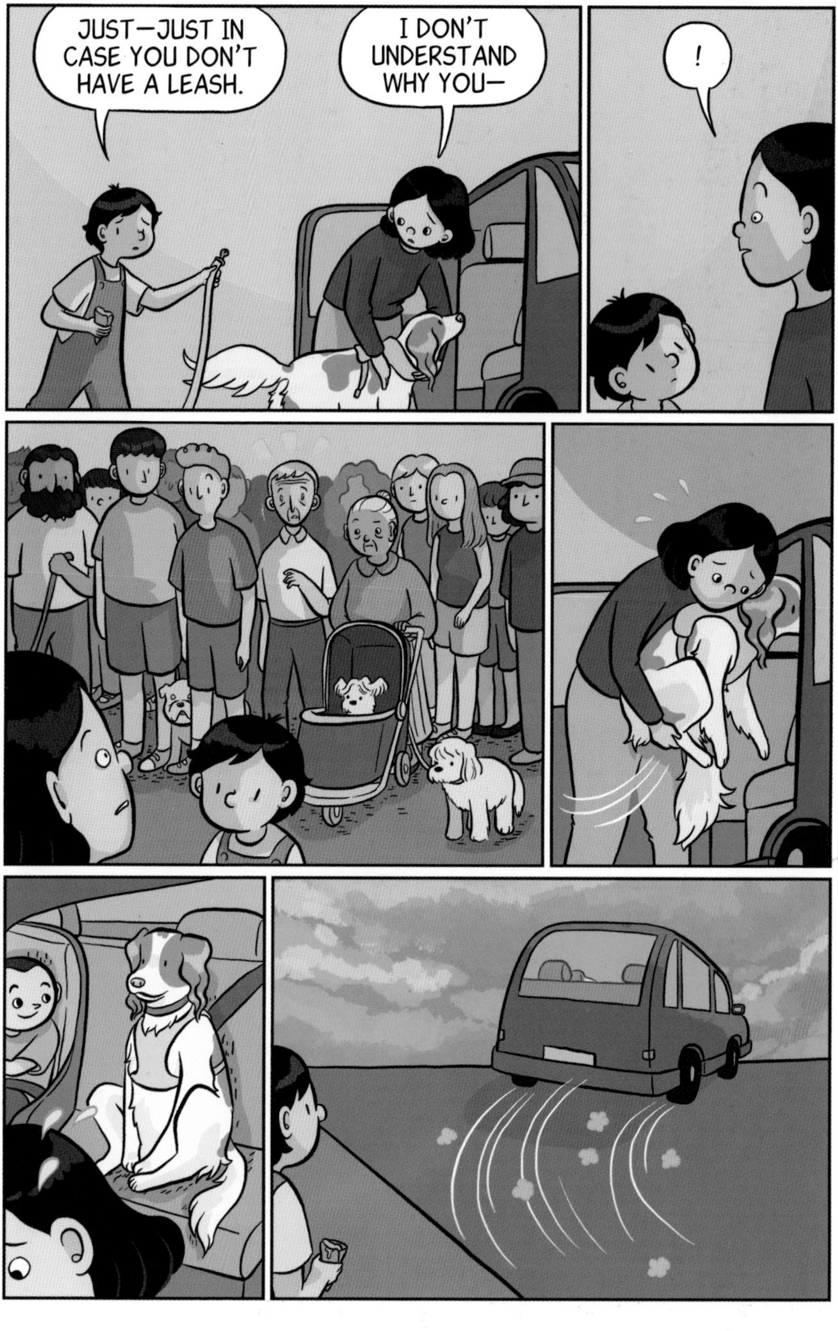
JUST—JUST IN CASE YOU DON'T HAVE A LEASH.
I DON'T UNDERSTAND WHY YOU—
!

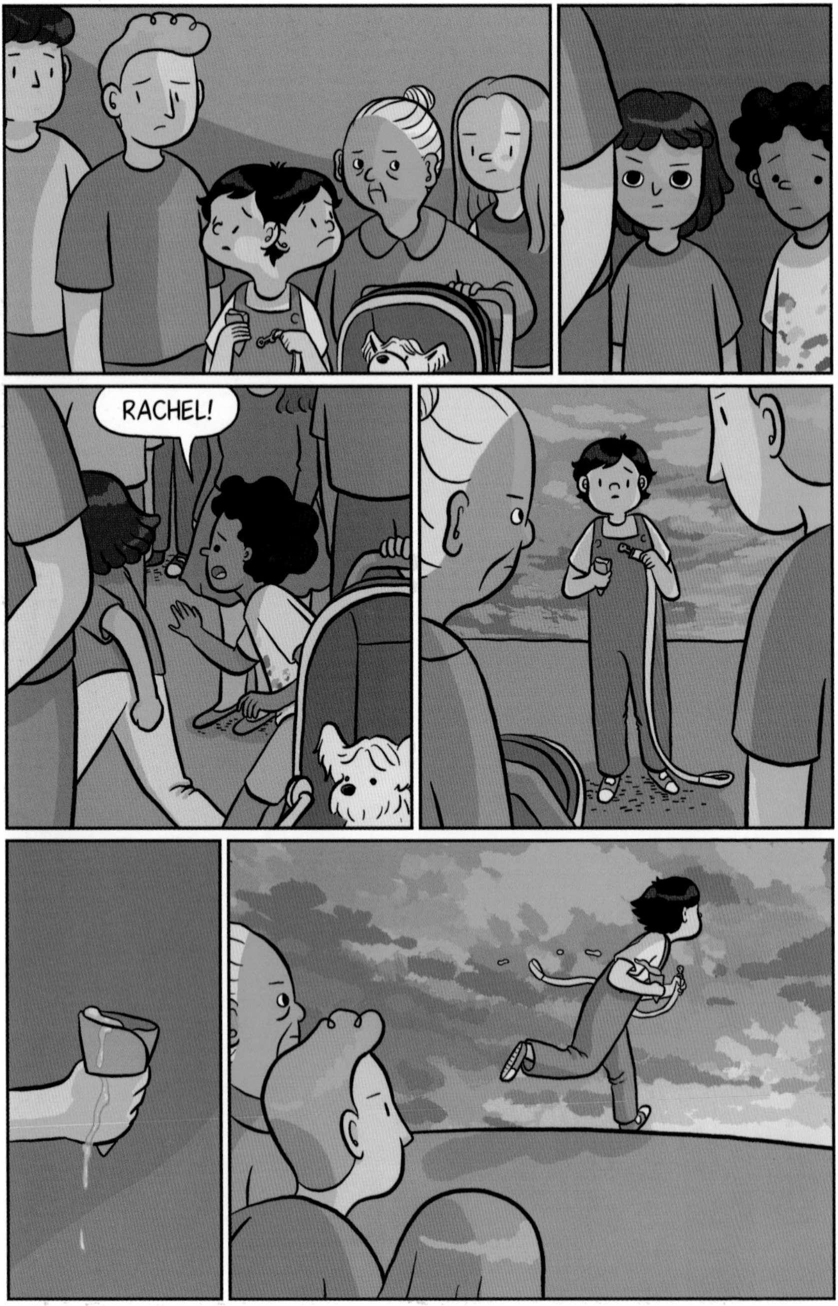
RACHEL!

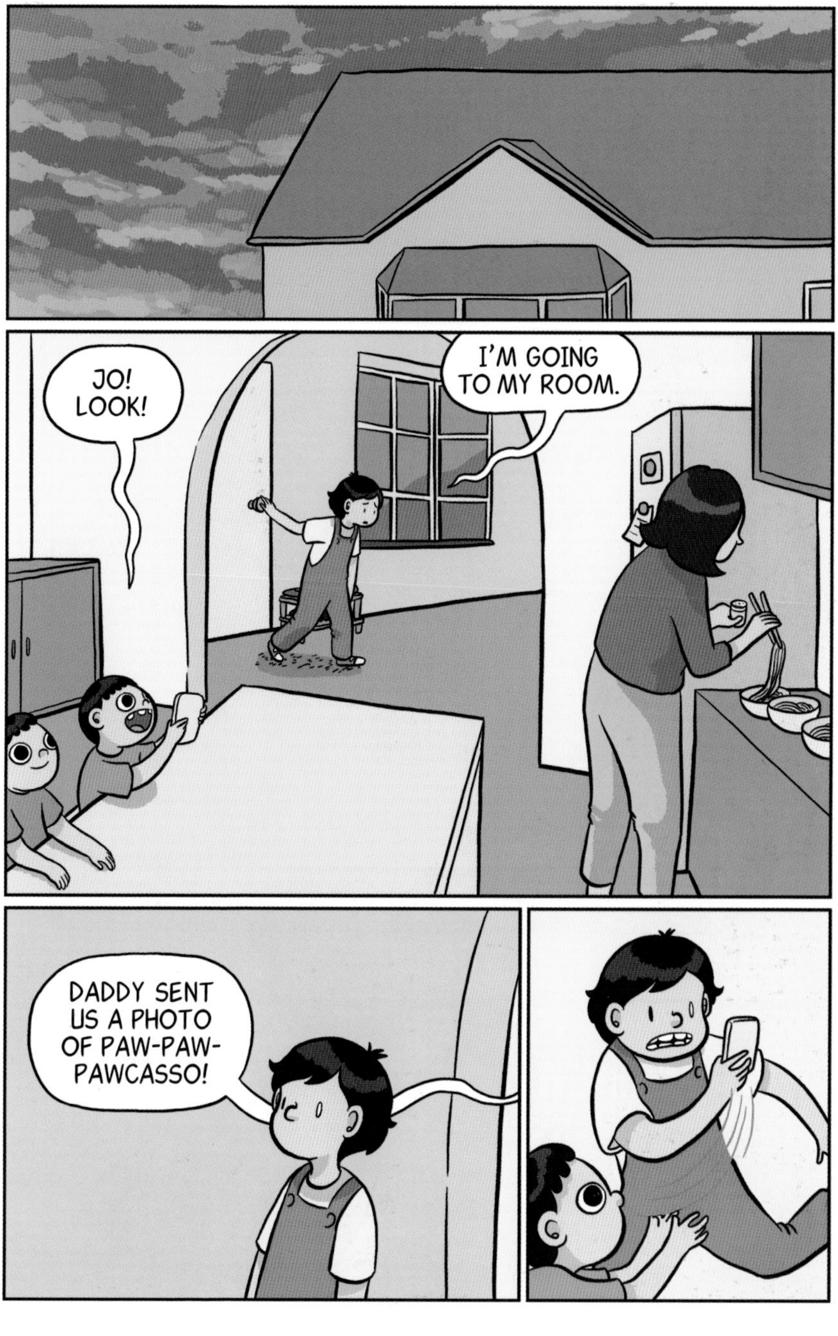
JO! LOOK!
I'M GOING TO MY ROOM.
DADDY SENT US A PHOTO OF PAW-PAW-PAWCASSO!

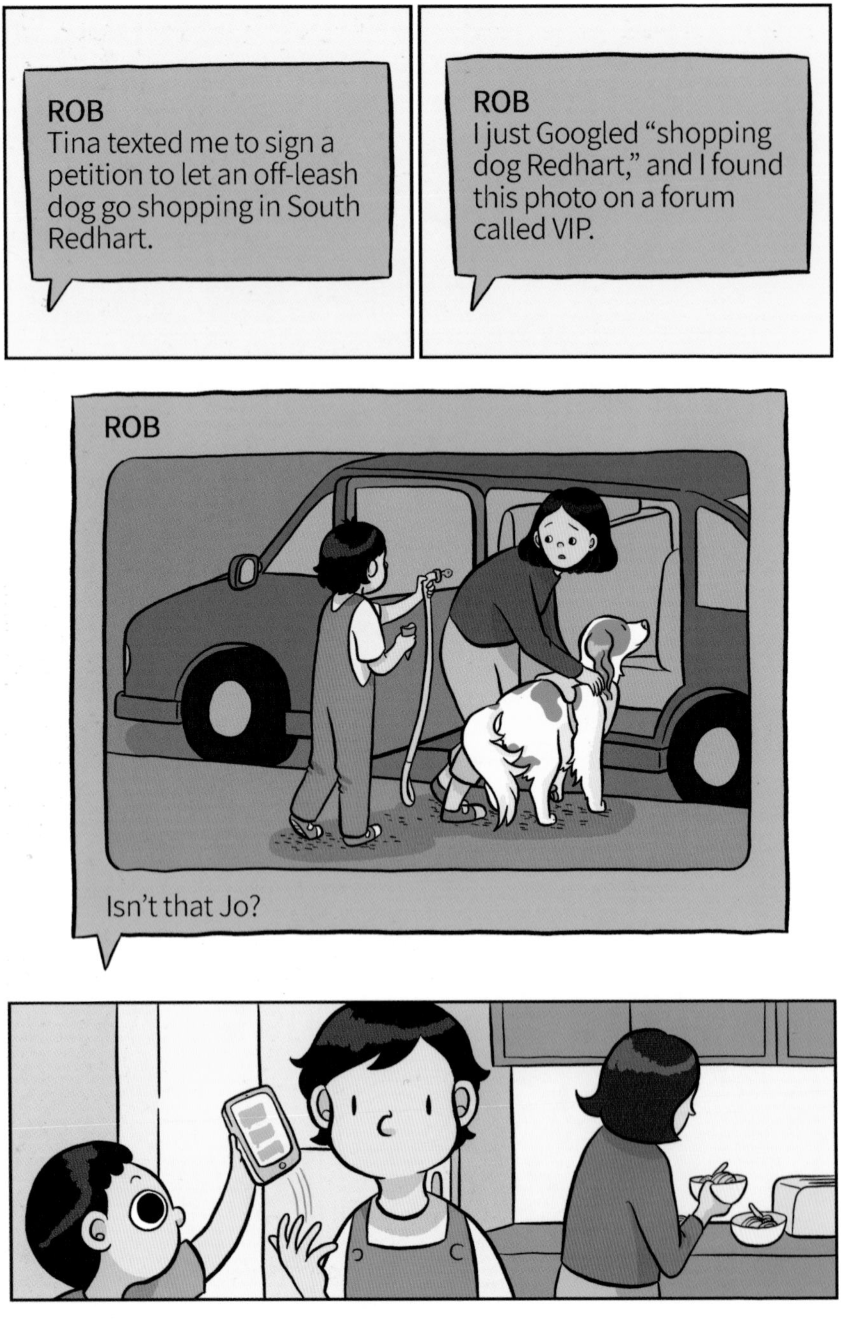
ROB
Tina texted me to sign a petition to let an off-leash dog go shopping in South Redhart.
ROB
I just Googled "shopping dog Redhart," and I found this photo on a forum called VIP.
ROB
Isn't that Jo?

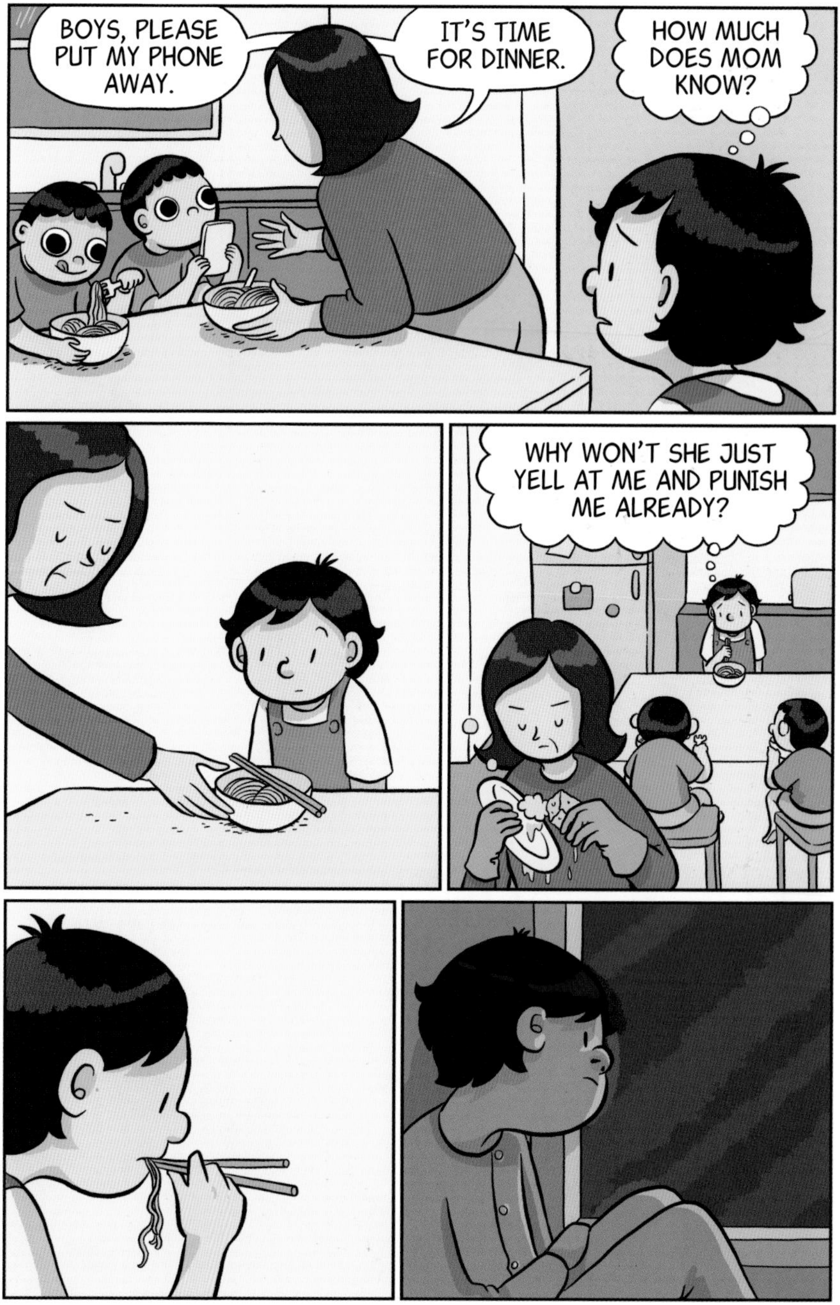
BOYS, PLEASE PUT MY PHONE AWAY.
IT'S TIME FOR DINNER.
HOW MUCH DOES MOM KNOW?
WHY WON'T SHE JUST YELL AT ME AND PUNISH ME ALREADY?

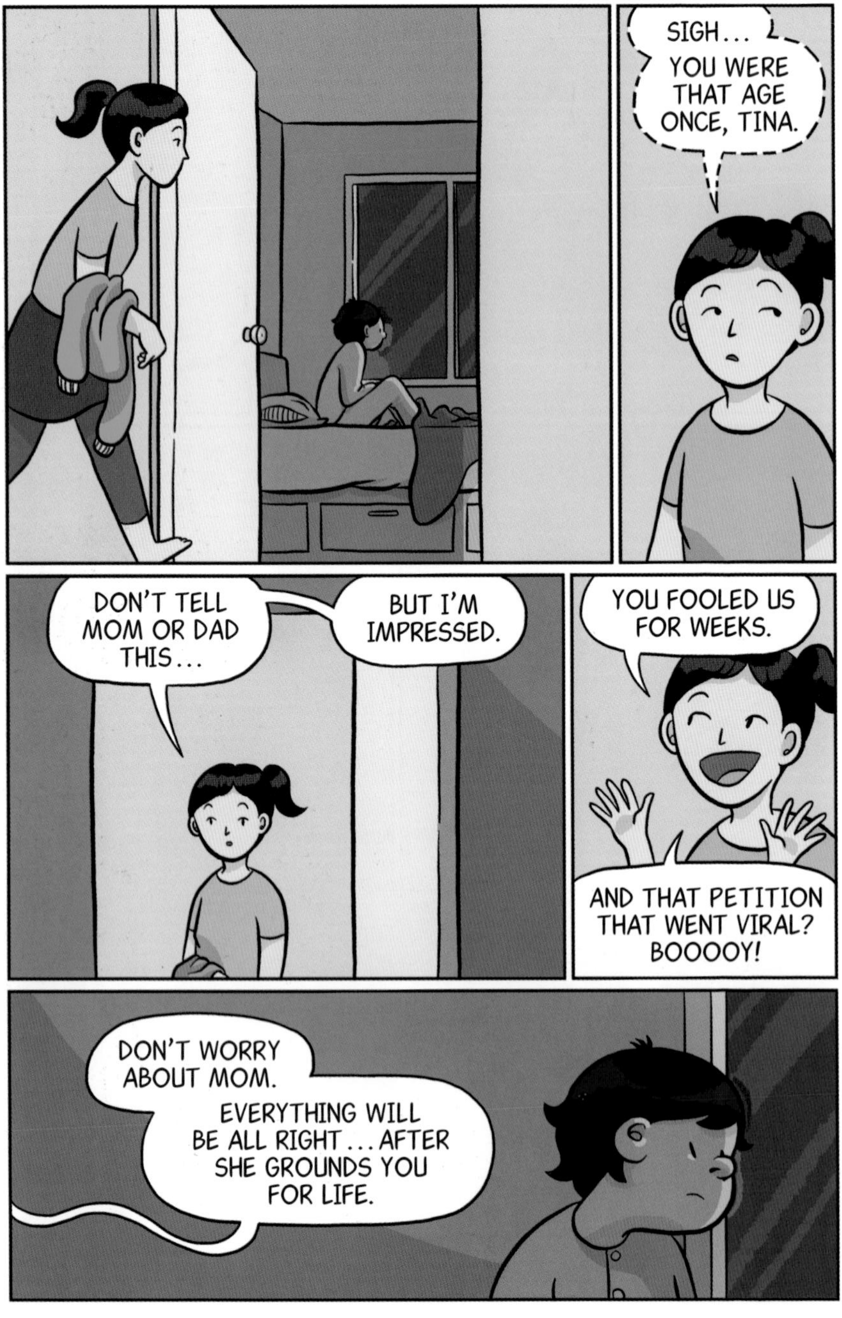
SIGH...
YOU WERE THAT AGE ONCE, TINA.
DON'T TELL MOM OR DAD THIS...
BUT I'M IMPRESSED.
YOU FOOLED US FOR WEEKS.
AND THAT PETITION THAT WENT VIRAL? BOOOOY!
DON'T WORRY ABOUT MOM.
EVERYTHING WILL BE ALL RIGHT... AFTER SHE GROUNDS YOU FOR LIFE.

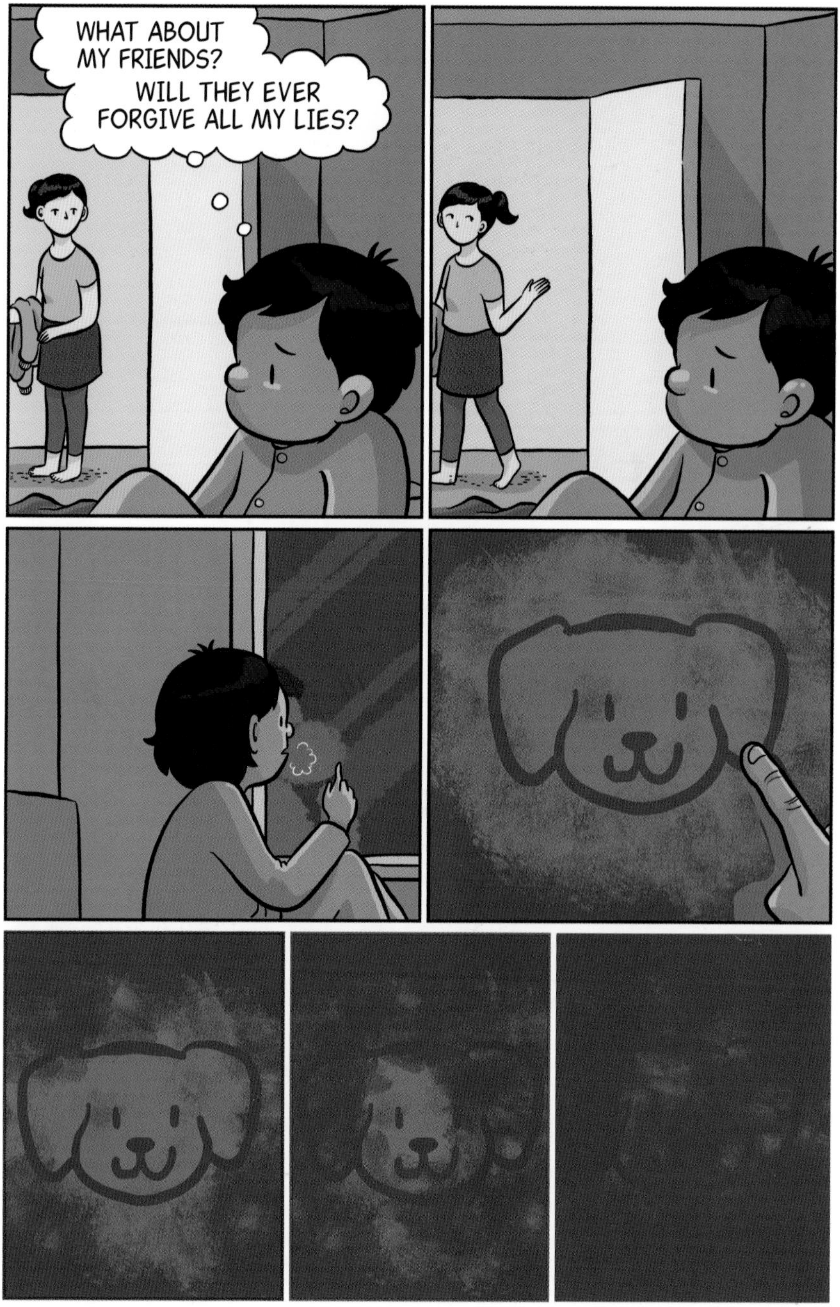
WHAT ABOUT MY FRIENDS?
WILL THEY EVER FORGIVE ALL MY LIES?

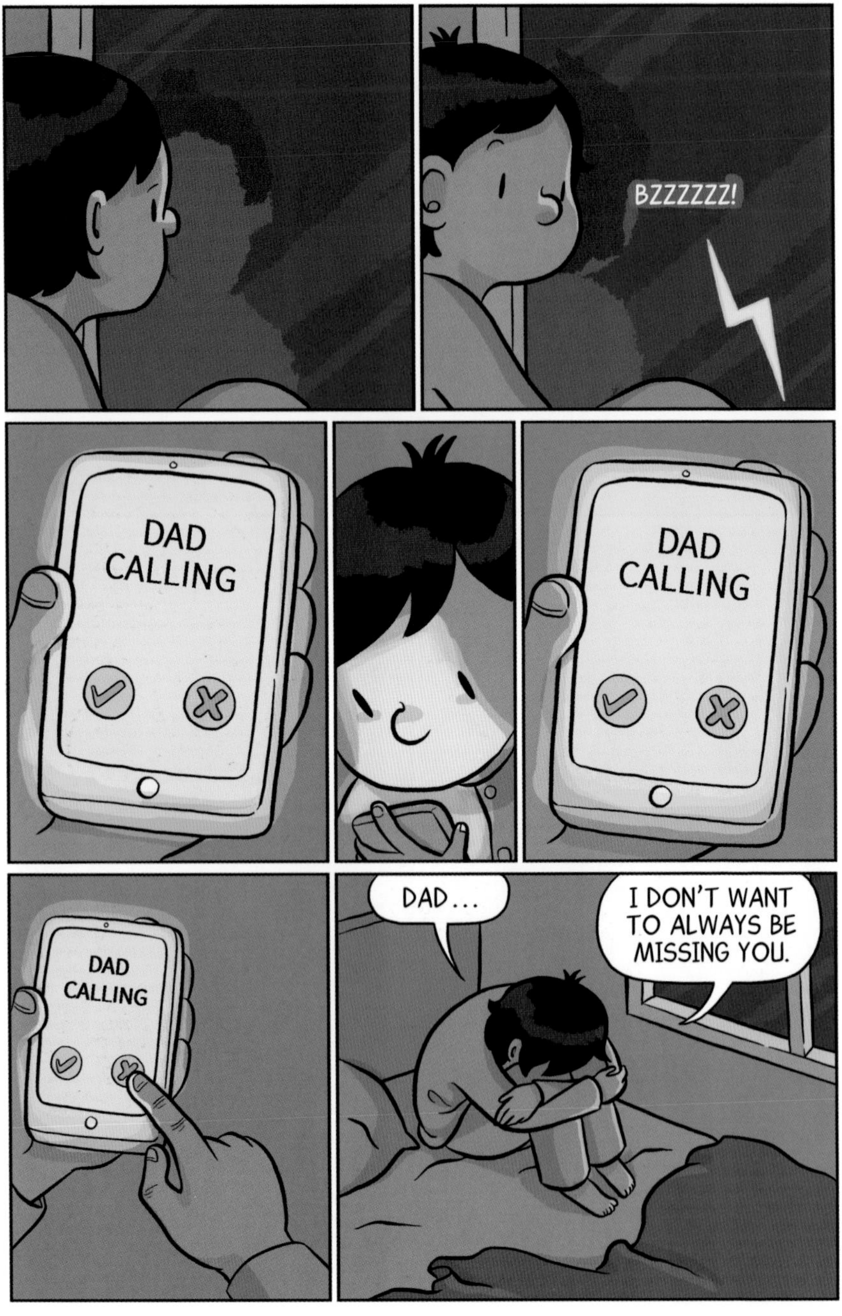
BZZZZZZ!
DAD CALLING
DAD CALLING
DAD CALLING
DAD...
I DON'T WANT TO ALWAYS BE MISSING YOU.

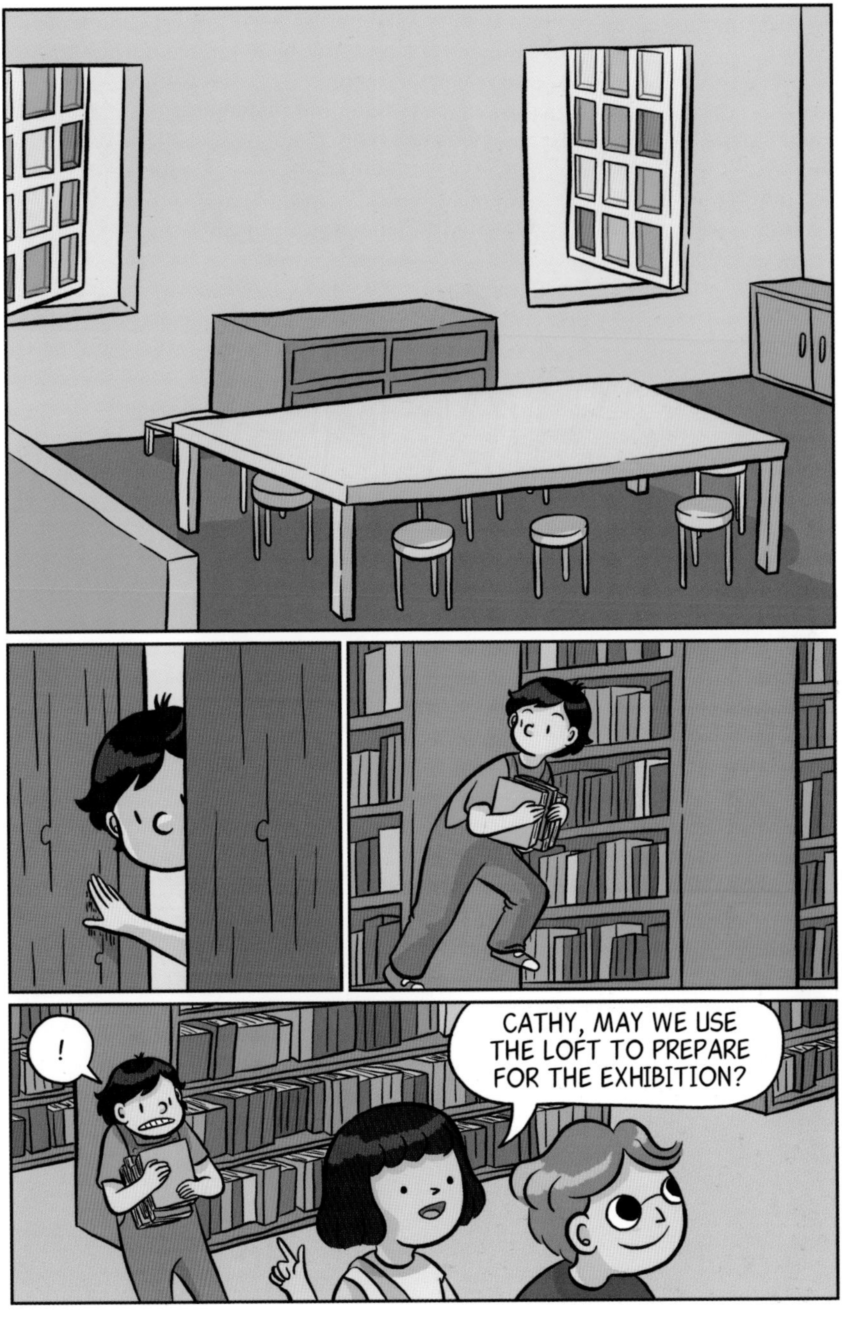
!
CATHY, MAY WE USE THE LOFT TO PREPARE FOR THE EXHIBITION?

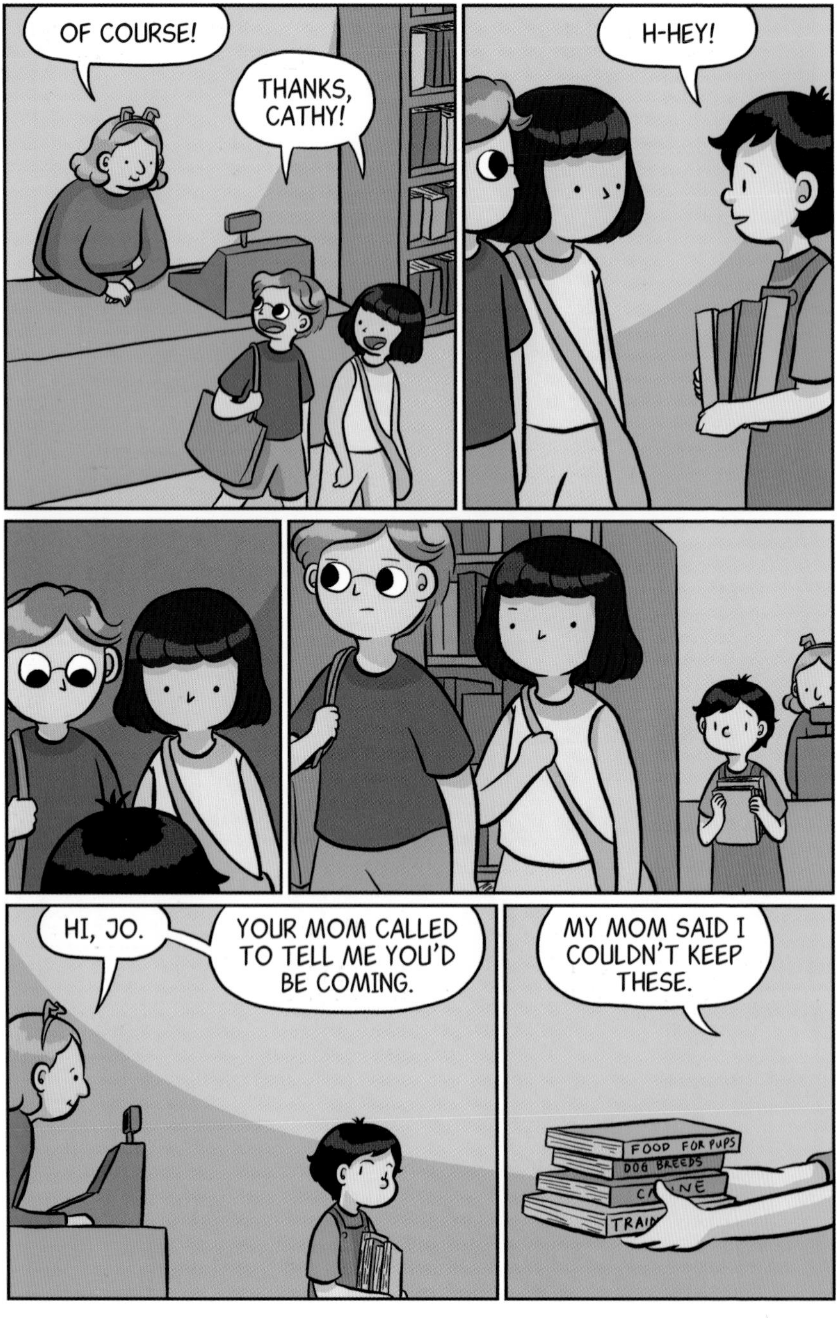
OF COURSE!
THANKS, CATHY!
H-HEY!
HI, JO.
YOUR MOM CALLED TO TELL ME YOU'D BE COMING.
MY MOM SAID I COULDN'T KEEP THESE.
FOOD FOR PUPS
DOG BREEDS

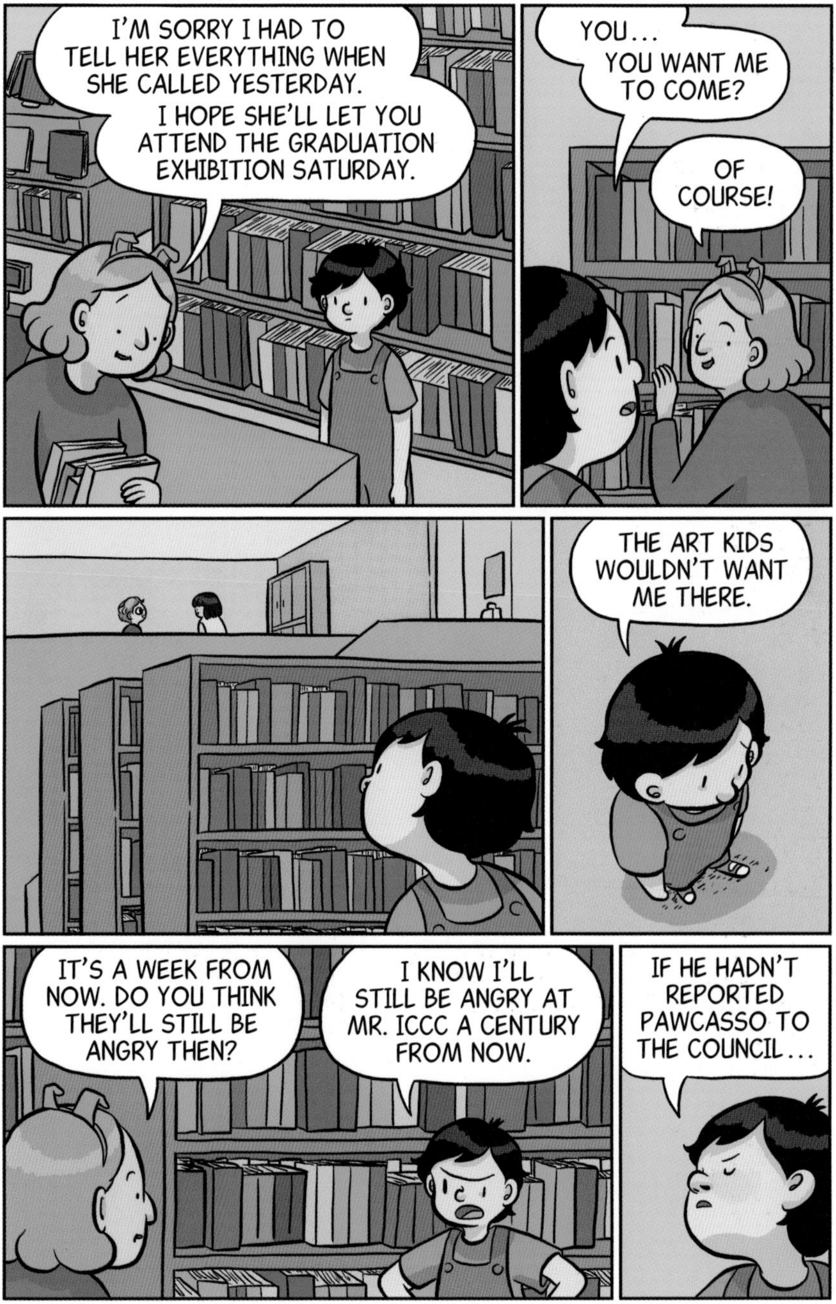
I'M SORRY I HAD TO TELL HER EVERYTHING WHEN SHE CALLED YESTERDAY.
I HOPE SHE'LL LET YOU ATTEND THE GRADUATION EXHIBITION SATURDAY.
YOU...
YOU WANT ME TO COME?
OF COURSE!
THE ART KIDS WOULDN'T WANT ME THERE.
IT'S A WEEK FROM NOW. DO YOU THINK THEY'LL STILL BE ANGRY THEN?
I KNOW I'LL STILL BE ANGRY AT MR. ICCC A CENTURY FROM NOW.
IF HE HADN'T REPORTED PAWCASSO TO THE COUNCIL...

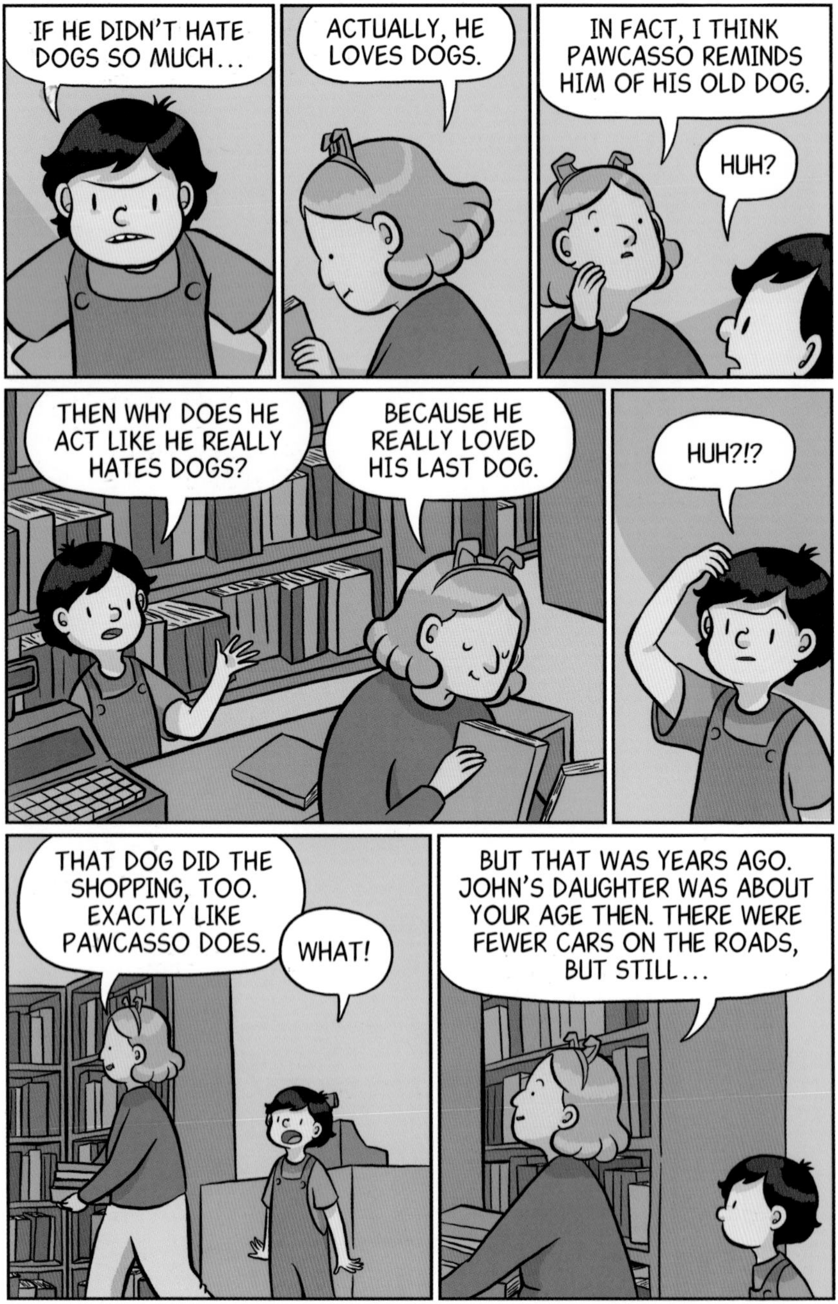
IF HE DIDN'T HATE DOGS SO MUCH...
ACTUALLY, HE LOVES DOGS.
IN FACT, I THINK PAWCASSO REMINDS HIM OF HIS OLD DOG.
HUH?
THEN WHY DOES HE ACT LIKE HE REALLY HATES DOGS?
BECAUSE HE REALLY LOVED HIS LAST DOG.
HUH?!?
THAT DOG DID THE SHOPPING, TOO. EXACTLY LIKE PAWCASSO DOES.
WHAT!
BUT THAT WAS YEARS AGO. JOHN'S DAUGHTER WAS ABOUT YOUR AGE THEN. THERE WERE FEWER CARS ON THE ROADS, BUT STILL...

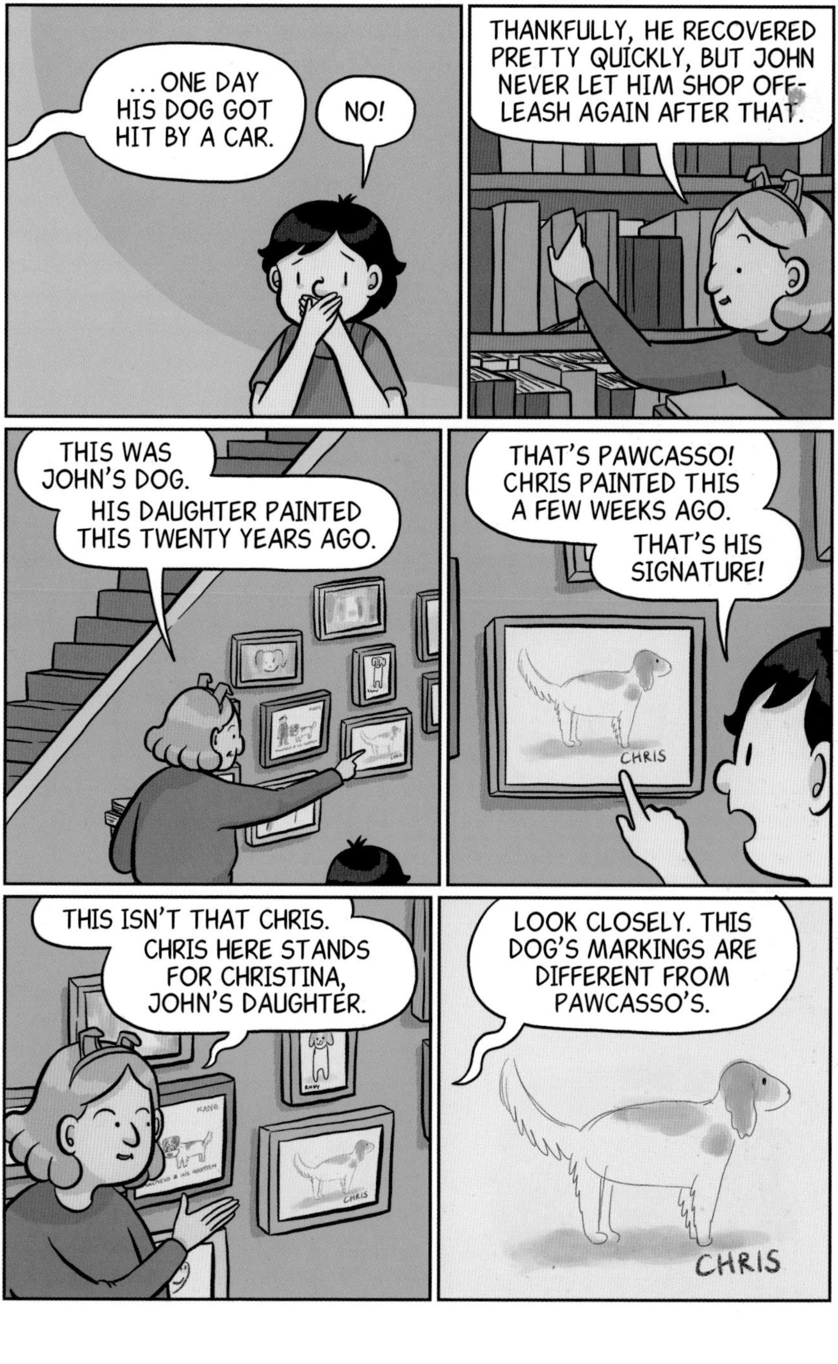
...ONE DAY HIS DOG GOT HIT BY A CAR.
NO!
THANKFULLY, HE RECOVERED PRETTY QUICKLY, BUT JOHN NEVER LET HIM SHOP OFF-LEASH AGAIN AFTER THAT.
THIS WAS JOHN'S DOG.
HIS DAUGHTER PAINTED THIS TWENTY YEARS AGO.
THAT'S PAWCASSO! CHRIS PAINTED THIS A FEW WEEKS AGO.
THAT'S HIS SIGNATURE!
CHRIS
THIS ISN'T THAT CHRIS.
CHRIS HERE STANDS FOR CHRISTINA, JOHN'S DAUGHTER.
LOOK CLOSELY. THIS DOG'S MARKINGS ARE DIFFERENT FROM PAWCASSO'S.
CHRIS

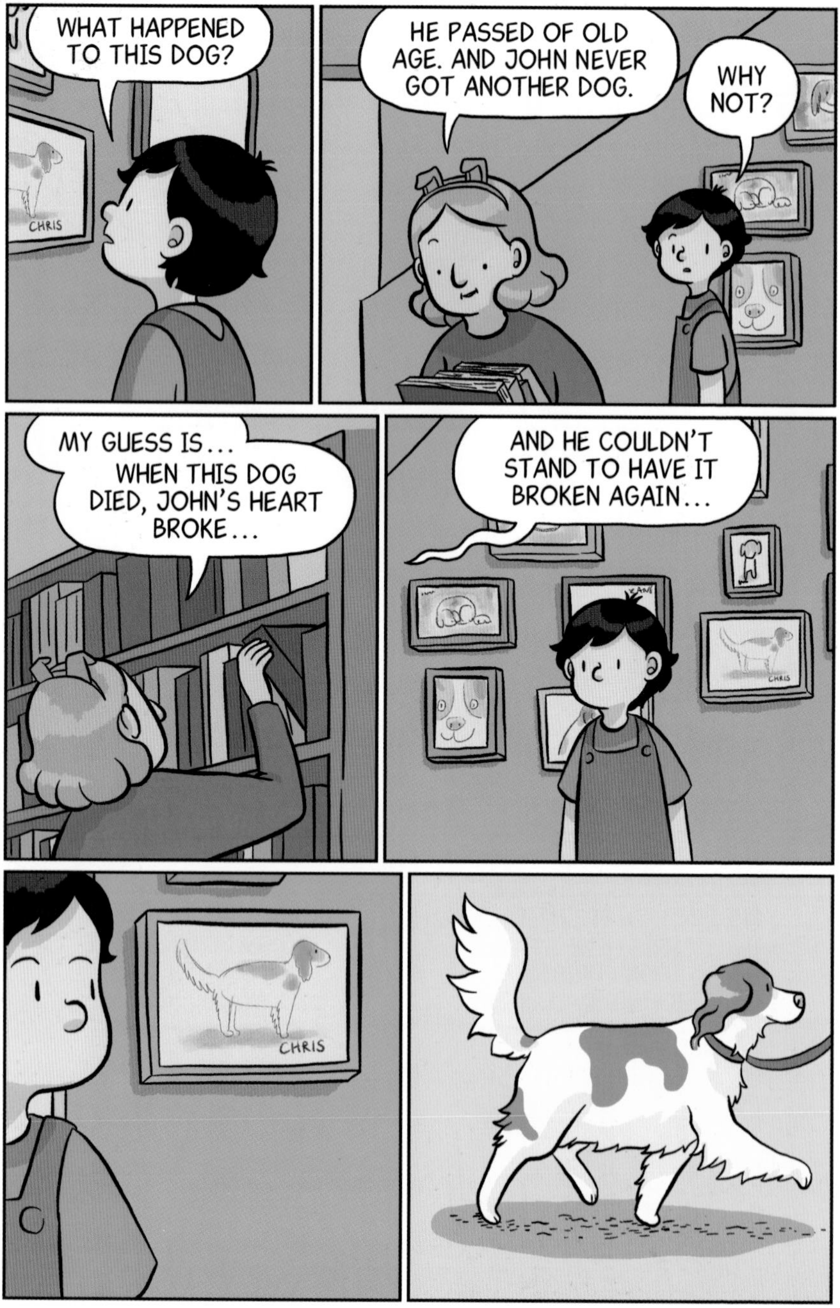
WHAT HAPPENED TO THIS DOG?
CHRIS
HE PASSED OF OLD AGE. AND JOHN NEVER GOT ANOTHER DOG.
WHY NOT?
MY GUESS IS... WHEN THIS DOG DIED, JOHN'S HEART BROKE...
AND HE COULDN'T STAND TO HAVE IT BROKEN AGAIN...
CHRIS
CHRIS

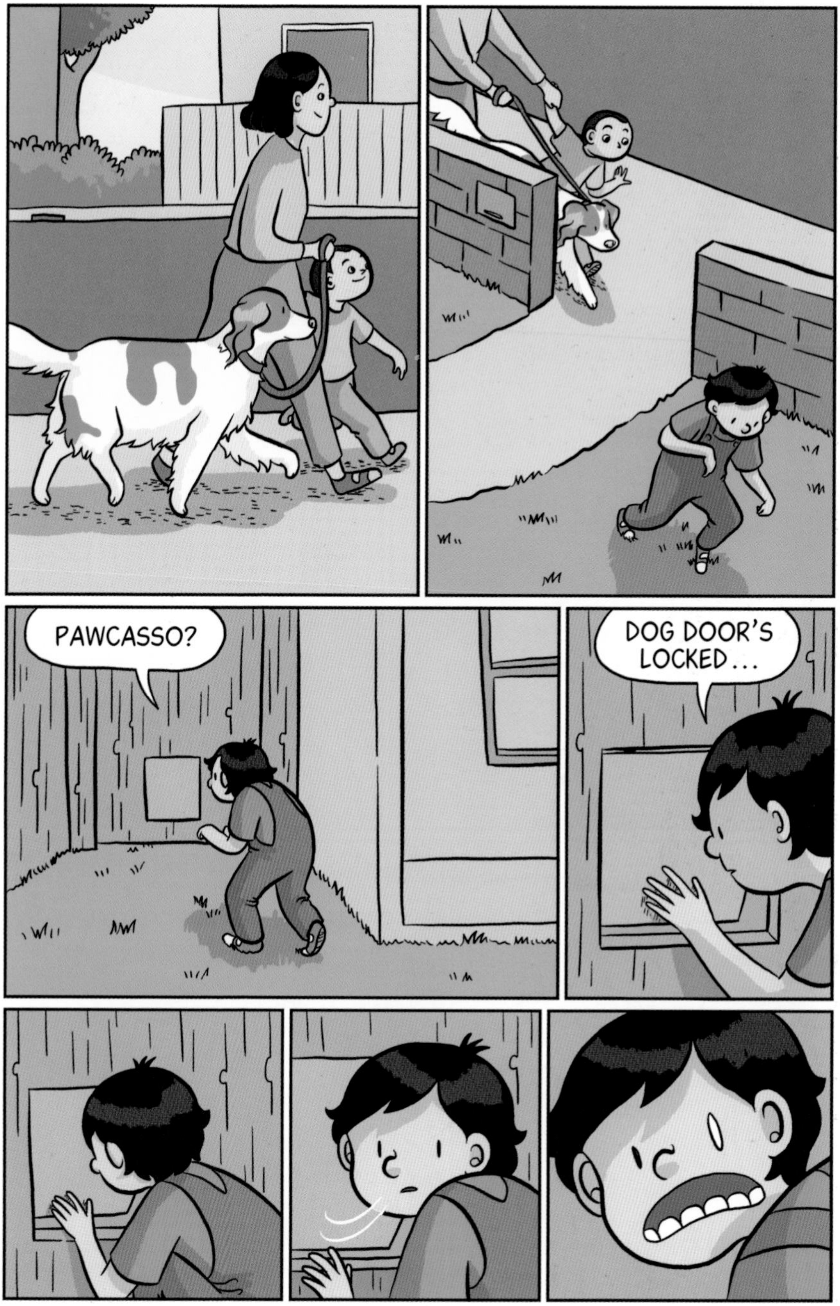
PAWCASSO?
DOG DOOR'S LOCKED...

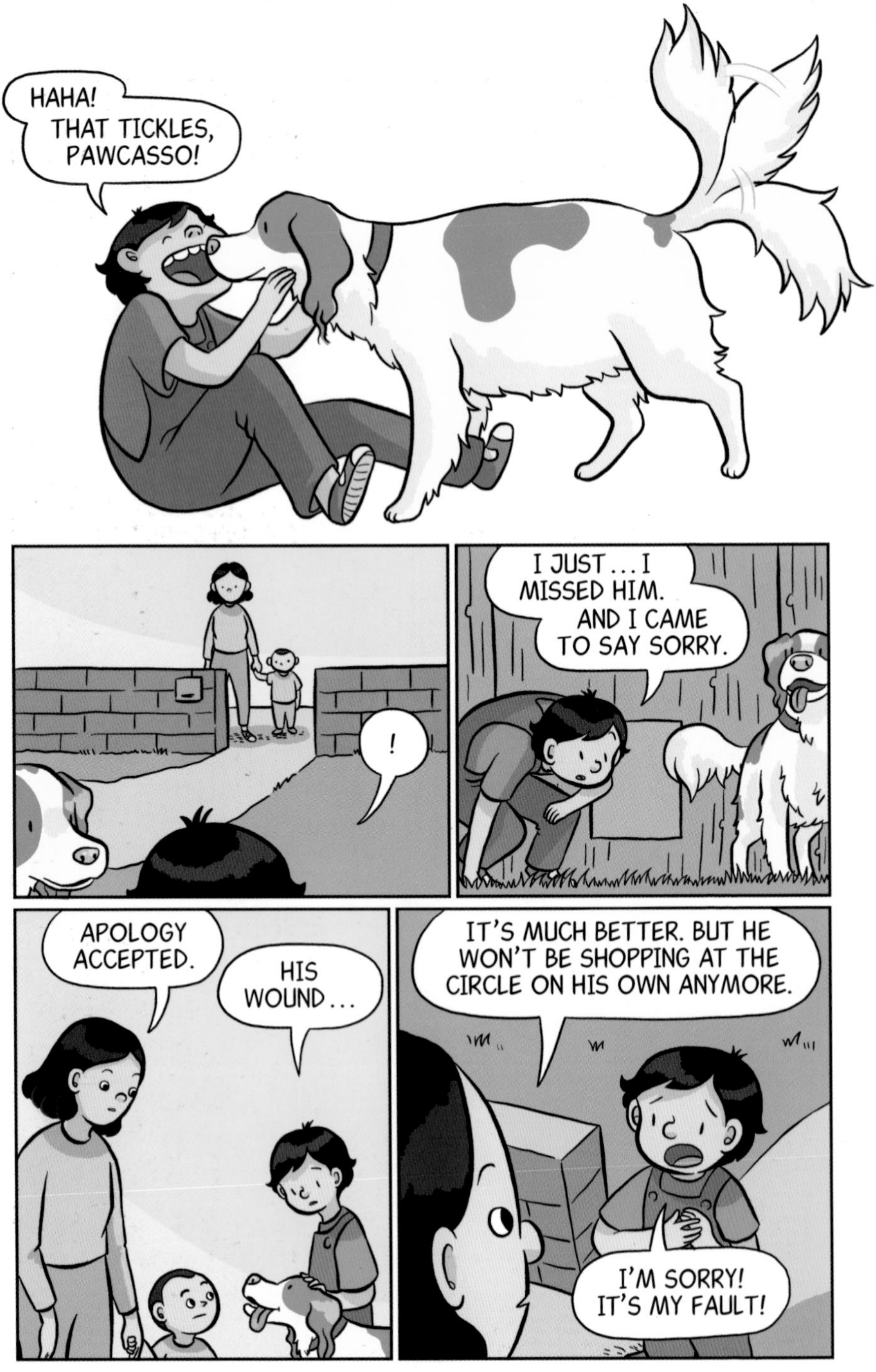
HAHA! THAT TICKLES, PAWCASSO!
!
I JUST... I MISSED HIM. AND I CAME TO SAY SORRY.
APOLOGY ACCEPTED.
HIS WOUND...
IT'S MUCH BETTER. BUT HE WON'T BE SHOPPING AT THE CIRCLE ON HIS OWN ANYMORE.
I'M SORRY! IT'S MY FAULT!

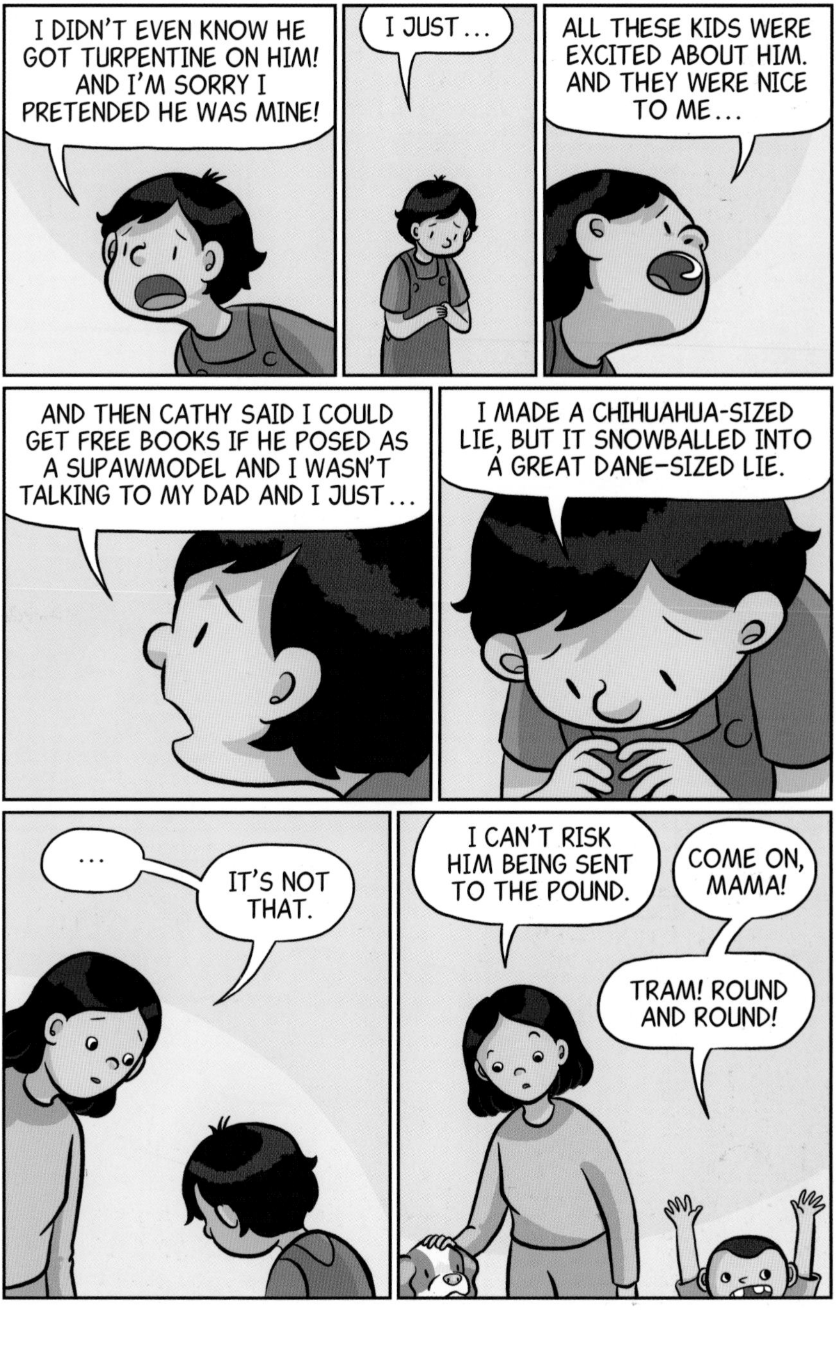
I DIDN'T EVEN KNOW HE GOT TURPENTINE ON HIM! AND I'M SORRY I PRETENDED HE WAS MINE!
I JUST...
ALL THESE KIDS WERE EXCITED ABOUT HIM. AND THEY WERE NICE TO ME...
AND THEN CATHY SAID I COULD GET FREE BOOKS IF HE POSED AS A SUPAWMODEL AND I WASN'T TALKING TO MY DAD AND I JUST...
I MADE A CHIHUAHUA-SIZED LIE, BUT IT SNOWBALLED INTO A GREAT DANE-SIZED LIE.
...
IT'S NOT THAT.
I CAN'T RISK HIM BEING SENT TO THE POUND.
COME ON, MAMA!
TRAM! ROUND AND ROUND!

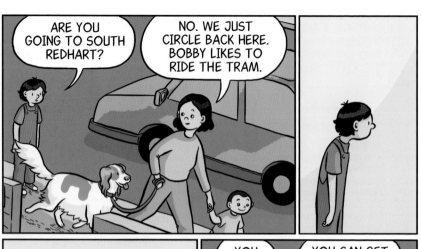

ARE YOU GOING TO SOUTH REDHART?

NO. WE JUST CIRCLE BACK HERE. BOBBY LIKES TO RIDE THE TRAM.

WOULD YOU LIKE TO COME ALONG?

YOU BETCHA!

YOU CAN GET OFF IN SOUTH REDHART.

I HAVE MY HANDS FULL WITH BOBBY. HOLD THIS TIGHT.

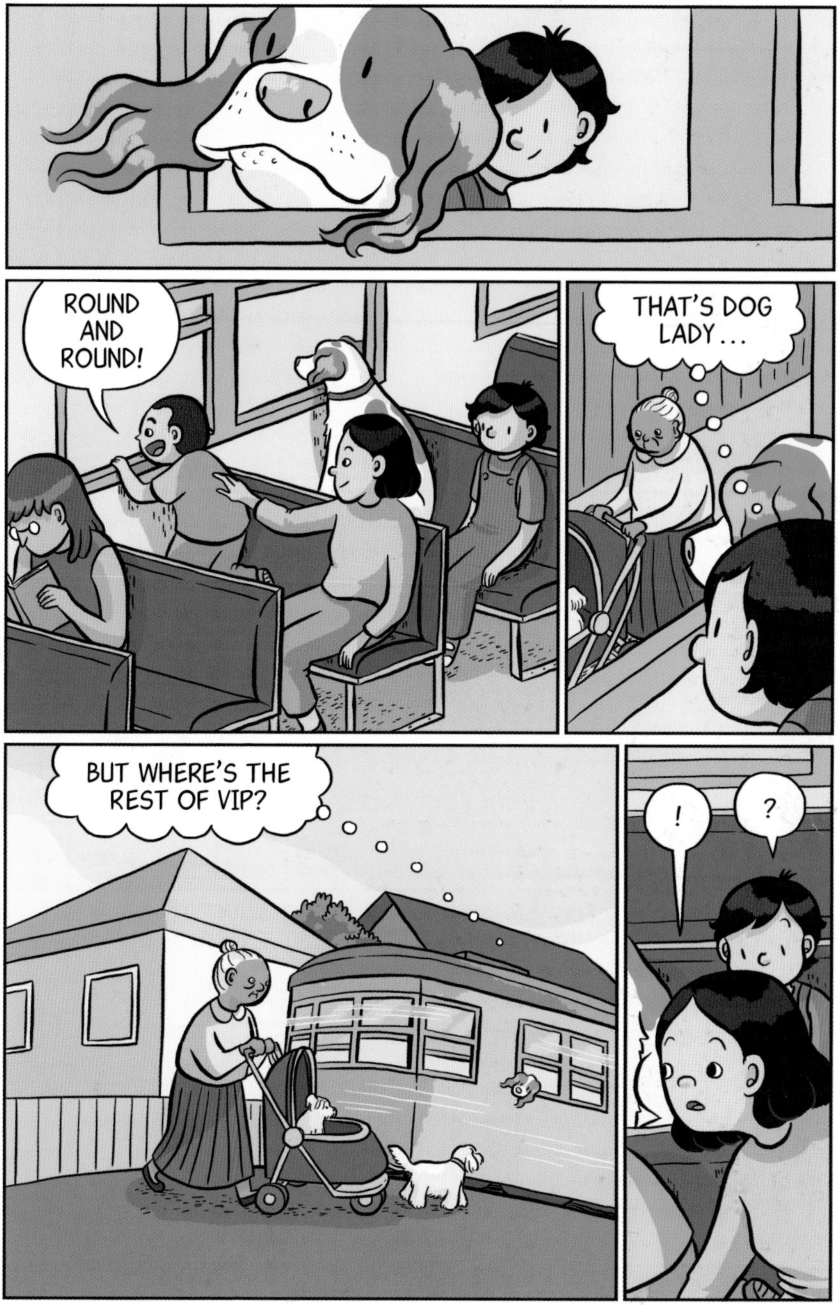
ROUND AND ROUND!
THAT'S DOG LADY...
BUT WHERE'S THE REST OF VIP?
!
?

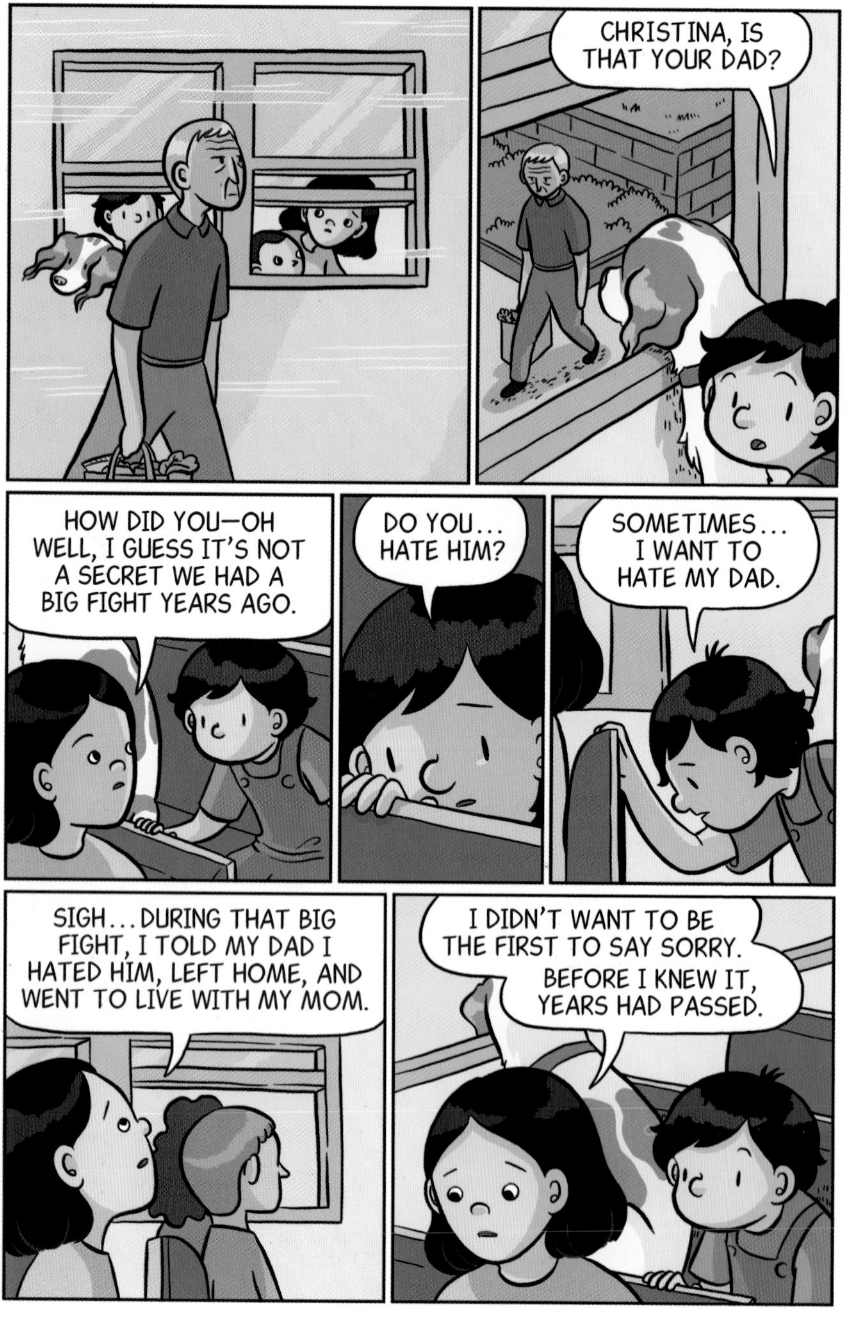
CHRISTINA, IS THAT YOUR DAD?
HOW DID YOU—OH WELL, I GUESS IT'S NOT A SECRET WE HAD A BIG FIGHT YEARS AGO.
DO YOU... HATE HIM?
SOMETIMES... I WANT TO HATE MY DAD.
SIGH... DURING THAT BIG FIGHT, I TOLD MY DAD I HATED HIM, LEFT HOME, AND WENT TO LIVE WITH MY MOM.
I DIDN'T WANT TO BE THE FIRST TO SAY SORRY.
BEFORE I KNEW IT, YEARS HAD PASSED.

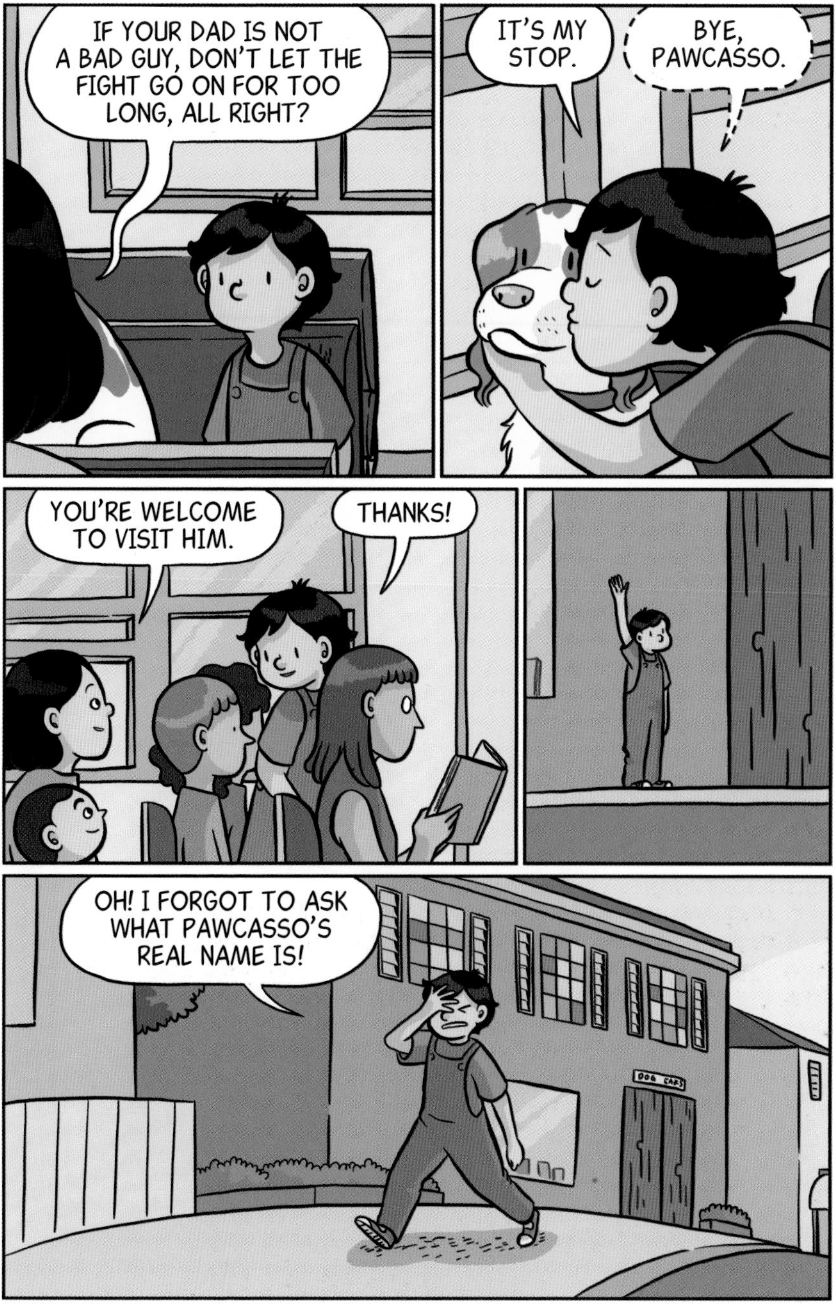
IF YOUR DAD IS NOT A BAD GUY, DON'T LET THE FIGHT GO ON FOR TOO LONG, ALL RIGHT?
IT'S MY STOP.
BYE, PAWCASSO.
YOU'RE WELCOME TO VISIT HIM.
THANKS!
OH! I FORGOT TO ASK WHAT PAWCASSO'S REAL NAME IS!

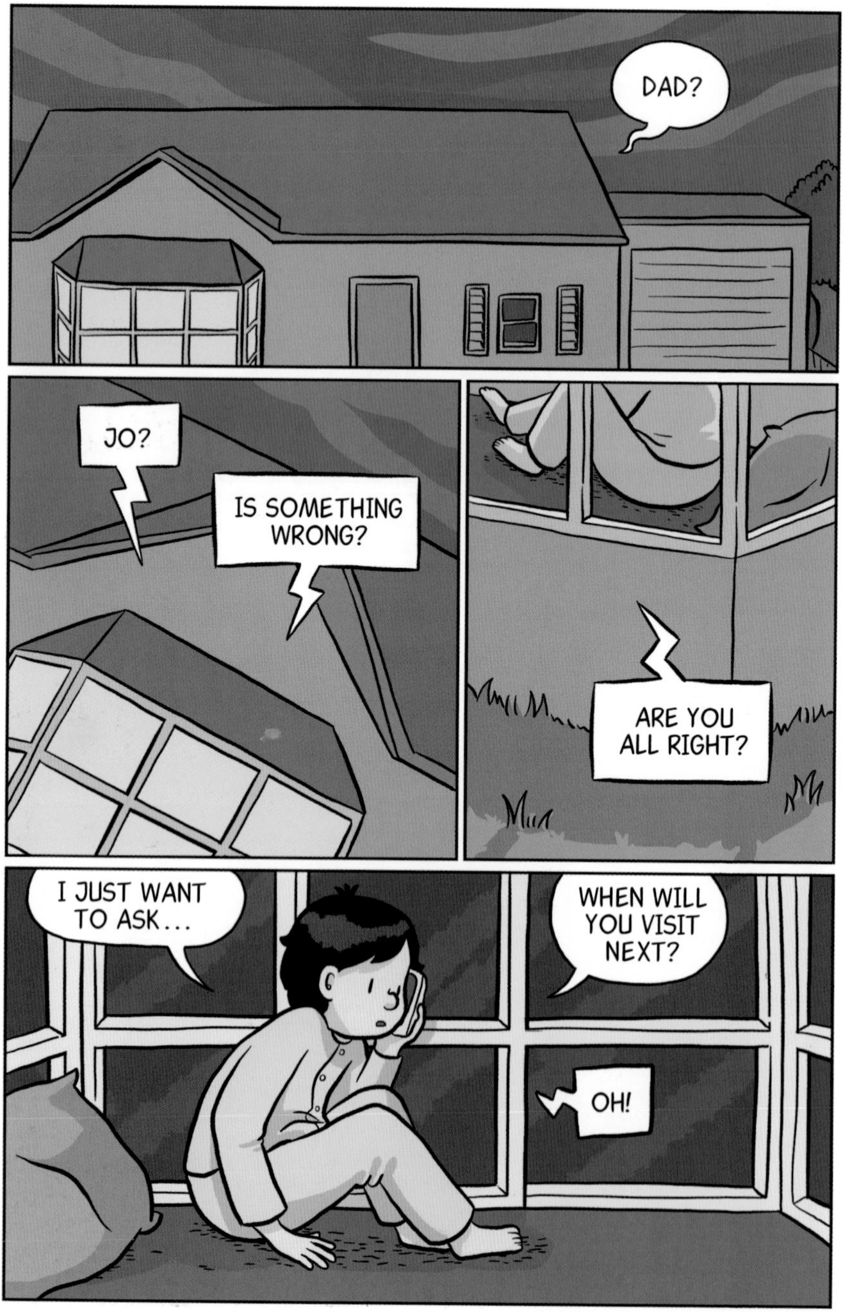
DAD?
JO?
IS SOMETHING WRONG?
ARE YOU ALL RIGHT?
I JUST WANT TO ASK...
WHEN WILL YOU VISIT NEXT?
OH!

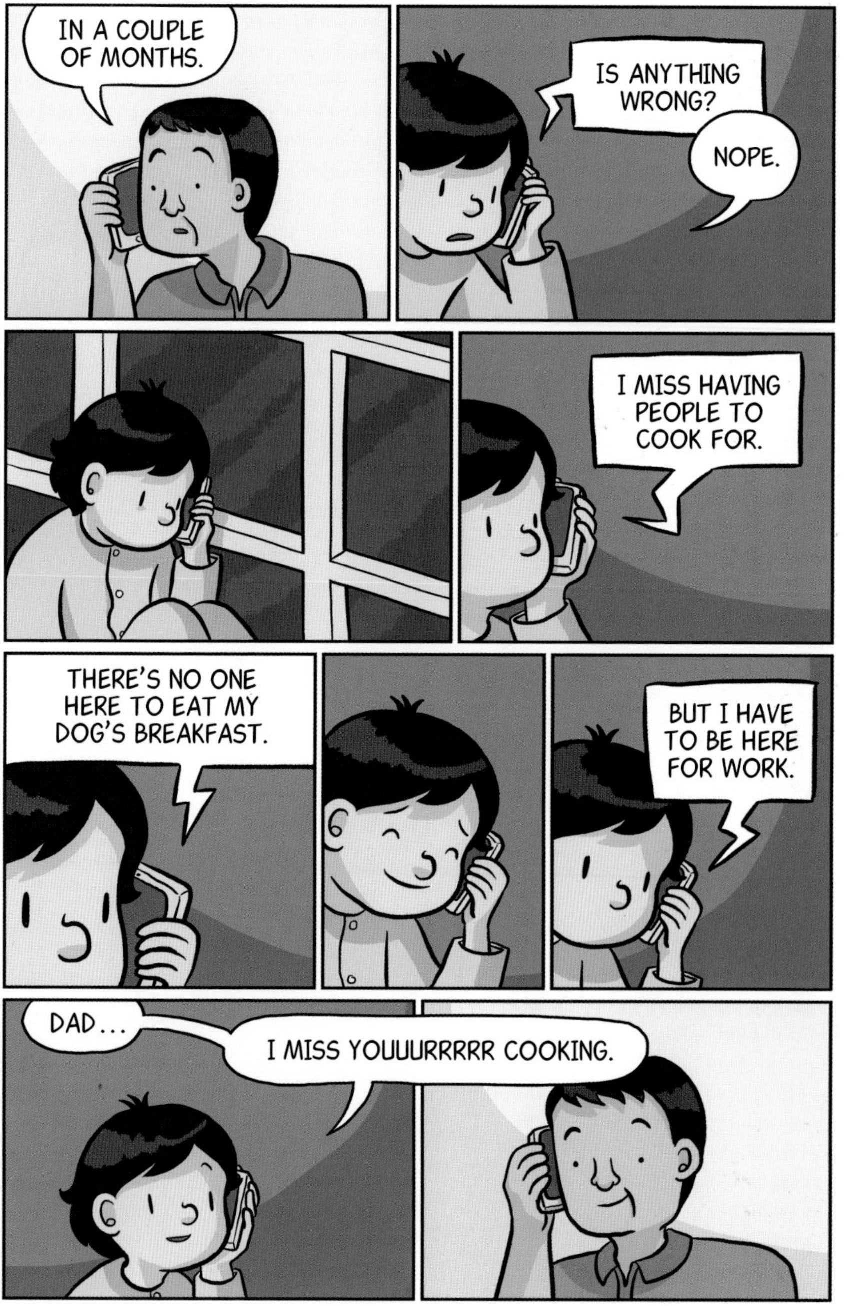
IN A COUPLE OF MONTHS.
IS ANYTHING WRONG?
NOPE.
I MISS HAVING PEOPLE TO COOK FOR.
THERE'S NO ONE HERE TO EAT MY DOG'S BREAKFAST.
BUT I HAVE TO BE HERE FOR WORK.
DAD...
I MISS YOUUURRRRR COOKING.

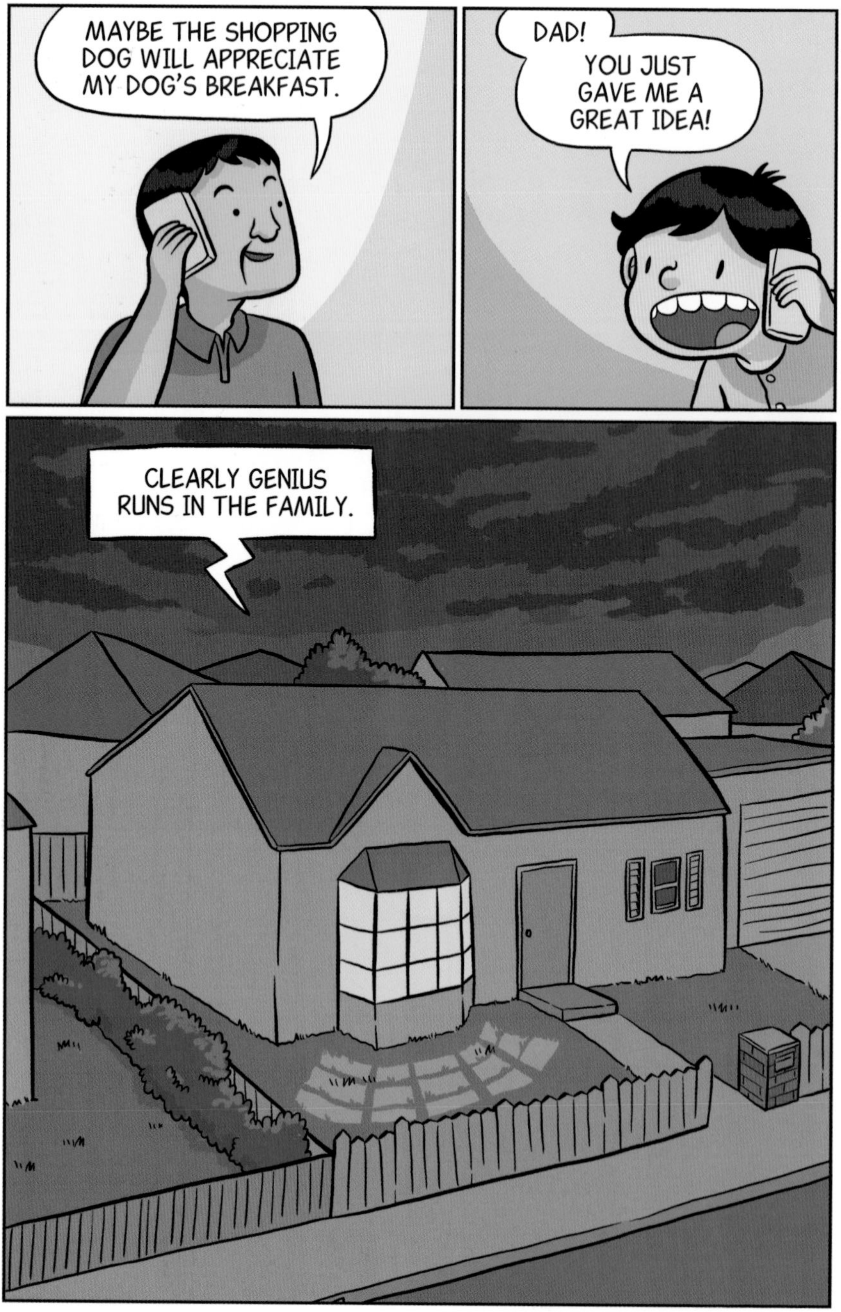
MAYBE THE SHOPPING DOG WILL APPRECIATE MY DOG'S BREAKFAST.
DAD!
YOU JUST GAVE ME A GREAT IDEA!
CLEARLY GENIUS RUNS IN THE FAMILY.

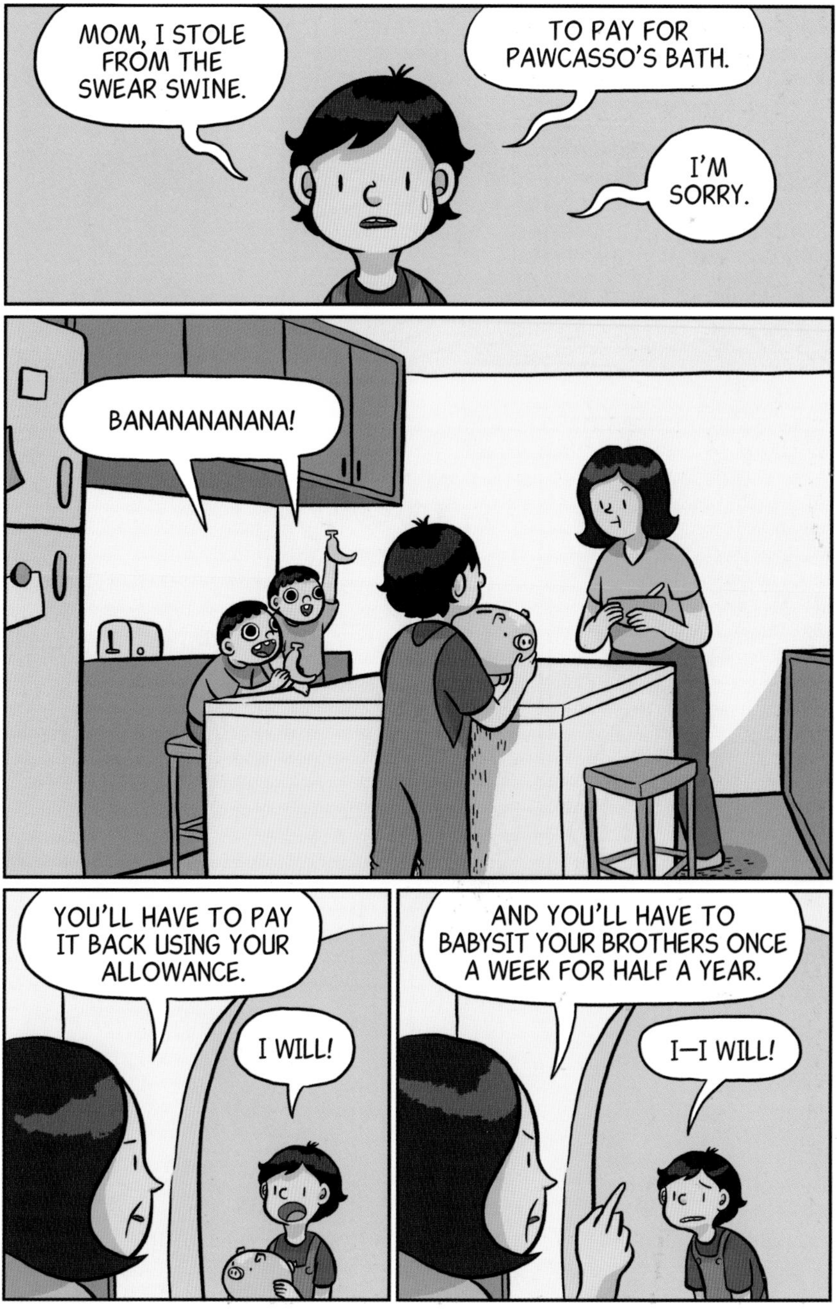
MOM, I STOLE FROM THE SWEAR SWINE.
TO PAY FOR PAWCASSO'S BATH.
I'M SORRY.
BANANANANANA!
YOU'LL HAVE TO PAY IT BACK USING YOUR ALLOWANCE.
I WILL!
AND YOU'LL HAVE TO BABYSIT YOUR BROTHERS ONCE A WEEK FOR HALF A YEAR.
I—I WILL!

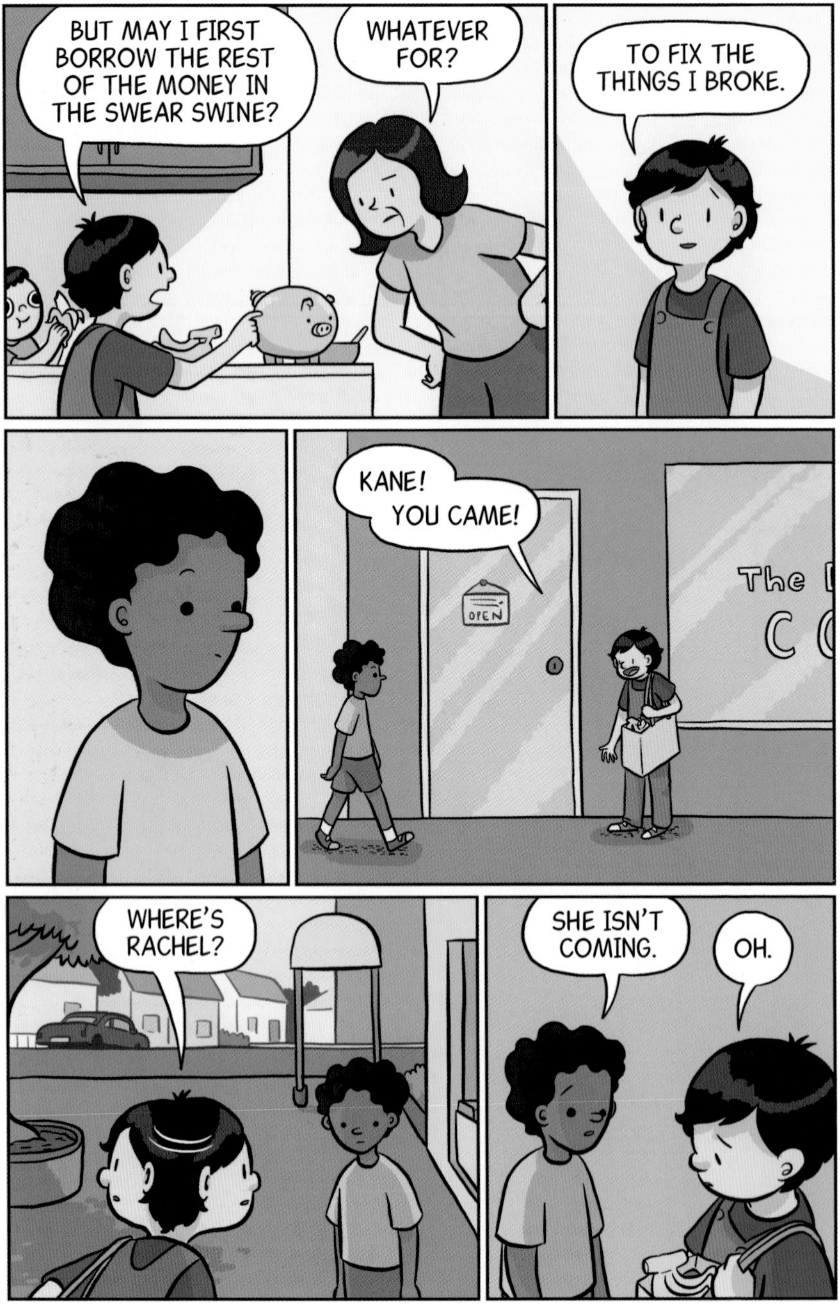
BUT MAY I FIRST BORROW THE REST OF THE MONEY IN THE SWEAR SWINE?
WHATEVER FOR?
TO FIX THE THINGS I BROKE.
KANE! YOU CAME!
OPEN
The
C
WHERE'S RACHEL?
SHE ISN'T COMING.
OH.

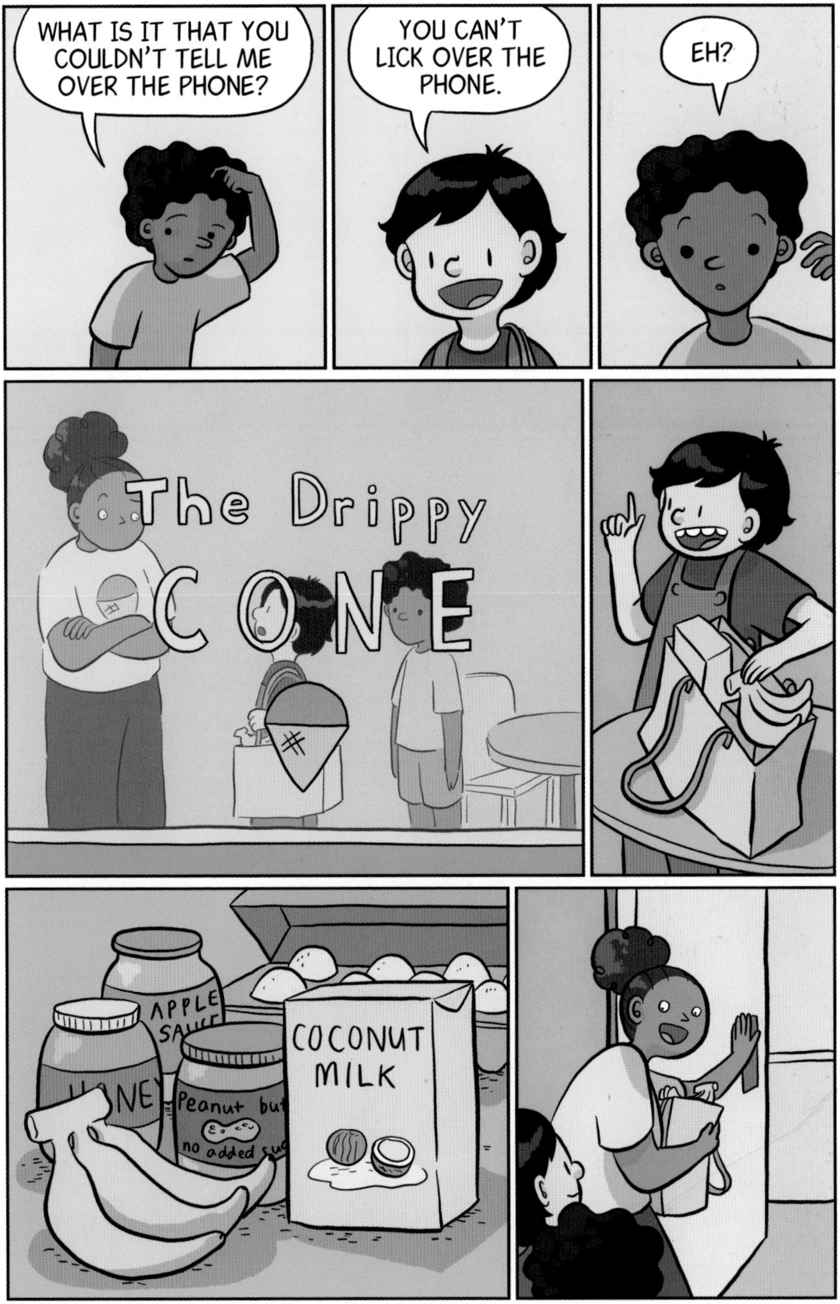
WHAT IS IT THAT YOU COULDN'T TELL ME OVER THE PHONE?
YOU CAN'T LICK OVER THE PHONE.
EH?
The Drippy CONE
APPLE
Peanut
no added
COCONUT MILK

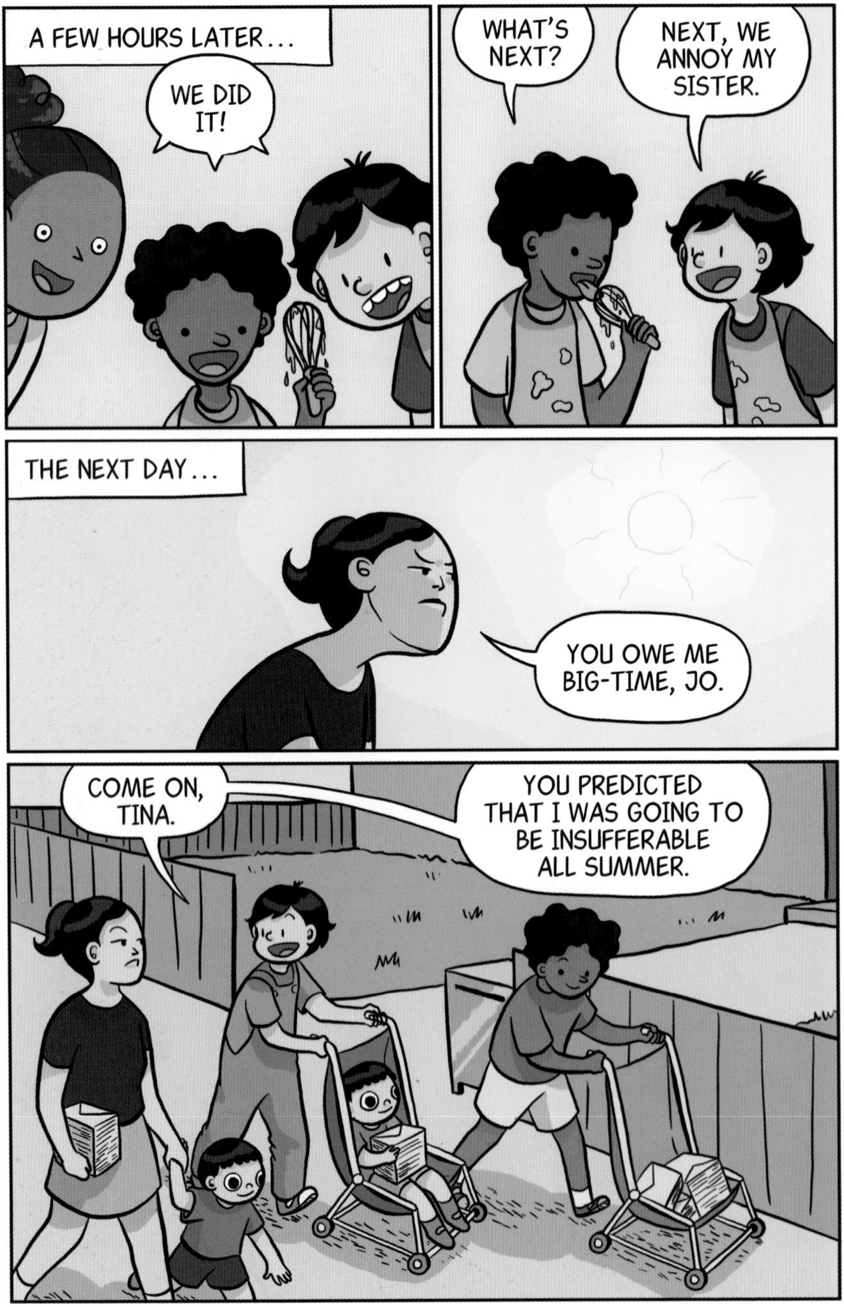
A FEW HOURS LATER...
WE DID IT!
WHAT'S NEXT?
NEXT, WE ANNOY MY SISTER.
THE NEXT DAY...
YOU OWE ME BIG-TIME, JO.
COME ON, TINA.
YOU PREDICTED THAT I WAS GOING TO BE INSUFFERABLE ALL SUMMER.

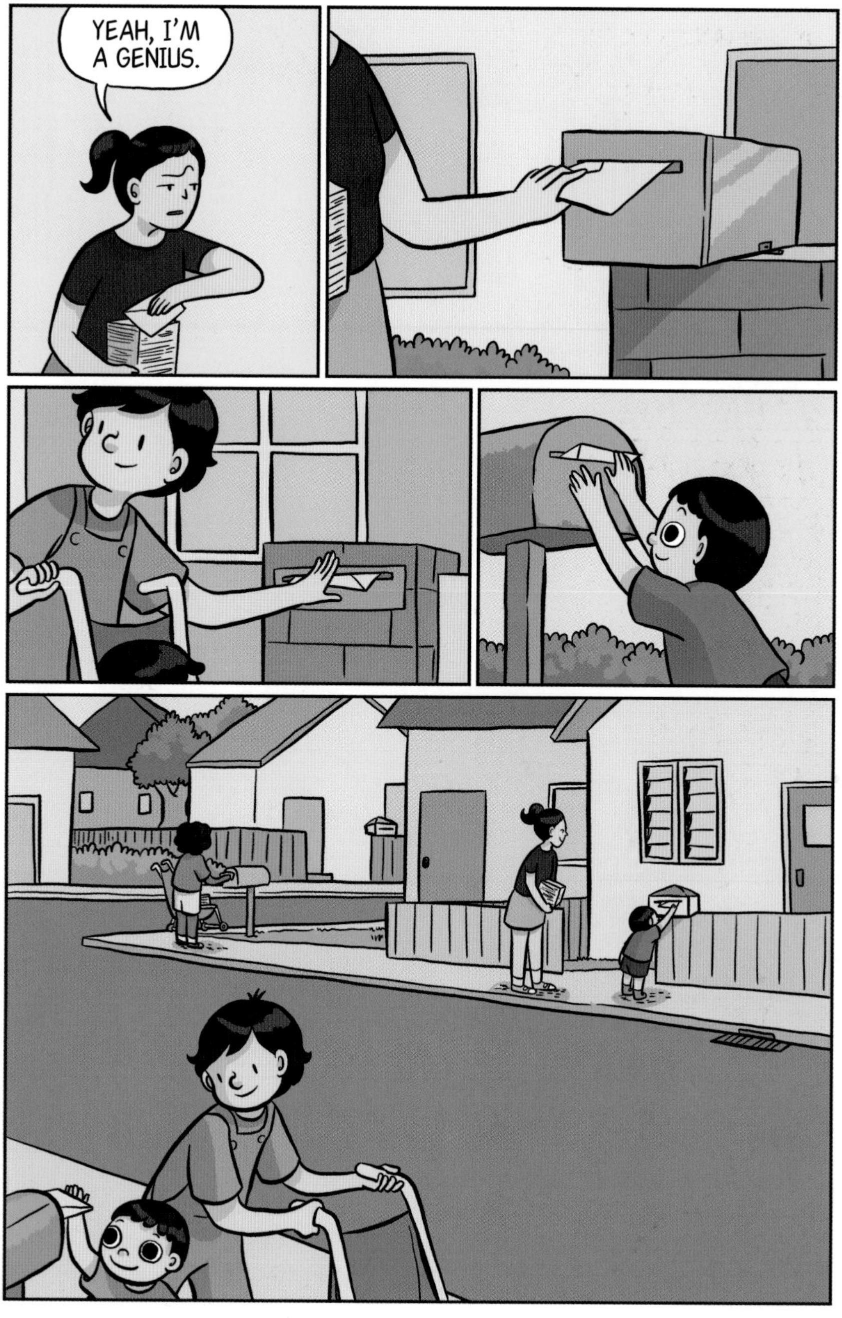
YEAH, I'M
A GENIUS.

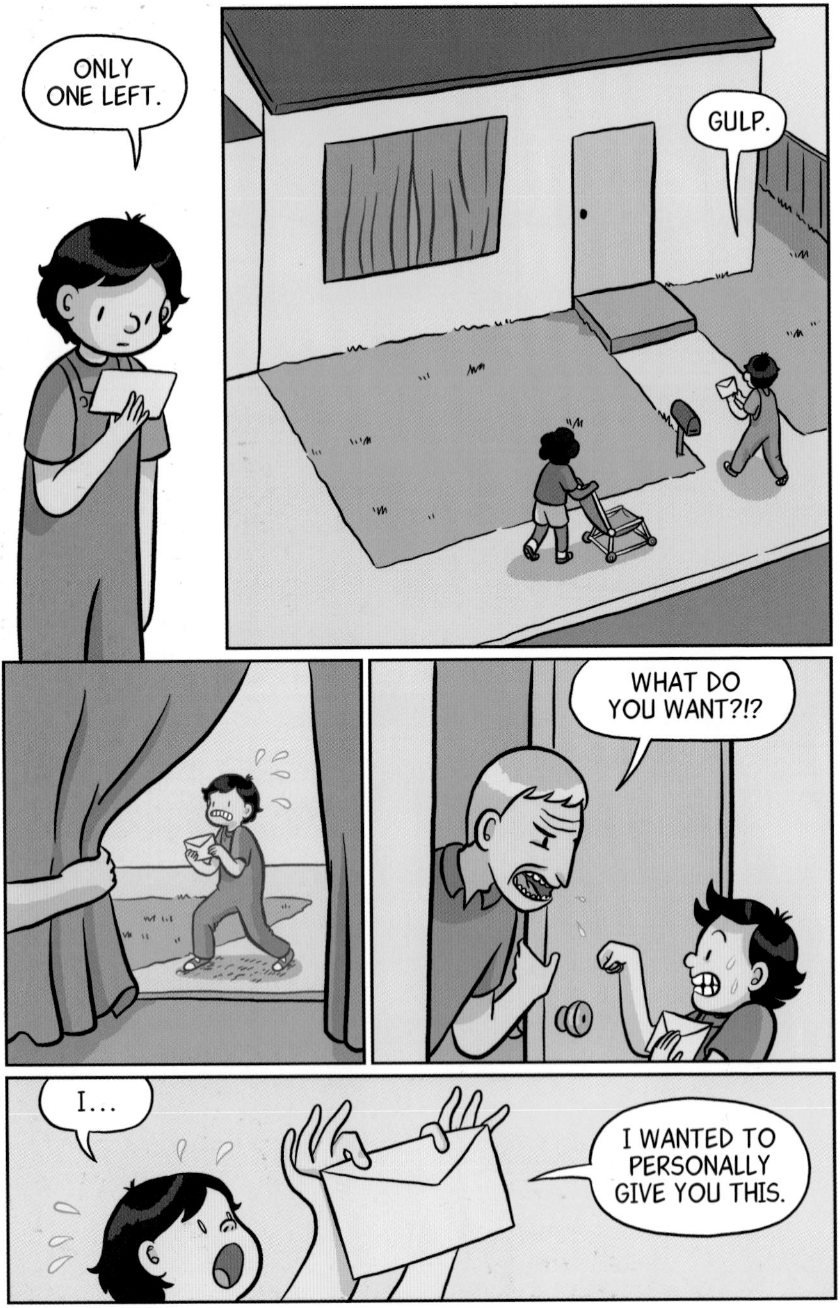
ONLY ONE LEFT.
GULP.
WHAT DO YOU WANT?!?
I...
I WANTED TO PERSONALLY GIVE YOU THIS.

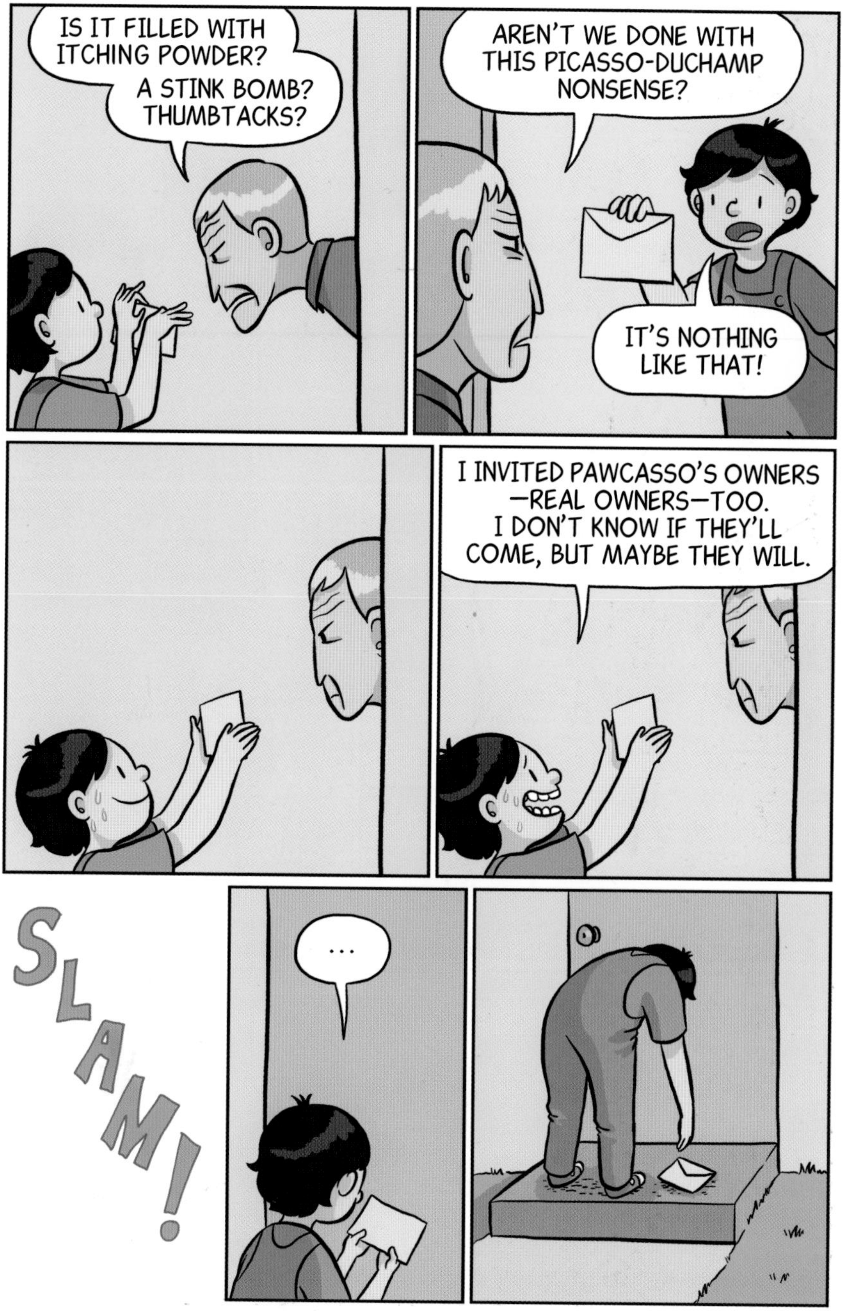
IS IT FILLED WITH ITCHING POWDER?
A STINK BOMB? THUMBTACKS?
AREN'T WE DONE WITH THIS PICASSO-DUCHAMP NONSENSE?
IT'S NOTHING LIKE THAT!
I INVITED PAWCASSO'S OWNERS —REAL OWNERS—TOO. I DON'T KNOW IF THEY'LL COME, BUT MAYBE THEY WILL.
SLAM!
...

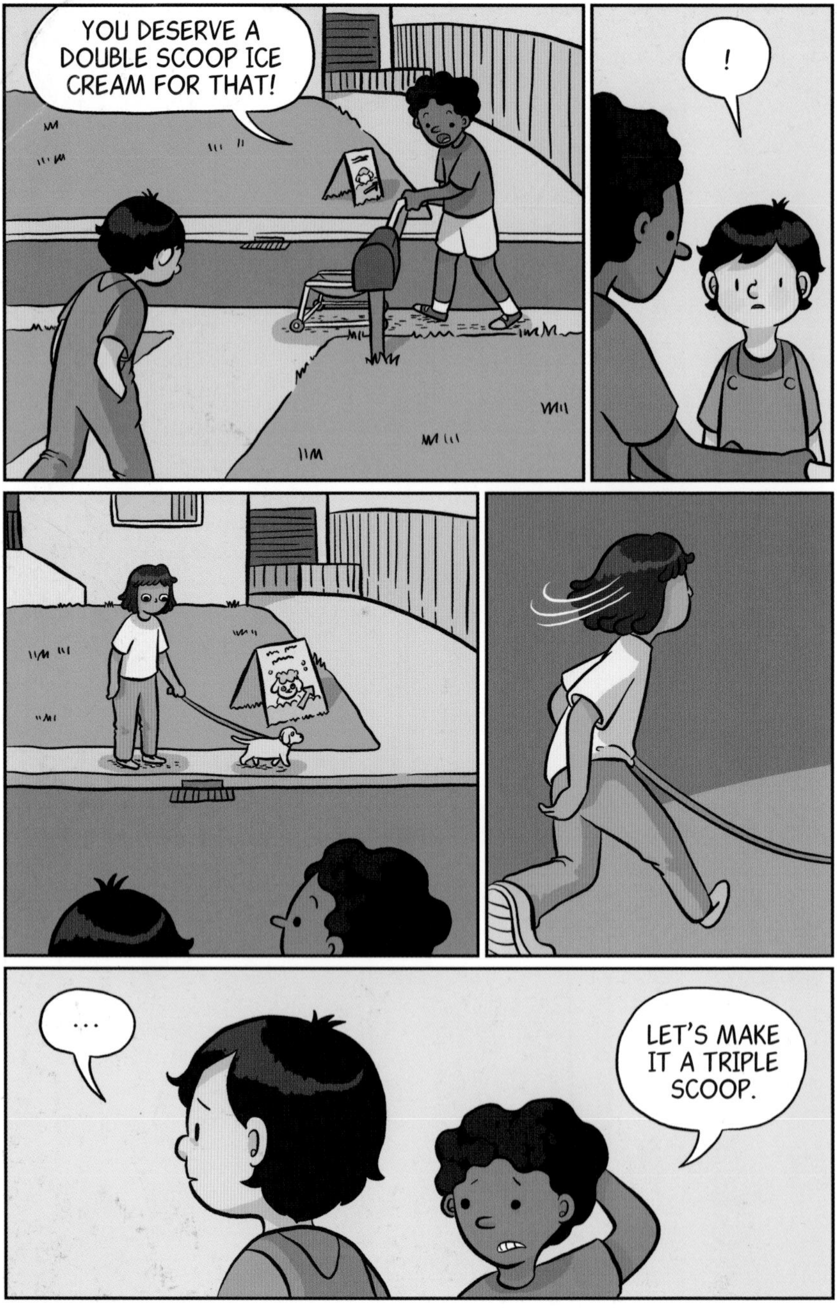
YOU DESERVE A DOUBLE SCOOP ICE CREAM FOR THAT!
!
...
LET'S MAKE IT A TRIPLE SCOOP.

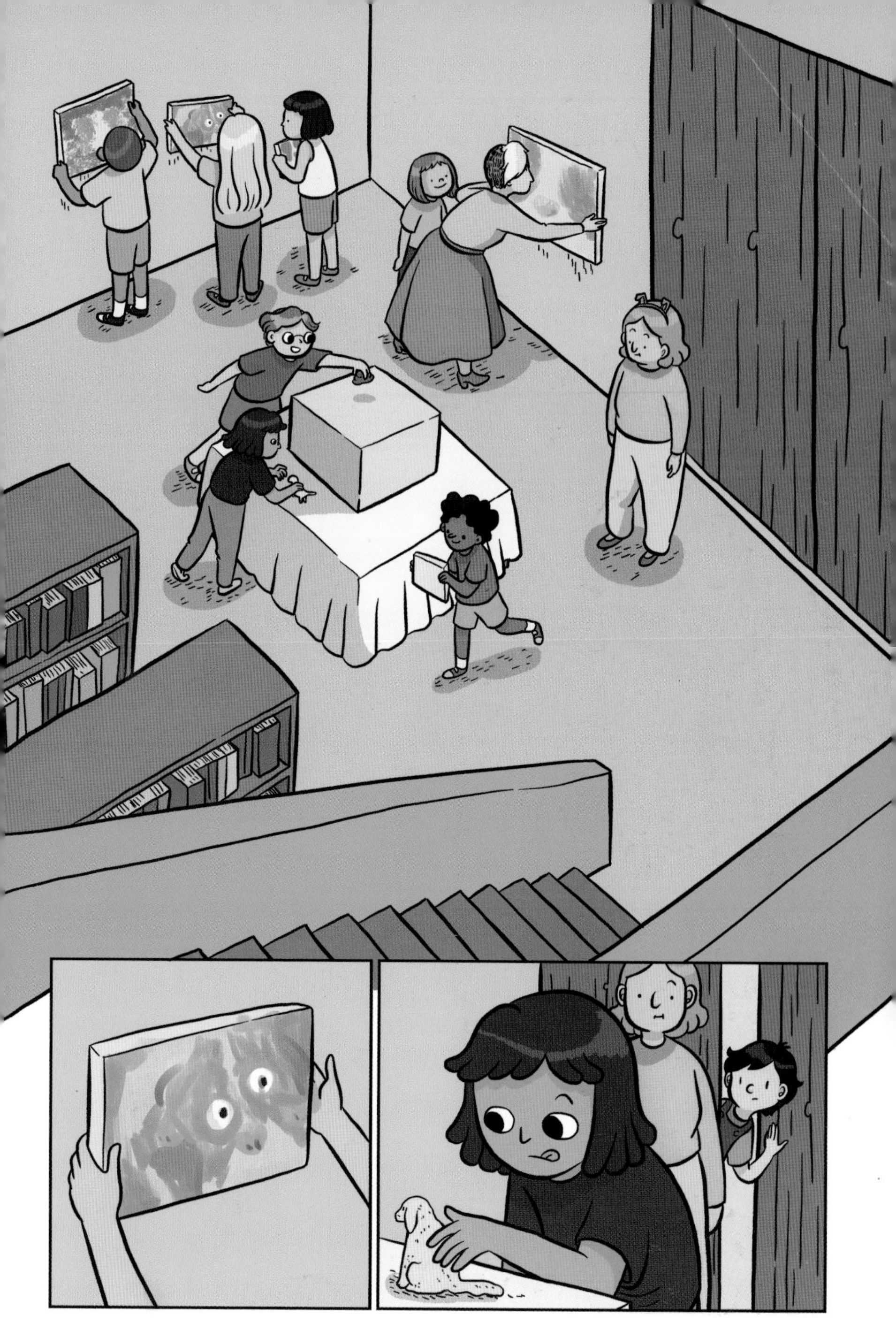

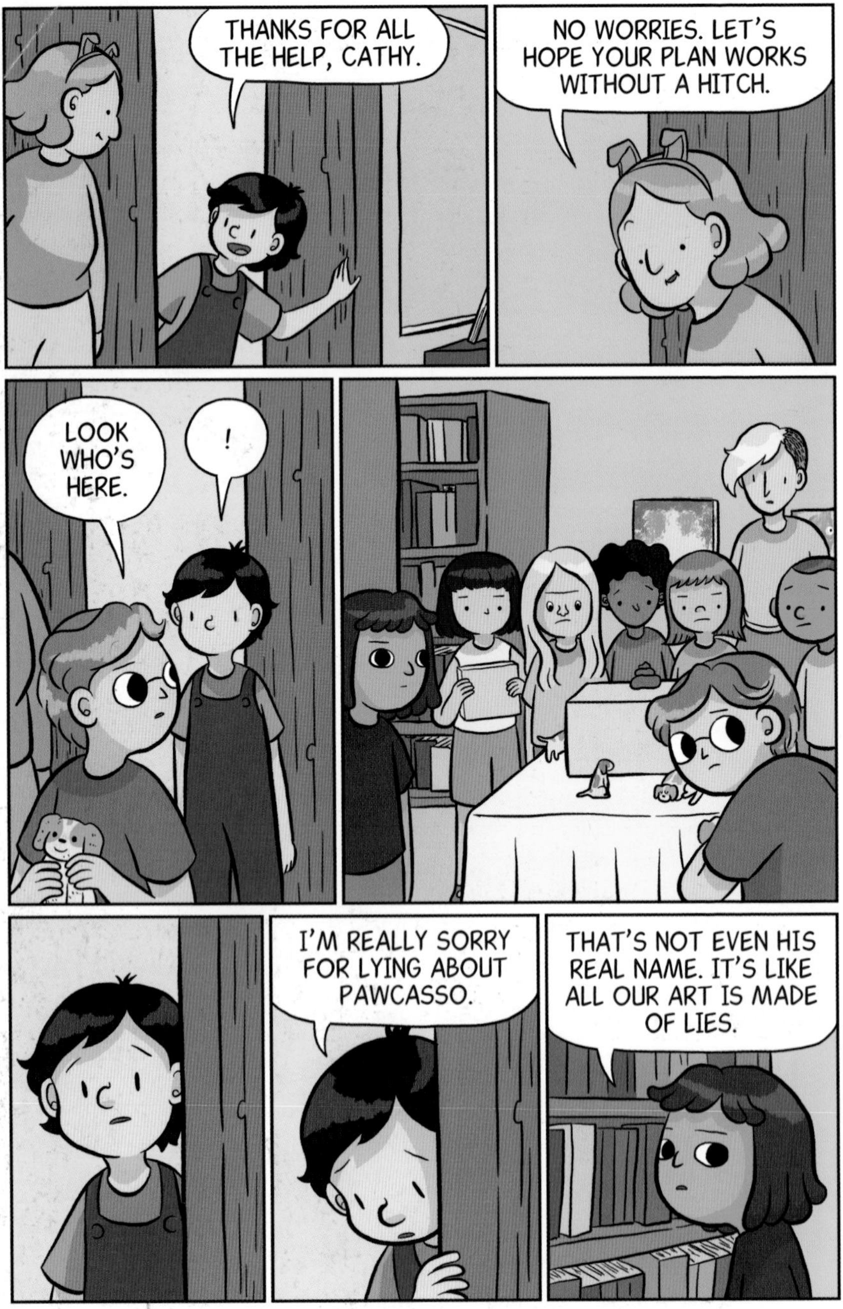
THANKS FOR ALL THE HELP, CATHY.
NO WORRIES. LET'S HOPE YOUR PLAN WORKS WITHOUT A HITCH.
LOOK WHO'S HERE.
!
I'M REALLY SORRY FOR LYING ABOUT PAWCASSO.
THAT'S NOT EVEN HIS REAL NAME. IT'S LIKE ALL OUR ART IS MADE OF LIES.

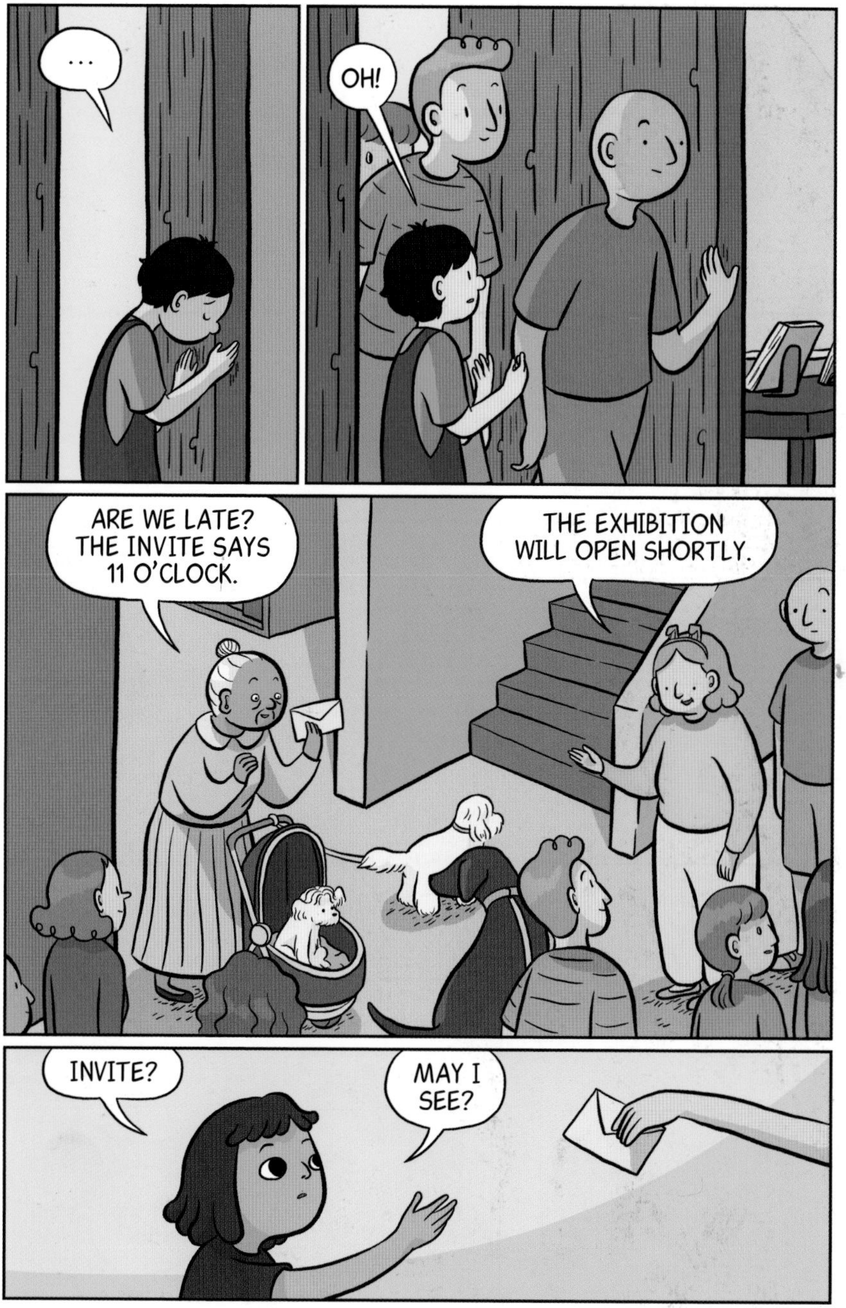
...
OH!
ARE WE LATE? THE INVITE SAYS 11 O'CLOCK.
THE EXHIBITION WILL OPEN SHORTLY.
INVITE?
MAY I SEE?

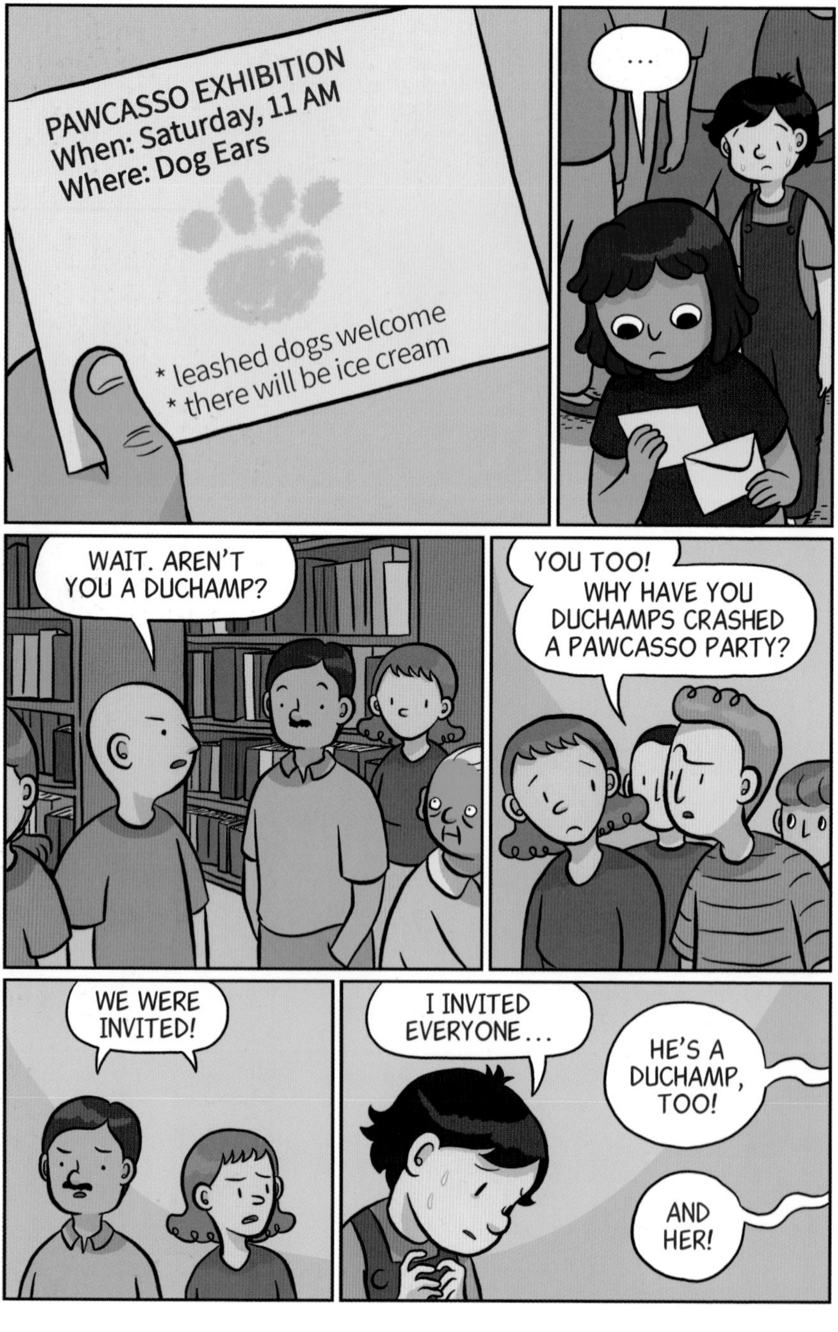
PAWCASSO EXHIBITION
When: Saturday, 11 AM
Where: Dog Ears
* leashed dogs welcome
* there will be ice cream
...
WAIT. AREN'T YOU A DUCHAMP?
YOU TOO!
WHY HAVE YOU DUCHAMPS CRASHED A PAWCASSO PARTY?
WE WERE INVITED!
I INVITED EVERYONE...
HE'S A DUCHAMP, TOO!
AND HER!

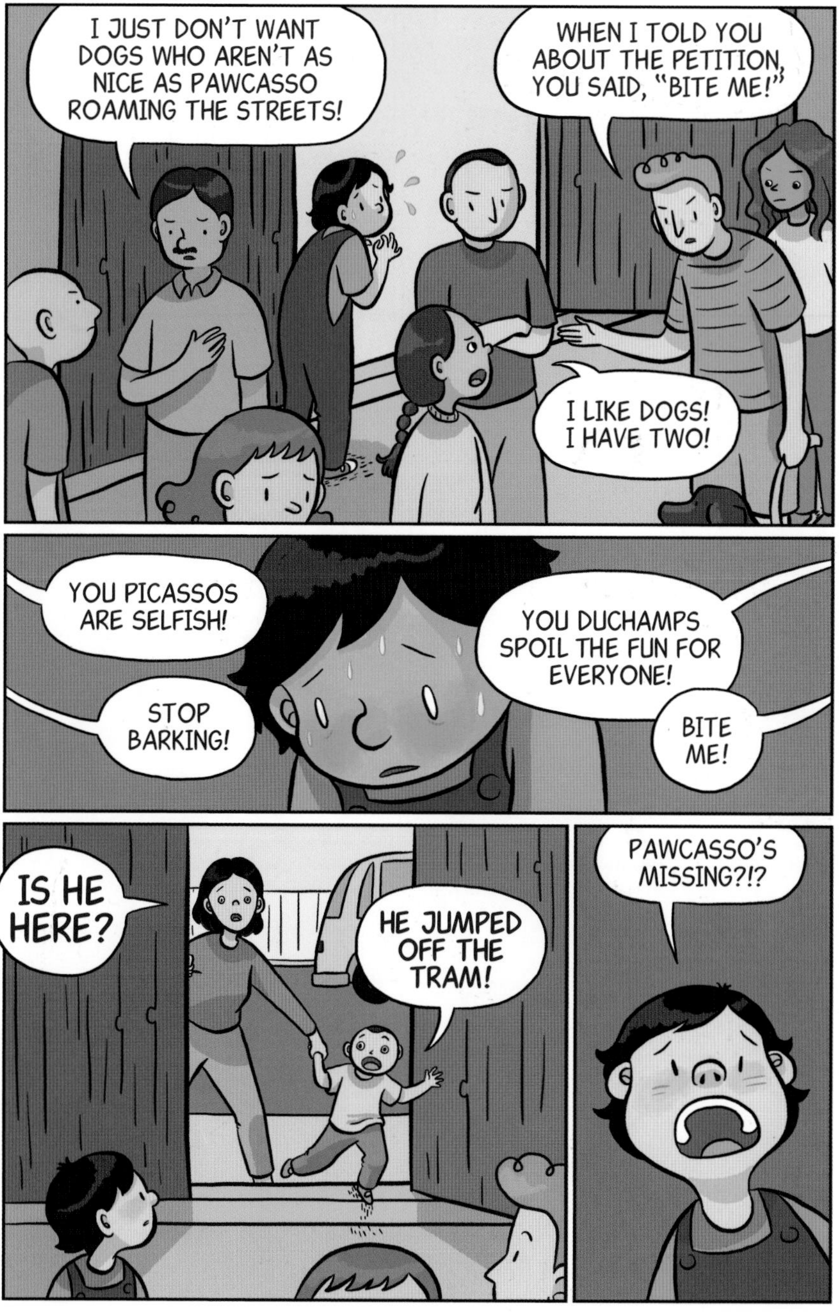
I JUST DON'T WANT DOGS WHO AREN'T AS NICE AS PAWCASSO ROAMING THE STREETS!
WHEN I TOLD YOU ABOUT THE PETITION, YOU SAID, "BITE ME!"
I LIKE DOGS! I HAVE TWO!
YOU PICASSOS ARE SELFISH!
STOP BARKING!
YOU DUCHAMPS SPOIL THE FUN FOR EVERYONE!
BITE ME!
IS HE HERE?
HE JUMPED OFF THE TRAM!
PAWCASSO'S MISSING?!?

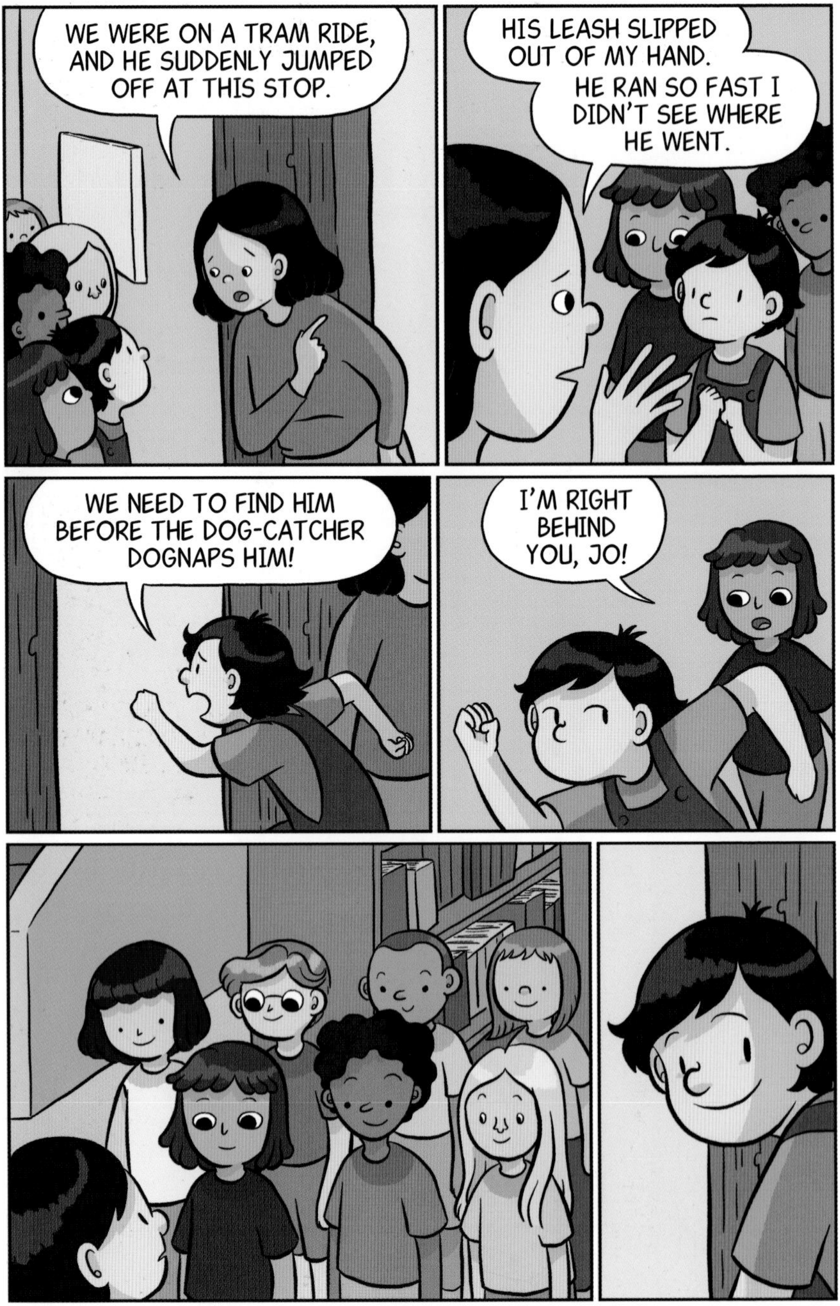
WE WERE ON A TRAM RIDE, AND HE SUDDENLY JUMPED OFF AT THIS STOP.
HIS LEASH SLIPPED OUT OF MY HAND.
HE RAN SO FAST I DIDN'T SEE WHERE HE WENT.
WE NEED TO FIND HIM BEFORE THE DOG-CATCHER DOGNAPS HIM!
I'M RIGHT BEHIND YOU, JO!

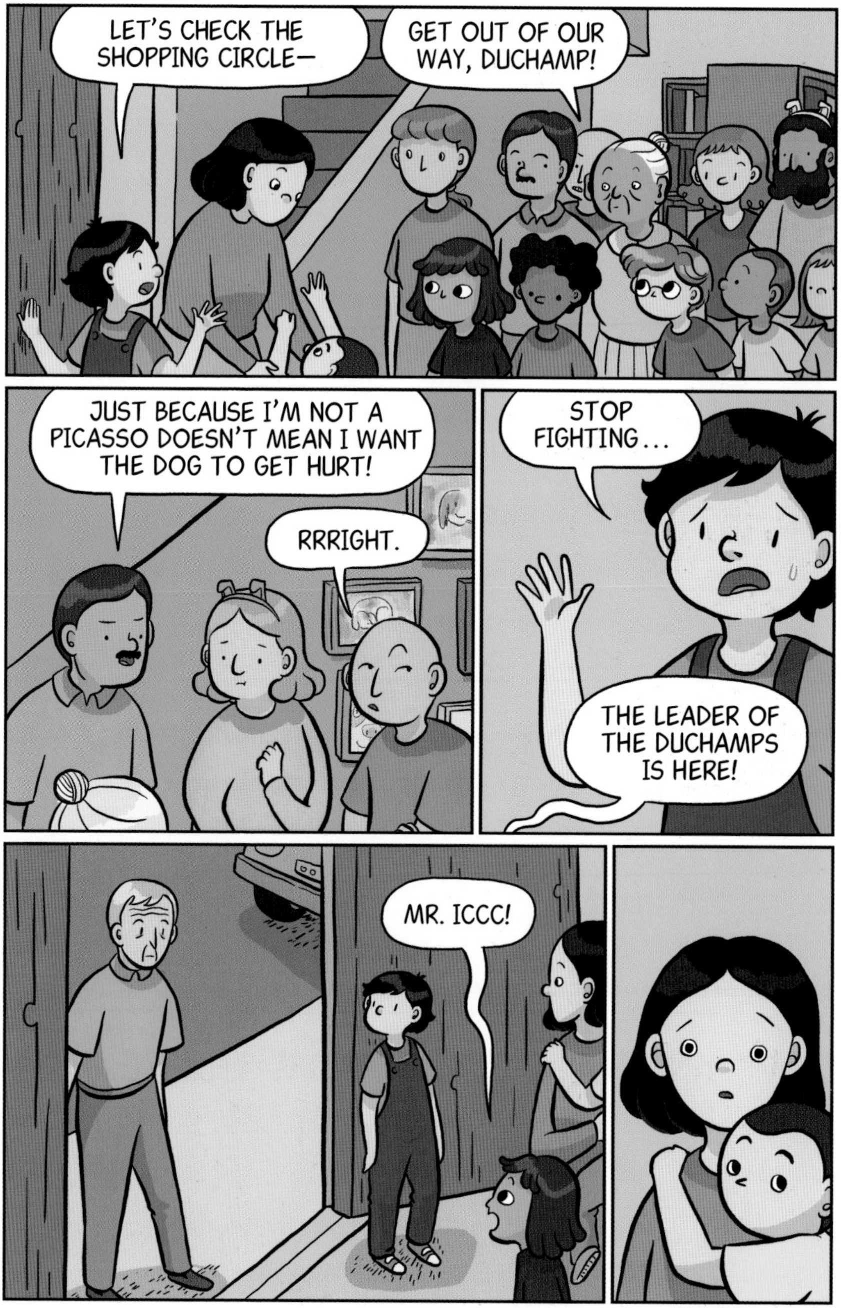
LET'S CHECK THE SHOPPING CIRCLE—
GET OUT OF OUR WAY, DUCHAMP!
JUST BECAUSE I'M NOT A PICASSO DOESN'T MEAN I WANT THE DOG TO GET HURT!
RRRIGHT.
STOP FIGHTING . . .
THE LEADER OF THE DUCHAMPS IS HERE!
MR. ICCC!

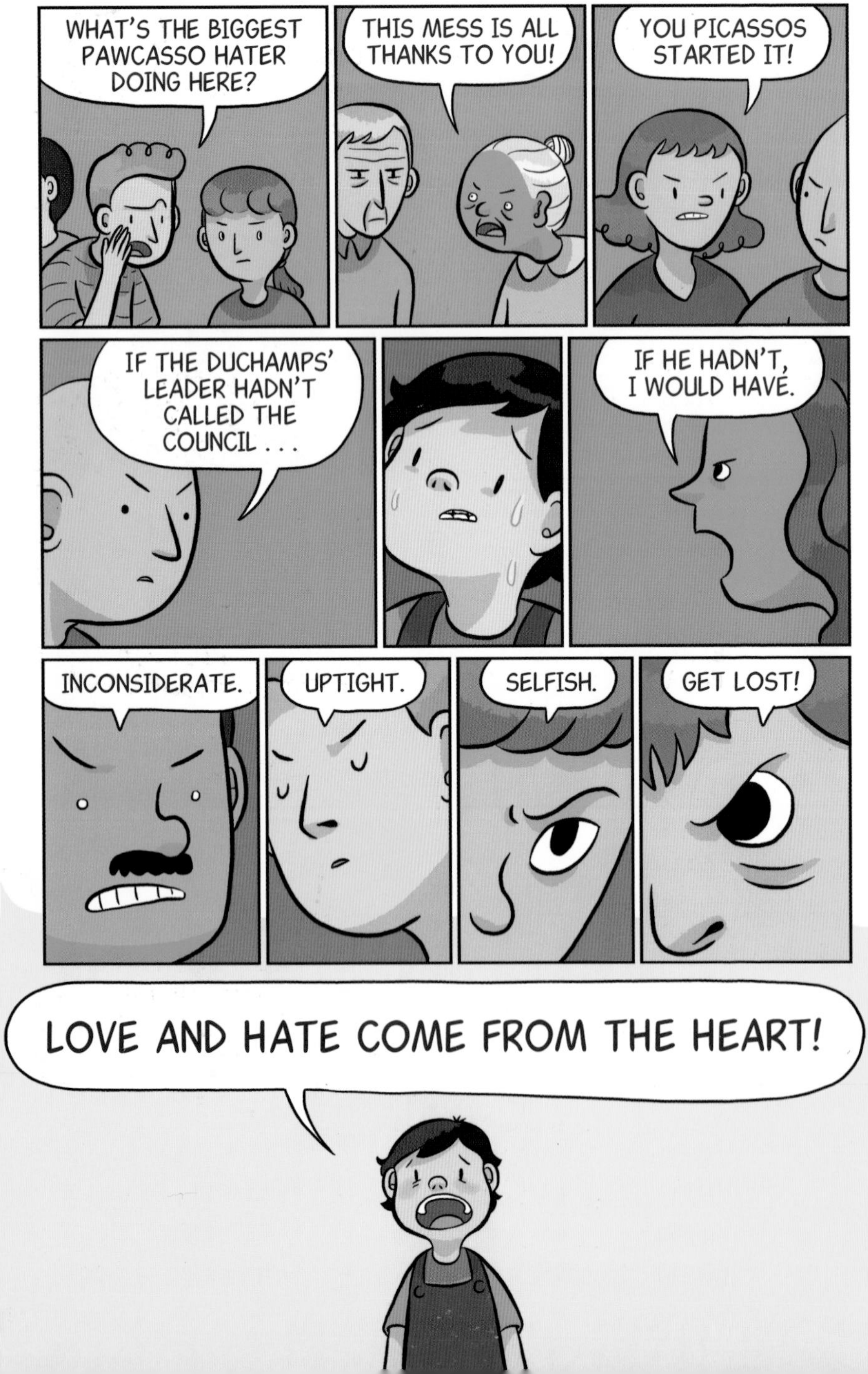
WHAT'S THE BIGGEST PAWCASSO HATER DOING HERE?
THIS MESS IS ALL THANKS TO YOU!
YOU PICASSOS STARTED IT!
IF THE DUCHAMPS' LEADER HADN'T CALLED THE COUNCIL . . .
IF HE HADN'T, I WOULD HAVE.
INCONSIDERATE.
UPTIGHT.
SELFISH.
GET LOST!
LOVE AND HATE COME FROM THE HEART!

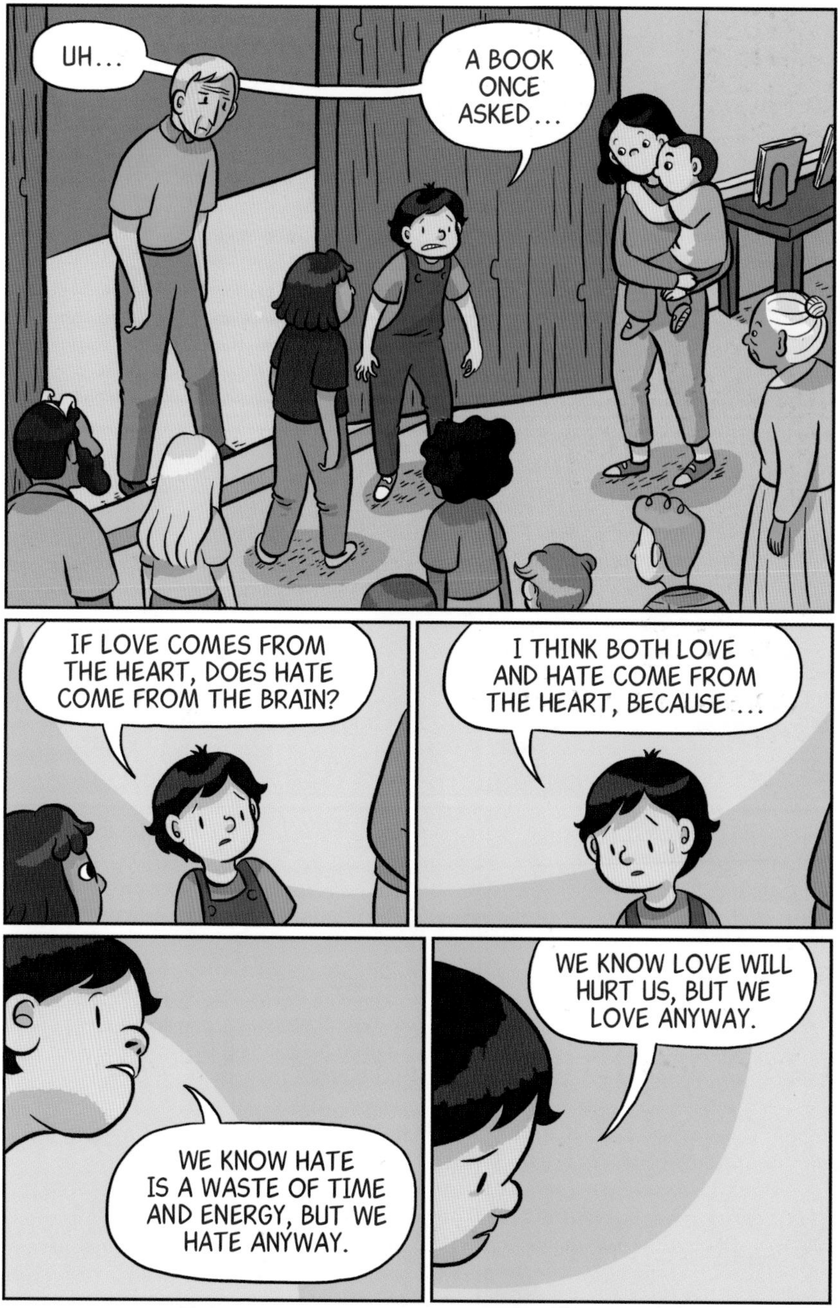
UH...
A BOOK ONCE ASKED...
IF LOVE COMES FROM THE HEART, DOES HATE COME FROM THE BRAIN?
I THINK BOTH LOVE AND HATE COME FROM THE HEART, BECAUSE...
WE KNOW HATE IS A WASTE OF TIME AND ENERGY, BUT WE HATE ANYWAY.
WE KNOW LOVE WILL HURT US, BUT WE LOVE ANYWAY.

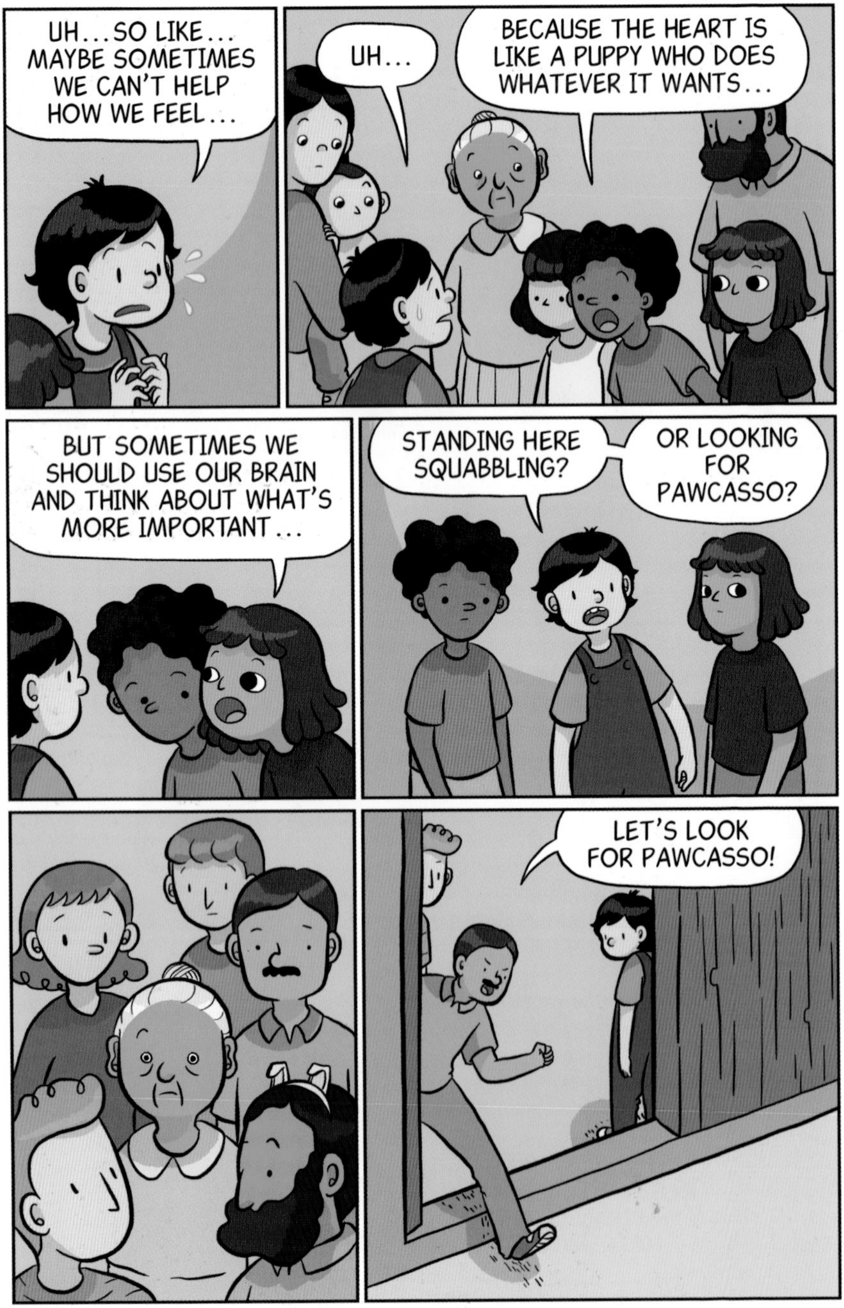
UH...SO LIKE... MAYBE SOMETIMES WE CAN'T HELP HOW WE FEEL...
UH...
BECAUSE THE HEART IS LIKE A PUPPY WHO DOES WHATEVER IT WANTS...
BUT SOMETIMES WE SHOULD USE OUR BRAIN AND THINK ABOUT WHAT'S MORE IMPORTANT...
STANDING HERE SQUABBLING?
OR LOOKING FOR PAWCASSO?
LET'S LOOK FOR PAWCASSO!

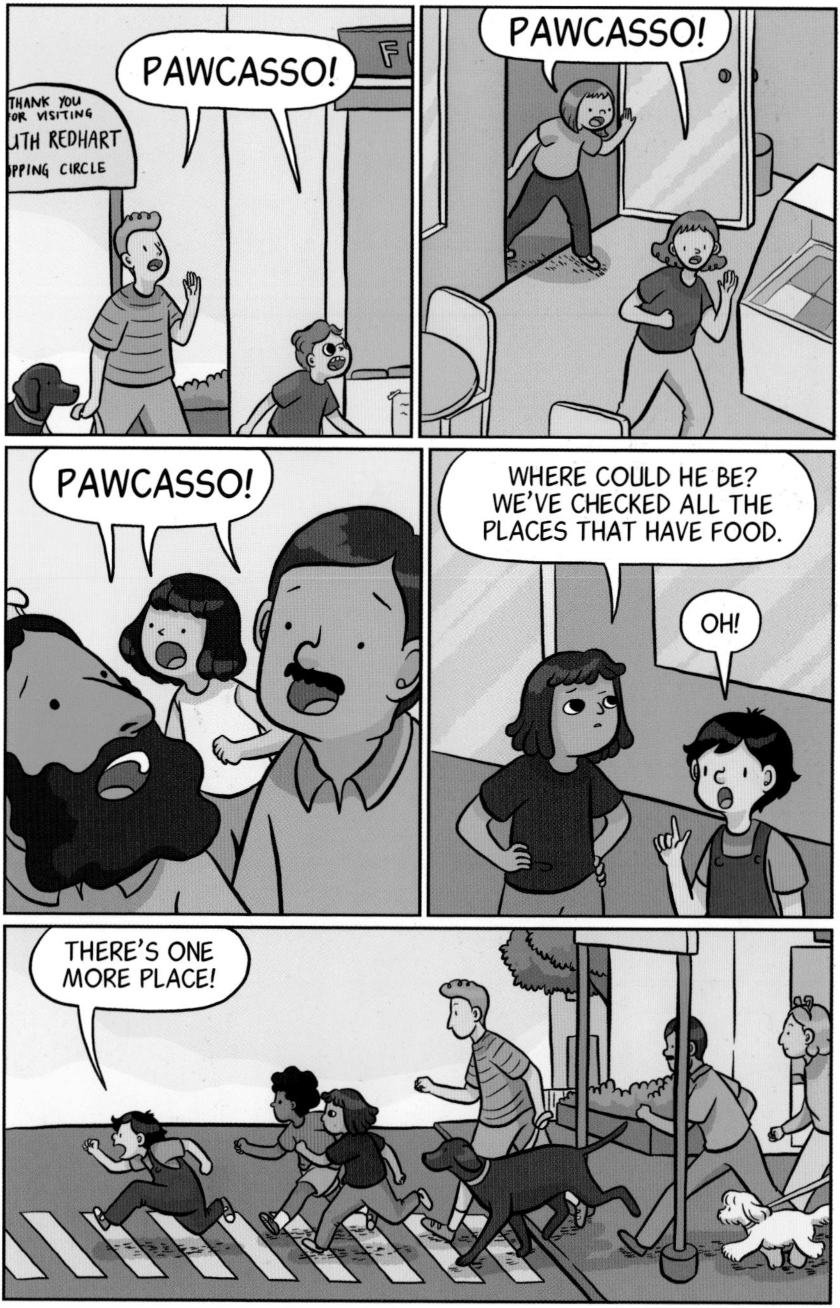
THANK YOU FOR VISITING
UTH REDHART
PPING CIRCLE
PAWCASSO!
PAWCASSO!
PAWCASSO!
WHERE COULD HE BE? WE'VE CHECKED ALL THE PLACES THAT HAVE FOOD.
OH!
THERE'S ONE MORE PLACE!

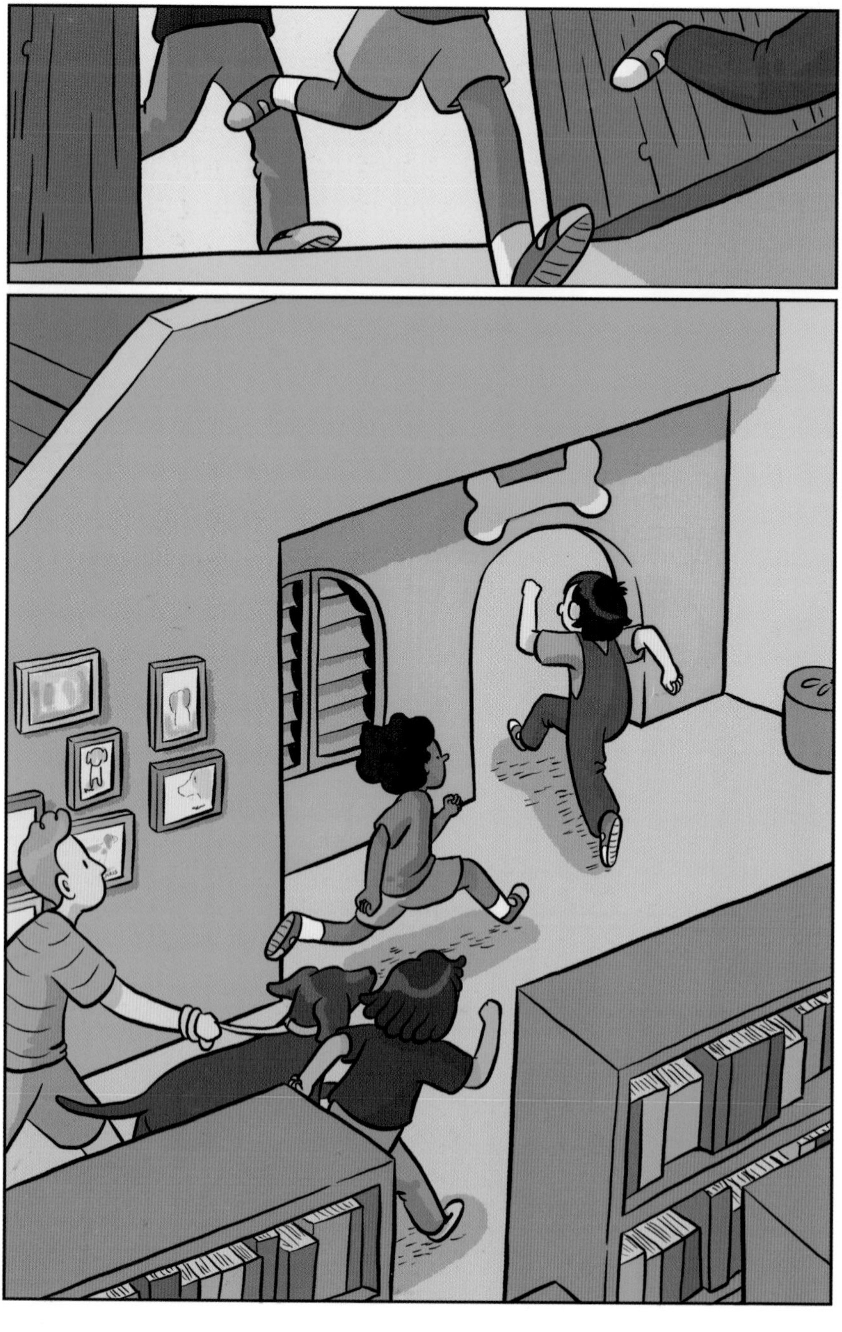

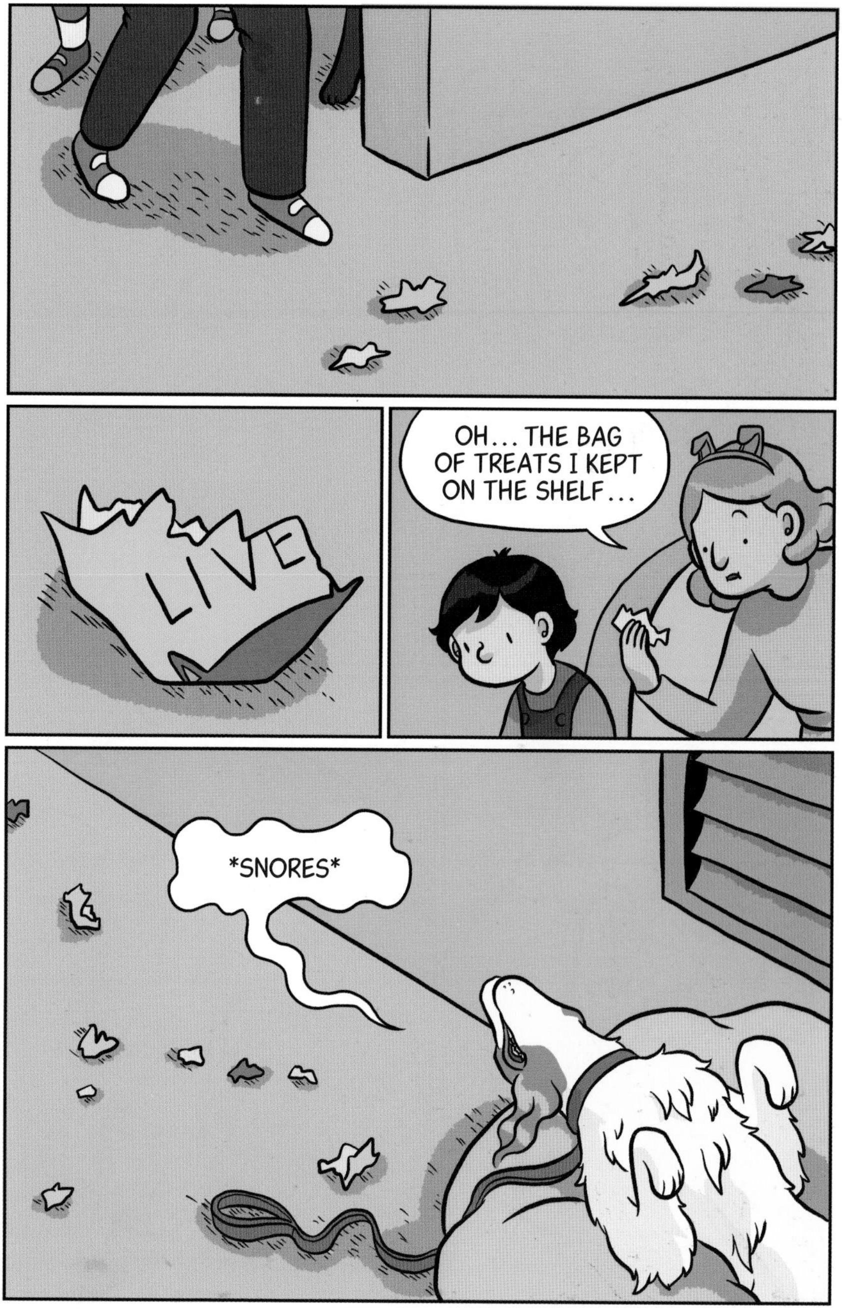
LIVE
OH... THE BAG OF TREATS I KEPT ON THE SHELF...
SNORES

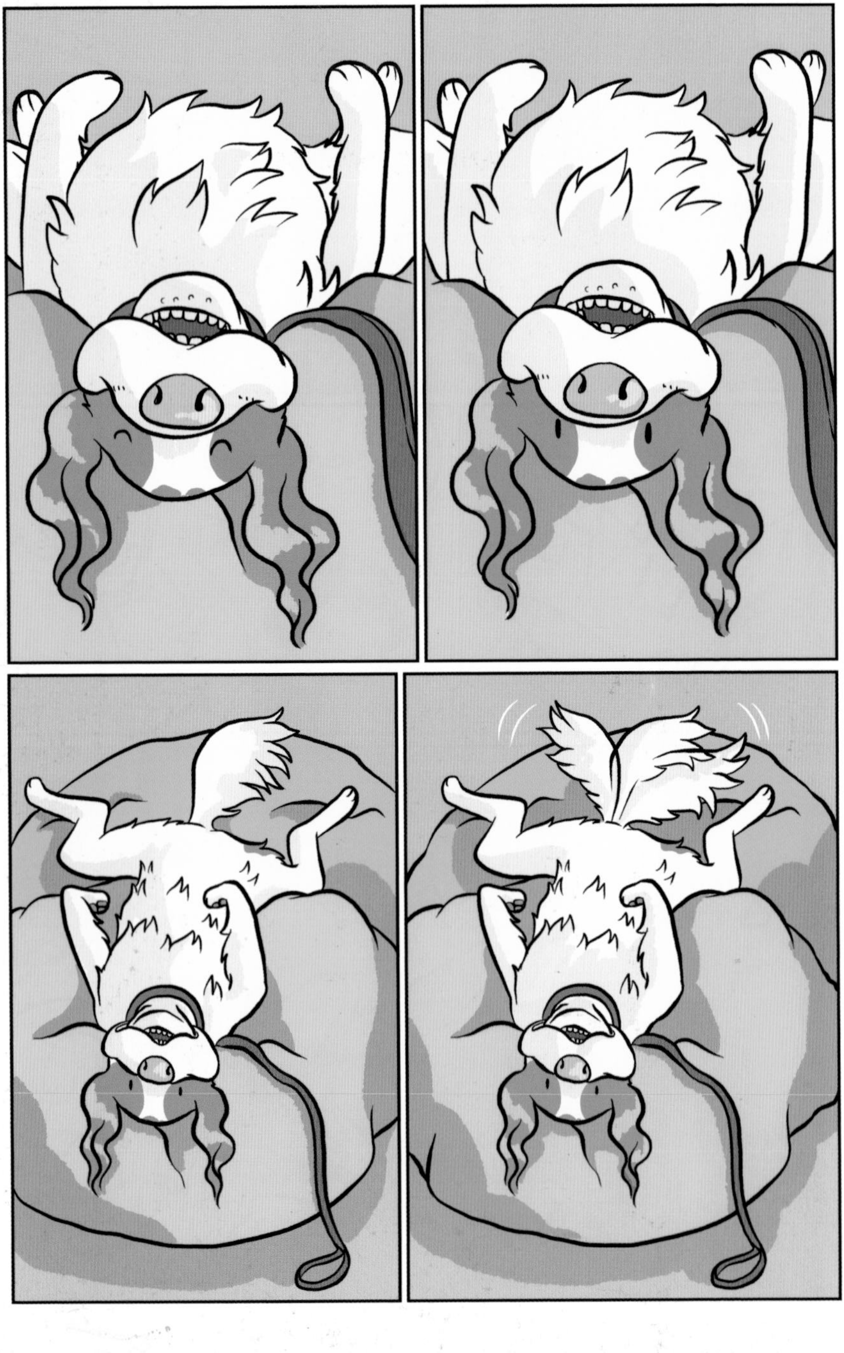

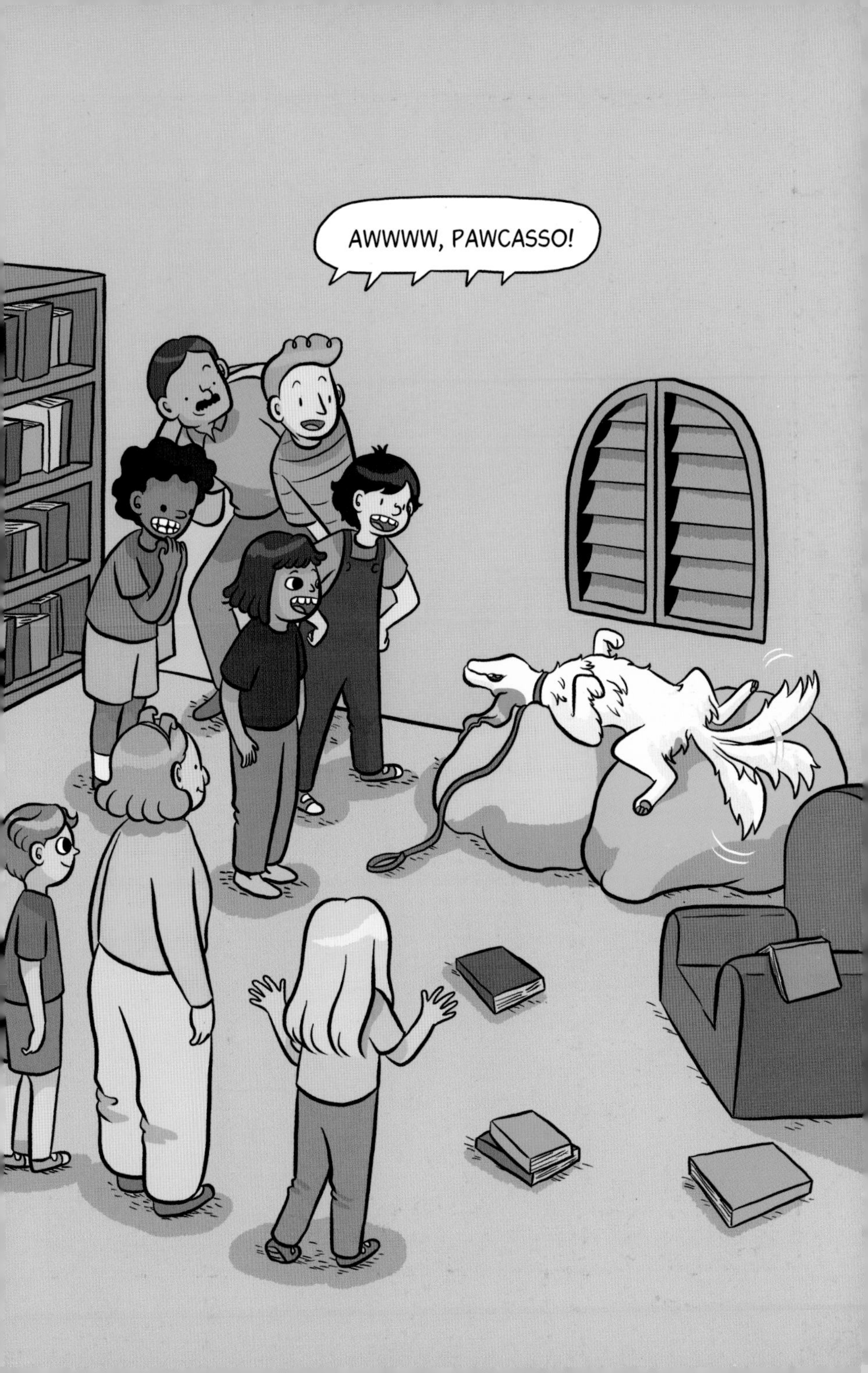
AWWWW, PAWCASSO!

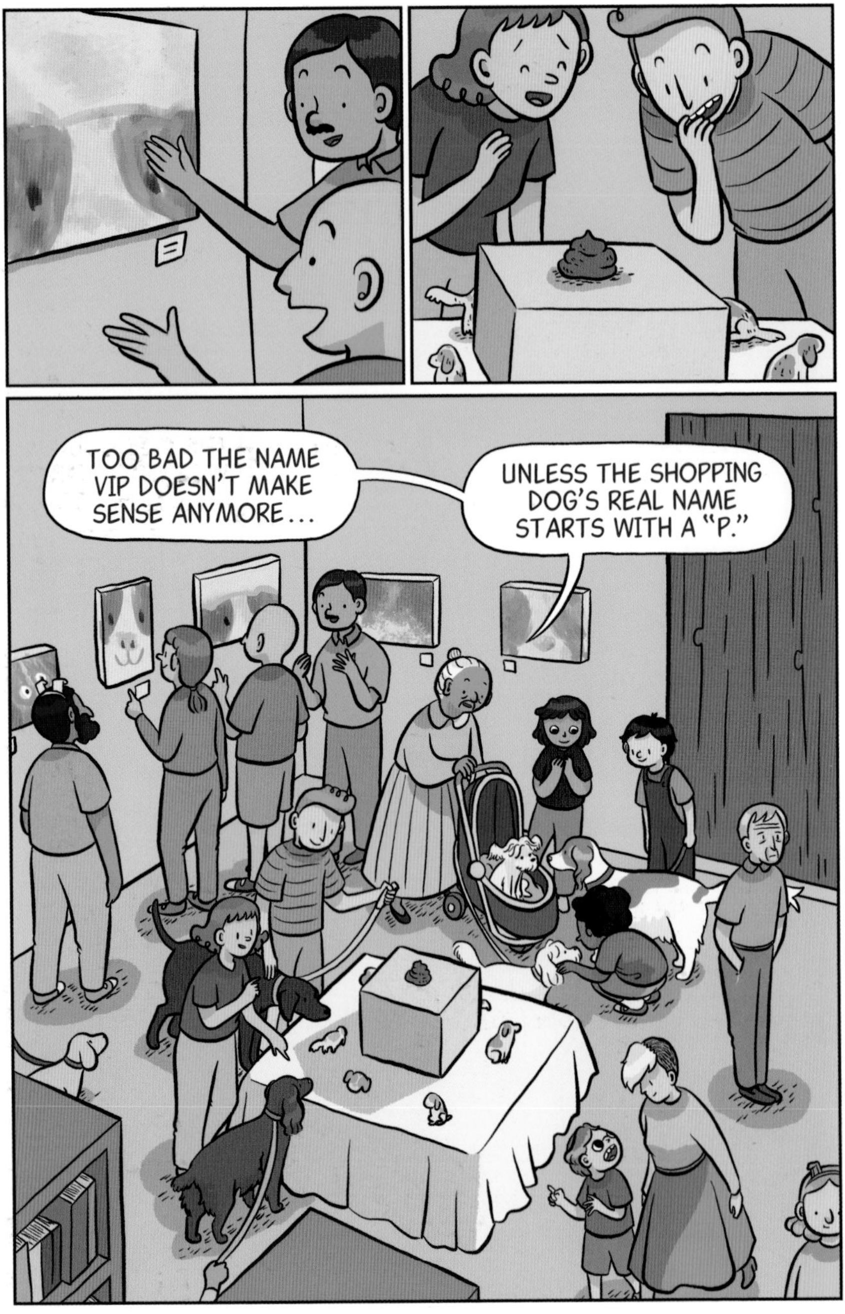
TOO BAD THE NAME VIP DOESN'T MAKE SENSE ANYMORE...
UNLESS THE SHOPPING DOG'S REAL NAME STARTS WITH A "P."

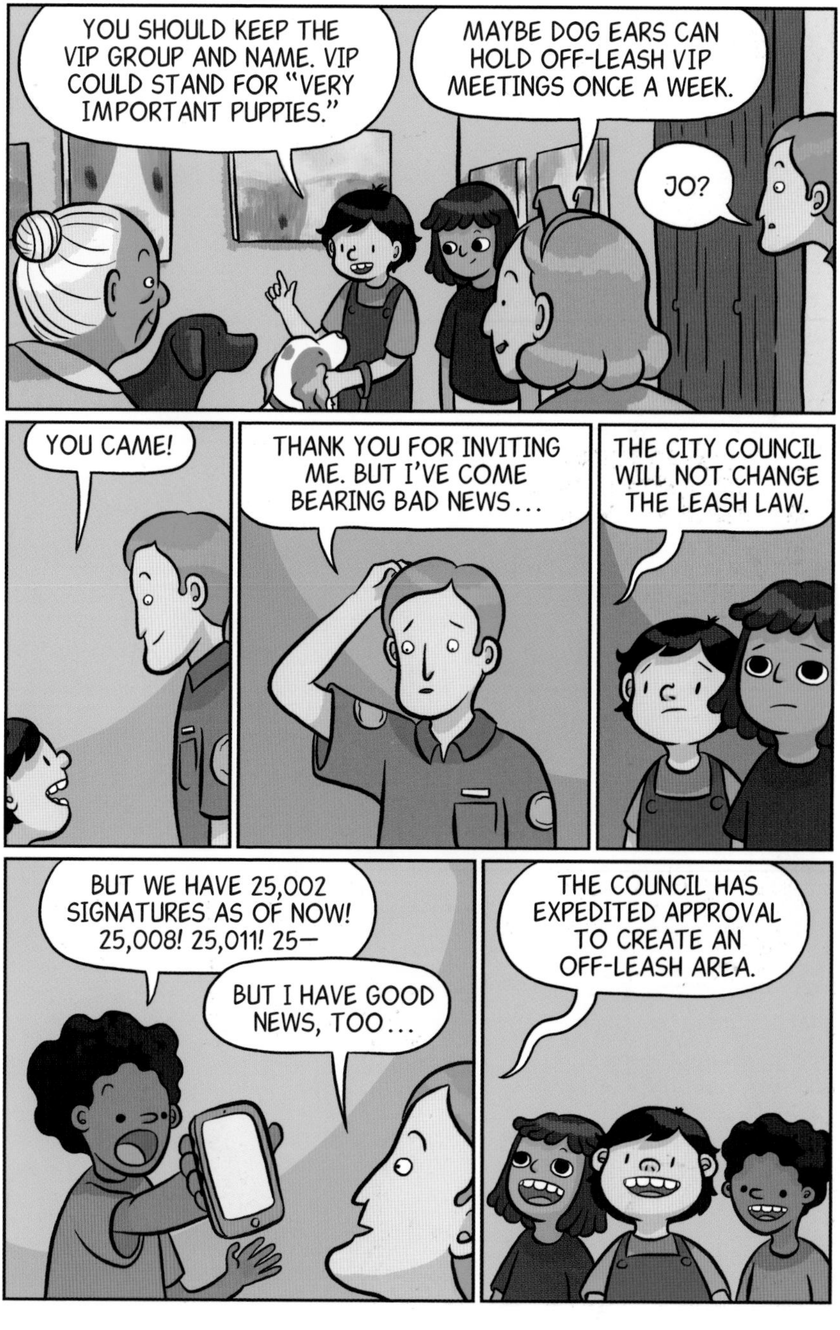
YOU SHOULD KEEP THE VIP GROUP AND NAME. VIP COULD STAND FOR "VERY IMPORTANT PUPPIES."
MAYBE DOG EARS CAN HOLD OFF-LEASH VIP MEETINGS ONCE A WEEK.
JO?
YOU CAME!
THANK YOU FOR INVITING ME. BUT I'VE COME BEARING BAD NEWS...
THE CITY COUNCIL WILL NOT CHANGE THE LEASH LAW.
BUT WE HAVE 25,002 SIGNATURES AS OF NOW! 25,008! 25,011! 25—
BUT I HAVE GOOD NEWS, TOO...
THE COUNCIL HAS EXPEDITED APPROVAL TO CREATE AN OFF-LEASH AREA.

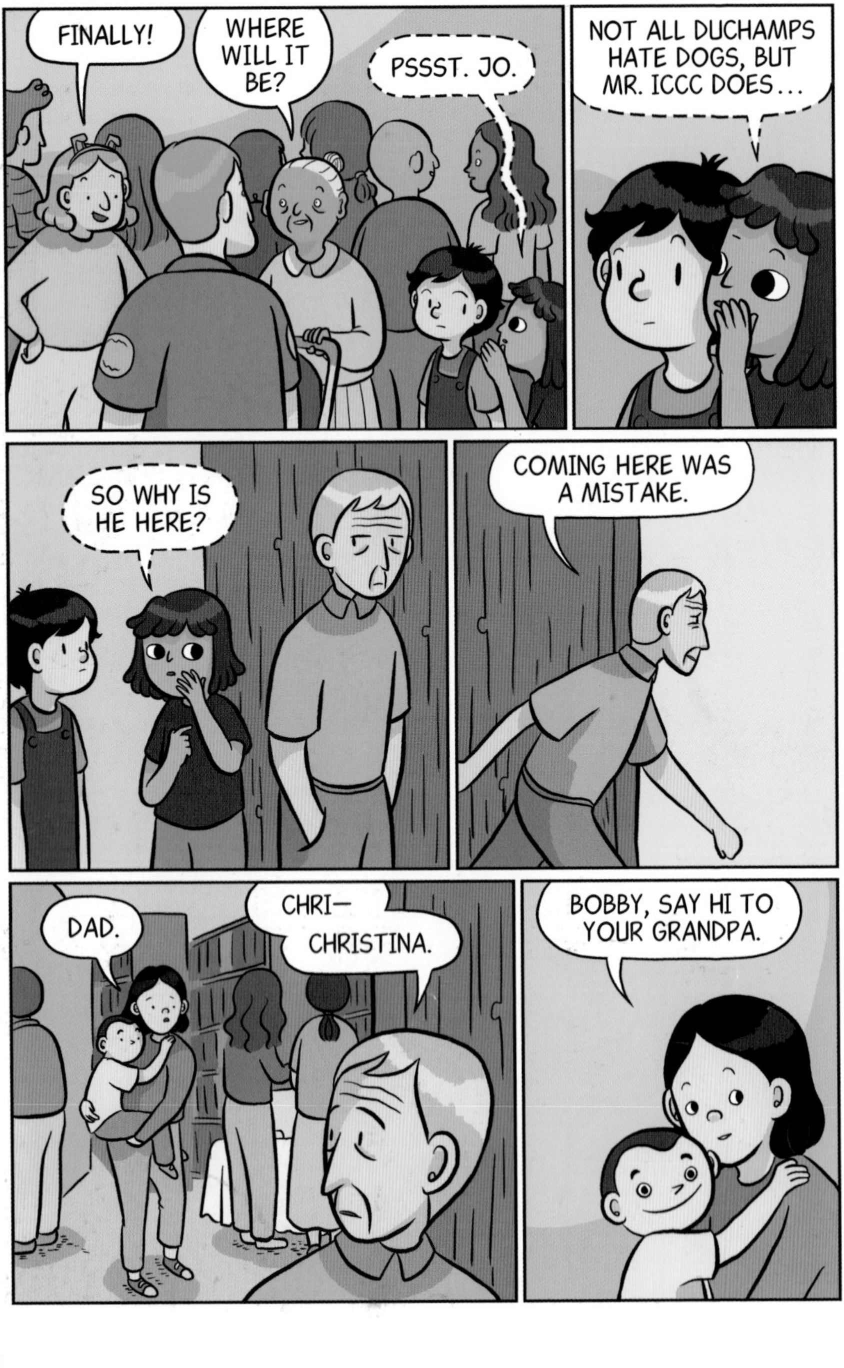
FINALLY!
WHERE WILL IT BE?
PSSST. JO.
NOT ALL DUCHAMPS HATE DOGS, BUT MR. ICCC DOES...
SO WHY IS HE HERE?
COMING HERE WAS A MISTAKE.
DAD.
CHRI— CHRISTINA.
BOBBY, SAY HI TO YOUR GRANDPA.

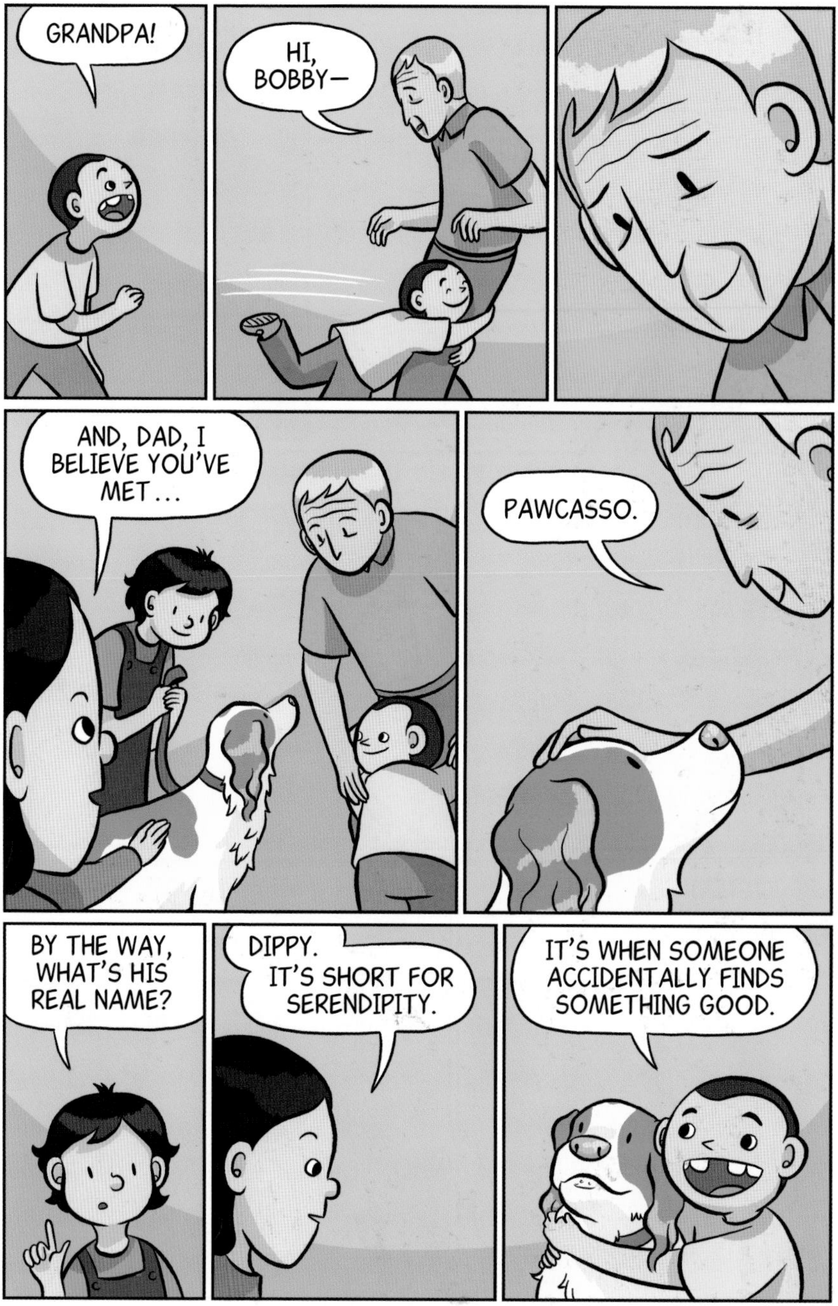
GRANDPA!
HI, BOBBY—
AND, DAD, I BELIEVE YOU'VE MET...
PAWCASSO.
BY THE WAY, WHAT'S HIS REAL NAME?
DIPPY.
IT'S SHORT FOR SERENDIPITY.
IT'S WHEN SOMEONE ACCIDENTALLY FINDS SOMETHING GOOD.

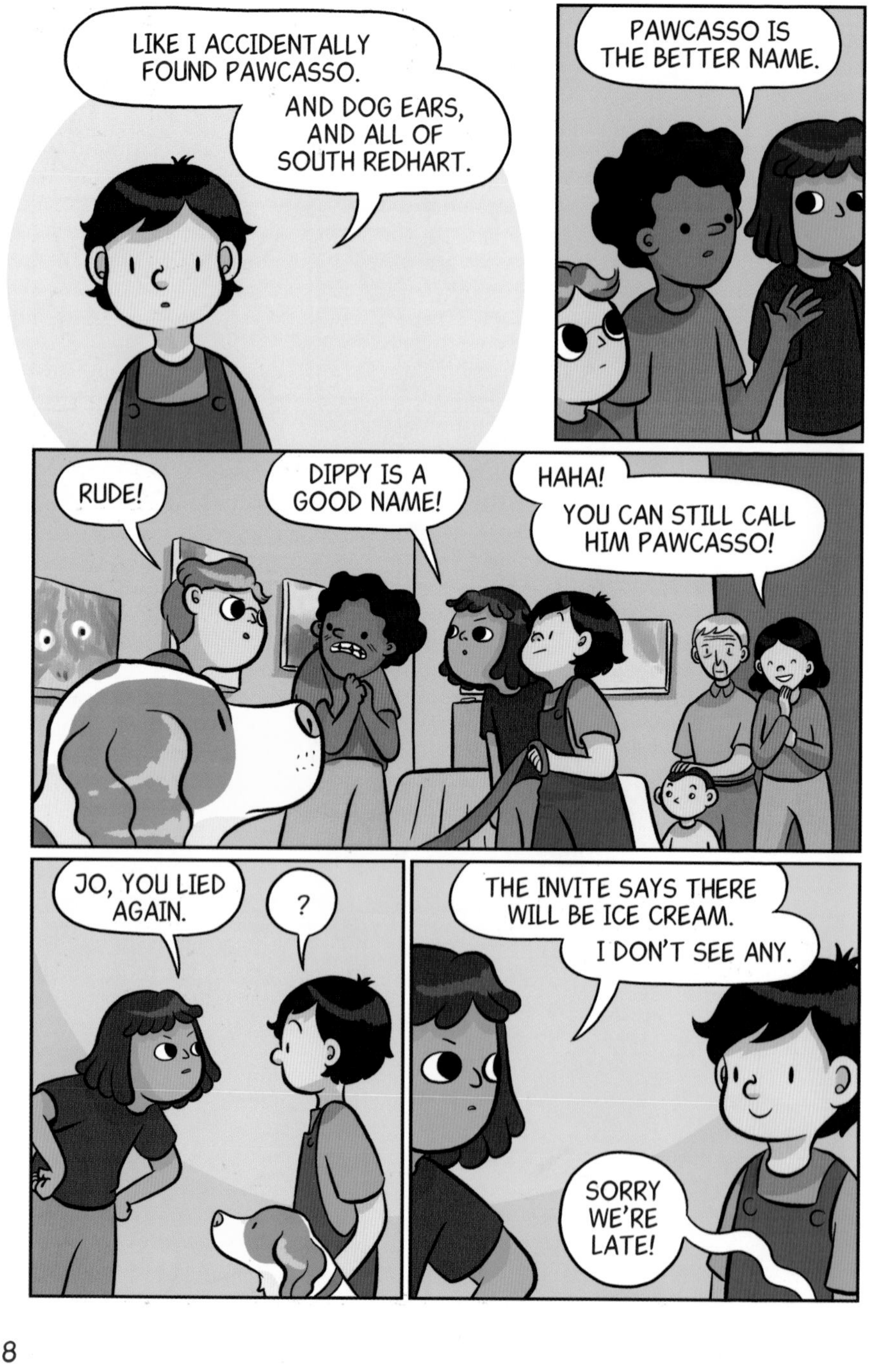

LIKE I ACCIDENTALLY FOUND PAWCASSO.
AND DOG EARS, AND ALL OF SOUTH REDHART.
PAWCASSO IS THE BETTER NAME.
RUDE!
DIPPY IS A GOOD NAME!
HAHA!
YOU CAN STILL CALL HIM PAWCASSO!
JO, YOU LIED AGAIN.
?
THE INVITE SAYS THERE WILL BE ICE CREAM.
I DON'T SEE ANY.
SORRY WE'RE LATE!

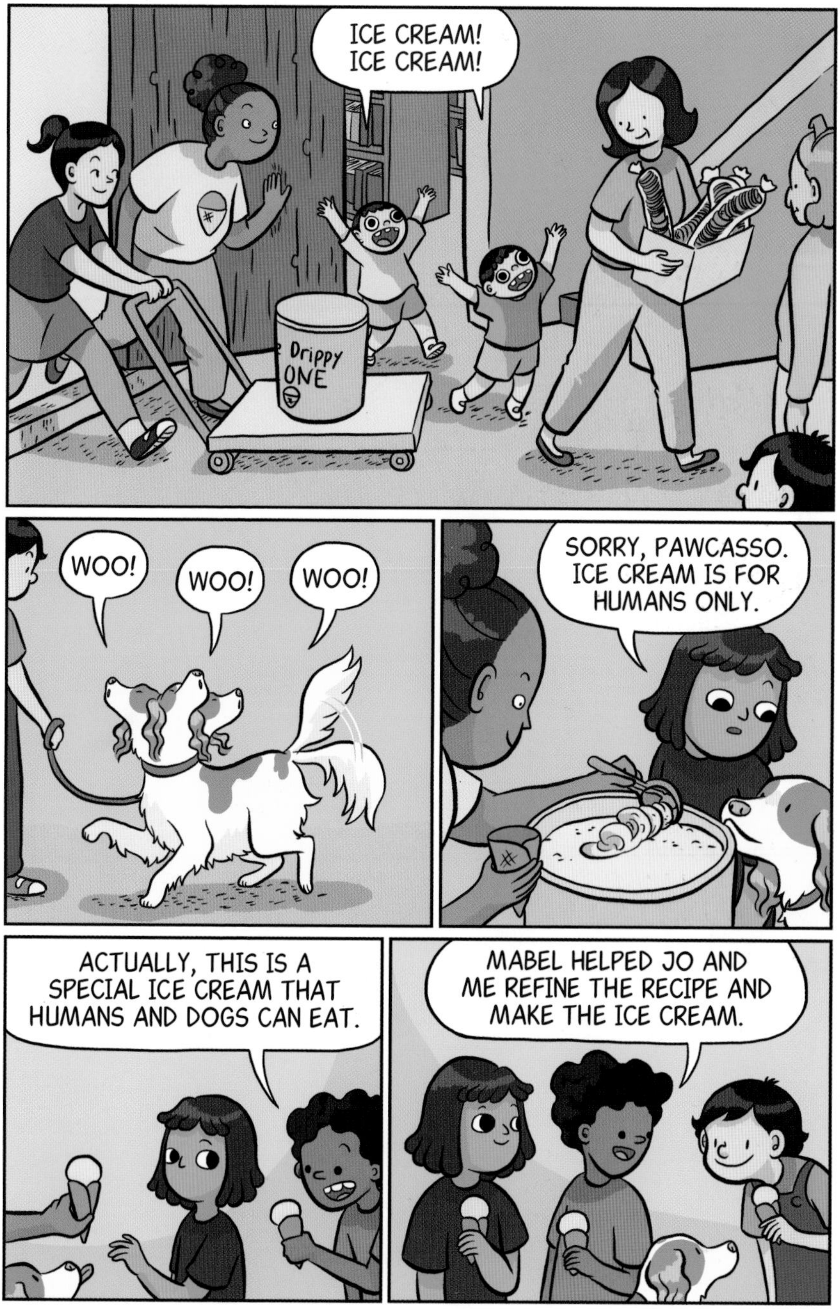

ICE CREAM! ICE CREAM!
Drippy ONE
WOO!
WOO!
WOO!
SORRY, PAWCASSO. ICE CREAM IS FOR HUMANS ONLY.
ACTUALLY, THIS IS A SPECIAL ICE CREAM THAT HUMANS AND DOGS CAN EAT.
MABEL HELPED JO AND ME REFINE THE RECIPE AND MAKE THE ICE CREAM.

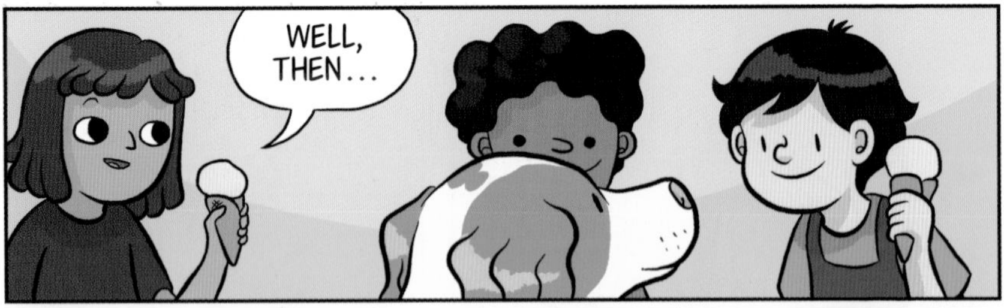
WELL, THEN...

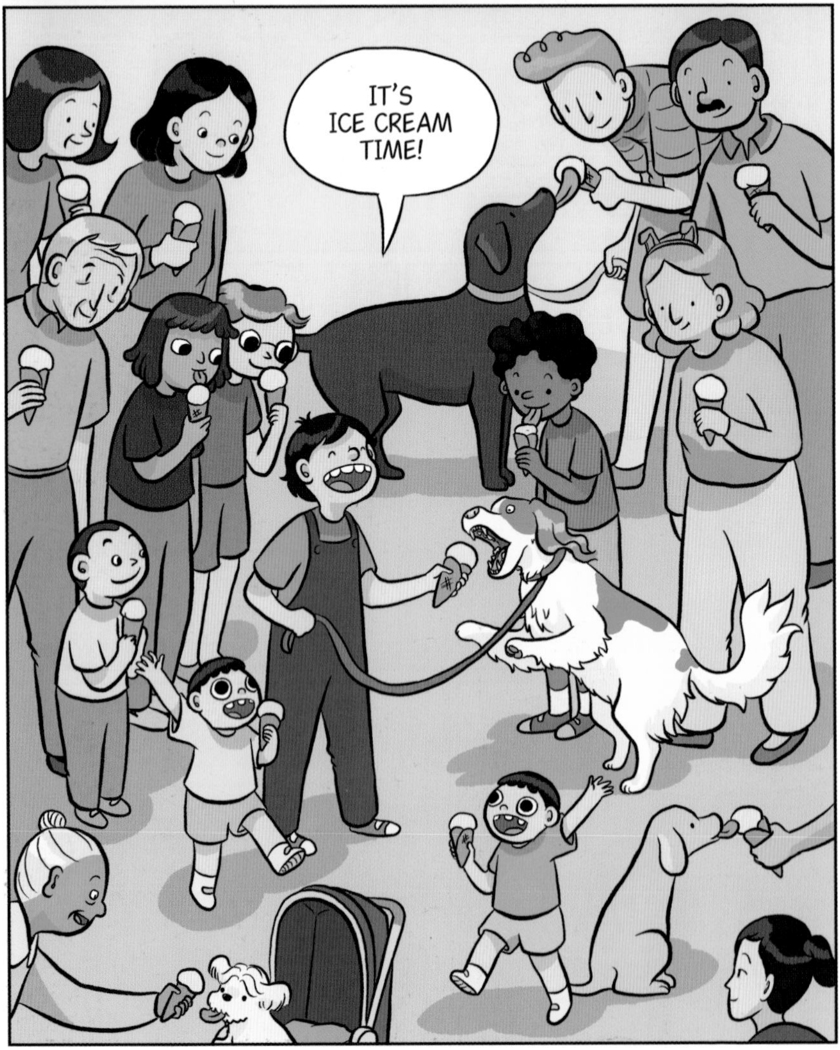
IT'S ICE CREAM TIME!

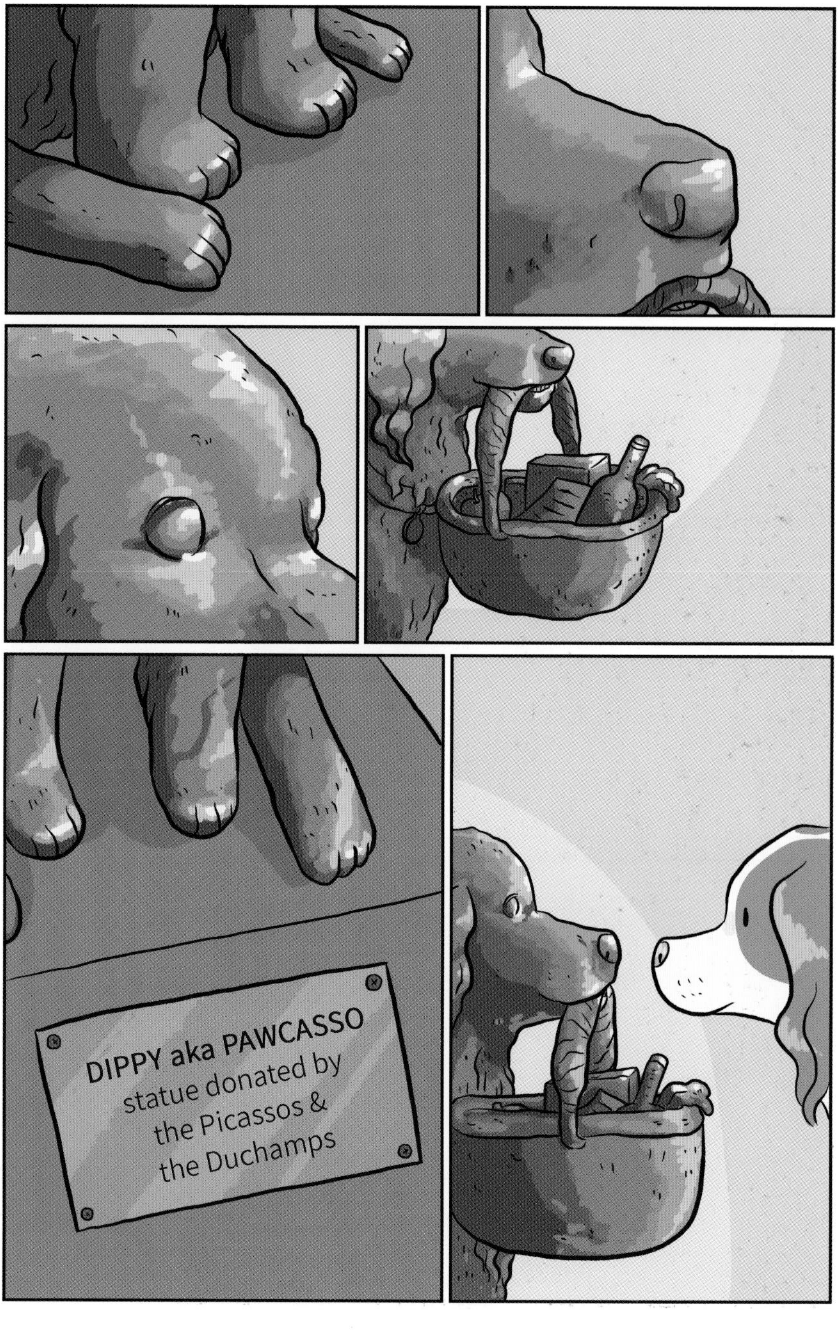
DIPPY aka PAWCASSO
statue donated by
the Picassos &
the Duchamps

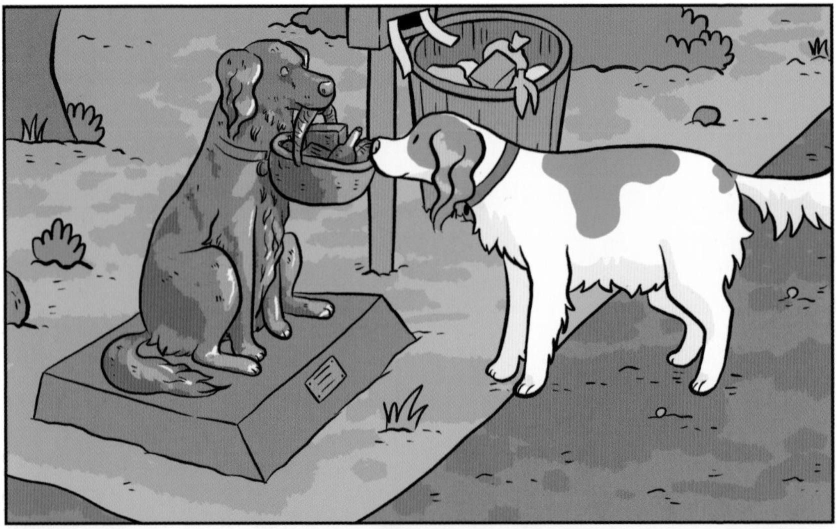

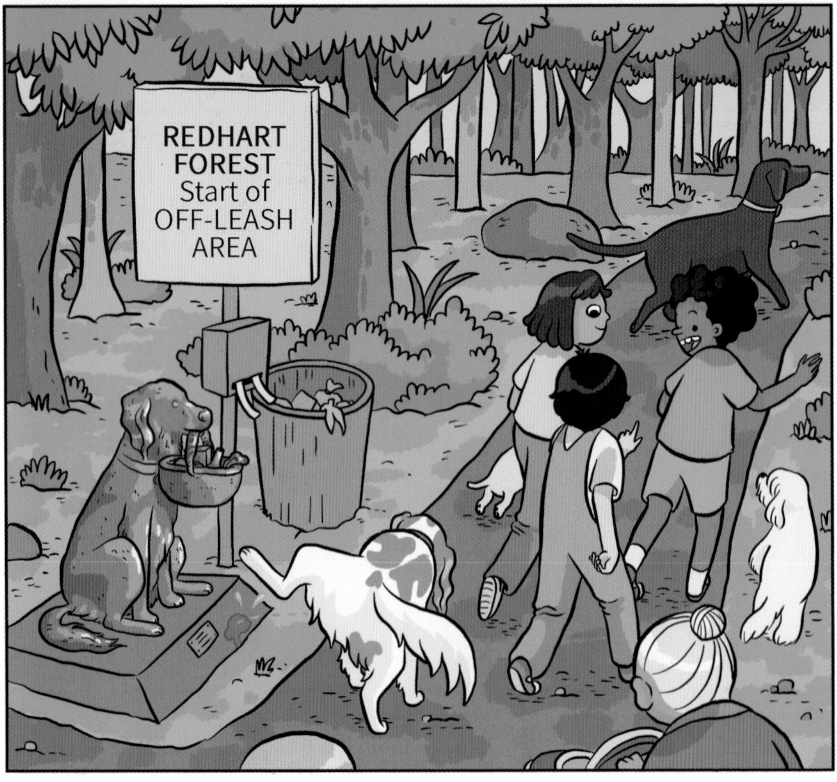
REDHART
FOREST
Start of
OFF-LEASH
AREA

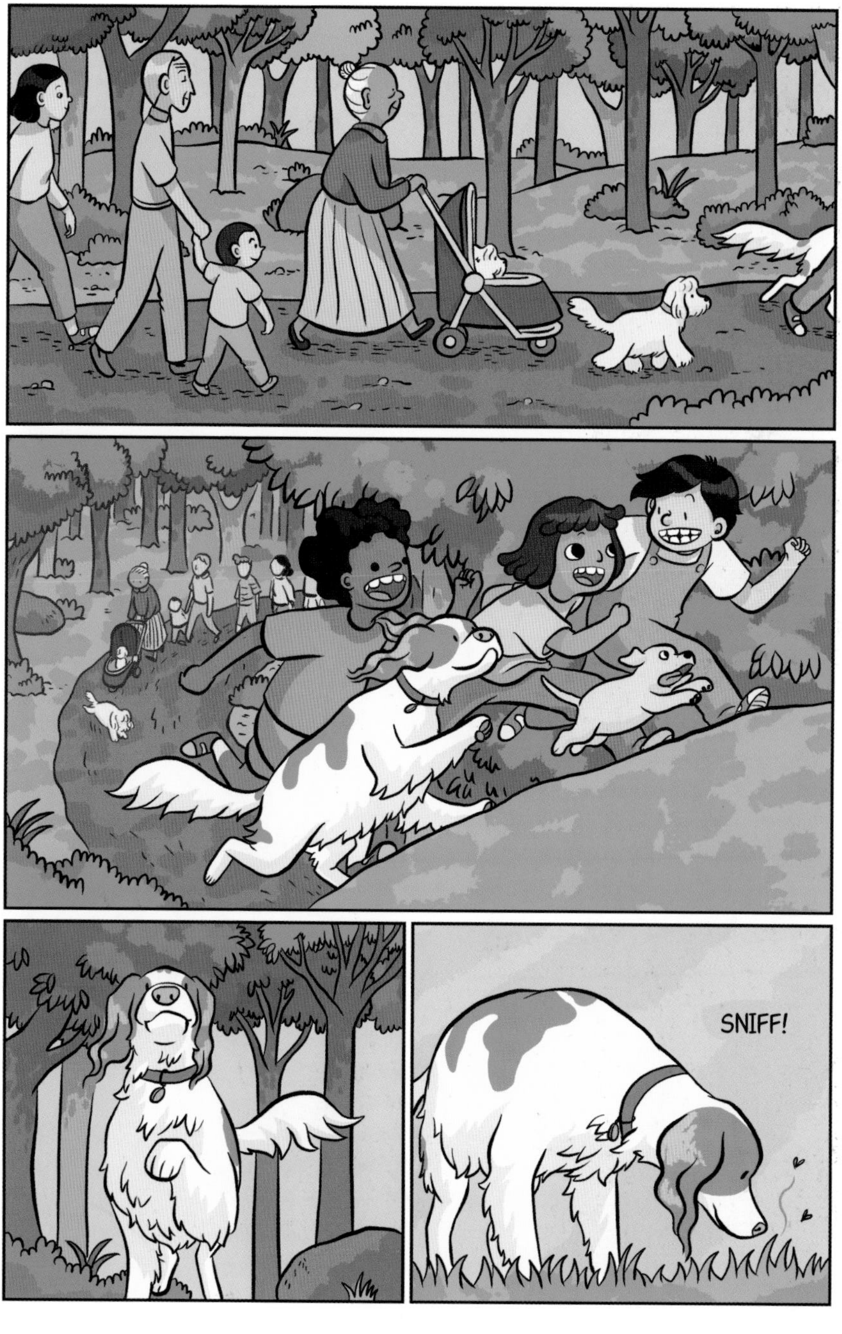
SNIFF!

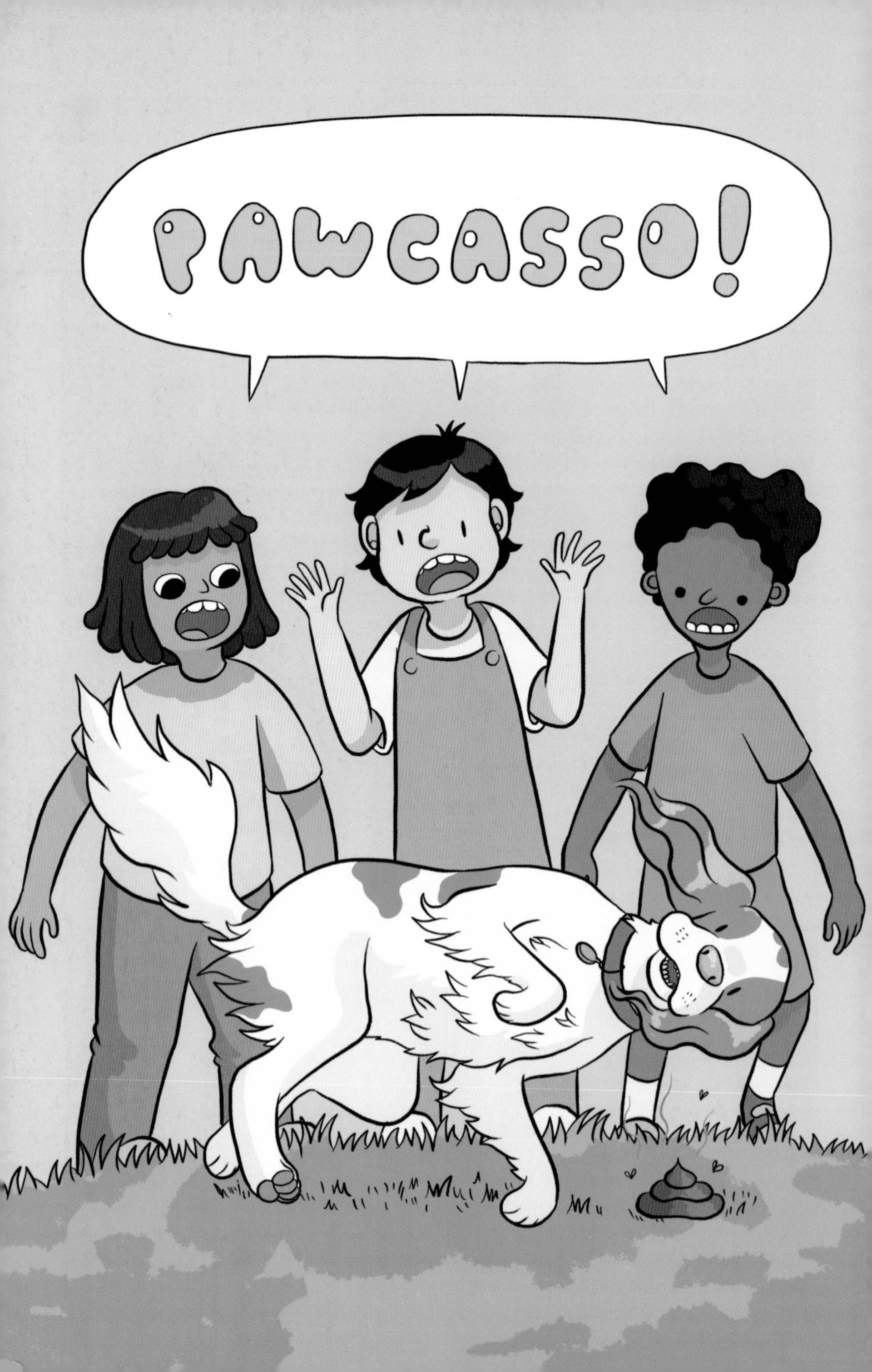
PAWCASSO!

ICE CREAM FOR DOGS AND HOOMANS RECIPE

① Slice 3 bananas and freeze overnight.

② 2 egg yolks

1 cup low-fat coconut milk

gentle heat

③ Whisk continuously for 7 minutes, or until the custard thickens and coats the back of a spoon. Let cool.

④ frozen bananas

coconut milk/egg custard

1/2 TBSP honey

1.5 TBSP unsweetened peanut butter

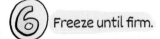

blender

⑤ Blend until smooth.

⑥ Freeze until firm.

⑦ IT'S ICE CREAM TIME!

THANK YOU
TO:

JIM McCARTHY

BRIAN GEFFEN

SAM BENNETT

MALLORY GRIGG

COLLEEN AF VENABLE

KELSEY MARRUJO

ALLEGRA GREEN

JON YAGED

ALLISON VEROST

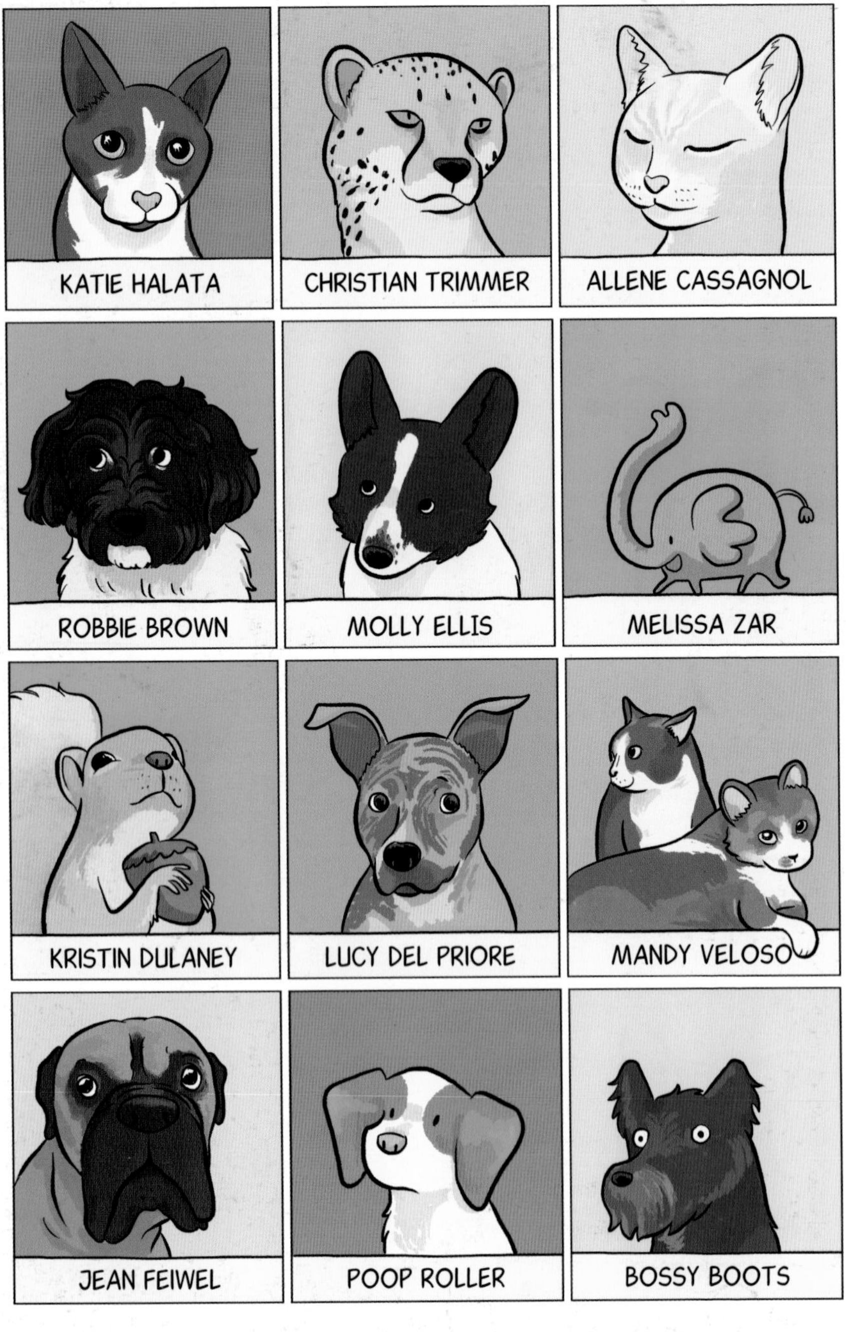
KATIE HALATA
CHRISTIAN TRIMMER
ALLENE CASSAGNOL
ROBBIE BROWN
MOLLY ELLIS
MELISSA ZAR
KRISTIN DULANEY
LUCY DEL PRIORE
MANDY VELOSO
JEAN FEIWEL
POOP ROLLER
BOSSY BOOTS

ALSO BY
REMY LAI

"Heartwarming and rib-tickling."
—TERRI LIBENSON,
BESTSELLING AUTHOR OF *INVISIBLE EMMIE*

PiE in the SKY

Remy Lai

When you buzz around school unnoticed,
it's easy to become a . . .

FLY ON THE WALL

Remy Lai

"A stunning debut."

—NPR

"Funny, enthralling, and a great reminder that being a little odd isn't a bad thing."

—Kayla Miller,
author of
Click and *Camp*

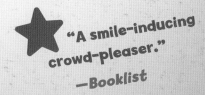

"Perfect for fans of Gene Luen Yang and Victoria Jamieson."

—*Shelf Awareness*

"A smile-inducing crowd-pleaser."

—Booklist

POOP ROLLER, YOU SMELL GOOD 99% OF THE TIME.
1% OF THE TIME YOU SMELL LIKE DEAD FISH IN A
ROTTING ZOMBIE. 100% OF THE TIME, I LOVE YOU.

Henry Holt and Company, *Publishers since 1866*
Henry Holt® is a registered trademark of
Macmillan Publishing Group, LLC
120 Broadway, New York, NY 10271 • mackids.com

Our books may be purchased in bulk for promotional,
educational, or business use. Please contact your local
bookseller or the Macmillan Corporate and Premium Sales
Department at (800) 221-7945 ext. 5442 or by email at
MacmillanSpecialMarkets@macmillan.com.

Library of Congress Cataloging-in-Publication Data is available.

First edition, 2021
Book design by Colleen AF Venable
Colors by Samantha Bennett
Printed in China by 1010 Printing International Limited,
North Point, Hong Kong

ISBN 978-1-250-77448-4 (hardcover)
10 9 8 7 6 5 4 3 2 1

ISBN 978-1-250-77449-1 (paperback)
10 9 8 7 6 5 4 3 2 1